H. W. Pierson

The Hahnemannian advocate

A monthly magazine of homoeopathic medicine and allied sciences

H. W. Pierson

The Hahnemannian advocate
A monthly magazine of homoeopathic medicine and allied sciences

ISBN/EAN: 9783741170959

Manufactured in Europe, USA, Canada, Australia, Japa

Cover: Foto ©Andreas Hilbeck / pixelio.de

Manufactured and distributed by brebook publishing software
(www.brebook.com)

H. W. Pierson

The Hahnemannian advocate

THE

Hahnemannian Advocate

A Monthly Magazine of

HOMOEOPATHIC MEDICINE

and Allied Sciences.

H. W. PIERSON, M. D., Editor.

VOLUME XLI.—JANUARY TO DECEMBER, 1902.

HAHNEMANN PUBLISHING CO.
CHICAGO.
1902.

INDEX.

MATERIA MEDICA.

MEDICINE.

SURGERY.

OBSTETRICAL.

NURSING.

PEDIATRICS.

PSYCHOLOGY.

EDITORIAL.

CORRESPONDENCE.

BOOK REVIEWS.

OBITUARY.

CONTRIBUTORS.

The Hahnemannian Advocate

A MONTHLY HOMŒOPATHIC MAGAZINE.

Vol. xii. Chicago, January, 1902. No. 1

Materia Medica.

ALUMINA.

When we look over the symptoms of Alumina we are struck with the wonderful *weakness* of the muscles, *weakness* of the limbs, *weakness* of the upper and lower extremities; *weakness* observed in the rectum, *weakness* in the bladder, inability to press at urine or stool; apparent weakness of the œsophagus when swallowing. So, going through all the regions we will find this diminished activity of organs and parts. *Slowness* of action; sluggishness; weakness; and this spreads on and on until we have *paralysis*. Sometimes it singles out one part, and sometimes it is quite general. Sometimes it is paralysis of the œsophagus so he can no longer swallow. Some-it is paralysis of the bladder, so he can no longer pass urine. The rectum is wonderfully affected, so he cannot pass the stool. If we look into these symptoms and compare them with the sickness we will see that *it affects the whole spine*.

It not only produces weakness, but it produces a *spasmodic* train of symptoms. It produces disturbances of *co ordination; tingling* in the skin; *burning* here and there; dreadful *itching* of the skin; *numbness* of the skin; *formication* in connection with this diminutive action—the whole state looks toward a paralytic breakdown. It has been said by those who have carefully looked into the subject that this remedy is quite suitable to the *complaints of old men*. When a sweeping statement like that has been made by someone well versed in materia medica it is because he has looked over all the symptoms and they appear to him like such complaints as occur in old people.

The mind takes on its share; just the same kind of tribulation. It will not work; forgetfulness; inability to reason; strange state of confusion of the mind.

The *mucous* membrane comes in for its share of trouble; *ulceration;* dryness; thick yellow and copious discharges.

The *skin* takes on terrible eruptions. The skin is, comparatively speaking, the outside of the body. That is all it is when looked upon as a symptom producer and disease manifestations *within* the body are relieved by setting up a discharge from the mucous membranes or by producing an eruption upon the skin. The one is equal to the other in relief. So when explosions take place, so to speak, in the body, in the blood, in the economy, in the fluids of the body, in the nervous system, they are likely to come to the surface as eruptions, and we have that brought out in this proving. In *Sulphur* and others of those deep-acting remedies, the symptoms are thrown to the surface. If it were not so the internal or deeper organs would be so greatly affected that the patient or prover would die, or suffer very greatly; but that is the method. Nature has provided for throwing things to the surface. Hence the catarrh of the mucous membranes, which the old fashioned doctor endeavors with all his might and main, by the use of salves and ointments, liniments and what not to check them and thereby prevent what we believe to be Nature's safety valve. These deep acting medicines show themselves in that way. This medicine exhibits itself by its wonderful action upon the *mucous membrane and skin.* These to a great extent, when taken together, show that it is a deep anti-psoric remedy; that it acts upon the innermost centers of life.

It has *infiltration* under the inflamed mucous membranes.

It has great *dryness* of the skin, *roughness;* rough *scaly itching* and it has been very useful in *psora.* "*Dreadful itching from the warmth of the bed.*" This is one of the exceptions of the remedy, because otherwise the *warmth is agreeable.* It has this feature of heat and cold running through—it is classed as a *cold* remedy; it is *sensitive to cold;* constitutional coldness; must be fairly well wrapped; wants warmth; wants heavy clothing in winter; wants to sleep in heavy clothing nights. A chilly patient; a low state of vitality; chilly; hovering around the fire.

This remedy then, if we take up the *mental* symptoms and go through the *particulars,* is quite rich in mind symptoms. "*Confusion of mind*" covers a great deal. It is a *weakness,* a letting down. "*No ability to reason or to think.*" A sort of confusion of mind is described, as an inability to settle upon the matter whether the things be true or untrue; an inability to form an estimate of common things. "*When people talk to her it seems strange what is said, and she is not able to say whether they are addressing her or somebody else.* When she talks it seems as if someone else were talking; as if she was making use of others' ideas." She cannot bring herself down to a realization of her existence, but there seems to be something strange about it.

"*Wondering, meditating over what is said.*" "*Consciousness of his personal identity confused*" is one of the ways of expressing it.

"*Great weakness of memory;* confusion and obscuration of the intellect." Then another feature rising in the mind is impulse. It is full of impulses. He becomes very nervous, excitable and sudden impulses come upon him. "Seeing blood or a knife, cutting instruments, instruments that can be used for suicide," she has an impulse to commit suicide; and this follows her a tormenting, persistent thought or idea. There are certain *persistent* thoughts in remedies, such as having impulses when they are not able to control them. Some are impelled to do one thing, some another. If the prover should go upon a high place he cannot resist that impulse to throw himself off and he goes away for fear he will carry it out. That occurs in certain provings. Certain convictions come to the mother on seeing her child and a fire—the impulse comes into the mother's mind to throw that child into the fire, and she must run away for fear she will carry out her impulse. It is the act of the involuntary system while the disturbed intellect cannot control the body as it does in a state of health. A perfectly healthy thinking mind will say to those impulse, "Be gone!" Individuals look upon *impulses* as things of foolishness. A clergyman of my knowledge cannot take a hatchet into his hands without the impulse comes into his mind to use it to cut off the heads of his children, and he grasps it and holds it behind his back until he gets the better of his impulse. *Aurum, Nitrate of Silver, Nux vomica, Natrum sulph.*, and such medicines are full of impulses. They are well to meditate upon because they are difficult to comprehend. It is on the borderland of insanity. These very states do lead up to insanity. We have insanity of the will as well as insanity of the intellectual powers. They are not sufficiently distinguished, though, in the literature on this subject. Quite likely many of the writers of our literature have not had access to the wonderful things developed in the human mind by provings. The provings point out the state of the mind to the physician so that he can perceive what is going on and how it goes on, as cannot be done in any other manner than to study the provings brought out in the mind symptoms of our provers. In *Nux vomica* the symptom is like this: *Though she love her husband ever so much she is disposed to injure him;* and though in *Natrum sulph.* she loves her own life, she says, "Doctor, you do not know how much I have to resist taking my own life." Many a case of suicide would have been prevented by this medicine, *Alumina.*

This medicine is full of these strange impulses—an impulsive medicine.

"Bad thoughts in the morning—*joyless and comfortless on waking.*" The love has gone. Joylessness. No love of his own life. No love of others. An inability to feel or to realize that affection. A loving wife loses all of her affection for her husband. Not intellectually; she is sound on the question, because she says "I want to love my husband; I want to love my children; they are lovable; my husband is kind and I have always loved him." She says, "Doctor, I am sick; something has come over me." *Sepia* leads all the medicines in this affection, but this medicine has it too. We see how everything is slowed down.

A premature old age. Wonderful remedy it is. It is deep acting.

And then come *fears*. Fear of evil—"*apprehensiveness*"—a fear that she will carry into effect the awful thoughts that come over her. She is burdened tremendously with these tormenting thoughts. "*Fears she will lose her reason; fears some dreadful thing will come.*" Fear in the evening, and she cannot sleep. Fears he has some incurable disease. Dread of death, with thoughts of suicide. Anxiety—variable moods—sometimes confident, sometimes timid. When the mind balance is lost the mood is always variable, always changing.

So many of these symptoms occur with *paralysis*, and after the paralytic condition is fully developed and the weakness in the lower extremities is established, the mental symptoms clear up.

These Symptoms are the Generals.

This remedy is *full of vertigo;* full of dizziness. As soon as he opens his eyes in the morning his dizziness and visual troubles come on, and as soon as he gets on his feet he is dizzy, and if he closes his eyes the dizziness increases. If it is in the dark and he attempts to move about the dizziness increases and compels him to sit down. If he closes his eyes to wash his face over a wash basin he pitches forward from dizziness. This is also sometimes found in spinal affections, such as sclerosis of the posterior zones. Ending in staggering, walking on a wide base. This medicine has enough of those symptoms to check that progressive disease, *locomotor ataxia.* When the disease has progressed somewhat it may be checked so that one will live much longer.

This dizziness is a marked feature of the remedy and a marked feature of the disease. "*Everything turns in a circle.*" *Dizziness continues until he becomes sick at the stomach.* This sort of dizziness ending in nausea is a different kind of nausea from that which comes from overeating. There is a series of modalities running through nausea from these brain and spinal troubles and from visual troubles. Nausea from visual troubles and from cerebral irritation and from spinal irritation is wholly different from that due to eating a boiled dinner.

"*Inability to walk except with the eyes open and in the daytime. Cloudiness and drunken feeling*, alternating with pain in the kidneys. *Easily made drunk, even by weakest spirituous drink," and he becomes dizzy. "When his eyes are closed his whole body totters; if not firmly held he will fall to the ground."* These symptoms have been confirmed over and over again. These conditions have been cured in disease.

Headaches. *Headache with vertigo and nausea.* Headache in the top of the head as if the head would be *crushed in, ameliorated by pressure.* Great heaviness in the head—pressure in the head. *Rending, tearing* pains in the head, through the eyes. Above the eyes.

There are all sorts of strange illusions of sensations running through this remedy. Illusions of feeling and of sensation, as if the head was too large; *as if one hand was swollen.* He looks at it and wonders if it is not so, and asks the doctor if it is not swollen. One leg he declares is longer than the other. Illusions of sensation. Sometimes when he becomes insane he has delusions of sensation. He believes they are so. When he looks at them and laughs at them and sees they are not so, and knows they are not so, he has illusions of sensation; but when he becomes deluded and believes they are so, that is insanity.

Eyes. "*Dimness, blindness. Loss of vision.*" The dim-sightedness begins in this way: "Dim-sightedness as if looking through a fog, or as if feathers were before the eyes." As a vail before the eyes. As if some white flocks were before the eyes. "Dimness of vision." These are all the same thing.

"Eyes inflamed, itching, ulcerating. Dryness of mucous membranes, smarting, soreness. Rawness of the edges of the lids. Eyes inflamed." Discharges from the eyes, thick, yellow. Eyes feel cold. Eyeballs feel cold as ice. From the itching and smarting the eyes will take on spasms, and the lids will close. Spasmodically close. "Strabismus. The eyelids become thickened, dry and burning. Chronic granular lids. Burning and dryness in the lids. Burning on waking, especially on looking up, with dread of light. Tottering and falling when closing the eyes. Eyes generally better from being bathed.

Ear. "*Stitching, roaring, aching* pains in the ear, in old *chronic* and *constitutional* troubles." No ear symptoms particularly that would be guiding to alumina as a remedy, only such as are to be taken in as little particulars. Ear symptoms of old chronic troubles, such as the buzzing and the singing and the roaring in the ears due to an atrophic condition of the middle ear is very hard to remove.

Nose. "Chronic catarrh of the nose. Very troublesome *Chronic nasal catarrh of long standing, of old people.* Discharge of *dry, hard, yellow green mucus in the nose. Violent pain in the root of the nose.* Copious yellow sour-smelling mucus. *The septum of the nose is swollen.* Redness of the nose. Swelling and hardness of the wing of the nose." In this study the question arises, *when will Alumina cure a patient who has those symptoms in the nose?* All of the *generals* will have to be brought up in every *particular*, in every *region.* We will have to recall everything that was said on the generals in the last lecture, and go over them. To give Alumina on those symptoms that I have read —and yet they are strong alumina symptoms, that is, in the make-up—*but you see there is nothing in there that is predicated of the patient himself.* Suppose you had a patient who was always roasting, always in a fever, a feverish state of heat. When he gets into a warm room he suffocates, and wants the windows open, and had just those symptoms. That would not be alumina, would it? And yet there are those in prescribing who would tell you that the fact of the patient being chilly and always cold, will say: "Why we are to take the totality of the symptoms, of course, and that is only one symptom." He gets down and figures through that and pays no more attention to that symptom that he would to a pain in the great toe or burning in the soles of the feet or burning in the back. *They would all stand on a level.* But I tell you it is simply nonsense to work out a case like that. Every *particular* that we come to in going through the symptoms, we are to be impressed with in the same way and in the same manner, and to recall the same condition with all these *particulars*, to reiterate all that was said about the patient. But you must remember that *languor*, that *weakness in body and mind:* that state of prostration; *slowness in coming on of disease;* the *progressive* complaints, if this remedy is to be a curative remedy. We see that brought out more in some of the particulars than in others. The general condition of the mucous membranes is illustrated by the state the mucous membranes must be in by the nasal discharge.

Face is withered and sickly. He looks sick, he looks nervously sick, because he is in a state of nervous prostration. He has been losing his flesh. Pain in the face, and feeling of tension. Many times you will see persons who have been in a better state of flesh who are very nervous. *Always brushing the face.* It is not because the face itches, not because it tingles. In this remedy particularly it feels as if *some thin dried skin* had been attached to it. Sometimes they will say as if *cobwebs were across the face;* or as if there were *dried blood on the face.* And if one has happened to be so unfortunate as to get dry albumen on the face it leaves a state of tension similar to that described. "Tension in the skin of the face, as though white of egg had dried on it." This sensation extends all over the skin.

Tingling upon the backs of the hands —you will very often see people rubbing the back of the hand as if there was something crawling on the back of the hand. It is a sensation of the creeping of ants in the skin—formication.

In Alumina is a *nervous tension*, a peculiar nervous *tingling;* not a constant tingling from a paralytic condition—a tingling in the skin. It is associated with this paralytic tendency, and hence the skin everywhere has tingling, but especially the extremities. Numbness, tingling, creeping, associated with the weakness, shows the irritation of the nerve centers of the spine and its prolongation into the brain, especially of the anterior roots.

"*Involuntary* spasmodic *twitchings* of the muscles of the face. Twitchings of the lids, twitchings of the face."

This remedy has another feature running through it that is common, the fulgurating pains. *Lightning* pains—pains that come like a flash of lightning, running from the shoulders to the ends of the fingers. Pains running down the back, down the crural and the sciatic, pains running to the toes. *Tearing, paroxysmal*, or when the same is associated with the disease locomotor ataxia these pains have always been called *fulgurating* pains. In the proving of the remedy you will find them as *tearing, rending* pains. The terms in the remedies do not conform to the terms in which disease is expressed. They have to be translated.

This is another peculiar symptom that is misinterpreted at times and misunderstood. You will find in provings a sensation of *bubbling* in the thigh, a sensation of bubbling in the muscles. Well, it is *quivering* and *twitching* in the muscles, it is a *rapid* jerking and twitching of the muscles on a very small scale, and it is likened to bubbling.

Throat. "*Dryness in the throat. Old catarrhal troubles, rawness; always taking cold and settling in the throat.*" In *alumen* like this one—the patient is always "*taking cold in the throat,*" so to speak. In *alumen* it is so common for the *tonsils to grow larger* and larger and larger with the colds. Every cold leaves an additional predisposition to another cold. While in this remedy it very seldom affects the glands, the tonsils, but very commonly the whole mucous membranes of the pharynx, extending up into the posterior nares, and down the entire throat; it smarts and burns, has granulations, varicose veins, and all the time a sensation of *sticking in the throat.* It is almost useless to prescribe this remedy in an acute soreness of the throat. It has *dryness in the throat, splinters.* But *Nitric acid* and *Hepar* and many other remedies have this symptom, and what are we going to do about it? No two are alike, even in their splinters. But we have to take the *whole remedy* together, the *whole patient* together. Now, in those violently inflamed throats that redden up in a hurry and ulcerate and threaten to suppurate in the night, you have "*sticks in the throat,*" that is similar to *Hepar.* Old ulcers in the throat, that linger, from syphilis and other causes call for *Nitric acid. Argentum nit.* has a sudden inflammation in the throat, also the splinters. *Natrum mur.* has a dry throat, and is the only one in the list that fits with this one. The symptoms are so similar that the only way we can tell between the two is to get the Natrum mur. *patient*, and that is the only way for you to have your materia medica, so that only one remedy comes up at a time. The one that comes up is the one that should fit the case.

As we pass downward from the throat, we observe *paresis*, a paralytic weakness. The throat may even *fill up with food*, and he *chokes* and *strangles.* It goes down the wrong way, it goes up into the nose. Or it may get part way down the œsophagus and *feel like a great lump.* The throat seems to have lost its power. This you will observe is indicative of the whole remedy. In this *particular* we find one of the features that helps to make up one of its marked *generals*, this *paralytic weakness.* The same as we will find in the bladder and in the limbs.

Appetite. We find some features clash with appetite, that are decidedly *general* because they relate to his *likes and dislikes.* He hates meat, does not want meat at all. An *aversion to meat*, an *aversion to beer.* Well, that is a good thing sometimes too. "Meat has no taste." In the old catarrhal states a loss of taste for certain kinds of food, but particularly meat. He might as well chew on chips, for he gets none of the old flavor he used to like; but he "*craves, starch and chalk and slate pencils*"—I should rather say, she does, because the complaints in which this is likely to come up are found in a nervous woman, the anemic, chlorotic woman who has almost lost her menstrual periods or when they come are very late—and she has a craving for *cloves, acids,* *coffee* or *tea* grounds etc., owing to the fact that in this paralytic weakness of these particular nerve centers there is almost no taste for anything. The tendency is to hunt for anything that has a *taste* and hence *highly seasoned* things are sought. He finally gets sick from a number of foods, and more particularly from eating potatoes. Potatoes cause flatulency, cause nausea, cause diarrhœa, and he turns against potatoes, because they make him sick. Indigestion, "colic from eating potatoes." He bloats up so that he is fretty and irritable and he has colic in the bowels from eating potatoes. He has an aversion to meat, and there is not much left for him to live on but to hunt for *highly seasoned* foods. It is a common thing for those broken down to get appetites for those things that do them the most harm. They go from bad to worse very rapidly. It would be supposed that the healthy man would use his judgment. Of course man has lost his intuition, his perception for food. He has become so perverted that he even craves things that devour him, the stimulants and the spices, and this is sometimes called "cultivated taste," but as a matter of fact it is a depraved taste. Man ought to be in such a state that he could from his instincts select his foods like the cow, the horse and the cat. I have no doubt but that he once was able to. But psora has crept into the human family and has turned him into disorder and he has not been for thousands of years capable of exercising his loves which guide him to his foods, but he is now compelled to use his judgment, his intellect—that is, to discover by experiment what is good for him.

Stomach. Eructations, bitter after eating potatoes. It is always useful because it is very similar to *lead poisoning*, it is useful in *painters' colic*. Lead colic; *great bloating in the abdomen, drawing in of the navel.* "*Cramping pains, violent cramps in the intestines*" As long as he would keep away from lead it has the power of counteracting the pains. When he has become predisposed to it from painting he may never be able to go back to it.

Rectum and Stool. One of the most important features of Alumina is *paralytic weakness of the rectum*. The rectum seems to be incapable of action. Until the rectum is full, greatly distended, there will be no action. *No urging to stool for many days*. Pressing down upon the rectum, as if the rectum were full of fæces, and yet no urging to stool. "*Inactivity of the rectum.*" No ability to urge or to force in the act of pressing at stool. Uses the abdominal muscles. When sitting at stool, strains until he is covered with sweat; becomes cold, exhausted. Sweats, becomes cold, becomes tired. Giving up in dispair. "He never will have a stool." Trembles from head to foot. Exhausted; and finally when he succeeds in passing the stool it may be hard, but very commonly it is soft—that is, such a stool as would be supposed to pass easily. So we find the *soft stool is expelled with great difficulty*. This, you see—this *paralytic weakness* of all of those parts made use of in expelling stool has gone with the *generals*, for this state seems to belong to all the muscles of the body. He is incapable of exercising without being prostrated. Paralytic weakness, or a general sort of paresis of the muscles.

Bladder. This same feature belongs to the bladder; the urine *flows very slowly in a small stream*, and he must *stand and wait*, or sit and wait for it to pass. It *dribbles* and dribbles in a small stream, and that effort that all healthy people can perform when the bladder is normal, that is, hurrying, is impossible in this remedy. Many times when straining to pass urine he will force out the stool; so that urine will flow sometimes *better without making an effort.*

Hard, knotty stools, like those spoken of in *alumen*, but more commonly its use is confined to the constipation, with inactivity of the rectum, when a moderately soft stool is expelled with difficulty, as I have described. "*Soft thin stool passing with difficulty.*" Alumina has a state in which the stool may be quite thin, yellow, fecal, which comes away in little bits of spurts; or it sometimes has the appearance that the peristalsis is reversed from straining. It seems to force it the wrong way. It does not do any good. A disorderly action of the rectum and anus. So, "diarrhœa when she urinates" is a symptom here, which I have expressed. "*Itching and burning excoriation and great sensitiveness of the anus.*" It has cured fistula in ano.

Now, these symptoms do not occur in *acute* sickness. When similar symptoms occur in acute sickness there are better remedies. But in *old, broken-down nervous constitutions*, those who have been getting sick and *progressing from bad to worse for some time.* Those who suffer from an *increasing debility*, from *loss of flesh*, from *loss of muscular power*, *loss of memory*, *loss of intellectual power.* Disturbance all through the nervous system. Going into a general break down. A general paralytic state.

Sexual Organs. Weakness of the male sexual organs, paralytic weakness. Of the female, the menstrual flow is scanty, pale and painful. After menses, exhausted in body and mind. That you would expect from the general nature of the medicine. At every menstrual crisis it seems to be that is all she can stand, and she dreads going through such another case. So exhausted, not from copious flow, but from nervousness. The general exhaustion. It is not a weakness from the copious flow, as in many remedies. Many remedies have great exhaustion from copious menstruation. But great exhaustion after scanty flow is a nervous exhaustion.

Copious leucorrhœa. Leucorrhœa is said to be so copious that it runs down the thighs when walking.

During pregnancy, and during the rearing of children these symptoms that I have already mentioned will bring to mind some important things. When you go to the bedside of a sickly baby, the nurse says, "Doctor, it never had a stool unless I gave it an injection" "Have you ever tried it?" Yes, she may say has tried. "Well, what did it do?" Then she will describe the action of the child when it had no injection. She will describe the little one getting into a sweat, it will strain and strain, and after a long time it passes with great difficulty a little soft stool. Alumina will cure that constipation pretty generally. You do not get a great many symptoms in infancy. And let me tell you another thing, the infant is much less complicated, has not taken so many drugs and can be cured much easier. When people have arrived at middle age and are greatly broken down with drugs you will have to select medicines far more carefully—that is, the medicine must be far more similar than in infancy. The infant, to a certain extent, resembles the animal more. Before its mind is cultivated and developed. And the more the mind is cultivated the more the system takes on, becomes complex, the greater degree of fineness, the higher degree of perception will be required to see with the eye of the artist and to individualize all of those medicines that seem to be quite similar. So with the horse, the cow, the animal, if you get a medicine that is partly similar to the complaints of the horse, if you get few symptoms and have to rely upon a few, you will cure the animal. So with the baby. But not so with highly wrought nervous people grown up, adult, middle age and advanced age. Take those highly wrought, nervous women, singers, artists, over sensitive ones. The selection here has to be the very choicest. They require ten times the care the farmer's wife does, though the latter appears to be equally nervous. Those who have undergone much strain, much worry and yet highly sensitive people, who have come down slightly from an elevated position, are harder to reach. They develop a complexity of the nervous system and of the nerve centers. Much more difficult to prescribe for. You can prescribe much more hastily for those of coarser fiber, who are not sensitive to every change of the weather and to every opinion of associates.

Full of dry cough, pain in the back, weakness in the limbs, disturbances of sleep, nervous exhaustion, nervous trembling, nervous weakness. But now you are prepared to read up as to the balance of these and make application of these principles.

J. T. Kent.

PULSATILLA—COMPARATIVE STUDY. (Concluded.)

For the past three months we have been making a study of the *particulars* of this remedy in comparison with a number of different remedies more or less intimately associated with Pulsatilla in some of its *peculiar* phases. This study has been *suggestive* instead of pretending to be complete in any of the details.

In this number we have endeavored to arrange a scheme whereby the *generals* of Pulsatilla may be selected at a moment's glance from which the *simillimum* may be found.

The *generals* and such *particulars* as seem to be most general in character are *alphabetically* arranged in the left hand column beginning with the mind. The *value* of each general being indicated by the type. In the parallel columns will be found twenty nine different remedies which are compared not only with reference to the *number* of generals in common, but also the *relative value* of each general. The study given to this comparison has been both interesting and profitable and a similar method may be adopted in analysis of different remedies.

With 42 *mental* and 35 *generals* Pulsatilla is given an aggregate value of 193; *Sulphur* 127; *Phosphorus* 118; *Lycopodium* 115; *Nux vomica* 111; *Calcarea carb.* 105; *Natrum mur* 104; *Arsenicum* 96; *Rhus* 94; *Sepia* 90; *Lachesis* 85; *Nitric ac.* and *Silecea* 83; *Ignatia* 81; *Graphites* 80.

Of the 35 *generals*, *Sulphur* has 30, *Phosphorus* 30, *Nux* 27, *Lycopodium* 27, *Sepia* 29, *Calcarea* 27, *Arsenicum* 26, and *Graphites* 25, while the remedies most frequently associated with Pulsatilla in its *particulars* have little in common, e. g. *Arg. n.* has 10, *Cimicifuga* 4, *Cyclamen* 9, *Lilium tig.* 5 and *Ipecac* only 20. Nearly the same results will follow the analysis in the *mental* generals. This shows the importance of securing a good foundation upon which the *particulars* are to be built, because the *generals* represent the *patient* while the *particulars* show the *effect* of environment. Each are important but the combination gives us the true *totality* upon which the *simillimum* must be based.

(The *italic* numerals indicate the limitation of our brevier figures and have no special significance).

PULSATILLA.

	Arg. n.	Arnica	Ars.	Calc.	Caust.	Cham.	China	Cimicif.	Cocc.	Conium	Cycl.	Ferr.	Gels.	Graph.	Ignatia	Ipecac.	Lach.	Lil. tig.	Lycopo.	Merc.	Nat. m.	Nit. ac.	Nux	Phos.	Puls.	Rhus.	Sepia	Silicea	Sulph.	Verat.
Absent Minded		2	1	1	3	3	1		2	1	1			2	3		3		2	3	3	1	1	1	3	1	3	1	1	3
Anxiety at night (fearful; timid)		1	3	2	2	3	3		1					3	2		3			2	2	2		1	3	1			3	1
" **during chill**																									3					
" *about future*				3	2		2						3	2			3				2		1	3	1					
Aversion to business										3							3								1					
" " *company*						3	2			3			3		2		2		3		3		3		1	1			1	
" " *life*			2	3			3										3		2		3	3	1	3	1	1		1	1	
" " **talking**		2	2		2		2	2					2		2				1		2	3	1	3	3	1		1	3	3
" " *work (mental)*							2											3	2		3	3	3	3	1	1		3	1	
Capricious			3			3																			1				3	
Confidence, want of							3												3						1			1		
Confusion after eating				2					2										3	2	3		1	2	3		1	1	1	
" *on waking*																	3		2						1				3	
Delusions (sees images etc.) on closing eyes																					2				1					
Despair	3		3	2	2				2	3				2	3		3	3	3		3	3			1	2			3	2
" *of salvation*			3	2													3	3	3						1				1	3
Discontent, dissatisfied, discouraged			2			2													3			1	1		1	2		3	3	
Dull, sluggish	2			3		2	3		2	3			3	2			3		3		3	1	1	3	3	1	3	3	1	3
Fear (compare, anxiety, frightened)	3		3	3	3				3	3			2	3	2				3		2		1		1	1			3	
" *nights*			2	2			3													2					1	3			3	
" *going into crowd*																			2		3				1					
" *death*		2	3	2	2			3	2		3		3				2		2			3	1	3	1	2				
" *insanity*				3				3						3				3		3	2		1	3	1					
" *people*																			3		2				1					
" *solitude*	3		2							3			3						2					3	1					
" **from fright**	3				3								3		3		3		3		2		1		3	2				
Grief (compare anxiety, weeping)					3									3	2		1		3		3				3					
Groaning						3			2						3	3							1		1					3
Hysterical—hypochondriasis	3		2	3	3	3		2	2	3		3	2	2	3			2	2	3	3	3	1	1	3	1	3	3	3	2
Indifference (apathy, indolence)	3	3	3	3		3	3		3	3	2		3	2	2		3	3	2	3	2	1		1	3		3	1	1	1
Irritable	2	3	3	3	3	3	3		3	2	2	2	2	2		2	2	3	3	2	3	3	1	1	3	3	3	3	3	3
" *during chill*			3	3	2					3									3			1			1				1	
Memory weak	3	1	2	3	2					3	3		3	2			3	3		3	2	1	1	3	1	1	3	1	1	3
Mildness		3	3	3				2							3			3	2		3	1		1	3	3	1	3		3
Morose		2								3	3					3			3	2			3		3				1	
Restless	3		3	2		3			2				3				3			3		1	1		3	3	1	1	3	
" **nights**					3	2					3				3				3					1	3	3	1		1	
Sadness, depression	2	3	3	3	3	3	3	1	3	3	3	3	3	3	3	2	3	3	3	3	3	3	1	1	3	3	1	2	3	3
" *during chill*							3			3	3			1	3			3			3				1					
Sensitive		3	2	2	2	2	3		2				3		3		2		3	2	2	1	3	1	1		1	1	2	
Suspicious		3	3		3				3								2		2	2		1		1	3	3	2		3	2

PULSATILLA.

	Arg. n.	Arnica	Ars.	Calc.	Caust.	Cham.	China	Cimicif.	Cocc.	Conium	Cycl.	Ferr.	Gels.	Graph.	Ignatia	Ipecac.	Lach.	Lil. tig.	Lycopo.	Merc.	Nat. m.	Nit. ac.	Nux	Phos.	Puls.	Rhus.	Sepia	Silicea	Sulph.	Verat.
Weeping				3	2	2		3				3		3	2			3	3		3	2	2	2	3	3	2		3	3
Air, desire for open		2																3	3		2				3				3	
Alternation of symptoms															2										2	1	1		1	
Anemia		2	3	2	2	1	3		3	3	2	3		3	2		2		1	3	3	3	3	3	3	2	2	1	3	1
Anxiety—physical	3		3	2		3	2		1	1		1			1	3			2	1	1		3	3	3	1			3	[illegible]
Asleep in parts		1	1	3	1	3	3		3	1		1		3	2	1			3	3	2	1	2	2	3	3	3	3	[illegible]	[illegible]
Band—sensation of—**internal**	2	1	1	1	1		2		2	3			1	2					1	2	3	3	1	3	3			3	3	
Bathing—refreshing			1		3	1																	1		3					
Bones softening				3								1				1			2	3		2		2	2		2	3	1	
Cold—tendency to take		1	1	3	1	3	1		1	3		1		1	1	1			1	3	2	3	3	2	3	3	2	3	[illegible]	
Congestion passive—venous		3			1		3		1		1			2			3		2		3	3	3	3	3	3	2	[illegible]	3	
Convulsions	2	2		3	3	2	1		2	2		1	3	2	3	2	1		1	1	3	1	3	3	3	1	1	[illegible]	[illegible]	[illegible]
" —epileptiform	3	1	3	3	3	2	1		3	1		1	3		1	2	2		3	1	2	2	3	1	3	1	2	[illegible]	3	1
" —*tetanic*		3	3	1	1	3			3	1			3		2	3	2		3	3			3	1	3	2	3		1	1
Distension bloodvessels		3	1	1			3			1	1	3		2			1		1		1		2	2	3	1	1	1	[illegible]	
Dropsy			3				3			3		3		3			2		3	3		3		1	3	1	3	1	[illegible]	[illegible]
Dryness—internal	2	3	3	3	1	2	1		2	1	1	1	2	2	1	1	3		2	2	3	2	3	3	2	3	3	[illegible]	3	3
Emaciation		1	3	2		2	3		2			3		3	2	2	2		3		3	3	3	3	2		1	3	3	[illegible]
" **of affected parts**			2											3							1	2		2	3		1	1		
Emptiness—sensation		1		1	1	1	1		3			1	1	1	3	1	1		1	1				3	3	2	3		1	1
Faintness	2	2	3	1	3	3	3	2	2		1	2	1	1	3	2	3	2	2	1	1	1	3	3	3		3	[illegible]	[illegible]	3
" **hot, close room**																2	2	1							3		2			
" **during labor**								3															3		3					
Formication		3	1	1	3	1	1		2	1		1		1	1	1	1		2	3	2	1	3	3	3	3	3	1	[illegible]	1
Hemorrhage passive—venous—dark	2	2	3	3	1	2	3		1	1				1	1	3	3		2	3	3	3	3	3	3	3	3	[illegible]	3	1
Heat—sensation	2		1	2	1		1		1		1			3	1	3	3			2	2		2	2	3	1			3	[illegible]
Heaviness		1	1	3	1	1	3		2	2		1	3	3	1	2	2		2	3	3	1	3	3	3	3	3	3	3	1
Induration		3	1	2	1	1	1			2	1	1		2	1				1	1			1	1	2		1	[illegible]	[illegible]	
" —**glands**		1	1	3	1	1	1		3	3	1	1		2	1				2	3		1	1	1	3	1	1	[illegible]	3	
Inflammation external—internal		1	3	3	1	3	1		1	1		1		1	1	1	3	1	3	3	1	1	3	3	3	3	1	3	[illegible]	[illegible]
Jerking—internal—muscles		1	1	3	1			3		1		2	1	1	1		2			2	1	1	2	3	3		3	[illegible]	3	
Mucous secretions increased	1	1	1	3	1	2	2		1	1		1		3	1	1	1		2	3	1	2	3	3	3	1	1	1	3	1
Numbness—external		1	1	1	1	2	1	1	3	3		1	3	3	2	1				1			1	3	3	2	3	[illegible]	1	1
" **affected parts**		1	1	1	1	3	1		2	2	1	1		1	1				2	1				1	3	3	1	1	1	1
Orgasm of blood	3	3	1	3	3	2	1		1	1		3	3	2	1		3	1	3	2	3	1	2	3	2	2	2	[illegible]	3	[illegible]
" " **after emotions**				1		3				3					3		2		1		1	2	3	2	3		[illegible]			1

H. W. Pierson.

SOUR STOMACH.

On page 212, second edition of "Leaders in Homœopathic Therapeutics," when writing on *Sulphuric acid*, I bring in by way of comparison *Robinia pseudo-acacia*. I refer to it here in order to impress upon my readers, that the remedies so introduced, are nevertheless very important ones, and though not treated separately are worth studying out more at length in many cases.

I have myself several times relieved this sometimes persistent and distressing symptom (sour stomach) in chronic dyspepsia where other remedies have signally failed. And with the removal of the *one symptom* have seen the patient generally improved.

Dr. Hunt in the New England *Medical Gazette* (vol. 6, page 12) says: "I have used the *Robinia pseudo acacia* with almost uniform success in acidity of the stomach, one drop of the tincture after meals."

Dr. E. T. Blake in the *Monthly Homœopathic Review* reports: "Constant dull headache < by motion and reading; at times dull *heavy aching distress in the stomach*, with sensation as if scalded; sour stomach every night preventing sleep." *Robinia* 6x cured.

Other cases might be quoted showing its efficacy in this connection.

Now some "key note charecteristic, one symptom admirer will exclaim, "Bully for Robinia," and "go for" the next sour stomach that dares to "sour on him," and very likely fail. Why? Because it was not the remedy that covered the case in its *totality*.

What about the other remedies that have the same symptoms as prominently as this? Such as *Sulphuric acid*, *Natrum phos.*, *Phosphorus*, *Ferrum phos.*, *Carbo. veg.*, *China*, *Lycopodium*, *Iris ver.*, *Magnesia carb.*, *Nux vomica*, *Calc. ost.*, and many others that might be added to this list.

The truth is in regard to *Robinia*, that while it has done some *good work* in sour stomach, it is not so well developed either in proving or clinical use as it should be to enable us to prescribe it with the accuracy of the other remedies. Here is a good field for exploration. After all, this does not bar its use if the others have failed. Many remedies have come to be known and taken their place to stay in our armamentarium in just this way.

Now we are on this subject, let us look at some of the above mentioned remedies for a moment. *Sulphuric acid* is particularly efficacious in three kinds of cases. First, in marasmic children with *sour stomach*, sour vomiting, and generally sour condition. *The child smells sour all over*, despite the greatest care in regard to cleanliness.

Second. In greatly weakened cachectic subjects who complain of a *sense of weakness and internal trembling*. This is subjective, for there is no actual trembling. Such cases are very apt to have indigestion and sour stomach, as I have observed.

Third. In old "topers," broken down constitutions as well as stomach troubles. This remedy has done wonders in such cases, especially in whiskey drinkers. *Natrum phos.*, one of Schussler's tissue remedies is also a good one for this acid condition of the stomach. I have greatly benefited some very intractable cases with it.

It has a very characteristic symptom, which if found in connection with the sour stomach indicates it before every other remedy, viz: *Tongue coated thickly yellow at the base*. It has a creamy look and may involve the roof of the mouth. It is noteworthy that *Kali bi.* which has a similar tongue is one of our best remedies for the dyspepsia of *beer drinkers.* (See Leaders 114). *Natrum phos.* will sometimes succeed where one might be led to *Sulph. acid* or *Rheum*, because it also, in a degree at least, has the sour smell of the body too.

Phosphorus, is also a royal remedy in sour stomach. It goes very deeply, and the temperament must come into the calculations, like *Calc. ost.*, *Sulph.* and the other temperamatic remedies. I have oftenest found it efficacious in chronic cases; and especially in aged people, where it often performs wonders.

The affection may range from simple acid conditions, to the worst malignant form of stomach trouble. There may be vomiting of many kinds and colors. Characteristic indications are: First, hungry or *weak feeling* in the stomach. Second, *wants cold things like Pulsatilla*; but, Third, as soon as they *become warm in the stomach* are vomited.

Ferrum phos. has similar sourness or sour stomach, or sour eructations, and is especially useful in subjects of the *Ferrum* constitution or temperament summed up in one word, *anæmic*.

Carbo veg., *China* and *Lycopodium* are all flatulent remedies, and in cases of sour stomach troubles this flatulent condition will almost always "stand-out" in the stomach or abdomen or both. Of course as is well known, *Carbo veg.* floats in stomach or upper abdomen. *Lycopodium* the lower, and *China* both. These three remedies are well proven and have their strict individuality as regards constitution and temperament, which must never be ignored. To undertake to fully compare even these three remedies would be to go over again what has been done in "Leaders," and even more.

In *Iris ver.*, the substance vomited is very *sour*, (so sour it sets the teeth on edge. *Sulph. ac.*) Burning in the alimentary tract is characteristic, from mouth to anus. (*Ars.* and *Caps.*)

Flow of saliva is also characteristic and it is of a stringy, slimy variety, like *Kali bich.*

Magnesia carb. especially useful in children, with *sour stomach*, stool and whole body smell sour, and especially if there is sour stool and much colic.

Nux vomica, like *Pulsatilla* is oftenest found useful in recent cases caused by errors in diet; but one can never take the place of the others. Individualization is necessary here as elsewhere.

Calcarea ost. Leucophlegmatic temperament. Everything in the whole intestinal tract seems sour. Eructations sour, vomiting sour, large sour curds. (*Aethusa*). Sour diarrhœa, but concomitants, temperament and constitutions more than all decide for this remedy.

But my article is growing too long, longer than I intended when I began. But I wanted to call attention to what I stated at the beginning, viz: that the remedies not appearing in the text, worked out under their repective names, were really valuable nevertheless, and should be studied as in the case of *Robinia*. All who possess "Leaders" will see that I have done little more than quote and re-arrange under this single symptom of sour stomach, which is after all *only* a symptom, but many times an important one.

Cortland, N. Y. E. B. Nash.

NATRUM MUR.—EUPATORIUM PERF.—MALARIA.

Miss M. W., age 30 years.

Oct. 16, 1901. "Chills and fever" last week; had an attack last June, as also in childhood. She now fears that another attack is about to come, is feeling so "miserable" and has a "numb headache."

, The treatment thus far has been quinine in the hands of an allopathic family physician. The quinine "poisoned" her, though, and another prescription was given (she knows not what) and the chills stopped.

History of the June attack is as follows: (the childhood attack she can remember nothing of)

Chill each day about 10 a. m.; preceded by headache and icy coldness of hands.

During chill, aching in bones, pain in back; pain in "bowels;" and *thirst* for *ice cold* drinks.

After chill; fever "high" followed by sweat; thirst for cold drinks in both stages.

History of present attack or rather "last week" attack:

Chill each day about 2 a. m. postponing half an hour or an hour each time, preceded by "hive-like" eruption (which only appeared after the quinine had been used).

During chill; aching in bones; pain in back;and thirst for cold drinks.

After chill; fever "high" and sweat, with thirst for cold drinks.

Physician's soliloquy: ———"Rather a mixed up case! Not very clear for any one remedy, though it looks somewhat like several. But here sits the patient; she has told you she is a dressmaker with a family to help support; she cannot afford to be ill any longer, has heard you can cure "chills" without quinine and so she has come to be "cured right off." The physician turns to the patient: "Now, Miss W., you want to be cured, you say?" "Yes doctor" says the patient, "right away." "You shall be cured," says the doctor, "but it will need a little patience, your case has been badly muddled by the quinine, and the quinine poisoning, as well as by the other prescription you used to break up your chills; we shall have to straighten out things first and then we will cure you. Do you understand?" "Yes, doctor, but I shant have any more chills, shall I, because you know I must get back to work?"

The physician explains matters and the patient consents to bear the results of the "straightening out" process!

Physician soliloquizing again: ——— "Taking into account the old school dosing (quinine etc) the *chill coming on at 10 a. m.* (about), the *thirst for cold drinks* in all stages, which constituted the primary attack (in June). Natrum mur. stands out strongly and it has all the headache and aching bones, etc."

Therefore *Natrum mur*[cm] goes on the patient's tongue.

Oct. 18.

"Chill" 6 a. m., yesterday; "a good hard shake for an hour and a half"

Headache.

< right side.

After chill—fever, not much sweat, *no thirst* with either stage.

Oct. 22.

"Chill" about 9 a. m. on the 19th inst. and again on the 21st.

After chill, fever and free sweat; very little thirst.

Headache.

< right temple.

Aching in back, intense and much aching in bones.

Physician's soliloquy:——— "Things are a little more orderly now for a prescription. The *chill comes at 9 a. m.; every other day; aching in bones* very marked, as also *backache*; the thirst is indefinite to be sure, but rather think upon close questioning, there is thirst, but a dread of drinking because of discomfort from it. *Eup. perf.* heads the list. Therefore *Eup. perf.*[cm]

Oct. 24.

Had a "chill" yesterday at 9 a. m.; less severe; but little fever following.

Eup. perf.[cm]

Oct. 28.

On the 25th felt a slight coldness, no other feeling of discomfort.

Has had no suspicion of a chill since then.

Feeling very well today.

Nov. 6.

Menses due yesterday, have not appeared yet.

On the 31st (which would be a third period for a chill since last feeling of coldness (Oct. 25th), had aching in limbs and backache, no sign of chill or fever.

Feels tired and "all gone."

Appetite poor.

Eup. perf.[cm]

Since the above report, the patient has been seen many times, not as a patient but through casual meetings; and at last meeting (Jan. 11th) she was feeling and looking very well. The menstrual period came a day or so after the last prescription of *Eup. perf.* and there has been a steady gain in every way since then.

S. Mary Ives.

Sepia—Sulphur—Malaria.

Mabel J., age 7 years.

Oct. 23, 1901. Tall, fair child, blue eyes; well built, but restless and languid in manner; skin a deep yellow; heavy rings under eyes.

"Chills and fever" for past three weeks; used to come every other day, now daily.

Chill commences about 3 to 4 p. m. used to come earlier.

After chill, fever and some sweat; but little thirst now, used to have much thirst.

Treatment—Quinine at first; past week one of "Humphrey's specifics."

Abdomen swollen and tense pain in back and legs.

Has emaciated since sick.

Urine "dark, reddish in color."

Moans in sleep and very restless.

The child is a hypersensitive little girl; cannot go to school or go anywhere in a crowd.

Sepia[cm]

Oct. 25

A pretty hard chill on the 23d, and another yesterday, "like she had when they first started;" a slight chill today, but not nearly so bad.

Used to sweat much as a baby; also now at times.

Craves sours, but especially sweet things.

Very nervous.

Nov. 2d.

Slight chilliness for few days after above; now has "blueness" about 1 p. m. each day; sleeps and wakes up crying.

Craving sweet things.

Irritable and fretful.

Sulph.[cm]

Jan. 2d, 1902.

"Much > in every way."

(Weekly reports since Nov. 2d fully justify this statement).

Appetite good.

Sleeping well.

Wants to go to school.

Jan. 14.

Still better; "wants some more powders, that's all."

Moral—Don't resort to Quinine and

"Humphrey's specifics" when you can get the indicated remedy.

In this case, there was the history of indefinite, long lingering "malaria;" the keen edge of the trouble had worn off, partially suppressed too by the quinine and "Humphrey's." The *Sepia* stepped in and brought back the original manifestation with relief to the economy. It also controlled that manifestation in its severity and opened up the way for the constitutional remedy, which proved itself to be *Sulphur*. The child at this writing (Jan. 22d) is a bright, healthy looking girl, full of fun and good humor.

S. Mary Ives.

From the Clinics of Dunham Medical College.

A CASE FOR LILIUM TIGRINUM.

Mrs. L. G., age 29, brown hair, dark eyes, face pale.

Very nervous < when tired.

Irritable; at times much depressed; sympathy aggravates; inclined to cry.

Pain in forehead over the eyes, often over one eye at a time.

< warm weather.

Palpitation < exertion.

Heart—pain as if squeezed.

< in morning.

Vertigo < stooping.

Stomach—sourness and belching.

< greasy foods.

Craves hot drinks.

Averse to sweets.

Constipation—stool large, hard; alternating with diarrhœa.

Diarrhœa—stool dark brown, frothy; lumpy at times.

Hemorrhoids which bleed some.

Menses very scanty, bright red then almost black; are very offensive.

Constant bearing down sensation in vagina, < when on feet.

< during menses.

Has had two miscarriages.

Leucorrhœa profuse, thick, greenish, acrid, causing itching.

Lower extremities—varicose veins, very troublesome after confinement.

Sleep—lies on stomach during sleep.

Dreams of friends who have died.

Anamnesis.

(a) Generals.

Sadness < consolation: *Bell.*, *Calc. p.*, Ign., *Lil. t.*, Nat. m., *Plat.*, Sep., Sil.

Menses scanty: *Ign.*, *Lil. tig.*, Nat. m., *Nit. ac.*, Sep., Sil.

—— dark: *Bell.*, *Calc. p.*, *Ign.*, *Lil. t.*, Nat. m., *Nit. ac.*, Plat., *Sepia*.

—— offensive: Bell., Calc. p., *Ign.*, *Lil. t.*, Nit. ac., *Plat.*, *Sil.*

Remedies running through all rubrics: Ign. 9; Lil. t., 8; Nit. ac., 7

—— through three rubrics: Calc. p., 5; Bell., 7; Plat., 7; Sil. 7.

(b) Particulars.

Bearing down sensation in pelvis: Bell., Ign., *Lil. t.*, Nit. ac., Plat., Sep.

Pelvis < during menses: *Bell.*, *Ign.*, *Lil. t.*, *Nit. ac.*, Plat., *Sep.*

Squeezing sensation in region of heart: *Ign.*, *Lil. tig.*, Nat. m., Nit. ac.

Constipation alternating with diarrhœa: *Ign.*, Lil. t., *Nat. m.*, Nit. ac., Sep.

Aug. 10, 1901.

Lil. tig^{m} and Sac. lac.

Sept. 25.

All symptoms were better but now returning.

Lil. tig^{m}

Nov. 25.

Leucorrhœa >

Scarcely any bearing down.

Headaches >

Sac. lac.

Bowels regular.

Dec. 10.

Bad spell with heart; could scarcely move.

Pain near left ovary.

Menses have been lighter in color; now dark again.

Leucorrhœa <

Lil. tig^{m}

Dec. 20.

Feeling better than ever before.

Sac. lac.

Dec. 31.

Somewhat stouter.

Face now wears a good color.

Leucorrhœa only after menses, and then only once or twice a day.

Sac. lac.

Hæmorrhoids gone.

HARVEY FARRINGTON.

Surgery.

MEDICINAL THERAPEUTICS IN SURGICAL CASES.

While it is true that the development of surgery in our branch of the medical fraternity has removed a reproach formerly attaching us as a class, yet it has had no small influence in exposing us to a reproach of quite another character, viz. the neglect of using the indicated remedy in cases readily curable, and a decadence in our skill as prescribers. In fact we have, unintentionally, arrested the development of homœopathic therapeutics. The transgressor here, or at least quite often, is not the surgeon, but his non surgical colleague. The whole medical world, yes and outside of it too, has for some years gone mad on the subject of operative surgery. Both lay and secular press has aided in this, until the ambition of most medical men is to be considered "surgeons." Happily, and none too soon, a reaction is setting in, and the amateur "surgeons" are slowly becoming convinced that specialism is a genuine necessity, and that no man can be *both* a surgeon and a general practitioner. But during the life of this fast declining craze much injury was done to both surgery and general medicine from lost opportunity. I have now been teaching surgery for nearly thirty years, and in that time have been called upon to make thousands of operations in clinical teaching. Two things have been borne in on me by this experience: One is wonder that any one was ever foolish enough to put his life in my hands, when I recall some earlier performances; the other is that probably a few years hence my present work will look to me as "impossible."

The same fact, however, both formerly and now, is still a potent one. I am handicapped by being robbed at times, of freedom of choice. Doctors bring cases to my clinic not for advice, and such treatment as I might prefer, *but for an operation!* They have, thanks to the prevailing craze, lost all conception of other methods of treatment. What! *prescribe* for an appendicitis? Absurd! The patient, filled with distorted interpretation of semi-professional literature, mind occupied with corruptions of the newspaper writer and fortified by the statements of friends, and doctors as well, not *experts* on operation, he will doubt the skill and knowledge (or courage) of the clinical teacher if he suggests some less formidable procedure.

More than this, the class, the students, they expect an operation. What a position the teacher finds himself in! He may *know*, as many of us do, that remedies can cure this case, he is not allowed to demonstrate it. He may desire to *test* the matter at least in certain other cases, but doctor, patient, and class say him nay. Of course if an operation is not capital in its nature, or contra-indicated, no great harm is done, perhaps, in yielding to the pressure. Under other circumstances of course the clinician has his own way. It must not be supposed that we are forced to make *useless* operations, for we do not yield to such pressure; we are simply restricted in our choice, as to two methods. This is not an exaggeration.

I lost my chair in a school some years ago, not from my inefficiency as a teacher, not from unsuccessful clinical work, but simply and solely because more cases were not operated upon. This is a fact.

So, rightly or wrongly, I have been a sinner. Believing with all my heart and mind, and with ample clinical experience to justify it, that many cases commonly operated upon could be cured by the indicated remedy, I have conformed to the teaching and prejudice of the times, and missed an opportunity to develope homœopathic therapeutics. All this was not in my mind, when I sat down to answer your letter, Mr. Editor, and it has quite exhausted the space given me. But I will let it go, nevertheless, as it is a confession that may do some good, and let us hope, assist us to hasten the recovery from the operation craze.

JAMES G. GILCHRIST.
Iowa City, Ia.

POST TRAUMATIC DISEASE CURED BY INDICATED REMEDY.

On April 25, 1901, a Miss D., age 30 years, small in stature, dark hair and eyes, sparely built, weak voice, very timid, and disposed to all sorts of fears, called at my office and told the following symptoms, for which she desired medicine.

She complained of much pain in left side, in region of the heart.

Pains were sharp and quick.

Pains came on whether she moved or not.

Often woke her out of a sound sleep.

She feels very weak.

Loss of energy.

Tires easily.

Has much headache, < in wind, < noise.

Gets very sick at the stomach at times.

Complains of much pain, at times, on right side, beginning in right ear, passing down into the throat, and involving the right side of her back.

Hands and feet always cold.

The least excitement causes headache.

Was often taken with paroxysms of vomiting that lasted for several days and nights.

Always < in winter and spring.

Bowels constipated — must often take something to evacuate them.

Menses only 25 days apart.

Suffers much pain at menstrual epoch.

Has much pain about two weeks after menstruating, always at night.

Discharges clots and threds with flow.

"Runs down" in winter.

Feet and hands perspire freely, but are cold.

Much backache.

Such was the case as presented at that time. In talk with the patient, I learned that *nausea* was one of the most, if not the most distressing symptom of which she complained. Something had to be done at once, so, before looking up the case in my repertory, I prescribed *Ipecac*[cm] three powders, one powder to be taken each evening on retiring, and a liberal *Placebo* to be taken every three hours.

May 10. Miss D. reported:

Pains in the shoulders.
Felt very tired this morning.
Nerves tingle.
Great weakness.
Nausea better.
Weak feelings come over me.
Dream much, usually scream or call for help in my sleep.
Always have headache just before menses.

She then told a history of peculiar traumatism. When she was a girl she called on one of her neighbors and was met in the yard by a large dog, which angrily leaped on her, striking her in the left side, and biting her repeatedly through her clothes, though inflicting no flesh wounds. The shock and injury were so severe that she was sick for a long time. She was then sent to Philadelphia where she was under treatment for one year without very much improvement. Then to Pittsburg, where she took treatment with like results. She then came west with her sister, hoping a change of climate would improve her condition. This was of no avail. The pains in her side continued. Sometimes they would extend into the pelvic regions and at times would resemble ovarian neuralgia; but the symptoms were not clear enough to conclude that such was indeed the case.

In short, all her symptoms seem to have resulted from fright and injury. Basing my opinion upon this hypothesis, I gave her one powder of *Arnica* the 200th and a *Placebo*, and requested her to report in two weeks. I saw nothing of her until June 1, when she reported her condition as very much improved. There was still some headache, and the menses had been a trifle early, but her general condition was very much better.

In July she was suddenly taken with an attack of malarial fever, when a peculiar loquacious delirium developed. She complained of nothing particularly at my first call but fever, yet her talking was so peculiar. I prescribed for her conditions and reduced the fever, but on my second call she seemed to mistake me for the old doctor in Pennsylvania, and began to laugh and joke and ask all sorts of questions about the folks at home, and about my girl—when I was to be married etc. On inquiry I learned she had been on a "tantrum" all night, spoke freely of her love affairs, though otherwise a very modest young lady, and the family with whom she was stopping was in a state of extreme excitement. They thought she would surely die. I talked with her a few moments, took part in her jokes to see how far she was delirious, then took from my case a vial of *Stramonium* the cm potency, placed a powder on her tongue, which she thought was very *sweet* of me to do, and then waited. She soon became quiet and I went about my business stating I would call again in a few hours. When I returned her mind was perfectly clear, she had no recollection of having seen me during the day, and said she felt very much better. I gave her a *Placebo*, and she continued to improve and in a few days was at her task of light art work. I repeated the *Arnica* in Sept., though there was no pain whatever, and the young lady has grown stronger ever since. When last seen just before the holidays, she was still growing stronger and is now taking lessons in art in Chicago.

There was really no necessity to repeat the *Arnica*, but because her pains were worse in winter than in summer, I supposed it might serve as a prophylactive which it seems to have done most effectually. I used no local treatments whatever, preferring to keep my case as clear as possible, in order to meet any turn the disease might take. Though given to doubt the efficiency of homœopathic remedies, after so many years of heroic treatment, she is now one of the most ardent admirers of the new system I have found for sometime.

There are so many things to be learned from a case like this, but I will waive the usual exhortation and permit the reader to form his own conclusions.

G. E. Dienst.

ENDOMETRITIS.*

In the region that is now the state of Washington, some hundreds of thousands of years ago, a great upheaval of nature formed the Cascade range of mountains, whose towering peaks catch the moisture borne on the chinook winds from the Pacific ocean, and make one-half of the state wet and the other half dry. In the same age and possibly at the same time, another upheaval occurred, where the long neck of Idaho stretches up between Washington and Montana, shaping the main ridge of the Rockies, and thus forming a vast basin between these two majestic ranges.

Some time after that, volcanic action occurred to the south, in the region of the present state of Oregon. Here poured forth the molten, hot, liquid, seething lava, in a stream, compared with which, that over flow seventeen centuries ago, which buried the cities of Pompeii and Herculaneum, was but a trickle down a window pane compared with the great Amazon. This stream, two hundred miles wide and more than that number of feet deep, flowed north, filling the basin between the two great ranges with liquid fire. Gradually this cooled and solidified into basaltic rock. As it grew colder, like all mineral substances, it contracted in volume, and shrank and broke away from the western side of the basin, leaving a deep crack along the irregular foot of the Cascades. Down this crevice now flows in smooth and winding current, or tumbles in mad and whirling rapids, the majestic Columbia, that river which, in places, literally stands on edge, being deeper than it is wide.

One summer's day I sat upon a projecting point of this basaltic rock and, marveling at the stupendous forces of Nature, gazed across the Columbia upon the vast piles of granite, towering up before me. As I watched and marveled, there arose from a pinnacled rock like a kite wafted before the wind, an eagle, that mounted in circles higher and higher, till it seemed as if he were about to build his nest amongst the clouds. Suddenly, like a thunderbolt from the heavens, he dropped straight, as if to plunge into the river, when, suddenly turning as he snatched his prey, he skimmed the surface of the water, and again, with the spray tipping his pinions, arose, till all that could be seen of him was the glistening in the sun of his broad wings.

We all have seen the gynæcological surgeon soar into heights more sublime than that of the eagle's flight. We have seen him descend almost to the level of a beast of plunder, and, from a river of

*Read before the Englewood Homœopathic Medical Society.

blood, with the cardinal fluid dripping from his finger ends, we have seen him snatch his prey in the form of a diseased ovary or a displaced uterus. The one he carried away, the other he fastened, as a spider might fasten a fly, for his future plunder. But, as the patient, who was borne out limp but living, proceeded to convalescence, the surgeon has again reached those dizzy heights where all we could see was his glistening fame shining in the light of modern surgery.

Let us descend from these lofty heights and wend our course, for a time, along a more humble path—a less pretentious way, by which pass the vaster stream of suffering women, and let us see if possible how, by gentler means, this class, that should ever be the object of our commiseration and our best thought, may not only be relieved of its pains and distress, but ofttimes cured of its ills.

Let me not be mistaken. I would not have you think I hold the fame of the surgeon of as little consequence as the glisten of the eagle's plumage in the sun. As the eagle, from his lofty perch, may more clearly discern the hiding place of his normal prey, and, as we admire him as he hovers among the clouds, we name him King of birds. So, as the surgeon can sometimes uncover what is hidden to the eye of the materia medicist, and, with a brilliant sweep of the knife, can remove a death carrying organ, we crown him imperial in the medical sciences. And, too, as the cunning fox skirting along the foot of the turreted heights, in his more humble way, tracks unerringly, with his pointed nose, the trail of the object of his hunt, so the materia medicist, with cunning questions and deep insight into the causes of disease, may certainly trace them to their source and prescribe the appropriate homœopathic remedy that will abate the pain, dissipate the disease and rejoice the patient, leaving her well and whole. But, as the fox, in his cunning, casts merely a glance at the seagull that is beyond his reach, so should the materia medicist, with certain judgment, be able to discern the purely surgical case, and giving it only a passing thought, leave it to the man with the knife.

It would take up too much of the valuable time of one evening of this Society's meetings to take you on a hunt after all the gynæcological "game in the wind" for the general practitioner. I shall be content if we run to earth one of the enemies of our sister beings. I have reference to hydra-headed monster—the *bete noir* of the gynæcologist, endometritis. Nor shall I expect to effect any extensive decapitation of the monster. I shall be satisfied to lop off one head, and leave it to some better steel than mine to administer the *coup de grace.*

The most frequent form of the disease is simple, non-septic, non-specific endometritis. It is usually symptomatic, seldom acute, and may be either atrophic or hypertrophic. The latter form is usually associated with those conditions that are characterized by general enlargement of the uterus, such as subinvolution, retro displacement, and fibroid; while the atrorhic form has for its chief cause imperfect development, with or without ante-flexion.

In the one there is an increase of the size, as well as frequently of the number, of the blood vessels, the follicles, and the lymph-spaces; the epithelium is thickened; there is general increased growth, often extending to the connective tissue. In the other there is general decrease of these tissues, except with the connective tissue, which may be very much relatively increased, constricting or totally destroying glands and ducts.

That we may treat successfully two such opposite conditions, though each is classed under the head of simple endometritis, it would seem necessary to be able to intelligently differentiate them.

For this purpose not always is it convenient or possible to use the curette and the microscope. Indeed more frequently must the general practitioner do without these means of diagnosis.

Fortunately we may well do so. The symptoms are usually characteristic. Bimanual examination reveals the primary lesion causing the respective conditions. Retro-displacements, particles of retained placenta, polypi, are producers of hypertrophied membrane. Here the menstrual flow will be increased in time and duration.

There may also be intermenstrual bleedings. The sound readily produces bleeding. The internal os is often exquisitively sensitive. The depth of the uterus is increased. The cervical mucus is tenacious and often milky. There is much leucorrhœa following the menses, especially if there are fungosities or polypi, or if portions of retained decidual membrane have formed excrescences.

Anteflexion, most frequently the result of imperfect development of the anterio-corpo-cervical region, and imperfect development without flexion, are frequent prime causes of atrophic endometritis. With the atrophied membrane the dysmenorrhœa is apt to be excessive, the pains commencing a few hours before the menstrual flow is established. This must be distinguished from ovarian dysmenorrhœa, where the pains precede the flow one to three days. The flow is scanty, often intermitting and in clots. The nervous reflexes are excessive, but the backache and "bearing down" are less prominent than in the hypertrophic variety, while sterility is more frequent.

If we could stop here—if this were all, the treatment of simple endometritis would be as easy as its name implies. Unfortunately these diagnostic causes and symptoms are only superficial. We must not pass over the too frequently unrecognized cause. Of not a little importance, even in these later days of advancement, I am sorry to say, are the results coming from the various maltreatments of surgeons and pseudo-surgeons as well as of general practitioners. One is horrified to think that the most unscientific treatment with the chloride of zinc pencil and fuming nitric acid is still in vogue amongst not only a large number of the rank and file, but also some of the authorities of the old school—and, must I confess it, some of our own school—poor imitators. As you will not forget the atrophic endometritis of the worst and most intractable form following this treatment, remember the frequency of the septic variety resulting from the use of carbolic acid and iodized phenol following curettement.

But let us go back on this trail. We are getting dangerously near the domain of surgery.

The very earliest history of these cases is often the most interesting and important to the general practitioner, and especially to the homœopathician. It would seem a waste of time to call attention to such frequently observed causes of the complaint under consideration as improper clothing about the waist of women and the legs of girls, insufficient neither protection, indiscreet habits, torpidity of the bowels, the laxative and purgative habit, all tending to produce pelvic congestion. Repeated pelvic congestion may, and does produce, first, simple congestive dysmenorrhœa, and later, gradually increasing endometritis, most often commencing as a slight endocervical catarrh. So, also, violent exercise during the menses (active congestion) and indolent lethargy of daily life (passive congestion). Masturbation—what shall I say of it? Nothing. It is a thread bare subject. But, keep it in mind, aye, keep it in mind. For this, more than any other one thing, is the cause, not only of the disease considered in this paper, but a hundred and one other ailments of the human female. Not only do I mean the innocent titillation of the little girl of three to five summers, or the profounder effect of the habit of her sister of thrice the age, but also the masturbation of the belly-dance of the weekly dance hall, and the masturbation of the married woman whose score of schemes she adopts to prevent pregnancy. We must not forget in this place to consider a prime factor in all these cases. It lies at the bottom of all the others. The constitutional discrasia. Do what you will, surgically, locally, internally, externally, you will get no *permanent* results if you forget the constitution and the constitutional remedy; if, while looking at the uterus, you forget the *patient*. You may relieve a nasal catarrh by cutting, burning and spraying. But in a year the trouble will have returned if the soil upon which the catarrh was first built is forgotten. Equally true, and for exactly the same reason, is it with uterine catarrh.

My excuse for dwelling so long upon, or even mentioning these well known causes of endometritis is because, while so understood in theory they are so seldom recognized in practice, because the advance in minor gynæcology so far lags behind that of all other branches of medicine and surgery, and because I believe the reason for this latter is to be found in the lack of adaptability of the treament to the special case in hand.

Only one more, so far as I know, unrecognized cause of simple endometritis will I mention. It is that of feeding. Do you expect to cure snuffles in a baby, you stop stuffing it. Do you hope to cure a hypertrophic catarrh in the pursy glutten, you regulate his diet; an atrophic catarrh in the walking corpse, you feed it. If your girl is overloaded with buckwheat cakes and syrup, chocolates and bon bons, ice creams and sodas, so that her tongue in the morning looks like the rough side of a tanned buckskin, and her breath is like the distal end of a sewer, while she has the snuffles at every breath of air, and coughs at the advent of every east wind, you cannot expect to cure her uterine catarrh, more than you can expect to cure her nasal, bronchial or gastric catarrh under the same conditions.

In this connection I wish to mention the effect of tea. In the backache of girls, enquire about the amount of tea drunk. You may find about the following history: Tea, backache, spinal irritation, general nervousness, functional dysmenorrhœa, cervitis. Not all tea drinkers will be thus affected, any more than all coffee drinkers will have headache, or all smokers will have tobacco heart. But I give you the hint, and ask you to watch future current medical literature, for lately I have seen some positive evidence that a few others are beginning to see the effects of tea on some of their female patients.

JAMES W. HINGSTON.

Nursing.*

Lecture No. 1.

Ladies: In this course of lectures we shall confine ourselves, as far as possible, to the consideration of the duties of the nurse in Obstetrical Nursing.

Obstetrical nursing is that branch of the art of caring for the sick which includes the nursing of the mother during pregnancy, parturition and the puerperal state, and also the care of the child.

It demands some knowledge of natural pregnancy and of the signs of accidents and diseases which may occur during pregnancy. It also requires knowledge and experience in the care of the patient during the labor and during her complete recovery, with the needs of her child. The obstetric nurse must also know how to help patient and doctor in the accidents and complications of labor, and has an important part to play in caring for mother and child in the diseases which occasionally attack them during the puerperal period. As wounds occur during labor, and as operations must often be performed during or immediately after labor, a thorough knowledge and drill in asepsis and antisepsis is absolutely indispensable.

To nurses gifted with good health and strength, who have opportunities for proper training and experience, and who are naturally fond of young children, obstetric nursing offers an exceedingly interesting and very lucrative branch of your professional work.

By the term "pregnancy" is understood the presence of the impregnated serum within the body of the mother.

Impregnation may occur in the fallopian tubes, and very rarely in the bursted sac of the ovary.

When the impregnated serum has lodged in has womb and develops there to maturity, the pregnancy is said to be normal, intra uterine, or eutopic.

When the impregnated serum remains in the fallopian tube or escapes thence into the abdomen or into the pelvis, the pregnancy is said to be abnormal, extrauterine, or ectopic.

Very often the expectant mother will consult a nurse before she engages her physician. One of the first things she will want to know is whether pregnancy exists, and you will need to be able to help her form an opinion. How shall you do this? By the signs of pregnancy, as they occur in the majority of cases.

The signs of pregnancy are classified as *relative* or *presumptive*, and positive and demonstrable signs. Upon one, or upon a number of the former, nothing more substantial, affirmatively, than probabilities of various degrees of strength can be predicated.

There are four signs which may be regarded as positive, namely, fœtal movements, ballottement, the sounds of the fœtal heart and recurrent uterine contractions.

In the diagnosis of pregnancy, subjective symptoms should receive due consideration, but objective symptoms must constitute your main reliance.

Items of importance may be gathered from a recital of the *history of the case*, which should include an account of the

*Course of Lectures delivered to the Nurses Training School at Maryland Homœopathic Hospital, by M. S. Douglass, M. D., Baltimore, Md.

mode of development, and the order in which the various observable and sensible signs were manifested.

The menstrual flow ought to be carefully inquired after. There may have been a regular return of it throughout the supposed pregnancy; or there may have been cumplete suppression. Should the former condition prevail, it will justly arouse suspicion. In that case, ascertain wherein the catamenia deviate from a normal standard. If menstruation has ceased, learn the circumstances under which it disappeared, and the peculiarities, if any, which characterised the last two or three "periods."

It is not very uncommon for a woman to menstruate once, twice or three times after impregnation, and cases are recorded wherein the catamenia returned with regularity throughout the full term.

Morning sickness—a sign of some value—is largely subjective, and concerning it strict inquiry should be made. When was it first felt? At what times, and under what circumstances, was it most troublesome? How long did it last?

When *quickening* is alleged to have taken place, try to fix the date, and the precise sensations experienced.

All of these symptoms are extremely liable to be misconstrued or misrepresented through either the woman's untruthfulness or mistaken convictions.

For our diagnosis we must depend, then, almost wholly on objection symptoms. The same common means of investigation are available here as in other cases where physical examination is required. They are, inspection, palpation (including "the touch."), percussion, and auscultation.

Inspection will aid very materially, in perplexing cases, in forming a correct conclusion. The abdominal contour of a woman who has reached the fifth month of gestation is quite diagnostic, even when purposely obscured to a certain degree by the apparel. The observer is often able, by inspection of it, to differentiate between pregnancy and simulating conditions. The precise outline of the gravid abdomen varies, but within limits which make all cases quite similar. As we take lateral view of a pregnant woman, the abdominal enlargement is seen not to be equable, but its point of greatest projection is near its superior boundary. This peculiarity becomes more and more characteristic as pregnancy advances.

This lateral view is of considerable value in the diagnosis of pregnancy.

A front view also of the abdominal tumor, taken when the woman is either standing or lying, reveals diagnostic characters, more marked in the erect posture. First shall be observed the absence of prominences and irregularities. It is not uncommon to find a difference between the two sides in point of fulness, but the elevation is not confined to a circumscribed area. This is generally due to presence of the fœtal trunk. Then, too, the tumor arising from pregnancy is narrower, and more prominent along the middle line than is a pathological enlargement.

During the first few weeks of uterogestation the abdomen, instead of being more prominent, is really retracted or flattened, and especially in the umbilical region. The uterus, from its uncommon weight, sinks in the pelvic cavity to an unnatural level, and in doing so drags upon the bladder, which in turn, through the urachus, causes the retraction mentioned.

Along a narrow line, extending from the embilicus to the pubus, there is darkening, the shades varying from light brown to black.

Foctal movements are often discernible. They are sometimes closely simulated by spasmodic muscular action, when as a means of differentiation, palpation affords positive aid.

Inspection of the breasts is a valuable means of diagnosis. The appearance known as the "secondary areola of Montgomery" should receive special attention. Briefly stated, it looks as though the color had then been discharged by a shower of drops. The appearance is due to the presence of enlarged sebaceous follicles devoid of pigment.

The purplish hue in the vaginal mucous membrane must be seen to be known, but when once familiar to the eye, will afford considerable aid.

Abdominal palpation alone is sufficient, in many ambiguous cases, effectually to dispel doubt. In early pregnancies it is not capable of achievements, but when combined with the vaginal touch it becomes a most valuable aid. Later, however, the uterus, with its developing foetus, rises within easy reach of the hand, and admits of minute examination. The fundus uteri is always easily distinguishable and its height can be closely determined.

If the examination be prolonged, the recurrent uterine contractions which are going on throughout the greater part of pregnancy will be felt under the hand; and during their prevalence, a pretty good outline of the gravid uterus can be distinguished.

In the intervals between contractions, when there is no muscular resistance, it is possible, after the middle of pregnancy to feel the fœtal form through the uterine walls. The fœtal movements, at this period, whether spontaneous or elicited are felt by the palpating hand.

"The touch" is a highly efficacious mode of examination, and on which in cases at all doubtful, ought never to be neglected. By means of it several important signs may be elicited.

A few years ago Hegar described a sign of pregnancy, of service in the early weeks, which bids fair to become generally recognized as positive. In the early weeks, development of the uterus is confined pretty closely to the body and fundus, and expansion is greater anteriorly and posteriously than laterally. At the same time while softening is just beginning in the lower part of the vaginal cervix, it is proceeding more rapidly in the supra-cervical uterine walls, so that there is soon a zone of uterine tissue at the uterine isthmus, which to the touch is softer and more boggy than the structures above and below. There, too, as a result of these changes, it is found that the uterine wall there becomes more prominent, so that the cervix feels as though it were set on the inferior surface of a small sphere. These changes can best be recognized through recto abdominal, or recto vaginal touch, while the uterus is depressed in the pelvis by means of abdominal pressure.

The sign is available as early as the fifth week of pregnancy.

At the close of the sixth or seventh week the lips of the os uteri communicate to the examining finger a slight sensation of softness. This softness begins at the lowermost part and progressively ascends. At about the sixth month this softening extends about half the length of the cervix, but not until close of gestation is the reduction complete.

There is a form of vaginal, or bimanual examination, the employment of which, at certain stages, will disclose a sign of pregnancy regarded as positive, namely, *ballottement*. It can be practiced by both hands upon the abdomen. To do so the woman must be placed on her side, one of the operator's hands resting above, and the other below the abdomen as she lies. By a sudden movement of the hand beneath the fœtus-the latter may be displaced or tossed, and the impulse of its return communicated to the sense of the operator.

Vaginal *ballottement* is performed by placing the woman on her back in a semi-recumbent posture, and then, with two fingers in the vagina, the uterine wall just anteriorly to the cervix is given a sudden push in the direction of the long uterine axis. This propels the fœtus away from the lower uterine segment, but it soon sinks again in the liquor amnii, and the gentle tap of its contact with the uterine tissues may be felt. When clearly elicited, it is regarded as a positive sign of pregnancy. It cannot be employed with satisfaction earlier than about the close of the fourth month, nor later than the seventh.

The fœtal heart beat is *the* positive sign of pregnancy.

The sounds have been compared to those of a watch under a pillow, but an infinitely better idea of them may be obtained by listening to the heart of a new-born child. The double stethoscope gives best satisfaction. The area of audibility varies considerably in extent. In one case the sounds can be heard over nearly the whole abdomen, while in another they are circumscribed to a small space. The rapidity of pulsation varies greatly, the average being about 135 beats per minute.

It is now well understood that, by auscultation of the abdomen of a pregnant woman advanced beyond the fourth month, we may hear the pulsations of the foetal heart, the *bruit de souffle*, and occasionally foetal movements and the funic souffle.

An exact diagnosis of pregnancy is often impossible even at the third month, but again it may be made with a reasonable degree of certainty. If the organ is found slightly anteflexed, and corresponding in size to the probable period of gestation, not painful to manipulation, of a peculiar softness, and moreover, the woman healthy, though her menses have not appeared during the time, then, every probability points to the conclusion.

It is highly important to know if the fœtus be living or dead. The circumstances which may give rise to a suspicion that the fœtus is dead are: 1—Absence of foetal movements. 2—Absence of the foetal heart sounds. 3—Diminished size and increased softness of the uterus. 4—Engorgement, succeeded by flaccidity of the mammæ. 5—Sensation of weight and coldness in the abdomen. 6—Debility and general ill feeling. 7—Peptonesia. (Peptones in the urine).

Only the last sign is quite constant, and the only reliable one, as the others may depend upon some other cause.

It is highly important to know, as early as possible after labor sets in, the *presentation* and *position* of the fœtus. If the presenting part has been driven downwards into the pelvic cavity, and the membranes have ruptured, this can usually be learned by a vaginal examination. Otherwise the diagnosis is not easily made.

In the examination papers of last winter, there seemed apparent a confusion as to the meaning of the terms presentation and position. A brief explanation may help this to be clear in your minds.

By "Presentation" is meant that part of a foetus which is felt *presenting*, on examination *per vaginum*. When the head presents, and especially the vertex or the feet, knees, or breech, the presentation is said to be *natural*; when any other part presents, *preternatural*.

By "Position" is meant the *manner* in which the presenting part is placed, in regard to the pelvis of the mother. For instance, in the first position of the vertex, the long diameter of the head occupies the right oblique diameter of the pelvis, the occiput being directed to the left iliopectineal eminence, and the forehead to the right sacro iliac synchondrosis. The back of the foetus is thus brought to the mother's left side.

The head is recognized from its shape and hardness which differ from those of any other presenting part. The breech may be mistaken for the head if you are not careful. The vertex will be distinguished mainly by its sutures and fontanelles. The bruck will be distinguished by the cleft between the two nates, the genitals, the anus, and the point of the coccyx.

The average duration of gestation after cessation of the menstrual flow, has been found to be 278 days. Various methods of calculation have been suggested, and sundry periodoscopes and tables have been given, with a view to facilitate the prediction, and make it more accurate than it could be without them, some of which are based on an average of 278 and some of 280 days.

Dr. Duncan's rule is: "Find the day on which the female ceased to menstruate, or the first day of being what she calls well." Take that day nine months forward as 275 days, unless Feb. is included, in which case it is taken as 273 days. To this add three days in the former case, or five if Feb. is in the count, to make up the 278. This 278th day should then be fixed on as the middle of the week in which the confinement is likely to occur.

Even when it is impossible to establish the date of the last menstrual period, the time of quickening can sometimes be recalled by the woman, in which case it is customary to add twenty-two weeks for the purpose of determining the proximate date of delivery. This is not reliable, as the time of quickening varies in different cases.

In the next lecture I will take up some of the duties of the nurse during pregnancy.

Personal Reminiscences.

HOW I BECAME A HOMŒOPATH.*

JOHN ADAMS WAKEMAN, M. D., PH. D., CENTRALIA, ILL.

The following sketch of my life, down to October 1st, 1901, is written by myself at the request of the Secretary of THE OLD GUARD, Chicago, of which I am one of the oldest members.

I was born in Hector, Tompkins county, New York, January 23d, 1816.

My parents, John Wakeman and Ruth Adams Wakeman, were both reared in Fairfield, of Greenfield County, Connecticut, and went to the state of New York before my birth, traveling the whole distance with all their worldly effects in a one horse wagon, selected and purchased a piece of heavily timbered land and built a log house, in which I was born, and in which I lived many years.

Schools at that early day were few and far between and very poor, seldom had more than three months, never more than four months in a year; and only the primary branches, such as reading, writing, arithmetic and geography were taught. As we lived one and a half miles from the school, and a part of the distance was across the lot and through the woods, with the extreme cold and deep snows and no roads at that early day, made it impossible to get a reasonable education.

At an early day I was taken from the farm and for six successive summers I was boating on Cayuga lake and the Erie canal from Montezuma to Albany,

*Written for "The Old Guard."

New York, with my father, and nothing being done for my education.

When about sixteen years of age, my parents with their large family came to the state of Ohio, settling in Huron county, Fairfield township, which was at that time a new country, few schools, few churches, few and very bad roads.

After reaching Ohio, I only went to school one winter; taught school about one year and boarded round; attended Norwalk Seminary for a time until it was destroyed, with all its chemical and philosophical apparatus and other necessaries, by fire, then returned home, borrowed Dr. Bell's Anatomy and Physiology of our family physician, and worked on the farm, spending all my spare time with my books, without any instructor or skeleton, doing the best I could for one or two years, before commencing my college course, which, as I found I was making but little progress towards getting a medical education, and now about twenty years old, I determined to do as soon as possible.

The place I selected was the Reformed Medical College of Worthington, Ohio, near Columbus, conducted by a board of trustees, and a faculty of five professors, as follows: Drs. Morrow, Paddock, Day, Mason and Jones.

We had a good, thorough, competent faculty; four or five lectures a day, and as many thorough quizzes. The fall and winter term continued six months, spring and summer, four months. I attended two full winter courses and nearly two full summer courses and graduated on March 24th, 1838. I married Miss Hulah J. Stills on the day following my graduation.

The examinations of the candidates for graduation were most thorough and protracted.

This school was afterwards moved to Cincinnati, and became the Eclectic College of Ohio. Both new and old systems of practice were taught.

At this time, there being no law to regulate the practice of medicine, the people were shamefully imposed upon by "*pretenders*," as any one so disposed might set himself up as a physician, and in his hands, calomel was most injudiciously used in doses varying from ten to sixty grains, and ptyalism, with all its destructive consequences, was of daily occurrence.

Fees were very low, visits including medicine in town, 37½ cents; an emetic, a purge, or a plaster only 12½ cents; the same for venesection, or extracting teeth. Obstetrical cases never more than three dollars, and no case could be attended without a bottle of whiskey, of which all must partake, the patient included, and as a consequence, many drinking and drunken physicians.

Blood-letting was the sine-qua-non, the *bad blood* must be driven off; and the limit of abstraction was only measured by the poor victim's power of endurance; bled so long as the blood presented the *buffy coat*.

All the attention deemed necessary for the parturient mother after delivery, was a little sponging with hot water, a compress to the vulva, a bandage and quiet, no disinfectants, no antiseptic douches, only perfect cleanliness, and almost never any trouble.

The poor babe came in for its share of nastiness; as soon as washed and dressed it was fed with a little of its Daddy's urine, sweetened, not to purge off the "*economy*," as in the case of Dr. William Dewees' babe, but to remove from its bowels the meconium.

Sixty-four years ago the practice was laborious, our drugs were most crude, rendering it necessary to administer remedies in infusion, in decoction and in syrup, and few remedies could be procured in powders or pills; must take the crude drug and reduce it to powder in our own mortars.

The fatality attending such practice was frightful to contemplate, and would drive a thinking man to look for and embrace a better system as soon as he could be satisfied in his own mind that one presented itself, although I think my success would not have suffered by a comparison with the best of country practitioners

It was instilled into our minds with religious care, never to allow our patients with fever or inflammation any cold water to drink; but this cruel predjudice was dispelled from my mind, on one hot summer day, most effectually in this way: Called to see the editor of the city paper, a stout, burley fellow, with a raging fever, and found him with a pitcher of ice water which he poured down his throat in unmeasured quantity, and a gallon bowl of ice water with sponge, and he as wet as a good Bapaist. I was alarmed and remonstrated. Doctor, said he, you attend to the medical part of this case and I will attend to the hydropathic. Agreed, we worked like good fellows, never saw a case do so well, I learned something that I never forgot, and I thank God that I learned it so early in life and saved much suffering for cold water. This occurred in the summer of 1838.

After I had practiced ten or twelve years, a Homœopathic physician came and settled in our county. Then professional bigotry led to all manner of ridicule of the man, and of his little pills; but truth is mighty and always prevails, and while I was as bad as others making sport, I was seriously investigating, hoping that there might be real merit and science in it.

I soon began to see that the physician was a gentleman and an educated man and light began breaking through my prejudice, and when my next door neighbor was a Homœopathic physician, an intimacy sprung up between us and seeing that his success in treating cases was far better than mine, and so much pleasanter and better every way, and that he succesfully handled cases in which I and all other allopaths failed and being at that time a great sufferer from pulmonary disease, he asked the privilege of treating me for three weeks saying if not relieved in that time, I need not continue it longer.

Well, in less than three weeks all my pain was gone, and all my foolish prejudice also and from that time I have been a true convert to the practice of Hahnemann, and to the best of my ability and in all candor and honesty up to the present time, am doing all I can for pure Hahnemannian Homœopathic practice, and am firm in the faith that we can find no better system.

When I announced myself as a convert to Homoeopathy very few of my old patrons left me, notwithstanding I was using the remedies as fast as my limited knowledge of the science would permit.

I continued to study and practice in this way nearly two years and the more knowledge I got the more I wanted, and in the fall of 1852 went to Philadelphia and attended a full winter course at old Hahnemann Medical College and in March, graduated in a class of 53, among whom was W. T. Helmuth, Sparhawk, Angell, Johnson, Brown of Texas etc. Our professors were Small, Williamson, Semple, Sims, Gardiner and Loomis, a strong faculty and all good men.

Now sixty-four years since I commenced practice; commencing in 1837; forty-eight of which has been Homoeopathic, have always been a close student, always strove to do the best in practice I could and posterity must render judgment.

A few years since, the Honory Degree of Doctor of Philosophy was conferred upon me by the faculty and trustees of

Ewing College, Illinois.

A church member seventy-two years.

Now nearly eighty-seven years old; two sons and one daughter, the latter the wife of Dr. William H. Leonard of Minneapolis, Minn.; first wife died in 1885; married Mrs. S. A. Willard in 1887, who is still living.

After my graduation in the spring of 1853, I located in the city of Portsmouth, Ohio, where I soon built up a good practice, but my wife's health failed in consequence of too much humidity at the junction of the Ohio, and Scioto rivers, she went into a decline, and hoping that a change of the country would benefit her, in June, 1859, moved to Centralia, Ill., on a farm adjoining town, where she soon got bilious intermitting fever, chills and fever, under which all the lung disease passed off, and she lived until 1885 and died of cerebral disease.

At this place have had several epidemics of cholera and in the winter of 1863 during the war, small pox was epidemic and I treated between ninety and one hundred cases with only one fatality; had charge of the hospital where we had 17 cases at one time, and Tartar emetic was the remedy for nearly every case, and in many the only medicine given.

All forms of the disease were presented and same of the confluent cases showed pox as large as a quarter of a dollar.

Have also treated several cases of yellow fever that came up from the south.

Since locating here, I think at least eight Homoeopaths have visited and settled here, but remained only a short time.

Drs. C. N. Dunn and wife have been here many years, and deservedly stand high in their profession.

I love my profession.

Editorial.

BETTER PHYSICIANS.

The Homœopathic profession may be roughly divided, according to an old physician, into four classes: (1) Sharpshooters. (2) Riflemen (occasionally). (3) Double-barreled shooters and (4) those who prefer bird shot, believing that the similar remedy must be there.

Of course these latter are a great improvement over the old blunder-buss and grape shot men. The advancement in therapeutics we all know is a question of education and experience, just as it was in Hahnemann's case. It took him about 40 years to get able to select the similar remedy and to depend upon the single dose of the 30th potency of some of the best prescribers we have were once allopaths or eclectics and depended upon the old unscientific method of treatment. *Gradually* they learned the better way.

Some of these sharpshooters even now are perplexed to find the similar remedy and are tempted to resort to palliation. If they are thus tempted to supply lack of knowledge with expediency what can be expected of those who are not so advanced?

How often does the question come up: Shall we resort to old methods or let the patient go into other hands?

This division of the profession who claim to be Homœopaths, is not presented with any idea of disparagement. It is presented simply to look our duty in the face. As the close prescribers have slowly learned the better way, it is a duty—a sacred duty—we owe to the other three classes to help them by instruction and example.

The pharasaical spirit will not help. It creates prejudice. Prejudice favors ignorance.

It is the earnest belief of those who have studied the profession for years, that all are striving to be better informed—all are teachable at times.

Our allopathic friends are making much of disease diagnosis. We infer that Hahnemann was equally expert, as the great London physician, for he spent an hour going over a lad with consumption brought to him from the London physician's hands before he could satisfy himself as to the diagnosis, the progress of the disease and the prospect of cure. The result proved that he could both diagnose the disease and diagnose the remedy that finally cured.

We should take the ground that any one who is a good disease diagnostician can be so instructed that he or she may in time become a close prescriber.

The great object of this journal is to help our less informed brethren. We want to put it into the hands of those anxious to learn the better way. We want our readers to send us the names of those physicians whom they know. We want to increase the number of the rifle shots in our ranks. In fact, this journal wants to help all to be better all round physicians.

THE EPIDEMIC WAVE.

In 1865 the writer, when a student, asked old Dr. Pulte of Cincinnati, then on a visit to Chicago, if we would have cholera that year. He replied at once, "No, cholera remedies are not called for this year; the genus epidemicus is met by other remedies." The remedies he mentioned, but they are now forgotten.

Eighteen months after the above conversation, in the fall of the year 1866, we had cholera and cholera remedies indicated. The collapse came early and *Veratrum alb.* was the remedy, when *Camphor* ceased to be of service.

In 1873 we again had an epidemic of cholera and that had been preceded by an epidemic of small pox. In 1871 we had the worst looking vaccination arms I ever saw. Of course, it was attributed to bad virus, smoke in the air, and water after the big fire; but such bad arms were not met again until 1882—in fact, for years, it was difficult to get the virus to work at all.

In 1893, behold small pox was again pervalent, and again we saw some awful arms.

During the past year small pox, in a mild form, has been more prevalent than for some time in this country. In London it is now very severe. Since May last 2,273 cases have been reported, and still the disease spreads. The medical officer of London declares that "there are reasons for believing that greater prevalence of the disease is to be expected for some time." He compares the recurrence of small pox epidemics to great waves. There was one in 1838 and another in 1871. He argues that another is now due, which will probably become general throughout the world, as did the previous epidemics. They have just built a new small pox hospital of 800 beds, making 2,540 beds in the various small pox hospitals.

What interests us is the recognition of an epidemic. A pandemic wave, without question, sweeps over us, perhaps around the earth, traveling in this latitude from east to west. This is an official recognition of what Hahnemann and other writers recognized as a genus epidemicus. Hahneman thought it was in action all the time. Some of the best prescribers took early note of the season diseases. For example, old Dr. O. H. Mann, of Evanston, a sharpshooter in his day, with a large practice, said he would study carefully the first few cases of summer diseases in children to learn the epidemic remedy, and after that the management of the next cases was easy. The complications only would need other remedies.

Just now we are having a great deal of erysipelas in Chicago, following measles and scarlet fever. It is the smooth variety, but very stubborn showing a severe type. *Belladonna* seems to be the remedy, but does not rapidly cure. One peculiar feature is the intense pain.

In the Cook County Hospital we have had one severe case of cerebro-spinal meningitis that was promptly controlled by *Veratrum vir.*, 1x every two hours. *Belladonna* and finally *Hepar* were necessary to clear up the case, a full report of which will appear in a subsequent issue. In the meantime the experience of the readers of this medical journal is asked to solve the question: What is the epidemic remedy now in your locality? The epidemic remedy is called for chiefly in acute cases.

Obituary.

DR. FRANCIS EDMUND BŒRICKE.

Dr. Francis Edmund Bœricke, a prominent homœopathic pharmacist, died on Tuesday, December 17th, at his residence at 6386 Drexel road, Overbrook, aged 75 years. He had been an invalid for the last fifteen years.

Born in Glauchau, Saxony, in 1826, Francis E. Bœricke came to this country during the Revolution of 1848, and made his home in this city. His father was a prominent manufacturer and exporter of woolen goods in Glauchau. Soon after his arrival here the young man obtained a position as bookkeeper with Plata, at Fourth and Chestnut sts., a well known dry goods merchant and the Saxon consul. Following this he became a partner in Andre's music store in Chestnut st. In 1852 he joined the Church of the New Jerusalem, and opened a store where religious books were sold in Sixth street below Chestnut st. A year later he was induced by Dr. Constantine Hering to turn his attention to the preparation of homœopathic medicines, and by his proficiency and industry soon gained the confidence of leading homœopathists in the country. In 1854 he married Miss Eliza Tafel, and in 1869 associated with himself in the pharmacy business as a partner Adolph Tafel, his brother-in-law, who had retired from the Civil war with the rank of major.

Dr. Boericke was graduated from the Hahnemann College in 1863. He received a scholarship and delivered lectures on pharmacy for some time. In 1864 he added to his business an establishment for publishing homoeopathic works, and soon enlarged his trade by establishing branches throughout the country. In 1895, Major Tafel died, and after that the firm consisted of Dr. F. A. Boericke, and Adolph L. Tafel, sons of the original partners.

Dr. Boericke is survived by his widow and nine children.—*Philadelphia Ledger*

Editor's Table.

Salicylate of Sodium Cause Blindness. Girl suffering with acute articular rheumatism was given Sodium salicylate. One day she awoke blind, ophthalmic examination revealed nothing abnormal. Next day when succumbing to endocarditis and pericarditis she was again examined with negative results. She died without return of vision. Total amount taken 140 or 160 grains in 60 hours. "Dr. Snell (*Ophthalmic Record*) thought there could be very little question that the Sodium salicylate was the cause of the blindness." It would be interesting to know if this was the synthical or that extracted from the winter green.

Air—Food—Drink.—This trio, rightly employed, is the catholicon, obvious and close at hand, yet unseen by many a narrow enthusiast, who, by the light of glimmering jack-o'-lanterns, is pursuing theories too ridiculous to merit the dignity of an argument. The wealth of no man is great enough to acquire it by purchase, yet it is the certain reward for the judicious practice of self-denial.

These are the elements of hygiene which are peevishly disdained by many an over-drugged and over operated invalid. And physicians are often at fault in not considering them sufficiently in their etiological investigations. With their minds overloaded with the latest contributions of the bacteriologist, they are apt to forget, or to deny the pathological influences of daily habits, temperaments and diatheses.—*Milwaukee Medical Journal.*

Before any physician should even hint of selecting a remedy for the treatment of any case of sickness, he should make careful inquiry regarding the *quality* and *quantity* of these *three* essentials used by the patient every day. Many disease conditions may be traced directly to improper environment and *cured* by securing the judicious co operation of these important agencies of Nature without the use of a particle of medicine. The common forces of Nature are the most potent factors with which we have to deal and cannot be ignored.—ED.

Thoracic Pain and Fat.—There is a thoracic symptom belonging to over fatness, to which I wish to direct special attention in the sub scapular and intra scapular muscles. This pain may be quite acute, especially on making a strong voluntary effort to maintain an erect posture or upon attempting to exercise the arms. It was described by one of my patients as a feeling as though the "flesh had grown fast to the bones." The pain may localized, although more commonly it extends across the back from side to side. In one of my patients it was excited by merely lifting the arms above the level of the shoulders. This patient also complained at intervals of a rather acute, though fugitive pain, which passed through the base of the right side of the thorax, especially upon attempting unusual muscular exertion. It is interesting to note that the fat deposit was decidedly larger on the same side of the thorax, and also that a reduction of the bodily weight entirely relieved the pain. These must be discriminated from other forms of pain, notably the rheumatic and neuralgic varieties, and in attempting this the etiologic influence of over fatness must be accorded due weight.—*Philadelphia Medical Journal.*

There is much valuable meat in the above hint. Not infrequent are the cases of fatty deposit over a nerve trunk, the innocent cause of socalled rheumatic or neuralgic pains which persist in spite of the most carefully selected treatment. A thorough examination of the physical condition along the course of the nerve or nerves involved will disclose the *cause* when of a *mechanical* nature and at the same time direct attention to a deeper *constitutional* cause when no visible cause can be detected.

Injurious Effects from Cold Baths.—Giacomo Rem-Picci concludes from his observations that people react very differently to cold bathing; the less robust and the thinner the individual, the more liable is he to albuminuria. This appears rapidly, sometimes within eleven minutes after the bath, and disappears after a few hours. The habit of cold bathing does not seem to prevent the appearance of the albuminuria, which, however, is slight. The albumin appears to be serum albumin. Hyaline casts are sometimes found. Polyuria usually accompanies the albuminuria, but the relation is not constant. The elimination of total solids is increased after cold bathing, whether or not there be albuminuria. Urobilinuria is not produced. Arterial pressure is increased after cold baths or douches of short duration, but after those of longer duration it is diminished for several hours. Prolonged and very cold baths cause rapid and irregular heart action, more or less diffuse cyanosis, and sometimes dilatation of the right heart.

A cold bath should never be taken by thin, anemic individuals unless they are surrounded by every needed means for bringing out a quick reaction. If the reaction is not *greater* than the action of the cold injury must follow as a logical sequence.

Eclectic Indications for Remedies.—When the face is flushed in color and there is prostration, nausea, exhausting discharges from the bowels, with cramps and cold extremities, *Camphor* is an effective remedy.

Green, watery, flatulent discharges with colicky pains and peevishness are corrected with *Chamomilla*.

When there is pain in the abdomen with a sensation of burning in the stomach, soft and flabby skin with inclination to fullness, *Arsenic* in very small doses is indicated.

When there is intestinal mucous irritation which causes any increase in the quantity of the normal secretions, with nausea, contracted tongue, vomiting perhaps with some passive hemorrhage, *Ipecac* is the remedy.

When the face is pallid and expressionless, with a yellowish hue around the mouth, with pain in the abdomen at the umbilicus, *Nux vomica* is the remedy. *Nux vomica* is also indicated when there is atony of the stomach or intestinal tract, with weakness of the nervous system.

When there is irritability of the mucous membranes of the bowels, with spasmodic pains, with cramps in the extremities, and diarrhoea, the movements large and watery and very frequent, with much prostration *Arsenite of copper* will control the condition, and *Arsenite of strychnia* will restore the strength.

Quick, sharp pains in region of liver, slight jaundice and yellowish green discharges from the bowels are indications for *Bryonia*.

Pain in the rectum, especially if accompanied by relaxed veins or a dark, purplish condition of the mucous membranes, will be quickly relieved with *Collinsonia*.—*Eclectic Medical Review*.

Do you see anything familiar in the above? Dr. Scudder knew a good thing when he saw it and came much nearer being a homœopath than many who sail under its banner today. The only objection to the above is that it is too crude for practical purposes. It does not equal "key note" prescribing.

Petroleum Alopecia Areata.—A young woman who had rebellious alopecia for more than a year was practically cured by washing the head twice a day with soap and then rubbing *Kerosene* vigorously into the bald patches. They soon became covered with soft hairs which by the end of eight months had almost all been transformed into adult hairs.—*Hallopeau in Medical Record*.

Petroleum causes the skin to *ulcerate* and under its action the scalp becomes sensitive to the touch with dryness and intense *itching*. The hair falls out in patches almost like syphilis, preceded by papular eruptions. The vigorous rubbing twice a day would have a stimulating effect without any applications of the kerosene.

Cereals vs. Starches as Foods.—*Fecula* and *flours* are often used as synonyms. Fecula are starches like that obtained from potatoes, corn, rice, etc. They are not digested in the stomach but in the intestines, and they are converted into anything else but sugar. On the other hand, flour, from whatever cereal it may be derived, contains all the constituents of the grain except cellulose, which is present in the husks. In addition to starch, therefore, it contains fat and mineral salts and proteids. Hence cereal flour resembles chemically the composition of eggs and contains all the elements of nutrition.—*Repertoire de Pharmacie*.

The immeasurable difference between the starches and the cereals as articles of food is clearly shown in the paper from which this abstract was taken and should be clearly understood by every practitioner. Any errors that may be committed in this matter will be due to a thoughtless acceptance of their similarity.—Ed.

Veratrum viride in Mania.—Any physician who has not employed *Veratrum viride* in acute mania has missed the best agency which is available for the cure of these distressing cases. It is one of the greatest advantages a physician can have to see the *feverish* sufferer, under the application of this remedy, pass from absolute sleeplessness into a state of quiet rest. That many cases which would otherwise go on to death are saved by the use of this remedy is a fact beyond question. The fear which many practitioners have of using Veratrum viride, on account of the varying strength of its various preparations, must, of course, be met when the drug is employed, by the use of Norwood's tincture.—*American Medical Journal.*

In large doses it has a more depressing effect than *Aconite*. A study of the provings will disclose the fact that its indications in mania are extremely limited e. g.: The delirium is only temporary, but while it lasts the patient may be quarrelsome and inclined to strike and kick vehemently, but the tendency would be to pass from a mania into a stupor or heavy sleep. There is a tendency toward intermittent *paroxysms* or spasms with *violent shrieking*, body bent backward with arms rigid and face dark blue with arrested respiration and followed by great prostration with cold clammy prespiration. The mania may have a *puerperal*, gastric or cerebro spinal origin.—Ed.

Iodine—Morn Sickness of Pregnancy.—F. H. Strauss (*American Medical Compend*) states that he has been able to confirm Dr. Eliot's experience with tincture of iodine. Eliot, in the *New York Medical Record*, reports a case in which five drops of tincture of iodine in a teaspoonful of sweetened water was given. The effect was magical, the vomiting ceased at once. Strauss continues, that in his own cases he has had most marked success in two cases in which he tried almost all the remedies except dilating the os. Many physicians have recommended the use of the compound tincture, but Strauss always used the ordinary tincture.

A purely empirical prescription in the hands of an old school physician, but with the following "totality" it becomes the simillimum: *Continued empty eructations;* sourish eructations with burning; heartburn, particularly after a heavy meal; *hiccough—nausea*; nausea immediately after rising with spasmodic pain in the stomach; inclination to vomit in *paroxysms* with heartburn; *vomiting* with diarrhoea; *vomiting of bile; despondency; increased sensitiveness and irritability*—Ed.

Pilocarpine in Eye Maladies.—Gratifying results are obtained in the treatment of interstitial keratitis, traumatic purulent iritis, vitreous opacites, and retino-choroiditis. Some place great reliance upon the drug in toxic insanity supervening upon influenza, auto intoxication, and similar processes, the brain rapidly clearing after two or three free perspirations. Apart from its action hypodermatically, pilocarpine (or the fluid extract of jaborandi) in small doses by the mouth, has been found of value in degeneration of the vitreous. The persistent nausea so common after the use of the drug is usually relieved by small doses of chlorodyne.—*Hansell, in Philadelphia Medical Journal.*

Cranberries—Thirst.—The pure, fresh juice of cranberries, given freely, either undiluted or with an equal part of water, is an excellent means of relieving the thirst in fever, and, moreover, is markedly antipyretic. In the thirst and vomiting peculiar to cholera it is even more effective. In fifty cases in which ice and narcotics failed to make the slightest impression, cranberry juice, in small but repeated doses, rapidly checked both vomiting and nausea.—*Coriansky.*

This practical hint is given for what it is worth. *Vibrunum opulus* has a wide range of action and is worthy a thorough proving. In Hale's *New Remedies* we have a suggestion of its scope of action but this is not sufficient.

Personals, News Items, Etc.

Dr. Samuel A. Kimball, formerly located at 124 Commonwealth ave., Boston, has moved to 420 Centre st., Newton, Mass.

Dr. W. C. Duncan, formerly of Colfax, Iowa, has moved to Dekalb, Ill., where he succeeds to the practice of J. C. Duncan, deceased.

Dr. P. L. MacKenzie, the well known physician of Portland, Oregon, is now attending the Post Graduate School of Homoeopathics at 370 South Wood st.

The use of orange blossoms by brides originated among the Arabs. Because the orange branch bears fruit and flowers at the same time, it is considered an emblem of prosperity.

Dr. E. Le Roy Biggs has recently located in Hot Springs, Ark., at 328 Central ave. As the doctor is well grounded in the principles and practice of pure homœopathy, there is no doubt of his success.

San Antonio, Texas, Hahnemannians met on September 20 at the office of Dr. Charles A. Wilson and formed a Homoeopathic Association. Dr. Wilson was selected as president; Dr. Wilbur A. Blauvelt, secretary and treasurer. Success and long life!

An Indianapolis dentist has given up the use of forceps for pulling teeth and has adopted the primitive method of the Chinese, using nothing but his thumb and index finger. He considers that the sight of the forceps themselves is responsible for much of the harrowing part of tooth pulling and that many nervous persons are greatly shocked by the sight of these instruments. The pain is also said to be less. He can take out the most firmly rooted double tooth in a few seconds. He learned this art from a Chinese practitioner.—*Scientific American.*

The Supreme Court of Indiana has recently decided that a physician is not bound to attend any patient by whom or for whom he is called, unless a contract for such service has been made. The fact that he is the family physician does not impose a legal obligation to answer a call. The effect of this ruling is to decide that the profession does not stand in such a quasi-public relation to the laity as to compel services against convenience or inclination.

Germany, the United Kingdom, the Netherlands, Sweden, Switzerland, Denmark and Norway are the only European countries in which there are more Protestants than Roman Catholics. In all Europe there are 160,165,000 Roman Catholics, 80,812,000 Protestants, 89,196,000 Orthodox Greek Catholics, 6,456,000 Jews, 6,629,000 Mohammedans, besides 1,219,000 unclassified. In America there are 58,894,882 Roman Catholics, 57,294,014 Protestants, and 130,000 Jews.

Eating should be incidental to the meeting of the family for a social hour together. Mere feeding is an animal affair. The brutes eat in silence, but meal time with civilized, refined humanity should mean an opportunity for pleasant chat, enlivened by good stories, interesting incidents, and laughter. Whatever pertains to business should be banished at this hour, together with all sad and depressing or troublesome thoughts. It is decidedly not the place to relate calamities and horrors. Everything that can cheer, amuse and entertain should be contributed to the meeting of families and friends. Refreshments of heart and mind should be considered equally important with refreshment of body, and thus would the fine art of living be promoted.—*London Family Doctor.*

Book Reviews.

International Clinics. Edited by Henry W. Cattell, A. M., M. D., of Philadelphia and published by J. B. Lippincott & Co.

It hardly seems necessary to more than announce the Vol. III of the eleventh series has come from the press and is ready to be distributed, because the profession have become so familiar with the valuable features of this work that many of them subscribe as they would for any other magazine. The advantage in this case lies in the fact that one volume appears every *three* months and is already bound and ready to be used. All of the topics discussed are of great practical value and represent the most advanced ideas upon the subjects under consideration. About 175 pages are devoted to *medicine* and therapeutics, while only about 100 pages are given to *surgery*. The different departments being: Therapeutics; Medicine; Neurology; Surgery; Eye and Throat; Laboratory.

The Standard Medical Directory of North America, consisting of twelve parts, including Directory of Physicians of North America, Medical Colleges, Medical Service of the United States, Medical Societies, Medical Practice Acts, Medical Publications, (including Books and Periodicals) Mineral Springs, Drugs and Medicines, Medical and Surgical Products, Manufacturers and Life Insurance Companies. Handsomely bound in red buckram, 824 pages, imperial octavo. Price $10.00. G. P. Engelhard & Co., Chicago.

ACCURACY is the great essential in a work of this character and the publishers are to be congratulated upon the exceptional manner in which they have gotten out their first edition. They have omitted one great essential which seriously impairs the usefulness of the present volume viz: The omission of the *alphabetically arranged list of physicians* There is no present means for determining the residence of any physician and that is a great purpose of a directory. This will undoubtedly be corrected in the next edition. The other valuable features are enumerated in the introductory.

A Dictionary of Practical Materia Medica by John Henry Clarke, M. D., London England. Published by the Homœopathic Publishing Co., 12 Warwick Lane, Paternoster Row, London, England.

This is a comprehensive work on Materia Medica and claims its right to the title of "Dictionary" because it *defines*. It might with equal right prefix the title of "Encyclopædia," because it not only defines but *describes*. It is made practical by reason of the fact that it gives many practical suggestions as well as facts not usually found within the covers of one book, e.g.: Under each remedy will be found the following grouping: (1) Synonyms; (2) Clinical applications; (3) Characteristics; (4) Relations; (5) Symptoms arranged in accordance with Hahnemann's scheme.

The reader will find many of the excellent features of *Jahr's Symptomen Codex*, Allen's Encyclopædia, Hering's Guiding Symptoms and many features incorporated in the different abridged works.

There is not a superfluous word and about the only criticism to be offered is the combining of *clinical* or cured symptoms with those recorded under the provings *without any distinguishing marks*. Opinions may differ on this subject but it does not seem wise to ignore the fact that they come from distinctly different sources, even though their values may be equal.

Another criticism to be offered may be disposed of in the same way, because there is an honest difference of opinion, but it seems to us that the editor of such a work ought to have such knowledge of the action of these different remedies as to be able to fix a *value* to each symptom recorded. Nearly every prominent contributor that has gone into this matter has arranged them under at least three groups and indicated the relative value by difference in the face of the type used. Experience has only served to increase the value of different symptoms, and at the same time shown a wonderful unanimity among the students.

There are in the neighborhood of 2000 pages in both volumes and the second edition will doubtless see this increased to a third volume containing a *Repertory*.

The question will be asked—in what way is it superior to other works already on the market? It is difficult answering this question because the relative superiority is based upon the mental guage of the individual. For me it would be difficult for any one to improve on *Allen's Hand book* for a single volume and still *Hering's Guiding Symptoms* seems to be incomparably better, but they occupy entirely different fields —the one does not conflict with the other.

The Dictionary most closely resembles the *Symptomen Codex* in its general make up but it contains a large increase in the number of remedies while some of the features that go to make the *Codex* untrustworthy have been eliminated in this new bidder for public favor. It will occupy a distinctive place in the library of every materia medica student.

The North American Journal of Homœopathy, Jubilee number. The editor and publisher of this excellent exponent of Homoeopathy are to be congratulated upon the beauty of the January issue, commemorating the fiftieth anniverrary of its birth. It is, typographically, a work of art; the practical nature of its contents is beyond question; and the history of the early efforts of the journal reads like the story of the struggle of Hahnemann's followers in America for existence.

The work of the North American for the advancement of Homoeopathy has borne fruit a thousand fold; may the recent semi-centennial celebration be the first of a long series.

Gray's Anatomy.—Some books are in fashion today and obsolete tomorrow, but the publishers of Gray's Anatomy have kept this masterly production up-to-date by frequent revision.

The last American edition, by Lea Brothers & Co., from the fifteenth English edition, is a classic exposition of this great subject. In details it probably surpasses all others, and therefore becomes a valuable reference book for the surgeon as well as a popular text book for the student.

The department of General Anatomy or Histology occupies over a hundred pages and presents a practical exposition of the minute anatomy of the human body, with excellent illustrations, and in addition to this there is a complete work on Embryology.

Homœopathic Pharmacopeia of the United States. It is known to all of our readers that this is the work of the American Institute of Homoeopathy and consequently has their seal of *authority* stamped upon it. No little criticism has been raised against the standard or unit adopted by the committee because it differed from the standard or rule adopted by Hahnemann and from which the provings were made, but a careful consideration of the subject will reveal other departures from the principles laid down by Hahnemann so it is eminently proper that the modern moulders of homoeopathic ideas should formulate a standard or foundation upon which a drug should be tested in the future and from which re-provings may be made when the College of Provers shall have been established. Taking it in all its bearings we believe the second edition is an improvement over the first and that the step has been taken in the right direction.

A serious of typographical error appears upon the top of each page whereby the old title Pharmacopeia of the American Institute of Homoeopathy is retained.

Review of Reviews for February. —This magazine, which has come to be regarded by every thinking man in the United States a necessary text-book, has exceeded its usual efforts in presenting practical matter in the current number. Several subjects of a practical nature are handled. Among those discussed editorially are articles on "Cuba's Immediate Needs" and "President Palma's Program for Cuba." In the former, liberal tariff relations with the island republic are recommended, this being in line with the President's message and with a sound trade policy —a careful analysis of President Palma's past achievements and the economical policy to be pursued promises much for Cuba's ultimate advancement as a nation, or an appandage of the United States. Why and how wireless telegraphy will reduce cable tolls is plainly told by Carl Snyder. How national punishment follows national crimes is illustrated in "The Turkish Situation," by one born in Turkey. Henry Holt presents a scheme for "The Treatment of Anarchism," in which he would exclude all of avowed anarchistic tendencies; would take the "red" at his word and withdraw all protection afforded him and his property; would exile all those now here who proved immune to the spirit of our institutions; the exiled anarchist returning without permission to be imprisoned for life; for the "red" assassin, the asylum. C. H. Matson tells of the organization of "A Farmer's Grain Trust" in Kansas, and how it succeeded in benefiting the members. "Coöperative Telephone Service: A Local Experiment in Wisconsin" is the title of an article telling how the business men of a town of about 5,000 inhabitants organized a company which furnishes to its merchant subscribers instruments at $2.25 a month and $1.00 for residences. At this rate the organizers earn an income of 25 per cent.

Besides the above, the number, as usual, contains a complete review of the world's important doings.

A TEMPERANCE LECTURE.

About the middle of the eighteenth century, a drunken swiss woman gave birth to several children. A few years ago Prof. Pelman looked up the number and career of her descendants, of 125 of them nothing could be learned. Of 709 the following data was obtained: of this number 106 were of illegitimate birth, 142 were beggars, 64 were supported by the municipality, 181 were female prostitutes, 76 had been sentenced for crime, seven of whom were murderers. The offsping of this one drunken woman cost the sate a million dollars.

"The bread earned by the sweat of the brow is thrice blest, and is far sweeter than the tasteless loaf of idleness."

"There are loyal hearts; there are spirits brave,
There are souls that are pure and true;
Then give to the world the best you have,
And the best will come back to you."

The Hahnemannian Advocate

A MONTHLY HOMŒOPATHIC MAGAZINE.

Vol. xii. Chicago, February, 1902. No. 2

Materia Medica.

THE PHYSIOLOGIC BASIS OF THE LAW OF CURE.

J. MARTIN LITTLEJOHN, PH. D., LL. D., F. R. S. C. (LONDON).

PROF. OF HERING'S PHYSIOLOGY AND PATHOLOGY, DUNHAM MEDICAL COLLEGE.

Previously we started out to demonstrate the physiological foundation of the Hahnemannian teaching. We laid down three laws or principles as the foundation of a rational therapy.

(1). *Similia similibus curantur*, the law of therapeutic action; (2) *contraria contrariis curantur*, the law of dietetic action, and (3) *ab ultima ad primam*, the regulative principle of all curative action.

We tried to elucidate a number of points, emphasized by the entire field of the physiology of the nervous system.

(1). The first pages of physiology bring out into prominence the *vital force* as that which lies behind the matter of the structure and the material functioning of the body organism.

(2). The basic principles that run all the way through physiology are *order*, *harmony* and *co ordination*, these being established by and through the nervous economy.

(3). There can be no organo-disease or organo-therapy, because no organ of the body is isolated and alone, the sympathetic relation of the nervous system making it imperative that the body be regarded as a common wealth of cells.

(4). The great media of therapeutic action are the cerebro-spinal and sympathetic systems (co ordinated), each system contributing an independent functioning to the united nerve mechanism; the former *controlling* especially in connection with its trophic function, exerted over all parts of the organism through sympathetic channels; the latter vaso motorly regulating the blood supply and, therefore, the nutritive condition of the cerebro spinal system. Any weakening of this united (co ordinated) nerve mechanism renders therapeutic reaction less certain and may render it impossible.

(5). The nutrition of the brain is the great central fact in all physiological functioning, this nutrition being a splanchnic function in connection with the peristaltic pulsations of the brain, corresponding there with.

(a). The rhythm of the heart.

(b). The rhythm of the lungs, and

(c). The co-ordinated activity of the vaso motors. These movements are regulated and limited by the cranium, the arterial and venous blood supply and the cerebro-spinal fluid.

(6). The fundamental theory of physiological life is that of *co-ordination* and *adjustment*. From the starting point of the embryological life we have the adaptation of the male and female elements in fertilization, the gradual progressive evolution of the embryonic layers and cells, embryonic tissues and organs, until, in the co-adapted organism we find the *structural and functional adjustment* of all the parts of the organism lying at the basis of vital manifestation. The structural framework is functioned in relation to the rhythmic activities of soft tissues; and these in turn are regulated by the *co-ordinated activities* of four distinct center motive powers, representing four definite planes of vital manifestation:

(a). The reflex,

(b). The automatic,

(c). The voluntary,

(d). The volitional center activities.

The vitality of the nerve tissue is the *basic life* of the physiologic organism and this manifests itself upon these four planes of activity in connection with all the organs and organic expressions of life. The co-ordination of these four central activities within the physically and physiologically conditioned material body constitutes what we know of actual life, the expression of the deeper life principle and the life force.

That system of therapeutics which takes account of all of these has upon it the stamp of perfection.

There are certain forces, sound, heat, light, electricity. The physical basis of all these is vibration. Vibration is an accepted fact in science. Solid bodies are composed of atoms which are vibrating at almost infinite velocities. One substance differs from another mainly in the modulus of vibratility, the different planes of substance representing the planes of gradually increasing vibratility. The higher vibratility governs and moulds the lower, just as the sun centralizes the solar system by emitting into every part of that solar system the most refined vibrations that mean life and light with all their accompaniments to the planets in that solar system. In man this vibratile characteristic also predominates, for within his organism he combines the higher and lower grades of vibratility in connection with mind, brain, bone, muscle, blood. So long as these combined vibratalities are in harmony the organism enjoys life and health.

In man there is a *vital force*. It is not the vital principle, or the soul, or the subjective mind. It is the vital force, that force which originates and remains in the body as the result of the union of spirit or simple substance with matter. It is the objective mind of the psychologist. The principle of this vital force is the *power of fluxion or of vibration*, which, as in the physical forces, can permeate the substance without affecting or modifying its substance. There are thus three planes, the pure *material*, the pure *spirit* or psychic, and the plane which originates in connection with the union of these other two, the *vital force* plane.

What is the plane of therapeutics? What is the plane of dietetics?

The plane of dietetics is that of pure matter, the food taken into the body passing through a metabolic cycle, terminating either in assimilation to the material tissues, or else in elimination as unassimilated or unassimilable. Here we are dealing with crude substances and the metabolic laws that regulate this cycle are two fold:

(a). Supply regulates the demand throughout the body, and

(b). Demand regulates the supply throughout the brain tissues, on a nitrogenous basis.

This makes it imperative to supply food substances in proximate principle or crude substance form, and this means the antidoting of hunger or thirst by the appropriate *contraria* substance, that will fill the void and satisfy the material craving and appetite.

In the therapeutic plane we are dealing with the *nexus* of spirit and body, and therefore, with those vibrations or fluxions that lie at the foundation of the force called vital. On this plane crude materials cannot be of any service, because they are foreign to the force to be affected, and as such cannot enter the field of the vital force.

In the crude drug substance, (a) there is nothing refining, but everything is crude and material as the material body substance, and as it is not the body material we are curing, as it is the vital force we are adjusting, there must be a refinement compatible with the force to be affected. (b). Increased vibratility is the principle of adjustment.

There are, it is true, the cruder forms of changes in the body, (1) the *metabolic cycle*, representing hunger, thirst, etc. These demand the crude. Why? Because the body has organs in which certain changing, refining and forming goes on, secretions being the products of this refining process. These secretions are the nutritive supplies of the higher forms of tissue.

(2). The *vital cycle* depends upon vibration. Waves of vibration pass along the tissues, especially from the nerves and the brain to and along the muscle tissues. There is no function of the body that does not have peristaltic or rhythmic vibration. How are we going to affect these? By affecting vibration in the substance used or in the treatment given. The potencies represent grades of vibratility, the higher potencies the higher vibratility. The time may come when we can measure the vital force by measuring its vibratality. We must approximate to this normal vibratility. There can be no life manifestation, except in relation to vibration. As the vibratility becomes less intensive man becomes less capable of reactive power, mental and physical decline follow. Homœopathically a *vehicle* is used to get the potent vibratility. Some call it magnetism, electricity, life or vital potentialization. Is there anything to lead to determine potency? Sympathetic life or visceral life is cruder and represents a lower plane of vibratility, although higher in the scale of rhythmic pulsation. The cerebro-spinal is more refined and represents a higher plane of vibratility, although more inhibitory in its nature. Therefore the higher potencies appeal to the cerebro-spinal system. As most, if not all, functional activities represent co-ordinated sympathetic and cerebro-spinal activity, the medium vibratility represents the normal, changes depending on the capacity to react.

The principle of determination is, (1) from last to first, symptoms disappearing in the reverse order of their appearance. Why? The last to appear is the least entrenched in the system.

(2). The pathway of least resistance is the pathway of curative effects.

(3). There is a normal degree of vibratile force in the organism. A certain portion may be over active or under active. This explains what seems to be organic disease. The curative principle is the economic distribution of these vital vibrations on the principle of adjustment such as is compatible with life. Disease causes are disturbers of this adjustment and in cure the vital force is directed to the orderly adjustment of the economy of vitality.

Symptoms are the voices of the patient or the vital force of the patient, expressing the internal condition through the outer or superficial plane of manifestation. At first we find in the organism a life force and it is constantly struggling against death forces or disease causes during the life of the individual. These disease forces are accentuated by unhealthy environment. These represent the *psora*, *syphilis* and *sycosis* of Hahnemann in the form of chronic miasms. The vibratile life force of the patient resists these. This vibratile life force represents the inherent rhythmic vitality of every organ and tissue. Everything superficial represents the expressions of the physiological life through or from under the pathological, demanding aid for the physiological life, to help perpetuate and keep up the struggle for existence and to determine it in favor of vitality. These expressions may be, (a) *subjective*, what the patient feels, reports; (b) *objective*, what the physician sees on the surface of the body or brings out by manipulations of the body or its parts in any form of deviation from the normal.

To meet these the law of cure is *similia similibus curantur*. All life represents force and the nature of this force is motile and vibratile The only way to meet the disease cause is by a similia, because the disorder is *mal-adjustment*, the two possible conditions being above or below par or normal, and vibratility or motility can only be changed by something of its own nature.

Is healing physiological or pathological? It is undoubtedly physiological. So long as life persists there is a tendency to the normal. This is represented by the *reactive vital force* of the organism. To this we must appeal. Here there is much of the confusion in the science and art of healing. It is not to the pathological state or condition we appeal, but to the physiological, to restore order and remove the pathological. Therefore all healing must be physiological in its nature. Are there any indications of this curative principle in physiology? It is this that lies at the basis of all mechanical systems of healing, the setting up of increase in or the checking of the vibratile impulses, the correction in the distribution of the normal vibrations sent out from the brain center of control and distributed by coordination from the different planes of center activity.

The curative work of any therapeutic system, if it is true. Curative action is threefold, (a) *corrective*, establishing disturbed adjustment; (b) *stimulating*, increasing the local or regional distribution; and (c) *inhibiting* or checking and decreasing the local or regional distribution of the vital impulses. What does nature do? *Nature does all the curing*. Every atom has a certain affinity for every other atom in the molecule. We call it chemical affinity. The law of gravitation has a centripetal and a centrifugal force, that is, drawing forces; and these forces whether chemical or physical, have their homologue in the field of biology. The simplest living substance has an internal force which keeps all its particles determined to the organism. Plants grow in fixed forms, the form being definite, different from the formlessness of the inanimate. Here cohesion is a determining principle. This is energy or force and it is derived from the formative intelligence of the animal organism. This keeps all parts of the animal body—from the simple amoeba up to man—in order and this order is the determining factor in functionings. On the basis of this energy or force the great governing principle of the animal life is *adaptation*. Dead substance cannot adapt itself to environment. This vital, operating and adapting force, which represents the *life principle* or soul, keeps the body continuously *constructed* and *reconstructed* on a definite and orderly plan, and this definite orderly plan is carried out by the executive officer of the organism, the *vital force*, in connection with the vital impulses sent from its center to every part of the body.

Here we have the foundation for, (a) the *psychic* cycle of the *will, understanding* and *emotions*, representing the volitional, voluntary and sensitive life of man; (b) the *metabolic* cycle of *anabolism, katabolism* and *rest*, representing the vegetative life of functional activity and development; (c) the *reproductive* cycle, in which certain organs are concerned in preserving the life from destruction, first, of the individual, and secondly, of the race, under the *vital force*, in connection with certain glandular activities, for example, the thyroid glands, supra-renal capsules, pineal gland, and the sexual reproductive glands. The most profound physiological principle illustrated in these glandular processes is *change of substance to the same character in order to assimilation, refining and double refining to reach the central bioplasmic life substance.* Poisons within the limits of the organism are detoxinated. If the system is overborne by poisons it cannot detoxinate. Then biological vitality gives place to chemical activity and the organism is in danger of dissolution and death, disintegration taking place from the central life force by the separation of the different planes of vital activity from the central force. In this case an antidote is demanded on the chemical plane, in order to prevent the central life principle and its forces from being overwhelmed by the toxic action of the poison.

One of the central facts of the physiology is, that the *organism acts as a unity*, consisting of a mass of unit cells. These cells all act in unison and harmony whatever takes place. Hence if the body is diseased there must be,

(1). *Lack of adjustment*;

(2). Reaction of the vital force in the form of disturbance, obstruction or impediment to normal activity;

(3). This reaction upon the vital force weakens certain functional activities and results in consequent tissue changes brought out in the field of morbid anatomy.

The greatest doctrine of modern physiology is that of the internal secretions. These internal secretions represent the most perfect and refined metabolic products in the body. The cerebro-spinal fluid is a secretion of the brain representing the most highly vitalized fluid in the body; the thyroid secretion and the supra-renal secretion represent respectively the stimulation to the vaso-dilator function of the cerebro-spinal nervous system, and the constrictor function of the sympathetic system. The meaning of these secretions we take to be, that a refining process goes on in certain glandular structures of the organism to prepare the most highly nutritive and vital fluids of the body, and on these depend the trophicity of the organism. It is being asserted very widely that physical and chemical processes fully explain the life of man. Even in some of the newer fields man is spoken of as a machine and all his activities are regarded as purely mechanical. Pure bioplasm is structureless, at least as far as the minute examination microscopically of it can show. It is free from granules, the broadest and most essential difference between bioplasm and non-living matter being that bioplasm has a remarkable capacity for movement. In fact mobility is the primary characteristic of bioplasm. Every form of living matter has mobility. This is not all. "Every nutritive act, every form of increase and multiplication, each kind of growth, the production of buds or offsets, the development, the formation and increase of every tissue involves active movement of the particles of which living matter is composed."

This movement in some forms of living matter is microscopic, but no living matter can exist apart from some movement, because *vital movements are essential to life.* When these movements cease life ceases. The primary movements that affect every part of a mass of bioplasm are undulatory or wavelike, producing continual changes in the mass of the bioplasm. In the development of the constituent elements of a mass of protoplasm, there is a movement from the center to the circumference, the nuclei and the nucleoli forming new centers of development internally to the bioplasm, these being vital centers growing out of centers of bioplasm already existing. As the constituent particles of bioplasm move from center to circumference, the fluid containing the nutrient matter or the non-living matter flows from the circumference to the center. As it reaches the center it becomes vitalized and then is determined in the movement from center to circumference and so on ad infinitum while life last. In the movements of one part of a mass of living matter in relation to the rest of the living matter, the movement is peripheral, the first movement being along the line of least resistance. Dr. Gideon Wells, writes, "All metabolism, may be considered as a continuous attempt at establishment of equilibrium by enzymes, perpetuated by prevention of attainment of actual equilibrium through destruction of some of the participating substances by oxidation or other chemical processes, or by removal from the body or entrance into it of materials which overbalance one side of the equation."

In connection with the formation of tissue the amoeboid or locomotive bioplasmic movement is noticeable. This is especially true of the nerve tissue, although it is equally true of muscle and probably of all tissues. The most essential movements in the tissue when developed are, (a) *the movement of living matter from center to circumference,* and as a result of this (b) *the movement of nutrient, non-living matter from circumference to center.* These are essential to life and life cannot exist and be perpetuated without these. The other movements are more or less accessory to these fundamental movements.

In explaining these bioplasmic movements from the centers of life, it is essential to remember that the primary constituent of bioplasm is water, the solid being held in solution in the fluid. In the most minute particle of bioplasm there is a center of vitality. To this center nutrient matter comes from the circumference to be vitalized and to enter the cycle of perpetual movement from center to circumference. New matter is formed in these vital centers, this matter previously non-living coming into contact with the living and acquiring its vital characteristics. There is no power of non-living matter at all comparable to this. A complex process goes on, (a) bioplasm selects the nutrient matter from the blood, (b) the blood in turn is tissue and as such is formed by bioplasmic processes. All the blood elements are in reality the white blood cells or their disintegrated products. The vital action in all cases is at some center of bioplasmic mobility. Hence vitality acts in bioplasmic centers only upon matter that approximates to these centers, preparatory to being itself vitalized. This center of life receives its illustration embryologically in connection with the nucleus of the fecundated ovum, the primary origin of vitality in the newly formed organism. Without this center of life and mobility the new organism would be impossible

Hence the *vital actions* are limited to already existing bioplasm, and this already existing bioplasm in the centers of life renders possible the physical and mechanical phenomena, which we call changes of matter. The bioplasm thus possesses a vital force which it can project into the non-living, drawing it closer to its center life and then projecting it outward towards the circumference of tissue and organ formation. Whatever the fundamental bioplasm in the fertilized ovum may be, as it divides and subdivides in drawing within and projecting out from its own center of vitality non-living matter which it causes to pass through formative changes, there still remains somewhere a great center of this vital activity and mobility. In man the tissues constituting the organism are definitely laid out, before the nerve tissue is developed or begins to act, nerve tissue being the last to reach full development. How then does this development take place? The bioplasm of the nuclei of the embryo represents the formative force at the center of the substance of the nucleus. This divides and subdivides, forming bioplasts that possess inherent vitality, taking in food and pressing it out to the circumference, until fully formed tissues are developed, the bioplasm being associated with the nerve tissue last developed and fully matured. Here lies the secret of that medicinal action which appeals to the centers of the vital force, because only in this way can the circumference of vital matter be reached.

This is equally true of disease. If the bioplasm increases too quickly, its developing power is impaired, resultant tissues are soft and feeble in functioning, because the period of formation has been too short to allow of maturing. On the other hand, if bioplasmic activity is too great there is no tissue development at all. This means that nutrient matter is too quickly rushed through the centers of vitality, to permit of the vitalizing process. Here we have what takes place in the inflammatory processes, an increased nutrition of the bioplasm of tissue or of the organism as a whole in the febrile states. Bioplasm lives very slowly, takes on nutritive matter and slowly projects it with vitalized power into the circumference of tissue or of the organism. In inflammatory conditions the bioplasm grows, becomes static, no new matter being formed to be projected outwards, with a probability of permanent damage being done to the bioplasm, preventing future new formation. This explains why destroyed organs or tissues cannot be reformed, because the formed or structural tissues cannot be reformed, because the formed or structural tissues and organs are developed from structureless bioplasmic atoms.

Connective and epithelial tissues are most liable to such rapid increase as is found in inflammation, but any tissue may thus pass into pathological motivity. And from every form of bioplasmic tissue, but especially connective and epithelial, pus corpuscles may be formed, these being the degenerated or degraded normal bioplasm corpuscles. Here development takes place pathologically, because all bioplasm tends to grow.

Now in these cases bioplasm is overfed, producing soft tissues, the bioplasm living too fast. The active agent in disease conditions is the degenerated bioplasm, or its particles. The pus corpuscles in connection with septic diseases and the bacteria in contagious and infectious diseases arise from the degenerated bioplasm. These so-called *materies morbi* are not the causes of disease, but are themselves the products of changes in the vital centers and the accumulation of the nutrient elements which favor the growth of the germ as soon as the disturbance of bioplasm exists. Probably in all cases vital action goes too fast, the vital center rushing through itself the nutritive matter with an increased vital activity—too much heat, too much fluid, too much nutrition favor those inflammatory, purulent and febrile conditions which present the conditions of bacterial development, namely heat, fluid and food. The primary starting point, therefore, in the disease condition, is the deranged vital activity; secondly, this reacts upon the metabolic cycle, causing the rush of nutritive elements from circumference to center, with the abnormal products in the bioplasm representing degeneration; thirdly, the pus corpuscles and bacteria are developed and propagated rapidly in the favorable medium.

In the highest form of tissue in the body, nerve tissue, we find all of these principles illustrated. Behind the simplest nervous action there lies a nerve current and this can be set free in connection with chemical change. Before such chemical changes can take place the material must be formed in connection with the central bioplasm. The current that passes along the nerve fiber is generated in the cell and in its nature it is analogous to electricity. These *currents* are undoubtedly associated with *nutritive acts*, these being governed by nerve force. The minute nerve filaments to the capillary blood vessels represent an automatic nerve apparatus connected with blood distribution. If the nutritive process becomes too active, these fibers in the capillaries communicate with the trophic nerve centers in the spinal cord (anterior horns), resulting in the transmission of efferent impulses to the circular muscle fibers of the arterial walls. This diminishes the caliber of the blood vessel and checks the flow of blood to the capillaries, diminishing the amount of nutrition allowed to pass to the tissues. The same nerve apparatus restores nutritive harmony, equalizes the blood supply and balances the nerve forces. In this way the supply of nutrition, the regulation of temperature and the balance of nutrition are preserved. All these nerve fibers and centers were gradually prepared for functional activity by a formative process in the bioplasm and only so long as bioplasmic vitality is preserved will the mechanical functioning of this nerve apparatus continue. The nerve force arises from the changes that take place in these bioplasmic centers. These centers are very closely associated with the sensitive peripheral terminators, especially in connection with the special senses and the terminal expansion of the motor fibers in muscles and other end organs of motivity. In comparison with these very few bioplasmic particles are found in connection with the nerve distribution in serous membranes.

We are justified, I think, in concluding, that the bioplasts at the periphery of the nerves, both superficial and central, have a threefold function, (a) in the formation, preservation and renovation of the complete neural apparatus; (b) in the development of the nerve currents of sufficient intensity to act as stimuli to the nerve centers, these nerve centers with their bioplasm being the great centers of neural impulse generation; (c) the same bioplasm is concerned in the thermogenic function, especially when an unbalance of the nerve economy exists. Heat is then generated instead of nerve impulses or rather the heat is not converted into nerve force or energy. This last will explain the relation of the nervous system to the development of temperature, whether physiological or pathological.

In the human subject, the activity of every organ and tissue of the body is subject to the higher parts of the nervous system, where the bioplasm is found in greatest abundance and complexity. Here we have nerve cells that continue to develop after the rest of the nerve mechanism and the body have attained their maximum. In the caudate cells of the gray matter of the brain we have the centers of fiber formation and the centers of nerve force generation. In the bioplasmic substances found superficial in the gray matter, where the interlacement of fine nerve filaments takes place, we find substance not enclosed in any cell wall, but supplied with such an abundant blood that the changes taking place within them are very rapid. These minute bioplasts are constantly changing during life and in all probability their close and intimate relation to the nerve filaments forms the basis of a *formative* function in connection with neural impulses. This is the center of the vital nerve activities.

In the principles we have laid down we have, the foundation of a number of laws, (a) nutrition moves from circumference to center; (b) vital activity with all its formative energy moves from center to circumference; (c) the central activities are the fundaments upon which peripheral expressions are built; (d) the only rational therapeusis is that which rests upon the central law, that the change in the current of activity must begin at the center, the *vital force*, distributing its curative effects along the pathway of least resistance in the nerve fiber economy, in order to reach the weakest part of all the organism and thus restore it to harmony with the rest of the organism; (e) *vital adjustment is the law of cure*, the purely chemical, physical or mechanical can never cure, unless in so far as these can be converted into a vital equivalent; (f) the nutritive law is that the proximate principle must be supplied in crude form, because this passes in the fluid stream from the circumference to the center of bioplasmic activity, while therapeutic action cannot be affected through the crude form, because the starting point of therapeutic action is in the central bioplasm; (g) order in the vital economy can never be restored by recourse to counter action or counter irritation, but only by the application of the law of *simillimum*. The vital force never decreases, never increases, therefore it can restore order only by an orderly distribution of that vibratile activity which from the center of life keeps every organ and tissue in rhythmic relation to the organism. The *vibratile adjustment* takes place on the scale of the existing mal-adjustment; (h) when dissolution takes place the central vital activities gradually, from without in, let go the material previously constructed under their formative action; if this dissolution is checked before it terminates in death, the reverse order must be followed in the reaction of the vital force upon the material parts of the organism. Hence *ab ultima ad primam* is the principle or law followed out in the rejuvenescence or restoration of the organism.

These are the basic physical, chemical and biological principles at the foundation of the true system of therapeutics.

HEPAR, THE PEACEMAKER.

F. E. GLADWIN, M. D., H. M., PHILADELPHIA, PA.

Hepar is in trouble; his friend Silicea is ill, in fact he is very ill. It is not an acute attack this time; it is his chronic trouble which seems to have reached a culmination.

Silicea's chronic condition has been long lasting and serious in its nature. He never has been well, he inherited a scrofulous constitution and has not improved upon it as he grew older. As a baby he had a great big head with open fontanelles and a little emaciated body, was threatened very strongly with rachitis, had enlarged glands, suppurated glands. His vaccination was followed by abscesses and convulsions. He had growing pains all the way up. When a little fellow his nurse dropped him, his hip joint was injured but no one knew about it, so it was neglected and hip-joint disease followed, then were suppuration, caries and fistulous openings, very sore to touch, the discharge was thin watery and very offensive.

Hepar and Silicea have been comrades since childhood and they have had many woes in common. Whenever you saw Silicea, Hepar would be likely to be somewhere around, he had either gone before or was soon to make his appearance. Hepar always had a soothing effect upon Silicea; that was curious, too, for Silicea was a quarrelsome fellow and obstinate, while Hepar became irritated from the slightest cause and became so furiously angry that he would like to kill some one.

Hepar has another friend whom he has known from boyhood; his name is Mercurius. Silicea and Mercurius could never get along together. I have a notion that they might have been a little jealous of each other in regard to Hepar, though I have never heard it so stated. Whenever Silicea and Mercurius came together there was sure to be a pitched battle. Hepar didn't like to have Silicea and Mercurius fight, for he was a friend of both; he was always on guard even when he was a little fellow and whenever it was possible he would stop in between the belligerents and prevent the fight.

Mercurius always did have a peevish, suspicious, quarrelsome disposition and showed lack of courage. To this day, Mercurius begins a dispute as soon as he comes into Silicea's presence. Silicea tries to keep cool, but Mercurius is so insulting in his remarks that Silicea soon loses his temper in spite of himself. He thinks Mercurius a great coward and he has no use for him.

Silicea has a loathing of life and would like to go and drown himself, but that is no wonder when you remember what a great sufferer he has always been. Hepar has the blues by spells, then he is extremely blue for hours; his pains discourage him, he becomes so sad that he thinks seriously of destroying himself. Mercurius is driven to thought of suicide by anxiety, he hasn't the courage to live.

Silicea and Mercurius are restless fellows—its a wonder they haven't tired Hepar out. Silicea is restless, fidgety, starts at the least noise.

Mercurius can't keep still. He goes hither and thither driven by anguish as though he had committed some crime, fears he will lose his understanding. Probably it is his conscience troubling him, because he has been so mean to Silicea. If Silicea could only understand the extreme anguish of Mercurius perhaps he would feel less like quarreling with him.

Mercurius considers everyone his

enemy. Silicea ought to make allowances for him, but Silicea is very sensitive and Mercurius has hurt his feelings too many times by his insulting manner, so Silicea can't understand nor forgive Mercurius, and Mercurius can't understand Silicea therefore they remain enemies.

Hepar is extremely oversensitive to pain, but his feelings are not so easily hurt; he is a great fighter, furious in his assaults, perhaps it's because neither Silicea nor Mercurius care to fight him that he is able to keep peace between them. Hepar's friendship for these two began way back when they all had hip-joint disease. Silicea had been longest ill. His case had been sadly neglected in the beginning; pieces of bone had worked out and there were several fistulous openings which were very sore. Mercurius was suffering all the pains of the disease which come when the pus is working its way to the surface. He suffered intensely at night. You know Mercurius always was such a restless fellow that he couldn't keep still, especially at night; yet when he had hip-joint disease walking made the pain worse and it seemed to him that it always happened that when the pain was at its worse that was just the time when he had the greatest desire to walk about.

Poor Hepar had great sympathy for Mercurius, he knew from recent experience what those awful nightly pains were; his hip was so extremely sensitive that great beads of perspiration stood out upon his forehead whenever the hip was dressed.

Silicea was Mercurius, next door neighbor. When Mercurius had been wrestling with pain and restlessness all night, he was naturally weak and irritable during the day, and when he saw Silicea limping around it gave him an angry feeling toward Silicea, so he sang out a disagreeable salutation as boys often will. At first Silicea was sorry for Mercurius, for in the long past he also had endured those nightly pains and he had not forgotten what they were, but Silicea was a boy that couldn't keep his temper more than three minutes under provocation, so Mercurius soon had him in a fighting mood, then the battle would begin, each throwing his plaything at the other in a most vicious manner at this point. Hepar would come in, catch the flying missiles and toss them lightly back or forward, as the case might be, and so turn the fight into a merry game. Ever since that time Hepar has been smoothing the way for either Silicea or Mercurius.

Mercurius couldn't resist the temptation to make annoying remarks about Silicea's feet. He said he knew Silicea never washed his feet, for just perspiration never made toes sore nor the feet so offensive and he triumphantly showed his own dampened stockings as a proof of his statement.

Silicea did feel bad about that odor of his feet and he washed them many times a day, but could not wash off the odor of the perspiration, finally in desparation he put something upon them and suppressed the perspiration, then he was in trouble, as people always are when they suppress a demonstration of disease. Indeed Silicea's present trouble has been much hastened by the suppression of that foot sweat.

The three children were all great sweaters from infancy. Hepar always perspired on the least exertion, it was frequently sour and offensive. Silicea sweat profusely upon the head and face, the morning would find his pillow wet with perspiration which was offensive. He too perspired on the least exertion, and now since he is so ill he has profuse debilitating night sweats which are sour and offensive. Mercurius always was a profuse sweater on the least exertion and his perspiration was offensive, but all of his sweating did not make Mercurius feel any better and at times it made him worse. Mercurius, night gowns were stained so yellow from perspiration that his mother couldn't wash them white, they always would look oily.

Hepar was a chilly little chap, his mother never had to call him back to get his overcoat, he doesn't like cold for anything. Mercurius doesn't want to be either too warm or too cold. Silicea says Hepar is right in regard to cold things in everything but the headaches, but Mercurius is sometimes right in the fact that neither heat nor cold is good for headaches.

Silicea had a felon, the pains were lancinating, stinging, burning, throbbing, severe;discharge watery, offensive. Hepar had been blessed with a felon every year for several years, so had much sympathy for Silicea. He said if Silicea could only stand the weight of a poultice the heat would make the finger feel better, but Silicea thought he couldn't stand the heat either, for even the heat of the bed made it worse. Mercurius told them they were both stupid in trying heat or cold, as either would make the pain worse; he had been through it all and knew.

So, mid quarrels and peacemaking the boys grew up and now Silicea is in consumption. He tried to learn the stone cutter's trade and it was too much for him. He had pneumonia which was neglected, tubercles, then abscesses formed, followed by cavities, hemorrhages appeared and now symptoms of septicæmia have followed; there are profuse, clammy, cadaverous, night-sweats covering the whole body; expectoration profuse, muco purulent, offensive and great weakness. Hepar can sometimes relieve the oppressed breathing. Mercurius came in once and stopped the nightsweats, thinking to do him a favor, but Silicea suffered so much more pain when the sweats were stopped that he was glad to have them return again. So Hepar hovers about him helping him when possible and keeping Mercurius away lest he should again do harm.

CONGESTIVE CHILLS—VERATRUM VIRIDE.

JOHN A. WAKEMAN, M. D., CENTRALIA, ILL.

In the congestive fevers which were prevalent in this section many years ago, characterized by severe chill of from two to thirty or more hours in duration, with violent headache, pains all over the body and limbs with nausea and vomiting, usually in a few hours diarrhœa with watery choleraic discharges, with cramping pains in stomach and bowels and not unfrequently bloody stools. The whole surface is cold and, with the extremities, is bathed in a cold, clammy sweat. Pulse small, hard and frequent; respiration, hurried and labored; the urinary secretion scanty and in some cases a complete suppression; the patient soon becomes delirious, often comatose—the thirst is great, so long as the patient retains sufficient consciousness to realize his wants, and involuntary discharges common.

None of the usual remedies for such a condition seemed to exert a controlling influence, and had much trouble with them until I prescribed Veratrum vir. (Norwood Tinct) in second, never above the third, dilution in from one to three drops in a spoonful of cold water every hour for 12, 24 or 36 hours, which would so relieve the condition that the remaining symptoms would be easily controlled by the usual remedies, and convalescence speedy. Many died under the usual treatment in such cases.

Called five miles into the country to see a case. Man aged 50 years, six to twelve hours after the chill came on, and found him unconscious and speechless, cold and clammy, with all the usual symptoms in such cases in an aggravated form and in spite of my best efforts and best remedies, there was not an advantage gained over his threatening disease and it looked as though the patient must die, when I turned him onto his face, and applied dry cups from the sacral region up to the cervical, when he called out *"Hold your horses."* This cupping aroused him and so relieved the brain that the needed reaction came up, accompanied with fever. Patient got warm, consciousness returned and in a few days convalescense was established by the indicated remedy.

The gastric or bilious remitting fevers characterized by commencing with a chill which is soon followed by a violent fever, is very different from these congestive cases, in which the system is so overpowered that no reaction comes up—a perfect collapse, not unlike that of cholora, is where the Veratrum vir. manifests its splendid effects, relieves the congestion, and enables the system to react and fever comes up for a time, but is soon controlled by appropriate treatment.

These cases are always alarming, always dangerous, and it is a great satisfaction to have such a remedy on which you can rely and almost never be disappointed.

Should my brother physicians take me to task for using the cups, I can only say in justification of my course that the case looked dark, all my remedies and efforts thus far (three days and nights) had failed to restore consciousness, or produce a reaction or relieve the congested brain and as a last resort I applied six or eight tumblers over the whole length of the spinal column, which so aroused him that he spoke for the first time during his illness and soon recovered.

(A physician must never be without resources).

Dr. E. E. Morley, informs us that "a *vitality modifying agency* is sometimes necessary," and in this case the cupping seemed to be that agency.

ANTITOXIN—VACCINATION.

W. W. GLEASON, M. D., PROVINCETOWN, MASS.

Boy. Fourteen years of age. Ten months ago was threatened with diphtheria. Antitoxin was injected twice. Made a slow and difficult recovery to health. Since that time ailing frequently with colds and glandular swellings, and subject to tonsilitis. Was attended allopathically through all these troubles. Eventually his father concluded with fear and trembling to have a homœopath examine "a tumor" as he called it, on the lad's legs. Thus I came too see him. "Please examine my boy" said the father, "and tell me what that humor on his legs is. Three doctors have seen it and will not name it." Then he told me of the boy's gradual emaciation, loss of appetite, growing weakness, loss of interest in things he had before liked. Questioning brought out the information regarding the antitoxin treatment, and the affirmation that the previous medical attendants had assured him the admininistration of the serum had nothing to do with the lad's ill-health. Symptoms were:

Spells of deep thought, or "brown studies." Thinks a disagreeable odor comes from his body, which nauseates him to smell it. Irritable. Fretty. Difficulty of thinking connectedly.

Morning vertigo.

Morning epistaxis, with red face.

Aversion to meat. No appetite.

Faintness in stomach, aggravated from 11 to 12 a. m.

Weakness and debility.

Indisposed to any study or work.

Aggravation of all symptoms when going from cold to warm room.

On both legs below knee to ankle anteriorly, dry, scaly, itching, sensitive, eruption, on dark red base, the whole anterior surface of the legs, dark red, and very sensitive, with the whole leg below the knee badly bloated.

Sulphur[m] three doses one week apart, cured.

The other case was that of a girl of fifteen. Had been vaccinated by one of the local physicians ten weeks before I saw her. She was a bright minded girl of naturally keen intellect. Condition as follows:

Sad. Anxious on awaking in morning as if some calamity was impending.

Quick of speech.

Peevish; quarrelsome; loquacious.

Mind wanders as if in what she calls "brown studies" and then she becomes very dizzy.

Forehead cold, drawing as if something pulled from eyes to back of neck.

Pains in throat and from throat to ears; swallows over a lump when drinking.

Thirst for large quantities of water.

Burning in stomach.

Urine thick, muddy, dark brown, scanty, frequent.

Stools very dark brown, cadaverous smelling.

Prolapsus ani.

Sleepless nights until early morning; tossing and moaning in sleep.

Shiverings over whole body, alternating with flashes of heat.

At the seat of vaccination (left arm) a large angry flat itching sore discharging yellowish pus, with coppery red areola, surrounded by purple discoloration, and on arm further from this discoloration numerous deep purple spots.

Right hand grows purple at times with prickling of ends of fingers.

Pain in right forearm, better from hanging hand down.

Lachesis[m] and cm cured in two weeks.

CARDIAC NOTES ON CARDIAC DIAGNOSIS AND THERAPEUTICS.

I often wish that I could be a quiet consultant just to assist in finding out the condition of the heart in many of the cases reported. I don't like to ask questions aloud (in this or any other journal) for fear of offending, but I am so anxious to learn more of remedy action on the heart that I make bold to write. So much is lost that need not be if more was known about cardiac diagnosis, say as given in my Hand Book of Heart Diseases. I often wish I could go over the heart with the attending physicians and make out just the condition before and after the remedy. Would it be out of place for me to offer to help in the diagnosis of these cases? I am firmly of the conviction that we can do so much more with our remedies if we knew what disorders they will cause, as well as what they have cured.

That Mania Aurum Case.

A forceful heart, I am convinced, is often the cause of mania, just as a weak heart leads to melancholia, and no doubt to a suicidal tendency.

Take the interesting and valuable case reported by Dr. Gleason. That young man had an active heart that took on hypertrophy. That restlessness points to cardiac weakness. The body and brain does not get the blood because the pump is weak and he must have artificial help by activity and finally heat, (e.g. sitting about the stove). His energy is at a low ebb. The outlook is dark. Rest is best for him which nature compels him to take. Now look at the dual action of Aurum and finally "the small rapid pulse." That young man doubtless had the athletic history that many young men are now passing through. We all meet them, sometimes cured by Arnica.

Possibly Dr. Gleason has some pulse or cardiac record that will turn new light on the action of Aurum in heart cases. The mental picture was gloriously snuffed out by Aurum. I am curious to know if he had this Aurum symptom: "Great anguish, coming from the præ cardial region, driving him from place to place; palpitation."

T. C. DUNCAN, M. D.

COOK COUNTY CLINICS.

REPORT OF CLINIC HELD BY PROF. DUNCAN.

This case (No. 257605 Mr. J. C.) was admitted to Cook Co. (charity) hospital, Oct. 30, 1901, and was diagnosed in the examining room as myocarditis. He was brought into Prof. Duncan's clinic in the amphitheatre the next morning and carefully examined by a section (Dunham students and post graduate physicians) of the class. The students found great difficulty in locating the apex beat. It was found to the left and downward, behind the sixth rib. The cardiac region was sensitive palpation and percussion. The cardiac area was enlarged due to hypertrophy. These was a re-duplication of second sound at apex. The other sounds were normal, but the cardiac action was weak. The action of the heart and the agony of face pointed to serious cardiac (doubtless myorcardial) disease that the record must throw light upon, which we here extract:

The man was 45 years of age with a negative family history. He drinks. Three weeks ago was taken with severe pain in the cardiac region (left side) with smothering and faintness.

In the meantime the appetite was fair and the bowels regular. He had a little dry cough. Liver and spleen negative.

He could not lie on the left side because of a smothering and crowding at the heart. No effusion could be found in the pericardium, nor friction, telling of an previous pericardial inflammation. The fact was emphasized by Prof. Duncan that inflammation of this serous surface could not occur without leaving roughening that would be revealed by a friction murmur heard on careful auscultation. The same is true with regard to the pleural surfaces following an attack of pleurisy.

It was ascertained that he had attacks of pain extending up the neck and down the left arm, and with them a fear of death. This pointed to the angina pectoris and doubtless of a myocardital origin, rather than spinal. The reflexes, however, were exaggerated. The remedies proposed in the class were *Bryonia*, *Spigelia* and *Cactus*.

From the subsequent record we learn that the remedies given the case were *Spigelia*, *Sulphur*, *Bryonia*, *Spigelia*, *Strychnine* and *Bryonia*.

It would look from all this as if there

was an early carditis, possibly from exposure, that developed the anginal attacks so well met by the remedies. He was discharged as improved Nov. 12, 1901, and the diagnostic record given of the case, while under treatment of Prof. Hood, was pseudo angina pectoris.

Nursing.*

Lecture No. 2.

Ladies. It is true that women in fairly good health during pregnancy seldom have the services of a nurse. There are, however, many things regarding which the pregnant woman often asks advice, and some respects in which she profits by special care and attention. This information you, as nurses, need to be able to impart.

When the fact of pregnancy has become known to the mother she naturally desires so to live as to secure not only her own health but also the health and development of her child. An abundance of properly selected food, an abundance of fresh air, gentle exercise and, above all, a tranquil and happy nervous state, with freedom from shock and disturbance, tend to produce the best development of the child. To obtain this mode of life is very difficult, and the mother who does so must give up some of the occupations and pleasures which she would otherwise enjoy. She must, for example, avoid crowded rooms, overheated buildings, excitement, indigestible food, late hours and fatigue, such as women often experience in prolonged shopping or at social functions.

The diet of normal pregnancy should be based primarily upon three simple kinds of food, namely: milk, fruit and bread. The quantity of meat taken must be small, and meat should not be used more often than once daily. All fruits and vegetables in season may be used, fruits being especially valuable because of their laxitive properties and of their stimulating action upon digestion. Rich foods, fried dishes, pastry, large quantities of meats, sweets, indigestible salads, nuts, pickles, large quantities of tea and coffee or alcohol should be distinctly avoided.

Some patients do not enjoy milk unless it is diluted with effervescing waters or unless it is prepared by rennet or is made into milk puddings, custards, koumiss, or is taken with gruels. Each pregnant patient needs from one to two quarts of water in twenty-four hours. The greater part of this should be taken between meals, especially upon retiring and rising in the morning.

So soon as the first weeks of pregnancy are past the patient will naturally desire to be freed from the pressure by her clothing upon the abdomen. This can be accomplished by a suitable waist, to which much of the underclothing can be buttoned at its lower border, and which obtains its support from the shoulders of the patient. In cold or cool weather thin woolen should be worn next the body. Circular garters should be replaced by long side garters. Shoes and slippers should fit easily, and wraps and all clothing should be loose and made with the greatest regard to comfort.

If a pregnant patient be suitably

*Course of Lectures delivered to the Nurses Training School at Maryland Homoeopathic Hospital, by M. S. Douglass, M. D., Baltimore, Md.

dressed she will be able to exercise, especially as her pregnancy progresses. Walking, or driving over a smooth road are best. During the first few months of pregnancy railway travel should be avoided.

The pregnant patient should have plenty of fresh air and her sleeping-room should be well ventilated. The best ventilator is an open fireplace, and a window containing a board which raises the sash from the bottom, having an air-space at the junction of the upper and lower sash.

The need of quiet for pregnant patients is very great. They should be relieved as far as possible from the cares and worries of daily life.

It is especially important that the skin of the mother acts freely during this period. She should bathe as often as she finds it comfortable to do so. The warm tub-bath at night and a moderately cool sponge-bath in the morning are the best combination for this condition. The warm bath is an excellent means of securing repose, and aids sleep, while the cool sponge bath is invigorating and prevents the patient from taking cold. Neither hot nor cold baths should be taken.

The movements of the fœtus within the womb are always a source of interest and sometimes of alarm to the mother. They are usually felt about the fourth month. The sensation is described as that of the fluttering of a bird held within a closed hand. In young patients, pregnant for the first time, the first movements of the fœtus are sometimes very terrifying and cause the patient considerable alarm. When their meaning is understood they occasion no disquietude. If the fœtu moves actively it excites contraction of the uterine muscle and hence brings about intermittent pains. In some cases movements are so active as to interfere seriously with the mother's sleep, and in other cases the movements give rise to such vigorous contraction of the womb that the patient suffers considerably. There is no way of controlling the movements of the fœtus except by having the mother avoid active, violent exercise. This will usually bring about a period of considerable repose.

Pregnancy is almost invariably characterized by abnormal sensations in the breasts, which in some patients are felt very early. They are described as tingling, pricking, or shooting pains, with great sensitiveness, and sometimes with itching or abnormal sensations about the nipple. The breasts are usually sensitive from the pressure of clothing, and the patient realizes that the breasts are increasing rapidly in size. In ordinary cases little is required in the care of the breasts if the nipples be sound and healthy. They should be examined early in pregnancy to ascertain whether the nipples can be drawn out by the thumb and finger or by the child in nursing, so that they can readily be grasped. The nipples should always be examined for cracks and fissures, and especially for evidences of soreness or sensitiveness or wounding.

The nipple should first be cleaned in a very gentle but thorough manner, to remove dried secretions and any foreign matter which may have stuck to the nipple from the patient's clothing. Then a mild and simple ointment should be employed, which will keep the nipple soft and further the growth of cells and thus put it in healthy condition for the child's nursing.

Among the early phenomena of pregnancy many patients experience what is called *morning sickness*, or the *nausea of pregnancy*. This is usually experienced as soon as the patient wakes, or in some cases so soon as she rises from bed. If the stomach be promptly emptied this often ends the nausea, and if the patient take a little liquid food or a cup of tea or coffee, or even of hot water, she goes through the remainder of the day in comfort. Other patients are nauseated for a longer part of the day, and in some cases the condition becomes a very serious one. All pregnant patients do not have morning sickness, but many do, and it is so common among patients who employ nurses that nurses are very likely to hear of it and should understand its significance.

In giving remedies for this and other abnormal conditions I shall confine myself to only a few remedies, which, in my opinion, are of the greatest importance. It is supposed of course that you understand the importance, as nurses, of reporting all such cases to the physician in charge of the case. However, it will sometimes happen that it is not possible to report to the physician, and the knowledge of the effects of some of the more important remedies by the nurse will often give the suffering patient great relief:

Apomorphia.—This remedy is used in cases that are obstinate and resist ordinary remedies.

Bryonia.—Nausea on waking in the morning. Her nausea is usually relieved by keeping quiet. Dry, parched lips, dry mouth and tongue. Splitting headache. Vomiting of food immediately after eating. She desires to keep still. The gastric derangement is ameliorated by keeping still. Stool of hard, dry feces, as if burnt. Worse on sitting up in bed, after being angry, in warm air, from warm weather or from warm food. Better in cool weather or from taking cool food.

Carbolic Acid.—One of the most prominent of the symptoms in all the provings was *morning nausea and vomiting*. It cures vomiting of ingesta during pregnancy.

Cocculus.—Burning in the œsophagus extending into the fauces, with a taste of sulphur in the mouth. She is scarcely able to raise herself in the morning from nausea and inclination to vomit, it makes her so faint. Worse from riding in a carriage or from sailing. Painful sensation of fulness in the stomach. Nausea which is felt in the head.

Gossypium.—It causes, and has also cured, *anorexia* and *nausea* at the time of the menses; *morning vomiting* in the early months of pregnancy, with violent retching, tendency to fainting, soreness of the uterine region; the nausea appears on *waking* and the vomiting on first *raising the head*; only a thick fluid and a little bilious matter is ejected, with passage of wind both ways.

Ipecac.—One continued sense of nausea all the time—not a moment's relief. Vomiting of large quantities of mucus. Disgust for food, empty retching; vomiting of food, slime or blood; sour vomiting. Cutting pains about the umbilicus.

Nux vomica.—Thinks she would feel better if she could vomit. Nausea and vomiting every morning, with constipation. Putrid taste low down in the pharynx when hawking up mucus. Food and drink have a fetid smell to her. Great depression of spirits. Aversion to water and bread. Longing for beer, brandy, etc. Bitter or sour taste. Belching eructions, hiccoughing, heartburn. Vomiting of food, of bile, of black or sour matter.

Oxalate of Cerium.—In very obstinate cases of vomiting during pregnancy.

Sepia.—Vomiting of milky water or milky mucus. Sense of emptiness at the pit of the stomach; the thought of food sickens her. Eructations tasting like spoiled eggs. Taste as of manure. Aversion to meat. In the morning nausea as if all the viscera were turning inside out. Inclination to vomit in the morning when rinsing the mouth. Disgust for all kinds of food. Vomiting of food and bile.

In ordinary cases the patient's bowels can be kept in fairly good condition by properly selected diet. This should comprise grains so prepared as to leave a portion of the husk or coarser part of the grain, which will act as a stimulus to the intestine. Oat meal, cracked wheat, fine hominy, breakfast foods of various kinds, and in some cases rice, are all useful for this purpose. Graham flour in the shape of bread or biscuit, and rye flour usually mixed with Graham flour or with white flour, are also useful. A liberal supply of fruit, of which the best are apples and oranges, should be afforded. The patient's appetite often craves large quantities of fruit, and this appetite should be indulged to the fullest extent, if digestion remains good. Grapes, rejecting seeds and skin, are especially useful. Strawberries do not agree with all pregnant patients, and some cannot take bananas. With some, uncooked fruit does not agree, although they do perfectly well when fruit is stewed or boiled. Many prefer apples in the form of puddings, and those who cannot use raw fruits may substitute dried fruits or peaches put up in glass. Most canned or preserved fruits, however, contain too much sugar to make them suitable articles for diet in pregnancy. In avoiding the constipation of pregnancy a liberal quantity of water must be employed, and this should be taken not only at meal times, but also on rising and before retiring, and between meals. Any sort of water which the patient prefers may be freely used. The free use of fruits or vegetables, or suitably prepared grains, and the taking of plenty of water, with exercise and bathing, will prevent serious constipation during pregnancy in the majority of cases. It is far better to be careful in this regard than constantly to employ drugs in the treatment of this condition.

Nux vomica.—In hypochondriacal persons, and those who are subject to hemorrhoids. Heat, especially in the face; congestion and headache; unfitness for exertion, disturbed sleep, oppression, ill-humor; sensation as if the anus were closed or contracted, with frequent and ineffectual effort to evacuate.

Opium.—Sensation as if anus were closed, but unaccompanied by frequent desire to evacuate, with pulsation and sensation of weight in the abdomen, dryness of the mouth; anorexia, congestion and headache, with redness of the face.

Alumina. — Obstinate constipation, dependant on a seeming incapacity or palsy of the expelling power of the large intestines, especially if augmented by the use of potatoes.

Bryonia.—Is especially suitable in summer, and to persons subject to rheumatism, or else when the constipation occurs in consequence of a disordered stomach, with chilliness, *congestion* and headache; irascibility; persons of an irritable, passionate character.

Pregnant women are often greatly annoyed by sensations of fainting, or syncope. In some cases this results from weakness, while in others it is entirely a nervous phenomenon, and is especially liable to result from an overheated room or some temporary excitement or a slight fright. Pregnant patients should avoid close rooms and excitement. When faintness occurs the patient should lie down, have the clothing loosened and remain perfectly quiet for a short time. The attack will speedily pass and usually occasions no serious complications.

Swelling of the legs and feet is very common during the latter months of pregnancy. If it is worst at evening, if the patient has little or no headache, if she does not feel dull or depressed, or profoundly melancholic, it is not a serious symptom. If, however, it is attended with very scanty secretion of urine, with violent headache, throbbing in the temples, impaired vision and great disturbance of mind, it is then a serious symptom and should be at once reported to the physician. Pregnant patients should wear loose and easily fitting slippers and stockings, all constriction about the limbs and waist should be avoided, and if the patient be easily fatigued she should take frequent intervals of rest in the recumbent posture. By this means swelling of the feet and limbs can be largely avoided. When such a condition is attended by obstinate itching, frequent bathing with cold water, and in some cases bran foot-baths, are especially efficacious.

Lecture No. 9.

Ladies: Cases sometimes arise in which it is necessary to empty the intestines by mechanical means. The mechanical relief of these patients is obtained by injections adapted to softening the feces and to remove them in a partially liquid state. It is occasionally necessary to extract with the fingers portions of hardened matter which otherwise could not be brought away.

In using injections for these patients care must be taken that the injections should not be too hot nor too cold, and that they be administered as gently as possible, as undue violence might result in the production of abortion. The simplest sort of injection is very dilute warm castile soap suds. This is useful for cleansing purposes, but is not well adapted to soften hard fecal matter. At least one quart will be necessary, and this should be given at a temperature of 100° F., by means of a fountain syringe, the patient lying upon her left side and having the hips higher than the rest of the body. Where it is desired to introduce the fluid as high as possible in the bowel it is well to empty a large-sized soft catheter, passing as far into the bowel as possible. The patient should be encouraged to retain the fluid as long as possible, and when the inclination for movement occurs the injection may be repeated, when the bowel will usually be emptied without much difficulty.

Preparations of oil are especially valuable in cases of obstinate constipation. It is not, however, easy to convey the oil without mixing it with some suitable vehicle. Either castor oil or olive oil may be employed, and the following combination is useful:

Castor oil or olive oil, 1 oz.

Castile soapsuds (at a temp. of 100° F.), 1 qt.

Mix together as thoroughly as possible; add one dram of spirits of turpentine thoroughly beaten up with the yolk of one raw egg.

This combination makes an unirritating and exceedingly efficient injection. If this does not run readily through a fountain syringe, a smoothly working piston syringe should be employed. Care should be taken to give the injection very gently, using as little force as possible.

Saline injections are sometimes given in combination with glycerine. The following is a useful formula:

Magnesium sulphate, .	2 ozs.
Glycerin, . .	2 ozs.
Spirits of turpentine, .	½ oz.
Castile soapsuds, .	1 qt.

When it is necessary to soften the hardened fecal matter ox-gall is often dissolved and injected and allowed to remain for several hours before the bowels are moved. The following combination is useful:

Powdered ox-gall, .	½ oz.
Olive oil, ...	1 oz.
Water (temp. 105° F.),	1 pt.

Thoroughly mix. A piece of Castile soap is then stirred about in this mixture, to make a light lather. The whole when thoroughly mixed is at a temp. of 100° F., which is suitable for the purpose. It should be injected into the bowel as high as possible through a large sized soft catheter or flexible tube, the finger being inserted into the bowel before the introduction of the tube. If the patient's pelvis be raised considerbly it will assist in obtaining a good result. Sometimes the knee chest posture is useful in this injection. If care be used the patient should suffer no discomfort, and should be able to retain the injection for several hours.

In giving injections to remove hardened feces, when it is desirable to carry the material injected high into the bowel, the knee-chest posture is often most advantageous. A few moments of this posture aids very greatly in promoting the passage of an enema high into the intestines. When it is inconvenient or uncomfortable for the patient to assume this position she may lie upon her back with the hips considerably raised by folded blankets or pillows, or she may lie upon her left side with the hips raised. In either case the result is good.

Considerable time is necessary for the thorough emptying of the intestines, because fecal matter is not readily softened. In some cases the softening material may be given at bedtime and an injection for cleansing the bowel administered on the following morning. In other cases several injections during the day are necessary for the purpose. Tubes employed for this purpose should be cleaned by boiling in soapsuds or by rinsing in hot soda solution.

Pernicious nausea of pregnancy is a condition in which the patient is profoundly depressed and nauseated during her waking hours. In many cases the food is rejected so soon as swallowed, and beverages are also rejected by some patients. The matter vomited consists at first of the food swallowed, then of a thin and glairy mucus, and finally, in fatal cases, of a dark coffee-ground-looking material. Patients usually lose rapidly in weight, become profoundly prostrated, and in some instances die of exhaustion.

In nursing these patients it is of great importance that a cheerful and encouraging mental influence be exercised. The words "nausea" and "vomiting" should not be mentioned to the patient. She should not be given a basin or towel in which to vomit, as many nervous patients are made sick by such a suggestion. All depressing and disturbing influences are removed, and the patient's room should be bright and cheerful and her attention should be diverted if possible from herself in any agreeable manner. She should have a soap-and-water sponge-bath once daily, and once daily a light massage, or an alcohol-and-water sponge or massage, accompanied by the innuction of olive oil. The mouth and teeth should receive attention, as patients are sometimes greatly annoyed by the formation of sordes and a very foul condition of the tongue. The mouth may be cleansed with boric acid solution, with dilute thymol, with lemon juice and water, or with ice water and a little alcohol.

The *preparation of food* for these patients requires the most painstaking attention. It is seldom possible to use solids, and barley water, beef juice, chicken, mutton and beef broths must be employed instead. Milk cannot be used unless pancreatized or peptonized, and in many cases in combination with barley water or lime water.

Barley water. Put two teaspoonfuls of washed pearl barley in a saucepan with a pint of water, boil slowly down to two thirds of a pint; strain.

Raw Beef-juice. Take one pound of sirloin of beef, warm it in a boiler before a quick fire, cut into cubes of about one-quarter of an inch, place in a lemon squeezer or a meat press and forcibly express the juice; remove the fat that rises to the surface, after cooling. *Never actually cook the meat.*

Chicken Broth. A small chicken or half of a large fowl, thoroughly cleaned and with all the skin and fat removed, is to be chopped, bones and all, into small pieces; put them, with salt, into a saucepan and add a quart of boiling water, cover closely and simmer over a slow fire for two hours; after removing allow to stand, still covered, for an hour, then strain through a sieve.

Mutton Broth. Add one pound of loin of mutton to three pints of water; boil gently until very tender, adding a little salt; strain into a basin and when cold skim off fat. Warm when serving.

Beef Broth. Mince one pound of lean beef, put it with its juice into an earthen vessel containing a pint of water at 65° F. and let it stand for one hour; strain through stout muslin, squeezing all juice from the meat; place this liquid on the fire and while stirring briskly slowly heat just to the boiling point, then remove at once and season with salt.

The patient should not be asked whether she desires food, nor should she know what is to be given her; nor should food be kept where she can see or smell it.

In cases in which the patient retains very little or no food when given by the stomach, feeding by the bowel must be employed. The success of this method of treatment depends not only upon the selection of the proper materials and their careful preparation, but also upon the care with which the injections are given and the especial attention to cleanliness which these cases demand. The most successful results are obtained with materials which a nurse can prepare. There are many preparations in market especially recommended for this purpose, but they are not so uniformly successful. Among those which are often employed are peptonoids, panopeptone, somatose, various beef juices and other similar preparations. The following formulæ have been found most useful:

1. Beef tea, three ounces;
   Yolk of one raw egg;
   Brandy, one-half ounce;
   Liquor pancreaticus, two drams.
2. One whole raw egg:
   Table salt, 15 grains;
   Peptonized milk, three ounces;
   Brandy, one-half ounce;
3. Beef tea, two ounces.
   Brandy, one-half ounce;
   Cream, one-half ounce;
4. Beef tea, two ounces.
   One whole raw egg;
5. Beef juice, one ounce.
6. Beef essence, six ounces.
7. Whites of two raw eggs.
   Peptonized milk, two ounces;
   Two eggs.

To give nutrient injections successfully the material employed must be at a temperature of 100° F., and should be introduced by a piston syringe which works perfectly smoothly through a soft catheter carried very gently as far into the bowel as possible. The patient should lie upon her left side, with the hips raised. She should be urged not to strain nor bear down, but to endeavor to retain the material injected. Neutrient injections are given, as a rule, at intervals varying from four to eight hours. Unless the tubes employed are kept surgically clean and the rectum is washed out daily with sterile water inflammation of the bowel may result, when the patient will fail to retain the injection. It is best to cleanse the below each morning by a copious but gentle enema of very mild soapsuds, followed by boiled water. Tubes used for rectal feeding should be boiled once or twice daily, and when not in use should be kept in a solution of boracic acid. To lubricate these tubes sterile glycerine or sterile olive oil should be used.

A small amount of nutritious matter can be introduced within the body by inunction in these cases. To accomplish this the skin must be kept in good condition by sponging with warm soap and water and by frequent light massage. The best time for inunction is after the soap and water sponge bath. The materials employed may be sterile olive oil or olive oil (two parts) and alcohol (one part), or sterile cocoa butter. From one to four drams of fat may be rubbed into the body by gentle but patient manipulation. The patient's strength is undoubtedly increased by such treatment.

Cases of pernicious nausea sometimes develop bed-sores very rapidly. To avoid this the patient should be turned frequently upon the side, the skin should be kept in good condition by frequent bathing, and when indications of a bed-sore appear pressure should be removed by such appliances or methods as are applicable to prolonged and wasting diseases.

In some of these cases the cause of the pernicious nausea is found in some abnormal condition of the womb. This may be remedied by local treatment, and the nurse in charge of such a case should be prepared to assist the physician in such treatment. She will require an abundant supply of hot water, antiseptic, surgical cotton or prepared wool, and in many cases antiseptic gauze.

Our next lecture will be "Preparations for a Normal Labor."

Medicine.

DIAGNOSIS OF CEREBRAL LESIONS.

E. R. McINTYER, B. S., M. D.

PROFESSOR OF NERVOUS DISEASES, DURHAM MEDICAL COLLEGE.

There are sufficient number of cases of mistaken diagnosis or no diagnosis and mistaken treatment in cases of cerebral lesions to prompt some discussion on this subject. True, we have books and books that tell us much about cerebral localization. Yet how few can locate a lesion within the cranium, much less diagnose its character, or probable termination. I am fully aware that some teach that to a true Homœopath a knowledge of pathology is useless; that he can prescribe as well without it. With this statement I am not prepared to agree, because (1) the totality of the symptoms cannot be obtained without considering the etiology and pathology; (2) there are many things to be done besides administering the Homœopathic remedy; and (3) the prognosis depends on the morbid anatomy. No one would think of treating a case of uræmic coma the same as one of cerebral haemorrhage, notwithstanding a similarity of symptoms. No one would expect to cure a case of syphilitic tumor of the brain with the appropriate treatment for tubercular meningitis, although they present many similar manifestations.

Not only is it important and even necessary to understand the pathological character of the lesion in order to make a scientific application of all the means of cure, but the location must be known, because not infrequently it is a case for the surgeon, and how shall he operate until he knows where to operate? Cerebral localization has attained great importance and received many additions since Ferrier first published his work on the subject. Still there is much uncertainty about many points in cerebral physiology, some of which will never be absolutely settled. However, we do know something of the functions of definite areas of the cerebral cortex. But that any area is exclusively motor or sensory many have grave doubts. The weight of authority seems to favor a sensory function in the motor area, so called, and that motion, per se, does not even originate in it, but the memory of motion.

We can easily conceive of certain cortical areas as memory organs, but we must remember that the thought of motion also contains sensation, motion being to the mind but a sensation of change of position. But space forbids a full discussion of this subject. The cut illustrates the results of the latest researches in memory localization. Not only do the symptoms vary with the location of the lesion, but also with its size and the rapidity of its development. There are cases on record of large intra-cranial tumors and abscesses revealed post-mortem that gave no head symptoms, the patient dying of some other trouble, their location and slow development accounting for it.

Again the symptoms vary with the character of the lesion as to its irritating or destructive nature. The tables of differential diagnosis will be easily comprehended. They are prepared for the purpose of teaching.

	Paralysis from Lesions of Cerebral Cortex	Paralysis from Lesions of Deeper Structures of the Brain.
Consciousness.	Rarely lost at the onset of paralysis except by extensive lesion, traumatism or an epileptic attack.	Sudden loss of consciousness is the rule, and convulsions are usually absent.
Pain.	Local pain in the head very common at the time of attack.	Patient usually unconscious at the time of attack. Pain in the head less constant after return of consciousness.
Percussion.	Percussion over seat of lesion elicits pain.	No pain on percussion.
Paralysis.	Transitory monoplegia, some muscles paralyzed more than others. The last group of muscles to show improvement will assist to locate the lesion. Sensibility usually impaired.	Hemiplegia or Hemianæsthesia, one or both, is the rule. Paralysis more permanent. Improvement uniform in all groups of muscles.
Muscular Rigidity.	Early rigidity of paralyzed muscles often present.	Early rigidity rare.
Choreiform Movements.	An infrequent sequel.	A frequent sequel.
Electrical Reaction.	Normal as a rule during and after the attack.	May be modified sometime after onset of paralysis.
	Lesions that Irritate the Cerebral Cortex.	**Lesions that Destroy the Cerebral Cortex.**
History.	The majority of cases have a history of syphilis.	Syphilis is not the most frequent of the many causes.

Convulsions.	Convulsions of an epileptoid type, followed by transient paralysis. The parts first to show rigidity during the spasm point to the motor area for that part as the seat of the lesion.	Convulsions are usually absent.
Paralysis.	Transient monoplegia not well defined, on opposite side from the lesion.	Well-marked monoplegia, more or less permanent according to the character of the lesion, on opposite side. The groups of muscles affected will point to the seat of the lesion.
Prognosis.	Good because of the frequency of syphilis as an etiological factor.	Depends on the character, location and extent of the lesion.
	Cerebral Hemiplegia.	**Spinal Hemiplegia.**
Form of Attack.	Onset usually sudden. Consciousness is often lost in central lesions.	Onset may be gradual. Consciousness is not lost.
History.	Some cerebral disease, as apoplexy, tumor, embolism, etc., on side opposite to the paralysis.	Some spinal disease located in cervical region and involving but half of the cord on same side as the paralysis.
Pupils.	Liable to be irregular.	Unaffected unless the cilio-spinal center in the cervical region be involved, when Argyle-Robertson pupil may be present.
Opthalmoscope.	May reveal choked disk or other signs of cerebral lesion.	Reveals no change in the eye.
Cranial Nerves.	Frequent involvement of some of them, crossed paralysis may exist.	Not involved unless spinal sclerosis extends high, late in the disease.
Reflexes.	Usually normal.	Some reflexes liable to be impaired or lost.
Spasms of Muscles.	Spasms of paralyzed muscles not common.	Spasm of limbs very frequent.
Electrical Reaction.	Usually normal.	Modified according to the parts of cord affected.
Sensation.	Anaesthesia or analgesia, when present, are on the same side as the motor paralysis.	Anaesthesia or analgesia, when present, are on the opposite side from the motor paralysis. Sensation of coldness, burning formication, pricking, etc., often exist at the onset. Hyperaesthesia may follow.
Respiration.	Seldom affected.	Difficult breathing, frequent when lesion is above origin of Phrenic nerve.
Sphincters.	Not involved as a rule.	Frequent paralysis of vesical and anal sphincters.
Sexual Function.	Sexual power commonly retained.	Sexual power is occasionally abolished or the passion is increased.

There are still other cases that will be difficult to diagnose without we know the relations of the different parts of the brain and the location of the cranial nerves, and their functions.

A person suddenly finds that he sees double when he attempts to look straight forward, or if the object is toward the right side, he soon finds that he can see single by turning the head to the left and lowering the chin. He has paralysis of the fourth nerve on the right side, which supplies the superior oblique muscle. By changing the position of his head in the way indicated above, the eye is brought to a position to see the object and the normal muscles of the sound eye rotate it to the same focus. The symptoms came suddenly, so it is probably a minute haemorrhage pressing on the nerve. But if he can see a single image by simply turning the head to the right, it indicates paralysis of the external rectus, by a lesion pression on right patheticus nerve. If by turning the head to the left he sees single the right third nerve is involved, and there likely will also be ptosis and a dilated pupil on the right side. In such cases as these of sudden development, tenotomy of the ocular muscles is the contra-indicated and will usually only do harm. A person presents himself with loss of the sense of taste. He affirms he can taste absolutely nothing. His mouth is normal as regards appearance and sensation. He is well, not another symptom to guide us. If we did not know that the sense of taste is controlled by two nerves, the trifacial and the glosso-pharyngeal, and that they are too far apart to be both involved in a lesion so small as to leave all other cranial nerves intact, we might stop here. But by carefully testing we find he can taste bitter, but not sweet, and this only on the back of his tongue. This tells us of some interruption of the lingual branch of the fifth nerve. If it were more central than this other sensory, symptoms of the face would appear, from involvement of some other of its branches. But if he can taste only pleasant or sweet substances, and only on the anterior third of the tongue, the glosso-pharyngeal is involved, and if it appeared suddedly we are justified in the diagnosis of a minute meningeal haemorrhage, since this nerve emerges from the side of the medulla without passing through other cerebral tissue. I once had a patient, who after a blow on the head complained of constant and increasing pain in the head, which persisted in spite of all allopathic treatment. Soon projectile vomiting ensued, which was also persistent. She became weak and emaciated. Some nine months after the first symptom, sight began to fail gradually. About this time she fell into the hands of a so-called surgeon, who operated on the rectum. This served only to increase her suffering, by adding the rectal trouble consequent on the operation. When I first saw her she could only see light, and this ceased after a few months, as did pupilary reaction. Neuro-retinitis was marked, and finally optic nerve atrophy. The vomiting improved as did the strength and weight. There was no involvment of any other cranial nerve. The pupils were widely dilated, but no ptosis. At first one might think of paralysis of the motor occuli because of the dilated pupil, but the absence of ptosis or any abnormality in the movement of the eye contra-indicated this condition. There was no syphilis. To my mind there is but one thing that could cause this array of symptoms, in a case giving this history; that is, a tumor of some kind pressing on the optic chiasm, since both eyes were involved. The age of the child would favor a Glioma, the blow might be the cause of a cyst. I had no opportunity of confirming my diagnosis. Another case I saw in consultation where gradual loss of memory progressed to general mental breaking down, without paralysis. He showed undoubted signs of syphilis. I diagnosed sclerosis of the cerebral arteries with consequent softening of the brain. This I confirmed by a post-mortem examination. Another case I was called to see about 2 a. m. He was in deep coma, like opium poisoning, but the pupils were not contracted. He had been for years a hard drinker. He worked at his trade (he was a sign writer) the day before all day. He died a little while after I reached his bedside. Post-mortem revealed very extensive softening of the posterior portion of the cerebrum, and cerebellum, with less marked changes in the medulla, which was probably attacked late and simply stopped the machinery of life.

Sanitation---Water.

BULLETIN OF THE HEALTH DEPARTMENT OF CHICAGO.

Last Saturday ended the twentieth consecutive week of the driest fall and winter weather ever recorded by the signal service at Chicago. Between Oct. 1, 1901, and Jan. 31, 1902, there was considerably less than one-half the usual rainfall. The total amount measured only 4.48 inches, instead of the annual average, 9.54.

Last year, 1901, was also the driest in more than thirty years—only 24.5 inches of rainfall, instead of the annual average of 38.6 during the thirty-one years of observation. The nearest approach to last year's amount was 26.5 inches in 1891, when there were 1,997 deaths from typhoid fever, and Chicago had the unenviable reputation of having the highest typhoid mortality of any large city in the civilized world.

There has been no sewer flushing rainfall since the 12th of last October. In November there was less than nine-tenths of an inch during the entire month; in December 1.7, and in January less than seven-tenths of an inch. Thus far this month there have been thirteen days on which snow fell, but the total amount measures barely half an inch.

Sewer flushing by the city was suspended at the close of November for lack of funds; some flushing of the main sewers was done in January, but there has been none this month. When rain comes after the twenty-odd weeks of dry weather and the sewers belch out their foul accumulations, and thousands of tons of filth are washed from roofs and streets and other surfaces into the lake and river it will behoove parents to safeguard their children against the use of untreated hydrant water for drinking purposes.

"Boil the water." The injunction was never more important than it promises to be this coming spring. It has saved hundreds of lives in the past before its novelty had worn off, and when it was better heeded than it has been recently. The department is seriously concerned over the situation.

There were thirteen fewer deaths from all causes reported last week than during the week before, and the mortality rate per 1,000 of population is substantially the same as one year ago. Fewer deaths from consumption were reported than in any week for several years—only thirty-seven, against sixty-one during the previous week and sixty-three in the corresponding week of last year. Influenza prevails as an epidemic, and to a greater extent than at any time since the great epidemic of 1891. The disease is assuming a more virulent form, and caused twice as many deaths last week as the week before.

Four new cases of smallpox were discovered during the week, three contracted from the bridewell case of Jan. 27 and one from a so-called case of "chickenpox."

Statement of mortality for the week ended Feb. 22, 1902, compared with the preceding week and with the corresponding week of 1901, estimated mid-year 1902 population 1,820,000:

	Feb. 22, 1902.	Feb. 15, 1902.	Feb. 23, 1901.
Total deaths, all causes	529	542	511
Death rate per annum per 1,000	15 11	15 52	15 16

Personal Reminiscences.

NOTES FROM PRACTICE.

Dear Editor: Homœopathy! You do not know what it is; you n ver prescribed crude opium or calomel. It is something grand; it cures everything curable. Our Materia Medica is so vast and my knowledge of it so limited that I often feel the "nihil" of myself, and still I can palpate the "ego" of Homœopathy. Why, in a couple of weeks all acute cases are cured—sometimes they are well in a couple of days—and the chronic ones, after the first dose, begins *"to change feathers!"* You should see how Homœopathy handles smallpox and diphtheria presently in our town. I have lost no cases of diphtheria, but I must tell that I was called to see them on the fifth day of the trouble. The others get well as they peep out. *Ant. Tart.* generally sweeps off every smallpox "germ," or "virus."

I must tell you that *Lyc.*, 50 m., given two or three times, has cured the boy I wrote to you about last summer. He wheezes no more, and last week *Kreas.* cm stopped his bed-wetting. He has had no *Lycopodium* for nearly three months. You should see how *Opium* worked on a man 73 years old, who woke up one Sunday morning with right hemiplegia. He can saw wood now. Three days after the first dose he could walk up to the village and take off his hat with his right hand.

What is the remedy? But I must tell you that I have a young married woman—the mother of the *Lyc.* boy—that keeps me worried. I cannot "strike" her. Her menses are irregular, thin, watery, acrid; not flowing nights. Pains before flow (in the pelvis). Always too warm. Can't stand heated room, where her feet get cold, bathed in cold perspiration, and her face hot. Can't bear tight clothing. Can't conceive since had her boy, 7–8 years ago, when she had milk leg and pelvic peritonitis. Uterus left retro-flexed and cervix lacerated; pelvic cellular tissue thickened. Woman is fleshy, fair complexioned, looks healthy. Has improved under *Puls.*, but I *can't cure her.* Had scabies when a young girl. Easily tires out. If I only could regulate her monthly as to time and quality it would be all right. *I need your help.* She is not a "weeping" woman; always gay, cheerful. General $<$ before and during menses; from warmth and when sitting; general $>$ after menses; cold on fresh air or motion. Aversion to milk, pork, fat and roasted meat. Desires meat soup, juicy or liquid food. Sweats easily in a warm room and on exertion. Crawling with itching all over $<$ scratching.

You are kindly requested to tell me something about that case.

Friendly yours, R. DEL MAR.

Centreville, Minn.

[Compare Silicea, Sulphur and Lycopodium.—ED.]

My Dear Doctor: I am very sorry indeed that I am so much afflicted with rheumatism that I cannot comply with your request to write an article for your journal. I have been confined to the house for a year; am in my 92d year; am still prescribing for patients at home nearly all the time.

I desire to thank you for your kindness shown me in sending your very good journal so long a time * * * * I think it the best published in the United States or any other country. And in these my last days I wish to say further and with all earnestness that "pure Homœopathy as taught by you is the very best system in the world today."

I say this after an experience of sixty-six years of close study and practice of the healing art by medicine—thirty the old school and thirty-six years in the new, or Homœopathic, school. * * You may publish this or any part thereof, or throw it in the waste basket.

Sincerely yours,

JNO. B. VIVION, M. D.

Galesburg, Ill.

[Such endorsement of Homœopathy and the merit of this conscientious exponent of the same gives us great pleasure and encouragement. Fortunately for us the conversion took place at an earlier period in our medical career and we therefore have the best period of our life to devote to the investigation of this all absorbing subject. The greater the study the more convinced are we of its superiority over every other system or method for *curing* the sick of their infirmities. Its superiority lies in the *breadth* of its application and *harmony* with *natural* law.—ED.]

Announcements.

AMERICAN INSTITUTE OF HOMŒOPATHY.

To the Members of the American Institute of Homœopathy.

The President of the American Institute is able to announce that it is now possible to forecast, to a great extent, the conditions which will attend the holding of the Fifty-eighth Annual Meeting of our National association, to be held in Cleveland, Ohio, June 17th to 21st, 1902.

The local headquarters will be at the Hotel Hollenden, which is one of the finest hotels in the United States, and in its arrangement and appointments is peculiarly well adapted to the purposes of the meeting. The house and its furnishings may be termed elegant, and its cuisine is of the best. A new addition is being built, which will be ready for occupancy in June. The hotel will accommodate 700 guests. A special reduced rate for rooms will be made for Institute members. The Hollenden is on the European plan. The "Colonial," across the street, is another first-class hotel, and can accommodate a large number. It is on the American plan. Other smaller hotels are conveniently near.

The hall for the meetings, in the Chamber of Commerce building, not far from the Hollenden, is splendidly adapted to the Institute's purposes. The hall is large—seating one thousand—it has attached to it numerous committee-rooms, and, what is of special interest and importance, it is quiet, being entirely out of hearing of the noises incident to traffic in busy city streets.

At the present time there is favorable prospect that the several allied Societies will combine with the corresponding Sections of the Institute, by mutual agreement between the officers of the various bodies, so that this year their work will practically be a part of the work of the Institute. This is looked upon as being a fortunate arrangement, and one which will add greatly to the interest of the coming meeting.

It is hoped to have as a special feature of the meeting a "College Alumni Conclave." This, if arrangements are completed, will be held under the auspices of the Institute authorities, and, while affording every opportunity for the enjoyment of the occasion, it will differ in important respects from alumni reunions which have been held in the past. The alumni of the various colleges will, upon arrival in Cleveland, register at headquarters, which will be provided for them by the committee of arrangements, at the Hollenden. On Thursday evening the general conclave will be held at the Chamber of Commerce hall. It is especially desired that the women graduates of our co-educational institutions shall take part. The program for the evening's entertainment will be arranged by the special committee, acting in conjunction with the Institute authorities. The entertainment will consist of appropriate music, orchestral and quartette, and the singing of college songs, together with brief speeches by representatives of the various colleges. In addition to this feature the local committee of Cleveland will, for the several days of the meeting, provide appropriate entertainments of various kinds which, while not conflicting with the Institute sessions, will afford diversion suited to all.

The location of Cleveland is especially favorable. It is easily accessible from the East, from the South, from the West, and from Canada. It is a convenient common meeting-place for all. It is, as yet, too early to announce the arrangements that will be made with the various railroads in the matter of reduced rates of fare. These will be made known in due time.

Cleveland is a city which is more than usually well adopted for convention purposes for a body the size of the American Institute of Homoeopathy. It is pleasantly located on the shore of Lake Erie. It has wide streets lined with many l e trees, beautiful drives and parks, fine hotels, golf links, club houses, and every attraction possible to offer by any place aspiring to entertain such a body as our National organization. The local profession is united, harmonious, and enthusiastic in he work that is given them to do. They are making every preparation and looking forward with anticipations of the greatest pleasure to becoming the hosts of the Institute on this important occasion. There is not a cloud in the sky. All promises well, and there is every prospect that our meeting in Cleveland will be a large one in the matter of attendance, harmonious in its labors, enthusiastic in the spirit that will prevail, and in all respects one of the most successful ever recorded in the history of the Institute.

The executive committee is thoroughly convinced, and more than ever satisfied, that in the best interests of the Institute it has made absolutely the wisest choice in selecting Cleveland for the next place of meeting.

CH. GATCHELL, M. D., Sec'y.

JAMES C. WOOD, M. D., Pres't.

THE OLD GUARD.

The next annual meeting will be held in Chicago in June.

"The membership shall include Homœopathic physicians who have been graduates in medicine for thirty years. The oldest member present shall preside."

The object of this organization is to guard Homoeopathy and to advance the cause.

At the last meeting it was voted that each member should write out for publication: "How I Became a Homoeopath," and send it to the secretary. It was also decided that each member be requested to give his experience with our various remedies in the treatment of disease, according to Similia, taking Jahr's "Forty Year's Practice" and Bayes' "Applied Homoeopathy" as guides. These experiences are to be published for the benefit of their less informed brethren, in such medical journals as members may elect.

In reply to inquiries, it may be said that any earnest, reputable Homoeopathic physician, anywhere above the age limit, may apply for membership.

Yours for the cause,

——— President.

W. W. Estabrook, M.D., ('47) V. Pres.
J. M. Gross, M. D., ('50) Treas.
T. C. Duncan, M. D. ('66), Sec'y.
100 State st., Chicago.

Editorial.

IN A DOCTOR'S WAITING-ROOM.

Have you seen that quaint collection of things of other days,
Which in any doctor's office meets the weary patient's gaze;
Which consists of battered numbers of three-year-old magazines,
And some illustrated papers of long-past battle scenes?
Have you seen those hoary relics of the antiquated past,
With which "trophies" and "mementoes" could be very fitly classed?
If you haven't, make a journey to that abode of gloom
Which is known to fame and patients as the doctor's waiting-room.

Through the pile you run your fingers, for you've nothing else to do,
And at last down near the bottom you discover something new!
Eagerly you pounce upon it, till disgustedly you see
That it's some prosaic treatise on applied pathology.
And if chance some other new one shall reward your wild pursuit,
You'll discover it's a record of the "Bilious Institute."
You can dig there for an hour, but whatever you exhume
Will be just the same old rubbish in the doctor's waiting room.

In a barber shop symposium of literature you'll get
At least this month's Standard or a late Police Gazette;
And, although you'll find their contents are perhaps a little bold,
They will have the signal merit of not being ten years old.
In a bootblack's stand the moments you'll be helped to while away,
With an illustrated paper of the mint of yesterday,
But like faint and shadowy faces from the past's unyielding tomb
Are the newest publications in the doctor's waiting-room.

Where they got them, what collector of remote antiques
Piled upon those shaky tables such fantastic shades as these,
Is a question never answered, for the doctors do not know
How they gathered these remembrances of days long ago.
But it seems to be quite certain that they'd stock a few small shelves
With recent works if they were forced to read those things themselves.
But they're not, and so their patients must their weary minds illume
With the faded, frazzled fiction in the doctor's waiting-room.

Is this picture true to life? Does *your* office resemble in any way the "bill of particulars" here filed against the profession?

If it be true (and who among all the readers of the Advocate has not seen its prototype?) there must be a reason for the same. Physicians do not differ from ordinary mortals. No great change comes over the character of the man with his transition from the student to the physician. The conferring of the degree of "Doctor of Medicine" will not transform a clown into a polished gentleman, neither will one of a strong vital-motive temperament have the mental characteristics of the student predominate. Each man will naturally adopt that line of work for which his development is best suited.

Naturally the majority of the profession starts at the bottom and become "general" practitioners. Their previous environment has in a large degree stamped its imprint upon their lives, and to the degree in which the vital, motive or mental temperaments predominate will we find their personality reflected in "the doctor's waiting-room."

The *vital* or full blooded physician detests an office practice; he dislikes study, and his books accumulate dust and grow old from neglect. His office is a lounging room in which he only spends such time as cannot be employed elsewhere. He enjoys women, horses and a good dinner. It is this sort of a man who seems to take delight in being positively gruff and discourteous to his patients, while at heart he may be as tender and sympathetic as a child. The description above reveals an occupant having the vital temperament in the lead.

If to this you add a strong *motive* temperment with good *perceptives* he will cultivate the *mechanical* side of the healing art. Will be a hale fellow, but earnest and aggressive; a good "mixer" and keen to operate. Cut and slash and almost brutal in his treatment of those who come under his care. His "waiting room" will be as large as circumstances will permit, and all the furnishings will be substantial. He will have a large clientele coming from all classes who will submit to any kind of a "waiting-room" so they can see "their" doctor. There may be books, papers and magazines on the table, but the new will be mixed with the old in hopeless confusion. He hasn't time to give it a thought. His personality is stamped upon every article in his "waiting-room" that was placed there by his own hands.

The third general combination—vital-motive-mental—equally developed, gives us the "*family*" physician. He has the *vitality* necessary for the arduous duties of his chosen profession—the desire for *action* that makes it a pleasure to be busy, and the reasoning, comparing, intuitional mind that finds its keenest delight in the study of human nature. He loves children; is kind and sympathetic in the sick room, and has a sufficient amount of intuition and reason to grasp the general indications of the disease at a glance. His "waiting-room" will reflect the image of his personality in a softening modification of the other two rooms. It may be large or small, as circumstances will justify. He would like to have it pleasant and attractive, but *cannot be depended upon to see to it himself*. He don't want to be bothered with the matter, but shows his appreciation of the efforts of others to keep him in shape, and generally will follow their suggestions, *if repeated often enough*. The above are *general* types. They continue along these lines until experience leads to *special* investigations due to development of *special* faculties, when we will invariably find the *peculiarity* of the man revealed in his "waiting-room."

We have another and rapidly increasing class—*the specialist*. He had positive opinions while yet a student. Took special delight in certain lines of investigation. His love of self, women, money or science so predominated as to govern his life. He selected this profession as the best means to satisfy the end in view, and bent every energy to the accomplishment of his purpose. He may be lazy or aggressive, as the vital or motive may predominate, but you can read his specialty by the general appearance of his office. It begins to proclaim his character as soon as you step across the threshold into his "waiting-room." If his dealings are exclusively with men you will find the walls of the "waiting room" covered with pictures illustrating various forms of disease terminations that will strike terror to the heart of the approaching victim. There may be cases containing plaster or wax figures so life like as to make a vivid impression upon the mind of the patient. The table will be covered with a collection of illustrated papers of the same elevating character usually found in barber shops. There may be a carpet or mat upon the floor or it may be void of ornament. This picture varies with the mental peculiarities of the physician, but the same general charater will prevail even though the "waiting-room" rival in the richness of its appointments the gilded temples of vice in which the disease may have been contracted.

The specialist whose practice is *limited* to diseases peculiar to women differs in no particular from the one who caters to the animal nature of man and, as a rule, include the two, but have separate waiting rooms. In both cases the *vital* temperaments predominate. The animal instincts rule.

The specialist who is worthy the name of surgeon is a man whose *motive* temperament predominates, with the *mental* a close second. His "waiting room" depends upon the relative development of the *perceptives* with the *mental*. The fine, delicate work of the dental or eye surgeon would naturally demand attractive waiting rooms, with refined appointments, while the surgeon who solicits major operations is dependent upon the appointments of the h-spitals and pays comparatively little attention to the minor details of the "waiting room."

The specialist who limits his investigations to the *causes*, direct and indirect, of the various disease manifestations and seeks to determine the means that must be employed for the cure of the same must have the *mental* in the lead, with the *vital* a good second. Many times he is the least *practical* of the three, and as the world counts *success* comes the nearest to being a failure. The "good things" (?) of this world offer little inducement, while the making of money for the satisfaction of accumulation will seldom tempt him from his favorite investigation. The world owes him much but pays him grudgingly. Again we repeat the question, is this picture true to life? If so, look at his "waiting room" for the answer. A small room, with perhaps a single window; a bare floor or an old, faded carpet; three or four nondescript chairs; an old, shaky table in one corner literally covered with a miscellaneous collection of old antiques completes the picture, unless we would note the dust that had settled upon everything, disclosing the fact that no patient had disturbed its peaceful possession. We must pass through the door into the "private" room, or "den," before the real personality of the occupant is revealed, because he has left nothing of self without. We find a room double the size of the outer room. Its walls are lined with books, while the floor becomes the resting place of those that could not be placed elsewhere. Seated in a large chair will be found a man with spare figure, delicate features, high forehead, with the upper part most prominent. The head sparsely covered with hair, while a long, white beard but partially conceals the pointed chin. A wonderful man—a walking encyclopædia—a charming companion, but impractical; a visionary delver into the mysteries of nature; a century in advance of his time. A shrewd man or woman, the complement to him, fits up an elegant suite of rooms, with everything that would make it inviting and restful. It would be easy for the same aggressive spirit to direct suffering humanity toward this wonderful interpreter of Nature's laws with the result that the whole world would rise up and honor his exalted memory.

How should a waiting room "be furnished." This question will be asked by everyone whose toes have been stepped upon, also by those who would cavil at the general tenor of the article.

"*To thine one self be true* and it follows, as the night the day, thou cans't not then be false to any man." If you have the furnishing of your waiting room it will be stamped with your personality—whether that representation be favorable or unfavorable. Like attracts like. You will draw to you and *retain* those possessing similar tastes. If you have no aspirations from a professional standpoint it will be made apparent in your waiting room and the people will call you "Doc.," show you no deference personaliy and question every suggestion made, will leave you without ceremony for any one who gives them reason to believe that his professional work is of prime importance. If your inclination leads you to select the most important field of the family physician, with its arduous duties and weighty responsibilities, carefully study your assets and determine whether you have the physical endurance and mental characteristics needed to win the confidence of *all classes of people*, and then see to it that your waiting room will inspire confidence and hope in all who may come within its confines. Make it neat, *cheerful* and comfortable. Add pictures, papers, magazines suited for all classes. You will not have time to attend to it but see that your instructions are faithfully carried out.

We have no dealings with the mercenary wretch who preys upon the credulity of human nature and counts every unfortunate as this legitimate spoil if by any means he weave his web about him; but you will know the character of the man by the furnishing of the waiting room with objects capable of exciting alarm and so developing the element of fear as to make the unfortunate willing to do anything to escape the impending room. *Shun such a man.*

The true physician possesses such elements of character as should make him a leader in every community for all that will uplift and better humanity.

If your natural inclination leads you to select that class of diseases for your special work which comes nearest to the animal side of man—abuse of the vital or selfish temperament through *amativeness* and *alimentativeness*, see that you occupy a higher plane so that your advise may carry the force of example, for you will then seek to secure *curative* effects instead of palliative. Make your waiting room true to yourself and give something to attract, elevate, excite hope in their breasts while waiting; illustrated papers, magazines, pictures of better class—neat and order.

The mind has a powerful influence over the body and nine-tenths of all the ailments that diminish the working force of the world has its beginning in *misdirected energy*. The correction of the same is a herculean task, so that no one man can hope to master all the intricate problems that must arise from the complexity of modern civilized (?) living. Hence the importance of division of labor. All must have knowledge of our common foundation. The specialist must, if he would be successful, give due prominence to the psychic side of the case and cultivate those faculties within that will enable him to see and analyze the underlying causes that have contributed to the present trouble. Much of this knowledge will be withheld by the patient until after his confidence shall have been secured and no one thing outside the personality of the physician himself contributes so much to this end as the first impression made by the waiting room. Make yourself master of the situation and then see to it that the most delicate sensitiveness of the most refined man or woman who may be attracted toward you is not painfully disturbed while taking their turn in your "waiting room."

The lessons to be learned are:

1. The world forms its first opinions from external sources—dress and general appearance.

2. The "waiting-room" does much to prejudice the patient for or against the occupant of the same. It becomes your silent but eloquent representative.

3. A pleasing environment will tend to the development of your higher and better nature.

4. Success depends upon a happy combination of the *mental-vital motive* temperaments. Study thyself, to know wherein the deficiencies may be found and then seek the best means for their development.

"A NEW SCHOOL."

Dr. Wm. Osler, a shining allopathic light, lately contributed an article to the New York Sun in which he says:

"A new school of practitioners has arisen which cares nothing for Homœopathy and less for so-called allopathy. It seeks to study rationally and scientifically the action of drugs, old and new."

Just what Hahnemann started to do about a hundred years ago, and what hundreds of Homœopathists have done since that time. So where is the newness about this "new school," except as an evidence of the fact that leading thinkers of all schools are beginning to appreciate Hahnemann's teachings of the use of drugs based on scientific principles.

OBITUARY—KIRKPATRICK.

Dr. John C. Kirkpatrick, a pioneer Homoeopathic practitioner of Los Angeles, Cal., died on Oct. 28. He first graduated as a regular, but becoming convinced of the superiority of Homoeopathy he took a course in the Cleveland Homoeopathic Medical College, graduating from that institution in 1877. For twenty years he was a member of the American Institute, and during his residence in Los Angeles, which dates from the year of his graduation, he took an active part in both the State and Southern California societies.

Considering the alleviation of suffering humanity his first duty and pleasure, Dr. Kirkpatrick literally gave of his vitality to save others, too often forgetting self in self sacrifice.

IS CANCER CURABLE?

Prof. J. E. Gilman has raised a storm by his claim, through the daily newspapers, that cancer is a curable disease by the use of remedies, aided by the use of the X-ray. At a regular meeting of the clinical society, held in the Hahnemann College amphitheater late in January, Dr. Gilman attempted to justify the statement theretofore made in the lay press, but the arguments advanced were not satisfactory to any of the brethren present. The conclusion reached seems to be that while Dr. Gilman's investigations may result in good, there is no ground for his present claim that cancer can be cured by internal remedies, assisted by the X-ray.

MARCH—OBSTETRICS.

The readers of the ADVOCATE will be treated to a sort of symposium upon the disturbances incident to the period of gestation and lactation, thus including certain phases of both mother and child. Among the papers will be found "Treatment During Pregnancy," also "Principles Underlying the Treatment of the Premature Expulsion of the Products of Conception," by Geo. M. Cooper, Philadelphia;

"Two Obstetrical Cases," by M. E. Douglas, Baltimore;

"Placenta Previa," by Frank C. Titzell, Chicago;

"Retained Placenta," by W. W. Gleason, Provincetown, Mass.;

"Nursing in Normal Labor," by M. E. Douglass;

"Medical Treatment of Endocervicitis," by J. West Hingston, Chicago;

"Marasmus," by G. E. Dienst, Naperville, Ill.;

"Homœopathy in the Cure of Children," by S. Mary Ives, Middletown, Conn.

Other papers have been promised that will make this number of special value.

THE REMEDY OR THE KNIFE, WHICH?

The above is the title of an article in the current number of the Medical Counselor, by Dr. Stephen H. Knight, professor of surgery in the Detroit Homœopathic College. Dr. Knight, while not averse to the use of the knife, claims that in almost all cases of appendicitis its use is not only unnecessary, but at times dangerous, and that the disease will be oftener cured by the use of the indicated remedy. Prof. Cowperthwaite, an authority, in his "Practice of Medicine," says:

"It may be a strange experience, but at the same time it is true, that I have had many cases of acute appendicitis, and never yet required the services of a surgeon, though I have always been ready to resort to surgical measures could I see the necessity. It is also a fact that I have several times taken patients from under the shadow of the surgeon's knife and cured them without an operation."

Materia Medica Miscellany.

SOME REMEDIES FOR COLDS.

Dr. Frank W. Somers, professor of Materia Medica, Cleveland Homœopathic Medical College, prescribes *Aconite* for a cold resulting from exposure to dry, cold winds. Chill followed by high fever; skin dry and hot; pulse hard and quick; thirst, anguish and fear of death. Great restlessness.

Belladonna.—Fever; free, bounding pulse; throbbing carotids; drowsy, or may be wakeful: throbbing headache; aching all over the body; head hot, feet cold; the tonsils, glands and muscles of the neck are involved; cough dry and hacking, with tickling in larynx, worse at night.

Gelsemium.—Chilly, can't get warm; sneezing, watery discharge from nose; no thirst; extreme languor and lassitude; limbs of lower extremities as if paralyzed; double vision; headache, beginning in nape of neck, extending over head to above the eyes; face dark red. Patient is dizzy and drowsy. Pulse full and compressible.

Rhus tox.—From exposure to cold and damp. Fibrous tissues involved. Sore, lame feeling, as if pounded. General relief from continued motion. Restlessness. Cough is dry and worse at night, and by uncovering any part of the body.

Camphor.—Chilly, surface of the whole body cold, nose cold, sneezing. Temperature sub normal.

Eupatorium.—Soreness and aching of the body. Bones ache. Thirst, with vomiting. Following the acute stage some of the following may be needed:

Pulsatilla.—Pulse loose by day and dry by night, with soreness in sternal region. Cough worse by lying down. Urine emitted on coughing. Expectoration is yellow or greenish yellow, thick and bland.

Hepar sulphur.—Cough loose, with rattling of mucus. Croupy cough, worse towards morning.

Hydrastis.—Cough, with discharge of thick, yellow, stringy mucus. Expectoration.

Phosphorus. —Tightness across the chest. Cough aggravated by cold air. Frothy expectoration. Expectoration tastes salty.

Drosera.—Arrested secretions in larynx. Cough paroxysmal, deep, hoarse and hollow. Tickling in throat. Cough worse by lying down and after midnight.

Rumex Crispus.—Traceolaryngical secretions scanty. Incessant cough and tickling in larynx, worse at night and in horizontal position. [Extract of article written for the Medical Counselor.]

To relieve the effects of lime in the eye, wash it thoroughly with plenty of warm water—a small quantity simply slacks the lime—then introduce solution of sugar and water.

Dr. J. R. Green of Chicago, in the Pacific Coast Journal of Homœopathy, says of *Cactus grandiflora:* Useful in the cure of certain heart affections; that the fluid extract is substantially useless. Two preparations only are efficient, the epressed juice of the plant (which is difficult to get and soon ferments and becomes inert) and an alcoholic tincture. This remedy, to be effective, must not be mixed with anything else. Dose, not to exceed one drop of the alcoholic tincture; preferably, one-fifth drop.

Arsenicum, 6 x., cured chronic headache of twenty five years' standing. Headache followed typhoid fever. Usually started during the night, lasted two days and two nights. Pain began in occiput, slowly extending to forehead during day. Attacks preceded by feeling of coldness in back of neck. Considerable nausea, but seldom vomited; no relief when he did. Motion and suddenly assuming a standing position made him dizzy. Scalp sore for several days after attacks subsided. As the years passed, patient became more sensitive to cold, drinking cold water made him worse. *Dr. Edward J. Burch in the Clinique.*

China, 15th, administered a dose a day for one month, an old Homœopath says, will prevent the formation of gall stones and the recurring attacks of gall stone colic.

Personals and News Items.

Dr. Fred'k W. Payne of Boston, Mass., has recently moved to the Colonial Theater Bld'g, 100 Boylston street, from 162 Boylston street. His office hours are as formerly, 11 a. m. to 1 p. m. and 2 to 5 p. m.

Redlands, Cal., offers a splendid field for a strict Hahnemann physician of good address. Any such desiring to locate on the coast can obtain full particulars by writing to Dr. S. H. Westfall, Redlands, Cal.

Dr. E. LeRoy Biggs, formerly professor of embryology of Dunham Medical College, is now located at 326 Central avenue, Hot Springs, Ark. Dr. Biggs must have had an unpleasant experience with the ubiquitous and irrepressible hotel drummers who swarm the incoming Hot Spring trains, as he warns all visitors to beware of them.

From the latest report of the condition of the Fourth National Bank of St. Louis, Mo., we are glad to learn that Mr. Frank A. Ruff, president and treasure of the Antikamnia Chemical Company is vice president and a director of that solid St. Louis financial institution, which has a capital of $1,000,000 and nearly as large an amount of surplus.

Dr. William A. Glasgow, 1901 graduate of Dunham, is now pleasantly located at Missoula, Mont. He is enthusiastic over the beauties of the valley in which Missoula is located, surrounded as it is by snow capped mountains. The doctor was the only Homœopath who took the examination before the Montana board, which is considered very rigid, ten out of a total of twenty-seven applicants for license failing to pass. As Dr. Glasgow is the only Homœopathic physician in Western Montana his prospects are exceedingly bright.

Winchester, Ky., a city of 5,000, 100 miles south of Cincinnati, who is said to be a good location for a Homoeopathic physician.

The St. Louis coroner finds that the board of health of that city is responsible for the death by tetanus of seven children who were treated with infected diphtheria antitoxin.

Dr. W. J. Prish of Niagara county, is now located at Fredonia, N. Y., having purchased the property of Dr. Evans who has taken up his residence in Pasadina, Cal. The doctor has been a reader of the ADVOCATE since 1887 and a graduate of Hahnemann, Philadelphia, class of '85.

The San Francisco dailies all have something to say anent the appointment of Dr. Ward, a Homoeopathist, as a member of the Board of Health. Some of the hide-bound papers regard the Mayor's action as a joke, but most of the editors seem to regard the matter as a step forward, which will result in good.

Liberty, Gage Co., Nebraska, wants a Homoeopathic physician very badly—none within fifteen or twenty miles from there. Only one allopath in the place. Population, 450, good surrounding country. Anyone desiring further particulars can obtained them by addressing Mr. C. F. Crocker, Liberty, Nebraska.

Dr. A. M. Duffield is pleasantly located at Huntsville, Ala., further proof, if any be needed, that Homoepaths can and do succeed in the South. Huntsville is becoming quite a resort for those wishing to skip the rigors of a northern winter. To all in need of a physician while in Huntsville the ADVOCATE takes pleasure in recommending Dr. Duffield.

The average human body contains between six and seven ounces of salt, about one-half ounce of which is eliminated daily.

Forty-three physicians were examined by the Illinois Board of Health at the meeting held at the Great Northern Hotel Oct. 9-11.

Dr. James Kraus, the Boston specialist in genito-urinary surgery and venereal diseases, has removed to Warren Chambers, 419 Boylston street.

Dr. D. W. Miller of Blackwell, O. T., and Dr. M. Ethel Reid of Eureka, Kan., were recently united in marriage. May the partnership result in happiness and prosperity is the wish of the ADVOCATE.

Any Homoeopathic physician desiring to locate on the Pacific slope should correspond with the Boericke & Runyon Company, 303 Washington street, Portland, Ore., regarding desirable locations.

A 150-pound man's body contains about nine and one-half gallons of water. Increase the amount of water in the body and power of increased activity will result. Its decrease causes sluggishness.

Homoeopathy is gaining ground in Washington, according to Dr. A. A. Pompe of Toledo, Wash. Any one desiring to locate on the Pacific slope might learn something of advantage by writing him.

The display of drugs, medicines and medical supplies was very meager. No doubt those having to do with the sale of articles relating to the physical welfare of the individual or the health of the community will prepare elaborate exhibits for display at the Louisiana Purchase Exhibition in 1903, especially if a suitable and attractive building, which should be provided, is set aside for that purpose.

Dr. W. A. Shappe, Xenia, Ohio, recently returned to his extensive practice after enjoying a two months' vacation.

The State department at Washington has been notified that the Central Sanitary Council of Tokio will not permit the practice of Homoeopathy in Japan. The general advance in thought resulting from Japan's intercourse with the outside world will, however, soon permeate the medical profession of that country.

The United States, of course, leads the world in the number of lady physicians, there being now over 6,000 in this country. In Great Britain and its dependencies there are 930; in France, 95. Women are not allowed to study medicine in Turkey, althose those graduated elsewhere are permitted to practice in the Sultan's dominions.

The Chicago Department of Health received a gold medal for its exhibits of appliances and methods at the Pan-American Exposition. Other Chicago individuals and firms exhibiting appliances and preparations used by the profession were A. H. Andrews, adjustable invalid bed, receiving a gold medal; Armour & Co., animal extracts, gold medal.

The Japanese are not meat eaters. The cow is an unknown quantity; milk, being an animal product, falls under the ban of their religion. But animals taken in the chase are excepted, as are fish. Mothers nurse their children until the latter are over five years old. The large mortality from tuberculosis in Japan apparently gives the lie to the theory that this disease is mainly caused by the consumption of tubercular cow products. A substitute for butter is made from a native bean rich in oil. The consumption of alcoholic liquors is almost unknown.

Book Reviews.

Dr. Ch. Gatchell has now in press a new work on "*Diseases of the Lungs; their Pathology, Symptomatology, Diagnosis, and Treatment.*" The book will be issued in a few weeks.

Success, the journal of inspiration, for March is, as usual, chock full of good things. To describe them all would be to enumerate every article in the issue. Especially noteworthy as showing what persistent effort, directed toward a certain end, will accomplish is Herbert Wallace's analysis of the life-work of Guglielmo Marconi. This is timely, as it preceeds by only a few days the inventor's feat of communicating on board ship across the ocean with his station at Poldhu, Cornwall, England, 2,099 miles distant.—The daily grind of hard physical and harder mental work of the West Point cadet is interestingly and truthfully told by Capt. W. C. Rivers, U. S. A.—President-elect Palma of Cuba makes plain that the very existence of that productive island is dependent upon friendly commercial relations with the United States. Present tariff on sugar prohibits its export to this country except at a loss, the seriousness of which is apparent when the fact that one half the people of Cuba are dependant for a livelihood upon the profitable marketing of the product of the cane fields.—Besides what might be termed leaders, terse, incisive articles abound, which cannot help but leave their impress for good on the mind of the reader.

A Handsome Group of Portraits.—About a year ago, within the short period of three weeks, four eminent and distinguished physicians departed this life. Two of these well-known men (Hunter McGuire and Lewis A. Sayre) were surgeons, and two (Jacob M. DaCosta and Alfred L. Stille) physicians, and three of them were ex presidents of the American Medical Association. Believing that the rank and file of the profession would appreciate and preserve portraits of these representative practitioners and teachers, the Arlington Chemical Company commissioned a competent artist to paint them in oil in the shape of a panel suitable for framing, and have reproduced the painting for distribution to their friends in the profession. This handsome and thoroughly worthy group of portraits is now being mailed, and if any physician is, perchance, omitted from the list a request will bring a copy.

Messrs. Boericke & Tafel announce the following books for publication within the next month:

Practical Medicine, by F Mortimer Lawrence, M. D. A work on modern Homœopathic practice brought right up to date, and of about 250 pages.

Therapeutic of Fevers, by H. C. Allen, M. D. A book in which the vetern author enlarges the clinical borders of this Therapeutics of Intermittent Fevers (now out of print) to include all fevers.

Leaders in Homœopathic Therapeutics, by E. B. Nash, M. D. A second edition of that Homœopathic classic.

Skin Diseases, by J. H. Allen, M. D. A book in which skin diseases are treated from the stricter Hahnemannian point of view.

Organon. Dudgeon translation. A new American edition of the "corner stone of Homœopathy."

The Hahnemannian Advocate

A MONTHLY HOMŒOPATHIC MAGAZINE.

Vol. xll. Chicago, March, 1902. No. 3

Obstetrics.

TREATMENT DURING PREGNANCY.

Hahnemann in his "*Chronic Diseases*" says: "Pregnancy in all its stages offers so little obstruction to the antipsoric treatment, that this treatment is often most necessary and useful in that condition. Most necessary because the chronic ailments then are more developed. In this state of woman, which is quite a natural one, the symptoms of the internal psora are often manifested most plainly on account of the increased sensitiveness of the female body and spirit while in this state; the antipsoric medicine therefore acts more definitely and perceptibly during pregnancy, which gives the hint to the physician to make the doses in these cases as small and in as highly potentised attenuations as possible, and to make his selections in the most homœopathic manner."

The intuitive mind of Hahnemann clearly perceived the fundamental principles of truth which combines to make the science of Homœopathy. He saw that pregnancy was not to be interrupted or prevented on account of disease, but that this most natural state became a means by which order could be established in a sick body, since the chronic ailments are more definitely portrayed at this time and the hypersensitive organism now more readily responds to the touch of the attenuated remedy.

Thus Homœopathy favors and supports this sacred function of wifehood and the true physician does all within his power to protect the woman to whom has been intrusted the birth of off-spring. In his endeavor to promote the Divine end the Homœopathic physician thus becomes a true healer and conserver of the human race.

The increasing tendency for physicians to advise the prevention or interruption of pregnancy must be most strongly condemned by the Homœopathist as being entirely contrary to sound reason and in discord with the spirit of true medicine. It would seem a blessing of Providence that the fruitful wife may at this time manifest symptoms of an otherwise deeply hidden miasm, and be given an opportunity to take on a state of health.

This teaching of Hahnemann has received but little notice by the medical profession. A case well filled with potentized drugs seems to be the only necessary acquisition in order to be considered a true disciple of Homœopathy. The time has come for us to insist upon an acknowledgment of *all* the fundamental principles of medicine and to require their strict application in practice. The cloak of Homœopathy shields many a false practitioner and our ranks must be cleared of them if our science of medicine is to be crowned with success.

Pregnancy is one of the natural functions of the female body. Divinely ordained, and its stages from conception to a successful termination are according to order and in harmony with the other life functions. It is evident that such a natural state can offer no obstruction to the action of the anti-psoric remedies, for they also act in the same direction with the life forces, that is, they turn disease into order, allowing the vital fluids to resume their free and unrestricted action.

Hahnemann saw that the state of a woman during pregnancy is different from what it is at other times. He says: "There is an increased sensitiveness of the female body and spirit while in this state." This agrees with our present day observations which give to the pregnant woman numerous physical and mental states unknown at other times. To explain this difference from a physiological standpoint based on merely natural phenomena will not satisfy the speculative mind. We know that man is as his mind is, that the body is shaped and governed by the interior and attenuated fluids of the highest regions, and these by the soul itself; therefore, during pregnancy the change must be looked for in this province of causes. In the spirit of the body is found an increased sensitiveness, and increased ability to bring to the surface hidden miasmata, an increased ability to show in signs and symptoms the slumbering inheritances of disease.

Every evil is counterbalanced by a corresponding good, consequently we find this over-wrought constitution now more definitely and perceptibly affected by the similar remedy and a cure of the existing complaints more easily brought about. Hahnemann points out that the indicated remedy in such cases must be toned to vibrate in unison with the oversensitive system, therefore the potency must be highly attenuated and the selection most homœopathic.

Such a gracious provision of Providence comes as a reward to the noble and true wives, who endure the long months of repeated pregnancies with fortitude and bravery, and who having passed through the throes of child-birth are ready to bestow their love and tender affection upon the little one at the breast.

The physician intrusted with the care of those in pregnancy bears a burden of great responsibility. He must use the greatest care in noting the development of the morbid symptoms and the selection of the remedies must be done with precision in order to make a curative prescription. His reward will be the satisfaction of knowing that he has acted from principle and been the means relieving human suffering and in this way of drawing a little farther toward the circumference, the hereditary tendencies which menace the unborn child and threaten the human race.

Geo. M. Cooper.

PREPARATIONS FOR LABOR.*

Lecture No. 4.

Ladies: Labor is that process by which the child is removed from the body of the mother. In natural, spontaneous labor the mother expels the child by the contractions of the uterus and abdominal muscles. When these forces fail the child may be removed from the body of the mother by various surgical procedures.

Labor also includes the removal not only of the child, but its appendages as well. These are the placenta the membranes, the umbilical cord, and the amniotic liquid. If any one or part of these is retained the labor is incomplete. This process must be a gradual one for the safety of mother and child, and may be conveniently divided into periods or stages. The first stage of labor extends from the first regular contractions of the uterus to the time when the membranes rupture and the greater part of the amniotic liquid escapes. The second stage of labor is occupied with the expulsion of the fetus, and the third stage comprises the removal or expulsion of the fetal appendages.

The accurate recognition of labor is an important matter which comes within the province of the nurse. To tell that a patient is in labor or not in labor the nurse should first wash her hands thoroughly with warm water and soap and then should place the patient upon a comfortable bed or couch, upon her back with the thighs drawn up. If labor be beginning the womb can be felt by the hand laid upon it to contract and then to relax at fairly regular intervals. If labor is not beginning, however, uterine contractions will not be especially noticeable.

The first stage of labor comes more under the care of the nurse than any portion of labor. The physician can do little or nothing for his patient, and the patient relies very largely upon the encouragement and care which the nurse gives her during this tedious time.

The rupture of the membranes and the escape of the "waters" marks the end of the first stage and the beginning of the second stage. This often occurs suddenly, and the quantity of fluid discharged may vary from a few ounces to several quarts. In young patients considerable alarm may be felt when the membranes rupture, and the nurse should explain this to the patient before its occurrence, that she may not be frightened. When rupture occurs the pains usually become more severe, uterine contractions are stronger, the patient strains and bears down to assist in the propulsion of the child through the body of the mother. Like the first stage, the second stage varies in duration from a few moments to several hours. During the uterine contractions the face becomes flushed, the heart beats very strongly, the patient often perspires, and she shows that she is making severe muscular exertion. In the intervals between the contractions the patient will often rest quietly and sometimes take a little nap.

When the head has been born there comes a cessation of a very few minutes in the labor, and then the patient has further uterine contractions and the

* Course of Lectures delivered to the Nurses Training School at Maryland Homeopathic Hospital, by H. H. Douglass, M. D., Baltimore, Md.

shoulders and body of the child are born.

The child is still connected with the body of the mother by the umbilical cord, which continues to pulsate, and through which blood passes from the mother to the child.

When the cord has ceased to pulsate it is tied by two ligatures and cut between them and the child is taken away and wrapped up. After a period of rest lasting from fifteen minutes to half an hour there occurs a return of the uterine contractions, and a second, smaller labor takes place. The pains come on again at regular intervals and are not very severe, the uterus contracts, there is a slight flow of blood, and then the edge of the placenta appears in the vulva. If the uterus contracts well the placenta is expelled entirely, the membranes coming after it in a rope or strand. There is but little bleeding, the womb remains well contracted and the labor has ended naturally.

In this process the mother is exposed to wounds and lacerations in the genital tract, the separation of the placenta leaves a wound as large as a small saucer within the womb, hence the parturient patient is exposed to the dangers of wound infection; or, in other words, to puerperal sepsis. If the uterus does not contract the patient will suffer from bleeding, and if she be extensively torn in childbirth, bleeding may occur from ruptured vessels. She must have much the same treatment which patients receive upon whom surgical operations are performed. There must be aseptic or antiseptic dressings to protect this patient from wound infection. Hemorrhage must be prevented or checked, and lacerations in the birth-canal will require closure by suture.

In addition to proper dressings the nurse must be prepared to take antiseptic precautions regarding her hands, her clothing, and any articles which she may use about the patient. There must also be at hand stimulants and anesthetics for a surgical procedure. While in natural birth assistants are not often required, in operative cases the physician needs an assistant to give ether, just as he would for a surgical procedure. Nurses who prepare themselves for surgical work do not expect to attend cases of infectious disease, and if they have a septic case are exceedingly careful to disinfect themselves before going to another operation. So the obstetric nurse must avoid infectious diseases and thoroughly disinfect herself before going from a septic to a non septic confinement.

In addition to the preparations for the care of the mother the child must be considered. Precautions must be taken to avoid infection in the child's body at those places at which it is most apt to occur. Its clothing must be provided, and it often requires a considerable degree of warmth.

In providing proper dressings for a patient to be confined the question of expense and of the work of the nurse engaged must be considered. Suitable dressings may be procured in one of two ways: Antiseptic gauze can be obtained at drug stores and instrument shops, from which dressings can be made. Such gauze, however, costs more than simple dressings. If the patient desires to avoid this expense the nurse can prepare dressings which are aseptic or can be made antiseptic at small cost. The choice of the method of preparing dressings should be left to the patient, and must be determined somewhat by the circumstances of the case.

A cheap and comfortable dressing is made from absorbent cotton and the cheaper quality of cheesecloth. Two thicknesses of the cotton as rolled are taken in a piece seven inches long and five inches wide. Each roll furnishes cotton sufficient for thirty-eight dressings. This piece of cotton is enclosed in one quarter of a yard of cheesecloth so folded as to be eighteen inches long and five inches wide. A roll of cotton can be purchased for thirty-five cents and cheesecloth costs five cents per yard. As a rule dressings must be worn for two weeks. Making a very liberal estimate of the number which may be required the cost of the simple dressings described will approximate two dollars. Dressings may be either sterilized or may be sterilized and made antiseptic as well. Three or four dozen are an ample supply for the first week. These should be put into a clean old pillow-case and the bundle put into an oven and the dressings baked for an hour or two. They should be left in the pillow-case, wrapped in a large, clean sheet of wrapping paper, labelled and put away until required.

If the cheesecloth contains starch it must be boiled in water to which sodium bicarbonate has been added, rinsing it in clean boiled water, and either drying it or soaking it in bichlorid solution (1:2000) after which it can be dried and cut into convenient lengths.

In addition to material for vulvar dressings, bandages will be required for the abdomen. Unbleached muslin is usually selected for this purpose. Sufficient should be purchased to make from half a dozen to one dozen abdominal binders. Each binder should be forty-seven inches long, of double thickness, hemmed at the edges and fifteen inches wide. In choosing rubber sheeting to protect the mattress double rubber sheeting should be obtained if possible. Two pieces, one yard square, should be obtained if the patient can afford them.

When a patient wishes to economize clean old linen may be employed to good advantage. This is soft and may be sterilized by boiling or baking, and made anti-septic by soaking in antiseptic solutions. With cotton-batting it can be used in place of cheesecloth.

A complete list of prepared dressings and medicines may be given as follows: Fifty tablets of mercuric chlorid, of which one to the pint equals 1:1000; lysol, three ounces; bichlorid gauze, five yards in glass jar; borated cotton, one large box; saturated sterile solution of boric acid, one pint; one large, new fountain syringe; rubber sheeting, two pieces, one yard square; one medium sized soft catheter; one stiff nail brush; one clean, new medicine-dropper; best brandy, two ounces; chloroform (Squibbs) four ounces; ether (Squibbs) two half-pounds.

Whenever possible the nurse should give to her patient assistance in selecting and suitably arranging a room for confinement. This should be in as quiet a part of the house as possible, where sunshine and air gain free access and, for the convenience of the nurse, on the same floor with a bath-room. The room should not have in it a stationary wash-stand nor any connection with pipes leading to a sewer. If possible, it should not have a register from a furnace opening into it. It is better if such a room have an open fire-place, in which a fire can be kept burning during cold weather. It is very convenient to have adjoining this room one or two similar rooms for the use of the nurse and the child.

The furniture should be as simple as possible and a high and narrow bed is preferable. A good hair mattress should be selected if possible. Old hangings should be removed and as little drapery as possible employed. The room should be thoroughly cleaned and aired, and it is better to fumigate the room, especially if any infectious case of disease has occupied the room. Carpet is unnecessay on the floor unless the weather is very cold, and a few rugs are all that is needed. Any expensive or highly finished furniture should be removed, as it may become soiled or injured from antiseptic or other material employed about the patient.

For the bed there should be in readiness an abundance of linen which has been repeatedly boiled. Old linen is preferable, as it may become soiled and it might be necessary to destroy it. Several pillows are required, and an abundant supply of towels and bed-linen should be in readiness. The bed for confinement should be made up with a rubber draw-sheet covered by a white draw-sheet in the center of the bed, and above the first linen and draw-sheet there should be placed a complete second outfit. This enables the nurse to take away the soiled linen upon the under or soiled outfit, leaving the patient comfortable. It is usually necessary to pin the draw-sheet and rubber sheet to the mattress with large safety-pins, to keep the sheet smooth beneath the patient. In the absence of the rubber sheet several thicknesses of newspapers may be used. You must learn to employ substitutes when you cannot have just the articles preferred. In short, learn to adapt yourselves to circumstances.

You will require several basins and toilet pitchers, a plentiful supply of hot water, a piece of new and pure Castile soap, several slop-jars and a small, clean agate or tin basin is also useful.

The patient may utilize old underclothing for her confinement. Unless the weather is very hot she needs to wear light woolen or silk-and-wool undershirts. Old night-dresses are useful for this purpose, and they may be slit down the front or the back for ease of application. When the patient begins to sit up in bed dressing-sacques are useful, and when she begins to get up a wrapper or bath-robe or dressing-gown is useful.

Some form of douche-pan or bed-pan will be needed. The ordinary earthen bed-pan usually answers the purpose, although agate-ware douche-pans are better. A commode will be needed when the patient begins to leave her bed.

In preparing for the child the nurse is often expected to provide ligature material for tying the umbilical cord. A thin, narrow tape, called bobbin, is sold in the stores, or a good ligature may be made by tying several strands of coarse linen thread together, boiling them thoroughly and keeping them immersed in boric acid solution.

The baby's outfit consists of toilet articles and clothing. The former are usually arranged in a basket, while the latter are generally prepared during pregnancy and put away in drawers. A simple but sufficient outfit for a baby would consist of the following:

One dozen white slips. Six flannel slips, with sleeves, for night. Six woolen woven shirts, with long sleeves. Six knit abdominal bands. Baby's hair-brush. Powder-box and puff. Four dozen diapers, not too large and made of cotton diaper, twenty-two inches wide. One dozen medium-sized safety-pins. Four soft wash cloths. One dozen soft towels. Two bathing aprons of flannel. Two light and soft shawls. One half-dozen pairs of knit socks.

A crib, or bed, for the child is usually selected. This should be without rockers or swinging motion, plain and simple, and one which if necessary can be thoroughly cleaned. In cases in which it is desired to keep the child especially warm and to move it about readily an ordinary clothes-basket lined with blank- and pillows makes an excellent temporary crib.

In our next we will take up the duties of the nurse during the patient's labor.

THE DUTIES OF THE NURSE DURING THE PATIENT'S LABOR.

Lecture No. 5.

The first stage of labor is especially that which comes under the care of the nurse. The nurse must see to it that the bowels are thoroughly and gently moved by a copious rectal injection. The formulæ which have already been given in treating of the constipation of pregnancy are suitable for this purpose. The bladder must be emptied at frequent intervals, and should the patient not be able to accomplish this the use of the catheter is necessary. The catheter should be passed by direct inspection, the hands of the nurse having previously been cleansed with soap and water, rinsed in hot water and then brushed with mercuric chlorid solution (1:2000). The catheter should have been boiled for fifteen minutes. For pregnant cases the soft rubber catheter is safest; the glass catheter should not be used as the urethra is often subjected to considerable pressure and the glass catheter might wound the parts. The tissues about the opening of the urethra should be thoroughly cleansed with sterile cotton and boiled water and then with bichlorid solution (1:4000). The catheter should be lubricated with sterile glycerin or sterile olive oil.

Vaginal injections before labor should never be given without the precise order of the physician. When such are employed they are usually mercuric chlorid solution (1:4000 or 1:3000), lysol (1 per cent.), and occasionally carbolic acid (1 to 2 per cent.) An excellent cleansing injection is composed of one quart of warm sterile water to which are added two and a half drams of lysol; or warm water, one quart; tincture of green soap, two ounces; lysol, two and a half drams. This combination is especially valuable to patients who have been annoyed by a profuse vaginal discharge during pregnancy.

In addition to emptying the bowel and bladder, if labor is just beginning, the patient should take a warm tub-bath. She should wash herself thoroughly with soap and water, washing the genital organs with especial care. Her clothing should be arranged so as to be as comfortable as possible. In cold weather a thin woolen under-shirt or vest, an old night-dress, a bed-room wrapper, woolen stockings and easy slippers should be worn. In warm weather lighter clothing is necessary. It is often customary to braid the hair in two portions, as it is thus most comfortable during the patient's labor.

It is well to avoid a heavy meal of solid food at this time. As labor proceeds and the mouth of the womb opens the patient is frequently nauseated and she may be obliged to take an anesthetic during labor, when the presence of solid food in the stomach is very undesirable. The best food for this period of labor is that which leaves no residue in the stomach. Chicken-broth, mutton-broth, beef juice, or other nourishing soups or broths, with a small quantity of bread, are suitable. An abundance of water should be taken and a moderate quantity of coffee or tea if the patient desires it.

If the labor is the first, during the early stage the patient should be encouraged to be up and about, because this favors the descent of the child. When pains occur she may lie down or sit, leaning the body forward and grasping a chair in front of her as a support. As the pains increase in severity the patient will be forced to lie down until the birth occurs. When the patient assumes the recumbent position in natural labor she should lie either upon her back or upon the left side, the head and shoulders slightly raised and the thighs flexed upon the body.

As many labors occur at night the nurse should watch closely to see that the patient does not become exhausted from lack of sleep. When the pains are simply nagging without increasing steadily in vigor the nurse should report this fact to the attending physician and thus give him the opportunity for prescribing something to give the patient rest. In some cases, where weakness is apparent, the physician may order stimulants at regular intervals during labor. They should not be given without his orders.

A most important function of the nurse during this part of labor is her mental control of the patient. Very frequently she is asked many questions about the course and progress of labor. She should give such explanations as good sense dictates, never relating anything of a depressing nature. She should never speak of possible complications or of severe cases which she has seen, nor of operations at which she has assisted, or of remarkable recoveries from dangerous illness. Her attitude should be that of patience and hopefulness, while she must absolutely avoid the expression of her own opinion. She must also carefully abstain from stating the probable duration of labor, as this is something which no one can absolutely foretell and regarding which the patient naturally desires information.

As the first stage of labor draws to its close the nurse must utilize the time in preparing for the second or active portion. A plentiful supply of hot water must be always available. Stimulants, antiseptics, dressings, utensils and the necessary articles for the child must all be in readiness. After the membranes rupture an antiseptic dressing may be worn over the vulva. Material should be in readiness for the cleansing of the doctor's hands, as upon his arrival he will usually make a viginal examination.

During the second stage antiseptics should be kept in constant readiness for the cleansing of the physician's hands, and also for cleansing the external parts of the patient at the time of examination. The physician is usually present at this time and the nurse's duties consist in having needed articles ready and in assisting the patient to sustain her strength. Many patients during the second stage of labor suffer from pain in the lower portion of the back, and frequently request the nurse to rub the back or support it by pressure. An anesthetic is often given to a very mild degree of anesthesia, and the nurse should be competent to assist in this. Just before the birth occurs the physician may give the anesthetic into the charge of the nurse, instructing her to use it freely at the moment when the head is born. If ether be employed it should be given in small quantities constantly inhaled, care being taken that the lips and face of the patient are not irritated by the ether. If chloroform is used much less is required to produce an effect. At the moment when the child is born the nurse should have in readiness a warm blanket, ligature for the cord and scissors should also be ready. When the child is born the nurse should be ready to receive it in a warm blanket as soon as the doctor has tied and cut the cord.

So soon as the head of the child is born a slight pause often occurs, and if the conditions are favorable the nurse may wipe the eyes of the child with a small square of very soft linen soaked in a saturated solution of boric acid. So soon as the birth of the child occurs the physician will allow a few moments to elapse before tying and cutting the cord. During this time it is well to wipe out the mouth of the child with soft linen soaked in boric acid solution, that it may be freed from mucus and that the child may not inspire mucus into its bronchial tubes. The discharge of matter from the mouth is much facilitated if the child be held by its thighs and legs with the head downward. Some physicians prefer to crush the cord with forceps before tying it, and apply forceps to the placental end of the cord to control hemorrhage. Two pairs of forceps should always be in readiness for those physicians who prefer this practice.

During the third stage of labor the duties of the nurse are to have ready a plentiful supply of hot water, at least two quarts of such hot antiseptic solution as the physician orders, to have antiseptic dressings available. As the physician delivers the placenta the nurse should hold a basin in which a towel is laid under the patient's thigh, to receive the placenta. The physician will usually remove clots from the vagina, placing them in the basin with the after-birth. If there are no lacerations requiring suture the physician usually instructs the nurse to clean and dress the patient, and the puerperal period may be said to have begun.

The majority of doctors have one douche given after each labor, to wash out thoroughly clots from the vagina and for antiseptic precaution as well. If the physician has confidence in the nurse he requests her to give the douche, if not he gives it himself. The nurse is responsible for the aseptic condition of the douche-tube and douche-bag, for the correct temperature and composi- of the fluid employed, and for keeping the douche-bag full, or at least partially filled, during the entire administration of the douche. She should warn the doctor before the fluid has entirely escaped, as otherwise air may enter the womb and a serious accident follow. The nurse is also responsible for the aseptic condition of the douche-pan, or bed-pan, employed in the giving of this douche. Some physicians prefer to place the patient across the bed, a rubber sheet beneath. After the douche has been given, or if no douche be given, the nurse should thoroughly antisepticize her hands and then exposing the parts should thoroughly sponge away blood and discharges with bichlorid solution (1:4000 to 1:2000). The doctor should order the strength of the solution. This should be done with gauze or cotton sponges. A sea sponge should never be used about a puerperal patient. When the parts have been thoroughly cleaned and dried an antiseptic dressing should be applied, attached to a binder or a T bandage, as the physician may direct.

The application of the binder is a matter which must be decided by the doctor. If there is danger of hemorrhage the binder should not be applied. If the nurse is told to proceed with its application she must first be sure that the uterus is well contracted, being hard and firm. To apply the bandage properly it must be fastened from above downward. The uterus should be brought downward and forward against the brim of the pelvis. The purpose of the binder is to carry the abdominal viscera down against the womb, and, pressing the abdominal walls gently but firmly to retain the uterus in position against the pelvic brim. If the binder be pinned from below upward it may push the womb up into the abdominal cavity and relaxation of the uterus and hemorrhage may result.

Cases sometimes arise in which the nurse is left entirely alone with the patient at the time of labor. The physician does not reach the case in time, the labor is precipitate and the nurse is called upon to deliver the patient. Fortunately in these cases there is no serious obstacle to the expulsion of the child, or birth could not occur so rapidly. Under these circumstances the nurse should place the patient upon her left side, or back, at the edge of the bed, drawing up the thighs and separating the knees, thoroughly cleansing the hands, and placing a basin of bichlorid solution (1:2000) at her side, with gauze or cotton sponges in the basin. The nurse should lay the hand across the perineum of the patient, a gauze or cotton sponge being placed over the anus. The hand should not completely cover the perineum, but leave a half-inch of tissue at the vagina uncovered. As the head comes down the nurse should gently support the perineum and pelvic floor, making pressure upward and backward. If the head comes too rapidly the mother should be told to open her mouth widely, not to bear down, and to breathe as slowly as possibly. The nurse must then watch her opportunity to let the head slip out before the mother has a hard pain. In this way a serious tear can usually be avoided. When the head has been born the nurse should pass the finger to the neck to see if the cord is around the neck. If it is it should be slipped over the head if possible. When the shoulders are born the head of the child should be raised up with the left hand, while the right protects the perineum. So soon as the child is born it is turned upon its right side. The nurse should grasp the abdominal wall with one hand and with the other feel the pulsation of the cord. If the cord is not beating it must be tied about two inches from the umbilicus, and in a second place just beyond and cut between the two ligatures. If the child does not breathe and cry artificial respiration must be employed. When the child breathes and cries it may be taken away, wrapped in a warm blanket, and placed upon its right side.

The mother must now lie upon her back and the nurse sit by her side holding her hand gently but firmly upon the uterus. She should make no effort to deliver the placenta until the mother has contractions of the uterus, or unless hemorrhage begins. If the doctor does not come in time to deliver the placenta, and if the mother has pains the nurse should assist the pains by pressing the womb downward and forward and by grasping it between the thumb and fingers placed behind it and compressing the womb from before backward. When the placenta appears at the vulva the nurse should grasp it and rotate it, drawing gently downward and backward, so that the membranes will twist into a cord. In this way all the membranes come away. The placenta must always be saved for the doctor's inspection. After the delivery of the placenta, the doctor still being absent, the nurse must see that the womb is firmly contracted and, if the patient does well, may apply the binder and clean and dress the patient as usual.

In our next lecture we will discuss "The Puerperal or Lying-In Period."

M. E. Douglass.

PLACENTA PREVIA.

It will be unnecessary for me to go into detail definitions regarding this condition any more than to say, as a sort of a starting point, that in these cases, the placenta is attached to a surface of the uterus, subject to dilatation both during the growth and development of the fœtus and during the subsequent parturition. In other words we may say that the placenta is attached to the lower segment of the uterus, instead of the fundus, as in normal cases.

The different varieties of this condition then, depend entirely upon the point and extent of the attachment of the placenta to this lower segment of the uterus. For instance, where the os is dilated and nothing can be felt with the examining finger, but placenta stretched across and covering the os, it is termed "placenta previa centralis."

When the os is dilated and there is a portion of the membranes, as well as a segment of the placenta, overlapping the margin of the os, it is called "placenta previa partialis." If the placental border comes to, but not beyond, the margin of the inner os, we have what is called "placenta previa marginalis." It is now pretty generally believed that such a thing as a purely cervical attachment never occurs. The idea of the older writers on this subject regarding this particular thing have been exploded by recent and more exact observation. Even exact central implantation is rare and according to the best authorities occurs only once in six cases. This leaves the majority of all cases as either partialis or marginalis, the most of them being of the latter variety, and on the left side. Why on the left side I am unable to determine more than that the majority of placental attachments in normal cases are on the left side.

It is also interesting to note the attachment of the cord to the placenta. It is usually eccentric, but in a great many cases it is marginal and in not a few cases it is only a velamentous attachment. When the cord is long, and it usually is longer than normal, we have prolapse of the funis added as another complication and danger to those already existing.

Placenta previa is a rare affection. Muller says it occurs once in 1000 cases. Hoffmeier of Berlin gives it as once in 750 cases. Crede of Dresden gives it in a pamphlet on the subject, as occurring as once in 700 cases. Schauta and Chrobak of Vienna, both of whom I had the pleasure of hearing on the subject, agree that its frequency is as about one to 750 cases. But be the figures what they may, certain it is it comes too often for the most of us, as is evidenced by the alarming death rate that occurs in the handling of the cases.

It is the most frequent in women who have borne children rapidly and it is six times as common in multipera as in primipera.

A few words as to the cause. In my opinion the majority of cases are unsuccessful attempts at abortion either induced or accidental. The conception has been disturbed and removed from its original point of attachment, and new villi or new attachments of existing villi develop and the fœtus goes on in its growth in its new position. I am convinced that if the clinical history of all cases of placenta previa could be truthfully obtained, it would be found that a large majority of them have been produced in this way accidentally or with the use of instruments or emmenagogues, in an effort to produce a miscarriage.

The clinical features of this condition are numerous and varied, yet sufficiently marked in most instances to materially aid us in making an early diagnosis that is so essentially necessary for the safety of the patient. As we all know, in normal cases of labor, the placenta is separated and thrown off by the contractions of the uterus, after the child has been expelled. In this condition the placenta must, from the very nature of things, be separated first by the stretching of the lower segment of the uterus, depending somewhat on the variety of previa and also on the size of the presenting part. Another important clinical fact to remember is that in normal labor the contractions close the open months of the blood vessels while in this they make them gap the wider and bleed more persistently and profusely.

Hæmorrhage then is unavoidable and is not necessarily limited to the time of parturition. As a matter of fact these women are liable to it at any time and to have it come on in any place. The least jar such as might come from a misstep or from alighting from a carriage, the straining at stool or while urinating are liable to cause a flood of hæmorrhage. These cases are never free from danger of a fatal hæmorrhage. This I wish to emphasize.

In the early months of pregnancy when they are small and more apt to come at the time when menstruation should appear, they may be taken for menstruation and thus throw us off our guard as to the real condition present. As a rule hæmorrhages come at about the 20th week and coninually recur at irregular intervals until parturition. They are not accompanied by nor followed with pain unless at full term. In the marginal variety however hæmorrhage is absent until labor begins or is about to begin, and is the first intimation that a placenta previa is on hand.

The diagnostic features of hæmorrhages are: They come on suddenly; they are not accompanied by labor pains; they come without warning and even during sleep and the amount depends upon the extent of the placental separation.

In speaking of diagnosis we are reminded that there are a few other things besides hæmorrhage to take into consideration. Upon digital examination we find the fornix soft and boggy and thicker on one side. It is only in the second half of pregnancy that we are to get this. As a rule this condition can not be diagnosed at all in the first half of pregnancy. Ballottement is obscure and of little value as a reliable diagnostic help. Pulsation of the vessels of the cervix indicate the abnormal circulation in the parts and point to placenta previa. A positive diagnosis can only be made however when the placenta can be actually felt. To touch, the placenta can be distinguished by its rough, spongy, granular feel, which is different from that of clots or anything else.

This naturally brings us to the question of prognosis. Statistics tell us that in one case in four the mother dies. Two out of three of the children die before birth is completed. One half of the children born alive die within a few hours or a few days.

The most of our deaths are in those that have had hæmorrhages all the way through pregnancy, and this of course means the partial and central varieties. However in cases with good vertex presentations, where the pains are good and dilation is rapid and with a patient having a constitution rugged enough to withstand a considerable loss of blood, the prognosis is much better than indicated above.

Now a few brief words regarding the treatment which is after all the most important part of the subject. We may speculate as to the cause, we can conjecture and guess as to the diagnosis and we can spin fine theories as to the pathology, but when it comes to the treatment it is not what it *may* be but what are we going to do, and do quickly, in order to bring these cases to a successful termination. There are a large number of conditions and diseases that affect the human body that when let alone, or even in spite of treatment, cure themselves. This is not one of that kind. The right sort of treatment is imperative and demanded, and not only this, it must be at the right time.

The history and clinical behavior of these cases force the fact into prominence that we must have one central idea, to be kept constantly in mind, and that is that there is no safety for the mother as long as pregnancy is not terminated.

Fortunately the great majority of cases that have hæmorrhage before the fifth month abort, and the treatment then is the same as for miscarriage in general.

From the fifth month to say the seventh, the earliest time at which we could hope to save the child if born alive, I have but one plan of treatment to offer. If you will remember, the statistics tell us that the child in only one third of the cases is born alive. Of these one half die in a few hours, so we have practically but one chance in six of saving the child, taking the cases as they run in all stages. The percentage is much smaller than this if we confine ourselves to this particular period of gestation, for most of them miscarry when hæmorrhages occur during this time, and then there is no hope, of course, of saving the child. The safety of the mother then should occupy our whole attention, and the treatment instituted should have that object solely in view. To meet these indications I do not believe there is anything else to do but to bring on labor artificially and empty the uterus as rapidly as possible. This I strongly advise and insist upon.

The best way to bring on labor perhaps is by the use of the Barnes dilators. The pressure they exert controls the haemorrhage, which is one of the dangers in doing this at this time. I am not particular however as to what means are employed to bring on labor, but will insist that the thing to do is to bring it on. My observation has been that the great fatality attending these cases, is not due to the inability of obstetrical art to cope with these complications, as much as it is due to the absence of obstetrical aid when most needed. I will quote Dr. Barnes on this point. "If the pregnancy has advanced to the sixth or seventh month it will as a general rule be wise to preceed to delivery, for the next haemorrhage may be fatal. We can not tell the time or the extent of its occurrence, and when it occurs, all that we shall have the opportunity of doing, will be to regret that we did not act when we had the chance."

To wait, to trifle, to tamper with these cases then is negligence and on theoretical grounds and for practical reasons the induction of labor is obligatory. To sit idly by with folded hands, is the best way to perpetuate the mournful tale as told by the statistics giving the death rate in these cases.

From the earliest time that there is hope of saving the child, we will say the seventh month, the treatment should still be of the same prompt and decisive character. We now have two lives, instead of one, to protect and any treatment that hazards either should be condemned. For this reason, we can only mention the policy of waiting the advent of normal labor to condemn it, because of the enormous risk of life to both the mother and child in so doing.

We should now follow the procedure in terminating the pregnancy that has the greater probability of being successful in saving both lives and has the least element of danger connected with it for either. This method I believe to be the induction of labor as soon as possible after we have had a hæmorrhage and we are sure of our diagnosis. There are two courses to pursue.

If our patient is of a rugged constitution and can withstand a considerable loss of blood, and if we have a good vertex presentation, we should induce labor, aiding it as much as possible by dilation and the use of tampons to prevent hæmorrhage, until the head becomes well engaged in its downward course, and then leaving it to terminate in the natural way.

On the other hand, in patients who have little reserve force, and who have already been exsanguinated to their limit, a more rapid method is advised. The Hicks method is perhaps the best. This consists in dilating with a Barnes, or other method, until two or three fingers can be introduced into the uterus. Version is then performed and the feet brought down making a plug for the uterus that effectually controls hæmorrhage. The delivery then is brought to an end as rapidly as possible. With this method there is some chance that the after coming head of the child, by pressure on the core, will prove disastrous to the life of the child, so no time should be lost in delivering this part of the infant.

This it seems to me is the best, the safest, and the most satisfactory way for all concerned to handle these desperate cases. We must first have in our mind a clear idea of the task to perform and then have the courage of our convictions with the necessary skill to carry them out.

In conclusion, I will sum up the treatment, as that is what interests us most, in a few words.

In cases that miscarry, treat them as you would miscarriages in general by emptying the uterus as rapidly as possible.

In cases up to the seventh month, where hæmorrhage has occurred, terminate the pregnancy at once, with no thought of the child, but solely for the safety of the mother.

After this time, make an effort to save the child as well as the mother, *but do not wait for the advent of labor.* Induce it as soon as a hæmorrhage has occurred, letting it terminate slowly and naturally in the one class of cases and by making version and a rapid delivery in the other.

FRANK C. TITZELL.

RETAINED PLACENTA.

I have in record a case which proves the power of the potentized remedy and the futility of the common scare because of retained masses of tissues. Mrs. S. called me for treatment of what she denominated "offensive whites." She was in seeming good health generally, able to attend to her household duties, but troubled greatly by the constant discharge from the virgina of purulent looking liquid so profuse as to necessitate the wearing of cloths which must be changed several times a day, both from the quantity and offensiveness of the discharge. Her abdomen showed some enlargement, but inquiry as to possible pregnancy was met with denial and that denial emphasized by the uncovering of a healthy pair of twins of six months growth sleeping in a cradle. I was not satisfied even by this evidence, and requested to be shown the cloths worn for the previous twenty-four hours. I collected from these cloths and carried home with me some relics not overpleasant, and close examination of these not only made me stronger in my suspicions of pregnancy, but shocked me by the conviction that some of these were portions of a dead fœtus. The presence of distinct pieces of bone, hairs, and flesh, all very small, to be sure, yet recognisable, were indisputable. Subjective symptoms were meagre. There were flushes of heat; cold feet; shooting in the vagina and mouth of womb; discharge burning and corrosive; burning in abdomen; slight hemorrhages at intervals of two weeks; gone feeling in stomach; weight in anus and constipation, with stools either knotty and hard or in very small round balls; colicky pains in abdomen; congestion of blood to head and face; great nervousness, uneasiness and worry of mind; greatly sensitive to any bad odors which caused the offensive discharge to be her constant annoyance; the neck of womb was closed tight; the abdomen was sensitive to pressure; the smell of food was repulsive. She was much better in all her feelings out of doors, and worse in a warm room. She had menstruated (as she thought) the second month after the twins were born, but not afterwards. (She had experienced flows of blood, as I have said.) Being a large, strong and robust, quite masculine woman, these hemorrhages had not weakened her, nor had the excessive vaginal discharge weakened her. This discharge had dated from the fifth month after the twins' birth. That is, she had had the offensive discharge over a month. Her symptoms pointed to Sepia, which was given in high potency. The offensiveness of discharge quickly lessened, and after three weeks' time a rotten mass was discharged which contained the better portion of a fœtus and quite a large portion of a placenta which might indicate a pregnancy of two months' growth. No further discharge occurred nor any untoward symptoms after the discharge of the dead tissues.

Another Sepia case is worth mentioning as showing how little danger there is of sepsis under Homœopathic treatment, even in severe cases, if no measures are taken to obstruct Nature's proper action. This was the case of a young, unmarried woman delivered of a twelve-pound fœtus at full term. There was some laceration, which was immediately and fully repaired with ten stitches. Aside from the laceration, which was unavoidable because of contracted pelvis, the birth was normal up to the last stage, when I found that the placenta was so firmly attached that it could not be removed, breaking down so readily that only pieces could be removed, and the woman suddenly showed such weakness that I preferred to repair the laceration while she could bear it and leave the placenta to Nature to expel. She was under China the first two hours, the symptoms calling for that remedy. The symptoms then changed. There came on shuddering with the after pains which for a first birth were unusually severe. She wanted to be covered thickly during these shudderings. There were fainting spells. She had pressing-down pains in abdomen and back. There was severe pressure at the anus. Yellowish spots came on her cheeks and a yellow shade on the bridge of her nose. There was frequent flushes of heat, chills following. Hands cold as ice. She had spells of laughing immoderately, closely followed by weeping moods. She dreaded being alone a moment. Everything irritated her, and she would then vehemently complain of everything and everybody. She had dizzy spells, followed by flushing of face. At times her sight became dim. Her eyes lachrymated constantly and were sensitive to the light. Here was a good place for that queen of remedies, Sepia. It was given in the two hundredth, and on the seventh day after confinement we had the entire placenta discharged, followed by a first-class recovery.

W. W. Gleason.

TWO OBSTETRICAL CASES.

A few weeks ago I was called to attend a charity case of obstetrics in one of our negro alleys. I found a young, single girl in labor, accompanied with convulsions. She lay on what passed for a bed, in a basement room that served as kitchen, dining, sleeping, living and wash room. She was living with her brother and his wife. The room was not over 10x12, and filthy as it possibly could be. Rags, filthy rags, covered the bed and practically covered the patient. Judging from appearances the floor had seen neither water nor broom for a long time. The space under the bed was filled with all sorts of rubbish, among which I saw several articles of cast-off clothing. For three months this girl had been staying here. On examination I found her limbs enormously distended; pitting on pressure and the pits remaining a long time; face badly swoolen; vulva swollen. Os dilated to about the size of a silver quarter of a dollar. Pains slow, and each pain accompanied by a convulsion. She hardly regained consciousness between the spasms. As far as I could learn she had had about sixteen spasms when I saw her. Knowing that if she remained where she was there could be but one issue, I took a high hand and summoned a police patrol and had her taken to the Maryland Homœopathic Hospital. In order to get her away I had to threaten her brother with arrest.

As soon as we got her to the hospital I had her put in a bath of warm water and thoroughly scoured with soap. Antiseptically preparing her and myself, nurse and instruments, she was chloroformed with the hopes to thus control the convulsions. In spite of this the convulsions returned with every pain, the only apparent effect of the chloroform being to soften the cervix and render it dilatable. With dilators I succeeded in getting the cervix dilated sufficiently to apply the forceps.

The presentation being vertex, but little difficulty was experienced in delivering a male child weighing a little over nine pounds. No lacerations occurred. The placenta was expelled by Crede's method. Considerable hemorrhage occurred, which was controlled by boxing the uterus.

For two days after the delivery the convulsions recurred at irregular intervals, and she received chloroform on three separate occasions. This, with the internal administration of Veratrum viride, and *time*, finally controlled the convulsions.

The œdema of face and limbs slowly disappeared. On the third day her temperature suddenly jumped to 104, she was slightly delirious, very restless. Aconite was given with prompt results. The patient made a good recovery and left the hospital with her infant at the end of three weeks, to return to her den of filth.

In the same hospital, the only accident of the kind I ever witnessed occurred. Everything had gone on apparently well, under the care of one of the internes up to a certain point, when the pains suddenly became so weak that for twelve hours no progress had been made. The membranes ruptured about fourteen hours before I was called, and pains continued for two hours with moderate severity, and then came on the weak, lagging pains.

On examination I found the os dilated sufficiently to apply the forceps. Presentation of vertex in third position. Administering chloroform I applied the forceps and delivered slowly a female child that would weigh about six or six and a half pounds. The placenta followed immediately. I had my hand on uterus, which was fairly well contracted, when the nurse informed me she was hemorrhaging dreadfully. I made an examination and found the bleeding came from the circular artery of the cervix. It was simply frightful the way the blood poured out. Catching the artery with a pair of artery forceps I ligated it, then another bleeding point was discovered in course of same artery, which was also ligated. The woman was very weak but made a good recovery. A slight laceration of cervix was repaired. In all other respects the case was normal.

M. E. DOUGLASS.

THE PATIENT IN DISORDER DURING PREGNANCY AND CONFINEMENT.

Mrs. X. is pregnant. Her mother and sisters are greatly concerned for her and likely to be extremely solicitous for her welfare until the period is ended. Who does not know what this means for Mrs. X.? Her husband, who perhaps has been a loyal patient for some time, wishes the doctor to call and see his wife and quiet the family anxieties. They have known of many women who aroused their sympathies with one and another distressing disturbance during pregnancy and confinement. They talk of these and hope Mrs. X. will be spared all the worst of them, but they are greatly concerned.

What ammunition has the Homœopathic physician with which to disarm this family concern and rout the enemy (disease) if it be really more than a fancied foe? What means to restore a peaceful atmosphere for the development of the precious new being in process of creation, providing for it the best conditions of its heritage? For such an undertaking there is nothing better in the way of preparation for the physician than a thorough understanding of health and disease afforded by the consistent philosophy of Homœopathy. With this perception of health, of what is to be *cured in disease*, the knowledge of things that *derange health and cause disease*, and perception of what is curative in drugs, the mental equipment is completed by the ever-needed tact, without which any undertaking might be frustrated. Thus armed the physician, better a woman than a man for such cases, may intrepidly encounter Mrs. X. and her solicitous friends and, provided they be reasonable people open to rational conviction, they may all be made allies, enlightened by a ray of truth, not alarmed with fear.

First of all is to be impressed a realisation that maternity is a wholly normal function. In an orderly state of the economy every function, not of the uterus alone but of all the organs dominated by a vital controlling force, is regulated to accommodate the constructive development of the new temple for the vital flame and preserve the old in its normal integrity. In this, the organism reaches its highest, grandest activity.

In every case where the functions are not performed in an orderly manner, when pelvic symptoms, digestive or circulatory disorder or mental derangement appear, the *whole economy* is to be considered and means used that will restore the equilibrium of the controlling force and bring about harmonious action of the various parts.

If Mrs. X., when first seen in the early

months of pregnancy, gives a clear record (tested by careful inquiries) of having been fairly well previously, assurances may be made that all apprehensions of alarming disorder, both before and during confinement, may safely be banished, if directions are followed. She is certain to do well, for storms of violence do not break from a clear sky and intelligent questioning will reveal, to a physician trained to seek them, even the early gathering of clouds that might later break, to the surprise of a less observant attendant. If during these early months, there be a more extensive symptomatic record, we need to be even more attentive. Perhaps the family solicitude rests upon a reasonable foundation, that the patient has been in evident disorder, subject to one or more kinds of "sick spells," or handicapped by general weakness expressed in various ways. They have already detected clouds in the sky and fear that a storm is threatening and will bring damage in its train. Here is the field for the true physician's usefulness. The attendant realizes more than the family what pregnancy means to such a woman.

Perhaps she has not been inconvenienced by much sickness or general debility, but has been "moderately healthy," yet the physician's inquiries bring forth acknowledgment of a few or many discomforts, not serious enough to prevent the ordinary performance of duties and pleasures, yet evidence that normal functions are disordered. There are various disturbances for which she has from time to time sought relief in this or that drug, or "home remedy" or druggist's prescription. Perhaps she has been in this same physician's care previous to her present state and a record is already made through months of attendance during her various sick spells and order has been restored more or less successfully. In either of the foregoing instances we are brought face to face with a problem which we must be prepared to solve completely to fulfill our usefulness.

The Disorders of Pregnancy.

To the physician whose deep concern is the greatest welfare of the patient, the periods of pregnancy and confinement are of great interest and importance. During these periods the organism reaches its highest activity, its fullest development; so also during this activity any disorder which exists has the fullest opportunity of expression. Symptoms are the external expression of the internal disorder, which those qualified to read the message conveyed are most desirous to see truly reflected, that the remedy demanded thereby may be administered to cure. In many instances pregnancy gives opportunity for new avenues of experience, symptoms not brought out except during this increased activity. In other cases affections previously existing are intensified at this time and their characteristics more marked.

Whichever may be the case, the true physician will not look upon any group of symptoms as an evil separately to be eradicated. Each manifestation will be taken as a partial index to the condition of the whole, and a remedy will be sought suited to the entire economy. Then, following the administration of that remedy, whether vomiting of pregnancy, albuminuria, varicose veins, cardiac disturbances, hemorrhage, malignant jaundice, convulsions or insanity be the prominent ailments they will be most promptly and satisfactorily dispelled. With this relief there is the immense satisfaction of having the patient thereby best fitted to continue and complete development without the manifestations of even more serious symptoms. There is no hesitancy about administering the needed remedy lest it bring about a forced abortion, for the remedy the patient *needs* renders the uterus more active in its normal functions and less liable to detrimental irritation. Furthermore, the physician need not seek means to force the uterus to expel its contents, because their presence irritates the system. The properly selected remedy will turn the economy into order and the normal function will not continue to be a dangerous irritation.

What a comfort and source of power (in the absence of mental anxiety and doubt as to the methods to pursue) is the knowledge that no manifestation can arise as a complication that is not dependent upon the constitutional disorder. Again, how much does this knowledge intensify the physician's care in seeking the remedy suited to the whole patient. He is aware that in so far as the disorder manifestation progresses, so *positively* is the remedy image intensified and the remedy when administered, going to the head of the disorder, will promptly arrest further progress.

Undoubtedly the best thing for the patient is that she should be under treatment before conception, or in the early months of pregnancy, that orderly action may be assured and the graver stages be prevented. But if when she presents herself first, marked manifestations are already developed the full history must be taken, and the present state treated accordingly, on the same plan. The physician must take patients as they come, unable to choose the time or the stage of the disorder, yet all this goes to express that the patient is to be taken into account. Though it may be to escape the evils of an abortion, already threatening, that consultation is sought, many other things must be inquired into, when little peculiarities will come to light that will help determine the remedy needed more than the fact that abortion is threatened. The remedy thus selected has often checked hemorrhage and prevented delivery until full term was reached, even when symptoms and examinations showed that preparations were well advanced for the actual expulsion of the fœtus.

Crude materialists will undoubtedly scoff at the idea of turning the fœtus in the uterus with an internally administered drug, but when it is realized that all mal-positions are the result of abnormal pressure in or on the uterus it is evident that if the muscles of the organ act properly the contents must take the position to which their shape naturally adapts them—that is, the normal position. The subtle influence of the Homœopathically indicated remedy so controls the muscle fibers to act in harmony that the form of the organ is changed to normal and the fœtus does actually change position to accommodate itself to the containing body. This is done far more adroitly than it is possible to turn the fœtus by external force of even the most skillful hands, in spite of the abnormal shape of the containing walls. Thus even the terrors of a cross-birth are removed by gently transforming it into a normal or more nearly normal presentation.

Let scoffers of medicines say what they will, when the indicated remedy is administered and then there is observed that change in a woman's condition whereby she ends her pregnancy in joy and comfort, whereas she had been suffering from any one of the aforementioned tortures, the satisfaction is not easily destroyed. When such results repeatedly and repeatedly follow the use of such remedies, who will jeopardize his reputation for sanity by claims of their inefficiency? Perhaps the most grateful patients are those who have gone through one or more difficult prolonged labors or tedious, agonizing pregnancies and then have received Homœopathic treatment through a succeeding period. The system is so improved that the labor this time is orderly, prompt and peaceful, almost without fatigue. The contrast, as she lies in comfort meditating on previous sufferings, is enough to arouse the gratitude of even mortal woman. She, and perhaps even her friends, are ready to admit that the medicine did have something to do with it.

We miss also the long sieges of gathered breasts and milk leg giving the patient weeks of suffering, when the story told by all the symptoms of the patient is accepted as the basis of the prescription. But it is difficult, well nigh impossible, to convince physicians and laymen of these facts so wonderful, unless they experience them or witness them in others. But to all who diligently seek, the evidence is clearly revealed.

Hygiene of Pregnancy.

It behooves the physician to understand what things derange health, likewise, to require obedience to hygienic laws. On these grounds the contents of a recently published book should be of interest to all physicians. Here is a point of hygiene brought to the attention of thinking people by one C. F. Bayer:* After much painstaking investigation of facts and circumstances, extending through many years, Mr. Bayer deduces the proposition that inflammatory condition of the uterus and pelvic organs in the course of pregnanancy and immediately following delivery, as well as nervous disorders (convulsions, mania, etc.,) and puerperal fever are chiefly dependent upon the habit of sexual intercourse during the period of child development, when the uterus and nervous system are especially sensitive.

So far as his careful inquiries and consultations with those in a position to know can determine, facts universally uphold this conclusion. It is only among civilized human beings that sexual continence in this period is not practiced. Among animals it is a law of nature followed, as we term it, instinctively; in reality, because they have no choice but to follow nature's laws. Among those usually considered unenlightened, *i. e.*, those living close to nature, some code, religious or other, demands obedience to this rule, and among such these disorders do not occur.

This point in hygiene has never been impressed, but to the Homœopathic physician who appreciates the logical relation of cause and effect and the interdependence of the parts of the economy, it particularly appeals. With this proposition accepted as a guide, it becomes plain at once that patients are to be advised of the importance of this means of securing the best conditions for the maintenance of health. Remove from child-bearing the thought of the suffering from various grades of congestion and inflammation in the uterus (with resultant abnormal attachment of placenta, subinvolution, painful labor and puerperal fever) convulsions and mental derangements, and you have dispelled the most dreaded feature of this function, normally as involuntary as digestion and circulation.

With these abnormalities of pregnancy and confinement removed, the average lying-in period becomes at once greatly reduced in time, and even civilized woman may look forward with hope of bearing children without cessation of the normal activities of life, and with a brief period for the restoration of tissues to ordinary quiescent state. It is herein impressed that *not* the normal

* Modern Researches. Scientific Publishing Co., Chicago.

function of child bearing, but the abnormal sexual relations during these periods, are responsible for the deplorable broken-down state of mothers when they should be yet hearty and sturdy. While it may take generations of continent habits for pregnant women, coupled with the observance of other hygienic laws and relinquishment of enervating influences, to restore civilized girls to the natural strength and reaction of the Indian woman, yet hers must be the ideal standard, and in this habit of continence she may well be followed. Among these people this is accepted as the only proper custom. When delivery takes place the woman is unattended, cares for herself and resumes her duties within a few hours. Even though she must interrupt her travel afoot in the course of a journey she soon overtakes her companions, perhaps at their next stopping place, carrying her hearty little papoose with her. Advocates of ardent antisepsis are at a loss to understand her escape from the undisinfected paraphernalia, but the more rational explanation is the above.

No less important is the effect of sexual intercourse on the developing child observed by the same author. He offers evidence which points to this as responsible for the vernix caseosa and skin and scalp eruptions. In cases of excessive indulgence he traces the development of sexual manias and abnormal sexual activity in the offspring.

Reflection on these matters, in association with the already accepted doctrine of transmission of psoric taint, comes with peculiar interest to the disciples of Hahnemann. It illumines a pathway, for the betterment of man's condition, where the door was but dimly outlined. Shall we not travel it and gather the fruits that grow therein?

JULIA C. LOOS.

PRINCIPLES UNDERLYING THE TREATMENT OF THE PREMATURE EXPULSION OF THE PRODUCT OF CONCEPTION.

In order that all things may follow each other in a proper series, it is necessary for us to proceed from general principles. These I have drawn by consulting the operations of the life forces in the body. They present to us all the laws governing the cure of disease.

That we may fully understand the subject it is necessary to review some essential points in the anatomical and microscopical structure of the Fallopian tubes, uterus and vagina. These organs are situated within the pelvis, outside of the abdominal cavity. The peritoneum folds about them from above, forming the Broad-ligaments. The free margin of the Broad-ligaments contains the Fallopian tubes, right and left, extending from each superior angle of the uterus to the sides of the pelvis. Each tube begins externally in a trumpet-shaped extremity communicating with the peritoneal cavity; it decreases in size and terminates in the uterus in a very minute orifice. In structure the Fallopian tube consists of three coats; the external or serous coat is derived from the peritoneum; the middle or muscular coat consists of an external longitudinal and an internal circular layer of fibres; and the internal or mucous coat, thrown into folds or rugae, is covered by columnar ciliated epithelium.

The uterus is composed of an external or serous coat, derived from the peritoneum; a middle or muscular coat, which forms the chief bulk of the substance of the uterus; and an internal or mucous coat, covered on its surface by columnar ciliated epithelium. Numerous tubular glands, lined with the same epithelium, are embedded in the substance of the uterus, their secretion serving to lubricate the internal surfaces of the organ. The mucous membrane of the cervix uteri is arranged in permanent longitudinal folds; the glands of this part are of the tubulo-racemose type, lined by columnar epithelium and secreting a thick glairy mucus.

The vagina is a membranous canal, lined with mucous membrane, covered with stratified squamous epithelium. In the ordinary contracted state of the canal this membrane is thrown into transverse folds. External to the mucous coat is a layer of erectile tissue surrounded by muscular and fibrous substances.

To comprehend the subject fully, we must next investigate these organs in relation to their several functions. All things produced are fashioned in anticipation of, and according to, the use they are afterwards to perform. The use of an organ determines its structure and position in the body. If we examine these parts therefore in the light of their use, we find that they are wonderfully adapted to taking up the first thread of a new life, conveying it to a suitable resting place, nourishing it until it is able to seek its own existence, and then giving it up to the freedom of the world. We see that the organs take on a form of motion; a motion beginning in the ovary, extending along the Fallopian tubes into the uterus, and finally to the vagina. It is a motion from within outwards and from above downwards. The natural and orderly operation of these parts depends on the preservation of this motion. If we examine it more closely from its inception in the ovary we find a center of activity deep in the ovarian stroma, which, at certain intervals, causes to burst forth on the free ovarian surface, an ovum ready to be carried on in the same vortex of activity. The Fallopian tubes are lined with numberless cilia in constant motion, but not without aim or determination. They take upon themselves this forwarding process from within outwards, being assisted by the two layers of muscular fibres forming the middle coat, which enter into a peristaltic or vermicular motion, extending in a wave—like manner to the uterine attachment. The uterus is formed to receive this motion, holding and jealously guarding it until the time is fulfilled, when it carries it on to its termination with such force that nothing can stay its progress. The ciliated epithelium and interlaced muscular fibres assume this motion in the uterus.

To attain a complete understanding of the use of any member, we must study its relation to all that surrounds it. Connection of structures in the body is also a connection of functions and forces. But slight consideration reveals the fact that the situation of these organs favors this expulsive motion. The uterus and vagina are placed between the bladder and its outlet, anteriorly, and the rectum, posteriorly; therefore they are situated within the very sphere of expulsion.

Again, reviewing these organs in relation to each other, we find the wide vagina below, receiving the motive wave from the less spacious uterus above, which in turn receives from the thread-like Fallopian tubes; thus it proceeds in perfect order and harmony from least to greater and finally to greatest, in a gradually descending series, from parts superior and interior to those inferior and exterior.

We can now foresee that any motion contrary to that outlined above must meet with resistance. The inner parts are most perfectly protected from outside influences. The external generative organs are fashioned in a manner to protect the inner parts; strong muscular bands encircle the vaginal entrance, and the vaginal walls lie in such close relation to each other that, at times, it seems as though the passage were almost obliterated. The cervix uteri is fenced in by rugae and valves turned downwards, which hinder the passage into the uterus, but not out of it. An army of uterine cilia challenge the way to the portals of the Fallopian tubes. Beyond this another host of cilia, enforced by a succession of valves, form an impenetrable line of defenses for the inmost recesses. Such is the construction of these parts that motion from without inwards is disputed with ever increasing vigor, the organs bringing into action every available action of cell protection.

The reception of the male by the female and the passage of the seminal fluid to the ovaries does not act contrary to this order of motion. The parts of the woman answer to those of the man just as though they had first been united and afterwards separated; so that the female offers no barrier to that which was created for conjunction; in fact the two parts so coalesce that in the moment of orgasm they are scarcely aware that they are not one. Following the course of the seminal humor to the ovaries, we see that its path nowhere touches the channel of activity described. Driven forth from its origin, it rests at the mouth of the uterus; it is then conveyed through small ducts in the uterinal walls into the ligaments of the ovary, and finally by an uninterrupted path of little canals it reaches the corpora lutea, penetrating with unerring determination into one ovum.

From the foregoing considerations it now becomes a self-evident proposition that health in these parts must depend on the preservation of this inherent order of motion.

Disease shows itself by disordered functions, interruption of natural currents of motion and disturbed operations. Each organ exerts its faculty of self-protection when attacked by corrupting influences; this it does by stimulating the powers impressed upon it by creation.

Such therefore is the structure of these organs that they are widely provided with the ability to meet the disturbances arising from a premature expulsion of the products of conception. Years of unscientific treatment, failing to embrace any of the fundamental principles, leave the medical world standing aghast at the word "blood poison," which has become intimately associated with an ill-timed ending of pregnancy. If the human race were free from all miasms, nature would be amply able to provide for all retention of fœtal parts that might result from accidental causes. Consult her and see with what skill she protects herself in such cases: ever on the alert, she seeks to drive from her domain that which opposes. This she does by increasing her motion from within outwards, goading it to the highest point until the offending material is cast from the body.

But we are living in a world of disease, surrounded on every side by influences ever ready to act contrary to the order of nature. These evils sometimes prevail and a reversed order of motion is impressed on the organs; a motion from without inwards. We now are led to seek that which will restore order in the place of disorder and establish the harmonious operation of the natural functions.

Homœopathy, rightly interpreted, exactly supplies that which is necessary; the similar remedy, the single remedy in a potentized form, acts in unison with the life forces and quickly turns them into the paths of order, so that disease gives way to health as the created forms of activity are restored. It is the experience of every true Homœopath, when guided by the above principles, never to see any of the troubles or complications pointed out by those who have no idea of the nature of disease in its origin, or of any of the modes and motives that rule supreme in the animal economy. The dangers arising from the retention of fœtal parts of its envelopes are reduced to a minimum when the curative remedy has been administered. So-called septic conditions fade away into nothing as soon as the vital force is allowed to proceed without interruption. Hemorrhages are controlled by nature's own method—muscular contractions—which are stimulated by the restored vital centers. The expulsion of all foreign substances takes place under the order of motion from within outwards, and health is again established.

All methods of treatment contrary to the Homœopathic are unscientific and harmful, for they act in a manner reverse to the orderly process of healing and protection from within outwards. Local measures of every kind from the radical curettement to the milder antiseptic solutions, for reasons now fully manifest, are to be condemned as highly injurious and liable to produce disease rather than cure it; since they proceed directly contrary to that motion which must be preserved in order that health may continue and disease be avoided.

GEO. M. COOPER.

SIMPLE ENDOMETRITIS—ITS TREATMENT.

[*Continued from the February Number.*]

As the lesser important part of the care of these cases I will consider first the local treatment.

The simplest case of endometritis, whether limited to the cervix or extending to the corpus, will require nothing more locally than the cleanliness of the vagina.

Cervicitis with erosion, strawberry granulations, and a glairy, transparent, or yellowish discharge will be much benefited by daily hot water douches, in the last half-pint of which is dissolved a teaspoonful of colorless hydrastis. But if there is offensive leuchorrhœa with inflammation of the vaginal mucous membrane, the purulency showing that pyogenic cocci have invaded the field, calendula should take the place of the hydrastis.

When the mucosa of the entire uterine canal is hypertrophied, with hemorrhages, fungosities, decidual tufts, or polypi, the sharp curette must be used. This minor surgical operation comes within the sphere of every general practitioner.

I cannot stop here to describe the procedure in detail. The salient points only will I give. They are these:

Complete anæsthesia;

Absolute asepsis;

Complete dilitation;

The sharp curette;

Gentleness of manipulation;

Complete removal of the mucosa, including that of the fundus and the horns.

Iodine as a swab where hypertrophy is excessive, mild cases requiring nothing.

The lightest of packing with sterilized or iodoform gauze.

Protection of the dressing from after contamination.

Here let me give you a few don'ts:

Don't use carbolic acid or iodized phenol after curettement, and thus induce a slough.

Don't try to substitute curettement in these cases with zinc chloride, nitric acid, carbolic acid, chromic acid, electrolosis, electric cautery; for each of these will produce a slough, and thus convert a simple endometritis into a septic endometritis, with all the consequences to the adnexia so well known.

Mild forms of atrophic endometritis will require packing with gauze (iodoform preferably). No anesthetic is required. Let the field and the cervical canal be made aseptic. Slight traction on the anterior lip with a dull double tenaculum will straighten the canal. With the applicator introduce a single, slender strand of gauze to the fundus. Do not pack. Protect the cervix with more gauze. Next day, and each two days thereafter, the size of the strip of gauze may be increased, as the cervix gradually dilates, and when the canal is sufficiently large the uterus may be swabbed with ichthyol before reintroducing the gauze. This treatment should be commenced about fifteen days before the menstrual period, and the last dressing removed two or three days before the expected flow.

If improvement is not manifest from this treatment from month to month, or in severe cases, the sharp curette should be used, and the after-packing should be left in the uterus for forty-eight hours.

During the course of any treatment for endometritis any displacements of the uterus must be cared for, as good results need not be expected if such prime factors in the cause of the disease remain uncorrected. What to do with displacements is a subject worthy of an entire paper, and I must not touch upon it now. Suffice to say here that every case of displacement does not require surgery to secure retention of the uterus in its proper position.

In taking up the subject of the Homœopathic treatment of endometritis, if I were to go into the details it would require a volume of space. Indeed, if I were to more than touch upon the subject it would occupy more time than could be allotted to one paper.

It is a foundation principle of Homœopathy that we must consider the *patient* and not the disease with which the patient is afflicted, when making a prescription. This is true in the disease we have been considering. We must not take into account the symptoms alone of the disease per se, because the symptoms which point out to us the distinct trouble is but the local manifestation of that indefinable, impalpable something which is within the patient that makes her sick. It is self-evident, therefore, that if I were to consider in detail the Homœopathic treatment of endometritis it would be necessary to cover half the symptoms of more than half the remedies in the whole Materia Medica.

It has been my observation that, of all the varied accessory symptoms of which these patients afflicted with endometritis complain, the mental are the most prevalent. Scarcely one of these patients, if indeed one, will be found who will not present a varied line of mental manifestations. Frequently the clew to the final decision between two or more remedies will be found in these mental symptoms. I therefore propose to give briefly some hints upon the more important of these that have enabled me, and I trust may enable you, to select the proper remedy. In doing this I will leave untouched those symptoms which are so common to so many of the remedies, such as, irritability, depression, melancholia, anger, suicidal mania, etc., etc., except where these mental phases take on some particular characteristic.

I will consider under the line thus marked out:

Aesc. Mental incapacity in the form of lack of concentration of mind, which must be distinguished from mental weakness; irritability when the bowel is loaded with fecal matter.

Aloes. Great disinclination to mental work alternating with great mental activity. Some days these patients will be full of ambition, full of mental activity, while during other periods of varied length they have a decided disinclination to make any mental effort, and use every excuse to avoid it.

Alumina. The patient cries against her will. She does not want to cry. She tries not to. (Different from *Pulsatilla*). Low spirited; little difficulties seem too great to overcome. Fears she will become insane. Time passes too slowly. Fretful. (I speak of this last symptom because of its so frequent occurrence when this remedy is indicated and the physician is so frequently led to think of *Phosphorus*, and other remedies having this symptom as a characteristic).

Ammonia carb. Forgetfulness particularly in the form of absent mindedness. She dislikes work, both mental and physical. There is a feeling of impending trouble. (In the evening, *Calcarea carb.*)

Aurum met. Religious mania—prays much. Melancholy. Has no confidence in herself, thinks others have none. Weary of life, and wishes she could die. Utter despair. Disappointed love.

Borax. She idles away her time, cannot settle down to one kind of work, changes from one occupation to another and from one room to another. She is fretful. All these symptoms are better after stool; there is much mental and nervous relief therefrom.

Bovista. The patient is awkward, drops things from her hands. (*Apis*). She is slow of comprehension and of understanding. She uses wrong words for right ideas. (*Calcarea carb.*)

Calcarea ostrea. Disinclination to work. Misplaces words. Thinking is difficult. The patient is melancholy, with apprehension, as of some misfortune; worse towards evening. Fears loss of reason, or that others will notice her confusion of mind.

Ferrum met. Inclined to weep or laugh immoderately. (She weeps and laughs alternately, *Phosphorus*). Disinclined to talk or study. The mind is confused, cannot collect her thoughts. Proud, self-contented look. (She feels proud, *Platina*).

Gelsemium. Cataleptic spasms; loquacity; hysterical delirium.

Graphites. Dim recollection of recent events. Slowness of thought. Hates work. Sad with thoughts of death; solicitous concerning her spiritual welfare. Timid; hesitates at trifles.

Helon. Dull, inactive, gloomy, irritable, etc.; all better when doing something to engage the mind.

Hydrastis. Cannot remember what she is reading or talking about. She is irritable—disposed to be spiteful.

Ignatia. Sad. Desires to be alone (*Nux vom.*). Changeable—from laughter to tears, and from tears to laughter (*Phos.*). Delicate, conscientiousness (*Sil.*). Disappointed love (*Aur. met.*)

Iodine. Irritable with sensitiveness; extreme excitability, worse during digestion. She feels as if she had forgotten something.

Kreosota. Stupid feeling with vacant

gaze; frequent vanishing or failure of thought. The patient is obstinate (*Sul.*).

Lachesis. The patient thinks she is under superhuman control; in her delirium she feels she will be damned. Great loquacity. Mania for overstudy. Jealousy. Fears being poisoned.

Lilium. The patient is irritable; disposed to curse or think of obscene things. She has a hurried feeling and hurried manner. She is much concerned about the soul's salvation. Apprehensive of disease, and thinks she has heart disease; fears she is incurable.

Lycopodium. Dread of men. Imperious and scolding. Weeps all day, (*Puls.*)

Mercurius. Homesickness; suspicious; distrustful; quarrelsome; hurried speech.

Natrum mur. Gets angry at trifles. Spiteful and vindicative. Jealous. Tired of life. Hurriedness (*Lil. tig.*) Awkward in talking, knows not what to say.

Nitric ac. Vindictive, attacks of rage with maledictions. Anxious about her disease.

Nux vomica. Insane desire when alone with those she loves to kill them. Desires to talk about her condition. Careful; zealous. Melancholy; oversensitive about external impressions.

Phosphorus. Indifference. Easily angered, with vehemence, from which she suffers much afterwards.

Platina. Great pride, thinks she is superior to others. After anger, alternation of weeping and laughing. She is religious; past events trouble her. Illusions—things seem small, persons inferior to herself. She is haughty; voluptuous. Alternation of mental and physical symptoms.

Pulsatilla. Religious mania; sees the devil, and world on fire at night. The patient is easily moved to tears or to laughter. Dyspnœa after emotions. Enviousness; covetousness. Frequent love affairs.

Sepia. Involuntary crying and laughing (*Phos.*). The patient is sad about her life and domestic affairs; dreads to be alone. (Desires to be alone *Nux. vom.*). Antagonistic mental states—imagines what she does not want to; uses wrong words when she knows she is using them. She is easily offended.

Silicea. She wishes to drown herself. Hysterical, with screaming. Over-anxious; conscientious about trifles. She is apathetic.

Sulphur. Stubbornness, obstinacy. Memory is especially weak for names. Foolish happiness and pride. Disgusted about odors about the body.

Thuja. Talks slowly as if hunting for her words. Hysterical or insane—will not be touched or approached when talked to. Scrupulous. Music causes weeping.

J. W. HINGSTON.

A CASE OF MARASMUS.

In the early part of last year, 1901, a lady called at my office to consult me about her baby, then four months old. This lady was well built, apparently well nourished, and to all appearance, a well educated lady. The family had recently moved into this state from Wisconsin, from whence they had brought a very feeble baby.

She told the story of an apparently healthy pregnancy, no serious trouble during parturition, the birth of a healthy child weighing seven pounds, a rapid convalescence, and the withering or fading of the baby when it was but two weeks of age. She seemed to have an abundance of milk, but as the child began to emaciate so rapidly, ceased nursing him and gave him cows' milk with some prepared food. Still the child continued to emaciate until it was nothing but skin and bone, very pale, almost blue from want of sufficient oxygen, almost helpless, and lay in one and the same position until changed by the mother or one of the family. At times it would make an effort to cry but its noise was so feeble that it was scarcely audible.

I examined this babe with more than ordinary care. It did not have that aged appearance that so many cases of marasmus present. It was very poor, so poor in flesh that one hesitated to handle the little fellow. Its face was not wrinkled, nor were the arms or legs, and the abdomen was slightly enlarged but not tympanitic.

I looked for a cause but found none. There seemed to be no disease present in this little one save progressive emaciation. The anemnesis presented nothing unusual, save in this one particular that this little boy, the youngest of six children, was the only one so sadly afflicted, the other children being strong and in good health.

There was little to encourage the mother, for the prognosis was a very unfavorable one. Some medicine seemed necessary, and the remedy that appeared to cover this case was *Argentum nit.* which it received, one dose of the 200 potency, and a liberal *Placebo*, with instructions to report in seven days if the child was alive.

The mother felt dejected, but could expect nothing but an unfavorable prognosis. At the appointed time she came, reported really no improvement. Again efforts were made to obtain the mode of living during gestation, when the mother said that nothing unusual occurred in habits of life or appetite save an inordinate craving for salt, great quantities of which she ate at different times. "Doctor," said she, "I seldom went to the pantry without taking a great pinch of salt." This gave me a foundation upon which to build a diagnosis, outline a course of treatment, and assure myself of a more favorable prognosis. *A Natrum muriatricum toxemia resulting in marasmus.* I gave two powders of *Natrum mur*[3x] trit, each powder to be dissolved in three teaspoonfuls of clear cold water, and a teaspoonful given each hour until all was taken, and repeat the following day. This was followed the third day with a liberal *Placebo.*

In a few days I was called by telephone to see the child as it was not expected to live. I drove through a drenching cold rain to find one of the most pitiable sights I had ever seen. A babe in which there was but a picture of life, cold, very pale, involuntary evacuation of the bowels of a slightly diarrhœic stool, yellow in color, and not of a strong odor; too weak to take much nourishment, and when one opened his eyes he could not close them, nor could he of his own strength close them when they were opened. He was carried on a pillow, was too weak to cry and as they placed him, so he laid. I saw at once we had one of two things before us, either a proving of *Natrum mur.* or impending dissolution. I said nothing favorable but chose the former view of the case, gave *Placebo*, and asked for a report by telephone the following day. The report came, "the child is better, diarrhœa slowly improving, slept better, and has an increased appetite." *Placebo* continued. I made no further calls. The child began to improve, and the former *Placebo*, globules No. 30 were continued, two globules every three hours. This lasted for some weeks when the mother reported in person that the child was growing, slowly 'tis true, but growing and increasing in weight. No more medicine was given until last September, when another powder of *Natrum mur*^m^ trit. (B. & T.) was given as before with no perceptible aggravation, but constant improvement, and the child, now almost one year since I saw him, is doing well and has a fair show for a long and healthy career.

G. E. Dienst.

Announcements.

ILLINOIS HOMŒOPATHIC ASSOCIATION.

The Illinois Homœopathic Medical Association will meet in Chicago, May 13th, 14th and 15th on the 17th floor of the Masonic Temple. A banquet will be given Wednesday evening at the Auditorium Hotel to the visiting members outside of Cook County by the resident physicians.

Edgar J. George, Sec'y.
80 Marshall Field Bld'g.
E. H. Pratt, Pres't, 100 State st.

MISSOURI INSTITUTE OF HOMŒOPATHY.

The Twenty-sixth annual session of the Missouri Institute of Homœopathy will be held in St. Louis, April 28, 29 and 30, 1902. An interesting program has been provided and indications point toward a large attendance.

Lewis P. Crutcher, M. D., Gen. Sec.,
423 Deardorff Bld'g,
Kansas City, Mo.
Willis Young, M. D., Pres't,
St. Louis, Mo.

THE LOCAL COMMITTEE OF THE AMERICAN INSTITUTE.

All arrangements are rapidly completing for making the meetings of the American Institute of Homœopathy in Cleveland a success long to be remembered. The local profession welcomes every member, and promises that in the matter of hotels, railways, entertainments and the like, no disappointment will be experienced. Every promise heretofore made will be fulfilled. One of the principal features of the week's meeting will be the coming together of the various college alumnæ forming a grand College Alumi Association, who will have special rooms assigned them in the Hollenden Hotel, and, on one evening, be given the large Assembly Room in the hotel for the "round up," with general jollification, music, singing and speeches. On another evening a reception, ball and banquet will be given at the Colonial Club on Euclid avenue. The usual first night opening services, addresses of welcome, President's Address, etc. will be held in the Chamber of Commerce building, where all the meetings of the Institute will be held. The Memorial Exercises are also suitably provided for.

On Saturday the Erie Railway has tendered an excursion to Cambridge Springs, Pa., where the visitors will be the guests of the Hotel Rider. During June, Cleveland is famed for its beautiful weather and its cool nights. It is justly called the "Forest City" with its miles and miles of paved and shaded streets, for driving, walking and bicycling—a boulevard system connecting its beautiful parks and waterways, and an unparalleled system of trolley lines. The meeting place and the hotels are adjacent and in the very heart of the city, accessible to the railways, places of amusement, the principal stores, and points of interest. A cordial and most hearty welcome is extended to every homœopathic physician—and his wife—to meet in Cleveland this summer with the American Institute of Homœopathy.

Gaius J. Jones, M. D.,
Chairman Local Committee.

Editorial.

HOMŒOPATHY IN OBSTETRICS.

Of all departments of medicine the greatest benefit may be derived by the obstetrician from the use of Homœopathic remedies during the periods of gestation and lactation.

Pregnancy is a physiological state and should be attended by no abnormal disturbances of health. Every additional demand of the normal product of conception should be met by forces that are held in reserve for just such requirements. Unfortunately for our boasted civilization, the period of gestation is looked upon with alarm by the majority of women, and a systematic attempt is made to defeat the plans of nature from the wedding night until the close of the menstrual period. Indeed, the foundations are laid for many of the ailments peculiar, to women at the birth of the child, through the ignorance of the mother by her unwilling acceptance of the responsibilities of motherhood.

By reason of the fact that the follower of Hahnemann is brought into close touch with the laws governing the phenomena of Nature through the study of the action of remedies, he is prepared to recognize and appreciate the significance of seeming trivial departures from the normal, or healthy, state and to bring influences to bear that will remove the cause, and allow the forces of Nature to repair the damages, and in the future maintain a healthy equilibrium.

It is a mistake to think that a foreign substance, either in a crude or potential form, is an indicated remedy for all the derangements incident to the period of gestation. The same rules must be applied here as in diseases from other causes, and only the *smallest* part of trouble calls for the exclusive employment of our Homœopathic remedies. This is no belittling of our law of cure, but the recognition of the law of cause and effect and a separation of the *mechanical* from the *dynamic* effects so that the picture of dynamic disturbances may be clearly drawn.

To the family physician is given the privilege and opportunity of detecting these departures in their incipient state, and upon him rests, in a measure, the responsibility for many a serious derangement that might have been "nipped in the bud" if sufficient care had been exercised at the proper time.

This surveillance should begin with the birth of the child, and should be directed to the detection of *tendencies* as development advances, and the correction of them by the most suited means possible. If they be due to errors on the part of mother or nurse, the mistake should be pointed out, with the effects liable to follow. It should not stop here, but your advice should be enforced under penalty of withdrawing from the case. Few will stand out against a logical presentation of the importance of the subject.

In many cases the correction of the errors of home education, atmospheric and sanitary causes, only serve to show that the cause for the trouble has a deeper origin than that of environment, and it is here that Homœopathy shines with refulgent glory. It is here that the Homœopathic physician has such superior advantage over all other systems of medicine that it is a mystery why the great majority of our schools do not study to become masters of the difficult problem of child development and make the same their specialty.

A prominent church authority says: Give me the first thirteen years of a child's life and I care not what influences are directed against it in the future.

During the same period of development, the conscientious physician can so mold and correct vicious tendencies as to lessen the mortality fully fifty per cent, and at the same time lay the foundation for a posterity whose standard of health will be very materially improved.

This is seemingly putting the cart before the horse so far as the topic of this editorial is concerned, but upon second thought the readers of the ADVOCATE will bear us out in the statement that the proper time to cure the child is to cure the mother *before* the child is born. If we can so impress the truth of our principles upon the child before she shall have reached the age of maturity there will be little work for the obstetrician outside of the mechanics of labor, and even these become unusually simple, as a rule, with the normal, healthy woman.

Homœopathy has to deal with disease tendencies, and if we cannot begin with the child it is well that we impress those about to assume the responsibilities of wedded life with the importance of starting out with definite knowledge of the nature of these obligations and the course that must be pursued if success crowns their efforts. Too many lives are wrecked at the very beginning of their new experience by reason of unjustifiable ignorance of the logical effects following the violations of Nature's laws. False modesty is responsible for much of this ignorance, and to a large degree the family physician is to be blamed, because he should possess that intimate relation with his families that would impel him to *protect* them against disease, instead of leaving them just as susceptible (if not more so) after a serious illness as they were before. It is in this field that Homœopathy wins her laurels, and all of this has much to do with the obstetrician, in lightening his load by lessening his responsibilities. Having established proper relations with the newly organized family, consultations will be made by both husband and wife *before* conception shall have taken place, and as soon after impregnation shall have become manifest the future prospects of the prospective offspring will be under his guiding hand. "*An ounce of prevention is better than a pound of cure.*" Homœopathy forces nothing, but in a mild, persuasive manner (in the hands of one who understands its principles) turns confusion into order and thus conserves *all* the vital energy of the organism, to the double purpose of providing for the additional obligations assumed by the prospective mother.

It is not our purpose to treat of the disorders peculiar to pregnancy, because this has received noteworthy consideration at the hands of the excellent corps of regular contributors to this issue of the ADVOCATE.

A happy suggestion comes to us at this moment. Write to such contributors as especially please or instruct you, telling of the good their thoughtful study has brought to your work. The work is a service of love, and a show of appreciation will encourage them more than anything else. Don't put it off, but write while the spirit prompts you. We will gladly publish such letters and try to make future contributions worthy of even higher comment.

DEATH OF A PIONEER, DR. J. R. HAYNES.

Resolutions passed by the Indianapolis Homœopathic Medical Society, March 12, 1902, upon the death of its oldest member, Dr. J. R. Haynes:

WHEREAS, it has pleased an all-wise Providence to remove from our midst by the hand of Death, our beloved fellow-member, Dr. John R. Haynes, and

WHEREAS, his loss is particularly felt by reason of his long and intimate association with this Society, and his unfaltering devotion to his chosen profession, be it

Resolved, that the Indianapolis Homœopathic Medical Society, hereby expresses its profound regret at the sad calamity which has taken him from among us, and extends to his family its deepest sympathy.

A. A. OGLE, Pres.
W. E. GEORGE, Sec'y.

W. R. STEWART,
C. B. MCCULLOCH, Committee.

Dr. John R. Haynes was one of the pioneers of Homœopathy, having been in active practice almost half a century. He was struck by a trolley car, in front of his home, in Indianapolis on the evening of March 11th and killed almost instantly. Dr. Haynes would have been seventy-nine years of age had he lived two days longer. His aged wife died of apoplexy on March 11th, 1900, exactly two years preceding his own death.

Dr. Haynes was a valued contributor to the ADVOCATE, his article on "Serpent Poisons" in the issue of August, last year, being extensively quoted in both homœopathic and allopathic journals. While he had passed the allotted three score and ten years, his mind was active and clear, and he labored for the advancement of the cause up to the day of his untimely taking off.

The ADVOCATE joins the friends of the late Dr. Haynes in mourning his loss, and trust his example may induce others to take up the work where he left off and carry it to fruition.

THE SPIRIT OF OUR LEADERS.

The spirit of the leaders in any cause make or mar it, hasten or retard it. In the old days of crowding to the front of true loyalty to the slogan of our wing of the medical army it was interesting to watch and note the influence of the valorous leaders. There were Hering, Lippe, Fincke, Dunham, Wells, Allen, Guernsey, Morgan, Hoyne, Phelan, Lilienthal, and others. Of the fighters who cut right and left were Lippe, Wells, Phelan, Fincke, and, in his early days, Hoyne, but later he and they became more politic. Hering, Dunham, Allen, Morgan and Lilienthal recognized the fact that men might be firm believers in the law, but from lack of knowledge of remedies be very poor prescribers, and they set themselves the task of gathering and teaching a knowledge of drugs. Hering, Allen and Dunham worked collecting the medical material; while Rose, Morgan, Lilienthal and others tested drugs, and these men strove especially to keep our profession abreast of the world in pathology as well as therapeutics.

The keen analytical mind of Guernsey, recognizing the fact that we could not learn or remember the mass of symptoms, emphasized the few that had been declared *characteristic* by Hering, and with rare tact captured the attention of the profession with his "Key Notes."

Those were easily learned, but they are only the stepping stones to the therapeutic temple.

Guernsey was a bold debater, but captured the good will of his opponents, so that at every medical meeting a goodly number would gather about him to learn of the better way.

The obstructionists of that day were those who clamored for the recognition of pathology, but they did not look for the pathology of similar drugs. That is a field awaiting workers today.

Another set of obstructors were those trying to introduce into practice drugs and compounds from allopathic sources, and to this day they will swamp us with this flood-wood if we will allow it.

What is a staunch believer in similia to do if he does not know or cannot readily find the similar remedy? He will "catch at straws."

The spirit demanded today is the one of the past that was victorious—kindly instruction. The leaders must capture the new generation of physicians. It cannot be done with vinegar, nor guns. Criticism arouses prejudice; prejudice blocks instruction. We want today at each of the great national centers—yes, in all states—kindly, captivating teachers who will take pains to show how to use our drugs aright in the active fight with disease. We also need others—able, learned and competent—to show the value and danger of any new drug.

We have today, as we had years ago, too much preaching and not enough teaching. We must have teaching that will capture the obstinate, and show even the dullest allopath how to select his drugs according to similia. To do this he must mingle with the masses, as did Dunham, Guernsey and other great leaders.

"Lead, Kindly Light." T. C. D.

THE ILLINOIS STATE MEETING.

In another column will be found announcement of the time and place of the next meeting of the Illinois Homœopathic Medical Association. While the attendance at these State meetings has always been good, there is room for improvement in that line. This year's Association officers are particularly desirous of securing a larger attendance than usual, as the program arranged merits it. It ought also be held as the duty of every Homoeopath, who can afford it, to attend his state meeting, as the coming in touch with the workers of his state cannot fail to help and broaden him in many ways.

To the hard-worked Brother in the city or country: Take a day or two off; allow your mind to relax and wander from daily cares: and receive enough instruction to inspire you to do better work until such time as you can attend another meeting.

CURED BY HOMŒOPATHY.

Although there have been numberless cases in which the efficacy of the law of similia similibus curantur has been proven beyond any question of doubt, it is always a pleasure to every Homœopathic physician to cure a case which an allopath had been unable to cure with several months' treatment, and to prove anew the law and convince those who did not believe in Homœopathy of its great value. Such a case came to my attention a short time ago, and for the benefit of Homœopathy I report it as it was told to me. Mrs. B., a lady of 29 years of age, was suffering with hysteria, which bordered on insanity, and at times she was insane. She had been in this condition for about three years, being first attacked when her husband was forced to undergo an operation for appendicitis. At that time she worried and grieved over her husband's illness until she became insane. An old-school doctor was called in, and since then has been treating her, but she did not improve to any great extent. She desired to change physicians and have a Homoeopath, but her husband was greatly opposed to a "little-pill man," and so no other doctor was called. A few weeks ago a brother of hers, who is attending a Homœopathic college in Chicago, heard one of the professors lecture on Ignatia, and it seemed to him that his sister was a typical Ignatia patient, as described in the lecture. He consulted with the professor, and on his advice prescribed Ignatia 8x four times a day. His sister gladly accepted the prescription, and in three weeks from the day she began taking the indicated remedy she had gained seven pounds and was rapidly becoming perfectly well. The drug was continued, and in a few weeks made a complete recovery.—*Dr. C. A. Harkness in the Medical Century.*

DOSAGE.

It appears to us that one of the problems to engage the attention of the twentieth century therapeutists and pharmacologists will be the action of drugs as influenced by the dosage. This part of pharmacology has been neglected too much. There are hundreds of drugs whose action not only varies under different dosage, but it is diametrically different. Ipecac in very small doses allays vomiting; in large doses it excites it. Cocaine in small doses excites the reflexes; in large doses it depresses them. In the case of a number of drugs it will therefore be insufficient in the future to attach a label—depresso-motor, excito-motor, emetic, etc. The different action in different doses will have to be stated.—*Merck's Archives.*

Materia Medica Miscellany.

A FEW USEFUL REMEDIES IN THE POST-OPERATIVE TREATMENT OF SURGICAL CASES.

The question is often asked by the laity, "Is there any difference between allopathic and homœopathic surgery?" Of course, the answer must be that, so far as mere mechanics are concerned, there is no difference, but you and I, as homœopathists, know that there is a vast difference in the post-operative treatment of all surgical cases. Personally, I should dislike to practice surgery without having at my command a class of remedies which have done for me yeoman service. The list is not a long one, but the few remedies which I have learned to use in dealing with the complications and sequelæ following operative work have served me so well that I desire to emphasize their value in controlling the pain, restlessness and inflammation incident to post-surgical treatment.

I do not profess to get on without certain agents which act in a purely eliminative way—the saline cathartics, for instance; or agents which are sometimes necessary to carry an enfeebled heart through the period of surgical shock. Occasionally, too, I find it necessary to resort to opiates, and sometimes most advantageously. However, the cases in which it is necessary to give opium are not numerous, and in the large majority of instances its administration is not only unnecessary but harmful. My object is simply to present a few of the remedies most commonly used by me for the condition under consideration. I claim no originality in either their selections or the indications calling for them. Nearly all belong to the polycrest group, and are well tried.

Two remedies, *Aconite* and *Hypericum*, are used by me oftener than any others for the restlessness which so frequently follows surgical work. With *Aconite* there is the agonizing desire to toss about, which is so characteristic of the drug. Where this condition is present, especially where there is fear of death, it is my practice to begin the drug just as soon as the stomach will tolerate anything. I give it in the third potency at least every hour until the nervous apprehension passes away. *Hypericum* is more useful if pain is a marked symptom, and particularly if the operation has been such as to cause profound shock. There is often cutting pains between the scapulæ with stitches in the small of the back. There may be tympanitic distension with cutting pains in the region of the navel. I usually give this remedy in the first decimal dilution every one-half, one or two hours, according to the urgency of the symptoms.

Arsenicum is one of the most useful of all remedies in aiding the system to care for the ptomaines and exudates incident to surgical work. There is great restlessness, prostration, weakness of memory, thirst, irritability of the stomach with nausea and vomiting. The urine is scant, and there may be retention of urine from bladder parlysis. As time goes on the urine becomes dark brown and turbid with approaching symptoms of uremia. With *Arsenic* the restlessness is one of prostration rather than of hypersensitiveness.

Apis mellifica is another remedy which has helped me out of many a tight scrape in abdominal surgery. It is, I believe, the most useful of all remedies at our command in cases of threatened uremia. There are renal pains with frequent and sudden attacks of pain along the ureters. The patient will experience a desire to empty the bladder often with the passage of only a few drops. The urine is scant, high colored, very often fetid, and after standing becomes turbid. A chemical and microscopical examination will show varying quantities of albumin and tube casts. There is loss of consciousness, stupor interrupted by piercing shrieks, impaired memory, with absent mindedness. The apis patient is unusually of an irritable disposition, hard to please, and exceedingly nervous. In all cases of suspected renal insufficiency, infusions and enemata with hot pack, and, if necessary, a hypodermic use of pilocarpine are to be brought into requisition. However, the timely administration of *Apis* will frequently make these measures unnecessary.

Rhus toxicodendron is also a most useful remedy where the restlessness is a prominent symptom and septic manifestations become prominent. It has a much lower type of restlessness we find in either *Hypericum* or *Arsenic*. There is incoherent talking with a low, mild delirium. The prostration is marked. There is a restless desire to change position in bed; the tongue is dry, red and cracked; the mouth is dry with much thirst; the breath is putrid. The patient is usually worse at night and seems to get relief in the change of posture. The abdomen is bloated and the patient will frequently complain of a sore, bruised sensation in the abdomen.

Cimicifuga is most useful for the intense backache which so frequently follows the dragging down of the uterus in gynecological plastic surgery.

Bryonia and *Belladonna* are called for in contending with peritoneal irritation following celiotomies. The usual head symptoms of *Belladonna* may be absent. The pain is always of a shooting, darting character, coming and going in quick succession. There is distension of the abdomen with loud rumbling in the bowels. The patient cannot bear to have the abdomen touched; tenderness caused by even slight pressure over the ovarian region.

In *Bryonia* the slightest movement will aggravate the pain. There is also griping pains about the navel, with rumbling and gurgling in the bowels. Respiration will frequently cause stitching pains in the abdomen. *Bryonia* is especially useful in the thoracic complications which sometimes arise as a sequel of the anæsthetic.

Colocynth is often necessary to overcome the cramp-like pains in the abdomen, which are relieved by the patient drawing the knees toward the abdomen. The colic of colocynth, unlike that of belladonna, is relieved by pressure.

Antimonium tart. is invaluable in contending with the bronchial irritation which so frequently follows the administration of ether.

Antimonium crudum is of equal value in overcoming the indigestion which is attended by pain at pit of stomach. With it there is belching with taste of what has been eaten, with a thick, white or yellow coating of tongue. Not infrequently the abdomen is distended with much rumbling of incarcerated flatus.

Magnesium phos. is often prescribed by us to overcome spasmodic pains in any part of the body, but especially if there are spasmodic pains in the bladder or urethra.

It is hardly necessary to say that *China* is the remedy above all others for anemia resulting from loss of blood. Later on, when it is necessary to build the patient up, *Calcarea phos.* is one of the best of all reconstructing remedies for anemia and prostration.

China and *Lycopodium* are of signal service if flatulence is troublesome.

Serpent poisons and *Phosphorus* are always to be thought of where blood degeneration is a marked symptom, particularly in septic conditions.

I think that surgeons too often take it for granted that general practitioners will understand that the indicated remedies are given in post-surgical treatment, and therefore, in reporting cases, say but little regarding internal medication. We cannot too often review the indications for certain remedies which, I believe, will aid us many times in saving life when death would result were such remedies not administered.—J. C. Wood, M. D., in *Era*.

ANTITOXIN—A PROTEST.

The above is the title of an article by Dr. W. B. Carpenter of Columbus, Ohio, in the February Medical Century. The grounds of the doctor's protest are the following:

1. Because it is an *unknown* agent.

2. Again, I protest against antitoxin as we know it because it is a *dangerous* agent for internal use.

3. Again, I protest against antitoxin as we know it because it has not given the measure of success warranted by its claims, showing a lack of merit in the drug or a lack of knowledge on the part of the prescriber.

4. Again, I protest because it is not a *proved* remedy, in the true Homœopathic sense, and it will never be known or manageable until it is.

Dr. Carpenter elaborates each of the

points made, and adds: "I would not be understood as saying that there is not any good in antitoxin, and there never was and never will be. We cannot utterly condemn the nosode remedies *a priori*, but if they are to be used at all we must insist that they be proved upon the healthy organism so that we shall have a definite symptomatology to apply. * * * After all this protest I hear the question, 'What are you going to do about the cures that follow the use of antitoxin?' I am simply going to admit that such no doubt happened in some instances. I do not take the stand that no cures are effected by this agent, but they come, when at all, inspite of its being imperfectly known and dangerous. * * * My contention is not that it has not done and cannot do any good, but that it has within itself so many elements of weakness, crudeness and danger that as antitoxin it must soon be superceded by something that will more safely and surely accomplish the work that this agent proposes to do. But be assured that no agent, no matter how well attested by *laboratory research and experiment alone*, will ever be found to cure diphtheria in the human being. The individual sick must be reckoned with, and noone agent will ever be found to cure all cases, even though seen in any early stage of the disease. Of the combination we have been considering, the serum element may be discarded as containing too many elements of danger. The Carbolic acid is a remedy that has a definite symptomatology, and ought to be more carefully considered when dealing with this dread disease. The toxin element should be more thoroughly proven, as has been done with the nosodes, psorinum and hydrophobinum. Then, as diphtherinum, our Materia Medica will possess another powerful remedy for some of the acute stages and chronic effects of malignant disease."

ENDOCARDITIS—TREATMENT AND REMEDIES.

Treatment.—Every means of resting the heart should be persistently employed, and even after the patient has apparently recovered, protection of the chest against changes of temperature should be secured by application of a light layer of cotton, wool or flannel. The diet should be simple and nutritious; an excess of liquid should be avoided in order to lessen intra-cardiac pressure. Warm baths should be given from one to three times in twenty-four hours. When pain is severe, hot applications should be made to the præcordial region. Endocarditis, when a complication of acute articular rheumatism, does not often require special treatment, as those remedies and general measures which best control the rheumatism will prove most efficient.

Remedies.

Colchicine on account of its action on the articular inflammation and its influence in the prevention of cardiac complications is highly extolled by many of our school and is worthy of consideration.

Aconite.—High temperature, anxiety, great swelling of the joints with acute pain, restlessness and pulmonary congestion.

Veratrum Viride.—The action of the heart is much more violent than under aconite; heart beats long and strong with great arterial excitement; constant dull burning in region of the heart; active congestion of the chest.

Spigelia.—Violent palpatation with anxious oppression of the chest; feeling in the region of the apices as though a dull pointed knife was slowly driven through it. Pulse weak and irregular.

Bryonia.—Is often indicated in connection with attacks of rheumatism; joints red, stiff and swollen, with stitching pains from slightest motion or touch. Pulse full, hard and rapid.

Cactus.—Sensation of constriction about the heart. Very acute pains and stitches in the heart; feeble, irregular pulse; palpitation; inability to lie with the head low.

Colchicum.—Endocarditis following acute rheumatism; tearing pain in the cardiac region, pulse small, rapid and trembling.

Rhus Tox.—Is called for in cases associated with acute rheumatism when the well-known rhus symptoms are present.

Belladonna.—Is sometimes indicated, especially in the rheumatic endocarditis of children.

After subsidence of the acute symptoms, administration of medicines having an absorbant and resolvent action, such as sulphur, iodine, spongia, and iodide of potassium tend to lessen the extent of the inevitable damage to the orifices and valves. In chronic cases with dilatation and threatened failure of circulation, alcohol should be given in moderate quantities, along with such remedies as arsenic, the indications for which are dyspnoea, weak and irregular pulse, with diminution of arterial tension, anxiety, mental agitation, anasarca, albuminuria; strophan — irregularity of heart's action, præcordial pains, palpitation, dyspnoea, valvular disease with regurgitation, oedema, general anasarca; apocynum—urine scanty, oedema, general anasarca, with great thirst; apis—oedema, retention or suppression of urine; kalmia—excessive action of the heart, rheumatic pains in the region of the heart, pulse irregular, quick and weak, hypertrophy; crataegus—præcordial oppression, rapid and feeble heart's action, valvular insufficiency, cardiac hypertrophy.—*F. C. Crawford in Cleveland Med. and Surg. Reporter.*

Cimicifuga will likely cure more "rheumatism" than any other remedy, for many symptoms commonly called rheumatism are myalgic pains without any rheumatism back of them, and Cimicifuga is specific in two classes of myalgic symptoms: 1. Those due to inflammation of the muscular substance (Arnica). 2. Those due to a loss of tone in the muscular fibres. Rhus suits tendonous pains and Bryonia corresponds to blood changes.

Nux vomica is an important remedy during convalescence from various diseases with no appetite, and with a lack of recuperative energy. After nostrums and various pain killers have been tried without result, Nux vomica will cure when there are twisting, stitching pains in the abdomen and pelvis, cramps in the bladder, ineffectual urging to urinate and defecate. It is to a fatigued and overworked mind what Arnica is to a bruised and overstrained muscular system.

Lachesis.—Hering says no remedy is so useful in breaking up of a quinsy in its incipiency or in bringing about resolution in advanced stages as Lachesis.

Vinegar in Smallpox.—Pure Cider Vinegar in tablespoonful doses four times a day will protect from smallpox; abort the disease, control the itching and, in fact, will do everything and more than vacination will do, so says Dr. C. F. Howe, the county health officer of Atchison, Kansas.

Chimaphila is a wonderful remedy in

the cystic irritation of old men characterised by a constant teasing desire to urinate, with little or no relief following micturition, the patient being frequently compelled to rise at night. The state best corresponding to the remedy is one of irritation rather than inflammation.

Personals and News Items.

If any of our subscribers wishes to secure a first class attendant for a patient for whom is prescribed a change of climate, Hermione W. Andreuus of Elmwood, Ill., will act in that capacity. No objection to going abroad.

Director of the Mint Roberts intimates that when peace in South Africa is established the world's annual production of gold will be $400,000,000. In 1900 the United States produced $78,000,000 worth of the yellow metal.

The negro's color is not even "skin deep." In a certain tannery human skins are once in a while tanned "to oblige customers." The process of tanning a negro's "hide" eliminates a very thin, black cuticle, after which the product cannot be distinguished from tanned "hide" of a white man.

A New York city newspaper which investigated the death rate of the twelfth ward, where the millionaires reside, and that of the thirteenth, where the common people herd, reached the conclusion that the mortality rate is higher in the millionaires' ward. One has sixty-one inhabitants to the acre, the other 539.

Marion, Iowa, enjoys the distinction of being the healthiest town of over 1,000 inhabitants in the United States, its death rate being 1.46 to the thousand. Citizens of that town aver that this statement made by the census bureau is misleading, out of the six deaths reported in 1900 two were not residents of that town, but were outsiders killed in a railroad wreck near there. The average death rate for the total of 1,190 cities reported was 17.47.

Michael Doran has recently awakened from his two years' sleep at the Binghampton (N. Y.) State Hospital. All previous efforts to awaken him during this time were unavailing, his only movement being to turn from one side to the other. He was fed artificially, and about six months ago, without any apparent cause, he "came to" and has since fully recovered, losing all desire to take such lengthy naps.—*Exchange.*

According to statistics compiled for the use of life insurance companies the average life of Americans is four and a half years longer than it was twenty years ago. If the insurance companies are inclined to do the right thing, premium rates will be materially reduced. As an illustration of the increased length of life, out of every 10,000 persons born in Massachusetts 1,266 now live to be eighty years old; in 1855 only 1,069 persons reached that age. Out of the same number born, 5,275 live to be fifty years old; only 4,400 lived to that age fifty years ago.

Governor Dockery of Missouri does not show in medical matters that liberality that has characterized his other official acts. A former governor, in order to compare Homoeopathic treatment of the insane with old-school practices, turned over the Fulton institution to the former. Gov. Dockery, years ago, was an old-school practitioner, and the illiberality of his time has evidently not given way to today's progress, as, for no fault of those in charge of the Fulton Hospital for the Insane, the management has been deposed, the vacancy to be filled by an old-school brother of the governor.

Book Reviews.

A Timely Treatise On Smallpox, to sell at $3.00, is announced for publication early in April by J. B. Lippincott Company. It is written by Dr. George Henry Fox, professor of dermatology in the College of Physicians and Surgeons, New York City, with the collaboration of Drs. S. Dana Hubbard, Sigmund Pollitzer and John H. Huddleston, all of whom are officials of the Health department of New York City and have had unusual opportunities for the study and treatment of this disease during the present epidemic.

The work is to be in atlas form, similar to Fox's Photographic Atlas of Skin Diseases, published by the same house. A strong feature of the work will be its illustrations, reproduced from recent photographs, the major portion of which will be so colored as to give a very faithful representation of typical cases of Variola in the successive stages of the disease, also unusual phases of Variola, Vaccinia, Varicella, and diseases with which Smallpox is liable to be confounded. These illustrations number thirty-seven and will be grouped into ten colored plates, 9½ x 10¼ inches, and six black and white photographic plates.

The names of Dr. Fox and his associates assure the excellence of the work, in which will be described the symptoms, course of the disease, characteristic points of diagnosis, and most approved methods of treatment.

Review of Reviews.—The March number of this great magazine is filled with just such matter as the intelligent citizen needs in order to keep in touch with the world's doings and progress. In connection with the visit of Prince Henry, the question of German-American diplomatic relations is gone into at length. England's attitude towards this country before and during the Spanish war is also discussed in the light of the revelations regarding the British Ambassador's actions just previous to the declaration of war. The Anglo Japanese treaty is dissected, and its possible effects upon the "open door" in China and the peace of the world are gone into. A review of what President Eliot has done for Harvard and the cause of higher education in America is timely. A feature of the March *Review of Reviews* is a very full and interesting account of the "Metaphysical Movement," by Paul Tynor. The article is the first complete and authentic account that has appeared of a movement that is having remarkable growth and influence among all classes of people. Mr. Tyner sketches the history of the cult, its literature and its purposes, with sympathetic understanding, and the article is illustrated by portraits of leading workers in the New Thought. Mr. Edwin Emerson, Jr., the American correspondent who served as a colonel of volunteers under Uribe-Uribe, gives an intelligent and clearly-written account of "South American War Issues." The article is illustrated from photographs of war scenes in Venezuela and Colombia. The author shows that the real trouble is the irrepressible conflict between liberalism and the heritages of Spain's clerical *regime* over her colonies. This inevitable war has been waged in Mexico, Venezuela and Central American countries, and wherever the war has been ended liberalism has been victorious, as it will be in Colombia. The above are some of the leading articles, but there are others, all discussed in that exhaustive philosophical manner always to be expected in the *Review of Reviews.*

The Hahnemannian Advocate

A MONTHLY HOMŒOPATHIC MAGAZINE.

Vol. XII. Chicago, April, 1902. No. 4

Materia Medica.

CACTUS GRANDIFLORUS.

Constrictions, contractions and congestions run through this remedy. The blood is always in the wrong place—determination of the blood to the head, coldness of the extremities; or, it may be, determination of the blood to an organ, the chest or the heart. There is never an equal circulation of blood in the body—spasmodic, irregular circulation, disturbed by contractions of circular fibers everywhere. When this comes in places where it can be felt and realized by the senses, it is felt as constrictions, and this gives us the key to Cactus. Where contractions cannot be felt, where there are no senses and no sense of feeling, it goes on as a spasmodic condition of circular fibers; but these contractions that are felt are more upon the surface of the body, in organs having circular fibers, as tubes and canals. These constrict, and this constriction is felt like a spasm. So Cactus has the sensation of tightness and constrictions about the head, about the chest, attachments of the diaphragm, all over the abdomen; and constrictions about the heart that are tonic in character, like a tight clutching. "Constriction felt about the heart." These constrictions are also felt about the throat, in the œsophagus, causing a spasm; in the vagina, causing vaginismus, preventing coition. In the uterus it produces the most violent cramps—clutchings and constrictions as if the uterus was grasped and held tightly, like a spasm. But at these times when these constrictions take place there are congestions. "Rush of blood to the part, with constriction." "Violent congestion of the uterus, with constrictions. Rush of blood to the chest, as if it was filled with hot gushes of blood, with constrictions, and constrictions of the heart." All these peculiarities run through Cactus, more markedly than most other remedies. Many remedies have similar things now and then, but in Cactus these manifestations are common. It is the nature of Cactus to constrict, so that constrictions occur in places where they have never been felt or thought of. These constrictions may cover the whole body, as if it were held in a vice or a wire cage; the scalp, the skin, as if it were growing tighter over the whole body. All this is in keeping with the nature of Cactus. Violent congestions that come on suddenly, as congestion of the brain, with hot head and flushed face. At the beginning of complaints, as pneumonia, a congestive chill comes on, a chill with hot head and cold body—like Arnica—with violent constrictions and tightness, as if the head were pressed and the membranes of the brain were too tight, or as if the brain were covered with a tight cloth which was being drawn tighter and tighter. In tubes and canals it is a constriction of a particular part, many times like as if tied with a string. In the uterus the constriction takes the form of an hour glass contraction. Cactus has inflammations, congestion, rush of blood to the part, gradually progressing to inflammation, and infiltration. These inflammations are of various parts.

Cactus has another thing running through it intermingled with these conditions—rheumatism. It is a rheumatic and gouty remedy, useful in old gouty constitutions; also very useful in acute inflammatory rheumatism, and in this instance the rush of blood, congestion, is in the joints that happen to be affected. Then again there is constriction, as if tied with a tape or as if bandaged. Tightness, tension, pressure are involved in that thought. It has a prolonged determination of blood to the heart, prolonged congestion, so that organ finally becomes disturbed in its functions, in its tissues. Cactus has a profound curative action upon the heart, and even cures organic heart diseases such as are produced from rheumatic congestion in rheumatic constitutions; also where the rheumatism has partially left the joints and the heart has become involved and there is constant constriction of the heart. Various efforts have been made by provers, and by patients, to describe this constriction of the heart. It is sometimes described as with an iron band, but this only illustrates the tenacity of the prolonged constriction. In these rheumatic troubles when the joints have ceased to be affected with this chronic congestion and enlargement of the valves so that we get murmurs about the heart—the patient begins to emaciate. The head is always hot; there is congestion of the heart—rheumatic conditions—and the patient gradually emaciates. Kidney troubles come on. The heart grows weaker and weaker, and then dropsical conditions set in—and this is the course of Cactus. Towards the last there are cardiac affections, along with kidney troubles, with emaciation, and then swelling of the hands and feet—dropsical conditions. That is the general outline, the very nature, of Cactus. It stands alone, by itself, and nothing in the whole Materia Medica can be found that reads like it. There is nothing to compare with it in the intensity of these things—congestion, constriction and contraction. These three run through the remedy, just as heat, redness and burning run through the whole of *Bryonia*.

The Pains of Cactus.

The pains in Cactus are violent, no matter where they occur. They compel the patient to scream, to make a big noise. The pains are clutching, constricting, often feel like tearing pains, but there is that idea of clutching as with a tape. Suppose a tape is tied round a violently congested organ, and it is drawn tighter and tighter, great pain will result. And this is the kind of suffering the patient experiences with that constriction of a congested organ. There are pains in the congested parts, in the sore parts; tearing, constriction, cramping. When pains occur in the intestines that are constricting, that are pains in the circular fibers, they are called cramps. But when the pains are in the long muscles they are not constricting pains; they are not the circular fibers but the long fibers that constrict and contract—and we call these pains cramps. So, in the circular fibers they may be called cramps. Cactus produces some spasmodic conditions in long muscles, but not to any great extent. With *Belladonna*, and with many of those medicines that have this nature of constricting, contracting and tightening of circular fibers, there is a convulsive tendency. The violent congestion of the brain in *Belladonna* will commonly be attended with cramps in the extremities, and convulsions of the muscles all over, or in parts. This is not the case with Cactus. There is violent congestion and the patient grows stupid under it; congestion of the brain, first with very red face, then darker from the venous stasis, and then stupor; he grows sluggish under the cerebral congestion.

The Mental State.

The mental state is that of fear, distress, because of the intensity of the suffering. The patient has never felt such suffering, and he does not see what it can all be about. So much suffering, so violent, so sudden, such cramps, such tearing, such constriction—what can it mean? When this constriction comes in the heart and about the chest, it makes the patient think he is going to die, and he is at once struck with violent fear, and this is depicted on his face. He fears death, and the pain is so intense that it seems he is going to die. But this wonderfully intense pain has nothing of the horrible anxiety of *Aconite*, which has similar constrictions of the chest and of the neck. The violent choking of *Aconite* makes him fear he is going to choke to death. Not so in Cactus. Screaming with pain is a common thing in Cactus, the suffering is so intense. "Taciturn, unwilling to speak a word or to answer." That often accompanies the Cactus state, and this is opposite to most of the medicines which have such violent pains. "Sadness, taciturnity and irresistable inclination to weep; fear of death"—that is, he thinks he is going to die from the severity of the pain. "He believes his disease is incurable"—that is, it seems to him such suffering must end in death. That violent, irregular action of the heart is followed out through all the blood vessels, because the circulation is so irregular, so spasmodic. He is so hot here and cold there. Heat in the head or heat in the chest. The circulation is that of determination to some particular part of the body. With all cardiac remedies we have violent dreams, great excitement of the brain during sleep, waking up startled and frightened and very commonly a feeling as of falling. He dreams of falling, his dreams full of excitement. These features run through Cactus, especially when the cardiac symptoms go along with it.

"Vertigo from congestion; face red, bloated; pulsation in brain. Feels as if he would go mad; and some anxiety. Vertigo, worse from physical exertion." With most of the cardiac remedies, or remedies where the circulation and heart are so much involved, we have much vertigo. If this remedy was well watched it would be found to cure a great many phases of vertigo along with cardiac conditions. "Vertigo; worse from physical exertion, turning in bed, stooping, rising from a recumbent position, and deep inspiration." Many of the complaints of Cactus are disturbed by irregularities of breathing. Here is seen vertigo coming on from deep breathing. If he holds his breath it seems as if his heart would fly to pieces, it would go so fast. Increased pulsation all over the body occurs when the breath is held. This shows what close relation there is between the breath and cardiac pulsation.

The headaches are such as can easily be predicted — constricting, pressing headaches. They are all violent, with intense heat of the head, for they are congestive. There is a pressing in of the top of the head, as if the top of the head would be forced in. But this is ameliorated by pressing hard upon the seat of the pain. "Heavy pain like a weight on vertex, better by pressure." Many times the patient may be wrong in the idea of pressure that is felt in the head. He often describes it in the most marked congestions as if the head would be crushed in, when the congestion in the brain can be seen to be the most violent, causing pressure from within out, and it would be thought that the patient would be better from some sort of support externally—and yet great soreness is felt, as if the head was being crushed in. Others with headaches feel as if the head is being crushed out. "Heavy pain like a weight in vertex; better by pressure, but worse from sounds, hearing talking, or strong light." This runs through the headaches. The sound goes through the head. The brain seems to be sensitive, as if the sound were a material substance hurled at the brain. The sensitive brain is affected in this way by quite a number of remedies. There are rightsided headaches; pulsating headaches; heavy pulsating pain in the head; tensive pain in the head—in the vertex. A tightness across the vertex, as if the scalp were being drawn tighter and tighter about the skull. There can be no doubt about a marked cerebral congestion with all these symptoms. The eyes show it; the face shows it; the heat of the head shows it. It has been recommended for threatened apoplexy, when the congestion is so violent, and the face is flushed and purple, or very red, and the pulsation is felt in the brain—the pulsation is felt all over.

Now this medicine has the violent congestion of the head found in *Belladonna*, but with *Belladonna* we have the intense heat of the body, fever heat, and this is not found in Cactus. In Cactus the heat is only a moderate fever; it is in the upper part of the body, in the head and neck. There is fullness, bloating of the neck; feels as if the head would expand from the pressure of blood in the head, but without any great rise in temperature. It has fever, but it has these without any fever. With *Belladonna* when you have these pulsations the patient is intensely hot, and he burns all over. There is some burning in Cactus, but not at all to be compared with *Belladonna*.

The above are some of the strongest features of Cactus, and many of the little things can be overlooked. The patient has choking about the neck, as if with a tight collar; constriction, tension of the skin and muscles everywhere. Choking about the neck, with constriction of the heart; in hysteria; globus hystericus; a lump or ball coming up into the throat, and she constantly swallows and chokes, and she goes into cramps; especially, cramping of the left arm; complete numbness of the left arm along with cardiac conditions in the history of rheumatism. The history of rheumatism goes well to fill up the Cactus case. The face is flushed bright red, becoming blue. With weakness of the heart it is blue; lips blue. We go to the bedside of a patient who has constriction about the neck, with congested head, blue face and lips — mottled; numbness of the left hand, constriction of the heart; the left hand hysterically weak, or is numb, tingling and crawling, like a formication.

Hemorrhage of Cactus.

Another thing running all through the remedy is, it is hemorrhagic. This is not surprising. Any remedy that has such cardiac and vascular conditions will at times have more or less relaxation of blood vessels, and it may be quite in the nature of it to bleed. These hemorrhages are of two kinds: Hemorrhage from vascular relaxation accompanying cardiac and muscular conditions; also from violent congestion of a part. The rush of blood to the head is of such violence in the moderately plethoric patient that he bleeds from the nose and hawks blood from the throat; congestion of the chest is so violent that he expectorates blood from the chest. This bleeding is from congestion rather than from tuberculosis. Congestion of the uterus, with bleeding; congestion of the bladder and kidneys, with blood in the urine, discharges of blood from violent congestion; in old cardiac conditions where relaxation is present in most marked degree—hemorrhage from relaxation. From this it will be seen that hemorrhage runs through the remedy.

Strong pulsations felt in strange places, like in the stomach, the bowels, sometimes in the extremities – feet and hands, as well as in the head. A throbbing all over. A feeling as if a cord was being drawn tighter and tigher around the attachment of the diaphragm, around the lower part of the chest. This is a strange symptom, and it clutches him around the waist line so that it takes his breath away, and he struggles for breath, becomes violent, wants to do something. It clutches him tighter and tighter for a while, and lets up when it gets ready. This clutching produces congestion of the bowels, inflammation of the uterus, inflammation of the pelvis, of the stomach; gastric inflammation, gastritis, gastric fevers. With all these symptoms it would not be surprising to her that it is a wonderful remedy for the cure of hemorrhoids, when it is taken into consideration how they are formed—the relaxation of the great portal system, the lower veins in the rectum, hemorrhoidal veins. The veins are in such a state of relaxation that constipation needs remain but a little while when great tumors will form, and they will bleed copiously. Bleeding hemorrhoids; constriction of the anus. It has very troublesome constipation—constipation in connection with hemorrhoids. It has paralytic weakness of the bladder; retention of urine—such a constriction of the neck of the bladder that the urine cannot be passed for a long time, and there is retention. In the kidneys there is such a congestion as favors suppression of urine, and no urine is formed. Bleeding; bloody urine; bleeding in clots. Cactus is a remedy that favors the formation of clots quickly; blood that flows clots so rapidly and so densely that it blocks up the way. Bleeding into the bladder blocks up the way; bleeding into the vagina, a great solid mass difficult to expel, and pressing so upon the urethra of the female that it is impossible for her to pass urine; like an immense great tampon. Hence the reading, "urination prevented by clots," which means by clots in the vagina as well as clots in the bladder. Inflammation of the ovaries, and of the uterus. Cactus is a medicine that you will need to know when a young, plethoric, vigorous woman comes down violently with congestion of the uterus at the menstrual period, and she screams because of the violent clutching and cramping of the uterus at that period. Before the flow starts, perhaps a day before, or just at the beginning, there is a violent spasm. The circular fibers clutch, and she will describe that as accurately as if a tape were tied around that sore and congested uterus. Then the uterus fills with blood clots when it does commence to flow, and the spasm to expel that blood is like a labor-pain, and she screams again, but it is some time before the flow becomes free enough to give her relief. We have a remedy in Cactus that will cure dysmenorrhea. It will relieve the most painful dysmenorrhea in which the excitement and the sharp scream can be heard by the neighbors. Then, suffocative attacks from these pains, because the heart suffers—constriction of the heart will commonly go along with constriction of the uterus. In cardiac conditions, it seems as if he will die for want of breath. There is constriction of the chest; it seems as if the wind will be choked out of him. There is oppression, as if a great load—he will call it a mill-stone—was on his chest crushing the life out of him, so great is the constriction and congestion. The congestion is sudden, and it comes on and subsides without inflammation, in many instances. There is a violent rush of blood to the chest, with constriction, awful dyspnœa, constriction of the heart, which passes away without inflammation. At other times Cactus has conditions like pneumonia, inflammation of the lungs, congestion ending in inflammation—pneumonia—with the usual expectoration, bloody and blood streaked. Cactus is also a remedy for what is known as hypostatic congestion of the lungs. He cannot lie down on his breast; sits up in bed, and there is a dullness of the lower part of each lung, gradually growing higher and higher from an effusion of serum into the lower portion of the lungs. This hypostatic congestion is due to cardiac weakness, a lack of pumping ability of the heart. Cactus will often relieve this a few times as it occurs in old broken-down cases toward the end of Bright's disease and the end of the old dropsical conditions; also, towards the end of heart troubles. It will postpone death. "Could only breathe with shoulders elevated and lying on back." "Lies leaning back, sitting quite upright." "Periodical attacks of suffocation, with fainting; cold sweat."

Some Heart Symptoms.

A few of the heart symptoms are, "Feeling as if the heart was compressed or squeezed by a hand. Cardiac rheumatism. Heart seemed to be held by an iron hand for many hours. Pain in the cardiac region. Great pressure at heart, going round under left axilla to back. Often this pain shoots down the left hand; is attended with numbness, and sometimes with swelling. Numbness, tingling, swelling. "Dull pain in the heart. Heavy pain in the heart, aggravated by pressure. Contractive pain in the region of the heart going down to left abdomen. At times felt as if someone was grasping the heart firmly. Paroxysms of pain in the heart"—that is, this kind of constriction comes in periods or violent paroxysms. "Acute inflammation of the heart. Chronic inflammation of the heart. Palpitation of the heart, continued day and night; when walking, and at night, when lying on the left side." These are the principal ones, but there are a great many others.

Another thing running through Cactus is, chest symptoms often come on—are exaggerated—at 11 o'clock, at that hour in the morning or at night. Its intermittent fever will bring on a chill with violent congestion to the head at that 11 o'clock hour. Regular paroxysms come on at 11 a. m. and 11 p. m. That is a general expression; sometimes it may be at 11 a. m. and at others 11 p. m. This remedy has cured intermittent fever of the congestive type, when the congestions are here and there, but particularly at the head, with constrictions, contractions.

J. T. Kent.

UTERINE DISPLACEMENTS COMPLICATING PREGNANCY.

"Of all the affections of the uterus with which we have to deal, displacements are perhaps the most common. Both as regards diagnosis and treatment, there is very much which ought to be thoroughly understood by the practitioner, *for nine-tenths of the cases of malposition which come under his observation are simple, and need only the ordinary application of common sense principles for their successful treatment.*" (Italics mine.)

I have quoted from a volume just from the press, entitled "Diseases of Women: A Manual of Gynæcology, designed especially for the use of Students and General Practitioners."

In the language of Dorothy Dix I am moved to exclaim, "Say, fellows, this Smart Guy has a capital cinch on how to corral wandering uteri. When it comes to making the obstreperous uterus know what's what, and understand the place the Creator intended it to occupy in the female economy, he has the whole bunch of the rest of us animals faded. As a gynæcologist, this fellow must be the Champion Monologue Artist."

I opine it has been the case with many of you, as it has been with me during the past score of years, that these "common sense principles" have been illusive. For, of all the troubles with which women are afflicted, I have found none more difficult to cure than are the varied uterine displacements. Judging by what I conceive the author to mean by the "ordinary application of common sense principles," and his success therefrom, I am led to wonder if it is possible that so many of our great intellects of the medical profession have had the blind staggers; for, almost with one voice they have declared that the usual treatments advocated for these afflictions have been unsatisfactory and disappointing. I am much inclined to surmise that the author of this new work must expect to run his crimson colored octavo up against a lot of gataboos from Rubetown, or he conceives that his well turned sentences will perhaps be sufficiently resplendent to bumfoozle the "students and general practitioners" to whom his work is dedicated.

If the treatment of uterine displacements were so easy and the cure of them so readily wrought, your chairman of this bureau would not have found it necessary to request me to present for your consideration a paper upon the uterine displacements complicating pregnancy. However, the fact remains that a great many of our ailing women are afflicted with some uterine displacement, and this is particularly true of the multiparæ. Thus is the affliction a frequent complication of the gestation period.

The most frequent form of displacement is retroversion. When it occurs as a complication of pregnancy, your attention will be called to its probable existence by the patient's complaint of pain in the back, constipation, painful deffecation, frequent urination, bearing down, weight, and general pelvic discomfort, in addition to the usual morning sickness. I wish here particularly to call your attention to a fact which is not generally understood, viz: that many cases of nausea and vomiting of pregnancy are due to retroversion and other displacements. Not infrequently correction of the displacement cures the morning sickness. Look to it in your stubborn cases.

The condition suspected, the diagnosis of retroversion is usually easily made by the bimanual method commonly recommended. When the dislocation is uncomplicated by adhesions, the treatment in the early months is simple. It will consist of the replacement of the organ and its retention in proper position by tampons of wool smeared with an antiseptic ointment. For this purpose, I would recommend an unguent consisting of boric acid gr. 10, lanoline and vaseline, equal parts, oz. 1. These tampons must be removed every three to five days, depending upon the existence of a leucorrhœa which may render the dressing offensive; after which the vagina should be thoroughly but carefully douched with a saturated solution of boric acid, and a tampon replaced as before. It will be necessary to continue this treatment until about the end of the fourth or fifth month, when the uterus will have risen above the sacral promontory and will remain in the abdominal cavity. With those patients who will be unable to receive this biweekly treatment, it will be needful to substitute for the tampon a properly fitted Hodge or Albert Smith pessary. The pessary has been given the credit of producing abortion, but I think closer observation would have shown that it was the uncorrected displacement for which the pessary was placed that was the cause of the abortion, for it is far from an unknown thing for a physician to have placed a pessary without first correcting the uterine malposition.

Where the retroversion is complicated with old pelvic peritoneal adhesions, the treatment will necessarily have to be considerably modified. It will usually be found impossible to correct the malposition at one sitting. Before this can be done, those adhesions must be gradually broken up; which may be done, if they are not too extensive, by gentle manipulation followed by the placement of a wool tampon of sufficient size to exert some extension upon the adhesions and which is advantageously saturated with an unguent consisting of ichthyol dr. 1, and equal part of lanoline and vaseline oz. 3. The ichthyol exerts an influence upon the tissues which favors absorption of plastic exudates in the seat of the adhesions.

What I have said of retroversion may be considered as practically true of retroflexion, but it must be remembered that as retroflexion favors abortion, somewhat more care must be used when manipulations for the correction of this condition are resorted to. It is the endometritis that so often accompanies the condition of retroflexion, and not the flexion itself, that is the most frequent cause of the loss of the fruit of the womb as well as the most frequent factor in preventing conception. However, where retroflexion exists, the fundus of the uterus is less likely to spontaneously rise above the sacral promontory as the organ enlarges in the course of gestation; but it is apt to remain in the hollow of the sacrum where it becomes wedged and permanently fixed. When this occurs there can be but one result unless the condition can be relieved, viz, abortion. When the uterus is thus firmly wedged in its malposition in the pelvis, and the fundus cannot be raised above promontory of the sacrum by ordinary methods, the patient should be anæsthetized, the cervix pulled well down by careful, steady and prolonged traction by double tenaculæ and an effort made to raise the fundus to normal position. Such efforts will usually succeed. The patient should remain in bed a few days.

In those old cases of chronic pelvic peritonitis with adhesions which the efforts of nature and those of the physician fail to break up or sufficiently stretch to allow the uterus to ascend into the abdominal cavity, abortion is the necessarily ultimate result before the end of the fifth month of pregnancy. Under these circumstances, and particularly where the complication is one of retroflexion, the abortion must be considered more serious than a similar condition under other circumstances. Infection from imperfect drainage due to the faulty position of the uterus, exacerbation of old inflammation from traumatism or other causes are prone to occur.

Of simple prolapsus nothing need be said. The application of the principles mentioned in the foregoing will be found to be all sufficient.

What may be said as to the prospects of cure of uterine displacements as the result of a pregnancy going to full term? I answer, a great deal more and a great deal less than has been claimed by individual practitioners. When women have been told off hand by their physician, who has encountered a stubborn case of malposition, that the bearing of a child would be the means of curing the condition, and so advises his patient to become pregnant, and follows it up with no further word of instruction, we must consider such advice as pernicious rather than tending towards any benefit. On the other hand, when we are told by others that in all their experience they have never seen any beneficial results from pregnancy upon uterine malposition, we at once conclude that they do not properly understand their subject and have left undone the principal part of their duty and of what might have been done.

If we will remember that most cases of anteflexion are congenital and due to imperfect development of the anterior portion of the uterus in the region of the internal os, it may be easily understood how, through the development and growth of the organ during the progress of gestation, the imperfectly developed anterio-cervical region partakes of this normal condition of growth conjointly with the rest of the organ. New life is given to the part, and more perfect nutrition is established, so that, after the termination of the pregnancy and involution takes place, the congenitally undeveloped portion assumes, with the balance of the organ, a normal state, and the anteflexion is cured.

But, in the case of retro-displacement, it will not be sufficient simply that the woman become pregnant and go to full term; for, if no further attention is given, it will be found that, when involution is completed the uterus will be found in its old mal-position. It may seem that, inasmuch as both a retroversion and a retroflexion are necessarily corrected during the period of gestation, a cure will be as readily accomplished here as in the condition of anteflexion already considered. Observation, however, shows that this is in no wise the case. For some unaccountable reason—or certainly for some reason not yet explained—a uterus once retroplaced is prone to assume the old position when involution takes place. Here is where the simple advise to the woman to bear a child for the accomplishment of such correction fails; but here too is just where much may be done.

The ordinary position that a woman assumes during the puerperal period is upon her back; which position she assumes and retains during almost the entire lying-in period. Is it not then plain to be seen that a uterus during involution, yet abnormally heavy, and with a tendency to retro-displacement, will readily fall back into the hollow of the sacrum? This position of the patient upon the back during the first days after parturition may not necessarily be harmful; but certainly after that time, it is reasonable to believe that if she is kept much of the time upon her face, or in a modified Sim's position, or certainly not farther towards a supine position than upon the side, this method will favor the assumption of a normal position of the uterus by the time complete involution is accomplished. This is not only reasonable in theory, but in my observation I have demonstrated it to be practicable. I have given my patients, who have been afflicted with retroversion or retroflexion, much encouragement to expect a cure of the trouble to follow gestation if they would carry out implicitly my instructions for two or three months following parturition. These instructions are along the line of suggestions towards keeping the patient in a prone position much of the time. It is not necessary that she should lie flat upon her face, but assume an exaggerated Sim's position, first upon one side and then upon the other, or allowing her for short intervals to turn as far back as completely upon her side, but in no case permitting her to lie upon her back at any time even for short intervals. I keep her thus in bed for at least six weeks, or until involution is completed, which sometimes, though rarely, requires eight to ten weeks. During all this time I watch my patient carefully to see that the uterus has no tendency to retro-displacement. Should it show any tendency in that direction. I use suitable manipulation for its replacement. I have the patient assume the knee-chest, or knee-elbow, or all-fours position from time to time, and, if demanded by the conditions, I have occasionally resorted to light tampons of the vagina during the latter weeks. When I first permit my patient to get up, I insist that her sitting position should be erect. I allow no reclining or rocking chairs, I permit no lounges, no semi-recumbent position. She sits straight up, walks, or lies down in the old position. The following out of this plan I insist upon for four to eight weeks longer, at the end of which time I have usually been able, to the satisfaction of my patients, to pronounce them cured of the old malposition.

It is possible that this method of treatment may sometimes fail, but I must say I believe that, in the very great majority of cases, such failure must be due to an imperfect carrying out of the minutiæ of the plan. If you have not tried it, I commend it for your consideration.

This article would not be complete from a homœopathic standpoint if I were to end it here. In all these condition, and while making all necessary applications and exercising all needful manipulations, do not forget the indicated remedy. Arctium lappa or Sepia may not lift a prolapsed uterus out of the vagina into the upper pelvis, but when indicated they will go a long ways in preventing a recurrence of the trouble after the uterus has been replaced by your efforts, or it has resumed its position after a night's sleep. A prolapsed uterus is somewhat like the lyre bird in its habits. It comes out to air in the day time, goes back to its home at night, and is a liar to you at all times. Caulophyllum or Fer. iod. may not reduce a dislocated fundus, but they may tighten the guy-ropes that help to hold it in place after gestation has made the reduction. Aletris or Conium may not take the bend out of the cervix, but they may exercise considerable influence in keeping the womb straight after the fetus has kicked the kinks out of it. Don't forget the indicated remedy. Don't confine your search for the indications to the pelvic cavity. Let your perspective take in the entirety of the case, particularly the mental manifestations and the neurotic knots. The key to the homœopathic remedy in these cases, as indeed I believe in all diseases, is most frequently found in the mental and other nervous symptoms.

J. W. Hingston.

THE TEETH AND THEIR HOMŒOPATHIC TREATMENT.

One of the most convincing proofs of the efficacy of homœopathic remedies in the early years of homœopathy, was their power to ease pain rapidly and effectually. You have all read of the young German student, who, after some years of careful study under the tutorship of Dr. Samuel Hahnemann himself, obtained such remarkable success in the city of Paris, France. His first success lay in being able to cure a toothache by having the patient take one deep inhalation from a small vial containing small white globules. For years I have longed to know how this was done, and what were the remedies so effective in stilling a throbbing tooth, or arresting the decay of those showing indications of becoming demoralized.

In a German book in my possession, "Dr. Arthur Lutze's Lehrbuch der Homöopathie," I found the long sought for information, and give it to the readers of the ADVOCATE to profit withal.

In prescribing, the 30x potency of the remedy is *always* understood, unless otherwise designated. The usual formula is to place 4 or 5 globules in a glass of cold water, and a teaspoonful taken every hour or every two hours until better, then at night and in the morning for four or five days, when the medicine is thrown away and nothing given for weeks in order that the remedy may do its work effectually. The rule is to use no cup or water glass that has had any strong acid, strong smelling medicines or coffee in it recently, unless very thoroughly cleansed before using it for this medicine, and the spoon—a horn is preferred—was always dried after giving a dose of medicine.

Again, no vial of medicine was left uncorked, not even for a moment, except to take from it what was needed, and never are the vials to be opened in a room containing strong odors of perfumes, drugs, or tobacco smoke. Among the things forbidden to persons suffering from toothache, or decay of the teeth, are coffee, tea, beer, wine, spirituous liquors; all sour and spiced foods and fat pork; all strong odors, as smelling salts, sulphur and strong smelling drugs. Absolute obedience to these and similar rules were required, and the results were very gratifying.

No. 1.

(a). If the pain was in a hollow or broken teeth, and passed from the affected tooth into the head or ears, with no tendency to swelling of the face, < in the cold, < inhaling cold air through the mouth, by taking cold drink; also < during and after eating, by touching the sick tooth, or when the tooth aches more at night, and especially after midnight.

(b). In teeth that turn dark, or decay quickly. In teeth where the enamel peels off easily.

(c). In such cases where the gums swell easily, protrude from the teeth, or where the gums bleed easily.

Give one strong inhalation from a vial of *Straph*[ma] when, in ordinarily acute cases, the pain will cease in from one to five minutes. Should the tooth or teeth persist in their aching, dissolve four or five globules of the same remedy, as already indicated, and prescribe as above.

No. 2.

(a). If the pain is in several teeth on one side, particularly the right side, so that it is difficult to locate the pain in any particular tooth; when the pains move hither and thither, the teeth seem too long, as if they protruded out of the gums more than necessary and were always in the way when closing the mouth;

heat in the face or pulsating heat in the head.

(b). When the pain is aggravated by heat and cold, or by a slight touch.

(c). When there is congestion to head or face.

(d). In one-sided pain of the face, especially the right side.

(e). In teething of children when the gums are swollen and very red, or when there is a tendency to convulsions. Also in spasmodic twitchings and cramps on the affected side.

Give an inhalation of *Belladonna*^{m}.

Example.

An example is given showing the manner of asking questions and method of treatment.

Question. "How is the pain?" Answer. "I really cannot tell which tooth pains me, it seems to be in the entire row of teeth and the pain moves back and forth."

Question "Are the teeth, in consequence of that, very sensitive?" Answer. "Yes, I can not endure to have anything touch them, and they seem elongated. I have also much heat in my head."

In a case like this I have them inhale from a vial of *Belladonna*^{m1} and the pain instantly ceases. Should it return, I dissolve a few globules in one half glass of water and give a teaspoonful, as already indicated."

No. 3.

Let the patient inhale *Chamomilla*^{m1} and give as indicated, when the conditions are:

(a). Pain aggravated by inhaling cold air, or sudden suppression of perspiration, and where the pain shoots into the ear. Especially indicated when ear ache complicates toothache.

(b). When the teeth seem too long, and have the sensation of being loose.

(c). In swelling of the cheek and gums with little or no fever, give *Chamomilla* internally, as already indicated.

(d). By aggravation of pain from warm drinks.

(e). In teething of children when accompanied by the characteristic green, fœtid stool with cramps.

No. 4.

Let the patient take a long inhalation from *Aconite*^{m1} or internally, as already indicated, when:

(a). There is throbbing pain in the tooth and accompanied by great restlessness and anxiety; or when there is fever, rapid pulse, dry glistening skin.

(b). There is repeated epistaxis, great dryness and heat of the skin then the medicine should be given in water every hour until relieved.

(c). There is difficult teething in children with the characteristic dry, hot skin.

No. 5.

Give one strong inhalation of *Arnica*^{m}

(a). In rheumatic toothache caused by sudden drenching from rain, sudden cold, or getting feet wet in cold rain.

(b). When caused by blow or bruise.

(c). When accompanied by pale, hard swelling of the cheek.

(d). By pains caused by extracting or filling the teeth. In such cases it is especially useful in cleansing the mouth with a solution of 8 to 10 globules in a glass of water In all cases calling for *Arnica* the skin should be kept warm.

No. 6.

Give *Pulsatilla*^{m}—a long inhalation or in water when:

(a). There are pulsating or boring pains in hollow teeth.

(b). There are irregular menses, or for toothache in pregnant women.

(c). There are fistulous openings. It may be necessary to follow this with *Hepar*.

(d). The pains are < toward evening, in a warm room, in bed, especially before midnight; > in cool air and towards morning.

No. 7.

Give an inhalation of *Nux vomica*^{m} or in water, when:

(a). The pains are caused by excessive use of coffee, wine or strong drink.

(b). Accompanied by obstinate constipation.

(c). There is a drawing, boring pain in a hollow tooth, as if it would be twisted loose, with severe shooting pains that cause one to shiver, especially < by inhaling cold air, and when the pains return each morning.

(d). Especially indicated in *all* persons who perform severe and prolonged mental labor.

No. 8.

Give an inhalation of *China*^{m} or in water, when:

(a). There are tearing or drawing pains in the upper teeth, or darting pains in the front teeth, < by a mere touch of the tongue.

(b). The toothache follows great weakness of the body caused by sickness or losses of vital fluids, or in women who have severe toothache before or after menstruation. Especially useful in women whose nerve force has been depreciated by hard work, excessive child-bearing or those who suffer from inconsiderate husbands.

No. 9.

Give an inhalation of *Hepar*^{m} or in water when:

(a). Toothache results from furuncles on gums or abscess in teeth.

(b). There are fistulous openings. (Puls.)

(c). There is a tendency to hollow teeth, or from bad effects of mercurialization.

No. 10.

Give an inhalation of *Sulphur*^{m} or in water:

(a). In long continued toothache of any kind, in drawing, tearing, jerking, boring, stitching pains with or without swelling of cheek. When the teeth feel dull, on "edge," or too long, and are < by night.

(b). When the gums recede from the teeth, the teeth loosen, and breath becomes very foul.

(c). In severe bleeding of the gums.

(d). When toothache results from suppressed eruptions, give the remedy in water, as already indicated.

No. 11.

Give an inhalation of *Mercurius*^{m} or in water:

(a). In toothache accompanied by excessive secretion of saliva, not brought about by salivation from mercury.

(b). In tearing, rending pains in the cheek bones, by retention of morbid matter due to allopathic drugging or in cases of syphilis.

(c). In oft returning ulcers in the mouth—cankers—give in water.

(d). When the pains as a rule are < after midnight and accompanied with excessive perspiration which does not relieve.

No. 12.

Give an inhalation of *Causticum*^{m} or in water:

(a). Where there are tearing, drawing and stitching pains and a stiffness of the articulation making it almost impossible to open the mouth.

(b). When there are all sorts of pains affecting the whole side of the head and face, bones and flesh, pains affecting the right side and > by night and by the warmth of the bed.

No. 13.

Give an inhalation of *Bryonia*^{m} or in water:

(a). In stitching and pulsating toothache which is > for a moment by cold water, then suddenly returns. Better by lying on the affected side, and out in the open air. Worse in the warmth, by going into a warm room, smoking, chewing, and when the food gets into the hollow tooth.

(b). In tearing and rending pains as if the nerve were exposed, as if cold air were constantly coming in contact with the nerve—the air seems to blow directly into the tooth. The teeth feel as if they would fall out when patient attempts to chew anything.

No. 14.

Give an inhalation of *Kreosote*[30] or in water:

(a). In drawing and tearing pains that affect the eyes and ears, or that pass down into the neck and into the shoulders. Especially indicated in left sided toothache that is > in the open air.

Special stress is laid on keeping the medicines well corked and away from all odors. Persons are cautioned not to exhale into the vial.

While these things may seem impracticable, they are worthy a trial. Country practitioners are often asked to prescribe for toothache and the above hints should prove useful.

It would also be of great interest and doubtless of great value to know the results of higher potencies of the same remedies, used as indicated above.

There is another point of value in the care of the teeth, as taught by Hahnemann and his associates, and that is the abolition of all perfumed preparations for the teeth. The only things used were a soft tooth brush, equal parts of medical charcoal and sugar of milk carefully triturated, to which was added a small bit of pure green soap, with which the teeth were cleansed night and morning, or after each meal, and the mouth rinsed in cold water.

G. E. Dienst.

RAPID CLIMATIC CHANGE NOT FAVORABLE TO INVALIDS.

Too much stress cannot be put on this subject. The tendency of the present day is to *get there* just as quickly as possible and, generally speaking, that means a change to an entirely different climate in two or three days.

Is it not unreasonable to try to circumvent Nature, which is the foundation of all cures? Why is it so few get well by going to Colorado compared to the number who used to be benefited? It is simply that they used to be obliged to travel by slow stages, and their lungs become used to the gradual ascent on the plains as they approached the high mountains in the West. They who traveled by wagon were the ones who made the reputation of Colorado, and who are living today hale and hearty.

Now the time tables are studied with reference to getting your tuberculous patient there by the quickest and most direct route, the result being frequently disastrous to the patient, and reflects on the judgment of the physician.

If a patient is sick enough to need a change of climate, consult the climatology of your own vicinity. You may be surprised to learn that your patient "is always better from a visit to Uncle John," who lives only a short drive or possibly a few miles away. If so, have the patient try the change which can be made easily and with slight expense, and you will be surprised to find "just what is needed" in your own county. When a radical change is indicated, then try a change of altitude at the nearest location, and note the result. And here I would advise that a change of not over five hundred or a thousand feet be attempted at the start. Watch the result.

When a patient shows improvement

in any particular locality, keep him there, and don't change until you know that improvement is arrested—just as you suspend your indicated remedy while its curative action is noticeable. Then change to a still higher, or warmer, location as you see is indicated. Make the migration correspond to the amount of improvement made.

Of course, it is not necessary to warn homœopathic physicians to avoid damp, malarious or marshy places. It is always well to keep posted on health resorts, and it is well to suggest that more attention be given this subject at our medical association meetings than has been done.

There are many places in the South of very great value as resorts for those whose health is undermined and, especially, for tuberculous patients. I have found one which has been very little noticed in the past, and yet it has a local reputation rarely excelled. I refer to Citronelle, Alabama, thirty two miles north of Mobile, and yet blessed with an entirely different climate from that of the latter city. It is free from malaria and very dry. Many have been cured of phthisis pulmonalis here; I myself amongst the number. I got sick in Mobile and by making this short trip got well again. Was in the last stage, weighed only 106 pounds, had forty hemorrhages in a year and cultivated Koch's bacilli by the pint. Gained twenty-four pounds in twelve weeks after coming here in September, 1886. After staying here four seasons was well enough to go into active practice in Huntsville, Ala., in the northern part of the state where I have put in eleven years of hard work and at one time weighed 152½ pounds. Have been married since 1896 and have three fine, healthy children, twin girls and a boy. What more does one want?

The inhabitants of the town are, mostly, Illinois people who came here sick and were made well, and have remained here to enjoy life. The advertising has nearly all been by word of mouth, not by flaming advertising sheets and broadcast literature.

In sending patients from the North to southern points, the best that can be done is to insist on getting off the train nights and stopping at a comfortable place on the way, thus giving the tissues a chance to be quiet for a normal sleep at the proper time. Make three or more breaks in the journey to well known healthy points like Asheville, Knoxville or Huntsville, Ala., Enterprise, Miss., Evergreen, Ala., Cullman, Ala., Thomasville, Ga., etc.

But the object of this communication is to impress upon the profession the need of less rapid migration. For it is well known that those who go from northern to extreme southern points hurriedly have to pass through a kind of acclimating fever, soon after arriving at their destination which would be avoided by less haste.

A. M. DUFFIELD.

MISCELLANEOUS THERAPEUTIC HINTS.

I am satisfied that vinegar should never be used on the person of a puerperal female, as I have seen several cases of death, apparently, from its use in such cases.—*Prof. Loomis.*

Never interfere with the action of a remedy, nor repeat it so long as improvement is going on; but fill up, as often as may seem advisable, with *Sac. lac.*, and let the remedy act as long as it will. This is the scientific Homœopathic rule, and should be held inviolable.—*Prof. Loomis.*

When improvement follows the use of a remedy, but patient immediately relapses as the medicinal influence passes off, you will frequently retain all the improvement by giving an occasional dose of Sulphur.—*Prof. Loomis.*

Guaiacum, most valuable in acute rheumatism; 3d or 4th attenuation in water will often greatly relieve in twenty-four hours.—*Prof. Williamson.*

Gamboge. Dysentery with retained scybala, with great tormina and tenesmus, attended with pain in the sacral region.—*Prof. Williamson.*

Aconite, the best remedy in the first stages of violent congestions.

Sulphur. One single dose in the first stages of ulceration of the cornea will, almost as certainly as given, cure.

Calcarea carb. Injudiciously given in cases of consumption will hasten death.

Caries. Is usually the cause of those abscesses which form near the bones, and not the abscess the cause of the caries.

Asafœtida and **Aurum** are useful in caries of the nasal bones.

Asafœtida, mammæ turgid as with milk in the ninth month of pregnancy, but patient not pregnant.

Kalmia, protracted and continued fevers, with much tympanitis, acts mostly on the brain.—*Prof. Williamson.*

Petroleum. Urinary troubles of children, often mistaken for colic, and the poor child not at all relieved by treatment.

Lachesis. Many years ago we had an epidemic of fever in a mild form and Lachesis cured all cases beginning on the left side and tending to the right; while those commencing on the right side were as promptly controlled by Lycopodium. It was very seldom that any other medicine was required to complete the cure.

In a neglected and bad case of quinsy on the left side, tending to the right, where solids could be swallowed much better than liquids, with pains shooting into the left ear at every attempt to swallow, Lachesis 30th, three doses at hour intervals, produced a great aggravation which subsided in a few hours, but no other remedy was needed, and recovery was speedy.

We are told the symptoms of this remedy are worse after eating; the patient *sleeps into* and *wakes in* the aggravation.

In spring intermittents, with thirst before the chill; chill and heat alternate and change from place to place; internal sensation of heat, with cold feet; profuse sweat after suppression by quinine the previous fall, worse in the early afternoon, with loquacity during the hot stage, will be quickly cured by one dose of Lachesis^{m} (Verified—W.)

Lac caninum. A case of chronic sore throat in an old syphilitic lady, of years standing, and could not be cured by her old school physician, with these peculiar symptoms: Disease on the right or on the left side today, but changes to the opposite side tomorrow, and thus keeps on changing sides every day, with many other symptoms of the drug. One dose 200th given and cured in three days.

Case of diphtheria relieved, but not cured, by other remedies; with this symptom: "*Ulcers shine like silver gloss.*" A few doses of Lac caninum^{m} cured the case speedily.

Arnica Montana. The best remedy in many cases of pleurodynia; have cured many cases with one dose of the 200th, often pain would cease in a few minutes. My first remedy, nearly always.

It is also a choice remedy in mental shock; where the patient has had a violent shock and can't get over it.

Prof. Walter M. Williamson says, when rheumatism begins low down and works up Arnica will cure.

Rhus tox. When a part is stretched or strained, as over-distension of the perinæum, give one dose 200th, and wait. One case of uterine hemorrhage, threatening abortion, consequent upon over-lifting, controlled by a few doses.

J. A. WAKEMAN.

A FEW MISTAKES.

I am not the fortunate man who never makes mistakes. I do, sometimes, make them, and will tell of a few. Though they may be of little interest generally, yet someone way take a "hint" and be benefited.

I was once consulted in the case of a boy about ten years of age with an eruption of scattering vesicles all over him, some of the patches being very thickly covered. They were umbilicated and fast changing to pustules, and in some places they were coalescing and forming crusts, with bad odor and much itching, there being very little fever. Otherwise the boy was well.

Now, the mistake was, *I didn't call it smallpox*, but I unfashionably inquired further and learned that he had been vaccinated over a year before and it did not "take." I pronounced his trouble "the development of the vaccination;" gave him the remedy, and he played about with other children until he scaled off and was well. A year after the same symptoms appeared, and with a still more carefully selected remedy he was well again. Of the many children, both vaccinated and unvaccinated who had been playing with him, not a one took the smallpox.

Had I said the disease was smallpox I would have had the glory of starting a smallpox excitement; the family would have had the pleasure of being quarantined, and Joseph the honor of being the hero of a pest house experience, if he had lived through it. As it was we all lost a chance of obtaining glory by my acting on the plain facts in the case.

Case 2. Rev. M., had been visiting a smallpox infected locality; came home; soon developed a rash, or vesicles, on face, arms and over body, with swelling, itching and burning, with fever. By carefully taking the symptoms a case of ivy poisoning was diagnosed. A little treatment, and he was well, no excitement. If I had called the disease smallpox it would have brought all parties into notoriety. Four other cases I now think of where the same mistake was made.

Case 3. Called to see Miss G., age 15 years; good sized girl; light hair, blue eyes. Sick two days; some fever; sore throat, a large thick, tough patch on left tonsil, a dark red base, very tender to touch and much difficulty and pain was experienced in swallowing. She got the remedy indicated, but no diagnosis. The next day the patch was gone with much of the soreness and dark color.

The mistake was that I not report a case of diphtheria, have the family honored with quarantine and myself the recipient of a notoriety. I can think of many cases of the same kind where I made the same kind of mistake—and lost the glory.

Here is another, more serious mistake: I undertook to treat a patient in a hospital where the resident physician and the matron were both deeply dyed-in-the-wool allopaths. The patient did not appear to be in a dangerous condition but, strangely, he would get bad spells late in the night. I was dismissed, and in a few days there was a funeral. I was dishonored, a scapegoat for the hospital, and the church was minus a minister. I should have kept out of the trap.

Here is still another. I allowed myself to be persuaded by some eminent Homœopathic physicians to permit the use of disinfectants in a room where diphtheria patients were. At their suggestion I directed Bromochloralum to be used, the fumes of which are death to microbes and, equally so, for animal life, even half dead children. The result was, a job for the undertaker—and I had to carry the blame. The good I got from it was I learned that men of fame should not always be taken as advisers, because they don't know it all. The lesson was dear, but very valuable.

And yet another. In my early practice I treated a few cases of venereal diseases without collecting the fee in advance—reason obvious. Another mistake was to promise not to charge until the patient got well. Of course they never got well.

Another grave mistake I have made in a few cases is to consent to the patient's taking those little black pills to keep the bowels open while under treatment. In such cases I always fail to cure and the patient soon becomes disgusted and leaves me, without benefit.

One of the worst blunders I ever made was to give free treatment to a "clever" party who was able to pay, in the expectation of gaining friendship—especially applicable to the clergy.

But the worst of all the mistakes I ever made—it was long ago—was when I found myself dealing with a hard case. I was persuaded to take some smart fellow's advice and gave a compound prescription of crude drugs, because recommended by some famous M. D., instead of working out the similar remedy by the symptoms. The patient always shared with me in the disastrous results.

Here is the record of a silly mistake. I asked a rival essayist and, by the way, a very clever fellow, to examine a paper and suggest changes for improvement, and I allowed him to strike out the most important sentence in it, and the spirit of it was taken out entirely. I learned my mistake when too late to correct it.

With all these mistakes I have learned much that is useful, but the most useful of all is, the surest, best and always the most successful method is to adhere to the text; follow the law; and practice what I profess, the Homœopathy of Hahnemann, according to his laws and the rules laid down by the old masters.

W. L. MORGAN.

INABILITY TO DRINK WATER CURED BY PLUMBUM, DULCAMARA, HECLA LAVA AND SILICEA.

Case I. A man came to me who could not drink water on account of the distress in stomach and a cough which set in and lasted several hours after each drink of water, he finally found a light beer could be drunk without distress and he had given up hope of ever drinking water again. He was a delicately constituted man and had some catarrh both of stomach and upper bronchial passages. In taking his case I also found he had been poisoned with lead and then had characteristic pain and retraction of abdominal wall at umbilicus, also he had been through the mercurial salivation (so fashionable again now as it was forty years ago by the allopathic school). I gave him one dose of *Plumbum*[cm] dry on tongue he to report in a week. This he did and said I have no abdominal pain now nor any retraction. As he was going East for two or three weeks, I gave him a dose *Mercurius Dulcamara*[cm] dry on tongue to report on his return. This he did and said "I can now drink water" and was very happy and has so continued to be, and yet some sneer at antidotal prescribing. All well, but can anyone do better? Answer.

Case 2. Was asked if anything could be done for a lady who was suffering from the beginning of an ulcerated root of a crowned tooth. "Yes" was my reply, but, said my questioner, the "Dentist and Doctor (allopathic) say nothing can be done." "That proves nothing" says I, "let me try and show you." I was given the case and *Hecla lava*[1m] hastened matters, caused pointing of abscess, lessened the unbearable pain in twenty-four hours, and then *Silicea*[m] cut out the pus and wound up the case in three days to the delight of patient and friends. Once before under the ministrations of the above Dentist and Doctor the same person had suffered three weeks, so they found out if anything could be done by the differance in pain, discomfort and suffering, three days or three weeks.

Case 3. I was called by a brother Homœopath to see a prominent clergyman. He had been a victim of one of these newly made so-called specialists for treatment of quinsy. First they tried to suppress the trouble, and failing to do so, had amputated one tonsil (a ruinous job when tonsils are inflamed) and had lanced the other to find pus and did not, Nature opening up the way herself later on, as is often the case. Rheumatism set in of a violent type. Ascites, œdema of legs from knee to feet. Sluggish kidneys and a weak heart. Such was the condition in which I found him, and the case seemed hopeless indeed. After looking the case over carefully, and believing that the meddlesome treatment of throat had infected system by pus, I prescribed *Pyrogen*[m] two doses a day and predicted a favorable condition of affairs in 48 hours, and surely enough he began to mend and slowly began to make a slow gradual but sure recovery. Question, when will physicians learn to assist Nature and not thwart natural processes?

A. G. Downer.

GASTRALGIA, CARDIALGIA NERVOSA.

Calcarea hypophosphite[cm] Sudden appearance of the pain, two to three hours after eating a regular meal; *entirely free* from all distress at *intervals*. This is a leading symptom; spreading of the pain upwards, from the epigastric region; *never downwards;* and relieved by taking a cup of hot milk.

Without this, the pain steadily increases, extends to the spine into the right chest more than the left; into the throat, and in some rare cases the right side of the head. Give one dose on the tongue and follow with *Sac. lac.*

Almost never necessary to repeat the dose, one of fifteen years standing cured by one dose.

Gastralgia. Mrs. J., aged 30 years,

mother of several children, now nursing a six months old babe, while she nurses is subject to severe attacks. Called in haste and found patient in bed flat upon her back, head very low, vomiting frequently of a glairy mucus, bad breath, sweating, with *intense* thirst; would *vomit* and call for *drink before lying* down.

With every movement, cutting pain running from *left to right* through the stomach and upper part of the abdomen with a clutching pain at the umbilicus; cold extremities and anxious face. *Ipecacuanha*[m] one dose given, and I seated myself to await results and in ten minutes, noticed patient manifested great alarm and presently said, "Doctor, am I not dying?" On being asked why she was alarmed, she replied, "I feel perfectly relieved in every respect, so perfectly easy, I thought I must be dying." Nothing more was given. Recovery was prompt.

A choice remedy in constant nausea, and frequent gagging of teething children, child thrusts its fist into its mouth and screams, with grass-green stools.

Also in dyspeptic pains in the stomach which return *at the same hour* every day or every other day, and may or may not be attended with nausea and vomiting.

J. A. Wakeman.

THE VALUE OF MENTAL SYMPTOMS.

Miss E. B., 23 years, spare, medium height, not strong. Has to be careful about overdoing, especially at her menstrual period. Menses too soon, never going over three weeks. Menses profuse and lasting a week. Has much menses; faints easily with palpitation; pain in heart, irritable before menses especially; tires with little exertion—hands cold, sleepless and restless at night. Dreams, very cross after bad night's rest. Her sister being present says she is impatient, easily excited to anger; insulting, uncivil, "hard to live with her, she is so cross."

The leaders in the group of cross remedies are *Chamomilla*, *Nux vomica* and *Staphisagria*. Of course *Chamomilla* was selected. Three powders of the 200th were given six hours apart. *Sac. lac.* three times daily for one month. Word came by mail that she was better and wanted more medicine. *Sac. lac.* was sent for another month. At the end of that time report came that she was well, which was a new experience to her. No more medicine needed. Time will tell whether this is a permanent cure.

W. H. Leonard.

Medicine.

PULMONARY TUBERCULOSIS.

At the invitation of the Chicago Medical College, Victor C. Vaughn, Dean of the Medical Department of the University of Michigan, conducted a clinic in the college amphitheater Wednesday morning, April 9. The subject of the clinic was *Tuberculosis*, and his purpose was to present such cases as would illustrate tuberculosis in its prebacillary state, but only partially succeeded in this particular. After presenting the views of Lænnec on the *unity of tubercular infection* and showing the mischievous effects of the contrary opinion held by Virchow, he paid high tribute to the patient investigations of Koch which demonstrated the fact that the *bacillus tuberculosis* was present, *either as a cause or an effect*, in every case of tubercular infection. At this point in the lecture a most forceful impression was left upon the minds of his hearers regarding the *curability* of tuberculosis in its early state, quoting from the statistics that go to show an infection of at least one-third of the entire population, while only one-seventh of all the deaths reported are attributable to tuberculosis, modifying this statement, however, with another statement that, undoubtedly, many deaths are attributed to other causes where a more careful examination would have revealed the presence of tubercles. Laboratory investigations have demonstrated the truth of the statement that normal, healthy tissue has been made to supplant tissue from which tubercular deposits have been discovered.

Assuming the statement to be true that all cases of hip-joint disease or Pott's disease have a tubercular origin, he made the statement that these forms of disease were as amenable to treatment as any other form seriously involving important tissues, *provided it was recognized and proper treatment instituted during the stage of unmixed infection.*

These preliminary statements led up to the point where the lecturer presented the best means for the recognition of tuberculosis *before* the bacilla appears in the sputum or other secretions from the body:

1. *Proof of the possibility of direct infection through personal contact.*

2. *Gradual loss of weight without any perceptible cause for the impaired nutrition of the body.*

3. *Presence of the characteristic temperature curve.*

Every disease in which abnormalities of temperature present diagnostic features, it will be noted that each possesses marked characteristics unless perverted by extraneous causes. The temperature curve of tuberculosis shows a characteristic rise during the afternoon, *reaching the highest point between the hours of 2 and 4 o'clock.* In order that the test may be conclusive the patient should be placed in a state of absolute rest and the temperature taken every two hours for a period covering the time between 8 o'clock a. m. and 8 o'clock p. m. If this is not conclusive after two or three tests the patient should be subjected to a certain amount of exercise, such as walking two or three miles, after which the temperature should be taken, when the thermometer will record an unusually high temperature for the amount of force expended.

4. *Feeble inspiration* in the apices of both lungs, with *prolonged expiratory sound.* This will be more marked in the first or second intercostal space, and generally more marked on the left than on the right.

These four diagnostic points may be supplemented by the deduction known as Fleming's laws:

(a). Idiopathic pleurisy always means tubercular infection, although followed by active infiltration in only about one case in three. (This was one of the methods employed for determining the proposition said to possess favorable soil for tubercular infection).

(b). Idiopathic pleurisy on one side indicates liability of tubercular infection in apex of the opposite lung.

Throughout the lecture an early recognition of disease tendencies was urged upon the profession. The simple fact that one death out of every seven was directly traceable to this cause, coupled with the further fact that many other deaths from acute infection owed their peculiar suceptibility to the insiduous progress of this general infection, ought to be enough to induce every member of the profession to become a master of every means that can be employed for its early recognition. While a systematic hunt for evidence of its indications should be made in every available case, with the hope that a vigorous and persistent following up of this method would result in the elimination of the same as a disease producing agent throughout the world.

Treatment.

In the beginning, a proper hygenic environment, supplemented by a liberal amount of suitable food, together with a sufficient amount of absolute rest in pure air are of greater value than any climatic changes unaccompanied by proper food and proper rest.

According to his experience a patient disclosing a tendency toward tuberculosis should be fed five or six times every day, and rich, juicy meats should be given at least at three of these meals. At the other meals eggs, cream and foods of a similar character have the strongest indications.

Surgery.

SURGICAL ITEMS—RAPID OPERATING.

At this time, it may serve a more or less useful purpose, to call attention to some clinical experiences from which even those engaged in surgical practice might possibly find something of interest.

The matter of particular moment that is now in my mind is the benefit that attaches to rapid operating in major cases. A few years ago the younger men engaged in surgical work were so deliberate in their actions that those of us who had training from men who did *their* work in pre-anesthetic days were not a little horrified. These old-time teachers of ours, from the stress in which they did their work—their formative age—acquired a deftness and dexterity that was little short of marvelous. Much of their work looked like sleight of hand, many an operation being completed before some of the onlookers thought it had commenced. Think of an Agnew who could make a double, absolutely synchronous amputation, a knife in each hand. Who can do that now? This speed was not *haste;* there is a wide difference in many. Speed, for distinction, includes a correct estimation of the magnitude and boundaries of the procedure, and a carrying out of the conception without hesitation or delay. Some there may be, even now, who are not cognizant of all the benefits of speed. Let us recall several facts.

Any agent competent to produce profound anesthesia and analgesia is not to be played with as an innocuous one. The taking up by the elimination in various ways is productive of various physiological disturbances, the gravity and significance of which are proportioned to the amount of the agent used, and this again is determined by the length of time the patient is kept under its influence. So *time*, therefore, is an important element in the anesthesia.

Shock is another item to be considered and dealt with. The most profound anesthesia does not eliminate the effects of traumatism, the reaction to structural damage. This is particularly true when the cavities of the body, especially the abdominal, are invaded. The less shock the quicker the convalescence.

In addition to shock and prolonged anesthesia, exposure to handling of viscera and to the air is harmful, and delays both reaction and convalescence.

Finally, economy of blood is a highly important consideration. Temporary hemostasis with clips etc., with permanent closure of bleeding vessels when the work is finished, will save much blood.

To insure rapid and clean operating the surgeon who is worthy of the name will have good eyesight, capacity to measure *with* the eye, manual dexterity and keen sense of touch, the *tactus eruditus* of the old pedantic school. He must be able to recognize by touch alone normal and pathological structures, and when he puts his finger into an abdominal wound recognize *at once* everything his finger touches, its construction and relations to other parts, and must make no mistake about it. A knowledge of anatomy is also necessary, and a clear conception of what he desires to do, so his work will be prompt, rapid and clean. If he is a clinical teacher he must cultivate the habit and ability to give his clinical lecture and make his operation without stopping the latter.

With no desire to deprecate asepsis, antisepsis or any or all of the modern technique of the operating theater, I say with emphasis, *rapid operation* compensates for much neglect in technique, and slow operating destroys much of the value of the antecedent preparation. For example, take an ovarian cyst. The surgeon who completes such an operation in from ten to fifteen minutes will get better results in insufficiently prepared patients than another who consumes from a half to an hour's time, and I have heard of those who consumed *more* time than this, with the most painstaking preparatory treatment.

JAMES G. GILCHRIST, A. M., M. D.

TREATMENT OF SCALP WOUNDS.

Case 9. This man fell on the ice last Friday and was attended by the ambulance surgeon. We have here an occipital scalp wound which is sewed up with black silk. It is about two inches long. His hair has been cut off from a large area, covering at least half of the occipital bone. I have taken out the stitches, and there seems to be just a little infection in the upper part of the wound. I will not disturb it; will simply put on a compress, hoping that will be the end of it. It is a great mistake to put sutures in a scalp wound. In some cases there will be no trouble, but in the majority of cases infusion follows. There is no part of the body so liable to suppuration as the scalp. The trouble is not in the hair, but in the hair follicles. I think a surgeon makes a mistake in shaving the scalp for an ordinary scalp wound. Try the simpler way. Get rid of all the blood, wash the wound thoroughly with a carbolic solution ½ dram to the ounce, then take a lock of hair from each side of the wound and tie them together. That will approximate the edges, yet not sufficiently close to interfere with the drainage. Then if you get an infection, there will be room enough for the pus to form and run outside rather than remain and dissect the scalp from the surface of the bone. There are a variety of ways in which you can bring the edges together by using an ordinary rubber adhesive plaster. Take a strip of this plaster and fold it with the sticky side in, then take your two locks of hair and lay them on the sticky side and fold them together. That will hold them in place. Then put on a compress wet with a two per cent solution, or five per cent if you have had contusion, and leave it alone. It will get well without any danger of infection. While if you shave the scalp and sew up the wound and then dust it over with iodoform powder, or any other kind of powder, you will have a pus pocket form under that, and a saturated powder. Turn back to Gross, and see how he cautions about scalp wounds because of the following. If you follow my method this will never happen. Another objection to the ligature is the fact that when you put your needle in you go down to the deep hair follicles and you are almost sure to carry infection in with your ligature.—S. D. Powell, in March *Post-Graduate*.

Nursing.*

THE PUERPERAL OR LYING-IN PERIOD.

Lecture No. 6.

Ladies: The time required for the complete recovery of a mother varies greatly. From six weeks to three months usually elapse before the patient is entirely well, and in some cases a still longer period. As the patient is in bed a part of this time, it has been termed the lying-in period, or the time of confinement. Formerly it was thought that one month was sufficient for the services of a nurse, and so obstetric nurses were called monthly nurses. During this time the womb and other portions of the genital tract are becoming smaller, until they are nearly in the condition in which they were before pregnancy occurred. This process is called involution. Wounds in the soft tissues during labor gradually heal. The abdominal muscles which were stretched contract and become nearly as firm as before. The secretion of milk is established and continues. Some patients lose in weight while nursing the child, while others gain after childbirth. The mother is never so small as before her pregnancy, unless artificial means be used to compress her body. She is larger about the waist and about the chest than before.

The lining membrane of the womb is shed off during the lying-in period, and with the discharge of other tissue from the uterus forms the lochial discharge. This is at first bloody, then serous, and lastly mucous. It is altered in cases of septic infection. The intestinal tract of the patient has been usually distended with feces during pregnancy. After the bowels have been emptied the intestines gradually regain their normal size and elasticity.

The first absolute necessity for the mother in the lying-in bed period is rest. It is sometimes very hard to persuade her friends and relatives that such is the case. Joy over the birth of the child, curiosity to see it, and general excitement disturb the mother very much. It is the duty of the nurse, however, to see that when the mother has been properly cleansed and suitable dressings applied, and her bed made clean and comfortable, that the room should be darkened, and that the patient should enjoy perfect quiet, and if possible several hours of sleep. Although the mother rests the nurse must remain watchful. She must know that the patient's pulse is good; that the flow of blood from the uterus is not excessive; that the extremities are warm; and that her sleep is a healthful and restful one, and not a dangerous unconsciousness caused by bleeding or fatal syncope. If the nurse is negligent, a mother may bleed to death while the nurse supposes her to be asleep.

While the patient sleeps the nurse will have time to wash and dress the child, to place linen and other articles

*Course of Lectures delivered to the Nurses Training School at Maryland Homoeopathic Hospital, by M. E. Douglass, M. D., Baltimore, Md.

soiled during the labor in cold water to soak, and to make the rooms which have been used neat and tidy. If linen and clothing has become much blood stained, they should be soaked in cold water containing sodium bicarbonate. If they be repeatedly rinsed, the blood will entirely disappear, and the clothing may then be washed in the usual manner. Clothing or other articles stained with blood should never be washed in hot water or boiled.

When the mother wakes from the first sleep her natural desire will be to see the child. If she is in good condition, and the child also, this desire should be gratified, and the opportunity should be taken to put the child to the breast. Before the child nurses, its mouth should be wiped out with a small square of clean linen dipped in a saturated solution of boric acid. The mother's nipples should be washed with Castile soap and warm water, and then with boric acid solution before the child nurses. After the child nurses the nipple should be sponged and dried with linen soaked in boric acid solution.

It is often difficult to induce the child to take the nipple for the first time. If the mother takes the child upon her arm and turns upon her side, the breast will naturally fall so that the nipple will come easily into the child's mouth. It is usually unnecessary to do more than simply moisten the nipple, when the child will nurse eagerly. But little fluid is present in the breast at first, and the child after trying for a moment may desist because it obtained nothing. As the secretion of milk increases the child will increase its efforts to nurse.

It is very important in the lying-in period that the mother should be kept clean, and that she should have abundant and proper diet and sufficient rest. Her room should be absolutely neat, the linen changed so often as necessary, the antiseptic dressings frequently removed, and in every particular the patient and her surroundings must be models of neatness. Each puerperal patient requires at least one thorough soap and water sponge-bath daily. This is best given in the morning usually about an hour after breakfast. The use of highly scented soaps is objectionable, and a wash-cloth is preferable to a sponge. Careful attention must also be given to the patient's hair that it does not become uncomfortably matted or tangled while she is in bed. If it is grateful to the patient, she may also have light rubbing with alcohol in the evening, about an hour before the time when she goes to sleep.

During the latter portion of the puerperal period massage is a most important method of advancing the patient's recovery. This should be given very gently at first, the back and limbs only being treated. Later on, the entire body, including the abdomen, may be subjected to massage with great benefit.

The posture of the lying-in patient is of importance. Immediately after delivery she should lie quietly upon the back, and remain so until she has perfectly reacted from labor and until all danger of hemorrhage or relaxation of the uterus is passed. So soon as the mother can move about comfortable in bed she should turn on either side. The shoulders are not usually raised from the bed for several days after confinement, and the patient may be gradually propped up in bed, with the doctor's permission, until she assumes very nearly the sitting posture.

So long as the patient is fatigued she naturally does not desire a bright light; but when she is not asleep the light in her room should be that best adapted to her comfort. Excepting in hot weather, abundant sunshine is an excellent thing for such a room, and should be admitted most freely. The ventilation of the lying-in room should be as perfect as possible. This may be accomplished by raising the lower sash of the window and placing beneath it a strip of board. An air space is thus formed between the upper and lower sash which prevents a draft. An open fireplace is also of the greatest assistance in securing good ventilation. Screens such as are used in dining rooms and other apartments may be utilized to avoid drafts.

The mother very naturally desires to have the child near her. Its presence, however, in her room is most undesirable. Many newborn children are restless at night for the first week or ten days after birth, and if they be in the room with the mother she must necessarily be disturbed and lose important rest. The child is often put in the room with the nurse, this arrangement enabling her to care for the child without disturbing the mother. The child's room may be near the mother's and adjacent.

While the lying in room should be well-ventilated, it should also be comfortably warm. Immediately after labor the patient experiences a considerable reaction and often complains of a chilly sensation. The best form of heat is an open wood fire. Next to this is an open stove burning hard coal; while worst of all is a register from a furnace, which brings heated and foul air from the cellar of the house.

Within the first forty-eight hours after labor the mother's bowels should be thoroughly but gently moved by an enema.

The diet of the mother after labor should be liquid. An abundance of water must also be taken. The use of liquids is necessary for the formation of milk, to stimulate the action of the kidneys and intestines and to appease the mother's natural feeling of thirst. Water and milk are the best beverages; the lighter forms of cocoa acceptable to some, but tea and coffee should be used in small quantities only. Some think that coffee lessens the secretion of milk and that tea increases it. There is no positive evidence that either belief is correct. Liquid food may be given every three hours and once during the night. After the bowels have moved and the flow of milk has been established, the diet may comprise soft eggs, custard, junket, milktoast, frenchtoast, light puddings, broths, soups, purees, calve's-foot jelly, partially melted ice cream, sponge cake, charlotte-russe, all vegetables in season, non-acid fruits, raw if perfectly ripe and, if not, cooked, baked apples being of special value if not too sour. At the end of the first week of the puerperal period the patient may add to this diet once daily the white meat of chicken or turkey, squab, sweetbread, lamb chops, oysters and fish. When she begins to be up and about her room, beef, bacon, and potatoes may be added. Fried dishes, shell-fish, pickels, nuts, candies, cheese, rich sauces, pastry, highly spiced food, and alcoholic drinks should be excluded at all times.

To cleanse the parts, the nurse, with antiseptic hands, irrigates or sponges the external parts thoroughly. Then separating the labia with the fingers of the left hand, she directs a stream of antiseptic fluid from a fountain syringe upon the external parts and the entrance to the vagina, washing these parts perfectly clean. If a syringe is not used, she should saturate a handful of gauze or cotton with the antiseptic fluid, and, holding the labia apart with the left hand, the right should be placed above the parts, the gauze or cotton squeezed, and the fluid allowed to run over the parts. No finger or instrument should be inserted within the vagina without the doctor's precise orders. When the parts are thoroughly cleansed the external parts may be gently dried with gauze or cotton sponges. The fresh dressing is then applied.

Soiled dressings when removed should be wrapped in waste paper and burned in the range or stove. The nurse should watch carefully for evidences of a foul discharge on the napkins, from inflammation or irritation caused by the dressings or antiseptic solutions employed. Dressings shall be changed and the patient cleansed whenever the dressing is stained through, whenever the bladder or bowel is emptied, and as often as the physician may direct.

After the baby nurses, the nipples should be thoroughly but gently cleansed with sterile water or with some antiseptic solution of boric acid. When the nipples are tender and a crack or fissure is feared, an antiseptic ointment may also be employed to advantage. Other physicians prefer a simple sterile fat, as sterile oil or cocoa butter.

It is often necessary to catheterize a puerperal patient, and this requires the strictist antiseptic precautions. The catheter must be boiled, the hands of the nurse made antiseptic, and the patient's parts gently but thoroughly cleaned with antiseptic solutions. No instrument or utensil or appliance which is not thoroughly clean should be used about the puerperal patient.

The regulation of visits made by outsiders to the patient is often a matter of difficulty. There are many reasons why but few people should call upon a case. It is usually best to limit visitors to the patient's nearest friends until she is able to go out. Importunate persons can often be appeased if the baby is shown to them. This satisfies their curiosity, and gives them an opportunity of comparing the child with their own and others of their acquaintance.

The question of the mother's getting up from confinement is one which is constantly brought to the attention of the nurse and her friends. Women usually expect to be up and about on the tenth day after the birth of the child when the confinement occurs among the poorer classes. It is evident that there is no fixed limit for the lying-in period, but that each patient must get up in proportion to her recovery and to her strength. It is for the doctor alone to decide when the patient shall leave her bed. So long as there is a free reddish discharge the patient should not be upon her feet. The average patient can leave her bed to use a commode at the end of ten days or two weeks, can be partially dressed and lying upon a couch during the third week, and up and about her room in the fourth week. Her going out of doors must depend upon the weather, upon her general strength, and upon the means at her disposal. She should go out at first in a carriage if this is possible, and begin to walk and take active exercise very gradually.

In our next lecture we will take up the care of the newborn child.

Pediatrics.

WHAT DOES HOMŒOPATHY MEAN TO THE CHILDREN?

Child study is one of the popular themes of the present day. Surely none can be more important and few more fascinating. Without the children, what of the future generations? We are learning how vastly important for the coming years of the world's history it is that the children be given every chance to develop wisely and well. To the children do we look for our encouragement. To them we look for the fulfillment of our hope and faith in a better future state of things; they must prove the workers in the battle for justice; therefore we aim to mould and influence them that they in their turn may influence others. This is the keynote to our future social reform, the development of the children, mentally and morally.

If this be true in an intellectual and moral sense, it is no less true in a physical and medical sense.

All are sick in this great world of ours, men, women and children, all. There are, it is true, degrees of sickness, but in each and every one lurks the hidden monster, disease, ready to make himself manifest whenever opportunity offers. Even the children are not exempt and herein lies the vital point of this paper; if only the mothers and fathers, the guardians of these little ones, could realize the significance of this truth, that in each and every child is the same demon, disease; very quietly he lies in some, so that we can hardly catch a glimpse of him, but in others he seems to be working sad havoc. In all he will sooner or later make himself apparent; some external, visible sign will be given forth of the internal disorder. How important it is to grasp this truth! It forms the groundwork of all future building; to understand clearly that every ailment exhibited by the child is but an external evidence of an internal disturbance. The cause of the ailment is to be sought for in the child's internal economy; the child is sick, therefore exhibits symptoms. It is true some exciting influence from without may cause such exhibition, but this influence could produce no deleterious effect, if the child was well. The physician is called to a new case, an adult patient, one who has been receiving medical attention for years. This physician, if a careful prescriber, travels back with that patient to the time of his earliest infancy, and then reviews the path by which this man or woman has journeyed, tracing step by step his progress in disease and its accompanying results. From the story of small disturbances foolishly treated, graver manifestations suppressed, skin eruptions, catarrhal discharges, etc., checked and suppressed until the system, no longer able to cope with such abuse, has fastened its disease upon some more vital portion of the economy, showing the life force is well nigh exhausted. How often the physician groans within himself when such a picture presents itself; could he have had that patient years ago, long before such havoc had been wrought. He must undo the wrong, in so far as this wornout, much-abused constitution will permit, and many times the results are delightful. But too often the physician must content himself with patching and surface mending, the giving of some comfort, yet we would wish to be able to rout the old ills and make new men and women of our patients.

To turn to child sicknesses, under homœopathy, is like a breath of inspiration. Here is a field of work worthy the devotion of a lifetime, in bringing out of these undeveloped portions of humanity men and women of health and vigor. How beautiful to watch the gradual unfolding of some poor, puny, sickly baby into a well-rounded, healthful child, who can enjoy life to the full.

How shall this physical reformation be brought about?

Again emphasizing the fact that all signs and symptoms of sickness are but the outward image of an internal disorder, that if the child were not sick primarily no manifestations of sickness would appear externally, the question arises what is the correct method of meeting such disease pictures? Shall we deal them blows from the outside and force them into silence, allowing the internal disturbance to continue unchecked, only to gather fresh impetus from this violence and vent its fury upon some other portion of the economy? Or shall we seek to restore order to this disturbed vital force, realizing that restored harmony within will result in a cessation of external disorder, with a consequent disappearance of symptoms and return to health? Of what use is it to quell a riot in one community, only to bring about a fresh uprising near by, and so on, time and time again. Why not set to work to root out the cause of the original revolt, and in this way secure peace.

All homœopathic cures are in direction of from within outward; treatment based upon any other foundation is absolutely futile and in addition most harmful; futile because it can never result in a cure, and harmful because it often places the patient beyond the possibility of a future cure.

Therefore, each child must be studied from the center of his being to the circumference; each and every individual separately, for each has his or her own peculiar characteristics, mental and physical. How absurd to imagine that all children with colic should receive the same medicine. What symptoms does the child exhibit, what are its peculiar manifestations? And from these symptoms we select the remedy. Each child receives the remedy, that is of all remedies, most similar to its particular case. Mark this clearly, the prescription is based upon the symptoms manifested by the child itself, and the colic is but a minor consideration; we, as homœopaths, have no specific for any disease. A medicine which aims directly at the colic, irrespective of its interior cause, simply produces temporary relief and stilles the cries, consequently there will shortly be a fresh exhibition of distress, which again must be forcibly hushed.

Take, for instance, an eruption on the skin; it is looked upon as an external disfigurement, a blood disorder, which must be removed, and usually by some outward application. No thought is given to the underlying cause. But what of the child meanwhile? The eruption has disappeared, but wait a little, and presently (it may take years) another effort will be made to gain relief from this inward turmoil, by an outward manifestation; and we find catarrhal discharges making their appearance in different parts of the body, a somewhat deeper form than the skin eruptions. These, too, are in turn suppressed, "dried up," by local applications.

We, as physicians, need the co-operation of the parents if we are to restore their children to health. They must understand the truth of homœopathy and its power. Then, when symptoms appear in the child, pains, eruptions discharges, fevers, etc., the parent appreciates the fact that such are merely images of an internal disorder and not to be trifled with, but rather carefully noted, each and every symptom, to report to the physician, that he may see a clear image of the internal disturbance and apply his remedy intelligently.

One must be a keen observer in order to read symptoms, and in dealing with children this is, perhaps, especially true; many times we must depend almost entirely upon what we can note and observe by close watching; the child cannot describe its sufferings, there is "no language but a cry" to guide us. The mother or nurse trained in watching and studying symptoms becomes expert. She has learned to report its mental state, the particular form of irritability displayed, the hours of aggravation, day or night, how affected by heat and cold and motion, the desires and aversions in the way of food and drink, all give most valuable information of the internal disorder and point to the curative remedy.

Passing from the things general to the things particular, the mother trained in homœopathy can now relate to the physician the symptoms she has observed as belonging to special portions of the child's body, its skin, head, eyes, ears, etc., etc. She can locate the seat of pain by having watched the child's actions; she will also have noted the time of aggravation of the pain; as to what gives relief, heat or cold, certain positions taken, rest or motion, etc. If vomiting or diarrhea is present, the mother can describe minutely the character of the ejected substances, their color, odor, consistency etc.

To the general features already obtained, we now add this image of the particular symptoms, and as the whole, clear picture of this sickness rises before us, this outward manifestation of an internal disorder, there stands out the remedy in strong relief, the one most similar to this disease picture, in other words, the symptom image produced by the proving of that particular remedy. There is no guess work, no try this and then that, and if they fail, try something else; it is work based upon a solid foundation, a perfect law.

And so, to the mothers or guardians of the little ones is granted a great privilege in being fellow laborers with the physician, who must have full control. No meddling can be permitted. This the friends of the little patient must understand; no little application made there, "just to help along." The handling of human sickness is a process requiring infinite delicacy and great skill. The readjustment from sickness to health cannot take place if in its process rude hands from outside displace and derange the work already accomplished.

The child from its earliest infancy begins to show forth expressions of disease; let us recognize clearly the significance of such expressions, and give the child a fair chance for life and hope in its richest and fullest sense. Do not let us thwart and cross nature at every effort she makes to relieve this already overburdened little economy, by suppressing each external condition, thereby laying up for the child untold misery. Shall we not rather seek to aid nature in her benevolent work, by restoring harmony to the disorderly force and assist the child to shake off its bondage of disease and thus be well equipped for life's warfare?

S. Mary Ives.

Correspondence.

THE BETTER WAY.

Dear Advocate: I want to respond to a hearty AMEN! to T. C. Duncan's short article beginning on page 112 of the March issue of your journal. Very little is gained by walloping the "out of lines" in our school, but to show them the "better way" at the same time shames them, and encourages to a course of right living. He says "another set of obstructors were those trying to introduce into practice drugs and compounds from allopathic sources, and to this day they will swamp us with this flood-wood if we will allow it."

True, and what about the compounds claiming to be homœopathic in the *combination* remedies now flooding the country? To be sure they are *labeled homœopathic specifics.* Let not the young homœopath be fooled by them. Where are the provings of such combinations? They may cure in some cases, but it is the *one* remedy that does it, in spite of the other two or three in the "mix," they cannot be too severely condemned. The pharmacy men had rather do straight work if the profession will back them up in it.

I offer my hand to Duncan and as many others as will stand by the guns with which Hahnemann, Hering, Dunham, Lippe, Wells, Allen, Raue and the long honorable list of veterans in earlier days made our cause glorious.

Let us get back to first principle, sound the tocsin for an advance all along the line against the foes of pure homœopathy, whether in our ranks or out of them. The rising generation in our school is looking to us to vindicate the truth of similia; our enemies to write "Requiescat" upon our grave. Whom shall we disappoint?

Cortland, N. Y. E. B. NASH.

AN ENVIABLE RECORD.

Dear Doctor Duncan: It was on one of the last days of the month of April, 1877, that Dr. Selden H. Talcott began his work as superintendent of the Middletown Hospital. The last week of April, 1902, will complete twenty-five years of service. It has been the intention of a few of us who were at the Middletown Hospital at that time to commemorate the occasion in some way, but so many other physicians wish to show their appreciation of the work and their personal respect for Dr. Talcott that our plans must be changed and enlarged.

When Dr. Talcott took charge of the Middletown Hospital it was an institution with about one hundred and fifty patients, its capacity is now more than fourteen hundred. At that time it was not self supporting; soon after, and since 187 , the income has paid the cost of maintainance. At that time there was no state homœopathic hospital in the world, now they are found on the Atlantic and Pacific slopes and in intervening states. The percentage of recoveries to the discharges has always been very large. The hospital has stood not only for Homœopathy, but for the Hospital Idea in the treatment of the insane, for the Rest Treatment, and for the individualization of patients. Such progressive work as this has been imitated and has raised the standard of the whole mass of state hospitals in the United States. It is most fitting therefore, that a quarter of a century of such advancement should be recognized and applauded not only by the Homœopathic profession but by all who love humanity and appreciate the suffering of those with minds diseased.

We propose to present to Dr. Talcott

a loving cup or other testimonial of such value as may be warranted by subscriptions for that purpose. These subscriptions, of one dollar and upward, were received by me until March 15th. Then the testimonial was decided upon and ordered, so as to be ready for presentation at the banquet.

The banquet will be held, probably in New York City, and all subscribers to the testimonial will be invited. The time and place with price of tickets will be announced about April 15th.

If you will write a personal letter of congratulation, addressed to Dr. Talcott, and will forward it to me, it will be retained until a suitable time for delivering with others to him; and these letters will be to him always a most gratifying additional evidence of the esteem and affection in which he is held by each individual friend.

Any suggestions will be gladly received by me.

Sincerely yours,

N. Emmons Paine, M. D.

West Newton, Mass.

Selden H. Talcott, M. D.,

Sup't Middletown Hospital for the Insane.

My Dear Doctor: It does not seem so long ago since the legislature of your state, the grand old Empire State, was annually besieged for a bill to establish an insane asylum under the benign system of Homœopathy. How earnestly did the Doctors work.

When you were appointed superintendent I remember the fear expressed that you were too young, but I am pleased to know that the Middletown hospital has grown in public esteem as you have grown in years, and that the State has steadily enlarged it to about ten times its original capacity.

The success of Homœopathic treatment under your supervision and consultants has emphasized it to all the world.

On this twenty-fifth anniversary of your superintendency I congratulate you upon your grand record. Regretting my inability to meet with you and the others at the banquet, I am,

Yours fraternally,

T. C. Duncan,

Chicago, April 4, 1902.

Dear Doctor Duncan: Acknowledging your favor of 28th ult., naturally, I am pleased at your interest in my case, and your kindly expressed desire to help. Frankly, my experience with "heart" cases is limited, and I am conscious that along these lines is my weakness. I would like to ask you to let me know the publishers of your "Hand-Book of the Heart" and the price, that I may get it without loss of time. I have Hale's Lectures on Diseases of the Heart, 2d edition.

1st. "G" stands for Gorton, the name of the President of our state association. This gentleman possesses a potentizer made in Philadelphia after the one owned and used by Dr. Kent. The potencies of *Cract-oxy.* that I used were made on this machine from B. & T's 30th. I enclose you grafts and trust they may be of service.

2d. The patient was not "old," aet 36.

3d. A rheumatic diathesis; I believe with a sycotic base, though I cannot obtain data that is positive. The last attack (two months old when she was brought to me) traceable to general unhygenic and malarial surroundings. *Rhus tox.* was the prevailing malarial remedy at this time—which fact helped to my first error in the case.

4th. Very anæmic—I attributed murmurs to this cause. They were mostly smooth, at apex, at least from deep cardiac region, because strong percussion was necessary to show dullness here. I could not follow these murmurs up by either ascending aorta or along pulmonary artery on left side. (Probably because my ear was at fault or my intelligence).

Sometimes I fancied, but was not sure, that murmurs had friction sound and then I suspected pericarditis; but at no time did temperature or other conditions (which I could see), confirm the idea of inflammation or resulting exudation. All this may have occurred before I had the case or, which I think likely, it was one of those cases of hydroperi, where pain, tenderness, fear and friction murmur are absent or very slight.

5th. I figured out the heart action as due to hydrothorax. When the heart worked better I expected to see a metastasis to limbs; but no œdema appeared here or elsewhere in the body, nor did bowel and kidney discharges change essentially in character, not more than the increased dietary would naturally show. If there was hydrothorax the fluid was absorbed and that in a surprisingly short time.

6th. There was a report of "palpitation" for an indefinite period before last attack of illness. I always found the pulse slow, soft, intermitting. I did not keep pulse and temperature record. Did not see the patient daily—only sent for when she was "bad off." Much of the prescribing was done by office reports. Always saw her on days when remedy was changed.

7th. Why did I not give *Bryonia* when the heart, arm and axilla pains appeared? Because of absence of fever, occipital headache, thirst and the general tumult or violence of a *Bryonia* picture. Hall says, "*Bryonia* of no alue in pericaraditis * * * when effusion is copious and aeration of blood deficient"—see page 84.

8th. On Nov. 6th, patient called at office (to pay bill), she was well and able to work, on farm. I noted pulse twice. First time thought her excited from rapid walk, ascending stairs etc. Pulse still soft, missing beats, don't remember the count. May not the intermittancy be congenital? Patient can not help to the answer, didn't notice it herself until attention was called to it.

9th. Patient lives on farm, 20 odd miles away and I shall not see her soon. When she calls again I will make that examination of heart as you outline. I gave one dose *Crat-oxy*[1m] on Nov. 6th. This on my own notion; patient did not ask for precripsion and I had no indications save the previous improvement under this remedy. I requested a report by mail if the dose caused any changes, but have received nothing.

Will you favor me with criticism on this outline. I have given it as clearly as I know how but hope to learn from you. And will you tell me if you share Dr. Hale's opinion that there is no such thing as a metastasis from the joints to the heart? (See page 70 of his book).

While I have been writing Dr. Gorton with whom I office, has been diligently putting up grafts and asks me to send you the enclosed with his compliments. All of them have been used with good results except the *Cracta*[1m] and cm which we have not used as yet.

Very truly yours,

JULIA H. BASS.

Austin, Texas, Dec. 4, 1901.

AN INLAND SURGICAL CLINIC.

Inland, because so far from the great centers of population where *seas* of humanity furnish such exceptional clinical advantages. Although not ranking as a large school, a glance at our hospital record with a visit to our clinic may impress the mind that the College of Homœopathic Medicine, State University of Iowa, is not without excellent opportunities for clinical instruction.

First, a glance at the record. The variety of material that has presented during the college year just closing has been all that one could desire. A partial list of conditions follows.

The emergency line is represented by fractures, dislocations, sprains, gunshot wounds, lacerations, contusions and foreign bodies.

Laparotamies were performed for appendicitis, salpingitis pyosalpinx, uterine fibroma and myoma, ovarian cysts and fibroma and uterine displacements with dense adhesions.

The male generative tract presented phimosis, stricture, varicocele, hydrocele of the cord, hæmatocele, hypospadia and prostatitis.

Beside the gynecological conditions mentioned, under laparotomies, the records show caruncle, adhesions of prepuce, labial abscess, lacerations of cervix and of perineum and cervical stenoses.

Tumors, internal and external and benign; malignant and have been presented to the class in a goodly number and variety; while hæmorrhoids, stricture, fissures and fistulæ have well represented their branch of orificial surgery.

Unclassified in any of the above, we find amputations, tenotomies in a variety of forms of talipes, caries and necroses, herniæ in all styles, empyæmia, coccydinia, harelip, floating kidney, hydrocephalus, spina bifida, morbus coxarius, genu varum and spinal curvatures. Jacksonian epilepsy and microcephalus have called forth demonstrations and explanations of cerebral localization, trephining and craniectomy.

A much valued feature of our work is the clinical lecture. On the day preceding the clinic the cases are brought before the class, examination by the senior members is permitted with full explanation by the professor in charge. This preliminery, with clear explanations by the operator of each manouver in the operation, makes our clinic one that for practical value to the student is unsurpassed. The writer has attended numerous clinics elsewhere and speaks advisedly.

The clinic itself is conducted with due regard to modern ideas of surgical cleanliness. Patients are prepared the evening before operation, given a full bath, and the field of operation thoroughly cleansed and covered with an antiseptic dressing. Under the anæsthetic this is removed and green soap, ether and alcohol with sterilized coverings complete the preparation. In this condition the patient is taken before the class, where nurses and assistants observe equal care to preserve asepsis in all wounds, *if* possible. Homœopathy is the rule after operations and the combination has given our hospital a death, or rather a recovery, record that is the equal of any like institution.

During the school year each senior has been privileged to act as clinical assistant at least four weeks, and to make the rounds of the hospital with the surgeon during that time.

The above sketch briefly outlines the methods and material by which surgery has been taught in a clinical way. The didactic methods are equally as good. Other branches of medicine are thoroughly presented.

After such instruction the graduates of 1902 join the ranks of the alumni feeling that they have received no mean preparation for their life work, and hoping therewith to contribute their quota to the relief of suffering humanity and to the credit of their Alma Mater.

B. E. FULLMER,
Senior Interne.

Iowa City, Iowa, April 1.

THE AMERICAN HAHNEMANNIAN ASSOCIATION.

MIDDLETOWN, CONN., April 1, 1902.

Dear Doctor: The time for our Fourth Annual Meeting is drawing near and I want to call your attention to a few important facts.

Our President and the members of Executive Board are aiming to make this meeting one of deep interest. To this end, a delightful program is in preparation which will combine intellectual feasts with social pleasures. A copy of the program will be sent to you a little later.

The meeting is to be held at *Narragansett Pier*, in the large, well furnished *New Mathewson Hotel, on July 1st, 2d and 3d*, (Tuesday to Thursday inclusive). You will notice that the date of meeting is somewhat later than has been our custom in the past; this is owing to the fact that it was impossible to secure accommodation in June. The rate, per day, at hotel will be $3.00. Narragansett Pier can be reached by way of N. Y., N. H. & H. R. R. Shore Line, changing at Kingston, R. I.

So much for time and place of meeting. Now, Doctor, a most cordial invitation is extended to you, and to your friends, professional or otherwise, who may care to join you. Will you not set aside these few days for a "summer outing?" It will be a restful, inspiring and joyful time to us all.

Yours very truly,

S. MARY IVES, Sec'y.

Editorial.

WHERE DO YOU STAND?

The practice of the art of healing has undergone many radical changes within the past hundred years; and the time has come when every member of the profession must be keenly alert to every vantage that may be gained through modern research. To no class is this so important as to the followers of Hahnemann. We have raised a sectarian banner and placed upon it a distinctive sign proclaiming the existence of a *law of cure* whereby disease manifestations may be removed in a *shorter, safer* and *surer* manner than by any other method known or unknown.

This bold assumption of superiority when combined with inexcusable ignorance of some of the simplest and most fundamental principles embodied in the relation between cause and effect has done more to retard the general acceptance of the principles of Homœopathy than any one thing in its history.

Do not misunderstand our position at the first introduction and refuse to read further, because by so doing you will be guilty of the same error committed by those who have condemned and at the same time refused to investigate the real claims of homœopathy. No one can be more positive in his belief that the selection of the *dynamic* agent capable of producing a *dynamic* disturbance most *similar* to the *effects* of some previous *dynamic* agent will restore harmony in a *shorter* time, *safer* and *surer* manner than by any other method known to man; but all disease manifestations are *not* dynamic in character and consequently do not come within the *curative* range of *dynamic* agents, hence, we must occupy a limited field or rise to a comprehension of the wonderful possibilities before us and occupy the field while it is yet ours.

The practice of medicine today consists in the applying of definite, clearly indicated means for the correction of certain equally definite defects. The competent physician must have *positive* knowledge (and the means at his command for readily acquiring the same) not only of the *nature* of the defects and the *cause* that may contribute to the same, but his knowledge must be *equally* exact with reference to the means that must be employed for the *correction* of the same. It doesn't stop there for the work is only begun when the disorder has given place to the harmonious working of this complicated mechanism. The greatest mission is to *prevent*.

Many cases of disease can be cured without the employment of drugs or any other substance foreign to the material organization of the body, viz: a fracture, a dislocation, the rupture of a blood vessel, the pressure of a foreign substance upon a sensitive nerve, all these demand employment of suitable *mechanical* means for correction of the same. The *tendency* toward fractures, dislocations, rupture of blood vessels, etc., is inherent with the organism and of *dynamic* origin and in a great majority of cases beyond the recuperative power of Nature unaided by skill of the physician skilled in the science and art of medicine.

Injurious occupation, vicious habits or modes of living, uncongenial social or domestic relations, the natural tax upon age and sex may contribute much to physical and mental derangements. Accurate knowledge of the relation between *cause* and *effect* will enable the physician trained to close observation to determine how much should be charged to *external* causes and how much is dependent upon individual *susceptibility* and consequently is of a purely *dynamic* or *vital* character. Errors in judgment in these cases is the cause for much of the opprobrium of the past and constitutes the basis of our plea for a more comprehensive knowledge of *all* the factors entering into the domain of disease.

It was thought at one time that the field of the surgeon was exceedingly limited—that all he had to do was to acquire that manual dexterity whereby a fracture might be adjusted, a dislocation reduced, or a diseased part amputated, but with increased experience came many problems calling for solution along conservative lines until the signs of the times point to a condition in which the skill of the surgeon will be measured by his comprehensive knowledge of the entire domain of disease and the relegation of the knife to its logical and legitimate place—*when indicated*.

The physician has given the surgeon such unsatisfactory support in the past, not only through his ignorance of disease tendencies, but of the best means to be employed *during* and *following* the surgical stages that he has been compelled to extend his investigations into the legitimate field of the physician. This is unfortunate, because there is enough for both, and can only be corrected by the physician rising to the importance of the occasion and making himself master of his profession. This can only be brought about by a rigid determination to refrain from the temptation of making an immediate selection of a remedy without waiting to carefully weigh cause and effect and determining *all the factors* entering into the case. The same conservatism is needed by the physician as has been recognized by the progressive surgeon and the cultivation of the same will do much toward placing homœopathy where it belongs at the "head of procession."

It is not an element of strength for the Hahnemannian to settle back upon the fact that the indication for the selections of the *simillimum* are not based upon the *diagnosis* but upon the *totality of the symptoms* because a proper study of the case will disclose the fact that the *true* totality of the symptoms can *never* be secured until all the *exciting* or *maintaining* causes have been *removed* or the *effect* of their presence determined and *eliminated from the picture of the dynamic disturbance.*

It is no element of strength for us to point to the equally palpable errors of others. First cast out the beam that is in our own eye then shall we see clearly the mote that is in our brother's eye. The recognition of the necessity for a reforming of our ideas must come from within. Each and every one of us has need for a careful introspection and to the degree that we act in accord with the results will in the advancement of the cause of homœopathy. *Where do you stand?*

STEPS IN MATERIA MEDICA.

Our Materia Medica is like a great city bisected by boulevards as well as streets. Some call it a Chinese puzzle. It is more. It is a tangled mass of symptoms tied into bones, skeletons. We are not given the course of the drug as it goes tearing through the body, vomiting, purging, paining and exhausting. What it does to the mind—eye, ear, nose, mouth, stomach and all the other parts, including sleep—is there more or less complete. What more it can do, who can tell? We read our several pathogeneses here broken to pieces, and get nothing tangible. Like the dictionary, the study is too disconnected.

Someone has discerned, for example, that Belladonna dilates the pupil and flushes the face; that Arsenicum wants to drink "early and often" and a little at a time. These striking and unusual effects characterize these drugs, like a glass eye or a Roman nose distinguishes the man. These peculiar things have been gathered together by a master hand. They are called Characteristics, Keynotes or Striking Symptoms. That seems to be the first and best available step in learning the labyrinth of symptoms.

There should be an earlier step, or foundation rather, for these Striking symptoms. Hahnemann knew this, so did Hering and other students of drugs. It is learned by provings and that is, when a dose is taken where away does it travel? What organs are disturbed? How, and why? We can jump clear over into disease technics and say it causes a gastritis, tachycardia, hæmorrhoids etc., but that mixes things. We want the picture of the drug with all its shades, forms and colors or, at least, an outline. That should be the next, if not the first study.

The very next step should be to know why the drug affects certain parts, and how severely. To learn this pathology of drugs we must now go into the realm of disease pathology. Here there is liable to be error. The removal of a disease is one thing; to cause a similar disease is quite another. So the genuine physiology and pathology of drugs are defective.

The next great step is that of classification of our knowledge and, to reach that, a comparative study is necessary. This work is in a fragmentary condition. Comparison is usually made, not with a similar or dissimilar drug pathogenesis, but with a disease which, in truth, is again misleading.

We group bullets, charges and guns long before we compare marksmen.

Is it any wonder so few get hold of drug action when these stepping-stones have been neglected? From characteristics to comparisons is a long hunt. The most elementary work we have on drug study is Regional Leaders.

Learn the peculiarities of one drug after another, then study out the WHY, and so on up to comparisons.

T. C. D.

College Items.

The homœopathic profession must never lose sight of the great obligation they owe to the medical colleges scattered throughout the length and breadth of this land where free speech is encouraged.

Twenty one colleges with an enrollment nearly reaching the two thousand mark present a power that will grow until the world is converted to Homœopathy, provided the graduates go out with such knowledge of its principles as will enable them to demonstrate its superiority over all other systems of medicine.

The results of this year's work is being made evident at the present time. We had prepared to collect such data from all the colleges as would give to our readers valuable information, but the reports at the present writing only imperfectly cover the ground, so the matter will be held over until the May issue.

For the present we can only publish such announcements as deal with commencement exercises to be held during the month of April.

Since the adoption of the four years' course, graduating exercises occur in most of our college during the month of April. There are, however, several exceptions to this rule. In the College of Homœopathic Medicine and Surgery, U. of M., which is a department of the University of Minnesota, the graduating exercises of the medical department are part of the general commencement ceremonies of the University, which occur June 5. The Hahnemann Medical College of the Pacific is another exception. The twentieth annual session began on March 6, and the graduating exercises will be held in the latter part of October.

Cleveland Homœopathic Medical College held its commencement exercises on April 9. Particulars regarding the size of the class are lacking.

The Twenty-fifth Commencement of the Homœopathic Medical College of the State University of Iowa occurred on the first day of April, in connection with those of the Colleges of Medicine and Pharmacy, at the regular convocation of the University. This is the last spring commencement, the term having been lengthened to nine months, commencing with this year. The following young gentlemen commencing with their degrees of Doctor of Medicine:

George H. Alden, Des Moines; Archie B. Clapp, Davenport; Charles H. Cogswell; Cedar Rapids; Arthur E. Crew, Marion; Burt E. Fullmer, Marshalltown; Gilbert T. McDowell, Woonsocket, S. D.; Clarence V. Page, Iowa City.

The eleventh commencement of the

School for Nurses was held in connection with the Hospital. Mrs. Jessie N. Fullmer, Miss Almeda B. Dean and Miss E. Marie Mether, received their certificates after a three years' term of study.

Later in the evening the faculty gave a banquet to the graduates and their friends.

Hering Medical College held its eleventh annual graduation exercises on April 10th, at Handel Hall. Fifteen members of the senior class graduated. A musical program enlivened the occasion. Vice President S. W. M'Caslin, Esq., conferred the degree. Rev. Fred. W. Miller delivered the oration. Dr. J. B. S. King, the registrar read an unusually interesting report.

The next evening, April 11th, a banquet was given in honor of the class. Dr. C. B. Hall of Hyde Park acted as toastmaster.

The third annual commencement exercises of the Detroit Homœopathic College will be held at the Detroit Opera House, Tuesday afternoon, April 22d, to be followed in the evening by a banquet at the Hotel Cadillac. Fine music and eminent speakers have been engaged for the occasion and an enjoyable time is expected. The college is in a most flourishing condition, having purchased during the past year a very fine property which they are now occupying. Although this is only their third year they have graduated a class of students each year.

Chicago Homœopathic Medical College holds its commencement exercises in Studebaker Hall, Tuesday afternoon, April 22d with banquet the same evening at the Auditorium. Doctorate Address will be given by Prof. John W. Streeter and the valedictory by Orlyn Lee Chaffee, M. D. A Special Alumni Course were held during the week preceding the closing exercises.

The Dunham Medical College and Post Graduate School of Homœopathics closes April 19th the most successful and satisfactory session in the history of the institution.

The graduating class, larger than on any previous year, well equipped to practice Homœopathy as promulgated by Samuel Hahnemann and upheld by the greatest modern master of Materia Medica and Homœopathics—Professor J. T. Kent, Dean of the college.

The commencement exercises will be held April 24th at 2:30 p. m. in Steinway Hall to which the public is invited. Professor H. W. Pierson editor of the ADVOCATE will give the Faculty address and Oscar Anderson, B. S., will respond as a representative of the graduating class, in the Pullman building by the faculty.

Personals and News Items.

Steps are being taken to establish a Homœopathic hospital in Milwaukee.

Dr. Fred'k A. Warner of Lowell, Mass., after nearly a half century's practice of his profession, will soon retire. He will devote most of his time to travel.

The ADVOCATE regrets to learn of the death of the wife of Dr. W. M. Follet of Seneca Falls, N. Y.

Dr. E. Mather, who formerly operated the Birmingham, Mich., Sanitarium, is now engaged in general practice in that city, and reports good success.

Dr. I. D. Foulon of St. Louis, Mo., former editor of the Clinical Reporter published in that city, died last month.

The Denver Homœopathic College, Denver, Colorado, will on the evening of April 24, graduate a class of ten, two ladies and eight gentlemen.

Dr. Howard Crutcher of this city has been appointed surgeon of the Chicago & Alton Raiload. Both the doctor and the company are to be congratulated.

The ADVOCATE is sorry to learn that on account of defective eyesight Dr. G. H. Anderson of Seneca, Kans., has not been able to practice his profession for over a year.

Dr. J. W. Hodge of Niagara Falls, N. Y., has an exhaustive, well written article on "Why Doctors Who Vaccinate Should Abandon the Practice" in the March Medical Counselor.

When the lawn is mowed use the damp grass for the carpet in the same way as you would employ tea-leaves. The grass revives the colors in a wonderful way, and removes all spots and dust.

Dr. W. L. Ray, who was deposed from the superintendency of the State Hospital for the Insane at Fulton, Mo., by Gov. Dockery, to make room for an old school brother, has located in Kansas City, Mo.

Because such a law is repugnant to many good citizens and because existing conditions in that state did not demand it, the governor of Wisconsin recently vetoed the Collins' bill making vaccination compulsory.

Do not forget the meeting of the Illinois Homœopathic Medical Association meeting to be held in this city May 13, 14 and 15, on 17th floor of the Masonic Temple. A banquet to visiting members will be served on Wednesday evening. A large attendance is expected.

The first woman to graduate in medicine was Elizabeth Blackwell, in 1849. In 1852 Philadelphia had three lady physicians, the increase from that number to over 6,000 in the United States being accomplished in less than a half century.

The New York Board of Health, on March 13, adopted a resolution against compulsory vaccination, as proposed in Assembly Bill No. 1,439, introduced by Assemblyman Fuller. This bill gives power to the State Commissioner of Health to compel vaccination in any county when it is, in his opinion, necessary.

According to the official reports of the Marine Hospital Service, there were 28,263 cases of smallpox in the United States during the week ending March 15. This is an unusually large number, and the officials are somewhat concerned about it. For the same period last year only 9,406 cases were reported. The deaths from smallpox during the last week have been 661, as against 136 for the same week of last year, the number being almost quintupled.

Topeka will be the meeting place of the Homœopathic Medical Society of Kansas, the date, May 7, 8 and 9. An interesting program has been provided. Any information desired can be obtained from Secretary Clay E. Coburn, Kansas City, Kans. Chairman of the different bureaus are the following: Sociality and Fraternity, Dr. Chas. Lowry, Topeka; Materia Medica and Organic Law, Dr. W. B. Swan, Topeka; Surgery, Dr. H. W. Roby, Topeka; Obstetrics and Gynæcology, Dr. W. A. Minick, Wichita; Clinical Medicine, Dr. J. W. Tiffany, Hiawatha; Legislation and Public Institutions, Dr. Chas. Lowry, Topeka; Dental and Oral Diseases, Dr. E. Baumgardner, Lawrence; Eye, Ear, Nose and Throat, Dr. S. C. Delap, Kansas City, Mo.

The Hahnemannian Advocate

A MONTHLY HOMŒOPATHIC MAGAZINE.

H. W. Pierson, B. S., M. D., Editor, 800 Marshall Field Building, Chicago.
Hahnemann Publishing Co., Publisher, 6704 Lafayette Ave., Chicago.
Benj. F. Swan, Business Manager.

Subscription price of the magazine in the United States, Canada, Mexico, the island possessions and Cuba, [illegible] a year, payable in advance; in Great Britain, continental Europe, India and other countries members of the postal union, [illegible] a year to be paid in advance. Unless otherwise specified, subscriptions will begin with January issue of the year in which order is received. Remittances should be made payable to the Hahnemann Publishing Co., 6704 Lafayette Ave., Chicago.

Address all articles intended for publication and books for review to the editor. All business and other communications should be sent to the Hahnemann Publishing Co.

Vol. XLI. Chicago, May, 1902. No. 5

Materia Medica.

ARNICA.

Taken internally Arnica will bring upon the body a state of soreness. The sorenesss begins in the muscles and gradually increases so that the patient is sensitive to pressure all over the body. He begins to feel as if he had been pinched or bruised all over. Where the pressure is pronounced, such as by lying on any part of the body, there is a feeling as if the bed or couch was too hard, and the patient is compelled to move off that part. Stiffness follows the soreness and it is especially noticeable in the joints while walking. When the pressure has been persistent for any length of time the skin will become black and blue, or purplish, in color, closely resembling a bruise in appearance. If the soreness continues for any length of time without any perceptible pressure or injury to the surface, there is a tendency to the deposit of blood beneath the skin without any special increase in the soreness of the parts. Arnica patients, before coming down with any acute illness, will complain of this soreness and wonder when and how they have hit themselves sufficiently to cause so many black and blue spots.

Is it any wonder then that the Old Masters selected Arnica for bruises, injuries, from being tremendously shaken up in accidents or when coming to a sudden halt while in violent motion? It is not only useful for injuries with this natural feeling of soreness, from bruises etc., but for that tendency to echymoses in debilitated constitutions. Just as they are about to have a fever a pinch of the skin that would amount to nothing in a good state of health becomes discolored and the discoloration extends for quite a distance from the place injured. There is a relaxation of the walls of blood vessels so that blood oozes out, instead of there being a proper tension and tonicity, and when this state comes on they bleed easily. Such patients are subject to venous hemorrhages.

When the injury occurs in mucous membranes the hemorrhage is free, but when the skin or the tissues beneath the skin are injured there is no opportunity for the blood to be eliberated, consequently it accumulates in the tissue, and we have what is known as a bruise.

This condition of the blood vessels

favors a form of apoplexy and, when the true state of the constitution is recognized, if Arnica is indicated, it will soon correct the tendency and prevent further extravasations of blood. It does more than this: It favors absorption and the disappearance of the blue spots upon the skin. But the absence of absorbents in the brain limits its action to the diminution in the size of the clots already formed.

In its action upon the vascular tissues Arnica has produced symptoms resembling intermittent, remittent and continued fever. It has chills, fever and sweating among its generals, hence it will be suitable for a great variety of slow fevers such as are associated with many forms of inflammation. The tissues of almost every organ of the body are in the same state of relaxation as will be found in the walls of the blood vessels, hence the ease with which they take on inflammation and the frequency of the hemorrhage. From this you will see that we may have hemorrhages from the uterus, the stomach, the liver, the lungs, the kidneys, the bladder and the heart. The greater the vascularity of the tissues the greater the hemorrhage. The peculiarity of the hemorrhage is in the fact that the blood clots so quickly that the various discharges from the body may be flecked with blood, as if pepper had been shaken on them. This "blood-flecked" character of the secretions is pathognomonic of Arnica. Children with whooping-cough have what Bœnninghausen describes as blood-flecked expectoration. Its power to promote absorption is made use of in preventing suppuration and will be frequently indicated in cases where a gland will take on inflammation through its great vascularity or from an injury which is characterized by great pain and soreness. Arnica given in time, will promote the absorption of the blood and thus prevent not only the induration but the suppuration and thus bring about a speedy restoration of the functional activity of that part. It does more than this, because it tends toward the permanent strengthening of the walls of the blood vessels. *Do not use Arnica locally* and never use it where the skin is off, for it has in many instances produced erysipelas of a most persistent and malignant type.

Having the clear indications you will be astonished at the relief from pain, soreness and tension following the administration of a few doses of Arnica in a suitable potency. Remember, you are dealing with a constitutional tendency and that you are seeking to leave your patient in a better condition than before the injury took place. It seems to act through the ganglionic nerve centers and the instant it is brought in contact with them the recuperative process begins. You will therefore note that the rapidity of the progress of the cure is in direct proportion to the vigor of the constitution and that recoveries are more prompt following injuries than shocks.

A study of the provings will show a condition very favorable to septic processes such as found in typhoid and scarlet fevers and in low forms of disease like erysipelas. It is a most wonderful remedy in septicemia, whether the result of injuries or following operative procedures upon septic constitutions. Do not think of Arnica for cuts or open wounds unless the after effects show shock and other signs of deep constitutional disturbances.

Mind. Arnica is full of mental symptoms: Fear—of instant death—of some impending danger — of being overwhelmed with excitement—emotion or horror. He is full of irritability and very obstinate. He will do nothing in his own acute illness that you want him to do; will not tell his symptoms; will tell you to go home, he did not send for you and does not want you. But as soon as you show signs of leaving and turn your back upon him he will begin to moan and cry and complain of being left to his fate. This is the ordinary type. I have seen a patient with malarial fever stop in the midst of his chill to tell me to go home; that he did not send for me; that he did not want me. The patient is liable to become delirious, very closely resembling those who have been drinking until violently drunk and then try to sober up. They must then drink some more and finally end in delirium tremens. When the Arnica patient once gets into a sleep it is very difficult to arouse him, and when aroused he does not know where he is. He tries to think what he is expected to say and is sure to wind up by saying something that will indicate his irritability or his obstinacy. On being aroused he forgets what he wanted to say. The words that would express his views will not come and it makes him angry and he turns over and says something outlandish. In the text there are a number of symptoms that point to grief. Results from fright, anger, excitement, emotion; susceptibility to shock. Mental or physical exertion disturbs and aggravates his symptoms. "All occupations have to be relinquished for the time, so great were the sufferings." Inability to perform continued active work. "Easily frightened; unexpected trifles cause him to start," and for some seconds he is not able to pull himself together sufficiently to tell where he is at; hence we say "confusion of mind" is a characteristic. In the first few days of typhoid fever the patient may have that sore bruised feeling that we have described, the confused mental state in all the zymotic conditions; stupid; benumbed; if aroused he can't think of what he wants to say; very irritable and stubborn. Most of the attacks come on by vomiting of blackish water. He is so sore that he cannot lie long upon any part of the body. These are general Arnica symptoms. They stand out in such bold relief that they distinguish Arnica from the rest of the materia medica. We get no such combinations anywhere else.

There is a general aggravation of the symptoms at night; on closing the eyes he seems to suffer all over; feels that he will become insane; becomes wild, dizzy. Everything seems to go around if he closes his eyes, and he becomes sick. During the wakeful moments the center of life and of all movements of the body is in the cerebrum. But when sleep is needed the activity is transferred to the cerebellum; hence persons who have diseases of the cerebellum suffer when they are asleep but not when they are awake.

Head. Among the head symptoms we find vertigo—when becoming erect—when sitting up in bed—when arising from a seat. Headaches too numerous to mention, all of a congestive type; headaches common to the zymotic and inflammatory diseases, and in this state one thing is important to remember about Arnica: It appears that the blood has all gone to the head, his head is so hot and the rest of the body so cold. Coldness of the body is astonishing; he is cold up to his neck and the head is hot; the whole brain in sensitive. There are violent throbbing, pressive congestive headaches. The scalp is so sensitive that he cannot have the hair touched.

Injuries to the Skull. Blows upon the head, with unconsciousness; vomiting and other evidences of internal hemorrhage. In basilar fractures that come on from injuries, with bleeding from the ears; most of them will die without Arnica. Arnica has cured meningitis, apoplexy, loss of consciousness with involuntary evacuations. Characteristic symptoms are boring the head into the pillow which means basilar head troubles in children and sometimes in adults; lying and rolling the head as if they were trying to get it backwards into the pillow. Bruised about the eyes as from blows by the fist; injuries of every sort; black and blue, with exudations of blood; a good deal of tumefaction and bleeding, with great soreness in the ball of the eye and around the eye. Sometimes, following injuries to the head, there is a crushed feeling as if in the bones or their articulations in which *Symphytum* will be the remedy. Arnica is more effective when the soft tissues are injured, but if the injury extends to the periosteum, involves the tendons, cartileges and ligaments, *Symphytum* comes in with its indications. A great bruise occurs sometimes on the skin and tissues where the flesh is thin, as over the tibia. Arnica will cope with the bruised condition of the soft tissues; but, if found upon further examination that the periosteum is injured, *Ruta* will then come in. The vasculars state of the periosteum gives indications that more clearly point to *Ruta* than to Arnica. Where the ligaments and tendons are relaxed, weak and paralyzed after an injury, we will think of *Rhus*, Arnica corresponding to an inflamed state while *Rhus* finds its indications in the paralytic state following an injury. *Rhus* itself is followed by *Calcarea*. The soreness has disappeared, but the weakness and stiffness remain. Every time they get wet they are stiff; old fractures and old injuries round about the joints are stiff. Then it is that *Rhus* greatly mitigates while *Calcarea* generally finishes the case.

Eyes. Arnica will cure a variety of eye troubles resulting from injuries when there is a disturbance of the iris with infiltration of the tissues, making a favorable condition for the development of cataract. There will be the highly dilated pupil; dull pain in the head with aching in the eyes etc.

Face. The Arnica countenance usually represents a besotted appearance like one who has been intoxicated. This will be noted in typhoid and other low forms of fever, erysipelas, injuries to the head etc. It will be accompanied by the characteristic mental symptoms. Arnica is useful for the hemorrhage from injuries to the gums or mouth following the extraction of teeth etc. *Sepia* is another remedy for nervous women who are greatly wrought up from having teeth extracted. It is indicated for the nervous shock following the extraction where there is little hemorrhage.

Throat. Arnica has few throat symptoms, but it will cure inflammation in any part provided the general state is as has been described. It has made a great record in tumefaction of the throat with great soreness at each menstrual period where there has been a bruised soreness throughout the body. The tonsils are enlarged and have a purplish hue.

Eructations. Very offensive to both taste and smell. Patient will often say he has eructations that taste like rotten eggs; putrid eructations. It is well to bear in mind these three characteristics:

Vomiting of putrid substances or blackish water.

Eructations bitter, sour or tasting and smelling like rotten eggs.

Sore bruised feeling all over.

Arnica has cured intermittent fevers where all that remained of the trouble was an inflammation of the spleen with great swelling and tenderness, together with sore bruised pain throughout the body. The history would show that this condition dated back to a malarial attack which had been suppressed with quinine, so at the present there would be little or no chill, scanty perspiration, but great soreness throughout the abdomen.

Abdomen. We find tympanitic distress throughout the abdomen; great soreness through the intestines. Inflammation seems to extend from the stomach into the pelvis. The stool will be violently offensive, smelling like rotten eggs; flatus also has the same odor. There may be indications of internal hemorrhage, dark fluid discharges, frequently involuntary, and other indications of profound constitutional disturbance; following injuries or operations where there has been much handling and bruising of the tissues or where the constitution was so vitiated as to produce a shock out of proportion to the injury of the tissues involved. If the operation necessitated no excessive handling of the tissues so that all of the injuries were clean cut, while the hemorrhage might be great and the shock profound, *Staphisagria* will more perfectly cover the indications than any other remedy.

Urinary Organs. In the provings we may have retention, involuntary urination or a complete suppression of the urine. Any one of these may follow injury to the spine or base of the brain or from shock following any serious injury. In the provings we have "urine thick with much pus, and some blood; bleeding from the urinary tract; blood in the urine; albumin in the urine." In all of these cases you will find indications of serious interference with the circulation.

Female Organs. "Uterine hemorrhage; prolapsus of the uterus; hemorrhage after confinement; abortion; profuse menstrual flow." In any of these symptoms you will find the generals which are so characteristic of this remedy. After delivery the woman goes into a state of collapse; pulse increases in rapidity; chill comes on; sore bruised feeling all over; great thirst during the chill; fever followed with no thirst; great prostration; lochia stopped. Arnica frequently comes in as a remedy of prime importance in this case, but it is important to study the complemental relations of Sulphur in the puerperal state.

In all of the cases calling for Arnica be sure that your generals have clear indications.

J. T. Kent.

A FEW APHORISMS ON THE MATERIA MEDICA OF SIMILARS.

It is pretty clearly demonstrated that neither this generation nor the next will reap much benefit from the reproving of drugs.

The value of any given symptom, or of any group of symptoms of any drug must be demonstrated empirically before it can be scientifically proven how effective the drug is in therapeutic use. On this common ground the two schools meet; but with difference: We have a finger-post that points distinctly toward the most probable road to the desired goal; the other party goes it blind.

At the present, every practitioner must to a large degree find out for himself the reliability or unreliability of any given symptom or any group of symptoms in any given drug. To this statement there are a few notable exceptions. These occur in those drugs that have been repeatedly verified empirically, the verifications of which have been so often published that the symptoms have become "reliable."

What is most needed is not a reproving of drugs, but a re confirmation; or rather a multitude of re confirmations gathered from the widest possible field, and from the greatest possible numbers. Such a course would tend to add constantly to the list of drugs that have passed the tentative stage; in other words such a course would tend to produce a thoroughly reliable and thoroughly practical materia medica.

There will not be in this generation nor in the next any reproving that will be worthy of the name. We are afraid to prove drugs in the way and to the extent necessary for valuable purposes.

It is like volunteering in time of war; only the very patriotic and very thoughtless volunteer. Medical patriotism is at a low ebb. We are willing that our second cousins should enlist, not our sons, nor ourselves. In all these years about reproving where is there a notable instance of success worthy the name? While reproving is difficult, from every standpoint, financial, personal, ability and genius—it is not so with *re-confirmation*. Thousands of intelligent men and women, urged on by hope of financial success, of personal fame, from a desire to gain the bread and butter of daily life, *are every day seeking re-confirmations* with all the ardor that their impulses inspire, and no greater motives can be appealed to for aid in this work.

So long as we fail to realize the magnitude of the wastefulness of the present time that lies in neglect to collect, classify, scrutinize and publish these confirmations in a reliable, practical manner, this wastefulness will continue.

Such a plan put steadily into practical use from a small beginning would be destined to great results.

It requires breadth of view, calmness and clearness of insight, patience and perseverence; above all it calls for united effort on a large scale.

It is the only practical road opened to the present generation, or the next—to greatly enhance materia medica.

We have already too many provings-socalled, and entirely too many drugs; at least until we know better the value or worthlessness of what we now have.

M. W. VANDENBURG.

Surgery.

LECTURE ON THE SUPERIOR EXTREMITY.*

We are to review this afternoon the upper extremity and to do so properly must briefly refer to the construction of the body as a whole. The bony skeleton is the frame upon which all the soft parts of the body are fashioned, and the spinal column, or backbone, is the foundation upon and around which this frame is reared. Composed of twenty-four true vertebræ placed one upon the other, and nine false vertebræ, united into two bones at its lower extremity, it forms an irregular, hollow cylinder, capable of limited rotation both to the right and to the left, as well as flexion in any direction. A little below the upper extremity of this flexible column are attached twenty four ribs, twelve on either side. These are long, slender bones, curved in the arc of a circle and very elastic. Their anterior ends are lengthened by cartileges, and through these cartileges the superior ten ribs on each side support the flat breastbone. The articulations of the ribs with the spinal column behind, and those of the costal cartileges with the sternum in front, are true joints capable of motion. On this skeleton you can see the bones mentioned and the construction of the frame

*Delivered at Dunham Medical College, by Professor F. H. Fahnestock.

of the chest, the shape and size of which can be changed by elevating the sternum and ribs, and its relative position to the lower part of the trunk altered by rotating or flexing the spine.

The nine false vertebræ are coalesced into two bones. The larger, or sacrum, articulates with the last lumbar vertebræ at a decided angle; the smaller, or coccyx, is redimentary and joins the inferior extremity of the sacrum. This low, and just as the spinal column is extended by a few true vertebræ above the articulations of the two superior ribs, so it is prolonged by four false vertebræ below the articulations of the two pelvic bones.

The four extremities are attached to this trunk. The legs, whose functions demand great strength and power, articulate with the strong and rigid pelvis, which is united to the rigid portion of the spine; the arms, whose use necessitates the greatest mobility, articulate with the ever shifting sternum, it in turn being supported by the movable and elastic ribs, which join the flexible portion of the spinal column.

In the bones of the upper and lower extremities we find a marked similarity as to number and general outline, but a difference in size, direction of axis and method of articulations. Omitting the scapula and clavicle, for the present, we find the humerus (arm) a long bone with head directed inward, and two tuberosities; a shaft slightly curved, with concavity forward, and an expanded articular lower end. The *femur* (thigh) is larger in every way. Its head is supported by a long neck set at an angle to the shaft. The trochanters, corresponding to the tuberosities of the humerus, are much larger. The curve of the shaft is convex forward. The lower end is much broader and the articular surface much more extensive than those of the humerus. The head of either bone corresponds in direction with the inner condyle. Both hip and shoulder have ball and socket joints.

In the forearm are two long bones, the radius and ulna, placed parallel, the former externally. These bones are relatively about the same in strength and size, each having one extremity more bulky than the other. The larger extremity of the ulna articulates with the lower end of the humerus forming the main portion of the elbow hinge, or joint. The smaller end of the ulna is below, but does not enter directly into the formation of the wrist joint.

The radius is reversed. Its smaller end articulates with the humerus, thus participating slightly in the hinge portion of the joint, and also with the ulna on the inner side, forming a rotatory joint. Its lower and more massive extremity articulates with the lower end of the ulna, forming a lateral hinge joint. It also forms the bulk of the articulation between the first row of carpal bones and the fore arm, thus carrying the wrist and hand with it when rotated.

In the leg are two long bones, the tibia, very bulky, with massive extremities bearing broad articular surfaces; the fibula on the outer side, very slender, slightly expanded at its extremities and having on the inner aspect of each extremity an oblique articular surface. The tibia alone articulates with the femur, forming a hinge joint of large bearing surfaces, the knee. This joint flexes backward and is guarded in front by the patella just as the elbow, which flexes forward, is guarded behind by the olecranon process of the ulna. The lower end of the tibia forms the major part of the ankle joint, uniting the leg and tarsus, while the fibula unites below with both tibia and tarsus. Although the fibula articulates both above and below with the tibia by true lateral hinge joints, it differs from the radius of the forearm in that it is not a very movable bone.

The number of bones entering into the hand and foot are the same, if you exclude the pisiform, which may be considered a sesamoid bone. The carpus and the tarsus would thus have seven each, the metacarpus and metatarsus five; the thumb and great toe, two; the four fingers and the remaining toes, three. The mechanical construction of the two members differs widely. The foot is placed at a right angle to the leg. The articular surface of the tarsus entering into the ankle joint is on the dorsum and behind the center of the foot. The bones of the tarsus and metatarsus form two arches on the plantar or lower surface, one longitudinal and the other transverse. These two arches are maintained by strong ligaments and support the weight of the body. The toes are short and by flexion and extension assist in balancing the body while standing or moving. The various movements of the lower part of the spine are not flexible. Articulating with the sacrum are the two innominate bones. These bones are very irregular in outline and joining with each other anteriorly and with the sacrum posteriorly form a bony ring called the pelvis. This pelvis is massive and strong and presents many roughened spots and prominences for the attachment of ligaments and muscles. The space surrounded by this bony ring is called the pelvic cavity and its axis is placed obliquely to the axis of the thoracic cavity.

You will notice as I point out on this skeleton the various bones described and which collectively make up the entire bony frame of the trunk, that if we take the five lumbar vertebræ as the anatomical center of the frame, the bones entering the chest wall are united to the true vertebræ above while the bones completing the circle of the pelvic cavity join the false vertebræ immediately beneath and its component parts are limited, compared with those of the hand.

The carpus formed of eight bones, including the pisiform, is so arranged in two rows as to resemble a ball and socket joint and because of its extensive articulation with the radius, it moves with that bone. The carpo-metacarpal joints permit but slight motion of the three middle bones, the fifth bone has some motion, while the first bone, that of the thumb, can be abducted, adducted, flexed, extended, and circumducted to quite a degree. The bones of the fingers are longer than those of the toes. They have greater range of flexion and extension in all their articulations. The joints between the first phalanges of the fingers and their corresponding metacarpal bones have the five varieties of motion, greatest in the forefinger, next in the little finger and least in the two middle fingers. The same joint of the thumb has only flexion and extension, the articulation of its metacarpal bone with the wrist being the one of versatile motion.

The shoulder which connects the arm with the trunk must be considered with the superior extremity, as it participates in and materially increases the extent of motion. The humerus articulates directly with the scapula by a ball and socket joint. This scapula is not a fixed bone, but articulates by its acromion process with the outer end of the clavicle and the clavicle by its inner extremity forms a joint with the superior extremity of the sternum. Both the scapula-clavicular and the sterno-clavicular articulations permit hinge motion and slight circumduction. These joints allow the scapula to be elevated and depressed, carried outward and inward over the ribs and rotated upon its vertical axis, they also permit the entire shoulder to be shifted forwards, backwards, upwards, downwards and to be circumducted, it moving upon the sterno-clavicular junction as a center. The scapulo-clavicular joint enables the scapula to change the direction of the socket in which the head of the humerus plays, thus giving greater freedom of motion, as well as affording a firm support to the arm in its different positions. It also enables the angle of the scapula to hug the ribs when the arch formed by the clavicle and scapula is raised or lowered.

As practitioners you will have to consider an extremity as a whole, and it will be impossible to detect the abnormal unless you are familiar with the normal. You will be able to compare the diseased or injured extremity with the sound one, a resource not to be forgotten. When dealing with the extremity in the living subject the surface only is exposed and to make practical use of your knowledge of general anatomy the surface lines, eminences and depressions, together with such deeper parts as can be felt or may become noticeable in certain positions are used as guides to the structures beneath.

The human hand and wrist is exposed and frequently injured. The hand is the most mobile and expert member possessed by the human being and distinguishes man from all other animals. The ability to touch every finger, from its palmer junction to its end, with the thumb is an attribute of man only. It is the hand that makes him powerful and master of all other animals.

The skin of this part is dense and thick over the palm and front of the fingers, while on the back it is much thinner. Sweat glands are exceedingly numerous on the palm. Hair and sebaceous glands are entirely absent on the palm, front and sides of the fingers and on the back of the last phalanges. For this reason these parts are exempt from any disease that attacks hair follicles and their glands.

The palmar surface is freely supplied with nerves and the pacinian bodies are more numerous than in any other part. The tactile sense of the palm and the pulp of the fingers, especially of the first finger, is developed in the highest degree. The subcutaneous tissue of the front of the fingers and the palm is dense, closely adherent to the skin and the parts beneath, while the fat is in little small lobules, lodged in small lacunae formed by its dense fibers. The subcutaneous tissue on the back of the hand is lax, loosely connected to the skin and the underlying tissues. The palmar aspect of the hand is free from veins, the blood being returned chiefly by the superficial veins on the back of the fingers and hand. From this we know that subcutaneous extravasation of blood is impossible in the palm, while it may be extensive on the back of the hand; that œdema would show markedly on the dorsum while the palm would not be infiltrated; that surface inflammations would be accompanied by swelling on the dorsum while little or none would be present in the palm; that inflammation of the dense and unyielding tissues of the palm would be accompanied by severe pain, while such would not be the case in the lax tissues of the dorsum; that cuts of the palm would not gape, but remain closed, facilitating rapid healing; that the palm is well adapted to resist the effects of pressure and friction.

The nails vary greatly in different individuals, and you may become familiar with the tubercular, arthritic and rachitic forms. There are several degrees of inflammation of the root of the nail and the soft parts about it. When a nail is lost by suppuration or violence, it will be reproduced, provided any of the deeper epithelial cells are left. During severe illness the growth of the nail is partly arrested and in convalescence a transverse grove appears, indicating the portion of the nail formed during the illness. The growth of the nail is about 1-32 of an inch per week. Each nail is supplied by a large branch from the corresponding digital nerve, as is made evident by the severe pain accompanying injuries to it.

On the back of the hand the distal heads of the metacarpal bones can be made out when the fingers and thumb are flexed. The palm of the hand is concave, more so above than below. The two middle fingers are longer than the first and fourth, hence to insure the strongest grip the handles of most tools are made larger in the center than at either extremity.

At the junction of the fingers with the palm a fold of skin extends from each finger to its neighbors, called the web of the fingers. It is best not to cut this web in amputating through the first phalynx, or in disarticulating at the metacarpo-phalangeal joint. On the front of the fingers are seen transverse creases in the skin. The first nearest the end of each finger is single and is placed a very little above the joint. Those next above are double and correspond exactly with the second joints of the respective fingers. The third creases are even with the free edge of the web of the fingers, single for the index and little fingers, double for the other two. They are about three-quarters of an inch below the corresponding joints. There are two single creases on the thumb corresponding to its two joints, the one nearest the palm crossing the joint obliquely. At the lower edge of the palm and opposite the clefts of the fingers are three elevations, made very distinct when the first phalanges are extended and the second and third are flexed. These are formed by the fatty tissue bulging up between the digital slips given off from the palmar fascia. The grooves that separate these elevations correspond to these slips. There are many creases in the palm of the hand, the most prominent forming a letter M. The second transverse fold above the fingers, marks, where it crosses the fourth metacarpal bone, the lowest point of the superficial arch. The first crease above the fingers crosses the necks of the metacarpal bones and marks closely the upper limits of the flexor synovial sheaths of the three fingers. The superficial palmar arch descends to a point level with the palmar border of the thumb when held at a right angle to the index finger. The deep arch is about half an inch nearer the wrist. The digital arteries of the palm given off from these two arches correspond to the spaces between the metacarpal bones. They bifurcate about half an inch above the clefts between the fingers, the branches running along the sides of the phalanges. The posterior carpal furnishes blood to the back of the hand. Its branches running along the intervals between the metacarpal bones and bifurcating to supply the fingers the same as those on the palmar side.

Beneath the skin of the hand is the dense palmar fascia. This fascia adds greatly to the strength of the hand and is comparatively free from vessels and nerves. It gives slips to the fingers and these slips send fibers to join the digital sheaths of the tendons, the skin and the superficial transverse ligament. The disease known as Dupuytren's contraction results from a contraction of the palmar fascia, especially its digital slips. Beside enclosing the muscles of the thumb (thenar eminence) and those over the metacarpal bone of the little finger (hypothenar eminence), it develops by strong walls a third space between the other two, which carries most of the flexor tendons. This cavity, formed by prolongation of the palmar fascia, is closed in on all sides, but is open above and below. Above it runs beneath the annular ligament of the wrist and along the flexor tendons of the forearm, while below there are openings at the roots of the fingers for the flexor tendons and openings at the webs between the fingers, giving passage to the lumbricales and digital vessels and nerves. When therefore pus forms in the palm of the hand it either escapes along the fingers or makes its way up into the forearm. So dense is the palmar fascia, that confined pus will often make an exit through the interosseous spaces and appear at the back of the hand instead of coming through the coverings of the palm.

The fibrous sheath for the flexor tendons extends from the neck of the metacarpal bones to the upper end of the third phalanx. Except opposite the joints these sheaths are firm and rigid and remain open when cut across. This explains the frequency of suppuration in the palm of the hand after amputation of part of a finger.

There are two synovial sheaths beneath the annular ligament for flexor tendons, one for the flexor longus pollicis, the other for the flexor sublimus and profundus. The sheath for the flexor pollicis extends about an inch and a half above the ligament and follows the tendon downwards to its insertion into the last phalanx of the thumb. The sheath for the superficial and deep flexors rises about the same distance above the annular ligament and ends in diverticula a little below the center of the second, third and fourth metacarpal bones, while the process for the little finger generally extends to the last phalanx. Thus there is an open channel from the thumb and little finger to a point about an inch and a half above the annular ligament. For this reason abscesses of the thumb and little finger are apt to be followed by abscess in the forearm. When these synovial sacks are distended by liquid they present an hour glass outline, the constriction being caused by the ligament. In one form of felon (whitlow), when the pus occupies the sheath of the tendon the suppuration can often be seen to end where the sheath ends, opposite the neck of the metacarpal bone. This is the case when the first, second or third finger is involved. In another form, namely, abscess of the pulp at the end of the finger, there being no tendon to cover the end of the bone, the periosteum is frequently involved and necrosis of the bone follows. It is seldom that the whole bone is destroyed, the base usually remaining sound, preserved by the insertion of the tendon of the flexor profundus.

The hand is very freely supplied with blood and hence will repair after most serious injuries. All the blood vessels leading to it anastomose freely, hence bleeding from the arches cannot be stopped by ligating the radial and ulnar arteries. If the bleeding vessels cannot be tied in the wound, pressure at the bleeding point and flexion at the elbow will often succeed in checking the flow of blood.

The lymphatics are mostly found about the fingers and at the back of the hand, hence inflammation of these vessels follows wounds of the parts where they are found more frequently than wounds of the palm.

From this general description of the hand, it is evident that all accumulations of pus should be opened early and drainage secured; that the free blood supply enables repair to follow the most severe injuries and so no part should be amputated save that damaged beyond all possibility of recovery; that in amputating at the junction of the finger with its metacarpal bone, if a strong hand is desired, the head of the metacarpal bone should be left intact in order to preserve the transverse ligaments at the lower part of the palm; that while neither flexor or extensor tendons are attached to the first phalanx, still when amputation is made through that bone, the divided tendons form new attachments and flexion and extension of the stump is quite strong; that when the third phalanx of the fingers or the second phalanx of the thumb is necrosed by delay in evacuating pus, if the soft parts are split, the dead bone removed, the part splinted and kept at rest the bone will nearly always be reproduced; that although the rule of saving all possible applies in full force to the hand and fingers, it is better to amputate just behind the articulation of the phlanges than to disarticulate and leave a club-shaped stump; that the skin from the palmar surface makes a better covering for a stump than the skin from the dorsum: that the hand and fingers are injured more frequently than any other members of the body and therefore a perfect knowledge of their anatomy and functions is absolutely necessary to enable one to manage correctly any given injury of the same.

The forearm in its upper third is much wider in the transverse than in the antero-posterior diameter. A transverse section through this part will show a cut surface practically oval. In women and children the arm in this part borders on the round rather than the oval, due to the accumulation of fat on the front and back as well as to the non-development of the lateral muscular masses. In the muscular arm the supinator longus makes a prominence on the outer border above, while lower the extensors of the thumb make a slight oblique prominence. The extensor communis is on the radial side at the back of the arm and on its inner side the ulna can be felt subcutaneous throughout its entire length. The upper half of the radius is so enveloped in muscles that it cannot be well felt, but the lower half of the bone is easily found beneath the skin. The course of the radial artery lies in a line drawn from the outer border of the tendon of the biceps to a point between the scaphoid bone and the extensor tendons of the thumb. The two lower thirds of the ulnar artery lie in a line drawn from the inner condyle to the radial side of the pisiform bone. The upper third would be represented by a curved line drawn from the middle of the bend of the elbow to join the upper part of the middle third of the artery. There is a most free anastomosis all along the arm between the two arteries so that in wounds of either vessel both distal proximal ends require ligatures. It is to be noted that large blood vessels and nerves are absent from the posterior aspect of the forearm, the part most exposed to injury, and for three or four inches below the elbow there are but few and very small veins. The bones of the forearm lie nearest the posterior surface and while in the center of the limb the two bones are about equal in strength, in the extremities, where one is more substantial the other is more slender.

Pronation and supination of the hand is the result of the peculiar articulations of these two bones. The center of motion is around an axis represented by a line drawn through the head of the radius, the lower end of the ulna and the metacarpal bone of the ring finger. The two bones are parallel to each other only in the position midway between pronation and supination, the position selected by the surgeon in the adjustment of fractures of the forearm. Of the two movements supination is the more powerful.

At the wrist the lower end of the radius and its styloid process can be well defined. The bone here is subcutaneous both in front and behind and the process lies more anteriorly and projects about half an inch lower than the corresponding process of the ulna. For this reason the motion of the hand is more limited outward than inward. The top of the styloid process of the ulna corresponds to the line of the wrist joint and a knife entered horizontally below that point would open the joint. The tip of the styloid process of radius corresponds to the scaphoid bone. A line drawn between the two styloid processes would slope downward and outward and would be about half an inch below the summit of the arch of the wrist joint.

Of the folds in the skin on the front of the wrist the lowest is the most distinct. It is slightly convex downward, is about half an inch above the carpo-metacarpal joint line and nearly three-quarters of an inch below the arch of the wrist joint. It indicates closely the upper border of the anterior annular ligament.

If the hand and wrist are flexed, the fingers being extended, about the center of the front of the wrist a tendon stands out prominently. It is the tendon of the palmaris longus. A little to the radial side is the larger though less prominent tendon of the flexor carpi radialis. In the groove between these two tendons lies the median nerve, that is, on the radial side of the palmaris longus. On the radial side of the flexor carpi radialis lies the radial artery. Towards the inner or ulnar side of the tendon of the palmaris longus the flexor carpi ulnaris is evident, appearing most distinctly when the wrist is slightly flexed and the little finger pressed closely into the palm. Just to the radial side of this tendon the ulnar artery can be felt pulsating. On the posterior side of the wrist the tendons are not so prominent as on the anterior. The chief interest lies in the change of the styloid process of the ulna in relation to the tendon of the extensor carpi ulnaris. When the hand is supine this process lies to the inner side of that tendon and when the hand is pronated the process is to the outer side of that tendon.

The number five runs through the hand and arm. There are four fingers and a thumb. There are five metacarpal bones. About the wrist joint there are five synovial membranes. There are five sets of muscles in the forearm working the hand and wrist, extensors, flexors, supinators, pronators and tensors of the palmar fascia. There are five bones entering into the frame of the arm and forearm, clavicle, scapula, humerus, radius and ulna. There are five motions of the thumb, fingers, wrist and shoulder, flexion, extension, abduction, adduction and circumduction. The brachial plexus of nerves supplying the arm has practically five spinal roots, four from the last cervical and one from the first dorsal nerve. There are five joints on the ulnar side from the last phalanx of the little finger to the wrist joint proper, and five along the same side of the arm above the wrist joint to the attachment of the extremity to the sternum. There are four flexors and a pronator taking origin from the inner condyle of the humerus and four extensors and a supinator originating at the external condyle. There are five bony processes at the elbow for the attachment of muscles, the two condyles of the humerus, the olecranon and coronoid processes of the ulna and the bicipital process of the radius. The chief flexors and extensors of the forearm, biceps and triceps, have together five points of origin. Five muscles run along the shaft of the humerus, deltoid, triceps, biceps, coraco-brachialis and brachialis anticus. Note also how the names correspond. Radius, radial nerve, radial artery, flexor carpi radialis, extensor carpi radialis; ulna, ulnar nerve, ulnar artery, flexor and extensor carpi ulnaris. The veins too have the same names. Note also that the flexors and pronators are on the anterior and inner aspect of the forearm, while the extensors and supinators occupy the outer and posterior part of the forearm.

On the anterior surface of the elbow three muscular elevations can be seen; in the center of the biceps and its tendon, below and to the outer side the supinator longus and extensors, while at the inner side the pronator radii teres and flexors appear. The biceps with the other muscular masses make two grooves shaped like a letter V, the open end above. In the innermost of these groves are the median nerve, the brachial artery and its veins. The tendon of the biceps can be readily felt. The bicipital fascia is attached and is continuous with its inner edge. A crease in the skin extends across the front of the elbow, not in a straight line, but convex below. It is placed above the articulation and its extremities correspond to the two tips of the condyles. This crease is obliterated on extension. In dislocation of the elbow backward the lower end of the humerus is about an inch below this fold, while in a fracture just above the condyles this crease is opposite or just below the upper end of the lower fragment.

The superficial veins, basilic and cephalic, formed by the radial and the ulnar, reinforced by the two branches of the median, can be seen on the anterior surface of the elbow.

The points of the condyles of the humerus can always be felt, the external being about three quarters of an inch above the humero-radial articulation, while the internal is fully an inch above the same joint. Hence the forearm, when extended and supinated, is not in a straight line with the arm, but forms an angle opening outward. Traction to reduce dislocation of the shoulder should, because of the above anatomical fact, be made from above the elbow. For the reason a line from condyle to condyle appears level when considered in relation to the arm, while viewed in relation to the forearm the internal lies at a higher level. The joint line at the elbow is not so long as the line between the two condyles. At the back of the elbow the olecranon is to be felt, lying nearer the internal than the external condyle. In extension its tip is above the line of the two condyles; when the forearm is bent to a right angle its tip is below the line of the condyles while in complete flexion it is wholly in front of that line. The ulnar nerve, crazy bone so called, lies between the olecranon and the inner condyle. There is a large subcutaneous bursa over the olecranon oftentimes found swollen and inflamed. Outside the olecranon when the arm is extended, is a pit present in those who are fat and also so in little children. This pit is regarded as a mark of beauty in the well shaped arm, but is of interest to the surgeon because in it the head of the radius can be felt and its rotation noted as the hand is pronated or supinated.

The lowest lymphatic gland is situated just above the internal condyle.

Remember, that in forced flexion of the elbow, the brachial artery is compressed between the muscles about the joint, and the supply of blood to the arteries of the forearm and hand greatly diminished; also that the synovial membrane of the elbow is prolonged under the olecranon process and that effusion in the joint will show about the edges of that process while the effusion of an inflamed bursa covers the process; that a bridge of bone connecting the radius and ulna, the result of improper adjustment of fractures of the forearm, totally destroys pronation and supination.

The outline of the arm is rounded and fairly regular in women and those who are fleshy. In the muscular, each individual muscle can be outlined from the surface. The biceps is especially distinct showing a groove on either side. The inner groove extending from the elbow to the axilla marks in the main the position of the brachial artery and and the basilic vein. The outer groove, ending at the insertion of the deltoid, indicates the position of the cephalic vein. The insertion of the deltoid is easily located. It indicates the center of the shaft of the humerus, is level with the insertion of the coraco brachialis and the upper limit of the brachialis anticus, locates the point of entrance of the nutrient artery of the bone and corresponds to the crossing at the back of the bone of the superior profunda artery and musculo-spiral nerve.

When the arm is extended and supinated the inner border of the biceps marks the course of the brachial artery, which is quite superficial and can be felt pulsating through its entire length. It lies on the inner aspect of the bone above and in front of the bone below. The relative position of the artery and bone must be considered in compressing the artery. The skin of the arm is loosely attached to the deeper tissues, and is frequently torn or stripped away in wounds of the part.

The musculo-spiral nerve, lying in close contact with the bone and winding around the humerus at the lower edge of the deltoid, is exposed to injuries in contused wounds, kicks, stabs and fractures of the shaft of the bone. In the latter case, even though the nerve be sound at the time of fracture, it may be so buried in the callus as to lead to paralysis of the parts to which it is supplied. Pressure of the head resting on the arm in the position of full supination and abduction or pressure of badly constructed crutches has caused paralysis of this nerve.

About the shoulder the clavicle, acromion process and the spine of the scapula are all subcutaneous and readily made out. The outer end of the clavicle is higher than the sternal portion. The roundness and fullness of the point of the shoulder depends on the deltoid supported by the humerus beneath. The part of the humerus felt beneath the deltoid is not the head but the tuberosities. The head of the bone can be felt in the axilla when the arm is abducted. The head of the humerus faces in the direction of the inner condyle. If the head of the humerus be diminished in bulk, as in certain fractures, or displaced from its socket as in dislocations, the deltoid, being no longer supported by the bone, will show a flattening and the acromion will be more prominent. In dislocations the head of the bone can be felt in an abnormal position.

The upper angle and vertebral border of the scapula are made accessible by carrying the hand as far as possible over the opposite shoulder, while to bring out the inferior angle and axillary border the forearm should be placed behind the back. The acromion, the external condyle and the styloid process of the radius all lie in a line when the arm hangs at the side with the palm forward.

The depression below the clavicle, subclavicular fossa, is worthy of attention. It is a guide to the amount of adipose tissue of the individual. It is obliterated in certain dislocations of the humerus, in fractures of the clavicle with displacement, by some inflammations of the wall of the thorax and by many axillary growths. In this region, within the coracoid process and about the middle of the clavicle, the axillary artery can be felt and compressed against the second rib.

The anterior and posterior folds of the axilla are very distinct. The depression of the armpit varies with the position of the arm being deepest when the humerus stands at an angle of 45 degrees from the side, as the arm is raised higher the axilla becomes more shallow.

The glands in the axilla, when normal, cannot be felt and when accessible to the touch, are indicative of disease. The large vessels and nerves in the axillary space render the free opening of deep abscesses of this part somewhat dangerous. The knife should be introduced midway between the borders and through the incision a pair of dressing forceps can be pushed into the cavity of the abscess, the blades being then separated to enlarge the opening.

From the extreme mobility and varied use of the superior extremity, we would expect frequent injuries of the part. The arm is always thrown out to break the force of a fall. For this reason the clavicle is more frequently fractured than any other bone of the body, the radius standing second in the list. Carefully estimating the exposure of the upper extremity and the number of fractures resulting, it is plainly to be seen that the great mobility and the number of joints between the hand and the sternum, together with the elastic and movable support of the ribs and spine are collectively a wonderful protection to this most useful member of the human body.

THE EFFECT OF PUBLIC SCHOOL EDUCATION UPON THE HEALTH OF THE COLLEGE GIRL.

Jane Kelly Sabine says that the type of the American student is better now than it was ten years ago, because of the influence of gymnastics and athletics in the lower schools. Bicycling, golf, and increased interest in all out-of-door sports have also done much to raise the standard. Nevertheless, the faults of the American type would still be marked; namely, flat chest, hollow back and prominent abdomen. Observation of 2,000 students in finishing schools showed defects in eyesight and hearing, and especially marked menstrual difficulties, 75 per cent. being found with irregularities dating from puberty, 60 per cent. had to give up from one-half to two days, and 90 per cent. had leucorrhœa. Since these defects date from the time when menstruation first takes place, when habit neuroses are most easily formed, when morbid sensitiveness keeps the girl at work in school, the reconstruction in her education must be made in the preparatory schools. For whatever position in life she is to occupy she needs good, sound health. Education at the expense of health is worthless. A sound mind in a sound body is a priceless possession; the college girl should represent that type.—*Medical Record.*

Nursing.*

CARE OF THE NEW-BORN CHILD.

Lecture No. 7.

Ladies: This evening we will discuss the care of the new-born child.

In our last lecture we left the child wrapped in a warm blanket and lying on its right side, while we attended to the mother. The next duty you have to perform is to bathe and dress the child. Get everything in readiness before commencing the process. The first thing select a warm place away from any draft. Cover your lap with a bathing blanket. Rub the child all over with warm sterile oil, vaseline, or even lard will answer if nothing better can be obtained, being careful to anoint all parts where there is a fold of skin or flexure. This softens the caseous material which covers the skin of the child. Now give a warm soap and water bath, using as much haste as you can, at the same time having removed every particle of the caseous material; dry quickly and thoroughly with a soft cloth. Castile soap is preferable to scented soaps. After drying use a powder to dust in the flexures of the limbs, in the armpits and about the genital organs, to prevent the child from chafing by the folds in the flesh or by its diaper or clothing. In some cases a simple ointment or sterile oil is preferred. Always use separate basins and wash-cloths for face and body.

The next step is to dress the cord. Some physicians prefer absorbent cotton, scorched linen, or gauze. My own plan is to anoint the root of the umbilicus with sterile oil, wrap the stump in absorbent cotton, and lie the whole upon the left side of the child's abdomen, and fasten securely in place with the binder. Next apply a soft napkin to protect the child's clothing from becoming soiled from any discharges. The next article to be put on is the shirt, and then the outer garments. The state of the weather will determine the amount of clothing to be put upon the child. After brushing the hair, the child should be wrapped in a soft blanket, and put to bed, lying on its right side. Usually it falls asleep in a few minutes. You can take this opportunity to tidy up the room.

The discharges from the intestines and kidneys are especially interesting in young children. The first bowel movements are dark, resembling tar or burnt molasses, and gradually give place to the bright yellow movements which are seen in health. The urine first discharged stains the diaper a reddish pink, sometimes a brick color, and this stain gradually gives place to a colorless state of the urine or to a faintly yellow tinge. The gradual change of the color of the discharges from the bowels and kidneys is an index of the activity of these organs and of the prompt establishment of the child's digestion. If the urine does not grow clear and the bowel movements remain black and thick, the child's digestion becomes established with considerable difficulty. During the first week or ten days the child is often jaundiced. This comes from the absorption of blood-pigment, and not because of disease of the liver. In healthy children it disappears in a short time.

At birth the stump of the umbilical cord is attached at the child's umbilicus

* Course of Lectures delivered to the Nurses Training School at Maryland Homoeopathic Hospital, by M. E. Douglass, M. D., Baltimore, Md.

and surrounded by an elevated rim of integument. The cord gradually withers, becomes black and shriveled, and finally comes away, leaving a small granulating surface, which retracts and is almost covered by the skin.

The healthy new-born child sucks vigorously, it cries actively, moves its limbs freely, and has considerable vigor in the grasp of its hands and feet. Although the grasp of the hands is much the better developed, still it tries to hold objects with the toes, and if the object be small enough it may partially succeed.

The craving for food which the child soon manifests is accompanied by considerable thirst. This is a wise provision of nature, as a free amount of fluid is necessary to flush the kidneys and establish the secretion of urine. Immediately after birth the mother's breasts rarely contain milk of an especially nutritious character. In most cases the fluid is thin, comprised of water, saline material, and young cells from milk-ducts of the breast. This is a laxative much needed by the child. It is called colostrum, and gradually gives way to the fully formed milk. If abundant water be given, so that the circulation of the child can have fluid and the glands of its body begin to act, the child will do well. It should not be fed by artificial means unless the coming of the mother's milk is delayed beyond the usual period. For forty-eight hours the child will do well upon colostrum and water if it be a strong and vigorous child. If it be prematurely born and weak, it may require additional nourishment or stimulus. The mother's milk forms gradually, usually by the end of the first three days after birth. In some cases it comes into the breasts so suddenly that the sensation is that of a rushing fluid. The secretion of the milk is greatly promoted by the stimulus of the child's nursing, especially if this be done at regular intervals. At first the child usually nurses once in four hours and once or twice during the night, for the first forty-eight hours. Then it nurses every three hours from six a. m. to ten p. m., and once during the night; and when the secretion of milk is fully established, every two hours between six a. m. and ten p. m., and once during the night. If the child is roused at regular intervals to nurse, in the course of a week or ten days it will form regular habits.

The capacity of the child's stomach gradually increases with the amount of food available. The natural measure of the infant's meal is the contents of one breast, and in the course of ten days or two weeks the secretion of milk will adapt itself to the appetite of the child, and sufficient, but no more, will be formed. The child should nurse the breasts in alternation, and before and after nursing the nipples should be cleansed with boric acid solution or sterile water. If there is danger that cracks or fissures will form, the nipple should be anointed after each nursing with an antiseptic ointment or with sterile oil. In some cases the child is slow in grasping the nipple in beginning to nurse, and the nipple must be moistened with water, or possibly with milk, before the child will grasp it actually. In some cases the breast is so dimended with milk that the child cannot cause the milk to flow freely. Here the tension must be lessened with the breast pump by drawing two or three drams of milk, when the child will be able to nurse. In some patients the first milk found in the breast is exceedingly rich in fat and does not agree well with the child. The use of the breast pump to remove this milk before the child nurses is usually all that is sufficient. The time occupied by a healthy infant in emptying a normal breast is from fifteen to twenty minutes. When the child drops asleep and cannot be roused to nurse, then the act of nursing shall cease.

In addition to the milk which the child obtains water should be given regularly by the nurse, two or three teaspoonsful every four hours unless asleep at night. The temperature of the water should be pleasantly cool.

The temperature of the new-born child is considerably above that of the healthy adult, and care must be taken that the infant does not become chilled. At the same time too great heat is most depressing and injurious. It is noticeable that infants that are not sufficiently warm almost immediately cry and fret, so that if a child is not hungry, and if its diaper does not require changing, we may suspect either heat or cold to be the source of its annoyance. The new-born child spends a large part of its time in sleep, and this should not be disturbed except for very good reasons. As the child at first has no consciousness of the external world, it is useless to disturb it with the idea that it is an intelligent creature which can give response. It may be with the mother sufficiently often to interest her, but otherwise it should be allowed to sleep and rest in quiet.

Infants' clothing should be as simple and as comfortable as possible. The number of garments actually needed is very small indeed. A thin, soft woolen undershirt, an abdominal band or binder, a pair of socks, a flannel slip which combines a jacket and skirt, and a diaper are the only articles of clothing necessary. For neatness, a white slip may be worn over the flannel one. Several small flannel wraps of different weights and sizes should be in readiness for use when it is necessary to carry the child from the crib to its mother or from one room to another. When the child is dressed its two slips may be put on together by drawing the sleeves one within the other. When it is old enough to go out a cap and heavier wrap will be necessary. The skirts of the infant's clothing should come but a short distance below the feet. All the clothing should be loose about the body, permitting the child to move freely. If the slips are too long, the movements of the feet are restricted, and the child does not develop so rapidly nor so perfectly.

If the child be bathed regularly, the bath is usually given in the morning, and the nurse must take care that the child is not exposed to chill. If possible, she should sit before an open fire, and should be surrounded by a screen to prevent draft. A bathing apron of flannel is especially desirable, and this should be double or having two layers. If the child is active and the nurse's clothing is likely to be soiled, she may put on first a rubber apron, and over this a double bathing apron which is of flannel, soft and thick. The child lies upon the under thickness of flannel while it is rubbed and dried. Care must be taken that separate wash cloths are used for the head and for the remainder of the body, in order to prevent the possibility of contaminating the eyes. Two wash bowls should also be employed, or else the head and face washed before the remainder of the body. The eyes should never be rubbed with a wash cloth, but should be cleansed by dropping sterile water in them from a medicine dropper which is perfectly clean. In bathing the child the stump of the umbilical cord and umbilicus must not be moistened. This should be covered by sterile gauze or cotton during the bath. Bathing should be followed by gentle massage over the entire body. If the child is puny and ill-nourished, massage may be combined with the inunction of oil by having the nurse anoint her hands with sterile olive oil or some other suggested by the physician in charge.

If the weather be excessively warm or the child be depressed from any cause and restless, it is often advantageous to give it a sponge bath or rub with alcohol just before it is put to sleep at night. A quart of water at a temperature of 100 degrees, to which are added two tablespoonsful of alcohol, makes a refreshing bath mixture when the child is fretful and has a tendency to slight fever. In bathing infants none but the purest soap should be used, and preferably without scent. Soft knitted wash-cloths, which should be boiled at least once weekly, may be employed. The child's body should never be entirely exposed during the colder months, but remain wholly or partially covered by the flannel bathing apron. Considerable care and skill are necessary to give the child the greatest comfort with the least exposure and risk.

To dress the umbilicus, the nurse should wash her hands thoroughly and brush them in a solution of mercuric-chlorid (1:2000). The soiled dressing should be removed very gently, avoiding traction upon the cord which might cause it to bleed. When the dressing has been unfolded and removed the umbilicus and cord should be very gently sponged with aseptic cotton and such solution as the doctor may order. The sterile dressing then prescribed should be applied, the stump of the cord being laid on the infants left side and held in place by a smooth bandage of soft flannel pinned about the abdomen.

The mouth of the infant must be kept aseptic by cleasing the mother's nipples before and after nursing, and by cleansing the child's mouth should grayish white patches appear upon the tongue and the sides of the mouth. The nurse must remember never to put a dirty finger or article into the child's mouth, as otherwise infection may arise. Should it be necessary to cleanse the mouth, the softest linen should then be employed which has been repeatedly boiled and has been dipped in sterile water or boric acid solution The eyes should be protected from infection by thorough cleansing at the time of birth by flushing them with boric acid solution or sterile water, as the doctor may order. After its birth the eyes may also be flushed with sterile water by the use of the medicine dropper, and any evidence of the formation of matter, sticking together of the lids, or redness about the eyes should be at once reported to the physician in charge.

Although the new born infant does not appreciate many of the sensations which adults have, it begins very quickly to form habits and to manifest a nervous, irritable, or quiet disposition. Very much of this depends upon the care of the nurse and the regularity with which she performs her duties. The child's habits are begun from the first day of its life. If the nurse is methodical, patient, and kindly, by the end of a week or ten days the child will form regular habits of eating, of sleeping, and of other functions of the body which are the basis of good health and physical happiness. When a child cries and frets it should be ascertained whether it is hungry, whether the diaper requires changing, whether the child is too cold or too warm, or whether something about the clothing is irritating it. If none of these causes is present, then the child will usually cease its crying if no attention is paid to it. Within a very few days after its birth, however, the infant learns that it can be taken up and obtain what it wants by making a disturbance and annoyance, and unless this is proved to be incorrect the child will soon have its parents and the nurse at its mercy. While children should never be neglected, and while the mother and the child should have the pleasure of being together as much as is consistent with the health of both, still discipline should begin at the same time that the care of the child first commences.

In our next lecture we will take up the accidents of pregnancy and of labor.

Editorial.

STATUS OF HOMŒOPATHY.

It is at this time in the year that the eyes of the profession are turned toward the colleges as they point to the results of their labors. Some important deductions may be drawn from a careful study of the reports as they come from the official representatives of the various institutions.

Boston University School of Medicine.

Dean, J. P. Sutherland, 295 Commonwealth ave. Boston.

Registrar, F. C. Richardson, 865 Boylston ave., Boston.

Courses and length, Four years, eight months each

Classes graduated since foundation 28

Students attending last year 181

Number of graduates this year, will not be known until examinations are held.

Alumni 837

Number Professors and Lecturers. 58

Value of College buildings and land... $200,000

Nothing can be given at this time concerning our commencement, as that does not occur until June and is then simply a part of the general University commencement.

Chicago Homœopathic Medical College.

Dean of Faculty, A. C. Cowperthwaite, 717 Marshall Field Building.

Dean for Students, A. R. McDonald, 338 Park avenue.

Registrar, W. S. White, 900 Marshall Field Bldg

Treasurer, S. H. Aurand, 780 Washington Boul.

Secretary, W. M. Stearns, 813 Marshall Field Blg

Business Mgr, E. J. George, 801 " " "

Courses and length, Four years, 7 months each, 28 courses altogether

Classes graduated since foundation...... 25

Students attending last year. 150

Graduates this year, Males 33; Females 3

Alumni, about 1,240

Professors and Lecturers... 65

Value of College property ... $5,000.00

Commencement exercises for the session of 1901—02 held April 23d at Studebaker Hall as follows:

Coronation March ......

Prayer............Rev. W. Craven, D. D.

President's Address......A. C. Cowperthwaite

Conferring of Degrees ... by the President

Prelude and Siciliana............

Doctorate Address. Prof. J. W. Streeter

Selection,......

Valedictory Address .O. L. Chaffee

Piano Solo.......

Address.............Rev. W. Craven

Selection........The Leffingwell Orchestra

Cleveland Homœopathic Medical College.

Dean, G. J. Jones, 824 Caxton Building.

Registrar, A. B. Schneider, 520 Rose Building.

Courses and length, Four, 26 weeks each.

Classes graduated since foundation 53

Students attending last year............ 119

Graduates this year Males, 27 Females 5

Alumni............ 2,300

Number of Professors.... 28

" " Lecturers.. 17

Value of College property $125,000.00

College of Homœopathic Medicine State University of Iowa.

Dean, Geo. Royal, Des Moines, Iowa.

Registrar, James G. Gilchrist, Iowa City, Ia.

Course and length, Four years, nine months each

Classes graduated since foundation 34

Students attending last year. 40

Graduates this year, Males. 7

Alumni ... 350

Number Professors and Lecturers 12

Value of College property $75,000.00

Has a Hospital of 54 beds, with a training school for nurses, three years course. Separate from College of Medicine. The normal class is from 75 to 80; this year for exceptional reasons, the class is very small.

College of Homœopathic Medicine and Surgery of the University of Minnesota.

Dean, Alonzo P. Williamson, 602 Nicollet ave., Minneapolis.

Course and length, Four years, 8 months each.

Classes graduated since foundation . 14

Students attending last year 24

Graduates this year 4

Alumni . . . 84

Number Professors and Lecturers 19

Denver Homœopathic College.

Dean, James Polk Willard, Masonic Temple, Denver.

Registrar, David A. Strickler, 706, 14th street, Denver.

Courses and length. Four years, 7 months each.

Classes graduated since foundation . . 6

Students attending last year . 33

Graduates this year, Males 8: Females . 1

Alumni. 56

Professors and Lecturers 31

Value of College property $25,000.00

Graduating exercises were held April 24th, at Trinity M. E. Church. Banquet immediately following at the Brown Palace Hotel. The exercises were the most largely attended of any in the history of the college.

The following program was rendered:

Organ Solo . . . Mr. F. Wright

Invocation Rev. E. J. Wilcox

Chorus. . . . . Trinity Choir

Presentation of the Graduation Class by the Dean . . . J. P. Willard, M. D.

Conferring of the Degree of Doctor of Medicine by the President, C. W. Enos, M. D.

Contralto Solo . . . . Mrs. W. J. Whiteman

Address . Hon. J. W. Springer

Male Quartette Trinity Male Quartette

Benediction . . . .

Organ Solo Mr. F. Wright

Detroit Homœopathic College.

Dean, D. A. MacLachlan, Majestic Building. Detroit, Mich.

Registrar, J. M. Griffin, 108 Miami ave., Detroit, Mich.

Courses and length, Four years, 7 months each.

Classes graduated since foundation, including this year. . . . 8

Students attending last year 15

Graduates this year, Males 4: Females 1

Alumni 35

Number Professors and Lecturers. 31

Value of College property $45,000 00

The following program was rendered on the occasion of the commencement exercises on April 23:

Overture .

Selection .

March Detroit Opera House Orchestra

Invocation . . Rev. E. B. Meeser, D. D.

Piano Solo. . Miss Georgia Richardson

Address. . Rev. L. S. McCollester, D. D.

Vocal Solo. . . . C. R. Hargreaves

Faculty Address . A. Graham, M. D., LL. D.

Vocal Solo. . . . . Miss Lottie Baier

Conferring of Degrees by the President, C. C. Miller, M. D.

Vocal Selection. . . . . A. Warington

Valedictory Address. . . C. S. Strain, M. D.

March. . . . . Orchestra

Dunham Medical College and Post Graduate School of Homœopathics.

Dean, James T. Kent, 92 State street, Chicago.

Registrar, J. C. McPherson, 92 State st. "

Courses and length, Four years, 7 months each.

Classes graduated since foundation . . 7

Students attending last year . 78

Graduates this year. 29

Alumni . . 103

Number Professors and Lecturers 31

Value of College property $40,000 00

Hahnemann Medical College and Hospital.

Dean, E. Stillman Bailey, 2811 Cottage Grove ave., Chicago.

Registrar, W. Henry Wilson, 2811 Cottage Grove ave., Chicago.

Number of courses and length, Four of seven month each.

Session begins September, ends April.

Classes graduated since foundation 42

Students attending last year . . 185

Graduates this year Males, 40 Females 7

Alumni (approximate) 2,400

Professors and Lecturers 68

Value of College property $250,000.00

There are about 12 Clinical assistants and demonstrators not included above. There are 22 Sub-clinics a week and 10 General Clinics.

The four years include nearly 4,000 hours of instruction, more than half of which in clinical or laboratory.

Hahnemann Medical College of the Kansas City University.

Dean, W. H. Jenney, Kansas City, Mo,
Registrar, Moses T. Runnels, Kansas City.
Courses and length, Four years, 7 months each.
Classes graduated since foundation 5
Students in attendance last year 48
Graduates this year, Males . 8; Females . 2
Alumni. 84
Number of Professors and Lecturers 29
Value of College property $5,800.00

The following program was rendered at the commencement exercises held on April 14:

Piano Solo. . . . . Mrs. E. C. White
Invocation, Rev. D. S. Stephens, D.D., Chancellor
Baritone Solo. . . . . Mr. Norris
Faculty Address . . . W. H. Jenney, Dean
Soprano Solo . . . . Glenn Wright-Hollenback
Annual Address . . Hon. L. C. Boyle
Duet . . . G. Wright-Hollenback, Mr. Norris
Conferring of Degrees and Presentation of Diplomas, L. G. VanScoyoc.
Soprano Solo . . . . Glenn Wright-Hollenback
Benediction, Rev. D. S Stephens, D.D., Chancellor

Hahnemann Medical College and Hospital of Philadelphia.

Dean, Pemberton Dudley, 1405 N. 16th Street, Philadelphia.
Registrar, Charles Mohr, Oak Lane, Philadelphia
Courses and length, Four years, 7½ months each
Sessions begin October 1, end May 15.
Classes graduated since foundation 54
Students attending last year 280
Graduates this year, Males. 67
Alumni 2619
Number Professors and Lecturers. . 67
Value of College property $823,000.00

The Fifty fourth Annual Commencement was held at the Academy of Music. The address to the graduating class was delivered by Rev. B. L. Whitman, D. D., LL. D., formerly President of Columbian University. The audience was large and appreciative.

Hahnemann Hospital College of San Francisco.

Dean, James W. Ward, 606 Sutter st.
Course and length, Four years, 7 months each.
Classes graduated since foundation 18
Students attending last year. . . 58
Graduates this year. . 5
Alumni. 167
Number Professors and Lecturers . 33
Value of College property $25,000.00

Hering Medical College.

Dean, H. C. Allen, 5142 Washington ave.
Registrar, J. B. S. King, 6718 Wentworth ave.
Courses and length, Four years, 7 months each.
Sessions begin Sept. 12, end April 10.
Classes graduated since foundation 10
Students attending last college year 79
Graduates this year, Males. . . 12; Females . 3
Alumni about 200
Number Professors and Lecturers 29
Value of College property . $85,000.00

Homœopathic Medical College of Missouri.

Dean, W. B. Morgan, 4208 N. Grand ave. St. Louis.
Registrar, D. M. Gibson, 241 S. Jefferson ave., St. Louis.
Courses and length, Four years, 7 months each.
Session began Sept. 10, 1901, ended Apr. 17, 1902
Students attending last year. 67
Graduates this year, Males. . . . 11; Females. . . . 1
Alumni. 678
Number Professors and Lecturers. 30
Value of property, real estate. . . . $65,000.00
Apparatus and appliance. 5,000.00
Institution chartered in 1857.

Homœopathic Medical College, University of Michigan.

Dean, W. B. Hinsdale, Ann Arbor, Mich.
Registrar, R. S. Copeland.
Length of course, Four years of nine months each
Classes graduated since foundation . . 25
Students in attendance last year. 72
Graduates last year, Males. . . . 15; Females. . . . 1
Alumni. 378
Number of Professors and Lecturers . . . 24
Value of College and Hospital property (exclusive of library). $150,000.00
Other information: Finest new Hospital, exclusively for clinical teaching in Homœopathy.

New York Homœopathic Medical College and Hospital.

Dean, Wm. Tod Helmuth, 504 Fifth ave.
Secretary, H. M. Dearborn, 146 W. 57th street.
Registrar, ., B. Bishop, 56th W. 49th street
Courses and length, Four years, 7 months each.
Sessions begin October 1st, end May 8th to 15th.
Classes graduated since foundation. 42
Students attending last year . . 105
Graduates this year, Males . . 23
Alumni, about 1800
Number Professors and Lecturers. . 41
Value of College property, about. $750,000.00

New York Medical College and Hospital for Women.

Dean and Registrar, M. Belle Brown, 80 W. 51st street, New York.

Courses and length, Four courses, 26 weeks each
Classes graduated since foundation 39
Students attending last year. 80
Graduates this year, Females. 7
Alumni 334
Number Professors and Lecturers. 43
Value of College property $40,000.00

Commencement exercises for 1902 will occur May 14th, in Astor Gallery, at the Waldorf Astoria. Seven graduates. Part of program will consist of an address by Mrs. D. McLean; Hippocratic oath administered by the Dean Dr. M. B. Brown. Music by famous Park Sisters.

Pulte Medical College.

Dean, J. D. Buck, 116 W. 7th St., Cincinnati.
Registrar, C. E. Walton, 8th and John streets, Cincinnati.
Secretary, T. M. Stewart, 704 Elm street, Cincinnati.
Courses and length: Graded Freshman, Sophomore, Junior and Senior Courses, seven months each.
Classes graduated since foundation. 30
Students attending last year. 40
Number Graduates this year, Males 8; Females 2
Alumni 578
Number Professors and Lecturers 31
Value of College property $200,000 00

Pulte Medical College has just completed a new Teaching Hospital. The latest improvements in plumbing and ventilating appliances have been introduced. All details have been arranged that will enable cases to be utilized for teaching purposes in a manner to bring the students in touch with the patient.

The Hospital is not intended to be the largest of any in existence. Its primary object is to serve as a Teaching Hospital. Cases will be sent to it that will illustrate types of disease which will include, of course, rare cases, as well as the common cases with which every physician must needs be familiar.

The Miami Valley Homœopathic Medical Society and Alumni Association of Pulte Medical College held a joint session on May 6, the scientific part of which convened in the college building at 10 a. m. The social session was held at the Hotel Sterling at 1:30 p. m. Besides the president's address, the program of the scientific session contained nine numbers, covering almost the whole range of medicine. As the authors of the papers all had something to say and are able to say it, a wager of a doughnut against a peanut would be safe in saying that the participants either missed their midday meal or had to forego the social session.

Pulte' commencement exercises were held on the evening of May 6th. Dr. Ch. Gatchell, Secretary of the A. I. H., delivered the Doctorate address; the faculty valedictory was delivered by Dr. Thos. M. Stewart and the degree of *Doctorum Medicinae* was conferred by President Thornton M. Hinkle, on two ladies and nine gentlemen.

Southern Homœopathic Medical College.

Dean, Geo. T. Shower, 431 Roland ave., Baltimore, Md.
Registrar, C. L. Ramsey, 819 Park ave., Baltimore, Md.
Courses and length, Four of seven months each.
Classes graduated since foundation, exclusive of this year's class. 10
Students attending last year 35
Graduates this year, Males. . . . 7; Females . . 2
Alumni 78
Number Professors and Lecturers. 33
Value of College property—Estimates cannot be accurately made without entering into tedious detail, as the basis of the holding has been changed.
Commencement will take place May 6th.

Southwestern Homœopathic Medical College, Louisville, Ky.

Dean, A. Leight Monroe, 904 Fourth ave.
Course and length, Four years, 8 months each.
Classes graduated since foundation 9
Students attending last year. . . 21
Graduates this year 11
Alumni 55
Number Professors and Lecturers. 25

The following summaries will assist us in making our deductions:

Homœopathic College.

Colleges	23
Time required for degrees (months)	28
Instructors	800
Students matriculated	1,693
Graduates	427
Alumni	14,250
Value of College property, endowment, etc. (approximate)	$3,000,000

Members of Inter Collegiate Committee 23

From the American Institute of Homœopathy for 1892 we find

Colleges	16
Time required for degree (months) .	18
Instructors	365
Students matriculated	1,389
Graduates	310
Alumni	9,141
Value of College property,	$1,000,000

From these summaries we learn that the number of colleges has increased almost 50 per cent; the length of time required 25 per cent; number of instructors over 100 per cent; the equipment more than doubled, while the attendance has only increased a trifle over 20 per cent. Better equipped colleges, longer course of instruction, and more efficient corps of instructors, when added to a definite *law* governing the selection of remedies for the cure of disease, logically ought to greatly increase the popularity of homœopathy with the public and bring to her colleges greatly augmented classes.

The fact that these classes have not kept pace with the improved facilities, compels us to carefully inquire into the causes with the hope that means may be brought to bear that will remove the obstacles and thereby put these institutions into a position where homœopathy will receive its just recognition and attract the brightest and best students of medicine to an investigation of its principles.

To make the fact more impressive that homœopathy is actually losing ground, we draw from *The Journal of the American Medical Association* the following summary:

For the year ending July, 1901.

Colleges	124
Time required for a degree .	28
Students matriculated . . .	23,846
Graduates	1,879
Alumni (approximate) . . .	160,000
Number of Instructors (approximate)	5,000
Value of College property (approximate)	$30,000,000
Members of American College Association	58

We have not the space to show the summaries from which the *per cent of gain* made by the dominant school for the past ten years may be drawn, but the fact remains and must be faced.

A study of these summaries reveals the fact that

1st. There are only five allopathic to one homœopathic college, although their alumni are more than ten to one.

2d. Their teaching force outnumbers our own, because their laboratories are more extensive and better equipped.

3d. Their average attendance is about one hundred and ninety, while we have only seventy five.

4th. The similarity in the course of study during the first two years naturally leads the student to select that institution offering the most comprehensive laboratory facilities.

5th. *The similarity in the course of instruction during the last two years naturally leads the student to stay where he is.*

We believe these five conclusions tell the whole story. There are too many homœopathic colleges for the present support, hence they are compelled to draw on private resources for the necessary means to carry on their work. Their laboratories are incomplete and clinical facilities inadequate. Only such students are drawn to their classes as have been impressed with superiority of homœopathic principles *before they become medical students.*

Why are there so many colleges? The answer is simple selfishness and ambition, two ruling passions. Most of the colleges are private institutions founded for the purpose of promoting the selfish interests of those directly concerned. Homœopathy was only an incident and generally was relegated to a minor place in the curriculum. How can we hope to successfully compete with the dominant school unless we bring to the front that for which our school stands?

The absence of a "law of cure" necessitates thoroughly equipped laboratories for experimental research and the earnestness with which these requirements are placed before the public secures the desired endowments, hence the superiority of the equipment over the homœopathic colleges. The homœopathic colleges have expended their resources in fitting up laboratories for the demonstration of basic principles and thus far *have not been able to secure the means necessary for that experimental research along the lines of materia medica provings.* This is the first step that must be taken if the school in general would occupy advanced ground. *It must be made compulsory* to be a success. We can only hope for preferment by the public when we have demonstrated the importance of this work.

We ought to be a militant body, earnest and aggressive, and our motto should always be carried in the front ranks and every member in the ranks sworn to defend and push its banner on to victory. Who are our opponents? A large body of men who have no principles to defend and no leader. They are divided into factions each one earnestly trying to discover the true way, but few are willing to listen to the feeble minority within our own ranks who insist that they have found it, because the great majority of the homœopathic profession show such indifference by their practice as to destroy the moral effect exerted by those faithful to the trust imposed upon them.

Homœopathy has been on trial seventy five years, and the truth of its principles demonstrated beyond the slightest shadow of a doubt. In all probability, nine out of every ten who have graduated from homœopathic colleges, believe the law of similars to be true, but their knowledge of the principles governing its application is too limited to enable them to make practical use of its efficient power. If all the colleges could be aroused to the importance of placing homœopathy where it rightfully belongs there would be no difficulty in securing such support as would raise the status of homœopathy to a plane where the whole world see and recognize its superiority and our classes would be filled by those who would not only be eager for the knowledge, but an honor to the profession they were seeking to enter.

The laboratories would include all that we now have and in addition one for determining the action of different agents upon the healthy by actual experiments. Homœopathic principles would have practical demonstrations and thus pass from theory to fact.

THE PHYSICIAN—PREPARATION—RESPONSIBILITY—REWARD.*

"And he digged deep, and laid his foundation upon the rock."

The value of a house depends as much upon its foundation as upon the superstructure. Few houses can be built upon a granite foundation, and few physicians have inherited from their ancestors that special fitness which naturally adapts them for the successful practice of medicine. Even as the foundation of

*Faculty address delivered by H. W. Pierson, M. D., to the graduating class of Dunham Medical College, 1900

a house should be carefully selected, so the child ultimately to assume the great reponsibilities of the physician should have the work necessary for the building of his character laid out at the very beginning of his development. Any man may plan the construction of a house, but experience has demonstrated the wisdom of entrusting this responsibility to the judgment of one familiar with all the details; and capable of so developing the imperfect ideas of the originator that additions may be made to the original plan without marring the symmetry of the whole or the construction of a new building more perfectly adapted to meet the contingencies of the time.

For a few moments, bear with me while I assume the responsibilities of an architect, employed by humanity to plan the building of a physician, capable of assuming the responsibilities of the present and of growing into the full measure of obligations that may be required in the future. Even as the rock represents the transforming effects of heat, air, moisture and time upon the primary elements, so the child becomes the embodiment of previous environments to which his progenitors have been subjected.

The child, to be selected, must possess certain mental with corresponding physical characteristics, in order that assurance may be given of his ability to withstand the pressure that may be brought to bear during the period of his development. In the beginning, as the rock upon which the foundation must be laid, we would have a positive development of the animal faculties, with evidence of strong physical vitality and every member of the body in perfect shape. Upon this as a base we would look for a particular combination of the higher mental and moral faculties linked to the physical or animal base by a prominence of the social nature. This foundation should be laid early in life, before the evils of an unfavorable environment may have perverted a naturally ideal character. And, unless Nature has been lavish in her gifts, especial direction should be given to the cultivation of a general love for humanity, because, if this is dwarfed or left out of the foundation, much of the symmetry of the superstructure will have been lost. Such a child as we have in mind will need little encouragement in the development of his perceptive or intuitive faculties, because his naturally strong vitality will enable him to see things and know people and be able to read and understand them at sight. But the sense of right and wrong is easily blunted unless frequent and positive direction be given to the exercise of this important faculty. It requires but a moment's consideration to recognize and appreciate the necessity for the positive development of a high moral character. His occupation naturally compels him not only to decide these questions for himself but to occupy the position of counselor and judge in many instances where the present and future destiny of an immortal life hangs upon his standard of morality.

At the same time that he is being taught to love his fellows and recognize the difference between right and wrong, his mind should be impressed with the fact that there is a force, a power, an energy immaterial in character but of greater import than anything visible to the naked eye—life. At first thought the importance of a looking for spiritual tendencies in the early foundation may be questioned, but experience has demonstrated the fact that a materialistic mind seriously handicaps the physician in his labor of love for humanity; and makes it the part of wisdom for the one possessing such tendencies to seek some of the more purely scientific fields of labor instead of lowering the standard of the true physician.

The first ten or twelve years of the child's life should be devoted to the specific cultivation of the above named essentials, leaving the other faculties to Nature. You can readily see that we are planning for a broad, generous foundation upon which a superstructure with noble purposes may be reared. All of this portion of the foundation naturally lies beneath the surface and must always remain there. It must become an integral part of the personality of the individual, otherwise the impression would be made that these peculiar traits were like a garment put on for show and, consequently, were artificial and lacking in sincerity, thereby destroying much of their power for good.

Special emphasis is also given to these suggestions by reason of the fact that the tendency of civilization at the present time looks to the cultivation of self and selfish interests, at the expense of those faculties which contribute to the general good of mankind.

The first logical sequence of this combination of social and moral faculties, with the natural intuitions of the child, will be the acquiring of a wonderfully keen knowledge of human nature. The child will seem, by intuition, to read and know people, because he has improved every opportunity for studying their natural and unguarded acts and words.

He is now ready for that mental discipline so necessary for the shaping and rounding out of a life prepared to assume the most comprehensive, and, at the same time, responsible position allotted to any member of the human family. The knowledge of cause and effect, the ability to draw logical deductions from certain causes—all that has gone before practically amounts to nothing unless it can be under the judicial direction of this important faculty.

The physician is a failure unless he possesses the natural impulses of love for humanity, keen sense of right and wrong, with intuitive knowledge of mankind in generous proportions. The man can never become a physician—a leader among men—until he has added to these that faculty of reason whereby he can determine cause from effect, or follow the logical sequence of natural causes and thereby reach the true interpretation of their meaning. It is at this stage in his development that the crowning glory of the foundation is placed. The physician must have the ability to draw careful distinction between the effects of different causes, because he is constantly being called upon to determine not only the nature of disease conditions but to select the true simillimum from a number of similars. This is best accomplished by the cultivation of the ability to make ready comparisons.

If you have the time to follow the process of logical reason the result may be conclusive, but an equally accurate method, with a great saving of time, comes by the combining of *intuition* with *comparison*. Intuition sees a thing at a glance and comparison enables the trained observer to see a number of pictures with equal facility and to select the one picture most closely resembling the one adapted to the case in question. This skill only comes as the reward of close application, but richly repays the student willing to make the effort.

You have now come to the time when the final inspection has been given to the foundation upon which you hope to rear a superstructure that shall crown your efforts with success and prove a living monument to which your friends may point with pride. Some have been following carefully drawn plans throughout life, while others have been their own architects; but, bear in mind the solemn fact that in every case each one has been compelled to lay his or her own foundation. To the degree, therefore, with which you have been wise in the planning and shown good judgment in the selection of material—improving your opportunities—will the foundation be suitable for the building you now hope to erect.

For the past four years you have been compelled to build under the guidance of experienced workmen. They have noted defects in the previous construction and, to the best of their ability, tried to show how the same might be remedied; but no one can lay a single stone for another. In their judgment, you have given evidence of a sincere desire to know what was for the best and have so improved your opportunities that we are pleased to welcome you into our ranks as master workmen, and bid you Godspeed in your future career. As you go hence, abundant opportunity will be given you to go over the entire foundation. You have better knowledge today of what should be required than when you commenced the building of a character from which the true physician is to be developed. If you are dissatisfied with the plan or the material, it were better that you begin at once to repair the same, because the defect will become more and more pronounced as the building goes on. It is always easier to look back and see where improvements might have been made, but it is a woeful waste of time and an expensive experience. It would be the part of wisdom for you to secure the services of an architect, even at this late day, and with him carefully study plans before continuing with the building.

At this point I am reminded that medical students are divided into two general classes: Those who have imagined that the practice of medicine offers exceptional opportunities for the making of money; and those possessing the attributes of the true physician and naturally following those inclinations to their logical conclusions.

If there be a single member of the first class present, let me say that your foundations are laid upon the sand, and that failure is as sure to crown your efforts as you attempt to build upon that foundation. Not only will the financial returns be less than could be secured by similar efforts in different lines, but you will be compelled to live with a man who has prostituted the nobler aspirations of life and laid upon the altar of a fickle goddess a never-ending sacrifice. She will never be satisfied but will demand his all and then laugh at his misery. But why should time be expended upon this class when calm reason must show conclusively that there is nothing in the principles of homœopathy that would harmonize with such aspirations, and those who might have thoughtlessly entered its portals would soon become convinced of their error and converted to higher and nobler purpose of the profession, or leave it for a more congenial environment.

During the past four years you have been studying the details of plans as presented by different builders, but now you will be compelled to make plans of your own and build in accord with the same. If it is possible, you are urged to begin those plans under the guidance of a competent builder—get a year or more of hospital or dispensary experience. Be where you can compare your plans with those who have demonstrated the success of their own—select for your model the one most perfectly representing your ideals, providing you are satisfied with the same; and, if that is impossible, select the best from a variety of plans, and build accordingly. Fine-spun theories and well rounded periods have no place in this plain talk. This is an occasion when the heart is tender and the mind most ready to receive hints that may be put into immediate use. To those who may be permitted to spend another year in the city, let me enlarge upon the suggestion of a moment ago: So arrange your plans that as great a portion of your time as possible shall be devoted to hospital and dispensary work. It follows, as a matter of course, that you will continue your studies in Materia Medica and the principles of Homœopathy under the guidance of the same masters as in the past. But whether you remain in the city or seek an independent location you have reached that point in the building of your foundation when your knowledge must be rounded out, and that can only be done by putting the teachings to the test.

In all that you do, be thorough. Do not measure your progress by the number of patients you can prescribe for, but by the exactness of your knowledge of each one. Unfortunate is the man or woman who acquires the habit of superficial work, of being satisfied with just enough to see the picture of the remedy. Begin by making records of every case, acute or chronic, and preserve the same for future reference. Make these records complete enough to show *all* the causes that may have contributed to the disease, with the reasons for the prescription, and they will become veritable gold mines to you in the future. Select a uniform style of paper, and work with an object beyond the present.

If you have any thought of ultimately limiting your practice to that of a specialist, wait until the foundation for a general practice has been laid and you have *demonstrated* the thoroughness of your knowledge of the *fundamental* and *exciting* causes of disease—what is curable in disease; the nature and action of your remedies—what is curative in medicine; and the principles underlying the selection of the one for the cure of the other. With this knowledge in hand you are prepared to give the natural inclination of your mind or the necessities of your physical nature full swing.

We have spoken of the importance of an early cultivation of the social and moral sides of your nature. Let us apply the same at this time. It is necessary for you to make friends. If the social faculties have been cultivated you will have no difficulty in this direction, because it will be natural. But, if yon have neglected this important element in the character of the successful physician by giving too much attention to books or the gratification of selfish desires, give them a rest and carefully cultivate people. Have an earnest desire to be friendly, and let sincerity be impressed upon every act. It will seem unnatural and the act of the hypocrite at first, but you must pay the penalty for early neglect, and the sooner you begin the better. Keep in mind the purpose and you will soon be worthy the confidence of your associates; and rest is assured they will not be slow in giving it because of the scarcity of the article. Remember that you are doing all this because of your love for humanity and that the great reward is only an incident. If you would have a practical working model, study the life of the Great Physician. He went about doing good.

Cultivate the habit of secrecy. Keep your own affairs to yourself. Never discuss your business with your friends in a general way. Be even more careful about discussing rumors or facts about others. Never, under any circumstance, discuss one patient with another, unless you have their permission. Remember, you are seeking to develop that element of character which will do most toward securing for yourself the confidence of others. This comes only after faithful and persistent efforts, hence the importance of rigidly following this rule. The reward will be appreciated when you are actually entrusted with secrets of great importance, the disclosing of which might mean the wrecking of human lives and the destruction of your hope for future confidence.

Avoid argument with the public. It is your business to listen, and every time you offer your services or your opinions unsolicited you only succeed in cheapening their value and developing lack of appreciating for the same when needed.

Of necessity, most of the consideration has been given to the *preparation* of the physician, but the *responsibilities* must not be overlooked, because much misunderstanding follows ignorance of the real duties of the physician. Beginning with the self-evident principle that the natural order is from *within outward*, we find that it is the first law of duty for the physician to be true to himself.

> "To thine own self be true,
> And it follows as the night the day,
> Thou canst not then be false to any man."

Carefully measure your physical and mental endurance. You have no more right to be reckless in the expenditure of your vital energies than to take from another that which does not belong to you without giving a just equivalent. "All work and no play makes Jack a dull boy," and the neglect of systematic recreation will take from you some of the necessary elements of a successful career.

You have consecrated your lives to the needs of the sick and distressed, and humanity has a right to expect from you the very best that you are capable of giving. Remember, the suffering of the poor is just as intense as that of the rich and their means for securing comfort and relief are correspondingly limited. It therefore becomes a sacred duty to minister to their needs to the very best of your ability. None can measure the value of a human soul, and the moment you assume the responsibility entrusted to your care any neglect on your part to become master of the means necessary for the preservation of that life become a crime in the sight of God, while man will not hold your guiltless if the evidence be clearly shown.

In your dealings with others the Golden Rule furnishes the best guide that can be followed. "Do unto others as you would that others should do unto you."

We now come to a consideration of that most important phase of the subject, the reward. What is the reward for this consecration of your life to the service of others? Is it commensurate with the great preparation required, and unparalleled responsibilities assumed? Let us see. If with this life all is ended then the compensation should be measured by the value of the living to mankind, which would be exceedingly small in some cases. But, if you are dealing with an immortal soul, the value of the services cannot be measured by any worldly standard alone.

In all cases there should be such a careful adjustment of the claim that it shall be so in accord with the double standard adopted that both parties to the transaction will feel that it is more blessed to give than to receive.

The laborer is indeed worthy of his hire, but if he demands in money full compensation for services rendered, the debt is canceled; and he has no right to expect the richer and more precious reward that comes to those who in the simple performance of their duty finds the way opened to the inner most recesses of the heart; and there learning the motives which prompts the very act is able to change the whole tenor of a life, and see it grow into the full measure and beauty of character designed by the creator. The rescuing of one human soul from the bondage to which sin, disease, or environment has condemed it should be sufficient reward for the arduous service of a life time.

So carefully plan your living that every phase of suffering humanity may feel that they have found one who can understand their needs and be trusted with the hidden secrets of the heart. It is only when you have reached this stage in your professional life that you are able to appreciate the blessed opportunities of the true physician or realize the richness of his reward.

STEPS IN RIFLE SHOOTING IN THERAPEUTICS.

Physicians who climb the hill of Therapeutics and become experts must do it step by step. Materia Medica is not the only study needed. The novice huntsman does not expect to be a "crack rifle shot" at once. There are several things he must learn first, and he usually begins with a shot gun. So does many a therapeutic. The hunter learns still shooting first. The habits of the animals whose lives are sought he must learn so he may know where to aim. Then he must be a good judge of distances and how far his gun will carry in all kinds of weather and conditions. So much for still hunting.

When he comes to moving targets the difficulties multiply. Some animals move rapidly, some slowly; some go in a straight line, others deviate from a straight line. A hunter may, with pride, bring down two birds at once with a shot gun, but the rifleman who take his game "on the wing" or running is a "rare shot."

This skill is not all acquired by practice either. There is an intelligent study that must precede this skill. This same is more than true in Therapeutics, which might be termed "firing remedies at disease." This disease may be an affection or possession, a plus or a minus; but the patient feels out of order. So we sit down and take the case: How he ails and where and how long; what makes him feel better, what worse, and when. Then we must dip deeper and bring out previous ailments and drugging, business pressure and dietetic discussions; does he sleep enough; if not, why, how and when disturbed. Having learned all we can, then comes the task of getting him to his normal condition according to his temperament and hereditary bias.

This may be a case of slight disorder, giving us plenty of time to take aim—select the similar remedy—and at the same time regulate the diet, work, private habits etc.

Is this trouble a result of a previous disease or of a drug, alcohol, tobacco etc., or of some bad habit? After proper directions have been given, then comes the selection of a drug that may be *the* similia, or only partially so, and another and still another drug must be fired at the case before the disorder is removed and the body is well.

Sometimes one rifle shot may do, but in cases where succession must be used the novice needs the electric light of experience *vide* Nash, Dewey, Hering *et al.* Those *still* cases—simple ones—are few, while the complicated ones are many, so many.

The active practitioner soon meets with disease on the wing (acute cases) and he must fire quickly and accurately to stop it. The course of the disease and the disease and the remedy must correspond. That may be easy to match in a hitherto healthy body, but in a chronically diseased body we may have the "wobbly," or up and down course. The sharp shooters here are few, but many are learning the proud art. This implies a greater knowledge than is taught in the books. It is hinted at when we are told to give an intercurrent remedy, when and why. The relation (comparison), as well as succession, of remedies must be known. How little of this is found in our literature!

The storm may have passed, and the relicts of this disease in the body upon the others gone before, with perhaps drug complications added, will take the crack shots who can "keep the trail." This, it will be seen, implies both knowledge and intelligent experience, and we look for it in this journal. The science of Homœopathy is easy compared with the art. T. C. D.

SCIENTIFIC VS. THEORETICAL MEDICINE.

A law of Nature is unchangable. It is forever the same. Anything that seems to demonstrate an exception, only goes to proven that something has been added to the working of the original law or rather two or more laws have been brought into intimate relations and the stronger has dominated.

A rule of action is noted for its exceptions and only serves to demonstrate its limitations and to prove that it is a makeshift until the law has been found which will govern absolutely. Opinions differ regarding the foundation upon which Homœopathy rests. One set of practitioners belief is limited by a *rule of action* that is applicable in a well defined sphere, while a smaller set of investigators profess absolute knowledge of a natural law which governs the *curative* action of every means applied to the removal of disease tendencies. Those who affirm the existence of a *rule* concede that there may or must be a *law* and believe it may be expressed by the motto *similia similibus curantur* but profess their knowledge does not permit them to affirm it to be a fact.

The arguments pro and con have been repeated so many times that they need not be repeated at this time. Our contention being that those who *know* their position to be true ought to be ready and willing to submit to any test that may be applied because truth courts investigation, and nothing but error is defeated in any such contest. The ADVOCATE stands for a *law of cure* and believes it can be demonstrated beyond the shadow of a doubt. At the same time it recognized that many of the demonstrations offered come far short of fulfilling all the requirements of a *scientific* demonstration. It also believes that the *seeming* stand-still or worse conclusion of actual retrogression is due to a spirit of indifference, even among the very elect, to the urgent necessity for aggressive work along the lines of winning new converts to the profession. It isn't enough to assume that a law has been established and offers clinical reports showing the picture of the disease manifestation with the indicated remedy; but these reports should show a true picture of the disease *and in addition* all the causes *fundamental* and *exciting* that may have contributed to the disturbance. An effort should be made to remove all *exciting* causes *before* administering the remedy, in order that the report shall *show* the *degree of susceptibility* and the symptoms that are *peculiar*. Many times the removal of the exciting causes will be followed by a *subsidence* of the *acute* manifestations, while the *susceptibility* remains unchanged, and only waiting a new exposure to burst forth into a flame. Many cases are reported as *cures* when the subsidence was due entirely to natural causes. The writer is deceived and the superficial reader accepts the statement as a fact and falls into a similar error. The close observer detects the missing links and condemns the whole thing. Every thing that is not for must be against. We have enough readers who not only understand the requisites for a *scientific* demonstration, but have the *facts* at their disposal from which such demonstrations can be made. The world needs these facts. Students are searching for the truth. It is your duty to give to the world such *facts* as you *know* to be *true*. Every time you put your records into such shape that they demonstrate something, the time is most profitably spent and the world may be made the better from your having lived in it. Let us give these facts to the profession through the columns of the ADVOCATE. The results will surprise even the optimistic. By so doing you can demonstrate the *scientific* basis of homœopathy and thereby stop in a degree the mad rush after the *ignis fatuus* of "rational" (?) medicine. The world wants to know facts and will accept the same when demonstrable.

Correspondence.

MORE ABOUT JAPAN.

EDITOR OF THE ADVOCATE—*My Dear Sir:* In the February issue of the ADVOCATE, page 79, you make mention of certain things Japanese.

It is true that in former years the Japanese were not meat eaters. Since 1889 there has come a great change in that country in this respect.

Mothers nurse their children until they are four or five years old, not because there is no use of cows' milk (for children are often fed on cows' milk) but to limit the number of children in the family.

As to the substitute of butter for table use, I never saw any.

As to "the consumption of alcoholic liquors" being "almost unknown," it would be nearer the truth to say in Japanese, "Sake wo nomanai mono g a sukuno gozaimasu," or in English, "Those who do not drink Sake" (native liquor) "are few." The great majority of the people take this Sake with their meals, and many persons take it between meals. The poor must be content with a poor quality, while the wealthier take a better quality. This Sake is brewed from rice and contains much alcohol and fusil oil. Besides the native drink, much beer is brewed in Yokohama, known as Sakurada beer and near the city of Tokio, there is another brewery where they manufacture the Ebiru beer. Imported liquors are used freely by those who can afford them, while many of the French and German wines are adulterated with a cheap quality of alcohol and sold to the poorer classes as Hakkurai Sake, or foreign liquor.

Tobacco is used universally, women and children not excepted. Of course due credit must be given many of the native christians who are total abstainers.

Very truly yours,

G. E. Dienst,

April 1. Naperville, Ill.

[The item to which Dr. Dienst refers was clipped from a London journal, and was printed by the Advocate as a curiosity, and we are glad to set our readers right by the insertion of the Doctor's letter, which, no doubt, is a true picture of present conditions in the "United States of the Orient."—Ed.]

Announcements.

AMERICAN INSTITUTE OF HOMŒOPATHY.

To the Members of the American Institute of Homœopathy:

All arrangements for the Fifty-eighth Annual Meeting of our National organization, to be held in this city, June 17th to 21st, are now complete. Present indications fully justify the assurance that in the matter of attendance, in its interest, and in its special features, it will greatly excel any previous meeting in the history of the Institute.

Cleveland is a summer city. In our week in June it will be at its best. It promises cool nights and pleasant days, while its shaded streets, its beautiful park system—which is Cleveland's especial pride—and its water-front, all combine to make it attractive to the visitor and refreshing to those who will next month enjoy its hospitality.

The spontaneous response that the special feature — the College Alumni Conclave—has brought forth, of itself guarantees a large attendance and an intense interest. It is thought that this occasion will do much to create increased interest on the part of each alumnus in his own alma mater.

Members of the profession should realize that the present is a critical period in our history. Events of great importance are at hand. In the law-making bodies of many states radical legislation is about attempted vitally affecting our interests as a school. The Institute is the most powerful guardian of your rights. Never before was a strong organization so important. Each one must do his part. Come and lend your aid.

The various social functions that have been provided by the local profession, while adding much to the enjoyment of the visiting members, will in no wise interfere with the serious work of the Institute. They are all planned to take place outside of the hours devoted to the business and scientific sessions. They will consist of the Conclave, a reception and dance, of drives and trolley rides, while there will be rare opportunity to indulge in golf and wheeling.

The Chamber of Commerce Building, in which the sessions will be held, is unusually well adapted to our purposes. The Hollenden Hotel, which will be Institute headquarters, is a first-class house, and the entertainment will be of the best. But, in addition to this, there are many other hotels of all grades and prices. Cleveland is very easy of access from all parts of the country, and the Committee on Transportation has arranged for a fare of one and one-third for the round trip from all railroad centers east of the Rocky Mountains.

On the part of the profession and the citizens of Cleveland a hearty welcome awaits all who may come.

James C. Wood, M. D., President.

Ch. Gatchell, M. D., Secretary.

REVISION OF BY-LAWS.

The Institute Committee on Revision of the By-Laws have, as per instructions, prepared a schedule which will be found in the Secretary's annual circular.

As space there would not permit of a thorough explanation of the plan proposed, we desire to present the same to the profession through the journals, that all members may study and understand the plan before the meeting.

1st. The schedule has been arranged so that all meetings may be held within the week.

2d. It has provided seven hours for the general business of the Institute—ample time.

3d. It has provided one whole day, six and one-half hours, for the sole consideration of Materia Medica—the keystone of our faith and without it we have no reason for our distinctive organization.

4th. It recognizes the fact that the majority of our members are general practitioners and that their rights must be protected. We have therefore provided for them, six and one-half hours of Materia Medica and one and one-half hours upon each department of medicine and in which practical rather than technical papers should be presented. They also have the right and privilege of attending any and all of the special societies they desire.

The Committee believe that any schedule providing for special societies alone should not prevail, because it takes from the general practitioner and adds to the specialists, the benefits of membership. The Institute cannot publish in any way the Transactions of all the special societies and their own without increasing its dues. This makes the general practitioner pay more than at present and the specialists less as it cuts off the dues of his special society.

Under the proposed schedule the Institute would publish its general business, statistics etc. All the Materia Medica meeting and the general scientific meetings held daily from 10:30 to 1:30 so that the Institute members would receive in return for their dues a volume of Transactions of about the same size as at present, while the special societies would be allowed to publish their own transactions.

5th. This schedule gives the special societies what they want, ample time to hold their meetings during the week of the Institute, and we believe will be entirely satisfactory to them.

Lastly. It does not saddle the expense of the special societies upon the Institute, which it cannot stand without increasing its dues, and we believe any increase of dues would greatly cut down our membership and in that way injure the life of the Institute.

THEO. Y. KINNE, Chairman.

REPORT OF THE TRANSPORTATION COMMITTEE, A. I. H.

The Committee on Transportation of the American Institute of Homœopathy is able to report that the various Associations of railroads have agreed to give a rate of one fare and one third for the round trip, on the usual certificate plan, for the meeting at Cleveland, June 17–21. This applies as well to the "allied societies;" and arrangements have been made for the presence of a special railroad agent on Tuesday, Wednesday, Thursday and Friday, so that any member who may, for any cause, be compelled to leave the meeting during the week, can have the benefit of the reduced rate. A large attendance is confidently hoped for.

Fraternally yours,
JOHN B. GARRISON, M. D.,
Chairman.

Personals and News Items.

There is a good opening for a Homœopath at Pretty Prairie, Kans., a town of 300 or 400. Population largely German. Any information will be given if inquiries are addressed to T. J. Clark, M. D., Castleton, Kansas.

The Hahnemann Medical Association of Iowa, holds its annual meeting in Waterloo, on the 21 and 22 of May. The excellent program prepared for the instruction and entertainment of the members and visitors ought to, and no doubt will, secure a larger attendance than usual.

The announcement of the fifty-eighth annual meeting of the American Institute of Homœopathy, to be held at Cleveland, June 17 to 21, containing the program of the Institute, together with the various sections, has been printed and distributed. The program is an exceedingly good one, and there can be no manner of doubt that every attendant will wish that he could divide himself into at least half a dozen separate entities, so he could be enabled to listen to or take part in all the proceedings of the various sectional meetings.

Dr. J. W. Enos, formerly located at Jerseyville, Ill., announces that he is now pleasantly situated at Boulder, Colorado.

The important post of Medical Director of the St. Louis World's Fair has been filled by the appointment of Dr. Leonidas H. Laidley, of St. Louis. Dr. Laidley was born at Carmichaels, Pa. He was educated with a view to the medical profession, and entered Cleveland Medical College, in 1866, Jefferson Medical College, 1868 and Bellevue Hospital Medical College 1872. In St. Louis he has made a successful career both as a practitioner and a medical teacher. He helped organize the Young Men's Christian Association, and organized the free dispensary which became the nucleus of the Protestant Hospital Association. He filled the chair of surgical diseases of women in the St. Louis College of Physicians and Surgeons, and later became Professor of Gynæcology and Pelvic Surgery in the Marion-Sims-Beaumont College of Medicine.

Materia Medica Miscellany.

Kali carbonicum. This is a splendid remedy in diseases of women. The menses are too early, to profuse and last too long; discharge acrid, odor pungent and accompanied with severe aching in the small of the back. It has the reputation of being frequently the only remedy needed to bring back health to a woman who makes a bad getting up. The pains of kali carb. are especially characteristic, being sharp, stitching pains felt in any part of the body. The pains remind one of Bryonia.—*Medical Visitor.*

Oil of Verbena (Indian Melissa Oil) to Prevent the Bite of the Mosquito. McIntosh recommends an application for this purpose in the *Medical Record* of November 16, 1901, which he has used for some years when out fishing or hunting in swamps where mosquitoes are prevalent, and in the evenings when sitting out-of-doors, and which he has found to be most excellent and efficient; it is the oil of citronellæ (oil of verbena, Indian melissa oil). It has a very pleasant odor, and is not expensive. The oil should be rubbed into the exposed parts, and repeated occasionally.—*Medical Visitor.*

Phosphorus. This drug is adapted to those tall, slender people, with fair skin, auburn hair, a decided blonde, whose natures are extremely sensitive and are quick-witted. These people are inclined to grow rapidly, and prone to stooping.—*Medical Visitor.*

Graphites. Do not forget that graphites is one of the best, if not the best, remedy we possess in erysipelas and the more difficult it is to find the remedy for any particular case the more surely is it indicated. In those cases where there is a tendency to relapses or where new centers of infection appear it stands above all the other remedies of the materia medica.—*Medical Visitor*

Lachesis. The aggravation of Lachesis are: After sleep; on rising; in the morning or evening or open air. The throat and body are worse from contact, patient cannot bear the least constriction around the throat or body. The aggravation in the text-book is not stated just right. It should be, the patient sleeps into an aggravation which arouses him.—*Medical Visitor.*

Antimonium Crudum in Callosities of the Feet. Dr. A. L. Blackwood in *The Clinique*, thus verifies an old characteristic:

Miss M., aged thirty nine, came to the clinic complaining of great tenderness of the soles of the feet, which pained her so that she could not do her work. This had been present for about three years. Examination showed that there were large, thick, horny callosities on the soles of the feet, especially close to the toes. The soles of the feet are very sensitive. The distress is most pronounced when walking upon stone walks. Antimonium crudum was given the patient at first in the 6x and later in the 12x. It is now nine months, and she considers herself well. The callosities have disappeared and there is no distress when walking.—*N. A. Journal of Homœopathy.*

Cure for Hiccough. A young girl suffered for four days withou cessation from singultus, about thirty spasms to the minute, the attack being due, apparently, to some gastric disorder. When she put out her tongue for a few seconds it was found the hiccough ceased. She was then ordered to stick out this member at regular intervals for a few minutes, at the termination of which only a few slight spasms followed. She was then ordered to repeat, when the singultus ceased altogether, and did not again return. It therefore would seem to be proper to try continuous or rhythmic traction of the tongue in these cases.—*The Family Doctor* (*London*).

White Wood as a Cure for the Tobacco Habit. According to the *Eclectic Medical Journal*, the Liriodenden tulipifera, also known under the names of white poplar and white wood, is probably the largest of the lumber-producing trees native to this country, excepting, of course, the giants of California. The inner bark has been used to a considerable extent, in years gone by, as a domestic remedy for malarial conditions, or infused in whisky as a tonic or bitters This bark also constitutes a very efficient cure for the tobacco habit. The fresh, inner bark may be chewed, or the powdered bark may be mixed with sugar and extract of licorice, and pressed into a tablet, say of five grains of the bark. These tablets are to be allowed to dissolve in the mouth whenever the desire comes to take a chew or a smoke. The man who made the discovery cured himself, and he was a most inveterate chewer. He also gave it to dozens of his friends, with fine results, finally selling his receipt to a large drug house for fifteen hundred dollars. While the remedy is cheap, it is also harmless, and at the same time a fine stomachic, resembling gentian in its action upon the gastric organs.

Book Reviews.

Dictionary of Domestic Medicine, by John H. Clarke, M. D., London. Published by Boericke & Tafel. Price $1.25 net, by mail $1.35.

This is a special edition carefully revised for the use of the American public.

The time will come when every village of any size will have its homœopathic physician, but such an ideal state does not exist now, hence the importance of having a *small* book sufficiently *comprehensive* and at the same time strictly *homœopathic*. These *three* important factors are very judiciously combined in this little book. We take pleasure in commending it to the notice of our readers.

International Clinics. Published by Lippincott's. *Volume IV. Eleventh series*, is before us for review.

The readers of the ADVOCATE know the high value placed by us upon this series of essays, lectures and especially prepared articles. Every thing appearing in the collection is classical in diction, concise in form and presents in a large measure the consensus of opinion upon the most advanced topics of under discussion. They differ from magazine literature in two ways. Every contributor is selected by reason of his special adaptability to some particular subject and is paid for services rendered. You get exhaustive monographs upon varied topics during the year. They are preserved in permanent form and in elegant style. It is no wonder that the list of subscribers is constantly on the increase. They are a credit to any library.

This number is of special interest by reason of the valuable lists of subjects treated under the head of *Therapeutics*—e. g., Remarks on Strychnine by Jacobi; Method of Investigating the Action of Drugs by H. C. Woods; Superiority of Small Doses in Treatment of Syphilis. Also a special article on Clinical Records by means of the *Card Index System*.

Diseases and Therapeutics of the Skin, by J. Henry Allen, M. D. Boericke & Tafel, Publishers. Pp. 535. $3.00 net.

The profession is indebted to the author of this valuable work because he has hewed to the line and given to the world a true expression of homœopathy with relation to disease of the skin. For convenience the commonly accepted *nomenclature* of the different forms of skin disorders is adopted, but this is followed by a characteristic *definition* in which Hahnemann's interpretation is followed as closely as possible. It helps to harmonize, and at the same time, direct the reader to a study of basic principles as found in *Chronic Diseases*. The *symptoms* presenting next come in for consideration followed by the *pathology*, *Etiology*, *Diagnosis* and *Treatment*. The arrangement and classification is simple and practical and the indexes are complete.

One of the most interesting features of the book is the concise arrangement of symptoms of every remedy mentioned in the book under a separate section known as *Dermatological Therapeutics*.

The author has shown great care in the preparation of this first edition and the work is to be commended because of its simplicity, comprehensive grasp of the subject and *faithfulness of the principles for which it stands*.

Abbott's Bacteriology. A Practical Manual of Bacteriology for Students and Physicians. By A. C. Abbott, M. D., Professor of Hygiene, University of Pennsylvania. New (6) edition, revised and enlarged. In one 12mo volume of 690 pages, with 111 illustrations, of which 26 are colored. Cloth, $2.75, net. Just ready. Lea Brothers & Co., Publishers, Philadelphia and New York.

Whether the physician looks upon "germs" as *causative* agents or the logical fruit developed upon suitable soil, they become of value in making diagnostic differentiations in many doubtful cases. *Simple*, and at the same time *complete*, directions are not easy to secure. This new addition is certainly up to date and practical.

Venereal Diseases. A manual for students and practitioners by James R. Hayden, M. D., and published by Lea Brothers & Co.

Two important facts are unintentionally made prominent by the author, viz: that under "old school" treatment venereal disease disclose a persistent tendency to complicate matters. Of course the relation of cause and effect is not dwelt upon, but the close observer cannot fail to see that their treatment is radically wrong. The book becomes of value to the homœopathic physician as a warning to avoid the method of treatment advocated therein if he would have his cases pursue an uneventful road to recovery.

The book is well written and the publishers have gotten it out in excellent style and the mechanical parts of the treatment clearly shown, but the treatment is abominable.

The editorial department of the *Review of Reviews* for May gives an excellent summary and exposition of the various measure before Congress. There are also illuminating paragraphs on foreign politics—the French elections, affairs in the far East, and the South African situation. Mr. W. T. Stead was an intimate friend and confidant of Cecil Rhodes, and for years was intrusted with the great South African's imperial secrets. Only a part of Mr. Stead's disclosures made since the death of Rhodes has been given to the daily press, but the whole story is told for the first time in the May number of the *American Monthly Review of Reviews*. There will be found the full text of the markable notes on world politics written by Mr. Rhodes in 1890, commenting with the greatest freedom on current American affairs, and giving some suggestion of the ideas which underlay the Oxford scholarship scheme. Nowhere else has been published so complete and authoritative an estimate of this modern Colossus of the English-speaking world. Pictures of "Groote Schuur," Mr. Rhodes' home at Cape Town, with excellent portrait of Mr. Rhodes himself, accompany the article.

An interesting feature of the May *Success* is Israel Zangwill's story of "What Have the Hebrews Accomplished?" "The Practical Process of Making Electrical Engineers" is described by Frank Hix Fayaret; Mary Lowe Dickinson discusses "The Value of Love," being number one of her "Culture in the Home" series. Besides these are a dozen other articles from masters' pens, any one of which is worthy of being the leading topic of a good magazine.

An important feature of the June *Success* will be an article by E. Benjamin Andrews, chancellor of the University of Nebraska, entitled "A Democracy of Learned Men," in which the celebrated educator shows the remarkable standing the United States has attained through their magnificent system of academic education.

The Hahnemannian Advocate

A MONTHLY HOMŒOPATHIC MAGAZINE.

H. W. Pierson, B. S., M. D., Editor, 809 Marshall Field Building, Chicago.
Hahnemann Publishing Co., Publisher, 6704 Lafayette Ave., Chicago.
Benj. F. Swan, Business Manager.

Subscription price of this magazine in the United States, Canada, Mexico, the island possessions and Cuba, $[illegible] a year, payable in advance; in Great Britain, continental Europe, India and other countries, members of the postal union, $[illegible] a year to be paid in advance. Unless otherwise specified subscriptions will begin with January issue of the year in which order is received. Remittances should be made payable to the Hahnemann Publishing Co., 6704 Lafayette Ave., Chicago.

Address all articles intended for publication and books for review to the editor. All business and other communications should be sent to the Hahnemann Publishing Co.

Vol. xii. Chicago, June, 1902. No. 6

Materia Medica.

REMEDIES THAT PRODUCE REDNESS OF THE PATIENT OR PART*

This paper is one in a symposium organized by the chairman of the Bureau of Materia Medica. A brief sketch of these drugs which have the property of causing redness of the skin, either general or local is the topic of the present essay.

Redness of the skin when it has passed the normal hue is a matter both of degree and kind, and expresses itself in a more or less inflammatory process from the mildest reddening of the surface due to hyperæmia or erythema to a bright scarlet or purplish color. Not only is the color of the skin changed, but according to degree of inflammation, involves the various structures of the derma, epithelial or follicular vesicles, herpes, blebs or blisters and pustules, or minute abscesses arise on the reddened base.

All toxic agents called drugs cause these manifestations on the skin to appear in the same manner and present lesions indentical with those induced by natural efflorescences affecting the same part. Each drug causes a specific alteration in and upon the cutis and all other things being equal, resolves its prototype, the skin then returning to its normal integrity. Furthermore those constitutional symptoms which are especially related to the outbreak on the skin in natural disease are seen to be exactly parallel in the artificially produced drug disease. Not only is the natural objective sign on the body surface indentical with the artificial one, so much so that the two are not infrequently confounded, but the subjective ones, such as itching, burning, tingling, smarting or aching are also experienced by the unfortunate patient. The similarity of the two is so apparent and the curative effect of one upon the other so well established that it would seem a deliberate denial of the senses to doubt it. It is of course understood that the present paper takes no note of chemical agents in their cauterizing effect, and are therefore excluded.

Belladonna, causes bright glowing scarlet redness of the skin, commencing in red, thick-set, red points, which

* Read by Prof. Chas. H. Evans, M. D., before the Illinois State Homœopathic Medical Association, May 15, 1901.

coalesce and then forming an even shining red surface. The eruption generally spreads from the neck and chest to the entire body and extremities. Associated with this redness is a high fever and sometimes cerebral symptoms.

Apis. The redness produced by this remedy is usually rose-colored or a pale pinkness. This modified redness is due to the œdematously infiltrated skin which is often enormously swollen; sometimes the features are swollen out of all recognition.

Aconite shows a flushed red skin. There is general redness of the skin which is generally roughened and harsh to the examining hand. One side of the face is red or the redness may alternate from one side to the other.

Arnica. The skin under this drug becomes erysipelatously red, hot and œdematously swollen, but the latter is not so great as that which is caused by *Apis.* The skin is involved deeply, even to the subcutaneous cellular tissue which is indurated and painful.

The *Antimonies*, both crude and tartarised, redden the skin, and large pustules arise on this inflamed base which closely resemble the pustulation of small pox, even to the umbilicated centre. Sometimes these pustules are very large, probably formed by the coalescence of smaller ones and then they are surrounded by a scarlet areola at their base.

Ailanthus. Patches of fine granular eruption having a dark purplish or mahogany color arise on the skin, similar in appearance to that caused by malignant scarlet fever. Other signs of malignancy are present at the same time.

Sulphur produces a rough reddened skin. An even redness covers the skin extending to all parts of the body, very greatly resembling scarlatina.

The use of this remedy in scarlet fever at some time during its course has given me the most gratifying results during our experience with scarlet fever, extending over many years. Circumscribed redness of the cheek is associated with redness and pulmonary symptoms. Vesicular herpes form on a reddened base.

Rhus tox. The redness caused by this drug commences in irregular patches, dull or dusky red in color. This inflamed surface is quickly studded with vesicles about the size of a pin head. When the face is attacked, the swelling closes the eyes. The burning heat and intolerable itching are almost unbearable and when large surfaces are involved nearly drive the sufferer frantic. *Rhus* also causes a measle like eruption.

Agaricus muscarius. Very great redness of the skin is induced by this drug with burning and intense itching. The general appearance, sensations and aggravations closely simulate that affection of the skin known as chilblains. I have cured some of the most aggravated cases of this disorder with the 30th attenuation of this remedy, that had long resisted numerous and heroic measures.

Sepia off. Under the influence of this drug there is redness and roughness of the face especially that of the forehead with more or less itching and burning. Redness of the skin occurs in irregular patches and herpes arranged in more or less circular form are seated upon it. These patches bear a marked resemblance to one of the varieties of "ringworm."

Secale cor. produces numerous petechiac ecchymoses and gangrenous redness in the substance of the skin. In such instances other toxic symptoms present themselves in consequence of this fungus.

Baptisia shows a hot, dusky-red, puffed face which gives the countenance a "besotted" appearance, which is heightened by the reddened, half-closed expressionless eyes.

It also causes a measle-like eruption on the skin and an erythema, like urticaria.

Pulsatilla. When the redness is more rose colored than bright, probably a dark pink describes it best.

It also causes a papular measle-like eruption having the same color and covering the skin of the whole body. More or less gastric derangement accompanies this eruption. Discrete pink, papular elevations, about the size of a large split pea, arise on the otherwise white skin, attended by some derangement of the stomach. This eruption mostly met with in children. I have always been able to cure this with *Pulsatilla* 30th in a very short time and with entire relief of the gastric symptoms.

Phosphorus exhibits a red face. It also causes red circumscribed patches on the cheek about the size of a silver dollar. This redness is the signal of hectic fever and points to tubercular or caseous destruction.

Phosphorus also produces purpuric spots and patches which are occasionally attended by hemorrhage from some outlet of the body. The ulcers which are produced by Phosphorus have a wide zone of redness surrounding them.

Sanguinaria can. also presents the same circumscribed red patches on the cheeks that have just been alluded to as being caused by Phosphorus and the same kind of pulmonary destruction is behind it. A general redness of the face is another of its effects.

Nitric acid. Broad dull red patches appear on the skin from which small suppurating pustules arise, and these are followed by rapid destruction of tissue. Various organs give signs of distress in connection or in alternation with the cutaneous application.

Mezereum causes an inflammatory redness of the skin, attended with eruption of large yellow pustules which soon suppurate freely. A red itching eruption is also developed by this drug, which is especially severe on the chest.

Cinchona and its alkaloid, Quinine, causes a bright scarlatinal redness of the skin of the entire body, which is followed by desquamation.

Stramonium induces a bright scarlet red color of the skin spreading rapidly over the whole body. The face is especially and excessively swollen. Cerebral symptoms are associated with this redness.

Lachesis. The dead and dying corpuscles of the blood, as a consequence of this toxic agent, so modify the color of the skin that it takes on a bluish-red color. Sometimes this bluish-red hue passes into a grayish-red. All forms of cutaneous inflammation take on this same color. Signs of malignancy also present themselves in other quarters.

Cantharis produces intense redness of the skin, with formation of vesicles, herpes, blisters and large blebs, often as large as a half dollar, filled with clear serum. Urinary symptoms are frequently associated with the cutaneous inflammation. The heat and burning in the skin are intense. I have observed that patients calling for this remedy are depressed and are in a generally "run down" condition. There seems to be an exhausted condition of the body or an imperfect nutrition from excessive labor.

Opium causes the skin of the face to become dark red and the features puffed, swollen, with sometimes a sweating surface. When this condition of the circulation has taken place there is also more or less unconsciousness, or even coma with dropped jaw and stertorous breathing.

Kali bromatum (potassium bromide)

causes a more or less thickly set eruption of acne, with redness of the skin; the eruption is most plentiful upon the face, shoulders and chest. Many of the acne form nodules, become pustular.

Melilotus off. causes intense redness of the face. This is due to cerebral congestion attended with bursting headache and hemorrhage from the nose.

Euphorbium produces intense redness and excessive inflammation of the skin, accompanied by the formation of vesicles or of herpes as large as peas, filled with yellow fluid.

Ammonium carb. A scarlet redness appears on the skin, especially over the upper half of the body. This efflorescense is frequently associated with cerebral symptoms.

Bryonia induces a dark smooth redness of the skin; the skin of the face is puffed and swollen but soft to touch. Although a high fever attends this circulatory disorder, the skin is bathed in sweat. A hot, pale, red, swollen skin also occurs over any painful joint.

This drug also produces a red, elevated, papular eruption.

Croton tiglium causes a dull redness of the skin in slightly elevated patches, which are soon thickly covered with pin head vesicles, containing first a clear, thin, cloudy fluid. Burning and intense itching are the subjective symptoms. I have found this remedy to be most efficacious in the treatment of Rhus poisoning.

Copaiba produces a pinkish-red eruption on the skin, like measles, and the resemblance to this disease is further heightened by the attendant sore throat, reddened watery eyes, etc.

Iodine induces various eruptions which in their general appearance are similar to those caused by syphilis.

Pix liquida, or tar, causes an eruption of acne, having a striking resemblance to acne and comedo, even to the black central points.

Veratrum viride shows a dark purplish swollen face. This color and appearance of the skin is due to an intense engorgement of the capillaries in the head, lungs, stomach etc. The skin of the face and at the entire body is more or less cold and clammy and the features, purplish and puffed, have a stupid appearance. Collapse may be present.

Salicylic acid causes an itching erythema similar to that of scarlet fever. These eruptions are bright and punctate, and soon become coalescent; there are also sore and inflamed throat, red conjunctiva and other scarlatinoid symptoms. An erysipelatous inflame with œdematous swelling and tension of the skin is also produced by this drug.

Iris vers has irregular patches of redness of the skin from which vesicles or pustules arise. The face and scalp are especially the seat of these eruptions, although they also appear on the body like herpes zoster.

Glonoine induces redness especially of of the skin of the face; the redness comes and goes. This redness is due to cerebral congestion.

Muriatic acid. Intense redness of the face. Eruption of red papules which dry into scabs. Red scabby, scurfy eruption on the skin.

Oxalic acid. Mottled red skin of the face appearing in more or less circular patches.

Viola presents circumscribed redness of the skin which becomes excoriated. This raw surface constantly discharges a yellow, purulent fluid. This soon dries into a thick greenish yellow scab, but the semi-fluid discharge continues to ooze and flow from beneath its edges. The skin is red far around the investing crust.

Natrum mur. A circumscribed red spot appears on each cheek. General redness of the face.

Sabadilla. There is fiery redness, burning and heat of the skin. Red spots and stripes of redness occur on the skin especially when in the open air.

Borax. Erysipelatous redness and heat of the skin. Red papular eruption, especially on the face. Redness and heat of the face.

Gelsemium produces a dark redness and puffiness of the skin of the face which has a stupid, "besotted" expression.

Terebinthina causes very great redness.

Antipyrine produces a measle-like, erythematous, scarlet eruption.

Arsenic causes redness and inflammation of the skin which is followed by desquamation.

Fuchsine, an aniline dye, induces redness and inflammation of the skin. Aniline dyed socks, stockings etc. have caused severe dermatitis and eczematous eruptions in hundreds of instances.

Nux vomica has more or less redness of the skin, with an eruption of papules like acne. There is a history of continuous alcoholic excess on the subjects calling for this remedy.

Calcarea carb. Red, elevated stripes appear on the skin over the tibia.

Kali bich. Redness of the surface in patches upon which papules and pustules form.

Dulcamara causes more or less general redness, but it is especially apt to take the form of urticaria.

Asclepias tuber., causes redness and inflammation of the skin over the entire body, with eruptions of papules, vesicles or pustules.

Silicea has a bluish redness of the skin in a wide margin around the border of ulceration.

ASAFŒTIDA.

"Fetty" has been a common household remedy for nervous and fidgety people for ages. If a person had a lump in the throat, acted silly, said foolish things and had a tendency to become hysterical the "Fetty pill" was brought out and given to her. It is not strange, therefore, that this remedy has been handed down to us as a nervous remedy and, under the proving, it sustains its reputation because it is so rich in nervous symptoms.

It is a deep-acting remedy and has a definite, well defined sphere of action. It acts through the cerebro-spinal nervous system. In some respects the clinical or cured symptoms have been of great value in determining the general scope of this remedy.

For example, the nervous manifestations following the suppression of mucous discharges, or the sudden healing of an ulcer by local means, will very frequently point to this remedy as the simillimum where the general indications for the remedy would have led to its selection without the nervous symptoms had the prescriber sufficiently accurate knowledge of its general scope of action to have studied its indications in the beginning of the case. The characteristic nervous symptoms are jerking, twitching of muscles, choking sensation—*globus hystericus*—a lump comes in the throat which is swallowed down and then returns immediately; palpitation of the heart, irregular pulsation aggravated by the slightest motion or the least exertion. Every emotion brings on this palpitation; epileptiform convulsions, chorea, fainting; the patient is so sensitive to pain that she faints. (Hepar). Many of the complaints for which this remedy is indicated have a paralytic tendency with weakness, numbness, tingling, pricking, twitching or jerking of the limbs.

It is generally supposed that there are no cardiac disturbances in pure hysteria. With the hysteria calling for Asafœtida the pulse is almost invariably weak and irregular; the patient is inclined to take a deep inspiration, because she has learned that this will restore the circulation and remove that feeling of faintness. Asafœtida is suitable for persons who look to be healthy and yet are easily disturbed by the slightest occasion. They are really sick, although many times they do not receive the sympathy to which they are justly entitled. One of the best differentiating points between true hysteria and the hysteria calling for Asafœtida is found in the characteristic disturbances.

Another general of this remedy is found in its tendency to attack the bones. The periosteum becomes inflamed, and the destructive influence extends to the bone with stitching, striking, tearing pains. These pains seem to begin in the shaft of the bone and extend outward; sticking, jagging pains, as if pieces of bone were sticking through the periosteum into the muscle. Another marked characteristic is found in the peculiar kind of bluish or purplish discoloration around the edge of ulcers. The face often has a sickly red or purplish appearance. This is due to the tendency of the destruction of tissue beginning in the center and working outward—deep seated ulcers—inflamed ulcers, ulcer, that have no tendency to the formation of granular or healthy tissue. The edges are elevated, hard, glossy, purplish, and the discharge is horribly offensive. The discharges, instead of being laudable pus, are really decomposed tissue that has been retained for a long time; putrid pus; putrid watery discharges from the nose, ears, or vagina; fistula etc.

The bones soften, and lose their calcareous deposits. In those constitutions calling for Asafetida we frequently find bony deformities, especially noticeable in the long bones and in the vertebræ. Asafœtida, therefore, overcomes this tendency and favors the deposit of lime salts.

Another general that will help to fix this remedy in your mind is activity at night. The mental symptoms are worse at night; the bone pains are worse at night, ulcers will start up and burn in the night etc.

Now, putting all these generals together we have a picture that closely resembles certain phases of syphilis—old syphilitic ulcers that have been too rapidly healed by local means when followed by excoriating pain and frightful, nervous manifestations, the Asafœtida will tend to re-establish the ulcer and thereby relieve the nervousness. Asafetida frequently acts as an antidote for the intense nervous symptoms following the administration of large doses of mercury, especially when bony structures are involved, or when it takes on the form of nervous manifestations instead of caries.

Another general characteristic of Asafetida is the tendency of complaints to return during rest. They drive the patient from bed, the ulcers are aggravated by the warmth of the bed, and he is forced to move. Asafœtida is one of the best indicated remedies in bone felon where the pains are aggravated by night, and the heat of the room compels the patient to seek the open air and walk until he almost drops from exhaustion. Has headache that is worse when lying down or sitting still. It compels him to walk incessantly, to seek the cool air.

You will see from the above that the mental symptom are not the leading features of this remedy; that they are always secondary, and have a sufficient cause for their manifestations, consequently you will never give Asafœtida for hysteria pure and simple.

Moschus.

Musk is another odorous substance having a powerful action upon the nervous system. Acting through the cerebro-spinal nervous system it stimulates three focal centers:

1. Motor.
2. Sexual.
3. Circulation.

There is a general state of excitement. Tremulous nervousness. Excited almost as if intoxicated—rapid pulse, slight feverishness, cerebral congestion, rapid, confused talking, pale face, easily startled, *fainting*, muscular twitching, tonic convulsions. Cries one moment, and bursts into uncontrollable laughter the next.

The most important indications from a nervous or hysterical standpoint are: Tendency to fainting or unconsciousness, with nervous attacks; coldness of the surface of the body; pale face when excited; suffocative paroxysms beginning in chest and rapidly extending to the larynx—spasm of the glottis; scolding until she falls unconscious.

In almost every case of hysteria, whether in man or woman calling for Moschus there will be found increased sexual desire, even though coition be followed by fainting or other nervous manifestations that make it seem impossible.

Ambra Grisea.

It is a fact worth noting that substances having a strong odor have a peculiar effect upon the nervous system. Ambergris is no exception to the rule. It acts through the cerebro-spinal nervous system with especial influence upon the spinal cord. It produces a sort of *hysterical hyperæsthesia* and seems to have as many indications for nervous men as women. It is because of this fact that we are comparing the remedy in this connection.

Reflex action is *increased*. There is *cramping* and *drawing* of muscles similar to what would be expected in spinal irritation—beginning in lumbar region and extending down legs. There is also marked susceptibility to *numbness* in both upper and lower extremities. A combination of tearing or drawing with paralysis in joint as if dislocated. These symptoms show the tendency of *functional* derangements to assume serious organic changes. It will therefore be indicated in nervous cases following a prolonged nervous strain with faulty nutrition. A slow or defective reaction follows efforts to recuperate. Ambra is a quick acting remedy and resembles *Psorinum* in some respects e. g., it is a morbid product of the whole, while Psorinum is a morbid product of the human family, and finds its best indications where there is a deep *constitutional* cause for the defective reaction.

In the mental sphere, Ambra is indicated where there is great bashfulness, timidity or easily embarrassed in the presence of strangers—almost impossible to urinate or have an evacuation from the bowels. Cough is worse from nervous excitement. There is discharge of menstrual blood between menstrual periods from any accident. There is hastiness of speech when talking. Slow comprehension. Cannot sleep at night—worries over inability to grasp ideas; anxious, troubled dreams and wakens in the morning more tired than on going to bed. *Nux vomica* has greater *irritability*.

The following peculiar applications

will be better understood when studied in connection with the remedies appearing in parenthesis.

Faintness—hysterical asthma(*Moschus*)

Defective reaction (*Asafet.*, *Castor*, *Psor.*, *Valer.*)

Bashfulness (*Coca.*)

Increased reflexes (*Kali br.* and *Nux vom.*)

Coldness in abdomen (*Calc. c.* and *Nat. c.*).

Thin, nervous people (*Nux vom.*).

Flow of blood between menstrual periods (*Bovista*).

Bad effects from over lifting (*Lach.*, *Sep.*).

Valeriana Officinalis.

The use of valerian as a "nervine" dates back almost as far as that of *Asafetida* and both remedies have been given indiscriminately for *hysteria* regardless of the causes that may have contributed to the peculiar mental symptoms.

Valerian is a typical "hysterical" remedy, but finds its best indications in those cases when the *intellectual* faculties predominate. It acts through the cerebro-spinal nervous system with the focal point directed to the centers of *special* senses.

There is a mental exhilaration with a great flow of ideas—a sort of joyfulness somewhat resembling the action of coffee. The patient seems "keyed up" and must talk incessantly. With this is a physical weakness or trementous restlessness which makes it impossible to sit or stand still. This feeling of expectancy may be likened to that of looking forward to a pleasant event with impatient longings. The effects are very similar. There is general weariness, especially in the extremities, with feelings of vague discomfort in various portions of the body.

In *true* hysteria we naturally look for disturbances in the *sexual* sphere. With the cat it seems to produce great *sexual excitement*, but it is a question whether this be not due to a stimulation of the sense of smell by the similarity of the odor of valerian to that of an erotic feline instead of any *primary* stimulation of the *sexual* center. Be the facts as they may from a clinical standpoint, Valerian has quickly controlled the mental excitability of women who have become hypersensitive and hysterical through delay in the coming of their lover, without the prostration that otherwise would follow.

Where the action is carried to the extreme there will be hallucinations in which the patient will fancy that he is not able to see, or that the walls of the room are enveloped in flames which seem to shoot out from his eyes—flashes of lightning seem to fall from the eyes. There is an exaggeration of the sense of hearing, smell, taste and touch, dependent somewhat upon previous *susceptibility*—those parts that have demanded greatest mental thought in the past becoming especially noticeable under the action of this drug.

It can be seen at a glance that the class of patients needing Valerian are those neurasthenics who are especially susceptible to mental exhilaration and whose suffering *follows* and generally affects the most vulnerable part.

There are characteristic motor disturbances due to the direct action upon the motor tract of the spinal cord—superficial jerking and twitching in various muscles throughout the body. Associated with this may be *drawing pains in many places like transient jerks.* The motor and sensory disturbances are generally *aggravated by trying to sit or stand still.*

Naturally with marked mental exhilaration in a neurasthenic patient there will be a corresponding disturbance of the brain and we will find a form of giddiness with a sensation as if *floating in the air*.

This hypersensitiveness is expressed in the peculiar hallucinations, disturbed vision, earache from exposure to *drafts and cold*, and sensation as if *a thread hung down the throat causing nausea.*

It is a specific for hysterical flatulency.

Nux moschata.

It is hardly proper to look upon nutmeg as belonging to the group of so-called "hysterical remedies" because it has a deeper action and is capable of producing profound disturbances, but many forms of disease are diagnosed as "hysteria" because the symptoms resemble in a measure those usually found associated with that form of disease manifestations.

Nux Moschata has a paralyzing effect upon the cerebro-spinal nervous system. Secretions throughout the body are arrested or suppressed and many of the socalled hysterical symptoms are attributed to that cause.

There is a peculiar mental state varying from absent minded to bewilderment—a feeling of strangeness—sleepiness and finally stupor. The mental state is vacillating—laughing immoderately—seems foolishly happy and then suddenly changes to sadness with loud weeping. This in turn may give place to an expression of stupidity.

There is a marked tendency to *fainting* with seeming heart failure—cold extremities and extreme *dryness of the mucous membrane*. Mouth is especially dry—tongue cleaves to the roof of the mouth.

H. W. Pierson.

IS THERE ANY VALUE IN MEDICINE?

Feb. 11, 1902. Mr. G. W., a man of 48 years, a German by birth, presented himself at the office, with a severe cough. He had been treated on these occasions previously, once receiving *Belladonna* for a peculiar headache "which took his thoughts so completely his mind seemed a blank and he could not answer questions." The second time he was suffering from a severe exacerbation of a peculiar affection of the diaphragm. He had evidently strained this muscle years ago in heavy lifting and reaching, and reported that every occasion of using the left arm for heavy work, since, was followed by a return of the lameness. *Nux vomica* seemed to master this quite promptly. The third time be had received *Mercurius sol.* for an attack of diarrhoea with bleeding hemorrhoids and perspiration.

At this date the following is gleaned:

Cough—rattling—has coughed much all winter, but has given no attention to it.

Has been < since going out in cold air after talking, in warm room.

< after being in wind, < night, > after midnight.

< lying right side, last night < lying on left side also.

< going in warm room from cold air; sore inside from coughing.

Expectoration thick lumps, dark.

Chest pain in line of trachea; burning, soreness, oppression on chest as if not room enough inside; lower chest feels sensitive to touch.

Right side < lying on right side, last night also on left side, twinging.

Larynx pain on talking—tickling in larynx.

> open air, cough >.

> keeping quiet.

< toward evening.

Sleeps usually < lying on left side.

Headache, scalp sensitive to touch.

Pain from cough.

Sneezing continues for awhile this morning.

Nose discharge thin, now—stuffy in doors, fluent in open air, smell is lost.

He reported having had two severe spells of pneumonia years ago, when his life was despaired of, (18 weeks one time) after that was sent to the country to strengthen his lungs and recover from malaria. Has lived in the country for seventeen years and has been much better there.

Sulphur^{cm}

Feb. 15.

Cough < first night after last report, second night *free*, rested well. Last night cough <lying on back, > lying on sides.

< in open air, > in warm room yesterday.

Whistling cough and respiration without expectoration, night.

Loose, rattling, today.

Expectoration now *free*—yellow, thick.

Chest oppression in lower portion, as if not enough room, breath seems cut off. Pinching pains have gone.

Head pain along sides in streaks.

Nose discharge >. Stuffy toward evening.

Back cold, wants heat applied.

Perspiration in bed last evening.

Sulphur^{cm} cont.

Feb. 20.

Jaw, left side sudden pain on 15th, extended though cheek, swollen 16th, > on 17th, swelling the left jaw, but appeared on right side of neck as a lump in throat, tonsil swollen 17th, with pain on swallowing.

Tired, unable to sit up on 17th. Inclination to lie down, tired even while lying, < sitting. Feels concerned because he is so languid, like malaria fatigue.

Cough, absent during pain in jaw and neck, returned when that was >.

Last night as bad as any time, with pain in chest.

From tickling in chest—lower end of sternum.

Whistling; rattling, moist.

Expectoration not so free last night, less yellow.

Perspiration from coughing.

Rectum—for eight to ten years, bleeding after stool—some stools of blood only—blood dark, free.

Before stool pain in lower abdomen.

During and after stool tenesmus.

Stool gushing at times— < after constipation if misses one day—bleeding < exposure to cold—< in cold weather.

< fat food: Rectal bleeding. < souer kraut; burning in stomach.

Malaria 20 years ago. Chills, first quartan, then tertain, then quotidian; shaking, morning and evening; spring to August. 8 to 9 a. m.

Fever after chill, with loquacious delirium.

Aching in bones.

During heat—headache; thirst, but water tasted bitter.

Chills ceased after drinking pint or more of clear raspberry juice: one chill up the back, stopped short and no more followed.

Cough came on after chills ceased—and after cough ceased chills returned in the spring.

> open air.

Sulphur^{cm} cont.

Feb. 22.

Cough bad all night, > after 3 a. m., perspiration during cough and in open air, although it is cold weather.

< Indoors.

Expectoration tight, difficult at night, freer in day time.

Chest, pain all through lower chest, heavy, choked, fullness.

Pain in right side on inspiration.

Head pain all through; hammering on left side during night.

< frontal.

< evening.

Looks very bad. Feels so bad it reminds him of the pneumonia siege, has never felt like this since then. Friends warn him that he has a consumptive cough.

As he sits in the office, time is taken to study the case with the repertory (that indispensable volume of Kent).

Cough lying down.
< evening.
> open air.
Perspiration from cough.
Perspiration in open air, in cold air.
Perspiration at night profuse.
} Generals first

Chest pain during deep respiration, on inspiration.

—— oppression.

—— constriction.

Respiration impeded, whistling.

Cough, entering a warm room.

—— whistling.

Inclination to lie down.

This brings the choice to one from *Bryonia*, *Sulphur*, *Lycopodium*, *Arsenicum*. Of these *Bryonia* alone is given under both *respiration in open air* and respiration in cold air, second degree in one and the highest degree in other. Further consideration determines that this covers the nature of the case throughout.

Bryonia 1m

Now comes the interesting part of the whole case. In four days he reported, "feeling good, am all right" and three days later said he was the only one of the family that was not tired. This man is one given to thinking and reasoning. He had experienced and witnessed a great deal of treatment by old school physicians and had come to the conclusion that the practice of medicine is all fraud and foolishness. He had determined to dispense entirely with any sort of medication for himself. After this experience he concludes there is some sort sort of medication of which he had known nothing before. He knew that he had been restored from a serious condition to one exceeding in health anything he had felt for years and that in a very brief time and under the influence of carefully selected medicine. He was given a copy of lectures on Homœopathic philosophy to read and found it consistent with his reasonable mind, and welcomed Homœopathy as a rational exposition of disease and method of cure.

The action of the medicine administered is interesting. *Sulphur* relieved the most recent cough etc., and at once instigated a general reaction in the system expressed for a while by symptoms that came and went and finally by a return of the old symptoms of pneumonia, results of which had never been fully eradicated during twenty-five years. The remedy which would have cured him then failed not when the system was turned into order and the old condition came to the surface. The *curative remedy* is irresistible when applied to the disordered system.

Julia C. Loos.

Harrisburg, Pa.

O SEPIA! THY NAME IS WOMAN.

[The man who can paint such a word-picture of the therapeutic action of remedies, should be compelled to write for the benefit of the profession.—ED.]

Wherever man, studying his kind with the keen instinct and self sacrificing industry of a student and benefactor, seeks to find a prototype or analogue in the wide field of Materia Medica, he opens up a mine rich and bewildering in the complexity of its elements, but eminently encouraging and helpful in its ultimate results. And when he divides the medical material for more careful and systematic study into three general groups, as, e.g., male, female, and common or neuter, he secures a somewhat cosmopolitan, but none the less characteristic, picture of each member subject to such investigation.

The distinguished member of the medical family selected for a brief biographical sketch, though presenting great similarity to many other drug-histories, stands out clearly and unassailable in its own special field. And as we become better acquainted and seek to classify it we unhesitatingly exclaim, *O Sepia! Thy name is woman!* Woman is written in her delicate, refined, hypersensitive organization; in her sad, tearful, irritable, contradictory moods; in her peevish and unwarranted fits of anger; in her restless, anxious, dissatisfied deportment. And especially in the disturbances peculiar to the female do we find *Sepia succus* proclaiming her womanhood. If other evidence were needed to establish her sex, one has but to recognize that element of superiority in which she stands pre-eminently above man, the ability to scold and heartily enjoy it.

Though a woman, she is by no means a Venus; neither has she the Godlike qualities of a Dorcas; and she is painfully deficient in those voluptuous and captivating characteristics that gave Cleopatra her power and her irresistible fascination. Notwithstanding these facts—conditions bequeathed her by her progenitors—*Sepia* reigns like a royal polychrest, proudly supreme in her own bailiwick. In her veins flows the dusky pigment of her ancestors. The blood of the cuttle-fish cannot be ignored.

Sepia is often ill, and her morbid imagination can supply any deficiency. It is not safe to make light of her complaints. She has mental strabismus.

When the physician is summoned to attend this lineal descendant of the "ink-bag" family, and smilingly approaches the couch upon which the patient languidly reclines, he sees a dark-haired, delicate, erethistic individual, usually of the feminine gender. When of the male sex his general characteristics are as essentially female as it is possible for them to be.

The doctor's olfactory sense need not be highly developed to detect an offensive odor emanating from his patient. The slight exertion she makes to be civil causes hot flushes to tint a cheek of questionable attractiveness. Her flesh is usually puffy and flabby, though an anæmic or jaundiced appearance is not uncommon.

Surrounding, and sympathizing with this invalid who "enjoys poor health," are several of her intimate friends, so much like her in many ways and yet so dissimilar: *Lil. tig.*, *Puls.*, *Murex*, *Act. rac.*, *Nat. mur.*, *Helonias*, *Sulphur* and others. As the physician grasps the patient's hand it feels cold and lifeless, though her feet are hot. At a subsequent visit her hands are feverishly hot and feet are cold. Her beauty is not enhanced by a yellowish discoloration across the upper part of her cheeks and nose. Her skin, though fine and thin, is often a dirty-yellow, blotched and disfigured. She seems so mentally depressed and apathetic that her sanity is not infrequently questioned; in fact, members of her family find it convenient to board in institutions for the insane. If one desires to present a first-class exhibition of hysteria, a word or act suggestion antagonism to her wishes may quickly develop it, or, what is infinitely worse, a family brawl. Notwithstanding she is so morbidly solicitous about her own health she is wholly indifferent to her household affairs, and even has an aversion to those nearest and dearest.

This marked indifference is so glaringly conspicuous that it seems to be the dominant factor in her life and tends to estrange her from her family and from active participation in the affairs of life. Her individual troubles always rule supreme. And whatever the nature of her disorder, morning and evening aggravation is generally noticeable.

Disturbed circulation is the bane of her existence and manifests itself through her whole economy. The portal and the female sexual system suffer most keenly. The chief local expression is upon the genito-urinary organs, the mucous membrane, and the skin. Disturbed circulation is seen in the intense, throbbing headache, often of a neuralgic character; in the sudden flushes of heat; in the attacks of vertigo; in palpitation of the heart; in the skin eruptions; in the engorged or hypertrophied mucosa; in the hepatic, abdominal and abominable pelvic derangements; in the painful, bleeding hæmorrholds; in her frequent and long-lasting calls to urinate, and in the marked and contradictory mental state. The chamber-maid informs you that madam's urine is thick and very offensive, and that it requires much elbow-grease to remove a clayey decoration from the sacred walls of the urinary containant. "When in the course of human events it becomes necessary" to attend other vulgar demands of nature, and the subjects of our sketch condescends to recognize its necessity, she is prone to deposit a sample of fæcal matter resembling the evacuation expelled by Mary's historical little lamb, or some other member of the sheep family.

To illustrate the ingenuity of this remarkable woman, and at the same time appreciate the pernicious activity of her sexual organism, one has but to observe how she improvises an external pessary by crossing her legs and squeezing them together to keep the contents of her pelvis or abdomen from masquerading in public. And when that dreaded function—menstruation—presumes to assert itself, her restless, melancholy state is so pronounced—until the flood-gates are open and the flow becomes free—that little or no freedom or comfort abides in that house for man or beast.

Whether matrimonial matches are made in heaven or not is a controverted question, but there can be no doubt regarding nature's intention for Lady Sepia. One has but to pass the hands over her skin to recognize her as foreordained to consort with some old gander, the "goose-flesh" skin standing up in beautiful geometrical array.

A suspicious morning nausea is not infrequent with *Sepia*, and if she has not passed that welcome age when the female is supposed to be immune she knows infection has occured. But wait until she has eaten a good breakfast, when the delusion is happily dispelled.

Anyone who is so unfortunate as to occupy a sleeping apartment with her, may rest assured that no rest or sleep will come to them after 3 o'clock in the morning.

She is so exquisitely sensitive to music that even the perfect and ravishing harmonies of an Orpheus throw her nerves into a family quarrel, and her various complaints—real or imaginary—are correspondingly aggravated. But, when the exquilibrium of the elements about her are disturbed, so that the earth trembles under the shock and glare of the heavenly artillery, she is greatly improved and fairly revels in an ecstacy of delight. This contradictory element of her nature is still further shown in the capricious appetite; it is usually excessive and never satisfied, but at times she manifests great aversion to food.

Though unwilling to cast reflections upon this dusky child of the deep, her reflex symptoms cause many an organ —near and remote—to groan under the tyranny of her despotic sway, and many a deluded follower of Æsculapius to pull out the wrong feather.

These very elements that constitute *Sepia* a woman; that stamp her as unique and peculiar; that make her, in many respects an undesirable companion, are the very expressions of disorder that so often confront the physician in the practice of his profession, whether a general practice or a specialist.

While *Sepia* is frequently indicated in diseases of the eye, ear, nose and throat, it was not the purpose of this pathogenic biography to present an exhaustive treatise for its exhibition in detail, but rather a general picture that shall assist the prescriber in utilizing the vast array of special indications, particularly when divorced from their context.

Whenever *Sepia* seems homœopathic to a given case, the degree of its success will depend largely upon its similarity to the general picture of the drug. And failure to secure expected results is not infrequently due to a non-realization of this vital fact. While this may be true of all of our remedies, it is especially so of *Sepia*. She is jealous of her rights, pardonably so. She cannot work well hitched to or with another. What she does must be done alone and in her own way. Associated with another she becomes a nonenity, or a disturber. Alone, free, and undefiled, she stands a beacon light on the tempest-washed shore of suffering humanity.

A few special indications in a general way will close this sketch of *Sepia*.

Though often indicated in ophthalmic disorders, it is in those cases depending upon disturbances in the female sexual system that it is effective. In blepharitis ciliaris it is an invaluable remedy. Also, in conjunctivitis occurring during warm weather, especially in strumous children, and when ameliorated by cold applications. Many cases of eyestrain, depending upon abuse of the eyes, secure relief from *Sepia*. Its reputation for arresting cataract in woman cannot be successfully assailed.

It should be thought of in aural affections when intolerent of loud noise or music. Also, when otalgia and toothache are associated, chiefly, however, in pregnancy. In eruptions upon or back of the ear, occurring in the *Sepia* patient it will promptly demonstrate its curative power.

It should be used in atrophic nasal catarrh, when dry crusts, yellow or greenish and often offensive, take up their abode in the nose or postnares. The nostrils may be inflamed, swollen and ulcerated.

Aphoria reflex from uterine disorders is not uncommon.

Remember, that *Sepia* is a great *finishing remedy*. When other medicines seem to have exhausted their usefulness, and the patient is not yet fully restored, *Sepia* gallantly comes to the rescue.

C. H. HUBBARD, M. D.

Chester, Pa.

THE PATHOLOGY OF ARNICA.

The pathology of a bruise is that of lacerated hyperæmic tissue. Tire, muscular and nervous, approaches it in a mild way. After a long walk or ride, where the muscles have been severely alternately contracted and relaxed, the tire, or soreness lasts a long time. The nerves are sore along their sheathes, and the muscle and its envelopes are tender to the touch. Go farther and the muscles become contractured and helpless! Walking can be continued until the person drops from lack of nerve and muscular power to "lift one leg before the other." The muscle is full of post organic matter, and the spine is weak from the surcharged blood. If there is an undue amount of blood about the cord the pressure constricts the cord and renders it helpless. The nerves of sensation are sore, while the motors refuse to work. They cannot.

A bruise is the same pathology in a more emphatic way. About the cord the blood vessels are dilated, and remain so. The same is true of the capillaries in the muscles. That is trauma. Like varicose veins, this condition may persist for years.

Arnica starts the heart until the capillary dilation is persistent. There is a sense of tire in the tissues of the cord, and that is the reason that Arnica, in its effect, is similar to a bruise. Its clinical effect proves that this similarity of pathology as well as symptoms may be reliable guides for its selection.

T. C. DUNCAN.

Medicine.

MIGRAINE.*

This is a neurosis characterized by a nervous disturbance occuring in paroxysms, at more or less irregular intervals, and of varying duration. The chief disturbance is headache, it is usually unilateral, but not always, and is frequently accompanied by nausea and vomiting, mental depression, vaso motor distubrance, flashes of light, tinitus aurum, vertigo and rarely by ocular paralysis.

It has been termed hemicrania, migrau, or sick headache, blind headache and bilious headache.

This disease is much more frequent in women than in men. It may begin at almost any age, even as early as two years of age, will continue at more or less regular intervals for any number of years and disappear.

The one great and all important factor in its etiology, that must never be overlooked in a single case, is that it is always the result primarily of a *neural* dyscrasia. That is, the patient is born with special predisposition to nerve trouble. Heredity, not at all necessarily direct, but as frequently indirect, is always present.

There are many conditions that may be immediate causes, or may help to determine this special neurosis instead of some other in the predisposed patient. Exhausting diseases of any character, poor feeding, or poor nourishing from any cause, over work, more especially mental, long continued sorrow or grief or very severe emotional shocks, long lasting worry of any kind, the "worry habit." Then there are physical immediate causes in any of the socalled sources of reflex disturbance. It is very

* Read before Illinois Homœopathic Association by N. B. Delamater, M. D.

rare to find a case of migraine in which there is not some ocular defect. There may be nasal or throat trouble of some form, or ear trouble. The genito urinary tract and the rectum are also frequently immediate exciting causes. Stomach and digestive disturbances are much more frequently *results* of this condition than causes.

Defective elimination is a source of trouble that in migraine is of great importance. In every case a full complete quantitative analysis of the 24 hours urine should be made.

It is hardly necessary to give here any outline of the sypmtoms farther than to call attention to the fact that these headaches are irregularly periodic, sometimes very regularly so. Many patients can tell the day and hour that an attack will appear. They nearly always run the same general course in each attack, lasting about the same length of time. Are usually unilateral, they attack the same region every time, or they may alternate between the two sides of the head or commence on one side and travel to the opposite side.

Treatment.

In the treatment the very first consideration is the putting of the patient in such condition as to render a cure possible. This means, first, the immediate removal of all possible sources of irritation of whatever kind or character. It means, as indicated above, the thorough and complete analysis of the 24 hours urine and the regulations of the excretions.

It has been my good fortune to see many cases recover from attention to this line of work in the treatment. There are many cases in which chronic uremic poisoning of some character is present, and in which there is nothing needed beyond full diminuation of these salts.

The nutrition is the next essential item to be considered and corrected. It must not be forgotten that worries, overwork and like causes must be removed so far as possible. After all these things have been attended to carefully and thoroughly, the real work for permanent cure begins. In those cases, and there are many of them, in which it is impossible to find any etiology other than the neural discrasia, of course the curative measures must begin at once.

This element in the treatment is exceedingly difficult to put on paper. The collation of a very large number of cases and results shows a very large percentage of cures by homœopathic physicians, and a very small percentage by the regulars.

There are two principal reasons for this, first, the "regular" as a rule depends almost entirely on immediate treatment for the individual attack, paying almost no attention, except possibly in regulating the diet somewhat, to the patient between attacks; while the physicians of our school pay most attention to treatment *between* the attacks. That is, we endeavor to prevent the attacks from appearing. We place the emphasis in treatment on the fundamental condition that is at the very bottom of the trouble, and undertake to remove. Then we have a clearly defined scientific method of reaching this dyscrasia, while the regulars have not.

Selection of Remedy.

The selection of the remedy will require time, patience and the most careful study. The physician who has the very best practical knowledge of Materia Medica will get by all odds the best results. I have many times been surprised at the results obtained by men who had no scientific attainments at all, but who did know their materia medica.

If you will take the time, care and study necessary to the affiliation of your remedy you will be more than paid.

You will never regret the hours spent in the study of your materia medica on these cases.

In this study you must bear in mind one thing. It is the patient that must be prescribed for, and not the attacks. To be sure you will necessarily take into consideration the special peculiarities or symptoms of the attacks, but only as aids in the selection of the remedy for the patient's individuality. It is a dyscrasia that must be removed, that must be corrected.

You must then know and consider the special hereditary influences that have come to your patient, then all the environments and modifying influences to which he has been subjected. The individual peculiar characteristics, mental or physical of the individual must also be met in the remedy.

The aggravations and ameliorations, in fact all that goes to make that particular individual mentally, emotionally or physically different from every other individual, must be considered in the selection of the remedy.

For instance the patient has a heredity of what had been termed scrofula or of dissipation from the use of liquor.

Has dark hair and a general tendency to rigid fiber, combined with a mild easy disposition.

Catches cold with the least change in the weather.

Rather inclined to indolence and indifference.

A tendency to sadness without adequate cause, many forbodings about the future.

A very sensitive nervous organism.

Frequent attacks of throbbing of the teeth.

Gums show a tendency to bleed easily.

Sudden craving for food and as sudden satiety.

Frequent sensations about the liver of various kinds, with a general bilious appearance.

Chronic constipation, excessive unsatisfied sexual passion, or excessive venery.

A heart that is easily influenced by emotions.

The pulsations in the head are worse when at rest, and a bursting headache, better when stooping.

There is morning depression, inclined to chilliness very early say from 3 to 6 a. m., with flushes of heat from 8 to 10 a. m.

Attacks come with great regularity. You will at once recognize that is a *Sepia* patient, and a careful analysis of the symptoms during the attack will show that this remedy also covers the totality of the attacks. If you use this method of fitting your remedy you will get results that will satisfy you fully.

In this paper I do not purpose to indicate *palliative* treatment, but simply to draw attention to the *curative*. So far as my own experience is concerned I have the most prompt and permanent results by using the 30th to the 200th potency in migraines.

A FEW THOUGHTS ON BELLADONNA AND SCARLET FEVER.*

That we are in danger of falling into routine prescribing, we are aware of, I dare say, and often to our sorrow and discomfiture.

During the spring of 1901, we had a great many cases of scarlet fever in East Des Moines and adjoining country. It was not severe; it was that red, smooth variety, with considerable of throat complication. For many weeks, cases after cases would fall into my hands, and so general was the rapid and complete re-

*Paper read before the Thirty-third Annual Session of the Hahnemann Association of Iowa.

covery under Belladonna 6x, that many adherents of the dominant school would call at my office and ask for that scarlet fever remedy I was giving Neighbor So and So. I would give Belladonna 6x, with proper instructions as to the care of the patient, to look out for the kidneys, etc., with the uniform result that they all recovered in a remarkably short time, and my fame extended a long way into the country as "The doctor who knows how to cure scarlet fever."

Whilst it is true that Belladonna will cure nearly every case in certain epidemics, it is also true that it will fail. I was not long in finding that out, as some time during the latter part of May, 1901, one of our well-to-do farmers drove up and said they had scarlet fever at his house, some ten miles out. They had had a doctor from a nearby town, who came twice daily to see the only child that was sick there. He was a bright and clever fellow of the dominant school, but somehow did not seem to get along with the case to suit the parents, so they came and asked me to send some of my remarkable remedy, with the parting words, "Will you come doctor, if we send for you?" Twenty-four hours passed, and no word from them. "Well," said I to myself, "Belladonna has again hit the case," but I was not long to rejoice. Twelve hours later, a telephone message said "Come as soon as possible." On arriving, I found case number 1 had nearly recovered and was doing nicely; but an elder sister, 9 years of age, was very sick, with high fever, sore throat, etc. As all the indications pointed to Belladonna, I gave it; found her better next day, but another sister, 5 years of age, had been taken sick meanwhile, though I had given her and a baby brother Belladonna as a prophylaxis. She got very sick under Belladonna, until the condition changed and *Rhus tox.* and *Apis mell.* were given, as the indication seemed to show. The 9-year-old seemed to do nicely on Belladonna, but this one got worse on my hands. I took my friend, Dr. Linn, out with me, and we concluded that I had better stay there all night, as the case was critical, and the kidneys were not acting well. The temperature at 6:00 p. m. was 105 2 10; at 7:00, 107; at 8:00, 107 8-10; at 9:00, 109; at 10:00, 109½. That was the last test, as the little sufferer passed quietly to her eternal rest at 11:10 p. m. Had I not taken the temperature myself with a good instrument, I would not have believed that such heat could be reached.

The 9 year-old, during the funeral of her sister, took a relapse. With the advice of the grand-parents, a change of doctors was made, but with the promise that I should return if called. That was Friday morning. On Sunday morning following, I was called to come at once and bring another doctor with me. My colleague, Dr. Holloway, accompanied me. We got there about 9:00 a. m. Found that not a drop of urine had been voided for 36 hours, and the case did not look inviting nor promising. After due deliberation, we prescribed *Digitalis.* She was then taking seven different kinds of drugs. Dr. Holloway gave me the good advice to stay with the patient, though we had a good, Homœopathic nurse who followed our directions well, with applications of warm water to the kidneys and over the bladder, and the remedy given often. At 1:00 p. m., or four hours after we again took the case, we were rewarded with a dram of urine, what the seven drugs had failed to do in 36 hours. At 4:00 p. m. we again obtained an ounce, and from that on the case made an uneventful recovery. The baby a year old entirely escaped.

Someone has said "That we learn more by our failures than by our successes."

I have learned never to call a case of scarlet fever not dangerous, but always warn the parents of the danger of complications, especially of the kidneys. I have learned to seldom send medicine without seeing the patient, when I am morally certain that it is scarlet fever or even scarlatina. I have learned that Belladonna will not cure every case of scarlet fever, even when it seems to be the indicated remedy; in that case, I have learned to change the potency, often with marked results. Although the 6x has, perhaps, given me the most satisfaction in my practice, though I have used it, and may again, from the 2x to the 500th potency. I always give Belladonna to the other children should there be any in the family, with good results, generally making the disease of a light form, and many entirely escaping it. That Belladonna will cure and prevent scarlet fever more than any drug known, there is no doubt in my mind, especially if we could always tell how sensitive our patient is to the drug, so we could give the high potency. I have no doubt we would make scarlet fever mortality very low, and the sequelæ comparatively nil.

As this paper is for the Bureau of Clinical Medicine, and on scarlet fever, it would be out of place and tiresome to the Association for me to expand the virtues of Belladonna as used by the true Homœopath. But I will say, use it in scarlet fever, not too low, especially in children, and more especially in those blonde, blue-eyed youngsters, who are, as a rule, very sensitive to the effect of the drug.

C. J. Loizeaux.

A MITE OF PHILOSOPHY.

He who builds his house upon sand must expect destruction when the storms come.

In medicine, particularly, it is imperative that a solid mental foundation be laid for the massive superstructure that should follow.

If our premises are right, our conclusions, if conducted by a proper process of reasoning, must be right also; if the premises are wrong, no process of reasoning will place one mentally in a sure and safe position. It is because of false premises that so many notions of cure exist, and for the same reason religious sectarianism is abroad in the land.

In the realm of medicine, with the many pathys, some one must necessarily be in error, for on matters so divergent as theory of diseases and their cure, as exist among physicians to day, some one or more than one must be in error; all cannot be right, nor can that accumulation of "good from all sources" be recommended as worthy the attention of a thinking or sound mind.

If disease is due to morbific substances in the human system, and to pathological changes in life, and to that only, as some teach; if *all* deviations from health or a normal condition of the functions of the body is due to the operations of micropic infection, they who turn their attention to the correction of these disturbances by morbific processess or the destruction of germs by massive doses of some material substance, by mouth rectum, or subcutaneously, are in the right and should and must succeed, and all opinions to the contrary must waive further right to recognition and a professional standing, and turn to the one only way, or suffer the stigma of being wrong and too ignorant to detect it. But is this correct? Let us see.

In the science of medicine there should be no "*pathy*," for that is sectarian, and sectarian means diminution of power. It is contrary to the spirit of this and all ages where, "in union there is strength." We say we are Homœopaths and homœopathy teaches us so and so. Thanks, a thousand times, to homœopathy for bringing unto us the *true* science of medicine. While our school is justly named homœopathic and our manner of practice and remedies used are styled homœopathic, still we are not, as some would have us be, a sect, and as such justly despised.

Homœopathy is *the* science of medicine, pure and simple, and represents, so far as man has been able to learn, the only rational method of curing disease. This is because homœopathy is based upon the impregnable rock of truth, and its doctrines and practices follow in logical order.

Let us ask: What do we understand by the term medicine in its broadest sense? By medicine we mean a *correct* knowledge of disease, its cause and cure.

What then is disease? It is a disturbance of the vital forces, impairing their functions, or the functions of certain organs or systems controlled by these forces, sometimes causing pathological changes, pain, deformity and death. This disturbance of the vital forces of health, indeed of life itself, is known by certain sensations called symptoms, and to certain aggregation of symptoms we give certain names which are known as certain diseases.

Suppose you were to see a man who began to yawn, he complains of debility and distress in the abdomen; he is weak, languid, listless, he begins to stretch, feels chilly, cold chills run up and down his spine; the blood deserts the superficial capillaries; he grows pale, his features shrink; he soon begins to shake, and in spite of his most urgent endeavor to keep quiet, he shakes until his teeth chatter, his knees strike together, and his back and limbs ache so severely that he feels as if he were being unjointed. His finger nails turn blue, his urine is diminished, his tongue is dry and white, his pulse is frequent but weak. This soon ceases and is followed by heat, first a gentle warmth, with or without thirst, and in 2 or 8 hours there may be a raging fever with delirium, which is followed in two or three hours more by another stage known as the "sweating" stage, after which the man feels about as well as usual. These brief symptoms show a peculiar condition known as ague. Ague or intermittent fever is the *name* given to these symptoms, but as the symptoms of intermittent fever vary so much in different individuals, in different countries and in different seasons of the year, you see at once how utterly futile it would be to say that, one remedy cured intermittent in Mr. Jones, in the spring of the year in Ohio, that it would also cure Mr. Smith in the fall of the year in Texas, when Mr. Jones had a severe chill with but little fever, and Mr. Smith had a light chill and severe fever.

But here is another case. A man says he is not sick, but every afternoon about four o'clock, he feels tired, languid and "mean," there is a slight tendency to bloating of the abdomen, he feels worse when he is warm or at rest, a glass of wine or a buggy ride would upset his feelings; he is one of those sensitive individuals that everything hurts and this is about all you can make out of his case. What is the trouble here? Can you name the disease? and yet we meet such almost daily in our practice, and find symptoms for which it would be difficult to find a name.

But no matter what the *name* of the disease may be, it is the result of abnormal or subnormal conditions affecting one's health, even life, changing the individual from a happy to a morose man, an affable to an irritable man, a sane man to an insane one, a painless condition of the body to a painful one, from health to sickness, from life to death: and the degree and nature of the symptoms which this disturbance produces, whether mental or physical, determines the name of the disease, as to whether it is simply melancholia or mania, a slight indigestion or severe gastritis, whether it is a mere eruption of the skin or the dreadful small-pox, whether it is simply a benign growth or the deadly cancer, no matter what nomenclature this disturbance may have appropriated to itself, it is the result of impeded vitality which is due to a sycotic, psoric, syphilitic or tubercular miasm, and in this impediment or disturbance, invisible, untangible and to some extent incomprehensible, we find the true germ of disease and the elements of death.

And, though some conditions are due to morbific agencies or micropic infection, to turn one's attention to these agencies as the sole cause of disease is misleading and results in the most faulty and often times fatal therapeutics.

Disease is a disturbance of life, an injury to the individual himself as well as his several physical parts, it is a sickness of the ego, and in many chronic forms as well as some acute attacks no satisfactory cause can be found. Why, then, in the study of so grave a subject as disease, do not men endeavor to search deeper into the mysteries of physical and psychical life for the source of some of the afflictions of mankind?

This is just what is being done today in colleges where the Organon gets the place it deserves in the curriculum of studies. As well might a physician of any "pathy" attempt to understand the true nature of disease without a knowledge of the Organon as for a clergyman to understand the true nature and efficacy of religion without a knowledge of the Bible.

It is only by a continuous study of disease as a disturbed vital principle; the peculiar nature of the signs or symptoms by which this disturbance is made known, and the agencies or remedies that will and do produce similar signs or disturbances that we get a glimpse of the magnitude of our calling as physicians and surgeons and a conception of the means an omniscient Creator has placed in our hands as curative agents.

Man is a Divine thought; disease, physical, mental or moral has impaired this divinity and man has become subject to pain, distress, discomfort, anxiety and death; but He who has created all things and holds sovereign control over matter and spirit has revealed to man the various means of relief from those distresses, and this is done by overcoming one force by another—not morbific but dynamic—by driving out—not suppressing—that element or miasm that has disturbed one's health, by a similar but stronger force—and anything short of this is irrational, unscientific, and when carried to the extremes, as is done by some prescribers, it is heathernish—barbarous.

G. E. Dienst.

Naperville, Ill.

A PECULIAR DISEASE.

Sometimes called "Black fever," "Spotted fever" or "Blue disease" by the laity in the country in which it is prevalent. This malady is an acute, febrile, non-contagious affection. It is characterized by an eruption of macules, which are first pink, afterwards gradually assuming a purplish or dark bluish color. It has been prevalent in the Bitter Root Valley in Western Montana since 1886.

Cause. This is a question that has excited much comment; all kinds of theories have been advanced by the various physicians in the valley, but none of them have been very convincing.

Time. Shows a casual relation as is manifested by the fact that the disease occurs in the months of April, May and June, the west side of the valley being most affected, in fact ninety per cent of the cases arise on that side, and extend into Idaho.

Age, sex and amount of vitality play but little part in causation. Fully ninety percent of the cases give a history of having been exposed to wet and cold, one to three days prior to the attack. Some claim the water is the cause, as in nearly every case a history of ingestion of the murky water coming down the mountain side, carrying with it decaying vegetation and other impurities is given.

Pathology. Little can be said of the pathology of this peculiar disease. In some post mortems, slight enlargements of the liver and kidneys were noticed, together with a slight fatty degeneration. In five or six case when the disease was at its highest, blood taken from the arm found to be dark and thick, and the power of coagulation entirely lost. However, after it was exposed to the air and shaken it regained a bright scarlet color.

These facts, together with the peculiar eruption, the frequent complication of gangrene, and the fact that the whole system is affected, would lead one to suspect the blood to be the part most affected.

Symptoms. The affection may be divided in three classes, mild, medium and severe.

The onset of the disease is on an average of about eighteen hours after the exposure. In a few cases, however, the disease seems to be preceded by a prodromal period of malaise for a few days. The attack comes on with a well marked chill, simultaneous with fever, general aching of the whole body and a flushed, dusky red color of the skin. The chill although most severe at the on-et often continues more or less throughout the attack, worse mornings, becoming lighter day after day until the disease runs its course. The fever comes on with, or rapidly follows, the initiative chill so that, upon the first visit of the physician, it is usually found to register 102 to 104 F. It gradually rises until it reaches its maximum in about seven to twelve days, when it registers ordinarily from 103 to 106 F. Some slight evening exacerbation, as in other fevers. The fever continues throughout the attack until death or recovery. In cases of recovery, which are rare in severe forms, the fever begins to abate about the fourteenth day and disappears about the twenty-first day.

Pain. Usually complains more of a general aching and soreness, worse by the least motion. The eruption appears about three days after the beginning of the sickness, first appearing on the back, later over the entire body. The color and form resemble measles, but are unlike the latter in being macular. The eruptions at first disappear on pressure, and very often are situated at hair follicles and vary in size from a pin head to that of a split pea. Gradually the eruptions become darker assuming a purplish or dark blue color, increasing in size and becoming confluent in places producing a mottled appearance. After the eruptions become dark they greatly resemble hemorrhages under the skin. In addition to the eruptions, the skin is congested and jaundiced. Later on in the attack there is desquamation, but only where the eruptions occurred.

The *Face* presents a very bloated and besotted expression.

The *Tongue* at first is coated white, later brown.

The *Pulse* is at first full and strong, gradually gains in rapidity and loses in strength.

Respiration is rapid, full and very labored and is worse in proportion to severity of the case; extreme vertigo, constipation and vomiting are present in nearly all cases in the early stages. In all severe attacks there is delirium, the speech is rambling and incoherent, and sooner or later there is como or death.

Complications are gangrene affecting the fingers and toes, hypostatic pneumonia and inflammatory rheumatism are not infrequent complications.

Prognosis. The prognosis depends on the severity of the attack, but is regarded as generally fatal, although a good many of the *milder* cases recover.

Treatment. The treatment of the old school is calomel in large doses, Magnesia, Sulphur, etc.

In one mild case that I have treated, *Bryonia* was indicated, but in more severe forms, *Rhus tox.*, *Baptisia*, *Lachesis* and *Crotalus* are to be thought of.

This disease, as you will see, mostly resembles typhus fever, but is not contagious.

I am greatly indebted to Dr. Gwinn, of this place, who has practiced in the valley over sixteen years, and has treated over two hundred cases, for the above data and information contained in this article.

WM. A. GLASGOW, M. D.
Missoula, Mont.

Nursing.*

THE ACCIDENTS OF PREGNANCY AND LABOR.

Lecture No. 8.

Ladies: The pregnant woman is exposed to very grave dangers through convulsions, syncope, and hemorrhage. In your capacity as nurse you may suddenly be brought to face these conditions, and be compelled to rely upon your own knowledge for the time being. It is well that you have some knowledge of these conditions, and what to do for the patient. The most common danger that threatens the pregnant woman is *abortion*, and its consequences. By abortion I mean the expulsion of the ovum before it has grown to the stage of viability; that is, practically before seven months. The symptoms of abortion are pain and hemorrhage. Bleeding may be so severe as to weaken the mother greatly, while if a part of the ovum be retained and decomposes she may suffer from septic infection.

The duties of a nurse consist in putting the patient at absolute rest in bed, not allowing her to assume the sitting posture for any purpose whatever, in removing all disturbing influences from

*Course of Lectures delivered to the Nurses Training School at Maryland Homœopathic Hospital, by M. E. Douglass, M. D., Baltimore, Md.

her, in keeping her absolutely clean and causing her to wear sterile vulvar dressings, and in saving for inspection all blood-clots or pieces of embryo. The vulvar dressings should be sterilized by baking or boiling, and the external parts should be thoroughly washed with soap and water, irrigated thoroughly, and then washed with bichlorid solution (1:2000). The nurse's hands should be made aseptic before the dressings are changed. Blood-clots and debris may be placed in cold water in a white vessel, where they can be examined most readily. The diet of the patient is usually liquid or light. It is often necessary to move the bowels by enemas. It may be necessary to apply local treatment in cases of abortion. The nurse must have in readiness an abundance of hot water, antiseptic solutions, clean linen, and in some cases an anesthetic must be given. If the patient is to be catheterized, the catheter must be boiled before it is used, and the nurse's hands and the patient's external parts should be made thoroughly aseptic.

If a nurse were alone with a patient who was having an abortion, and bleeding became so severe as to threaten the patient's safety before the doctor could arrive, the nurse would be justified in lowering the patient's head and in giving a vaginal injection of sterile water at a temperature of 110 degrees F., and the indicated remedy. Stimulants may be given in small doses only. I will give you a few prominent symptoms of those remedies most likely to be useful.

Sabina is a prominent remedy; the hemorrhage is rather profuse, of a bright red color, and is accompanied with clots.

Pulsatilla in those cases where the sudden spurts of blood are unusually profuse, with only a moderate flow in the intervals.

Ipecacuanha when the hemorrhage is profuse, and blood bright red, especially if accompanied with nausea.

Aconite with its great fear of death, and of air, or bustle.

Nux moschata with its hysterical symptoms and syncope.

Belladonna with its bearing down sensation, and bright red blood, which feels hot to the parts over which it flows.

The question of diagnosis does not rest with the nurse; but she must remember that pregnant women may be seized with signs of weakness which, she has been taught, indicate bleeding, either internal or external. When such symptoms are present the patient should be put at absolute rest in bed and the doctor summoned as speedily as possible. The nurse will find the patient's pulse rapid and feeble, her color pallid, her skin relaxed and clammy, a desire for more air or water, and dimness of vision present. If possible, the nurse should have in readiness hot sterile water, and an abundance of clean linen by the time the doctor arrives. If there is an antiseptic in the house, it must be in readiness for his use. Whiskey or brandy and ice should also be ready. The nurse must expect that some form of obstetric operation will be done, and should be prepared for this if possible.

The veins of the lower extremities often become considerably enlarged during pregnancy. Should such a patient bruise her limbs a vein might rupture and serious bleeding follow. Should the nurse be present at such a case before the doctor could arrive, she should place the patient on her back, elevate the limb from which the bleeding is coming, and apply over the point of bleeding a perfectly clean compress several inches square. This may be held by the hand until the doctor arrives. The nurse must be careful to have an absolutely clean compress, as septic infection might follow the use of soiled material. *Hamamelis* externally and internally should be used.

Before rupture, however, the vein should be supported by the use of flannel bandages. It shall begin at the toes and cover the lower extremity completely, omitting, of course, the heel. The bandage should extend beyond the joint where the veins are enlarged. It may be removed at night when the patient retires, and the limb bathed and the skin kept as clean as possible. In some cases obstinate itching accompanies this condition, which is greatly relieved by bathing with warm water and sodium bicarbonate, or by using some lotion which the attending physician may prescribe.

In reporting any occurrence to the physician, if the nurse cannot telephone to the physician personally, she should write a note stating as accurately as possible what has happened. This will enable her to avoid unnecessary alarm to the family and will greatly aid the physician.

A pregnant woman may be suddenly seized with convulsions. The patient becomes suddenly unconscious, moves the limbs violently, froths at the mouth, becomes blue in the face and neck, and after a few moments slowly regains consciousness. Occasionally convulsions begin with acute mania. The patient becomes violent, and may attack a friend or relative.

In the presence of convulsions, medical help must be summoned at once. The nurse should try to open the patient's jaws and get between the back teeth a pad composed of a folded napkin or towel. This will prevent the patient from seriously wounding the tongue. The patient should be put to bed and undressed as soon as possible, and the nurse should prepare for an obstetric operation or a labor. An abundance of hot water, clean linen, stimulants, a syringe for injections into the bowels and a syringe for vaginal injections, blankets, rubber sheets, and several clean pitchers should be placed in readiness. Upon his arrival the physician may give medicine by hypodermic injection or in the rectum, and may desire to give the patient a hot bath or hot pack. Should the convulsions return before the doctor arrives, the nurse should keep the patient upon the bed and keep the jaws asunder by the pad above described. No more serious complication for mother and child can arise than convulsions, and the nurse is justified in insisting upon the immediate presence of a doctor.

Among the curative remedies for this disease, none occupies so prominent a place as *Belladonna*. The patient has the appearance of being stunned; convulsive movements in the limbs and muscles of the face; paralysis of the right side of the tongue; dilated pupils; red or livid countenance; renewal of the fits at every pain; more or less tossing between the spasms, or deep sleep with grimac s; or starts and cries with fearful visions.

Other important remedies are Cicuta virosa, Gelsemium, and Veratrum viride.

Pregnant patients sometimes have attacks of syncope which are alarming, but which are not often dangerous. They result from fatigue, from being in a hot and close room, or from exposure to the heat of the sun, or from some sudden fright or shock. If the nurse is called upon to take charge of such a case, she should make the patient lie down with her head as low as possible, loosen her clothing, give her plenty of fresh air and a little stimulus. A teaspoonful of whiskey or brandy in a little hot or cold water, or a teaspoonful of aromatic spirits of ammonia in water, is usually sufficient. The patient should lie quietly until she has completely recovered, when she may be taken to her home in some suitable conveyance.

Should bleeding occur during labor, all that the nurse can do will be to send at once for the physician, to have ready a copious supply of hot water, and to give the patient not more than a teaspoonful of whiskey or brandy every hour. The same remedies may be employed as have been noticed in hemorrhage during abortion.

After the child is born the nurse should watch the patient for signs of bleeding, and if she sees the mother suddenly becoming pale she should at once place her hand upon the abdomen and try to outline the uterus. It should be a hard mass reaching to the umbilicus. If the abdomen feels like a pan of dough, and if blood is coming from the vagina, the physician must at once be informed, and must take steps to secure the prompt expulsion of the placenta. In such a case as this a hot vaginal douche will be necessary, and in some patients a hot intra-uterine douche as well.

After the placenta has been expelled the doctor will usually satisfy himself that the womb is well contracted. Should he not do so, the nurse should watch the patient as carefully as possible, placing her hand upon the uterus at frequent intervals and watching closely for the general signs of bleeding. When the nurse is told to clean and dress the patient, if the flow is very bright in color and is excessive, she must at once warn the doctor. Should bleeding come on very soon after the birth of the child, the physician is usually present, and will assume the active part in the treatment of the case.

Post-partum bleeding usually occurs within the first three hours after the birth of the child. The patient becomes pale, feels like fainting, complains that the room is dark, that she is thirsty, is restless, and may have slight pain in the abdomen. Blood may flow very freely from the vagina; or but very little blood may escape because a clot forms in the neck of the womb, like a cork in the neck of a bottle, and holds back the blood. The abdomen feels like a mass of dough, the womb cannot be distinctly felt, the patient's pulse is from 100 to 130. The condition is one of great danger, and the nurse must not simply send for the doctor, but must act at once. She should do these things in the order given: First. Rub the abdomen from above downward until she can feel the uterus. Then grasp it firmly by carrying the fingers behind the womb as deeply as possible into the pelvis, and, placing the thumb firmly upon the anterior surface of the womb, the womb should be bent forward over the pubic bone and brought as closely against the pubic bone as possible. Second. The nurse should have anyone who can help her bring the douch-pan or bed-pan in use, a fountain syringe, and three or four toilet pitchers of water at a temperature of 112 (F). Without removing her hand from the uterus, with the other hand she should introduce the douche-nozzle into the vagina, having first thoroughly soaked the douche-nozzle in the hot water, and, having her helper hold the douche-bag and pour in the water, she should give a hot vaginal douche of one gallon. She should rub the uterus gently while giving the douche, and continue to carry it downward and forward.

While she is doing these things a messenger should go for the doctor as rapidly as possible. Meanwhile the nurse must not become frightened or alarm her patient. In most cases what we have described stops the bleeding or makes it much less. If the doctor does not come promptly, the nurse should continue to grasp and massage the uterus gently; and should bleeding return she may repeat the hot vaginal douche. She cannot leave the patient, because she must control the contraction of the uterus.

If at the end of an hour the doctor does not arrive, and the uterus shows a tendency to relax and to bleed, if the nurse has with her a hypodermic syringe she may give an injection of strychnine (1-15 grain). The patient may also have a teaspoonful of brandy in hot water, and the brandy may be repeated in one-half hour. The patient must be kept absolutely still. Her bed may be wet and soiled, but she must endure this discomfort rather than have bleeding set up by moving her. Blankets should be wrapped about her legs, a hot water bag covered by a piece of flannel, or a towel should be placed under the back of the neck at the base of the brain, her head should be as low as possible, and she should be encouraged to believe that in a short time she will be comfortable and well. Usually, in the hands of good nurses, the physician who comes to a case of post-partum bleeding arrives to find the hemorrhage stopped by the prompt and skillful action of the nurse.

To prevent a return of the bleeding some form of binder especially adapted to hold the womb in contraction must be applied. A boxbinder is made as follows: Three large towels are rolled firmly and the rolls pinned or stitched. The uterus is made as small as possible by massage, and is carried down against the pubic bone. One towel is placed across the abdomen above the uterus, and one towel is placed upon each side of the uterus, so that the womb is put in a box, one side of which is the pubic bone, the other three sides being the three towels. The abdominal binder is then pinned over the womb and these towels, beginning from above and pinning downward. This holds the womb firmly, while the pressure upon the abdomen is of benefit to the patient in a general way.

In some cases the physician performs transfusion of normal salt solution, introducing it beneath the skin or directly into a vein. The nurse should understand the preparation of normal salt solution for this and other purposes. It is not necessary to make the solution chemically exact, and in an emergency one teaspoonful of salt to a pint of water may be employed. Some physicians prefer one teaspoonful of table salt and one teaspoonful of pure sodium bicarbonate to a quart of warm water. If the solution be prepared at a temperature of 110 (F), before it can reach the interior of the body it will usually fall to 105 to 100. The nurse must take care that vessels in which this fluid is placed have been thoroughly scalded, and that the water has been thoroughly boiled before it is introduced into the body.

Physicians sometimes introduce antiseptic gauze within the womb to prevent the return of hemorrhage. For this the nurse should place the patient across the bed, her hips at the edge of the bed, her feet and legs on chairs. The patient should be moved as gently as possible. The physician will require an antiseptic solution, a perfectly clean or sterile towel, and materials for cleaning and making antiseptic his hands, while the few instruments required shall be boiled before they are used.

A patient who has had severe bleeding recovers slowly from her confinement. If she becomes infected, she is usually very ill. During her recovery she will require very careful feeding and the best of nursing to bring her back to health. After severe bleeding, sudden excitement and all disturbance of the patient must be avoided. She must not sit up suddenly, nor rise up quickly in bed, lest a serious accident to the heart or brain should occur.

Next week we will have something further to say along this line.

Editorial.

THE DRIFT IN THE COLLEGES.

It will be seen by the figures, as given in last month's ADVOCATE, that the average attendance of the 121 allopathic colleges has been a fraction more than 113.

Of our colleges, those in Philadelphia, Boston, New York, Cleveland and two in Chicago exceed that number. But the eight hundred instructors, if fired with the old zeal, would have at least a student apiece each year. That would give for the four years 3,200 students. And if the zeal of the old guard of the long ago still obtained we would have 12,000 times four, or 48,000 students. Even if one-half of the members of the profession sent a student each year that would give 6,000 new students each year. All this leads to the conclusion that the enthusiasm of the profession, for its own progress, is not what it should be.

Here are some interesting facts: Hahnemann of Philadelphia leads with 269 students and fifty-seven instructors. Hahnemann of Chicago comes next with 185 students and forty-eight teachers. The Chicago Homœopathic follows close with 150 students and sixty-five instructors. Then comes Boston University with 131 students and fifty-eight teachers. Cleveland is the fifth with 110 students and forty-five instructors. New York had 105 students and forty-one instructors. Then comes a great drop—Hering reports seventy nine students and only twenty-nine teachers. Dunham had seventy-eight students and thirty-one instructors. The Homœopathic department of the University of Michigan reports seventy-two students and twenty-four teachers. St. Louis comes next with sixty-seven students and thirty teachers. Detroit reports forty-five students and thirty-one instructors. Kansas City University reports forty-eight students and twenty-two teachers. The Homœopathic department of the University of Iowa and Pulte of Cincinnati each report forty students, the former having twenty-four instructors and the latter thirty-one. San Francisco reports thirty-eight students and thirty-two teachers. The New York College (for women only) has thirty-six students and forty-two teachers. Baltimore has thirty-five students and thirty-three teachers. Louisville and Denver tie with thirty-three students each, the former having twenty-six instructors and the latter thirty-one. The University of Minnesota (Homœopathic department) brings up the procession with twenty-eight students and nineteen teachers.

It would seem to be an easy matter for the Chicago colleges to merge, Hering to unite with Hahnemann, which would bring the latter's number of students up to 264, with seventy-seven instructors, and the west side schools, by uniting, would have 228 students and ninety-seven instructors, which would about equal the faculty of Rush.

If the two New York schools united, the result would be 141 students and eighty-three teachers. If Detroit would unite with the Undversity of Michigan the latter would then have 117 students and fifty-five instructors. It would seem that Pulte might take in Louisville, which would give the Ohio college seventy-three students and fifty-seven teachers.

Large vs. Small Colleges.

When the prospective student who wants to be thoroughly educated in medicine gets several "circulars of information" he scans them carefully. He finds some with a long faculty list and large classes, and others with few teachers and smaller classes. Why? He lives in a land where majorities rule. His education is his capital. It should be the best obtainable, the most comprehensive, otherwise he is being cheated. He cannot afford to spend time and money to get an inferior article. He scans more closely what is offered beginners, and so does his preceptor. The best is none too good for him, and he goes where he thinks he will get that. The large faculty, according to the ADVOCATE'S figures, evidently draws the students.

T. C. DUNCAN.

THERAPEUTIC INDEX.

It would give us great satisfaction to know that every reader of the ADVOCATE keeps a careful record of the treatment of every case coming under his professional care. It would give still greater satisfaction to know that each record was so systematically arranged or indexed that the physician could at a moment's notice turn to a record showing *what* every prescription had been and *why* it had been made. We would never have any difficulty in securing ample clinical verifications for any remedy to be considered if such was the situation.

A vast amount of useful information is lost to the profession as well as to the individual physician, by reason of the fact that the results of thorough investigations are locked up in case records.

It is a simple matter to keep this index when you start one with a clear idea of what is to be secured. If started right this index becomes of so much value that its influence extends back to the moment when the record is to be made and insures greater care in preparation of the record and more thorough study for the simillimum because of the fact that it is to be preserved as evidence of the character of work performed.

The following *essentials* must be on hand before a satisfactory Therapeutic Index can be successfully secured.

1. **A Vertical File Case.** The lower drawer to the ordinary roll-top desk usually has the right proportions for a Vertical File Case. A substitute for this may be found in the common letter files that flood the market until your cases become so numerous that it is poor economy to put up with their inconvenience.

2. **A Set of Manila Envelopes** large enough to fit the Vertical File Case and numbered consecutively from 1. The envelopes should be stout and have printed on one side near the top the following: File No.—. Name and address. There should also be printed upon this same side the following card:

CASE RECORD INDEX.

Name *File No.*

Address

Date	*Remedy.*	*Potency*	*Directions.*	*Result.*

3. **Paper cut in a uniform size to fit envelopes.** This paper be blank or ruled to suit the taste of the individual. It is needless to state that it is upon this paper that the "Records" are to be kept. It is not our purpose to discuss the method of keeping a record because the pages of the ADVOCATE contain abundant illustrations.

Every inquiry, also the prescription, with date and directions should be recorded, not only within the Index upon the envelope every time there is a change of remedy, potency or directions.

4. **A set of Cards** about 3x5 inches in dimensions ruled and arranged after the following plan or something similar:

THERAPEUTIC INDEX.

REMEDY

Date	*File No.*	*Diagnosis.*	*Duration of Action.*	*Results*
......	......	....	....	......
......	......	....	....	......
......	......	....	....	......
......	......	....	....	......
......	......	....	....	......

Upon these cards should be written in large letters the name of the remedies to be found within the various records, e.g. File No. 1 may be the record of a case of *suppressed menstruation* for which *Pulsatilla* was selected. The result was the re-establishment of the flow. *Duration of action* was one day. *Pulsatilla* was given as an *intercurrent* in Case No. 4 for "After Pains" with excellent result. The next case calling for *Pulsatilla* was File No. 10 for *Constipation.* By means of this card you will have an index directing you to all the cases in which you gave *Pulsatilla* with something of a suggestion as the reason for its selection. All you have to do is refer the case to see the indications upon which the remedy was selected, also the relation this prescription bears to the case in general.

The advantages to be gained by this systematic method are so many that it is a wonder that every careful prescriber has not improvised some method by which the results of his faithful efforts may be put to some use.

We will suggest but a few of the many reasons why this should be made universal.

1. Incentive to faithful, conscientious work.

2. Promotes careful preparation of every "record."

3. Promotes careful study of record before making a prescription.

4. Discourages frequent changes in prescription, because the reasons for each change is shown upon the "record."

5. Enables the physician to study action of various remedies from a practical, clinical standpoint.

Announcements.

AMERICAN HAHNEMANNIAN ASSOCIATION.

The American Hahnemannian Association will this year meet at Narragansett Pier, R. I., on July 1, 2 and 3. Following is the program:

BUREAU OF HOMŒOPATHIC PHILOSOPHY.

Edward Adams, Toronto, Canada, Chairman.

Treatment of Mental Diseases ....
James T. Kent, Chicago.

Repetition of the Dose, H. W. Pierson, Chicago

The Vital Test, H. A. Cameron, Philadelphia

The Woes of Babyhood, ...
Fredericka E. Gladwin, Philadelphia.

How to Make a Homœopathic Prescription.. ..
Stuart Close, Brooklyn.

The Value of Pathology and Diagnosis to a Homœopath, H. Farrington, Chicago.

The Philosophy of Disease Prevention.... ....
F. S. Davis, Quincy, Mass.

The Significance of Symptoms, in Relation to Patient, Disease and Remedy ....
Julia C. Loos, Harrisburg, Pa.

The First Cause. The Cure ....
W. L. Morgan, Baltimore.

The Vital Force, Its Relation to Health and Disease, G. W. Cooper, Philadelphia

Subject not announced ....
F. W. Patch, S. Framingham, Mass.

Subject not announced ....
Ed. Carleton, New York

Subject not announced, R. L. Thurston, Boston.

BUREAU OF CLINICAL MEDICINE.

John Dike, Melrose, Mass., Chairman.

A Few Clinical Cases, Edward Adams, Toronto.

The Constitutional Remedy, with Illustrative Cases, S. Mary Ives, Middletown, Conn.

Clinical Cases with a Moral ....
H. W. Pierson, Chicago.

The Indicated Remedy in Collapse..............
Julia C. Loos, Harrisburg, Pa.

A Study of Materia Medica. Secale—An Illustrative Case, F. E. Gladwin, Philadelphia.

Can the Tubercle Bacillus be Removed by the Potentized Remedy? H. Farrington, Chicago

JULIA C. LOOS, President,
Harrisburg, Pa.

S. MARY IVES, Secretary, Middletown, Conn.

THE I. H. A.

The Twenty-third annual meeting of the International Hahnemannian Association will be held at the Chicago Beach Hotel in this city, on June 24, 25 and 26.

The following excellent program has been prepared:

BUREAU OF HOMŒOPATHIC PHILOSOPHY.

Alice B. Campbell, Chairman.

W. W. Gleason, Provincetown, Mass. "In Service of Homœopathy.

B. Fincke, Brooklyn. "The Domain of Similia, by J. P. Dake, as Introductory to the new Hahnemannian Monthly, published by Boericke & Tafel, 1879."

S. L. Guild-Leggett, Syracuse, N. Y., Dynamic Drug vs. Vital."

W. H. Leonard, Minneapolis, "Know Thyself."

H. C. Allen, Chicago, "Susceptibility to Medicinal Action."

BUREAU OF OBSTETRICS.

E. E. Reininger, Chairman.

B. Fincke, Brooklyn, Homœopathic Tokology.

W. H. Leonard, Minneapolis, Treatment of Children.

A. McNeil, San Francisco, Answers to Questions in Circular.

T. D. Stowe, Mexico, N.Y., Care of Mothers and Children.

Leslie Martin, Baldwinsville, N. Y., Obstinate Case of Nausea and Vomiting. Prenatal Treatment. Ischuria of New Born Infant.

J. Fitz-Mathew, West Sound, Wash., Abortion at the Third Month.

C. M. Boger Parkersburg, W. Va., A Gelsemium Case.

J. B. S. King, Chicago, Albuminuria.

D. C. McLaren, Ottawa, Can. A Tough Case.

S. F. Shannon, Denver. "Along Line of Hints in Paper Sent Me."

L. C. Fritts, Chicago, Puerperal Mania. Two Cases.

P. E. Krichbaum, Montclair, N. J. Labor Made Possible and Easy.
Alexander Donald, St. Paul. Personal Experience in Obstetrics and Care of Children.
H. A. Moméw, Elkhart, Ind. Prescription During and After Labor.
Ansley Quackenbush, Ottawa, Can. Obstetrical Work.
E. E. Reininger, Chicago. Labor Complicated with Malaria.
Edith T. Clarke, Chicago. A Paper; Subject Chosen from Among Ideas Suggested by Circular Letter.
Lydia Scholes, Chicago. Prescribing for Baby.
W. W. Gleason, Provincetown, Mass. Breech Presentation.
L. M. Stanton, 102 W. 89th st., N. Y. Cases.
J. N. Lowe, Milford, N. J. A Lycopodium Case.
W. B. Kilnetop, Charles City, Iowa. Cases.
Jean I. Mackay-Glidden, Los Angeles. Cases.

BUREAU OF MATERIA MEDICA.

A. R. Morgan, Chairman.

A. R. Morgan, Hippomanes.
E. A. Taylor, Chicago. "Kali Iodidum."
J. A. Tomhagen, Chicago. "Bromine."
H. C. Allen, Chicago. "Proving of Malandrinum." "Dulcamara and Verifications."

SURGERY.

Mark M. Thompson, Chicago, Chairman.

Mark M. Thompson, Chicago. The Relationship Between Surgery and Materia Medica
C. E. Fisher, Chicago. "Homœopathy and Surgery."
Frank C. Titzel, Chicago. Surgery of To-day.
Pauline E. Lange, Chicago. Cleanliness and the Indicated Remedy in the Treatment of Wounds.

BUREAU OF CLINICAL MEDICINE.

P. E. Krichbaum, Chairman.

P. C. Majumdar, Calcutta, India. A Paper.
S. L. Guild-Leggett, Syracuse, N. Y. Clinical Cases.
Alice B. Campbell, Brooklyn. In Praise of Platina.
B. Fincke, Brooklyn, X Ray Cases.
E. E. Case, Hartford, Conn. Clinical Experiences.
F. W. Payne, Boston, Neuritis. Two Cases Cured.
A. Villiers, Dresden, Germany. X-Ray, C. M. (Finke).
Josephine Howland, M. D., Auburn, N. Y. Suppressed Rheumatism--Cure Results.
Belle Gurney, Chicago. Some Nervous Reflexes in Women.
L. P. Munger, Hart, Mich. Small Pox.
C. M. Boger, Parkersburg, W. Va. Membranous Croup.
Leslie Martin, Baldwinsville, N. Y., Dysmenorrhœa.
E. H. Wilsey, Parkersburg, W. Va. Clinical Cases.
J. C. White, Port Chester, N. Y. Clinical Experiences After Surgery.
J. B. S. King, Chicago. Arterio Sclerosis.
T. D. Stowe, Mexico, N. Y. Croup.
A. McNiel, San Francisco. Cured Cases.
L. M. Stanton, New York. Clinical Cases.
E. A. Taylor, Chicago. Clinical Cases.
E. E. Reininger, Chicago. Malaria Cured Homœopathically.
J. A. Tomhagen, Chicago. Clinical Cases.
D. C. McLaren, Ottawa, Can. Clinical Cases.
H. P. Holmes, Omaha. Clinical Experience.
J. H. Allen, Chicago. Clinical Experience.
J. W. Krichbaum, Danville, Ky. Note Book Cases.
C. W. Butler, Montclair, N. J. Clinical Cases.
J. Fitz Mathew, West Sound, Wash. Clinical Cases.
W. L. Reed, St. Louis. Clinical Cases.
H. C. Allen, Chicago. Insanity.

Society Reports.

WISCONSIN MEDICAL SOCIETY.

Wisconsin always has a good Society meeting. The writer did not get to Milwaukee until President Forsbeck made his speech. He spoke for a broader liberality, and advised physicians to learn all that had a bearing on medicine. That was all right, but when a speaker at the banquet said that "Homœopathy was doomed, unless we bestir ourselves," the good doctors were the next morning horrified to read in glaring headlines that "Homœopathy Was Doomed." That was rebuked next day, but it shows how earnest words can be distorted. One of the speakers at the banquet recalled the grand enthusiastic heroes of the past: Drs. Douglass, Ober, Pierce, Patchen, Bowen and last, but not least, Dr. H. P. Dale, of Oshkosh, (father of Harvey B. Dale) in whose office the State Society had its birth. Next year they go to Oshkosh again for their annual meeting, and as this will be a sort of jubilee for the cause it will likely arouse more enthusiasm. The attendance, considering that most of the doctors were unusually busy for this time of the year, was good. Some thought there was not the usual activity among the members. This was, however, more of a Wisconsin meeting than ever before. There were fewer outside physicians attending, Chicago not monopolising things as she sometimes does when the colleges are represented. Some fancied that Milwaukee was given too much prominence, but the hostess must do herself proud, as she certainly did. The Mayor made a fine speech, giving us a bit of advice, i.e., that on the witness stand the physician must answer as to facts, but is not compelled to give his opinion or professional conclusions.

The committee on Materia Medica had a good report. "Remedies in Gestation" by Ella C. Chaffee of Whitewater was practical and full of new hints for remedies.

The paper on "Organic Cell Salts" by Dr. J. H. Bidler of Monroe was a relation of experience with Schussler's remedies which, according to the members, are best given according to the law as emphasized by Dr. Hering years ago. Similia must guide in remedy selection.

It seems that the Eclectics and progressive Allopaths take readily to abridged therapeutics. It is a stepping stone to better things.

The paper on "Suppressed Symptoms" by Dr. Evelyn Hoehne of Milwaukee was excellent. She cited a case where eczema of the face was suppressed and the fat child, with open fontanelles, died later of brain symptoms. One speaker emphasized the necessity for a better understanding of the course of disease as this child illustrated. A fleshy child, with open fontanelles, with eczema, was on the road to hydrocephalus. From first to last it was a case of obstructed lymphatics. The remedy to head off this condition was given as Calc. phos.

The bureau on Pediatrics, led by Dr. A. P. Andrus of Ashland, made a good report. The paper on "Cross, Cry Babies" by Dr. W. B. Webb of Beaver Dam was good, barring the expedients.

Dr. S. R. Stone of Rhinelander read a paper on "Phimosis as a Cause of Reflex Neuroses," which was well illustrated and received.

"The Commoner Diseases of Infancy," by Dr. R. K. Paine of Manitowoc, was very practical.

Dr. Harvey B. Dale of Oshkosh read a paper on "Capillary Bronchitis," citing the value of several remedies, among them Tart. em. One speaker cited the fact that Tart. em. was interdicted in 1863 by Surgeon General Hammond. The army surgeons were prohibited from using it in pneumonia. They gave it in large doses, ten grains or more. This raised a howl of protest, and Dr. Hammond was desposed. After that he brought up animal extracts, then criticised by the regulars but since adopted by them.

The committee on Surgery, presided over by Dr. G. W. Patchen, brought out several fine reports, showing that Wisconsin has able surgeons.

The bureau of Clinical Medicine, Dr. M. G. Spawn of Beloit, chairman, brought out papers on "Summer Diarrhea" by Dr. R. K. Paine of Manitowoc; "Diphtheria" by Dr. Harvey B. Dale, of Oshkosh; "Smallpox" by Dr. J. Buckeridge of Beloit; "Cases from Practice" by Dr. C. H. Hall, of Madison; "Diagnostic Significance of Facial Expression" by Dr. A. R. F. Grob, of Milwaukee; and "Tonsillitis" by Dr. M. G. Spawn of Beloit. The value of antitoxin was emphasized, but one speaker had used small doses of Carbolic acid hypodermically with equally good results.

Smallpox had been extensive in Wisconsin, and the mild cases made quarantine difficult. The value of Tart. em. should not be overlooked. "The Diagnostic Value of Facial Expression" as an especial guide in remedy selection was well brought out, and should be elaborated still more. For cardiac dyspnœa referred to Aconite was suggested.

Anacardium was spoken of by one writer as a remedy in endocarditis. Speaking of whooping-cough, one member (Dr. Sutherland of Janesville) gave his experience with the chestnut. Other remedies, as Corral. rub. 30th, Chelodonium and Drosera were also mentioned. One speaker, who had seen many epidemics of this disease, emphasized the fact that no two were exactly alike, and that we should choose the *similar* remedy for the *genus epidemicus*.

The officers selected for the ensuing year were: President, Dr. E. Everett, of Madison; Vice President, Dr. A. P. Andrus of Ashland; Secretary, Dr. M. A. Barndt of Milwaukee; Treasurer, Dr. G. W. Patchen of Manitowoc. It is expected that this wise selection of the officers and chairmen of bureaus will result in a good attendance next year.

It seems, from the data at hand, that the oldest homœopathic physician in Wisconsin is Dr. Warner of Waukesha, who graduated 1842, and the secretary was instructed to send him congratulation on reaching the sixtieth medical anniversary.

The cause grows in Wisconsin, and there are still many towns where a physician guided by similia would do well.

D.

Personals and News Items.

Under the provisions of a law recently passed, the Iowa Board of Medical Examiners now issues licenses to osteopaths who are graduates of approved osteopathic colleges.

It has been reported that Hahnemann College of this city will discontinue holding three terms a years, returning to the old plan, the same as in vogue in the other homœopathic colleges.

The State of Michigan, at the University at Ann Arbor, provides both allopathic and homœopathic educations. During the past six years, five students matriculating with the homœopathic department, have deserted to the "regulars." In the same time thirty-nine of the "regular" matriculants deserted to enlist under the banner of Similia.

The American Institute of Phrenology, Incorporated 1866, opens its next session, September 3d, 1902. For particulars apply to the Secretary, M. H. Piercy, care of Fowler & Wells Co., 24 East 22d street, New York.

Judge Samuel Greene, of the Criminal Court at Birmingham, Ala., has decided that osteopathy is the practice of medicine, and that any person engaging in the same in Alabama can be forced to procure a license for practicing medicine. His decision was based on the dictionary definition of the word "medicine," which is: "Science which relates to the cure, prevention or alleviation of disease." The defendant claimed that osteopathy was not the practice of medicine, as no drugs were used.—*Medical Times.*

Dr. H. V. Wall, formerly of Kansas City, Mo., is now located at Crawfordsville, Ind.

Mrs. Annie Botsford obtained a verdict of $500 against the Presbyterian Hospital before Justice Gildersleeve of the Supreme Court, because the hospital authorities performed an autopsy on the remains of her husband, Albert Kent Botsford, without authority from her. The verdict is said to be the first of its kind in this State. The institution does not perform autopsies without consent of the relatives, and it set up that a brother of Mrs. Botsford had given this consent. The court would not permit evidence to this effect, on the ground that the widow was the only one who could give the authority.

Dr. A. H. Wales has decided to leave his practice in Chicago and enter into partnership with his father, Dr. H. W. Wales, of Lanark, Ill.—*Medical Visitor.*

No doubt this move will give Dr. Henry a partial rest. It would appear that he needs and deserves a surcease from the strenuosity of his labors for nearly forty years. In the late 60's and in the 70's, when the highways around Lanark for about four months of the year were almost impassable, it was a common sight to see Dr. Henry, seated in his coffin-shaped buggy, behind two long-limbed racers galloping over the country to visit some patient in the "barrens," six or eight miles from Lanark. No night too dark, no roads too bad, no condition of fatigue too great to keep him from the bedside of a sufferer. Hopelessness of monetary reward was no hindrance to professional visits—the poor were just as certain of the best treatment as the rich.

Verily, he hath earned a rest, but it is doubtful whether his hundreds of patients, who, after years of association, have become his personal friends, will allow him to take it is another question.

OBITUARY:

Dean William Tod Helmuth, M. D., LL. D., of the New York Homœopathic Medical College, died suddenly on May 15, aged 69, of angina pectoris.

Before appointed dean of the N. Y. Homœopathic Medical College, Dr. Helmuth was for many years professor of surgery in the same college. He had also been connected with several hospitals as surgeon, and was an active member of his state and the national Homœopathic societies. Dr. Helmuth's scholarly attainments, coupled with his thorough knowledge of surgery and medicine, made him an important factor in the upbuilding of homœopathy, and his place in the medical world will be difficult to supply.

Homœopaths in America join their British brethren in mourning the death of Richard Hughes, which occurred on April 3, in the sixty-sixth year of his age. Early in his medical career he joined Drs. Drysdale and Dudgeon in editing the British Journal of Homœopathy, publication of which was discontinued in 1884. In 1867 was brought out his "Manual of Pharmacodynamics," upon which his fame as homœopathic author may be said to chiefly rest. This was followed by "A Manual of Therapeutics," and "Cyclopedia of Drug Pathogenesy" in four volumes, with index.

Besides being a learned physician, Dr. Hughes was a man of large sympathies which found vent in the free treatment of the poor of Brighton and vicinity, the principal seat of his practice.

Miss Clara Schmat, daughter of Fred. Schmat, merchant in Attica, N. Y., gave an informal party on the evening of November 20th last. About thirty of her friends were invited. Among the refreshments served were tinned cans of oysters, which had been opened and allowed to stand for two days. Before midnight all of the guests were taken violently ill with ptomaine poisoning. Physicians worked all night, trying every means to counteract the poison, but Miss Schmat died early next morning, and Frank Harrison died two hours later.—*Medical Times.*

There seems to be sound judgment in the verdict of the jury in a Philadelphia court in setting aside the will of a man who had bequeathed the residue of an estate of $30,000 to an Association of Spiritualists. The will was contested by a daughter of the decedent on the ground that her father was of unsound mind and under the influence of Spiritualists. For the defence it was contended that the decedent was not of unsound mind, and that his belief in Spiritualism was as reasonable as the opinions of many on religious and social subjects.

Materia Medica Miscellany.

The Action of Arsenic on the Skin. Brooke discusses arsenic skin eruptions due to disturbances of the vaso-motor centers, phenomena due to the action of arsenic on nerve trunks and disturbances of nutrition. The first mentioned consist of more or less extensive diffuse erythematous eruptions, scarlatiniform, or erythrodermic, of very unequal intensity in different parts (like all arsenic eruptions), but usually preponderating on the trunk and upper limbs. The phenomena due to the action of arsenic on nerve trunks consist of flushing, cyanosis and edema, so frequently observed on the face and extremities, and the transient edema on other parts of the body, herpes, pemphigoid eruptions, hyperidrosis, etc. The disturbances of nutrition consist of those changes that affect the normal growth of the skin apart from any inflammatory change, pigmentation, hyperkeratosis (erythromelalgia of the palms and soles, combined with hyperkeratosis and more or less hyperidrosis, being the most invariable symptoms among the victims of the epidemic investigated), stimulation of the growth of the nails etc. The drug at first produces stimulation of the skin and leads to hyperkeratosis or profuse desquamation, or both, to hyperpigmentation and to hyperidrosis. If continued the hypertrophy passes to atrophy, the cellular growth being almost completely inhibited, but the tendency to hyperkeratosis and hyperpigmentation remains almost to the final stage, in which all the tissues are wasted beyond recovery. — *British Medical Journal.*

The Action of Arsenic on the Healthy Tissues. Roberts (*British Medical Journal*), discusses the universality of the distribution of arsenic, its dynamic action and normal distribution within the human body, and the effects of arsenic oxidation on the tissue of the skin. He believes that there may exist in the body certain functional elements of which very few have yet been discovered, but which may be essential to the performing of certain specific functions. Thus, manganese is said to be essential to the oxidizing ferment; iodin to the thyroid; phosphorus to the nucleins; fluorin to the bone cells. In the list of these functional elements some appear to play the part of principal act-

-ors in the body, while others may be styled substitution elements or under-studies, so to speak, of these. Thus arsenic may, to some extent, take the place of phosphorus in relation to nucleins; selenium is said to be capable of acting for sulphur; copper, zinc or manganese may replace iron, while phosphorus, arsenic, vanadium, bismuth may play the role of nitrogen. But one thing we have at least attained to, namely, the knowledge that arsenic is not merely a drug possessing curative powers; that it is not necessarily an irritant poison; that it is not a poison in itself, but that its action is initiated and determined by the tissues themselves; that its effects are essentially of a nutritive order brought about by the agency of active oxygen; that these effects are beneficent to the organism when the oxidation is slow, and injurious when too rapid; that the more highly organized the cell, the more stable its protoplasm, and the more rapid its metabolic processes, the more readily does it feel and manifest the action of arsenic.

Alcohol and Tobacco.—It cannot be doubted that when evil effects ensue upon smoking tobacco they are very much intensified by indulgence in alcohol. Further, though even after a more than moderate indulgence in tobacco no toxic symptoms such as headache and stupor may supervene yet such would probably be the case if alcoholic drinking was practised at the same time. The powerfully solvent action of alcohol is sufficient explanation of this. It is, of course, well known in pharmacology that the active constituents of drugs are, as a rule, readily soluble in alcohol though not in water, and hence the class of preparations known as tinctures. Similarly nicotine and the pyridine bases are very easily soluble in alcohol. The chief poisonous constituent of tobacco smoke is pyridine and not nicotine. Pyridine is a poisonous base not so easily soluble in water as in alcohol. Pyridine bases can be easily traced in the mouth of an immoderate smoker, and especially the smoker of cigars. An alcoholic drink is therefore calculated quickly to wash out this poisonous oil and to carry it into the stomach, absorption of the poison ensuing, giving rise to definite toxic symptoms, due not so much to alcohol or pyridine bases alone as to the combined action of both in the manner indicated. Such symptoms would probably be avoided if smokers would abstain from drinking alcohol at the same time that smoking is being indulged in. Many a headache or malaise would thus be guarded against if at the time of smoking no alcoholic beverage were taken. An alternative plan would be to pass all the smoke through an absorbent, such as water, as in the hookah, and thus to exclude the poisonous oils. In such a case the accompaniment of an alcoholic drink would doubtless be much less injurious.—*Lancet* (London).

Argentum nit. Girl, 14, dark hair, blue eyes, rosy complexion, no menstruation. While in school, grew languid, lost color and appetite, was irritable and nervous. Became greatly emaciated, legs weakened and trembled when she walked. Received Phos. ac., as she had been growing quite tired. No benefit. Then tested urine, but found no albumen or sugar. Was going into a decline. Tried Helonias, with no result. Finally learned that, coupled with loss of appetite for food in general, was an *irresistible desire for sugar.* Then gave one dose Argentum nit. 200, and within a month she was the healthiest appearing girl in town.

An examination of Argentum nit., will disclose the fact that all her symptoms were covered by that remedy. But there are other remedies that cure all but this one just as well. This case is reported not only as a case of remarkable cure with a potency, but to impress upon all the value of what are called in the Organon peculiar and characteristic symptoms (Organon, p. 153). Also to prove that it is not necessary to name a disease condition in order to cure the patient.—E. B. Nash in *Homœopathic Recorder*.

Thuja—For warts of all kinds, especially venereal. Treatment.—Touch the warts two or three times daily with the mother tincture of Thuja, and give one tablet of the third decimal potency four times a day. The growths will soon begin to decrease in size, and a month or two of this medication will usually complete a cure.

Hahnemann taught that the outward manifestation of an internal disease or dyscrasia should never be suppressed or removed forcibly, but should be allowed to remain as an evidence of the curative work of the similar remedy. This rule applies as well to chancres, the discharge in gonorrhea, leuchorrhea, otorrhea, nasal catarrh, the eruptions in skin diseases, as eczema, urticaria, etc.

Why do we homœopaths use Thuja? some of you ask. Because it is homoeopathic to warts of all kinds, and especially to the venereal. In many provers warty growths appeared while taking the remedy, and clinical experience has verified thousands of times that warts rapidly disappear under the influence of Thuja. In Hering's Guiding Symptoms in the pathogenesis of Thuja we read: "A surplus of producing life; nearly unlimited proliferation of pathological vegetations, condylomata, warty sycotic excrescences, spongy tumors and pock exudates organize hastily; all morbid manifestations are excessive, but appear quietly, so that the beginning diseased state is scarcely known."

I have repeatedly removed large, unsightly warts from the face and hands, and have seen areas containing several hundred warts on the pudenda cured with Thuja. It is painless, harmless, leaves no scar, benefits constitutional troubles at the same time and, like a popular patent medicine, "works while you sleep." Several cases are on record in our journals and text-books where Thuja has removed warty growths weighing several pounds from cattle, leaving no scar to mark where the tumors had been. On horses it had done the same good wook and, strange to say, in the same strength, or mildness, of dose as used in the human family.—Dr. Horace P. Holmes, in *Medical World*.

Homœopathic Remedies in Diphtheria.—The writer has seen very severe cases yield to the homoeopathic remedies. A careful study of the indicated remedy should be made in every case.

In virulent cases of diphtheria most cases have been cured by *Mercurius* cyanide. In putrid diphtheria, in which the membrane extends all over the mouth, fauces and pharynx, with salivation, there is extreme prostration, the breath, is fetid, and tongue heavily coated. *Mercurius cy.*, seems to be indicated most in those cases that are malignant in type; the gangrenous membrane seems to melt away from the action of the remedy; give three powders and repeat every two hours, using gargles freely.

Mercurius corr., when the vulva is swollen, and there is intense burning, worse from pressure; constriction of the throat, swallowing causes spasm.

Mercurius biniodide when there is dryness and great soreness in the throat; the patient is obliged to swallow constantly, and there is great soreness and swelling of the glands externally. The diphtheritic deposits begin on the left side, with accumulation of thick, tenacious mucus in the throat; the tongue is coated yellow at the base, the tip and sides being red. The glands are very much enlarged, and the patient has high fever.

Kali bich., has great swelling of the glands and ulcers which secrete a purulent discharge: there are diseased follicles which exude a caseous matter; the coating of the tongue is yellow at the base; the discharge is very tenacious and stringy.

Lachesis has great difficulty in swallowing, great fever and exhaustion, infiltration of the tissues about the neck, membrane more confined to left side. The writer has given this remedy in several cases, but cannot remember receiving any decided improvement in the symptoms; and, the indications for the remedy have been very clear at the time. Perhaps other men have had better results with the remedy in these cases.

Arsenicum is indicated when there is a dynamic fever, feted breath, and the membrane looks dark and gangrenous, where the pulse is rapid and weak; the patient restless and prostrate, with throat swollen both externally and internally, and the membrane has a dark and wrinkled appearance, and where there is considerable edema about the throat.

Apis, phytolacca, Rhus tox., Ailanthus and *Belladonna* are especially applicable to the inflammatory symptoms of pseudo-diphtheria.

Mild diphtheritic anginas yield quickly to the *Mercurials, Belladonna, Apis* and *Ignatia*.—*Homœopathic Journal of Pediatrics.*

Local Use of Arsenic.—The application of Arsenic triturations to the surface of malignant ulcerations was exploited with considerable success by Dr. J. S. Mitchell, of Chicago. Instead of the arsenical pastes and powders so commonly used, he applied Homœopathic triturations of the drug of sufficient power to cause disintegrating effects, combined with continuous internal medication. The 2x was applied locally, three to six times a week, while the 3x was given internally, usually about three times a day.

Dr. G. L. Van Duersen reports in the *N. E. Medical Gazette* three cases cured or greatly benefited by this treatment, which he claims is Homoeopathic. He sustains his positions by the following quotations from Allen and Farrington:

Allen, in his "Handbook of Materia Medica," says: "Arsenic is above all a tissue drug, ranking with Phosphorus and Antimony. An irritant poison . . . the skin irritated, and violent itching and burning are followed by eruptions and finally ulceration. Glandular action is first excited then diminished."

In studying the symptomatology of the drug we find, "skin white and pasty, or dark and livid, dry and rough. Eruptions around the mouth, burning and painful, itching, worse from scratching. Red herpetic eruptions around the mouth. Ulcers on face with burning pain. Fleshy excrescences spring from ulcers, soon became gangrenous. Ulcers with thin bloody pus coming from under thin scab. Indurations and tumors becoming ulcerative."

Farrington, in his wonderfully written "Clinical Materia Medica," tells us that arsenic alters the blood. It is useful in low types of disease when blood changes are serious. The inflammations of this remedy are characterized by their intensity and by the tendency to the destruction of tissue.

In these local inflammations Arsenicum you will find burning, lancinating pains the characteristic sensations. It tends to produce induration or hardening of the skin, rendering it a valuable remedy where there is thickening of the skin with copious scaling." — *N. A. Journal of Homœopathy.*

An Extraordinary Case of Quinine Susceptibility. — At the recent meeting of the American Dermatological Association, H. W. Stelwagen (*Journal of Cutaneous and Genito-Urinary Diseases*), reported a case of this nature. The individual, a young man, had a severe attack of cold some years ago, when a physician prescribed quinine in the ordinary dose. The first dose the patient took was followed by a severe constitutional disturbance, simulating typhoid fever, and by an erythematous eruption, and finally desquamation. Some time after that he took some patent medicine which contained one-eighth of a grain of quinine to the dose. He became the victim of another attack just exactly like the first one. The same thing took place every time he took quinine or any of the cinchona derivatives. The patient was made painfully aware of his susceptibility to quinine on different occasions, the most unusual of which was a typical attack following the application of a hair tonic which contained quinine. It was not due to any neurotic disturbance, because the eruption appeared no matter whether the patient was conscious of taking quinine or not. Some of his medical friends administered quinine unknown to him, but it was invariably followed by a typical attack.

Staphisagria — Is deserving of especial mention for pains following surgical operations about the abdomen, particularly that of appendicitis. It seems to soothe in a marked degree pains in wounds made by sharp cutting instruments.

Agaricus — Is a useful remedy in intemperate persons who are excessively nervous, have loss of appetite, insomnia and constipated bowels. The remedy is also most useful in diarrhoea in wet weather, with much rumbling; worse mornings after rising and after eating. Stools slimy, thin and yellow.

Nux vomica — Is the greatest remedy in dysentery when it occurs in a regular hæmorrhoidal sedentary subject, or when due to debauchery and high living. Straining, changeable stools, aggravation from drafts and hæmorrhoidal complications are good indications. Do not always prescribe Mercurius corrosivus and Arsenicum for dysentery.

Hepar sulphuris — Given a history of scarlet fever, a perforation of one or both membranes of the ear, a purulent discharge and a deafness that is really pronounced, and we have a group of indications that can be proved to be reliable and that call for Hepar. It is in the restoration of hearing that Hepar shines with much brilliancy. — *Medical Century.*

Complete Absence of Vagina. — Mrs. D., married, 28 years of age, of medium height; thin of flesh, masculine breasts and hips, vulva and clitoris normal, hymen absent; fourchette well developed; a cul de sac 2.8 c. m. in depth, apparently formed by the continued assaults of the male organ, exists in the location of the vaginal os.

Examination, under complete anæsthesia, per rectum, demonstrated the absence of the uterus, tubes and ovaries — a small nodule, about 2 c. m. in diameter, situated between the rectum and bladder seemed to represent the termination of the genital cord. The patient claims to have keen sexual desires; but signs of ovulation or menstruation are negative. Her temperature is decidedly of the nervous type, and her character, voice and face are quite juvenile. — Dr. Samuel J. Stewart, in *Medical Sentinel.*

The Hahnemannian Advocate

A MONTHLY HOMŒOPATHIC MAGAZINE.

H. W. PIERSON, B. S., M. D., Editor., [illegible] Marshall Field Building, Chicago.
HAHNEMANN PUBLISHING Co., Publisher, 6704 Lafayette Ave., Chicago.
BENJ. F. SWAN, Business Manager.

Subscription price of the magazine in the United States, Canada, Mexico, the island possessions and Cuba, [illegible] a year, payable in advance; in Great Britain, continental Europe, India and other countries members of the postal union, [illegible] a year to be paid in advance. Unless otherwise specified, subscriptions will begin with January issue of the year in which order is received. Remittances should be made payable to the HAHNEMANN PUBLISHING Co., 6704 Lafayette Ave., Chicago.

Address all articles intended for publication and books for review to the editor. All business and other communications should be sent to the Hahnemann Publishing Co.

Vol. xii. | Chicago, July, 1902. | No. 7

Medicine.

REPETITION OF THE DOSE.

The universal rule with medical practitioners of all schools is to repeat their remedial agents at *suitable* intervals until a *cure* has been effected. The only question to be determined is the *interval* that shall most perfectly accomplish the desired result.

The ultimate result of all medication should be a *cure*. Anything short of that result is but little better than the unaided efforts of Nature, which tends to limit the duration of disease manifestations. A fountain can never rise, without outside aid, to a level above its source and the same may be predicated of Nature. When we speak of Nature in this connection, reference is made to the *vital* energy which pervades the human organism and seeks to *maintain* a *normal* or healthy activity throughout the various organs and functions of the body.

It may be well for us to define disease, because much misunderstanding can be traced to the tendency of looking upon the *material effect* as the real and fundamental disease when back of it all must be a *dynamic cause* which serves to *perpetuate* the disturbed functional activities of the organism.

Disease may be defined as a deviation from the healthy or normal condition of any of the functions of the living body—the *effect* may be temporary or permanently manifest in change of tissue.

Medicine can never in and of itself restore harmonious relations or substitute healthy for diseased tissues. *It must act in conjunction with the vital force and always occupy a subordinate place.* The great cause for disease being *overaction*, constant vigilance is required to prevent the substitution of a *drug* disease for the *natural* disease.

With these preliminaries understood, we will lay down the following proposition:

The highest mission of the true physician is the rapid, *gentle* and permanent restoration of the sick to health—to be satisfied with nothing short of a *cure*. Permanence is the most important factor, and the combination of the three measures the *skill* of the individual practitioner.

The discussion of this question must

therefore take into consideration all three factors, although special prominence will be given to the first because of the limitations of time.

Acute disturbances are as a rule self-limited, with a tendency to return to the *condition which existed prior to the exposure.*

It will be generally conceded that the suitable remedy should be repeated sufficiently often to enable the disturbed vital force to resume its normal activities, when the medicine should be stopped until the observations of the physician shall enable him to determine whether the vital force will be able to secure a normal or healthy state or only the *conditions which existed prior to the exposure.*

We should bear in mind the fact that in *acute* manifestations of disturbed functional activities, the *first* thing is to determine the nature of the *exciting* cause and remove the same if possible *without the aid of drugs*, because the addition of every drug tends to *complicate* a natural process. This is true in *acute* diseases, but in *chronic* diseases the vital force is absolutely incapable, through its own inherent power, of overcoming the *complications* that previous exposure has brought about. It must therefore depend upon the addition of a *new* force that will most perfectly co-operate with the vital force in securing *harmonious action.* This addition must be so carefully adjusted that there will be no *overaction* and at the same time *too little action* will retard the progress toward a cure. Here again do we find a test of the physician's skill. Theories and beliefs must surrender to positive knowledge; and it was with the hope that definite, positive data might be brought to you at this time that a systematic course of investigation was commenced one year ago.

For the purpose of thoroughly testing this matter every new case coming under our observation during the past year has been assigned to one of the following groups or classes, dependent in a measure upon their degree of *susceptibility* to environment.

Group A. Included such cases as showed a tendency to *over* action—stimulation, congestion—inflammation etc.

Group B. Included such cases as showed a tendency toward *under* action—depression—anemia—paralysis etc.

Group C. Included such cases as showed that the *primary* or *fundamental* cause was *constitutional* and dependent upon a dyscrasia that involved the *constructive* or *nutritive* functions of the body.

This classification was somewhat arbitrary and occasionally led to complications, whereby a case was transferred from one group to another, but in the main it proved a very satisfactory method for making comparisons.

To these we adopted the following rule for the repetition of the dose.

a) Give a single dose of the indicated remedy dry upon the tongue and wait for results.

b) Put the equivalent of a single dose into from two to six tablespoonfuls of water and direct that one tablespoonful be taken at regular intervals until gone.

c) Repeat the dose, either dry or in water, at regular intervals until action was recognized by an *aggravation* or *improvement*, when the remedy was stopped.

d) Repeat the remedy at regular intervals until indications called for a change of remedy, when the same rule was continued.

Our purpose in the test was to determine:

1st. The class in which improvement was *earliest* noted.

2d. The class in which improvement would be marked by the most *steady* progress as shown by *least change in remedies* or use of *intercurrent* remedies.

3d. The class showing the greatest *permanence* of action.

4th. The comparative values developed by potentisation.

The fact that nothing but *chronic* cases of a *complicated* nature come under our observation explains the further fact that the *lowest* degree of potentization employed was the *thirtieth* (centesimal scale).

The length of time given to these observations is too short to determine the *permanence* of action, consequently our report is incomplete and loses much of its *practical* value; but we hope to bring out a discussion that will impel every member present to put the matter to a thorough test and thus confirm or refute the *conclusions* drawn from our investigations.

Conclusions.

Group A. *Rapidity of action* was more uniform in the *lower* potencies when dissolved in water and given at *frequent* intervals for only a *few* hours.

Gentleness of action followed the single dose, either dry upon the tongue or dissolved in water; but it was at the expense of time, requiring in some cases double the time to complete the *curative* action of one remedy.

Intercurrents and *antidotes* were most frequently called for when the remedy was given "so long as improvement lasted."

Permanence of result cannot be determined at this time, but the general effect leads us to believe that in the majority of cases it will remain with that class who were instructed to repeat the remedy until action was established. This latter class was under closest observation, because the opinion of the patients could not be depended upon.

Group B. There can be no question about the rule to be adopted in this class of cases. The *lower* potencies must be employed. The *frequency* of the repetition depends upon nature of the disturbance, but as a rule, night and morning is sufficient for ordinary cases. *It should be continued, however, until positive action is established.* Prognosis must be guarded, because you get little direct assistance from the patient. This was the only class that offered the least encouragement for the persistent use of remedies and none of the cases in which this was followed has been discharged as cured; although in some cases the improvement has been of such a character that we can lengthen the interval between doses.

Group C. This is the most complicated and, consequently, the most difficult class to analyze. *Rapidity of action* is not to be thought of. The unexpected tempts the superficial prescriber to wander off into by-paths until he is hopelessly lost.

The class of remedies are *deep acting*, as a rule, and should be *undisturbed in their action*. Great care must be exercised to reduce *exciting* causes to the minimum and to surround the patient with a suitable environment. The skill and ingenuity of the physician is taxed to its utmost, but the results are most satisfactory. *Permanence* may be secured with both high and low potencies provided the remedy is carefully selected and *permitted to act*. The *single* dose apparently works better than when frequently repeated for a long period of time, and leads to fewer complications, but requires greater care and observation. A safe rule to follow is to repeat the dose every night or morning until action is manifest and then carefully note results *without interfering with its action*, unless compelled by the exigencies of the case.

H. W. Pierson.

AGAINST VACCINATION.

There is an initial difficulty in the way. To try to state the case against vaccination is to start with Alice a-hunting of the snark. For the snark, regarded as biological product, is quite as well known as and far more justly popular than the active organism of vaccine lymph, which has never yet been beheld of mortal man. Every inducement has been offered for the finding of him. Like some other notorious criminals, there is a reward for his capture of no less than £1,000 the amount offered by the Grocers' Company of London for his indentification and domestication, but the thousand goes begging, and there is none to claim. What "vaccination" is and how its alleged miracles are performed no man knows. Theories abound, but no two are alike and the fury with which the theorists attack one another is only exceeded by the fury with which they all assail me for the unpardonable offense of agreeing with all of them at once. The "exhaustion of pabulum theory, the "secretion of antidote" theory, the "identity" theory—all have risen like bubbles blown by a child at play, to win a moment's admiration from the unscientific public, and pass away. Of the last named, one of our greatest pathologists has said that we have heard the last of it from any man with a scientific reputation to lose—which is true, though we still hear a good deal of it from the ruck of medical practitioners, who have not. For better or for worse, vaccination remains an unexplained mystery. Medicine can tell us nothing of the rationale of its own faith. The whole thing is a crude empiricism, to be judged by results alone.

A Question of Statistics.

Thus it is an entirely false pretense to talk about vaccination as a medical question. Of results any man can judge. It needs no medical training to calculate a percentage, and when medical men, abondoning the attempt to render a pathological explanation of the matter, turn to tell us of what "statistics prove," they must descend from the tripod of the medical oracle and argue on level terms with the man in the street. The pretense that vaccination and its alleged benefits constitute a medical question, which none but medical men have the qualifications to discuss, was abandoned forever in the best, because the most honest, defense of vaccination ever penned, when Dr. Guy, F. R. S., told the Royal Statistical Society that "to the question whether vaccination is or is not a preventive of smallpox there is, there can be, no answer save such as is couched in the language of figures." A training in statistical science forms no part of the professional curriculum of a medical man, and those candid words shifted the venue from the pathological laboratory to the study of the statistician. There is nothing left but to compare the claims set up on behalf of vaccination with the actual observed facts of the case.

Jenner's Declarations.

But even so, the change benefits us little. What are the claims set up? The difficulty is not met, it is but shifted. For here we face the changelessness of never ending change. Year by year the claims made for vaccination have dwindled, till already, as Paddy would say, the vanishing point is well in sight. When, in June, 1798, after the three months of perfunctory investigation which the medical historian is accustomed to represent as "thirty years of incessant thought, watching and experiment," Jenner published to the world his "Inquiry Into the Causes and Effects of the Variolæ Vaccinæ." He therein wrote, "What renders the cowpox so extremely singular is that the person who has been thus affected is forever after secure from the infection of the smallpox; neither exposure to the variolous effluvia nor the insertion of the matter into the skin producing this distemper." In 1801, in a subsequent pamphlet, he repeated in even stronger terms, "The human frame, when once it has felt the influence of the genuine cowpox in the way that has been described, is never afterward at any period of its existence assailable by the smallpox." This was the declaration which won for Jenner his thirty thousand pounds; this the promise which elicited the first of our long series of compulsory vaccination laws from the English parliament.

That such pretensions were accepted, practically without question, seems wonderful to modern minds, but the wonder ceases when we reflect that vaccination is not the first but the second of the remedies to which the medical profession had pinned its faith. Inoculation, the predecessor of vaccination, was being found out for the deadly failure that it was, and the profession, that had been spreading the disease by the very measures they had so enthusiastically promoted for its suppression, found themselves in pressing danger of being found out with it. "Medicine," writes Sir John Simon, "was baffled and helpless." What was to be done? "Inoculate my way," said Jenner, "with cowpox instead of smallpox." And the profession wept on the neck of the man who rescued medicine from the ugliest fix it had ever been in.

Claims for Vaccination.

Little wonder, then, that the doctors of that day were delighted, and that, to adopt the paradox of the Solemn League and Covenant, "each ran before the other in their zeal" to read their confession of faith in the new creed of the cow. In 1800 John Ring, Jenner's henchman, published his "Testimonial," for which he had secured the signature of nearly every London doctor, wherein it was declared "our opinion that those persons who have had the cowpox are perfectly secure from the future infection of the smallpox." But these extracts from the fountain head cannot now be used as the basis of controversy; they only make the vaccinists angry, as reminding them too strongly of the altitude from which they have ever since been steadfastly engaged in climbing down. Not that the mass of accumulated post-vaccinal smallpox now recorded has diminished the assurance—it has but changed the terms—of the official language. As late as 1887 the *Lancet* pronounced it "within the power of every person to absolutely protect himself from all attack of smallpox;" and again in 1892 the same paper wrote in a leader: "No one need die of smallpox; indeed, no one need have it unless he likes—that is to say he can be absolutely protected by vaccination, once repeated." And the denial of any possible drawback has been neither less positive nor less emphatic than the assertion of the alleged benefits. "Against this vast gain," writes Sir John Simon, "there is no loss to count."

But in England at last the royal commission came, and promptly the doctors were seen falling over one another in their eagerness to disclaim these excessive assertions. Called to give evidence on which their reputation would be staked, the experts were suddenly smitten with an epidemic of carefulness. "Primary vaccination," admits Dr. Gayton, "is a very fleeting protection indeed—it is not absolutely protective up to any age; it would not ward off an epidemic." And the proper practice is in its every detail as difficult to run to earth as the theory on which it is supposed to be founded. Every possible number of marks, from a single insertion to something like a tattoo, finds adherents. The instruments to make these marks withal vary from a darning needle to a "three-pronged scratch," and the sapient authority which enjoins the treatment of the vaccine wounds by covering them with a vaccine shield is trampled on the heels by another, who declares that vaccine shields "restrict the circulation, rub off the scabs and are a fruitful source of danger." Of lymphs the name is legion, cultivated on a menagerie of divers beasts. As late as 1895 in England "fresh lymph from arm to arm" was the only variety sufficiently in favor with the government to earn the bonus, which was the official reward of what the wiseacres of Whitehall were pleased to call "efficient" vaccination.

Purity was Assured.

This lymph, you were assured, you could get absolutely pure—whatever that assertion might mean when applied to a material whose essential constitution was utterly unknown. It was all guaranteed by the government, we were assured, until the guaranteeing official, Mr. Farn, was examined before the commission, and admitted that he had never in his life guaranteed any lymph at all. And now our arm-to-arm lymph is all abandoned, and we are to have calf lymph, glycerinated. Why glycerinated? In order to destroy the "extraneous germs commonly present" in it. Commonly! Extraneous germs "commonly" present in the lymph to whose purity all officialism had been calling all its gods to witness through all the years in which the registrar general had been recording the confessed slaughter of a child every week on the average with lancet, tube and point! No detail of doctrine or administration but is divergent and disputed. Yet through all this diversity one unity prevails. For every kind and degree of failure there is always a ready fertility of excuse. Call as we may the witness of the vaccinated, who have had smallpox of every degree, even unto death, and they were always vaccinated either not widely enough or not often enough or too soon or too late. "Quackery," said Cobbett, "has always a shuffle left," and we must follow it through endless windings if it is to be thoroughly exposed.

Figures Against Vaccination.

To begin at the beginning—Do the vaccinated take smallpox? Certainly, in many thousands of cases. On this point it is enough to adopt the words of the dissentient report of the late Royal Commission: "It is superfluous to cite further evidence at this stage to prove, what is no longer denied by anybody, that smallpox attacks the vaccinated." But supposing a place to be well vaccinated, can smallpox prevail in that place? Certainly. The year 1888 found few places in England more thoroughly vaccinated than Sheffield. Between 1876 and 1888 Sheffield had earned £2,603 of bonus over and above the ordinary fees, for the excellence of her public vaccinations. That was the bonus of thirteen years, and in the thirteen months' epidemic of smallpox in 1887–88, Sheffield reaped her reward of 6,088 cases of smallpox. And five years later unvaccinated Leicester had her turn—the Leicester against which all the vials of medical prophecy had been poured out for many an expectant year. And while in Sheffield 192 persons were attacked in every 10,000 living there, in Leicester the attack rate was but 19 per 10,000 of the population; so that the man in the street in well-vaccinated Sheffield had just ten times the chance of taking smallpox as had the inhabitant of almost unvaccinated Leicester. Then will it preserve from death by smallpox? Certainly not.

Cities not Immune.

Warrington and Leicester had an outbreak of smallpox within a few months of each other. Warrington, vaccinated up to 95 percent of its births, had a mortality of fourteen per 10,000 of its inhabitants; Leicester's mortality from the cause was but little more than one per 10,000. But at least it will protect you for the first ten years of life, if it has been performed in infancy? Not a bit. In the one epidemic alluded to in Sheffield it is found that you may cut up the period of ten years into portions as you please, and still into each portion you can fit a vaccinated case of smallpox, whose record is contained in the returns of that one epidemic. Between 1865 and 1874 Berlin had 3,273 cases of smallpox in confessedly vaccinated children under 10 years of age, and of these 870 were fatal. But revaccination at the age of 12 is now the cry; and surely this will preserve you! Well, it is hard to see how it could have preserved the 870 of Berlin who were dead of smallpox before they were 10. So that the 12-year old plan is already given up by some of the best authorities. Dr. Birdwood of the smallpox hospital ships, London, has already declared in favor of revaccination every two years, and vaccination promises to join the ranks of movable feasts before long.

Sanitation Expels Smallpox.

But smallpox has declined. If it was not vaccination that caused the decline, what was it? Well, let us look at the history of London. London is not a little place and offers a fairly large sample of what is in the barn. From 1871-85 London was well vaccinated, only seven births in every 100, on the period average, escaping vaccination. And in that period the average smallpox mortality per million was 400, and the great epidemic of 1871-2 killed 2,422 per million. Then came a great change. In 1885 the system of extra mural isolation was adopted, the cases being removed to the hospital ships down the Thames. And from 1886-95, with an average vaccinal "default" of 15 per cent, that is, with more than twice as many births escaping vaccination, the average mortality sinks to ten per million, and the worst that smallpox could do in any one year was only forty-eight per million, thus showing that it is our sanitary measures that have stayed the steps of smallpox, even as the same measures have overthrown others of the same zymotic tribe, driving out plague, typhus and leprosy forever and depriving the other fevers of all but a fraction of their terrors. — *Chicago Record-Herald.*

Alfred Milnes, M. A.
London, England.

FIVE HUNDRED CASES OF SMALLPOX—NO DEATHS.

The smallpox epidemic of the past few years has been of a very remarkably mild type. The cases I have seen were taken very much as if they were coming down with la grippe—great aching, with chilliness, followed by fever which grew higher each day for four days, and began to recede as a very fine red eruption appeared, first on the forehead and face, then neck and chest, coming out on the pelvis and soles. At this latter stage the patient felt good, aching all gone and, although weak and exhausted, felt perfectly easy. These little fine red points soon enlarged, filled with a clear watery fluid and became raised. The contents of the pock soon turned yellow and began to discharge and dry up, commencing with a small depression or umbilication at the center. As the fluid turned to pus the patient had a recurrence of the fever, depending on the number of pocks and their size. In some cases the secondary fever was hardly noticeable while in others the patient raved in violent delirium.

The number of the pocks varied from a single one to many thousands. I counted seventy-five on one side of a lady's nose, not a very large nose either.

The cases were very contagious, usually every member of the family would have it, but there were many exceptions. Children were the most readily infected, but my worst case was a young lady twenty-two years old. While none died, some were very sick.

The treatment was, of coarse, the indicated remedy. Belladonna and Bryonia were often indicated in the pre-eruption stage, while Pulsatilla, Arsenic, Sulphur, Rhus tox. and a wide range of remedies were called for during the secondary fever.

Vaccination or the administration of Variolinum did not prevent. A great many were vaccinated and never exposed. Quite a number who were vaccinated took the disease, so many coming under this class that some of my old school brethren declared it could not be smallpox, because no vaccinated person could have smallpox.

It might be well to notice that faith in vaccination had a very rude shock in this community. I had one case, an Indian, about forty-five years old, who had been successfully vaccinated three times, and he had a pretty rough case. Others had it a week, two weeks, six weeks, or any time, after vaccination, and I could see no difference between these and others who had not been vaccinated.

As regards pitting, it is my experience that a large majority of cases, being mild ones, did not pit; but that where the ulceration was deep, through the true skin, nothing would prevent the little white scars showing for life. Some old practitioners may criticise this statement and think I should have done something to prevent it. And this reminds me of a lecture of the late Dr. J. S. Hoyne who said, "we tried everything to prevent pitting." Dr. Small, then of Hahnemann College, conceived the idea that by puncturing the vesicle with a fine needle pitting could be prevented. It seemed to work in some cases, but one day he was called to attend a lady who was very anxious to keep her good looks on account of her position in society, and Dr. Small went all over her face, carefully puncturing every one of the thousand or more vesicles; and," added Dr. Hoyne, "she was the worst pitted case I ever saw." I give it up; I know of nothing and I do not believe there is anything that will prevent the scar forming on the face when the ulceration is through the true skin, and, more especially, when the disease is of the confluent type. The scales that come off after the pock has discharged and dried up are of a dirty brownish color, and when thrown into the fire snap and crack like pine needles. Where pitting has not occurred a large purplish spot is left, the size of a dime, which remains for many weeks.

Isolation or quarantine is the true preventive. I do not believe in the smallpox suit to prevent the physician carrying the disease around, but do think that the physician should wash his hands after handling the patient.

I think actual contact is necessary to communicate the disease; that is, a person must come near enough to a case to be within the influence of the poisonous exhalations which are always given off by a sick person. And I think the most contagious period is about the fourth day, when the eruption is first appearing and the fever is very high.

In conclusion I would say that the discharging pocks have a most disagreeable odor and a bad case will destroy one's appetite for quite a while. I attended about five hundred cases, with no deaths, the most of the cases being mild ones.

L. P. MUNGER, M. D.

Hart, Mich.

THE SUBVERSIVE FORCES.

Nature has its obverse and its reverse sides. Generally speaking, this is true in a material as well as in a spiritual sense. Nature, we believe, was originally governed by harmonic forces only. What is harmonic is true; what is unharmonic is untrue. Some of the characteristics of harmonics are completeness, law, government, system, proportionality, time, concordance, true relationship in all things and under all conditions. In the movements of the planets there is an attempt at disharmony by a slight wavering from the paths of their orbits due to the influence of other bodies; but the law of gravitation re-establishes them, and harmony reigns in that adjustment that is provisional in nature. Harmony has its perfection of sounds, of stops, rests, pauses, rythms, progressions, scales, curves, axes, chords, vibrations, melodies and euphonies. All the harmonies of the universe have their special tones, rythms, keys, pitch. All true nature's songs are musical and restful to the true ear of music. When we see perfection in music, in form or color we say it is divine. So we may say of all nature; as it assumes perfection it is clothed and hallowed by divinity and, in proportion as it is perfect, it magnifies its creator. It is then freed from the influence of all subversive forces, and endowed with power to resist the influences of their presence.

So it is in a perfect organism, he is neither conscious or in any degree subservient to their influences. If the elements clash he feels them not. The temperature may rise or fall, but he accommodates himself to it. That power which tempers the conditions to the shorn lamb lies often within the organism itself, a genetic principle, in the way of some provisional, a concomitant of himself, and in that way man becomes a law unto himself by his obedience to law. The subversive forces are but the outgrowth of broken law—error quaked and fled away under the mutterings and condemnations of Sinai when the law was written for the people of this earth. The stilling of the waves of Galilee was but a rebuke to him who is the father of all subversion.

When we study the relationship between sin and disease we see they are quite parallel—"The wages of sin is death;" so, often disease destroys or overcomes the life. Sin is progressive, so is disease. Sin hates law, so disease hates life or physiological law. Sin robs us of physical and spiritual strength, so does disease. Sin degrades, so does disease; in fact, disease is but the sequela of sin. In the many expressions of disease we meet with, we see in them but the characters and expressions of the different forms and expressions of sin. Take, for instance, one of the chronic subversive forces, such as syphilis, and we see stamped upon the whole of its endless phenomena a character peculiar to itself, seen in no other disturber of the organism, presenting phenomena progressively, a tiara of potencies, each growing in intensity of power in the order of its progression, each expression seeming quite different in form from the other, yet partaking of the same genetic principle of nature and action innate in its parent, *incertum lues*, with its periods of pauses and rests, progressions and polymorphic lesions, which have no similar in the category of disease.

So, then, we see that the study of all disease is the study of the character of sin, the disease being the physical expression of a certain form of sin. As sin is the transgression of the law, so is disease a transgression; as the germ begotten of one sin begets another, so the germ begotten of one disease begets another; a vital principle is undermined that weakens another, and makes vulnerable parts and processes once invulnerable. If we inoculate our bodies with a death dealing element, as is seen in vaccination virus inoculation, we must expect a death-dealing process to follow. It is a false hope of overcoming one special subversive force, that may never appear, by another and by so doing undermine a thousand and one health processes. It is like using an old worn-out gun to shoot at a mark, when the gunner too often becomes the mark. A physician's constant effort should be to strengthen life processes and to fortify the truth at all times, for we know there is no end to the destructive processes or developments set up in some organism, especially the tubercular one, through this vicious method of vaccination. The organism is always disturbed in the direction of the action of the predisposing miasm. If the organism is sycotic in its nature, then the developments will be of that order, with its attending phenomena. Yet this is true of anything that disturbs the life force, whether it be due to crude drugs or to the effects of acute diseases. The sensitivity of the organism is intensified in disease, especially if the circulation is increased and there is a weakened eliminative process. It is when there is extra work to be done, when the physiological powers are overtaxed, the eliminative channels clogged and energy is not being housed in the tissues that the subversive forces take undue advantage of us. In our moments of weakness they insinuate their new processes, changing the life forces or their mode of action, and we know that changed momentum gives us new processes. Excesses come in both structure and those physiological reagents that have to do with food changes, so we become a prey not only to the subversive forces themselves, but to all the processes and changes to which the organism is subservient, until the life forces are no longer able to free themselves from the new bond, and they at once begin to adapt themselves to the new order of things, and there follows a history of endless subversive changes and disease phenomena peculiar to each type or order, whether it be of syphilis, psora or sycosis, or any of their blendings, from the initial lesion, as in syphilis, to the tertiary destructive processes of the body structure of the body. Few are the physicians who have not noticed the sudden and mysterious appearance of disease in the human organism, coming, as it seemed, from nowhere and developing with no plausible reason or apparent cause, remaining either as a functional disturbance or developing into some pathological condition after causing untold suffering or, many times, endangering the life of the sufferer. How few have come to any positive solution of this subject in their own minds. *But Hahnemann has solved this mysterious problem for us, and if we will but listen to his words of wisdom, we may know where commenceth the sudden pain, the rheumatism, the neuralgia, the eczema, the ulcer, the new growth, the stasis to internal organs, the cough, the spasm, the convulsion—yes, all the phenomena that is tabulated under what is known as disease.* All this falsifying of its processes, these anatomical and physiological deflections from what is true can be reasonably shown to be caused by and have their origin in the chronic miasms, either singly or combined with each other, in their various degrees of combination. As a cause of disease, sycosis today outnumbers all the miasms. It is said that fully eighty percent of all disease today depends upon it as a primary cause, with its countless manifestations, its inflammatory processes, its cystic degeneration, its fibrous changes, its rheumatism, its gouty concretions and its thousand and one manners of attack. It fills our jails, our prisons and houses of correction and lies behind much of the criminality of our country.

The early appearance of mental phenomena is so indicative of sycosis. That monarch, The Mind, is overthrown. HE THINKS, HE WILLS, HE ACTS, and out of that triune develops the lust disease. A precept of the Decalogue is broken and he falls, by virtue of the loss of that genetic principle which is a part of the character of his Creator after whose image he is created, and at once he becomes subservient to the false disintegrative power of subversion, and the true physiological processes cease at that moment. Then a false one is set up in that organism, whether moral, spiritual or physical, and to some degree take on a retrograde action, and a miasm becomes consistent with the life force. Therefore the life forces are from that moment propelled forward in the direction of its influence, and that which was first a mental process, an unholy thought implanted the seeds of death within the life; first functional, later on it becomes an organic disease, the *fons et origo et mali* of so many of the diseases of the present day.

The first order of subversive forces affecting the human organism are the chronic miasms, syphilis, psora and sycosis, which are directly or indirectly the origin of all diseases affecting the human organism, the cause of death and decay of body and all those false and unnatural processes of that which is known as disease.

The second order of subversive forces are the acute miasms, as seen in typhoid fever, the exanthematous diseases, diphtheria, la grippe and many others that present themselves from time to time, often so dangerous and destructive to life. We notice that they do not attack all individuals alike or with the same degree of intensity, and herein is revealed one of the mysteries of one of Hahnemann's discoveries, which might be called the mystery of iniquity, or the bond between sin and disease, for we find that the second order of subversive forces (acute miasms) depend upon the first order (the chronic miasms). See Organon, paragraph 31.

Speaking of morbific agents, Hahnemann says:

"We do not fall sick beneath their influences before the economy (the organism) is sufficiently disposed and laid open to attack of morbific causes." By this we understand that the organism cannot contract a new acute disease or come under the influence of a contagious element (acute miasm) unless the soil (system) has been first prepared for it by the first order of subversive forces, syphilis, psora or sycosis. There must be in that organism a prepared aura, or an agreement to an acceptance, a conjugality of concomitants, a marriage with the subversion, as the organism has made an unholy alliance or has been born with one, a treibund, as it were, with the allies, and it is now in bond to the new subversion, both as to its character and its phenomena; for its phenomena is its character, soon to be known to all men, and that prophecy can no longer be fullfilled: "If they drink any deadly thing it shall not hurt them." We can say with Hamlet: "Observe my uncle; if his occulted guilt does not unkennel in one speech, it is a damned ghost that we have seen." In the beginning man was given dominion over everything that creepeth upon the earth. There was no limit to it. There was no power left out that was not his, not even death. But now we see this is not the case, for by sin we became subservient to the first order of subversive forces that had within themselves the power to allow the second order to come in which in themselves are but condemnation of the first order.

The third order of subversive forces to which humanity often becomes a slave or bondman too, may be divided, for convenience, into terrestrial, and celestial, or influences in the earth and those of the heavens. Sometimes one form is modified by the other. Throughout all the chronic miasms are these seen. Thus we find in our drug provings that their modalities depend on the existence or influences of something else, as to their periodicities < and > idiosyncrasy, predisposition, susceptibility, atmospheric, electro-thermal and solstic changes. The sycotic patient trembles at the moving wheels of the Zodiac as it unwinds its solar problems. He wanders about the earth for relief; we find him in the bath and the steaming-tub. Every mineral spring of any importance on the earth has seen his face. He goes up and down for help. When the seasons change he suffers with pains of every character—rheumatism, gout etc. He is super-sensitive to pain, and writhes, twists and squirms under it. Why should he be subject to a falling barometer or to planetary fluctuations. Because he has violated law or, by heredity, has become subservient to a broken precept. As long as he fulfilled these precepts or, by a true recognition of them he was protected by all that power that was behind these laws and precepts, the principles so involved are insignias of power and truth. He has lost now his power of resistence that before his fall was a genetic principle in the life force. If it rained he heeded it not. If the atmosphere was surcharged with moisture it mattered not to him. The storm came and the heat, and the summer and the winter passed, but he suffered no special inconvenience. But now he is no longer fortified. The rain, the snow, the rising and falling barometer are his enemies, his peace disturbers, his combatants, where before they were his friends, his supporters in life. He now has many enemies, yea, nature cries out against him. He is like the tides of the sea that, subject to the vacillating moon, rise and fall at her august command. His fever, his pains, his feelings, his strength rise and fall with its ebb and flow. Yea, the conjugations of the far-off moving planets assist in bringing about his subversions, his pains and his sufferings and changes in his own little system that is no longer obedient to that higher law of life or true harmonics. The law governing harmonics is the law of life; the rebellion began within himself. The touch of nature which makes all things kin is no more, *hence he cannot help himself, and in his weakness and distress he must cry out for help*, since all nature, every precept and every law condemn him, of which he was once coexistent of and cooperative with. Out of his distress, out of his need, has arisen all the schools of medicine, sciences, pathies, antipathies, creeds of healing, orders, sects, systems that mortal man could invent, even out of the darkness, out of his distress came the fourth order of subversive forces. Out of the man-made helps and systems with their venesections, counter-irritants, cauteries, blisters, tonics, stimulants in their multiplied forms, the plasters, the splints and the bandages of tradition, until he crieth, "Whence cometh my help? Is there no balm in Gilead?"

Yes, these death processes come in the place of life, and we see them in the animal and vegetable also. But my first answer to his question, "Is there any balm in Gilead?" is that a new life must begin in himself with each individual. We must live, think, act, eat, even hope aright. This is divine healing. If we look up the word Health we find it to be an abstract noun, from the word *whole*, not from heal. *Whole* is hale, sound, entire, complete. "They that are whole need not a physician." The original form of the word *hale* is hal, a descent from hal, hool, whole, Norwegian, "hel," (the w being in use only during the past 400 years). Hel, hale, holy, health, thus it runs, hal, hol, hool, holy, holiness. Got ist mein heil: Isa. 12: 2. So we see that to be healthy is to be holy.

The second answer to the human cry is that we offer to them this God given gift of Hahnemann—Homœopathy—a system of medicine that stands alone in the broadness of its scope, in the perfection of it as a science, not man made nor man-limited. A system that has no marks of man's fingers upon it, nor stamped with the insignia of his mind. To the earnest student a thing of beauty, a wonder and a power of the God who gave it. But there are many who would limit its power and insist upon perverting it by the alteration of remedies and the use of crude drugs, never willing to admit that it is a system of dynamics and not of chemistry, expecting much and receiving little; for he who uses the crude drug or the lower potencies cannot expect to be classified above his power. There are changes and movements and actions in the clockwork of organisms that are not catalogued under the third potency; yea nor under the thousandth nor the millionth. It requires instruments of the highest power to follow all the movements of the subversive forces' actions upon the life force that to the mind which has not studied potentiality is invisible, and tracings that are divine, responding only to law and to potency. They speak to him in unknown tongues and out of temples unseen. A thousand years of syphilis, or psora of hereditary transmission, has produced a potential in that so-affected organism that cannot be measured but by potency and by law; the dynamics that may meet it under similia may not yet have been conceived. Then let us not entrammel law, nor seek to follow those infinite subversions except through the gateway of *similia, simplex, minimum*.

The *higher* homœopathy is growing; the *false* is falling into decay. Some have gone after false gods and associated themselves with error and believed a lie; therefore they must return unto the dust from whence they came, by the same road by which they came up out to their man-made science and their man-made system of medicine that only has faint tracings of the good, having not the seal of the law nor the insignia of similia and of power. Even now we can say with the poet.

"The world with this faith is filled,
Then let come the fervent zeal,
The hearts of fire and of steel;
The hands that believe and build.

"For the past is dead to their prayers.
Out of the shadow of night,
The world wheels into light,
And it is daybreak everywhere."

J. H. ALLEN, M. D.

Chicago.

APHORISMS REGARDING CONSUMPTION.

Massachusetts is the only state operating a sanitorium for the cure of consumption.

It is not sufficient to prescribe rich food; the prescription will not take the place of the thing prescribed.

The sooner the patient puts himself under the care of a competent physician the greater are his chances of recovery.

Thousands are dying of tuberculosis, not because their disease is incurable, but because there is no place to cure them.

A tonic to increase the appetite will be of no avail to the poor man whose means will not allow satisfaction of even a poor appetite.

Malnutrition is a predisposing cause of tuberculosis. To cure this trouble the factory and shopgirl should be educated in housekeeping.

Cincinnati, Boston, New York and Buffalo are the only municipalities in the United States having special institutions for the cure of consumption.

Pulmonary tuberculosis can be cured in almost all climates lacking too pronounced extremes of temperature, and where the air is relatively pure and fresh.

During 1901, American citizens donated for educational, religious and philanthropical institutions the sum of $107-300,000. A part of this could, with great benefit, be diverted to the erection of decent habitations for the poor of every large city.

In Europe royalty and aristocracy have created hundreds of sanitoria; the kings and queens of American finance could perform a much greater amount of good.

The erection of unsanitary tenement houses should be prohibited by proper legislation. Without the better housing of the poor the tuberculosis problem will never be solved.

There are now enough largely endowed colleges, plenty of libraries and general hospitals; but there is a penury of good model tenement houses; too few public baths; a scarcity of decently kept places of amusement.

The most modern and most successful methods of treating consumption consist exclusively in the scientific and judicious use of fresh air, sunshine, water, abundant and good food, and the help of certain medicinal substances when the just mentioned hygienic and dietetic means do not suffice in themselves to combat the disease.

It should be the duty of every physician to exert his influence with municipalities, statesmen and philanthropists to induce them to build and maintain sufficient sanitoria in which to place immediately all cases of consumption which either constitute a source of infection to their kin and neighbors, or who cannot receive in their homes the proper treatment which their condition demands.

Compiled from paper of S. A. Knopf, M. D.—*Medical Record.*

Materia Medica.

MALANDRINUM.

Malandrinum is a nosode from the disease called grease in horses. Grease conveyed from horses by grooms to the cows appears as cow-pox and the same disease carried to sheep is known by the name scab.

Malandrinum, potentized, is a useful medicine in the treatment of variola and given as a prophylactic, it proves to be of so much greater power that vaccination does not "take" on persons who have taken a few doses of Malandrinum in the five thousandth potency at intervals of two to seven days, going about their work in the midst of an epidemic.

Dr. I. Bosowitz, of Brooklyn, recommends the virus of the malanders, or the grease of the horse, either for the inoculation, instead of the cow-pox virus, or for internal use in a high trituration. Dr. Raue in his admirable work, Special Pathology and Therapeutic Hints, page 999 says: "The successful application of Malandrinum as a preventive has been confirmed this season (1880–81) by Dr. R. Straube, several others and myself. It prevented the suppurative fever, or lessened it, to a considerable degree and took away all offensive exhalations. Cerebral symptoms, such as delirium and hallucinations, necessitated the interposition of Stramonium, while great soreness of the throat and cough required Belladonna."

Dr. R. Straube wrote an article containing a partial proving of this remedy for North American Journal of Homoeopathy, August, 1881. He says:

"Malandrinum produces aching in the lower part of the upper third of the forehead. This was shown by several persons December, 1899, under my own observation and care, taking Malandrinum the ^{mm}."

Some Cases.

Dec. 9, 1899. No. 1. J. M. H., age 50, light complexion, blue eyes, farmer.

Head—Ache in frontal region.

Abdomen—Pain in bowels, worse riding on horse back.

Skin — Itching; sensation as if burned.

No. 2. Mrs. J. M. H., age 43, dark complexion, wife of No. 1.

Head—Ache in upper frontal region.

Stomach—Sickness in stomach.

Neck—Tired.

No. 3. Nellie, age 4, daughter of Nos. 1 and 2.

Mind—Lazy, tired.

Skin—Itch.

No. 4. J. H. F., age 28, blacksmith, light complexion, employed as guard during an epidemic of variola.

Sensorium—Dizzy like a drunken man.

No. 5. Mrs. J. H. F., wife of No. 4. Nursing a baby.

Head — Frontal headache above the center all the way across the head.

Chills—Feels cold. Says, "I do not know whether I am taking a chill or not."

No. 6. H. G. L., age 30, farmer, robust.

Took one dose after dinner which was at noon.

Head—Ache in upper frontal region at 7 to 9 p. m.

Chill, fever etc., coldness at night.
Skin — Itching; sensation as if burned; itching on legs.

Dec. 10.

No. 7. Mrs. H. G. L., wife of No. 6.
Took one dose, tablespoonful of solution of 6m in water after dinner.
Noticed that evening at 7 to 9 o'clock:
Head—Ache in the upper frontal region.
Mouth—Inside of mouth sore.
Drinking—Water sickening to the taste.
Stomach—Sick at stomach.
Neck—Tired.
Sleep—Wakes up often during the night, thinks it will never be morning.
Nerves—Sensation of being tired.
Extremities — Upper and lower limbs ached on the 14th.
Skin—Itching, burning.
Chill—Coldness at night.

No. 8. S. C. F. Light complexion, grain buyer, 6 feet high, weight 200 lbs. A remarkably healthy man; one who never calls a doctor. Took a tablespoonful of a watery solution of Malandrinum[1m] on the morning of the 10th before breakfast.

The next morning at 8 o'clock, about 22 hours after taking the dose he experienced:

Head—Ache in the upper frontal region; forehead a little warmer than usual.
He says, "I am never sick and never had such a headache and have no indigestion to account for it. It was just a genuine ache. Ceased about 4 p. m.
Chill, fever—A feeling of coldness at night.

Dec. 11. Mouth and lips sore.

Dec. 10.

No. 9. Mrs. S. O. F., dark complexion, age 43.
Took one dose dry on her tongue about 4 o'clock p. m. After dinner she felt sick at her stomach. Did not think at first it was caused by the medicine.
Head—Ache afternoon and evening one day until about 9 p. m. above the center of the head; all the way across the forehead. Could not tell how it felt. She said: "It seemed to make me sick at the stomach. It was made worse by motion."
Upper extremities — Pains in the arms at night.

Dec. 14. Skin—Itching of the body at the back of the neck.

No. 10. Miss G. F., age 20, complexion fair, daughter of Nos. 8 and 9.
Head—Ache in frontal region just a little above the center, all the way across the forehead. She could not describe the sensation.
Sensorium—Dizziness, inclination to fall forward. Thought she would fall if she did not sit down.
Mouth—Taste like the smell of sour milk.
Throat — A little sore at night. Worse swallowing drinks than food, but even empty swallowing aggravates it. She says, "My arms and legs ached so Monday (Dec. 11) I thought I was taking la grippe." She thinks she did not notice the aching so much when going around as when sitting.

J. S. WATT, M. D.

Brookville, Kansas.

THERAPEUTIC HINTS, TAKEN FROM MY NOTE BOOK OF OVER FORTY YEARS' PRACTICAL OBSERVATION.

When called to a person who feels he has cold chills running up the spine, yet to the touch is hot, there is no remedy equal to Gelsemium, frequently repeated. Again, if pain or aching all through the body is so severe that he cannot be quiet, Gelsemium.

If there is severe chill, catarrhal condition of bronchi and head, and soreness of chest, Gelsemium.

If called to a person whose head is hot, extremities cold, no particular pain, stupor, dull, desires to be let alone, Gelsemium.

Many children will be dull, stupid, not much fever nor any very positive phenomena, Gelsemium.

Many persons, especially women, have a headache for months, just enough to be annoying, top and back of head, Gelsemium three times a day will relieve in a short time.

When you find a person subject to spasms of glottis, no remedy equals Gelsemium.

If called to see scarlet fever, measles or any eruptive disease, I have never found any equal to Gelsemium to allay the irritation of the mucous surfaces, relieve the head and drive to the surface the eruption.

Again persons will come stating that they wake up in the night with a nervous feeling in fleshy part of the legs and arms; cannot go to sleep; muscles in continuous commotion—not a cramp, but a nervous feeling of unrest—not troubled during the day, Gelsemium upon retiring and upon awakening will soon relieve.

On the first days of all malarial fevers Gelsemium is an important factor, as it prepares the system for other remedies, breaks the force of the attack as well, and many times does all the work.

When a woman at the time of one or two days before the menstrual period is nervous, spasmodic dysmenorrhea, severe pains, increasing until flow is established, Gelsemium has always given relief, quieting the pains and producing a normal flow.

In nearly all cases of maiden ladies of a nervous temperament, whose lives are spent largely in society and upon whom there is a constant nervous strain, when some act or function has not met expectations, and the high tension has met a mountain of difficulties, they collapse into a discouraged condition of hysteria, for such nothing is equal to Gelsemium.

To some women whose menstruation is regular but scant, the day the period comes on they will have severe pain, cramp, sense of nausea, pale, pulse and heart weak, nervous prostration, extremities cold, give Gelsemium.

In a large per cent of cases of insomnia from mental overwork, feel as though could not get themselves together, or remain still long enough to quiet down, want of nervous control, Gelsemium.

In gonorrhea, old cases, discharge moderate though constant, with but little burning in urinating, has been drugged and locally burned out, Gelsemium, constitutionally and locally, restores to normal conditions more surely than any other treatment I have found.

In eclampsia either before, during or after delivery in nervous temperaments of a hysterical make-up, and when the convulsion is severe but assumes normal after each attack, Gelsemium is almost a specific.

Any unexpected thing or condition, as ringing of a night-bell or anything that causes sudden alarm and relaxed condition of the sphincters is quickly relieved by four or five drops of Gelsemium.

In facial neuralgia, of the teeth or head generally, if caused by a cold or sudden change of the weather, and pains from fatigue or severe exertion, running, jumping or over muscular excitation, pain in the eyes, ears when from a cold, a lame stiffness of any part of the body, or muscular rheumatism, all of which have been caused by change of weather or getting wet or overwork, is relieved by Gelsemium. In short any and all conditions of mucous and catarrhal conditions from above causes.

Pains of nerve origin are relieved by Gelsemium.

The action of Gelsemium in all the above and kindred conditions is rapid, and leaves no constitutional effect. It does its work and passes off. I have verified the action of this remedy so often in the above conditions during a forty years' busy practice that I used it with the same confidence one expects rest from sleep, and with a feeling of certainty that cannot be had in using the new remedies now flooding the market.

J. E. King, M. D.

Eldora, Iowa.

BACILLINUM.*

A nosode of tuberculosis named and first described by Dr. Burnett, for whom it was prepared from tuberculous sputum by Dr. Heath. As this preparation has been experimented with separately, I think it, on the whole, advisable to give its symptoms apart from the other nosodes of phthisis.

Clinical.—*Addison's disease.* Alopecia. Consumptiveness. Growth, defective. *Hydrocephalus.* Idiocy. Insanity. Joints, affections of. Phthiriasis. Pityriasis. *Ringworm.* Scrofulous glands. Teeth, defective; pitted. *Tuberculosis.*

Characteristics.—This remedy has been used largely in infrequent doses (at intervals of a week or more) of the 30th and upwards chiefly on diathetic indications in the affections named above. In acute affections it has been found useful to dissolve a few globules in a wineglassful of water and administer a teaspoonful every four hours. In the provings, a severe headache, deep in, < by motion, was a constant symptom; also a slight cough with easy expectoration of phlegm. In cases of acute tuberculosis it has not done so well as in more chronic cases. Dr. Cartier has found it particularly useful in cases where there was excessive muco-purulent bronchial secretion threatening to occlude the lungs. It must be compared with *Bacillinum testium*, *Tuberculinum* of Swan, *Aviaire Tuberculinum* of Koch. Dr. Burnett has shown that ringworm of the scalp and pityriasis versicolor on the body are indications of tubercular diathesis, and they respond to this remedy. Also they are leading indications for it when present in combination with other affections. A case of insanity with pityriasis yielded rapidly to the remedy. Phthiriasis has been cured by it when all attempts to kill the body-lice by parasiticides were useless. Dr. Young has recorded the cure of several cretinous idiots. An inter-current course of *Bacillinum* will often make a wonderful change in patients who have a personal or family history of chest affections. I have found an eczematous condition of the margins of the eyelids a strong indication for it. < Night and early morning; < cold air.

*Reprint from Dictionary of Materia Medica, by John H. Clarke, M. D., London.

It is a diathetic remedy of vast importance. The symptoms of the *schema* are taken from the provings by Burnett and myself recorded in the last edition of Burnett's *The Cure of Consumption by its own Virus*, together with some from a proving by R. Boocock.

Relations.—Calc. phos. goes with this remedy very well. So do Lach. and Kali c. I know of no antidote.

Symptoms.

1. *Mind.*—Taciturn, sulky, snappish, fretty, irritable, morose, depressed and melancholic even to insanity.—Fretful ailing, whines and complains; mind given to be frightened, particularly by dogs.

2. *Head.*—Severe headache, deep in, recurring from time to time, compelling quiet fixedness; < shaking head.—Terrible pain in head as if he had a tight hoop of iron round it; trembling of hands; sensation of damp clothes on spine; absolute sleeplessness.—Meningitis.—Ringworm.—Alopecia areata.

3. *Eyes.*—Eczematous condition of eyelids.

6. *Face.*—Indolent, angry pimple on left cheek, breaking out from time to time and persisting for many weeks.

7. *Teeth.*—Aching in teeth, especially lower incisors (all sound), felt at the roots, especially on raising or projecting lower lip; very sensitive to air.—Grinds teeth in sleep.—Imperfectly developed teeth.

9. *Throat.* — Tickling in fauces, compelling cough.

11. *Stomach.*—Windy dyspepsia, with pinching pains under ribs of right side in mammary line.

12. *Abdomen.*—Fever, emaciation, abdominal pains and discomfort, restless at night, glands of both groins enlarged and indurated; cries out in sleep; strawberry tongue.—Tabes mesenterica; talks in sleep; grinds teeth; appetite poor; hands blue; indurated and palpable glands everywhere; drum belly; spleen region bulging out.—Inguinal glands indurated and visible; excessive sweats; chronic diarrhoea.

13. *Stool and Anus.*—Sudden diarrhoea before breakfast, with nausea.—Severe hæmorrhages from bowels, cough.—Obstinate constipation.—Passes much ill-smelling flatus. — Stitchlike pain through piles.

14. *Urinary Organs.* — Increased quantity of urine, pale, with white sediment.—Has to rise several times in night to urinate.

14. *Respiratory Organs.*—Slight, tedious, hacking cough.—Hard cough, shaking patient, more during sleep but it did not waken him. Pricking in larynx with sudden cough. — Single cough on rising from bed in morning.—Cough waking him in night; easy expectoration.—Expectoration of non-viscid easily detached, thick phlegm from air passages, followed after a day or two by a very clear ring of voice.—Sharp pain in precordial region arresting breathing.—Very sharp pain in left scapula, < lying down in bed at night, > by warmth.

20. *Neck and Back.* — Glands and neck enlarged and tender.

23. *Lower Limbs.*—Pain in left knee whilst walking; passed off after persevering in walking for a short distance.—Tubercular inflammation of knee.

24. *Generalities.*—Great weakness, did not want to be disturbed.

26. *Sleep.*—Drowsy at day; restless at night; many dreams.

27. *Fever.*—Flush of heat (soon after the dose), some perspiration, severe headache deep in.

ON THE PATHOLOGY OF ARSENICUM.

Acute gastritis has a clearly defined course. The irritation produces an excessive amount of gastric juice that overcomes, on its way down, the alkaline current from the liver and the pancreas, yes, even of the intestinal succus, so that enervation is retarded, digestion is imperfect and the body weakened. The thirst for water increases the gastric irritation and an anæsthetic like alcohol is preferred, but the subsequent heat and burning is distressing. This condition produces a restlessness of body which, as emaciation goes on, is attended with a mental foreboding that becomes agonizing. The heart is taxed, and rushes the lessening blood current so that the brain is drained to supply other vital organs and functions. The appearance of the body is that of starvation. Emaciation, nervous, restless apprehension, with coldness of the surface, is the outward expression of the internal gastritis, whose pathology is inflammation of the stomach and of the intestines also. The secretions are deficient and the excretions defective.

Arsenic taken in palpable doses produces effects that correspond to that pathological picture. The nausea, vomiting and diarrhea are the early effects; while thirst, emaciation and restlessness are due to the systemic drain going on. The brain does not get its proper supply of blood, and mental vagaries and apprehension come on *passi passu*.

The small dose only can produce these later symptoms, so in therapeutics, according to similia, we select an attenuated dose and give it to match them. "Die milde macht ist gross"—and similia is its guiding star.

T. C. D.

A GELSEMIUM CASE.

Mrs. H. P. C., pregnant five months.

- Sick headache, pains ascend from neck, accompanied by profuse urination.
- Sleepy faintness, sometimes fainting, better from motion in open air.
- Constipated; much flatulency.
- Deep yellow, acrid, adhesive leucorrhoea.
- Formerly had diarrhoea from emotions.

Has lately returned from the tropics; Gelsemium[cm] cured.

After delivery the child showed severe brain symptoms, rubbing the head, screaming constantly and vomiting hard curds of milk, æthusa helped for a little while only.

I now found great dread of downward motion present, sleeplessness also appeared, part of the mother's Gelsemium state seemed to show in the infant, for this it received Gelsemium[cm] B. & T. with prompt relief.

We are accustomed to look upon the symptom as distinctive of Borax, but from several late experiences, I am persuaded that it is equally characteristic of Gelsemium, provided of course that the other symptoms confirmed the choice.

While making a practical application of our materia medica, I have found many symptoms of pronounced value upon which doubts and aspersions have formerly been cast; it is therefore to be earnestly hoped that none of us will be guilty of casting out these provings until their unfitness has clearly been proven, the pathogenesis is a rich mine and it is our plain duty to develop and determine its drift; the gold is there, but we must mine it.

C. M. Boger.
Parkersburg, West Virginia.

HYPERTROPHY OF HEART WITH GASTRIC CATARRH.

TOLEDO, WASH., June 30, 1902.

Dear Doctor Duncan: Having noted your offer to help in some cases, I beg your assistance on inclosed case.

I think the patient has functional heart trouble.

I live in hopes to be able, before long, to come to Dunham and learn how to cure sick people. I told the party I would send his case to you as I was sure he could be cured and saved to his family.

Thanking you in advance, I remain,

Yours very truly,

A. A. POMPE, M. D.

Mr. J. D., age 36; farmer, short, thick-set; Dane; forehead wrinkled; red cheeks; mournful, woebegone expression of face.

Cannot breathe well, has to draw long breath; feels tender in pit of stomach; has to hawk, and secretion seems to come from stomach, feels better when it comes up; nearly chokes him to get breath sometimes, has to stoop over to get breath. This trouble passes off when he gets dizzy spells in the head, when very dizzy can breathe easily.

On further inquiry elicited the following:

Head—Dizzy, worse ringing after stooping any time of day or night; blood seems to rush to head when stooping over, and everything goes in a circle, has to catch hold of something to keep from falling.

At another time I obtained:

Head—Pressure on side of head (temple); head feels heavy; sometimes holds head with both hands for a minute, but that does not give much relief. When he has the dizzy spells, feels heat coming up from stomach, and sweat breaks out of all pores; feels as if needles were stuck into all pores. Feels sick at stomach, with dizzy spells, but cannot vomit—feels as if he would feel better if he could vomit. When dizzy spells come on has ringing or sizzling in left ear, as of steam blowing out of safety-valve; sometimes ringing like cowbells. Has these symptoms to a less degree when not dizzy. When dizzy feels weak in the knees, as if he were going to sink down. Feels good in the morning when he arises, but when he starts to move around dizziness commences. Sleeps well; dreams of his work.

Mind—Feels disgusted and as if he wanted to be dead. When dizzy spells come on feels blue and discouraged; cries easily; sympathy makes him angry. Feels as if he would be better off if he were dead.

Wants his food tolerably salty.

Eyes—Can hardly see, flickering like heat waves; seems as if he saw things far away which were near by.

Mouth—Feels thick; thick spittle in morning, white and milky-like, tastes like chalk and water.

Heart—Lying on left side makes his heart palpitate, feels as if it were beating in his throat.

Amelioration. Feels better when he moves about.

Have given him Nux vom., Bryonia, Glon., Puls. and, last, Cactus. No results from any prescription except Cactus c. c.—made him much worse, no amelioration afterwards, that is, better than before prescription.

At times patient feels fairly well; is always worse in spring and summer—in warm weather.

He is a poor man with a large family

and can do little work, and I have looked after him free of charge.

Examination of heart, as far as I could discover, was negative.

This is an interesting case. We will analyze it a little.

"Tenderness at pit of stomach" is a significant symptom, and leads one to go over all the diseases which have epigastric sensitiveness.

The hawking suggests chronic gastritis, but the tongue would decide. It is coated white, brown and flabby. The fact that he spits up white mucus would lead to the inference that it is a case of chronic gastric catarrh. But what is that due to? We must look farther. "He feels worse after walking; must stoop over, and gets dizzy." That dizziness may be due to lack of blood to the head. When the pulmonary circulation gets the most blood he can breathe better. The lack of blood in the head makes vision imperfect. After dizziness, then rush of blood to the head would relieve. There is partial nausea with the head symptoms.

"Lying on left side makes heart palpitate, and feels as if it beat in the throat." "Heart negative on examination." Doubtless this latter refers to the regularity. That heart is enlarged, presses on diaphragm on standing, and stomach, then we have the train of symptoms of stomach, throat and head.

Cactus increases the heart action, and aggravates.

The history of the case may throw light upon it. He is "short and fleshy." That tells of a hyperæmic spine and a heart above the natural. *Sulphur* would act well; then should follow *Kali carb.* or *Arnica*, as the conditions then demand.

T. C. DUNCAN.

SELENIUM.*

Mind.—Great debility and relaxation caused by extending mental labor far into the night. Extraordinary forgetfulness when awake, but a clear recollection when half asleep. Extraordinary loquacity and talkativeness.

Head.—Violent sticking headache over the left eye, excited by walking in the sun and strong odors. Headache from lemonade, wine and tea. Falling of the hair. (Also from the eyebrows, beard and genitals.)

Eyes.—Itching vesicles on the margin of the eyelids and the eyebrows.

Ears.—Increased earwax.

Nose.—Inclination to bore into the nose. Fluent coryza in the evening. Yellow, thick, gelatinous nasal mucus.

Face.—Greasy, shining skin of the face. Extraordinary emaciation of the face.

Teeth.—Boring pain in the molar teeth with tearing in the lower jaw. Teeth covered with mucus.

Appetite, etc.—Want of appetite with white coated tongue, early in the morning. Aversion to strongly salted food. Great desire for brandy.

Taste.—Repulsive, sweetish taste on the lips after smoking.

Eructations.—Hiccough and eructations when smoking.

Hypochondria.—Pains in the liver during inspiration. Miliary eruption in the hepatic region. Stitches in the spleen when walking.

Abdomen.—Sensible throbbing in the arteries of the lower abdomen and in the entire body after eating.

Stool.—Hard stool. Constipation.

Urine.—Urine dark, diminished. Urination after every stool. Urinary sedi-

*Reprint from advance sheets of Boenninghausen's Characteristics and Repertory, by C. M. Boger, M. D

ment like coarse grained red sand.

Sexual Organs.—Slow and insufficient erections, with too rapid emission of semen and long continued voluptuous thrill. Discharge of prostatic fluid during sleep and stool. Impotency with lasciviousness.

Respiration.—Frequent, sighing, deep breathing. Tightness of breathing from stitches in the side.

Cough.—Cough early in the morning, straining the chest, with expectoration of bloody mucus.

Respiratory Organs. — Hawking of bloody mucus. Hoarse, husky voice.

Throat.—Stiffness of the nape when turning the head.

Back.—Paralytic pain in the small of the back, early in the morning.

Upper Extremities.—Nightly tearing in the hands. Itch vesicles on the margin of the hands and between the fingers. Biting in the palms.

Lower Extremities.—Itching about the ankles and feet in the evening. Cramp in the calves and soles of the feet. Flat ulcers on the legs.

Skin.—Heat like a fiery glow, in single spots on the skin of the body. The spots which have been scratched open remain humid a long time. Flat ulcers.

Sleep.—Late falling to sleep in the evening. Awakened by the least noise. He always awakes at the same hour. Irresistible inclination to sleep, after which all of the symptoms are intensified.

Fever. — Constant chill alternating with heat. He sweats easily from the least exertion. Sweat during the afternoon sleep.

Generalities.—Great emaciation, especially of the face, hands and thighs. He is intolerant of draughts and easily cold, which is followed by tearing in the limbs. All of the symptoms are aggravated after sleep whereunto he has a great inclination, especially on hot days. China intensifies the symptoms, until they become unendurable.

Allied Remedies. — Alum., Bov., Bry., Calc. c., Ign., *Merc.*, Nux. v., Puls., Sep., *Sul.*, *Thuj.*

HAHNEMANN AN EPIDEMOLOGIST—HOW TO MEET THE NEW DISEASES.

Those who read Hahnemann's writings carefully are impressed with a breadth of knowledge, not always appreciated by his most enthusiastic admirers.

After a study of "The Coming Cholera," then in Russia, from the symptoms given in that epidemic, he picked out *Camphor* as the most similar remedy to the onset of that epidemic of the disease. At the same time he looked upon *Camphor* as a prophylactic or, as it would be said today, a drug, that would render one immune from the infection of the comma bacillus. For the subsequent symptoms and in other epidemics, following the *Camphor* phase, he selected *Arsenic*, *Verat alb.* and *Cuprum*. These have (with *Secale*, *Aconite*, *Phos.* etc.) been the chief remedies, called for in every epidemic since 1832.

In one epidemic of typhus fever he found *Bryonia* and *Rhus* the chief remedies, but in other epidemics other remedies proved most similar.

In scarlet fever he thought, at one time, that *Belladonna* was *the* remedy; but subsequent epidemics of this disease presented different phases, and *Aconite*, *Rhus*, etc. more closely corresponded.

Old writers, before Hahnemann's day, recorded the fact that succeeding epidemics were not always typical, so they same to refer to the *genius epidemicus.* This he discovered in treating cases of intermittent fever, however transmitted. Now one remedy would be the similar, and again in another year a different one, and they cured. The observations of Hahnemann on the epidemic constitution, to Dr. Ægidi, etc., show a wide research into this influence upon diseases and remedy indications, and every physician should have their help.

In the 60's spotted fever made its appearance in the United States after a long absence. The high fever was relieved by *Aconite* and profuse perspiration, but the subsequent cerebro spinal inflammation demanded other remedies, as old physicians will remember.

It would seem from the reports that are coming in (vide p. 222, June issue) that we are to be visited again by this disease. It may be a type of plague, typhus or meningitis. However transmitted, it is of atmospheric origin or predisposition. The epidemic remedy should be carefully studied out and given to the profession. We are among the years of severe epidemics "that seem to follow each other around the world in pandemic waves." (Smith) Dr. Glasgow should report some cases for close study.

From my study of epidemics the type of the epidemic constitution seems to be found at the very onset of the disease. After that the disease may or may not be typical, but in the third stage or convalescence the constitutional bias of the individual will be manifest and may need typical or individual remedies, as in chronic diseases.

The early symptoms seem to determine the remedy (similar) for the genius epidemicus.

T. C. DUNCAN.

Nursing.*

THE ACCIDENTS OF PREGNANCY AND LABOR.

Continued from June Number.

Lecture No. 9.

Ladies: We will resume to night our talk upon the accidents of labor. There is one other accident I wish to call your attention to, namely, asphyxia of the child. When the child is born it usually breathes and cries within a few moments after the umbilical cord ceases to beat. If the cord is not beating when the child is born, the child must breathe and cry if the action of its heart is to continue. When breathing does not commence help must be given at once. The treatment consists in performing artificial respiration, in stimulating the action of the heart and the lungs by placing the child in a hot bath and sprinkling its chest with cold water, and by using stimulus by dipping the finger in whiskey or brandy and inserting it into the child's mouth, to stimulate the movement of breathing. It is especially important that the child's mouth be cleansed before the effort is made to induce breathing. The infant should be firmly grasped by both legs and held with the head downward. Placing one hand upon the forehead and raising the head gently, the mouth should be thoroughly wiped out with the other hand with a small bit of soft old linen dipped in boiled and sterile water. The child must be kept suspended by the legs for

* Course of Lectures delivered to the Nurses Training School at Maryland Homoeopathic Hospital, by M. S. Dunglam, M. D., Baltimore, Md.

several minutes until mucus has had a chance to come out of its mouth.

There are several methods of making artificial breathing suitable for a child. I will describe one which you would be justified in employing. Some methods should be carried out by physicians only.

The child should be grasped by the two hands, one hand placed across its back at the shoulder-blades, the fingers coming upon the anterior surface of the chest. The other hand grasps the body by the thighs and pelvis. The child should be held with the hips considerably higher than the head. It should then be folded and unfolded, bending the trunk of the body forward very gently but firmly until the abdomen is distinctly squeezed and forced up against the chest. Then the body is unfolded or unbent until the child is bent slightly backward. This should be done at regular intervals, counting four, between the movements. After making six of these movements the nurse should pause a moment to see whether breathing does not begin. The constant tendency must be to keep the child's head low and its hips high, so that blood may be kept in the brain and mucus may find its way out of the mouth. If the child begins to make movements of respiration, it should be placed in a warm bath and its body gently rubbed until the skin becomes thoroughly red. If breathing continues, the child may then be taken from the bath, quickly dried, wrapped in warm blankets and turned upon its right side.

So long as the child remains red in color there is good hope that it will live. When, however, it is pale and bluish, its limbs making no resistance to movement, it is in great danger of death. If the finger-tips be placed over the heart and the child's body bent forward, the heart can usually be felt to beat if life still continues. So long as the child is red or reddish in color we must not give up hope nor discontinue efforts to bring about breathing.

We will now turn to the subject of *obstetric operations.*

Obstetric operations are performed to save the lives of mother and child; or if the life of the child cannot be saved, to rescue the mother if possible. As many of these operations are done in private houses, the obstetric nurse must prepare from the furniture of the private house a suitable operating table or bed, and other appliances furnished by hospitals. The low, very wide bed commonly found in private houses is exceedingly objectionable for obstetric operations. Neither doctor nor nurse can work to advantage with the patient upon such a bed. If a narrow, high bed cannot be procured, it is much better to use a table the size and shape of the ordinary kitchen table. This should be clean, and covered with a blanket, rubber sheet, and clean linen; and after the patient has been anesthetized in her bed she may be lifted on to the table.

In an addition to an operating table, small tables are useful, upon which sterilizers, basins, and dressings may be placed. Tables used for cutting out clothing are very useful for this purpose. If suitable tables cannot be obtained, kitchen chairs having a large, firm wooden bottom will be found convenient. The nurse should avoid in obstetric operations damage to the patient's furniture. If instruments be sterilized upon a highly polished table, the varnish of the table will often be ruined. Antiseptic solutions may be spilled or may spatter upon it, injuring the polish. It is always much better to use the kitchen furniture if it is reasonably clean. Carpets are in danger of injury from the same cause, and the floor beneath the edge of the bed must be protected by rubber sheeting or by thick layers of paper, or by an old thick rug, or any other convenient material.

Domestic utensils must often be employed for obstetric operations. All pitchers and basins must be thoroughly scrubbed with soap and hot water, rinsing, and then scrubbing with bichlorid solution (1:1000). Water should be sterilized by boiling.

In obstetric hospitals, sterile clothing is prepared for the lower extremities of the patient during an operation. In private houses the lower limbs are covered with long stockings, and the thighs wrapped in clean sheets or in large clean towels.

To secure an abundance of light in a private house is often difficult. A candle in a firm candlestick should be in readiness if light fails, as it may often be utilized for the examination of lacerations or to insert stitches.

To prepare a patient for an obstetric operation, the nurse should ask the physician what method of preparation he desires, and whether he wishes the nurse to catheterize the patient. If he gives us definite instructions, and if he tells the nurse to catheterize the patient, she may proceed as follows: The external parts, including the hair above the pubes, should be very thoroughly washed with soap and warm water. The hair about the labia should be trimmed short with scissors curved upon the flat. The parts should be very thoroughly rinsed with hot water; and if the patient's bowels have not been emptied by enema the rectum should be very thoroughly washed out with hot soapsuds. Then the parts should be scrubbed with cotton or gauze dipped in bichlorid solution (1:2000). Having sterilized the catheter by boiling, and having very carefully scrubbed and made antiseptic her hands, the nurse should then catheterize the patient. After this the tissues about the meatus should be again thoroughly douched with the bichlorid solution.

The anesthetic for an obstetric operation should be administered by a physician with the same precautions used in any other surgical procedure. The difficult extraction of the child is as serious an operation as the removal of an ovarian tumor. Hence the same precautions in the care of the patient should be taken. The anesthetizer should have a hypodermic springe with tablets of strychnin, atropin, and other stimulants, whiskey or brandy, should be in readiness, several small soft towels and a small basin should the patient vomit. Considerable suffering may be avoided if the nurse rubs upon the patient's lips and about the nostrils a little cold cream or vaseline before the anesthetic is administered. The nurse can do much for her patient in encouraging and comforting her. Many women fear that the operation will injure the child. The nurse should explain that the operation is undertaken in the interest of the child as well as the mother, and that it is far better for the child than to delay. In this way the nurse can give great assistance to the patient and to the physician as well. During obstetric operations no one should be present, if it can possibly be avoided, except physicians and nurses. Occasionally some self-possessed person may be useful as an assistant.

The nurse must have ready hot water bags or water bottle to secure a good reaction after the operation. It is much better to remove the patient from her bed for the operation, as she may then be placed upon clean, dry linen immediately after. If the family do not realize the fact, they must be told that she will not recover from the effects of the ether for a short time, and so their apprehension may be allayed.

The physician will bring with him his

instruments and the sterilizer in which they are to be prepared. The most convenient and simple apparatus is a tray or pan covered by a second slightly larger than the first. Instruments can be boiled in such by the use of an alcohol lamp or by placing the pan upon a stove. Some physicians prefer to add a tablespoonful of sodium bicarbonate to the water in which their instruments are boiled, while others use a one per cent solution of lysol. Some employ carbolic acid in one or two per cent solution. When the instruments have been boiled the upper pan or tray is removed, turned over, and placed beside the first. This gives the operator two sterile trays or pans in which he may arrange his instruments. Occasionally the nurse will find that a physician comes to an obstetric case without a sterilizer. Instruments must then be boiled in some domestic utensil, which is a very unsatisfactory procedure. Nurses must also exercise caution in the use of alcohol lamps, placing them on metal trays if possible.

Delivery by Forceps.

When a nurse is told to prepare the forceps for use it is meant that she should sterilize them. They should be kept in the solution in which they are sterilized until the physician applies them to the child. If they are not sterilized, the physician will sometimes order them placed in a toilet pitcher of antiseptic fluid, the larger portion downward and the upper part, or handles, apart. The pitcher is covered with a clean towel, and is placed upon the floor at the side of the physician. Cases in which it is necessary to deliver by forceps are often those in which a laceration of the mother's tissues is inevitable. Physicians usually prepare instruments for closing lacerations when they prepare the forceps. These are needles and needle-holder, hemostatic forceps, scissors, tenaculum forceps, and uterine dressing-forceps. As it may be necessary in these cases to give a douche, a douche tube should be boiled with the other instruments. Suture material is often sterilized with the instruments. If possible, instruments should be boiled for from twenty to thirty minutes.

For forceps operations, the patient is usually placed upon her back at the edge of the bed or table. Beneath her should be a rubber sheet or Kelly pad, and a slop jar to receive douche-water and discharges. Occasionally the patient is turned upon the side, usually upon the left side. In hospitals, where there is an abundance of assistants, each lower extremity may be held by a nurse. In private house it is well to use some simple device which will support the limbs. Of these, the best is a sheet folded in the longest way, so as to make a band six or eight inches wide. When the patient is anethetized and placed in position, her legs are flexed upon the thighs, and the thighs upon the body. Stockings and clean or sterile sheets or towels are applied to the limbs, and the sheet is then placed across the patient's shoulders just below the neck, passed on the outer side of each lower extremity, and tied around the leg just below the knee. In this way the limbs are drawn backward and rotated outward. Assistants are not required to hold the limbs, and the posture is a convenient one for the operator.

Beneath the edge of the bed or table should be placed some material to protect the carpet. The physician's forceps and other instruments in the sterilizing pans should be placed upon chairs or table at his right hand, and a basin of antiseptic solution with gauze or cotton sponges should be in readiness. The nurse should prepare the antiseptic solution ordered for the douche, and also boil the catheter. The physician will usually order the nurse to prepare the patient for the application of forceps, and this is done as already described. During the actual delivery of the child the nurse can sometimes assist with the anesthetic or occasionally follow the doctor's orders in rubbing the uterus and causing it to contract. She should be ready as soon as the child's head is born to wipe out the eyes and to cleanse the mouth, as is done in normal cases. The child is often asphyxiated for a few moments after such a delivery, and then the nurse may assist in causing it to breathe. When the placenta has been delivered and saved for examination, a thorough vaginal douche is given as ordered by the doctor, and he proceeds to close any lacerations which may be present. During this portion of the operation the nurse may cleanse her hands and assist the physician by threading his needles and sometimes by sponging the parts. The usual dressings are applied after the stitches have been taken.

Symphysiotomy.

When the pelvis is too small or the child a little too large the pubic joint may be severed to allow the child to escape. This operation is called symphysiotomy.

The instruments required are a scalpel, a probe-pointed bistuory, a sound, hemostatic forceps, needles and needle-holder, scissors, uterine-dressing forceps, antiseptic gauze and a roll of surgeon's adhesive plaster, an abdominal binder, and often a catheter to which is attached a long piece of rubber tubing. These instruments must be sterilized and the patient prepared as described. Several assistants are required. The patient is placed upon her back at or near the edge of the table. The limbs are usually extended at first, but afterward flexed. After the opening of the joint the delivery of the child is usually accomplished by the use of the forceps. These should have been sterilized with the rest of the instruments and kept in readiness. Lacerations often occur, which are closed as usual. The wound made above the joint must also be closed by suture.

When the joint is opened the two halves of the pelvis gape asunder. When the child is delivered these two portions must be brought together, and some apparatus is required to maintain them in that position. A good and simple dressing consists in a strip of surgeon's adhesive plaster, six to eight inches wide, long enough to go around the patient and to overlap. The pelvis of the patient is pressed together by two assistants, who grasp her body at the hips. An antiseptic dressing is placed over the symphysiotomy wound. The strip of adhesive plaster is carried underneath the patient, and is pulled tight and smooth by two persons holding the ends. The adhesive strip is brought up and around the patient in such a way that the center of the strip is directly over each trochanter of the femur. The strip is made to overlap. Over this is placed an abdominal binder. A catheter is often inserted into the bladder and allowed to remain.

After the symphysiotomy the patient must lie upon her back for at least two weeks. Her bed must be kept very carefully, and attention paid to the skin to avoid bed sores. It is often hard to make the patient realize that it is absolutely necessary that she remain upon her back. Such patients require the use of a catheter. When the patient is dressed two strong persons stand upon each side, press firmly against the sides of the pelvis, the old strip of plaster is quickly removed, the skin bathed with soap and water and with alcohol, and a new strip is applied. This opportunity may be taken to apply alcohol or alcohol and water to the skin which is just beneath the plaster, and in this way soreness can usually be avoided. The symphysiotomy patient who does well can usually turn upon her side at the end of three or four weeks. The plaster strips may be removed, and the patient can wear a canvas belt with straps and buckles. She is usually well in six weeks after operation.

In our next we will continue the subject of Obstetric Operations.

Psychology.

"KNOW THYSELF." *

We are approaching an age when the hidden shall be revealed, when the unseen shall brought to light and the without shall be viewed from the within. This cannot be except to "know thyself."

"The proper study of mankind is man."

Anatomy, Physiology and Psychology are inclusive in the consideration of the whole man. Neither part can be properly studied except standing upon the view-point of the whole. Science recognizes man as dual, with mind and body. Theologists assume man to be soul and body. Scientists are afraid to include soul in the study of Psychology for they might not prove its existence by any known theorem; so scientific Psychology is without a soul. We cannot have an effect without a cause. Hahnemann not only brought out the theory of "similia" but he developed a method of reasoning from generals to particulars. He recognized the subjective in man as well as the "Spirit-like force" in the remedies. He laid the foundation for the study of Psychology.

Let us study the whole man by finding his parts. Mesmerism, Hypnotism, Suggestion, Spiritism, etc., are means to an end; but it is only the border-line that has been reached. The so-called "New Psychology" or "New Thought" has developed a "working hypothesis" which has awakened thought on the subject, with the added interest of healing the sick. This is based upon the classification of the "objective" and "subjective" mind; "conscious" and "subconscious;" "conscious" and "superconscious" or "inconscious;" "intelligence" and "volition;" reason and intuition; and may we say, "positive and negative;" male and female.

Speaking of the objective and subjective it is good thinking to differentiate between them as being a discreet degree: the subjective higher and the objective lower; the higher resting in the lower. This will be found to be the basis of union between mind and matter, or better, spirit and matter. We speak of matter as being the ultimate or lowest in creation. Man is dual, and more than that, to reach his full composite character, we have reached the cube of two which is eight. To do this scientifically we must learn something more about the so called "subjective."

Let us entertain the thought that man is a composite being. The eastern cult teaches that there are seven principles in man. If so he must be a composite. The western new thought movement has not entertained this old theory of man. The church has only the dual character, body and spirit. A recent christian writer has made a fuller statement adopting the Budhist division of seven principles:

1st. "The body or external shell."

*Read before the International Hahnenmannian Association, Chicago.

2d. "The form of the natural vitality, the *anima mineralis*, *anima vegetabilis*, *anima animalis*—three in one, or as modern medicine expresses it, the 'vital force.'"

3d. "The third body is the natural human soul, or body of desire, this constituting a natural self and what Swedenborg calls "proprium"—in no sense spiritual, but earthly and of the earth."

"A fourth body, which is not however an organism in permanance, which has an impersonal identity of its own, neuter in character between good and evil, and entering into the character of neither; which has a specific function in the formation and direction of the life of the man, but which serves merely as a satellite, and which floats in its own *habitat* with its own species after the earthly shell is pierced and dissolved; this is the double, the *ghost*, the shadow form, the memory form, the astral image."

"The fifth, the first of the spiritual series; this is the spiritual self ego, or proprium image; the body of human self-will, self-intelligence, self-desire, self-delight, self-life."

"The sixth body is the Soul of the Spirit, the sensitive organism of the psychic personality, termed also the spiritual body, and is, while the human personality endures, not merely a body for it, but also its form of existence, its form of identity, its form of consciousness, of operation, of delight."

"The seventh body of the full series is that of the inmost, the Psychic Germ."

It may be observed that the six elements of the human are in three pairs. Here is a suggestion of a law of all living beings—a body and a soul. The soul or spirit is a medium of connection with the cause world. Even the human body is composite in structure, being the microcosm of the macrocosm—a little Universe holding all the elements of the larger—the cosmic whole. Each cell is interdependent with the whole cellular system and corresponds to a similar relation of planet to the planets of the universe. The cell-life like the planet-life has its soul or spirit, so that there shall be an orderly connection with their dual environments. This duality pertains to all forms of life. There can be no life without *form*. But what about this seventh principle? Where is the duality that exists in the six lower elements? Here is something that the "New Thought" apostles have not considered. Neither theologists nor scientists have entertained it. May not the tenets of regeneration as held by christians, and of re-incarnation by the theosophists, here find an explanation to their statements? Does not regeneration and re-incarnation mean the same when fully understood? Is not this "Psychic Germ" the seed placed in the Human for the purpose of forming a new body to be born into a spiritual life as a fitness for the future world? The Human was born into this life; why not into a future one?

Human intelligence is a derivative from the higher Intelligence. "Let us make man in our image, after our likeness." The "New Psychology" cannot afford to leave the old basic truths. It is in old books that we find considerable knowledge which cannot be ignored until found useless. In the study of the mind we are dealing with that which is from God; and shall we not recognize Him who through Mind created all things?

In our study of this subject the ethical must be foremost. We cannot toy with it. It is for legitimate and good use. A steady and an upright influence is necessary, that our association with others may be for good; hence healthy association will be a success in society. Following in this line of thought and action will lead to a healthy mental state.

Thought comes from the understanding and intuition, and is often a revelation. The mind like the stomach must be fed. Teachers and books are the source of supply and the food should be good. Here is the field of so called "suggestion."

The law of regeneration in nature indicates that when a positive and negative come together, a union is formed and the result is something new. The intellect and volition come together as positive and negative, or male and female, the result is "a thought struck me," a thought comes for consideration and there is an expansion of the understanding. Herein is the basic principle of "Suggestion." The understanding is in the objective world; the intuition is in the subjective sphere; both receiving suggestion on their relative planes. If we live in nature alone we are materialists. There is no revelation without intuition or volition. The divine Mind is in rapport with our higher selves; hence the source of revelation. Mind is the medium of all generation or creation, hence the law of what Swedenborg calls "molecular motion."

"All structures originate in motion and the motion determines the configuration of the structure" or form. The universe and all things in it is held in an orderly condition by the Creative Mind; shall not the intellect in Mind acting under law have a controlling influence on its environments? The human Mind, though finite, is in the image and likeness of the Infinite Archetype; and the finite is subject to the Infinite under a spiritual law. May not there be revelation to this end, which shall be strictly scientific?

"Revelation, if revealed, would be the comprehensiveness of the all-science." There can be no true science without the consideration of Cause and Effect; spirit is the Cause, and the objective world is the Effect.

The incarnation of the Divine into the human is involution. The reincarnation of the human into conscious life is evolution. The ethical is the internal element in the lower and love in the higher.

"Ye must be born again" is a scientific statement. The will, or love is a well of water in us, springing up into everlasting life. Here, will is the organ of love. To be born again is to "know thyself," then we shall know God, which is to know of the philosophy of life.

W. H. Leonard.

Minneapolis, Minn.

Editorial.

INTERNATIONAL HAHNEMANNIAN ASSOCIATION.

The twenty-third annual meeting of the I. H. A. met at the Chicago Beach Hotel, Tuesday, June 24th.

It was the best attended meeting the Association has had in a number of years, nearly one hundred members and visitors being in attendance during the session. It was almost a Chicago Society, by virtue of the fact that over seventy-five per cent were residents of Chicago. This demonstrated that the Homœopathic center of the world is now located in this city.

The familiar faces of Drs. Stowe, Mexico, N. Y.; Nash, Cortland, N. Y.; Campbell, Brooklyn; Butler and Krichbaum, of Montclair, N. J.; Boger, of Parkersburg, W. Va.; Reed, of St. Louis; Glidden of Los Angeles and Leonard, of Minneapolis, showed the widespread interest manifested by the older members. Most of the old wheel horses who have been fighting the battle of pure homœopathy for the past quarter of a century and more were content to send in results of their experience to be read by the Association or not as circumstances might warrant.

The Chairman of each bureau had been faithful to the trust imposed with this result: The number of papers was so great that none of the papers was read where the author was absent, except as a mark of special courtesy to the writer. As it was, the sessions were so crowded with papers that adequate discussion was an impossible thing. Seven sessions, each of about three hours length, were held, and there were enough papers referred to the Publication Committee to have kept the Association occupied for another day. One of the strange characteristics of such meetings is the almost insane desire to rush the work through, as though the cost of an additional day at the hotel would be extravagant or the demands of business made a longer vacation out the question. Fewer papers, arranged with a definite purpose, would attract greater attention, bring out better discussions and add valuable information to our current literature. This plan would require much work on the part of the Chairman of each bureau, but the remuneration would amply repay for the time expended.

The next place of meeting will, in all probability, be Boston, and there is a strong effort being made to transfer the membership to the American Institute of Homœopathy, and thus endeavor to make the Section of Homœopathics—Materia Medica, or whatever may be the title in the organized scheme, a strong exponent of the Homœopathic teachings of Hahnemann.

Dr. E. B. Nash, of Cortland, N. Y., was elected President and will do much to harmonize the different interests.

It is to be sincerely hoped that the way may be prepared so that both the national societies standing for pure homœopathy may become affiliated with the American Institute, and it seems as though this new plan would provide a way whereby this might be carried out. It would be a great mistake to drop the old organization until the new plan has been thoroughly tried, because it would have been as difficult for the materialistic homœopath of the past to fraternize with those who believe in the dynamic nature of disease as for oil and water to mix. A vital principle is at stake and there is no common ground upon which all may stand. It furnishes all the elements of a spirited, if not *spiritual*, discussion and truth is sure to triumph if her advocates are capable of presenting truth in a proper light.

AMERICAN INSTITUTE OF HOMŒOPATHY.

As was to be expected, Ohio came to the front and covered herself with honors. The same spirit that has made her sons and daughters famous throughout the world was manifest in every phase of the entertainment prepared for the guests of the institute at its recent meeting in the most beautiful city of the state—Cleveland.

Centrally located, she drew from the east and from the west. The hotels were ample and convenient, The Chamber of Commerce offered fairly good accommodations for the different sections and committee meetings. The weather was perfect and the people who entertained were simply untiring in their efforts to make the visit to the "Forest

City" an event long to be remembered.

The attendance was the largest of any meeting of the institute since the "World's Congress" in Chicago, in 1893, about 800 members being present and an even greater number of visitors.

The character of the papers was above criticism and Homœopathy was the most prominent theme and received the most uniform consideration of any meeting of the Institute within the past twenty years. This is saying much and has a significance that should be recognized and made the rallying cry, calling the members of the profession to the support of this powerful instrument for good.

The Institute is what the members make it; and the followers of Hahnemann ought to be sufficiently numerous to dictate the policy that governs the body. The canker that is eating at the heart of the organization is politics, or at least that is the impression that has been permitted to go forth. The truth of this assertion may be questioned and a strong plea for the present policy advanced. It depends altogether upon the viewpoint of the observer. If the prime purpose of the organization is to secure adherents to the cause of Homœopathy the methods employed will not bear investigation. If the colleges are the legitimate channels through which Homœopathy is to be perpetuated then the Institute is clearly within its legitimate sphere when it seeks to promote exchange of opinions upon all the branches of medical science. If Homœopathy is something *added to* the general foundation of a medical education, it becomes a specialty, and should take its place with other fields of special investigation. All physicians cannot succeed as homœopathic specialists, their mental and physical make-up positively puts them into a different class. It is nothing more than right that they should select that line of work in which their talents will be given greatest opportunities for development. Homœopathy should be taken as the foundation of every specialty, simply because it is based upon law and gives the *safest, surest* and *speediest* method for correcting the *dynamic* manifestation of disease. It is indicated for that part which lies beyond the range of every other department of medicine; but it certainly requires a master mind to grasp the significance of the many phases of dynamic disease and select the *simillimum* in each individual case. We therefore believe the policy adopted by the Institute this year is a step in the right direction and that it is up to the specialists in Homoeopathics to make good their claim for recognition as specialists in Homoeopathic Materia Medica. The time has come when the Hahnemannian Associations should be merged into a great, powerful Section of the American Institute of Homoeopathy. They can hold a session covering as many days as their papers will permit—one, two or three days before the general meeting of the Institute, and then come into the meetings of the Institute filled with a zeal that would reach *through* the Institute into every part of this great nation.

For fear the readers of the ADVOCATE may not thoroughly understand the significance of the plan for reorganization adopted at the recent sessions of the Institute we will briefly state that the work of the coming session will be divided into two general divisions: Specialists and General Practitioners.

Each special section or department will have its own organization and arrange its program, as though it was separate and independent of the Institute. It will work through its organization to build up its section in every particular, but all of the business of the section will be reported to the general business session of the Institute for ratification, in order that there be uniformity of action; and, through the union of these different sections, the real strength and dignity of Homœopathy will be felt and appreciated.

Immediately following the sessions of the First Division will be held the general sessions of the Institutes in which Homœopathy will be the special feature, Medicine, Materia Medica and the Best Methods for promoting Homoeopathy being the work of this division.

You will see that this is a radical departure and that much earnest work will be required of the executive committee to get all of the machinery in good working order within the next ten months. The end to be accomplished, however, is so great that they should have the hearty co-operation of every practitioner of medicine who sails under the banner of Similia.

The officers elected for the coming year are:

Joseph P. Cobb, Chicago, President.

H. F. Bigger, Cleveland, First Vice President.

Chas. Gatchell, Chicago, Recording Secretary.

J. Ritchie Horner, Cleveland, Corresponding Secretary.

T. Franklin Smith, New York, Treas.

The place of meeting will be selected by the members of the Institute by postal card vote next October, but it is almost a foregone conclusion that Boston will be selected.

LARGE VS. SMALL COLLEGES.

There is no question but that numbers beget numbers, but it doesn't follow that the large college with the large faculty is the most satisfactory or the most profitable institution for the acquirement of an education. There can be no question but that the plan of *individual* instruction is the most desirable form, but it is out of the question because of the *excessive cost.*

The purpose of an institution of learning is to provide the means necessary for the acquirement of knowledge by the *individual* student. The *earnest* student will put himself in harmony with his environment and utilize the means at his disposal for the development of mental faculties that are within. *The work of development depends entirely upon the student. Large* classes in *small* institutions work a loss to the student, but there are few *small* colleges today that are not thoroughly equipped for *double* the number of students that enjoy their privileges. This means that the individual student has greater advantages in the small college than in the large.

A word about the small faculty. If all the departments are well filled there must be greater uniformity in the instruction than possibly can exist with large faculties. The burden rests upon the individual members of the faculty and to the advantage of the student; e.g., we will take DUNHAM MEDICAL COLLEGE: She only has thirty-one instructors but they give 858 hours time during the first year; 976 hours during the second year; 1,058 hours during the third year; 1,012 hours during the fourth year and 570 hours during the fifth or post-graduate year.

During the first year 209 hours are given to Anatomy, descriptive and dissections; 128 hours to Histology; 166 hours to Physiology, Biology and Zoology; 187 hours of Chemistry, general and inorganic. In addition to this, the student receives 165 hours instruction on Materia Medica and Homœopathic philosophy. Could a student get any more or any better instruction if the college had one hundred instructors?

While we are on this subject, it may not be out of place to call attention to the following facts: Out of nine hundred and seventy-five hours instruction, the student gets one hundred and thirty-seven hours of Materia Medica and forty hours of Homoeopathic philosophy during the second year; the same amount of time during his third year and in addition 342 hours of *Clinical* work, while in the fourth year there are 190 hours of Materia Medica and 479 hours of clinical work. Where can you find a college of any school giving so much time to the study of Materia Medica and the practical demonstration of the same?

In conclusion, neither the size of the college nor the *number* of instructors or its faculty offers a guide for determining the *quality* of instruction imparted.

UNION OF KANSAS CITY COLLEGES.

The ADVOCATE is glad to learn that an agreement between the members of the faculties of the Hahnemann Medical College of the Kansas City University and of the Kansas City Hahnemann Medical College has been reached, whereby the two schools will pool their efforts in the attempt to establish one good school, instead of wasting energy to keep alive two weak ones.

The faculty list of both colleges contained many able homoeopaths who have been and are doing yeoman work for the cause in the Missouri valley. Now that the friction necessarily following rivalry is removed, better work may be confidently expected, and there is no reason why a great school should not be built up at the Kaw's mouth.

Dr. Samuel H. Anderson will be dean of the united colleges and Dr. M. T. Runnells, registrar.

We have no doubt the ADVOCATE voices the sentiment of the profession everywhere in wishing success to the new college.

CANCER VS. MALARIA.

An article appearing in the *British Medical Journal* urging the inoculation of patients suffering from carcinoma with cultures containing the *plasmodium malaria;* and offering as the basis of their suggestion the old idea of incompatability between certain well known diseases—e.g. quartan fever and epilepsy; carcinoma and tuberculosis etc., etc.

The discussion of this question by Hahnemann covers the entire ground and shows why certain diseases *are* inimical to others and why one disease will give place to a *dissimilar* disease, but proves exclusively that the *weaker* dissimilar disease is only held in abeyance until the subsidence of the *stronger* disease where it reappears with all its original power. It is safe to select a remedial agent whose action is known by proving same upon the healthy and whose power can be more easily regulated than to attempt the inoculation of that patient with the virus or poison of any experimental disease.

It is a mystery why any one who has knowledge of the action of remedial agents secured through the application of the law of similia will be lead away from the *sure* indications by a purely *speculative* theory, when said theory is in plain opposition to the demonstrated truth.

Epilepsy is never cured by ringworm; itch is never cured by scurvy; phthisis is never cured by smallpox; smallpox was never cured by vaccination, and cancer can never be cured by malaria. Any or all of these conditions may be held in suspension by a *dissimilar* disease that is more *intense* in action, but there is nothing in the history of medicine to prove that a *permanent* cure ever followed the substitution of a *dissimilar* disease.

VACCINATION.

We publish with great satisfaction the report of Alfred Milnes, M. A., London, England, upon the mooted question of vaccination, because it comes from one who has had opportunities for knowing the actual value of vaccine virus as a prophylactic against smallpox.

It takes courage to stand by one's convictions on questions in which a majority of the medical profession are agreed. It does not follow however that the majority is right because there was a time when the majority was opposed to vaccination. The curse was fastened upon the people when they were face to face with a greater evil—poor hygienic environment and a most vicious form of medication.

Today, sanitation is a science and smallpox a disease of slight mortality.

It isn't our purpose to discuss the value of vaccination, but to raise a protest against *compulsion* in the use of it.

Homoeopathy stands for individualization. Its advocates ought to stand united against the idea of indiscriminate vaccination. They lower their standard every time they endorse any form of medication for the prevention of any form of disease. We believe the patient alone is to be treated and that the indications for treatment are disclosed by the total picture of disease manifestations or the constitutional tendency toward certain types of disease.

It is extremely difficult for a healthy individual to get smallpox or any other form of disease, hence the importance of securing a healthy environment and then select those individuals who show a tendency toward smallpox or other eruptive diseases and treat such individuals symptomatical with the indicated prophylactic, *provided they were willing.* Those who are healthy suffer no risk, and those wishing a logical protection would likewise secure immunity, so the risk would be borne by those willing to take the risk. It is among the possibilities that vaccine virus would have a legitimate field when thus employed, but even then the Homoeopathic physician has something better in that remedy whose power has been thoroughly guaged and consequently becomes the servant of the physician instead of his master.

Obituary.

THOMAS C. DUNCAN, PH. D., M. D., LL. D.

Died at his residence, 590 W. Adams street, Chicago, July 16, 1902, of heart failure after an illness of only a few hours, age 62 years.

Such in substance was the notice appearing in the paper Tuesday morning, July 17th. Altogether unexpected and apparently without the slightest warning. The doctor was down town on the 14th and in seemingly perfect health with many plans for aggressive work during the coming winter. It seems quite probable that he has had evidence of danger in this direction, because for a number of years he has been a close student of the actions of the abnormal heart and the therapeutic indication found in his materia medica for the same. It would be interesting to know which antedated the other, because it is not an infrequent occurrence for a physician to die of that upon which his special study has been directed—the power of the mind over the body.

Dr. Duncan was born in Kinross, Scotland, in 1840 and came to America with his parents seven years later settling in Wisconsin. He graduated from Milton College in 1862, and the same year enlisted in the army as a private in the 1st Wis. Vol. Cavalry. His promotion was rapid and at the close of his service, he retired with the rank of major.

In 1864, he married Miss Emma Osborn, of Kenosha, Wis., and moved to Chicago. The same year, he entered Hahnemann Medical College and graduated from the same in 1866.

The doctor was of a kind and loving disposition, but very earnest and aggressive in character—a natural leader among men by reason of the fact that he was always ready to work for anything that met with his approval. He believed in Homoeopathy and was untiring in his efforts to advance its cause with the publ c. Shortly after leaving college he became editor of the *U. S. Investigator* and in the same year was enrolled as a member of the American Institute of Homoeopathy.

He was not an original investigator and his writings do not show that care and study that mark the student but he looked for results and appeared at best advantage when planning the accomplishment of some definite plan.

For about twenty-five years he was prominently engaged in college and hospital work and during this time wrote and published several books and contributed very liberally to the medical literature of the day—his latest official position being that of associate editor of the HAHNEMANNIAN ADVOCATE.

A wife and son, Dr. Frank Duncan, survive him.

A TRIBUTE TO DR. TALCOTT.

It is with a keen sense of sorrow that we write of the demise of that great man, our oldest superintendent of homoeopathic insane asylums, Dr. Selden H. Talcott, who died so soon after the complimentary banquet given him at the Waldorf-Astoria on May 14.

His profound study of the therapeutics of the insane, to which his time and best efforts of his intellect had been given for a quarter of a century, will be more thoroughly appreciated as the years go on. For years he wrote little except in the way of disease diagnosis but, like a true scientist, he was not satisfied with knowing the course of mental diseases. Like Hahnemann, he studied his cases to select the similar remedy for each. Recently, in the maturity of his study, he has given us some valuable literature on this most difficult branch of medicine. At the Atlantic City meeting of the Institute he surprised the writer, as well as others attending the session of the Bureau of Neurology, by the breadth of his diagnostic acumen and therapeutic knowledge.

"Canst thou minister to a mind diseased?" Hahnemann answered, "Yea, verily." Dr. Talcott declared, "Most assuredly, not only in a single case, but in many cases," and in the institution over which he presided the percentage of cures grew larger year by year, even when the cases were not of his own choosing. We were told that the homoeopathic asylum was crowded with "chronic incurables," and still the number that was improved increased. The reputation of the Middletown Asylum, like that of the New York Opthalmic Hospital, has furnished the argument that has given to our school asylums for the care of the insane in Massachusetts, Minnesota, Wisconsin, Missouri, California and Illinois. The result of the work in these states should furnish convincing evidence of the superiority of homoeopathic methods in the treatment of the mentally weak upon which the authority of all the states should act. Homoeopathy must go from conquering to conquer. All that our men have to do is to quote the record made by Dr. Talcott.

We regret the departure of a man who has been a good manager of an asylum and a skillful physician among the insane. He was modest, conservative and sensible, an honor to the profession and a blessing to the world.

T. C. D.

DR. JOHN B. VIVION.

Died Tuesday, July 1, Dr. John B. Vivion, aged 91 years, 8 months and 8 days, at his home in Galesburg, Ill.

Dr. Vivion was born in Clark Co., Ky., where he lived until he was eight years old, then going with his parents to Warren Co., Ky. There he remained six years, moving to Howard Co., Mo. His father died at the age of seventy-nine, his mother reaching the extraordinary age of ninety-five. His education was obtained in country schools and while teaching, which he did for several years. His early decision to become a physician was definitely carried out by beginning to study under able preceptors at the age of twenty-two, when almost from the beginning of his regular studies, he practiced under the guidance of his instructors. Later he attended lectures in the medical department of the Transylvania University at Lexington, Ky., and on May 1, 1836, in Dover, Mo., he began to practice regularly, the same year marrying Maria Jane Atkinson, who died in 1887. To them were born eight children, those surviving their father being John G. Vivion, Cashier of the Second National Bank, of Galesburg, and E. L. Vivion, of Galesburg. Dr. Vivion married again in 1888, Lucy Neeley, who survives him.

After passing the half century milestone, Dr. Vivion was so thoroughly convinced of the superiority of homoeopathy that he attended the Hahnemann Medical College in Chicago, where he was duly graduated, and has ever since been a consistent practitioner of the truths formulated by Hahnemann.

While not a politician in the vulgar sense, he was in the true meaning of that word. He never sought office, but served the communities in which he lived when called upon. A whig, until the dissolution of that party in 1856, he threw his lot with the democrats, but was never a strong partisan. While in Missouri he was elected to the state legislature. After going to Galesburg he served a number of years as health commissioner, was for two years city health officer and five years city physician. He served his profession by being elected first temporary and later permanent president of the State Medical Society, later resigning the latter position in favor of a younger man.

In his youth, Dr. Vivion received a christian education, and his whole life was a following of the teachings of the Master. He became a member of the Christian church in 1843, and in the same year was elected an elder. When he removed to Galesburg there was no organization of the Christian denomination. In 1871, a small company of believers was mustered, meeting in the Doctor's office. Later a hall was secured, and in 1872 a church organization was effected, Dr. Vivion preaching to the congregation until 1890, when a pastor was secured.

To show the appreciation in which the Doctor was held in the city, where he labored so long and conscientiously, we quote from the Galesburg *Republican-Register:*

Dr. Vivion will be long remembered for his faithful, untiring work as a physician, for his sterling, upright qualities as a man, and for his devotion to his church and his religion. He was an exemplar in what is good and best in a community.

In the death of Dr. Vivion the homoeopathic profession has lost one of its brightest lights, a member whose work was always honest and pointed to as an example to be emulated by the younger members. The example of his life is not lost. He has gone to his reward.

Personals and News Items.

Dr. Ralph D. P. Brown, Dunham, 1902, will locate in Pueblo.

Dr. Emil Kober announces his removal on July 1 from 212 East Twelfth street to 423 East Sixth street, New York City.

Dr. E. Mather who for so many years has been practicing in Birmingham, has moved to a larger field, and is now located at 80 Park Place, between Clifford st. and Grand River ave., Detroit, Mich.

The American Institute of Phrenology, Incorporated 1866, opens its next session, September 3d, 1902. For particulars apply to the Secretary, M. H. Piercy, care of Fowler & Wells Co., 24 East 22d street, New York.

To illustrate what is by many homoeopathic physicians thought to be the deplorable trend of meetings of the A. I. H.—to make all else subservient to "politics"—the following dialogue is reported:

Physician No. 1.—Been to the Institute?

Physician No. 2.—Yes.

No. 1.—What did you learn that was new?

No. 2.—(After thinking a moment). Don't know as I learned a thing—but we elected our president?

No. 1.—Is the Institute becoming a political gathering, the chief business of which is to elect officers?

No. 2. ———

A commercial man who attended the recent meeting of the American Medical Association recently held at Saratoga described the gathering as "two-thirds picnic and one-third medical politics, with a little science mixed in here and there."

The fifteenth annual meeting of the American Association of Orificial Surgeons will be held in Chicago, September 10th and 11th, 1902. A program is being made up of lectures and papers by the leading specialists and practitioners in rectal, genito-urinary and gynecological work, and in the treatment of all chronic diseases. The orificial surgeons are the workers in the great field of the reflexes and the profession generally is every day being brought closer to a realization of the fact that the reflexes play a most important part in the chronic manifestations of disease. Papers and discussions will cover the entire scope of the work, preparatory, operative and therapeutic, and the sessions will be of great benefit to all who attend. H. C. Aldrich, M. D., of Minneapolis, Minn., President. Ralph St. J. Perry, M. D., Secretary, Farmington, Minn.

The following prescription to cure the disease known as poverty, taken from the *Pacific Coast Journal of Homœopathics*, is good enough to bear many repetitions:

In a New Hampshire city there dwells an octogenarian physician who, in addition to his wide medical skill, is known far and wide as a dispensor of blunt philosophy. The other day a young man of his acquaintance called at the office.

"I have not come for pills this time, doctor," said the visitor, but for advice. You have lived many years in this world of toil and trouble, and have had much experience. I am young, and I want you to tell me how to get rich."

The aged practitioner looked through his glasses at the young man, and in a deliberate tone said:

"Yes, I can tell you. You are young, and can accomplish your objects if you will. Your plan is this: First, be industrious and economical. Save as much as possible, and spend as little. Pile up the dollars and put them at interest. If you follow out these instructions, by the time you reach my age, you will be as rich as Crœsus—and as mean as h—l."

The following officers and chairmen of the American Institute of Homoeopathy for the year 1903, were elected at the recent meeting in Cleveland:

President, Jos. P. Cobb, Chicago.
1st V. President, H. F. Biggar, Cleveland.
2d V. President, M. Belle Brown, Cleveland.
Secretary, Ch. Gatchell, Chicago.
Recording Secretary, J. Richey Horner, Cleveland.
Necrologist, C. A. Weirick, Chicago.
Censor, Millie J. Chapman, Pittsburg.

CHAIRMEN OF COMMITTEES.

Organization, Registration and Statistics, T. Franklin Smith, New York.
International Bureau of Homoeopathy, Geo. B. Peck, Providence, R. I.
Drug Provings, H. P. Bellows, Boston.
Publication, Geo. F. Shears, Chicago.
Medical Examining Boards, H. H. Baxter, Cleveland.
Transportation, C. E. Sawyer, Marion.
Press, Dewitt G. Wilcox, Buffalo.
Resolutions, B. F. Bailey, Lincoln, Neb.
Memorial Services, E. B. Hooker, Hartford, Conn.
Proposed Change in Publication of Transactions, Chas. E. Walton, Cincinnati.

CHAIRMEN OF BUREAUS.

Materia Medica, G. Royal, Des Moines, Iowa.
Clinical Medicine and Pathology, J. W. Dowling, New York.
Pedology, Anna Spencer, Batavia, Ill.
Homoeopathics, T. Y. Kinne, Paterson, New Jersey.

The Hahnemannian Advocate

A MONTHLY HOMŒOPATHIC MAGAZINE.

H. W. Pierson, B. S., M. D., Editor., 809 Marshall Field Building, Chicago.
Hahnemann Publishing Co., Publisher, 6704 Lafayette Ave., Chicago.
Benj. F. Swan, Business Manager.

Subscription price of the magazine in the United States, Canada, Mexico, the island possessions and Cuba, $[illegible] a year, payable in advance; in Great Britain, continental Europe, India and other countries members of the postal union, $[illegible] a year to be paid in advance. Unless otherwise specified, subscriptions will begin with January issue of the year in which order is received. Remittances should be made payable to the Hahnemann Publishing Co., 6704 Lafayette Ave., Chicago.

Address all articles intended for publication and books for review to the editor. All business and other communications should be sent to the Hahnemann Publishing Co.

Vol. xli. Chicago, August, 1902. No. 8

Materia Medica.

PYROGENIUM.

[We cannot render the readers of the ADVOCATE better service than by giving them the following indication for *Pyrogen* from a therapeutic standpoint as well as an addition to the list of remedial agents. At the same time the profession are made familiar with some of the many valuable features of the new *Dictionary of Materia Medica* for which a review appears in this issue of the ADVOCATE.—ED.]

Pyrogen. Pyrexin. Sepsin. A product of the decomposition of chopped lean beef in water, allowed to stand in the sun for two or three weeks. Dilutions; (which should be made, according to Burnett, direct and *without* glycerine).

CLINICAL.—Abscess. Anus, sweating near. Bed-sores. Bright's disease. Constipation. Diarrhoea. Dysentery. Eczema. *Enteric fever*. Fistula. Headache. Heart, rapid action of; consciousness of; failure of; obstruction of. *Labour; puerperal fever*. *Ovary, abscess of*. Peritonitis. Phthisis. Phthisis pulmonalis. Ptomaine poisoning. Puerperal fever. *Pyæmia*. Sepsis. *Spine, Pott's curvature of*. Tabes mesenterica. Tuberculosis. Typhilitis. Ulcers, varicose; obstinate. Varicosis.

Characteristics. John Drysdale was the first, in 1880, to suggest the use of this substance as a medicament (*On Pyrexin or Pyrogen as a Therapeutic Agent*, Bailliere, Tyndale & Cox). Burdon Sanderson has stated (*B. M. F.*, February 13, 1875) that "only liquids which contain bacteria or have a marked proneness to their production" are capable of setting up pyrexia. This remark struck Drysdale, and though, of course, he could not endorse the "only" of the statement—many drugs known to homoeopaths set up fever—he saw that the fact might be turned to account. Sanderson further defines *Pyrogen* as "a chemical non-living substance formed by living bacteria, but also by living pus-corpuscles, or the living blood or tissue-protoplasms from which these corpuscles spring." In Sanderson's experiments with *Pyrogen* the following effects were observed. (1) From a non-fatal dose: The animal shivers and begins to move about restlessly. The temperature rises from 2 to 3 degrees C., the maximum being reached in three hours. Thirst and vomiting come on, followed by feculent and thin mucous, and finally bloody diarrhoea and tenesmus. In five hours these symptoms begin to subside, and the animal recovers with wonderful rapidity. When death occurs it is from heart failure. In *non-fatal* cases with gastro-enteric symptoms the temperature gradually rises for four hours, and as gradually subsides: in *fatal* cases it rises rapidly to 104 degrees F., then rapidly declines to below normal. (2) From a fatal dose: There is intestinal hæmorrhage, purging, collapse, and death. After death extravasations of blood are found in heart, pleura, and pericardium; the spleen is enlarged and full of blood. Mucous membrane of stomach and small intestines is intensely injected with detachment of epithelium and exudation of bloody fluid, which extends the gut. The blood is dark, the corpuscles being in clumps instead of rolls, and being dissolved in the liquor sanguinis. White corpuscles partially disintegrated. Drysdale prepared a tincture of *Pyrogen*—which he preferred to call *Pyrexin*, since it is not a mere fever-*producer*: others have called it *Sepsin;* but this is too close to *Septicæmin*, a name given to a related and perhaps identical nosode: I have chosen to retain the name *Pyrogen*, by which the remedy is best known in homoeopathy—and put his own suggestion into practice. His success was very encouraging, but as he continued to use the tincture and lowest attenuations the difficulty of keeping the preparation was not small; and the remedy did not come into extensive use till Burnett published his pamphlet on *Pyrogenium in Fevers and Blood-poisoning* in 1888. Burnett used chiefly the 6th centesimal dilution, which is perfectly harmless, and which will keep indefinitely. Heath, who made one of the preparations used by Burnett, gave some of it to Swan, of New York, who ran it up into the high infinitesimals. Much of the American experience is with Swan's attenuations, including a proving by Sherbino (*Med. Adv.*, xxv. 369), whose symptoms I have marked (S) in the Schema. The remainder of the symptoms of the Schema are for the most part clinical. Yingling (*H. P.*, xiii. 402) collected symptoms from many reported cases, and arranged them with the symptoms of the proving. (Yingling erroneously describes *Pyrogen* as prepared from "pus from septic abscess." This is *Septicæmin*. He refers, however, to Burnett's pamphlet and to cases cured with *Pyrogen*, leaving the actual substance referred to not in doubt. H. C. Allen, who published the proving and most of the cases in *Med. Adv.*, rightly describes *Pyrogen* as a "Product of Sepsis". Drysdale's original cases include a number in which threatened typhoid was averted, a case of tabes mesenterica cured, and one of ulceration of the colon greatly benefited. Burnett's were cases of fully developed typhoid all cut short at the height by *Pyrogen* 6 given every two hours. In his pamphlet is included a successful experience of Dr. Shouldham's with *Pyrogen* 6 in two cases of diphtheritic sore throat. I have had ample opportunity of observing the power of *Pyrogen* over typhoid fever, and typhoid and hectic states, including one of discharging abscess connected with Pott's disease of the spine. T. M. Dillingham reports (*Med. Adv.*, xxvii. 367) the case of a young German Jewess who had been under treatment at various hospitals for Bright's disease, and at the *Hahnemann* Hospital of New York among others. To this she was readmitted on March 14, 1890, when she first came under Dr. Dillingham's care. The urine showed an enormous amount of albumen and a variety of casts. Feet and legs greatly swollen, face puffy. Throbbing headache, often accompanied by profuse nose-bleed, nausea, and vomiting; < motion and light; abnormally bright eyes, widely dilated pupils. *Belladonna* gave temporary relief; but on May 31st the condition was desperate. Dillingham then learned that the trouble dated from a large abscess resulting from a lanced, badly cared-for felon of the left thumb. She was ill six weeks with this abscess, having, as her doctors said, "blood poisoning." Soon after this her face and feet began to swell. On May 31st the condition was this: Feet, legs, and genitals greatly swollen. Frightful throbbing headache, > by tight band constantly worn. > By heat; very fond of the *hot bath*. Headaches had terrible aggravations lasting two to four days, during which time she could neither lie in bed nor sit up, but was in constant motion, groaning and crying piteously for help. *Pyrogen* cmm, Swan, one dose given, and no other medicine, although the patient, on one occasion begged for something to stop the pain. In the course of June she began to mend, and on October 20th was discharged cured. In Sherbino's proving he was cured incidentally of a consciousness of the heart and its working, and palpitation from least excitement or anxiety, < beginning to move; congestion to head as if apoplexy would ensue. *Cactus* had done no good. Sherbino cured: (1) a case of puerperal fever with *Pyrogen*, being led to its selection by the very high pulse rate. (2) Relapse of typhoid, pulse 140, temperature 102 degrees F.; both were normal in twenty-four hours. (3) Young lady, 17, fever, aching bones, bed felt very hard. Numb, paralytic feeling. *As the fever left the pulse kept mounting up.* *Pyrogen* cmm, Swan, repeated as often as effect ceased, cured. —*Pyrogen* is one of the *germinal* remedies of the materia medica. When once the idea of its essential action is grasped an infinity of applications become apparent. As Drysdale put it, "The most summary indication for *Pyrogen* would be to term it the *Aconite* of the typhous or typhoid quality of pyrexia," and wherever poisoning by bacterial products (*e.g.*, in the hectic of phthisis) is going on *Pyrogen* will be likely to do good. *Sepsis* is the essence of the action of *Pyrogen*. H. C. Allen gives this indication for its use in septic states: "When the best selected remedies fail to relieve or permanently improve"—analogous to the action of *Pso.* and *Sulphur* in other conditions. Also: "Latent pyogenic process, patient continually relapsing after apparent simillimum." As *Pyrogen* is a product of carrion, the carrion-like odor of bodily emaciations, secretions, and excretions is a keynote for its use. Other leading indications are: Restlessness; must move constantly to > the soreness of parts. "Constipation, from impaction of fæces in fevers; stool large, black, carrion-like." "Chill begins in back, between scapulæ." "Severe general chill of bones and extremities." "In all cases of fever commencing with pains in the limbs," Swan. "Pulse abnormally rapid, out of all proportion to temperature." *Pyrogen* 5, five drops in water night and morning, assisted in the cure of a case of anal fistula in a case of Burnett's (*On Fistula* p. 66). Under its action a sweating at the seat which the man had had for many years disappeared; and the skin of his hands, which were subject to dry eczema, assumed a much cleaner aspect. J. S. Hunt (*H. W.*, xxxi. 54) reports five cases of varicose ulcers, all of which healed quickly under *Pyrogen*. Bellairs (*H. W.* xxxiv. 298) gave *Pyrogen* 200 to an elderly woman who suffered for years with an ulcerated leg, which was riddled with deep, burrowing wounds, extremely painful and discharging freely. *Hep.*, *Sil.*, *Ars.*, *Ham.*, did no good. Under *Pyrogen* once or twice a day "a large boil" formed on the calf of the leg and discharged its contents, after which the various ulcers healed up directly. The symptoms are > by heat (drinking hot water; hot bath). > Tightly binding head. > Stretching out limbs; walking about; turning over or changing position. Heart's action and cough < by motion. Eyeball < moving eye. Cough < motion and in a warm room. < Sitting up in bed; rising. (Cough > sitting up; < lying down.)

Relations.—*Compare:* Septicæmin (B. Sanderson says bacteria and pus cells produce the same chemical result; Pyrogen and Septicæmin may therefore be identical, but I think it best to keep them distinct"): Malar. (the *vegetable* Pyrogen); Lach. In typhoid with soreness, bed feels hard, Bap., Arn., Rhus. > Motion and stretching limbs, Rhus. Cough < by motion and in a warm room, Bry. Uterine hæmorrhage, Ipec. ("if Ipec. fails when indicated give Pyrogen," Yingling). Offensive diarrhoea, Pso. Black stools, Lept. Constipation, Op., Sanic., Pb. Lochia thin, fetid, Nit. ac. Vomits water as soon as warm in stomach, Pho. Throbbing headache, Bell. Varicose, offensive ulcers of old persons, Pso. Skin ashy, Sec. Suppuration, Hep.

Causation.—Blood poisoning. Ptomaine poisoning. Sewer-gas poisoning. Typhoid fever (remote effects of). Dissecting wounds.

Symptoms.

1. *Mind.*—Loquacious; can think and talk faster than ever before (S). Irritable (S).—Delirious on closing eyes; sees a man at foot of bed.—Whispers; in sleep.—Sensation as if she covered the whole bed; knew her head was on the pillow, but did not know where the rest of her body was.—Feels when lying on one side that she is one person, and another person when turning on the other side.—Sensation as though crowded with arms and legs.—Hallucination that he is very wealthy; remaining after the fever.

2. *Head.*—Staggers as if drunk on rising in morning (S.)—Dizziness on rising up in bed.—Pains in both mastoids, < right; dull throbbing in mastoid region (S).—Great throbbing of arteries of temples and head; every pulsation felt in brain and in ears; the throbbings meet on top of brain (S).—Painless throbbing all through front of head; sounds like escaping steam (S).—Frightful throbbing headache > from tight band.—Excruciating, bursting, throbbing headache with intense restlessness (often accompanied with profuse nose-bleed, nausea, and vomiting).—Sensation as if a cap were on.—Rolling of head from side to side.—Forehead bathed in cold sweat.

3. *Eyes.*—Left eyeball sore, < looking up and turning eye outward (S).—Projecting eyes.

4. *Ears.*—Loud ringing, like a bell, left ear (also right) (S).—Ears cold.—Ears red, as if blood would burst out of them.

5. *Nose.*—Nose-bleed; awakened by dreaming it and found it was so.—Sneezing: every time he puts hand from under covers; at night.—Nostrils closing alternately (S).—Cold nose.—Fan-like motion of alæ nasi.

6. *Face.*—Face: burning; yellow; very red; pale, sunken, and bathed in cold sweat; pale, greenish, or chlorotic.—Circumscribed redness of cheeks.

8. *Mouth.*—Tongue: coated white in front, brown at back; yellowish brown, bad taste in morning (S).—Tongue: coated yellowish grey, edges and tip very red; large, flabby; yellow brown streak down centre.—Tongue clean,

smooth, and dry; first fiery red, then dark red and intensely dry; smooth and dry; glossy, shiny; dry, cracked, articulation difficult.—Taste: terribly fetid, as if mouth and throat full of pus (produced by dose of *Pyrogen* cm, Swan); sweetish.—Breath horrible; like carrion.

9. *Throat.*—Diphtheria with extreme fetor.

10. *Appetite.*—No appetite (S); or thirst.—Great thirst for small quantities, but the least liquid was instantly rejected.—> Drinking very hot water.—Thirst and vomiting (dog).

11. *Stomach.*—Belching of sour water after breakfast (S).—Nausea and vomiting.—Vomiting: persistent; brownish, coffee-ground; offensive, stercoraceous; with impacted or obstructed bowels.—Vomiting and purging—Vomits water when it becomes warm in stomach.—> By vomiting.--Urging to vomit; with cold feet.—Stomach feels too full (S).

12. *Abdomen.*—Full feeling and bloating of abdomen (S).—When on lying on left side bubbling or gurgling sensation in hypochondria, extending back to left of spine (S).—Pain in umbilical region with passage of sticky, yellow stool.—While riding in a buggy aching in left of umbilicus; < drinking water; > passing flatus downward.—Soreness of abdomen so severe she can hardly breathe, or bear any pressure over right side.—Very severe cutting pains right side going through back, < by every motion, talking, coughing, breathing deep; > lying on right (affected) side; groaning with every breath.

13. *Stool and Anus.*—Feculent and thin mucous, and finally bloody diarrhoea and tenesmus (dog).—Two soft, sticky stools, 8 to 9 a. m.—Involuntary escape of stool when passing flatus (S). Profuse watery, painless stools, with vomiting.—Stool horribly offensive, carrion-like.—Stool very much constipated, large, difficult, requires much effort; first part balls, last part natural, with streaks of blood; anus sore after (S).—Constipation: hard, dry accumulated fæces; stool large, black, carrion like; small black balls like olives.—Congestion and capillary stasis of gastro intestinal mucous membrane, shedding of epithelium, bloody fluid distending intestines (dog). —(Sweat about anus removed; fistula relieved.)

14. *Urinary Organs.*—Urine scanty; only passed twice in twenty-four hours (S).—Urine: yellow; after standing, cloudy with substance looking like orange peel; red deposit on vessel hard to remove; deposits sediment like red pepper (S).—Got up three times in night to urinate (S).—(Bright's disease of kidneys.)--Urine albuminous, containing casts, horribly offensive, carrion-like.—Frequent calls to urinate as fever comes on.--Intolerable tenesmus of bladder; spasmodic contractions, involving rectum, ovaries, and broad ligaments; [cured in a case of Yingling's with *Pyrogen* cm Swan (and higher); patient's next period came on naturally and painlessly, whereas before menses had been painful and extremely offensive.]

15. *Male Sexual Organs.*—Testes hang down relaxed; scrotum looks and feels thin.

16. *Female Sexual Organs.*—Puerperal peritonitis with extreme fetor; a rotten odor.—Parts seriously swollen (Bright's disease).—Menses horribly offensive; carrion-like.—Menses last but one day, then a bloody leucorrhoea, horribly offensive.—Hæmorrhage of bright red blood with dark clots.—Septicæmia following abortion; fœtus or secondines retained, decomposed.—(Has cured prolapsus uteri, with bearing down, > by holding the head and straining as in the act of labor.)—Abscess of left ovary, acute throbbing pain, great distress, with fever and rigors (*Pyrogen* cm, Swan, produced an enormous flow of white

creamy pus with general >).—Lochia: thin, acrid, brown or fœtid; suppressed followed by chills, fever, and profuse fetid perspiration.

17. *Respiratory Organs.*—Wheezing when expiring (S).—Cough: with large masses of phlegm from larynx; < by motion; < in warm room; cough = burning in larynx and bronchi; = pain in occiput; = stitching in small of back, only noticed in the chair; coughs up yellow sputa through night (S).—Cough > sitting up, < lying down.—Expectoration: rusty mucus; horribly offensive.

18. *Chest.*—Pain in right lung and shoulder, < talking or coughing.—Neglected pneumonia: Cough, night sweats, frequent pulse, abscess had burst discharging much pus of mattery taste (rapid recovery under *Pyrogen* cm. three doses).—Chest sore, purple spots on it. —Severe contracting pain within lower sternum, sometimes extending to rib-joints and up to throat, as if œsophagus being cramped.—Ecchymoses on pleura (dog).

19. *Heart.*—Pain in region of left nipple, as if in heart; increased action: pulse 120 (S).—Heart tired as after a long run; increased action < least motion (S).—Every pulsation felt (painlessly) in head and ears (S).—Sensation as if heart enlarged; distinct consciousness of heart (S).—Sensation as if heart too full of blood.—Feels as if the heart were pumping cold water (Yingling).—Violent, tiresome heart action.—Palpitation or increased action without corresponding increase of temperature.—Palpitation < by motion.—Loud heartbeats; audible to herself and others.—Could not sleep for whizzing and purring of heart; when she did sleep was delirious.—Cardiac asthenia from septic conditions.—Ecchymoses on heart and pericardium (dog).

20. *Neck and Back.*—Throbbing of vessels of neck running up in waves from clavicles.—Weak feeling in back; stitching on coughing (S).

21. *Limbs.*—Aching: in bones; all over body as from a severe cold; with soreness of flesh, head feels hard; > motion (S).—Cold extremities.—Numbness of hands, arms, and feet, extending over whole body.—Automatic movement of right arm and right leg, turned the child round from right to left till feet reached the pillow: repeated as often as she was put right (cerebro-spinal meningitis).

22. *Upper Limbs.*—Pain in shoulder-joint; in front, passing three inches down arm (S).—Hands and arms numb.—Hands cold and clammy.—Dry eczema of hands.

23. *Lower Limbs.*—Aching above knees, deep in bones, while sitting by a hot fire; > by walking (S).—On going to bed aching in patella; > flexing leg (S).—Aching above left knee as though bone broken (S).—Aching above knees in bones, > stretching out limbs (S).—Tingling in right little toe as if frost-bitten.—Feet and legs swollen (Bright's disease).—Numbness of feet.

24. *Generalities.*—Cannot lie more than few minutes in one position, > change (S).—Debility in morning, staggered on trying to walk [S].—Nervous, restless [S].—Aching all over, bed feels hard.—Great muscular debility; rapid recovery in few hours [dog].

25. *Skin.*—Skin, pale, cold, or ashy hue.—Obstinate, varicose, offensive ulcer of old people.

26. *Sleep.*—Slept awhile; woke to roll and tumble in every conceivable position [S].—Unable to sleep for brain activity and crowding of ideas [S].—Restlessness > after sleep.—Cries out in sleep that a weight is lying on her.—Whispers in sleep.—Kept awake by purring of heart.—Dreams: of various things; of business.

27. *Fever.*—"In all cases of fever

commencing with pains in the limbs" [Swan].—Shivers and begins to move about restlessly; temperature rises gradually and as gradually subsides [dog]. —Temperature rises rapidly to 104 degrees F., and sinks rapidly from heart failure [dog, fatal dose]. —Chilly at times and a little aching; a little feverish [S].—After dinner, ache all over, chilly all night, bed feels hard [S].—After getting into bed, chilly, teeth chatter; woke 10 p.m. in perspiration on upper part of body; > motion [S].—Feels hot as if he had a fever, but was only 99 degrees F., feels like 105 degrees.—Cold and chilly all day.—No fire would warm; sits by fire and breathes the heat from it; chilly whenever he leaves it; at night when the fever came on he had a sensation as if lungs on fire, must have fresh air, which gave >.—Frequent calls to urinate as soon as fever came on; urine clear as water.—Every other day dumb ague.—Perspiration horribly offensive, Carrion-like; disgust up to nausea about any effluvia arising from her own body.—Cold sweat over body.

MATERIA MEDICA—A STUDY.*

"When the mind with great earnestness, and of choice, fixes its views on any ideas, considers it on all sides, and will not be called off by the ordinary solicitations of other ideas, it is that we call intention or study."

When the word study is used in this paper it will imply the mental effort of understanding, and an earnest and protracted examination of the materia medica, by reflection, collection, and scrutiny of evidences obtainable.

By the way of prelude it is well to repeat again the first, the most wonderful and magnificent truths of the philosophy of homoeopathy; the foundation upon which our materia medica is constructed, without which there can exist no science of therapeutics.

First.—"The body of man in health is animated by a spiritual, self-moving, vital power, which holds it in harmonious order."

Second.—"The spirit-like power to alter man's state of health (and hence to cure disease) which lies hidden in the inner nature of medicines can never be discovered by us by a mere effort of reason, it is only by experience of the phenomena it displays when acting in the state of health of man that we can become clearly cognizant of it."

To the earnest and true physician the study of materia medica is one of the most fascinating works that can be imagined. Its field is so broad and varied that any student can easily be satisfied, for it takes into account the boundless creation of God, with man as its chief concern.

Its importance can be fully realized when it is taken into consideration that when medicines are *properly* selected and applied, it precedes, accompanies, and follows every procedure used for the relief of suffering humanity.

A review of the study of materia medica is quite in keeping at the present time, as a wave of discontent has again swept over a few of the homoeopathic ranks.

For this I am truly glad, for such a feeling is a certain indication that the lesson has not been *thoroughly learned*, or properly applied—errors have crept in, or evidences are lacking.

In the re-proving of the materia medica there can not exist the least doubt in the minds of any of its great value in the thorough study of the inherent dy-

*Read at meeting of American Institute of Homoeopathy.

namic property of each drug in question, providing the rules laid down by Hahnemann are strictly followed.

The method presented by the founder of homoeopathy stands today pre eminently above all others. Every means known to man must be used to ascertain the entire sick-making properties of a drug, for it is then only that the exact fulfillment of his matchless methods are fully realized.

In section 141, Hahnemann tells us the best way to study a remedy is for the physician to make a proving upon himself, providing he be healthy, sensitive, and has an unprejudiced mind.

"By such observations upon himself, he will be brought to understand his own sensations, his mode of thinking and his disposition, (the foundation of all true wisdom) and he will also be trained to be what every physician ought to be, a good observer."

In the examination of the true sick-making powers of drugs, Hahnemann demands on the part of the physician an *unprejudiced mind*, some understanding, attention, and fidelity in observing the images produced in all the drug trials.

An unprejudiced mind! Sound understanding, attention, and fidelity in observation! An unprejudiced mind is hard to find—the majority of us are full of prejudice and endless shades of belief. It is very evident that they are not all facts but they come from what each one has laid down as facts. Each one desires to have peculiar ideas, facts, etc.

Here we see cropping out the worst kind of prejudice. A true man is certainly one freest from prejudices, and one who can observe evidences. The unprejudiced mind is the one to occupy the seat of judgment and make decisions.

An unprejudiced mind can only be attained by learning all the truths and doctrines of homœopathy.

If we study carefully that part of the Organon included in the sections 118 to 145 we can learn how the materia medica was formed, and also its best methods of study.

In section 118, it is clearly pointed out to us that each remedy must be treated as an individual, and that one individual can never be taken for another, which should ever put an end to substitution, alternation, or combinations. It should be clear enough to any of us when the founder of homoeopathy said when speaking of the proving and study of drugs, "that everything conjectural, all that is mere assertion or imaginary, should be strictly excluded; everything should be the pure language of nature carefully and honestly interrogated."

Having materia medica constructed upon the above principles, it can be readily noted by repeated provings that all the different phases of the drug are not brought out in one prover, but it takes many provers to fully note the entire sick-making powers.

This peculiar fact will teach the close observer that each one of us is living on a certain plane and in a certain atmosphere of his own.

Of the many methods employed in the study of the materia medica from Hahnemann down to the present, there is one that surely takes the lead of them all; while at this same time any method which gives us aid must not be ignored.

The method to which I refer is the getting of the complete symptomotology of a drug, as the totality of the symptoms is the *ne plus ultra* in the homoeopathic materia medica.

It will not take an observer very long to note that the symptoms can readily be arranged into different classes according to their importance and occurrence. These different classes of symptoms can best be divided into those that are general, those that are common, and those that are particular. These classes in turn are sub divided into first, second, and third grades according to their degree of importance.

The general symptoms of any remedy stand first in importance. All symptoms that are predicated of the patient himself are general; all symptoms predicated of any one organ are particular.

Those symptoms which appeal closest to our very being, our vital force, are things that are strictly general, but those symptoms which become less and less general are particular.

When the ego is brought into use the symptoms mostly are general, for example when he says, "I see," "I do so and so," "I feel so cold," or "I feel so hot," "I am thirsty," "I am wakeful," or the lady says, "I menstruate," referring to her general condition and not to any special organ.

To illustrate: One of the general symptoms found in Apis is a burning, stinging sensation. The patient says, "I have a burning, stinging sensation all over my body" "I feel a neuralgic pain in my temples like a bee sting." "I have a burning, stinging in my eyes." "I have a burning, stinging in my face." "I have a burning stinging along the edges of my tongue."

So these symptoms of burning, stinging pains are noted all through the remedy and constitute the general symptoms. The generals are the ones which control the army of symptoms noted in Apis, and in like manner all other remedies. The generals are the ones related to the patient himself, to his very being. And these very important symptoms are just the ones that so many want stricken out, "the would-be chaff," as they call them. What do you think would be left if these chaff-blowers could have their way in this matter?

The common symptoms are those which any one would naturally expect in a remedy. Take for an example, remedies which produce fever. We naturally expect thirst, and thirst would be a common symptom.

I have heard it repeated so many times that such and such a symptom can be found under a dozen different remedies, and they should be expunged from the books, they are all worthless.

The cavilers did not recognize the fact that these were all common symptoms and belong there naturally, and that the symptomotology would not be complete without them.

Again, all remedies which produce eruptions are classed as a common symptom. What would we think of the symptom of dragging down in the pelvis? Why it would be a common symptom, common to many remedies—but to study out the exact place of each one of them we must get the generals and possibly the particular, strange, or uncommon ones.

Now as to the particular symptoms. They are the ones that cause you to stop and meditate. You naturally would say to yourself, "this is strange," "this is something peculiar indeed." Take in the case of Apis again. This patient has a high fever but does not drink. How strange that is. That would be a peculiar symptom, or as the students of materia medica would say, one of the characteristic symptoms of Apis.

The general, common, or particular symptoms can be arranged according to degrees. In either class, those symptoms found the most frequently or constantly, are of the first degree, those less frequently of the second degree, those occasionally, of the third degree.

Now if we diligently study all our remedies in the above manner we shall be able to get a very clear picture of all well-proven remedies. Then to verify or prove them homoeopathically by the correct application of them, we fasten those images so that they can be recalled when their use is required.

At this place in my paper I feel like the minister who attempted to make a speech before a large audience and his hearers were very anxious to hear another gentleman in his stead. When the minister arose the crowd began to hiss and shout "sit down!" He did not sit down but raised both hands in the air as if he were in the act of pronouncing the benediction and said, "Keep quiet! I do not want to make a speech, but I want to tell you something."

I want to tell you that the materia medica is studied very little by the mass of homoeopathic physicians of today. You can go into three-fourths of all offices of this fair land and not see a materia medica in sight, or if it is you could write your name on the covers.

Further, how many repertories will you see, and how many know how to use them? How many do you suppose have studied one remedy thoroughly this year. You know very well that many materia medicas are not opened once a week or once a month by the majority of physicians.

These are the men that want to use the pruning hooks, and blow 'chaff—principally the latter—blowing all the time.

In those offices you will find the combination tablets, and if the dispenser happens to run out of them he will put two or three remedies in a glass or give half a dozen remedies in two days.

Then there goes up a great howl about the pharmacists selling all kinds of combinations. Why is it these pharmacies make these combinations? Simply because they have sale for them; a demand from their patrons. Who buys them? These men who never study their materia medica—the lazy man.

"When we have to do with an art whose end is the saving of life, any neglect to make ourselves thoroughly master of it becomes a crime." May the good Lord have mercy on the criminals of this country!

It is only constant effort that leads towards perfection in any calling in life.

Those of you who take part in the reproving of drugs with unprejudiced minds and will look up all the original matter upon the drug in question, especially that of Hahnemann, will then learn to know the greatness of the men who formulated the laws of "similia similibus curantur," and that he was one of God's grandest noblemen.

J. C. Fahnestock.

Piqua, Ohio.

A LYCOPODIUM CASE.*

It has been our experience to achieve such marvelously good results in many cases, of apparent *Extremis*, or when rapidly merging into such a condition, that we shall never cease to remember, and to be grateful, for the masterly therapeutic action of this seemingly in-insignificent, but really magnificent remedy.

The indications impressively suggesting its use, the "during labor pains, must keep in constant motion with weeping." "Labor pains run upward," declares "that she cannot stay in bed; weeps and must get out of bed." Pain goes upward, and sometimes from right to left, across hypogastrium and abdomen. "I can't stand it. I must get up, or I'll die." When this state prevails, give Lycopodium at once, and you

*Read at meeting of International Hahnemannian Association.

will be surprised and charmed at the instantaneous calmative effect that it will have on this tempestuous outburst of misery. And not only this, but the case goes on in harmonious energy, efficiency and comfort until labor is normally completed.

We had a case of premature labor, which during its course, developed the above cited symptoms, until convulsions were plainly imminent.

The patient was about to lapse into unconsciousness. She said, "I feel so queer; I am losing my senses; I seem to have no feeling, am numb. My brain is numb. O, doctor, can't you help me."

We said to her, "Have you any pain?" "Yes, a little; it goes from my right side across my abdomen to the left side."

Quickly as possible I gave her Lycopodium 30th, tongue, dry. Response was simply immediate and all that could be desired. Silently within our heart we said, "Glory to God, who has given us this eternal and immutable law of cure."

This case cleared up, for good, rapidly, after the use of two or three powders of Lycopodium 30th. It was indisputably the true-*simillimum* for this case. Suppose that we had not given the always demanded simillimum in this case. What then? A limping progress of wretched results must have eventually followed, perhaps a fatal issue at its close. Amazing and wonderful is the power of the *true* homœopathic similar.

Do not let us forget Lycopodium, when we are confronted with the sometime desperate straits and emergencies of the lying-in room. In many instances it may not be suitable or required at all, but when it is you will need it extremely. If you do not, have it in your pocket case, for no other remedy can take its place.

J. N. Lowe.

Milford, N. J.

INDICATIONS FOR A FEW REMEDIES USEFUL IN LA GRIPPE.

In the beginning, dry fever, Acon., 1 to 3, often repeated.

In the beginning, the coryza being dry, Nux or Sticta.

Excessive dryness of nasal passages, Sticta.

Nose dry at night, damp during day, Nux.

Headache, with dry cough, Nux.

Watery secretions, Cham., Puls., Sulph.

Cough, with wheezing, rattling in the trachea, catarrhal hoarseness, with dryness of the eyelids, Cham.

Young children, nervous irritable persons, Cham.

Patient, mild dispositioned subjects, Puls.

Much sneezing and nightly cough, in horizontal position, Puls.

Mucous discharged is thick. Puls., Sulph., Merc., Bry.

Inflammation, cough, with sharp pain in chest, Bry.

In cases advanced beyond Bry., especially if secretions are profuse, greenish; thick with night sweats, Merc.

Nasal secretions, corrosive, Ars., Merc., Gels., Cepa.

Cough provokes vomiting of food, Ipec., Phos., Bry.

Cough ceases only after vomiting, Kali-bich.

Cough provokes spurting of urine, Caust., Kreos.

Most simple cases will require Acon., or Bry., Nux., Puls., Ipec., Merc., and Hepar, during stages of expectoration.

Bronchitis fully established, give Ant.-tart.

Great headache, Bell., Stam., Hell., Glon.

Coma, Opii.

Flowing tears, corrosive nasal flow, bland, Euphrasia.

Mucus bloody, Cham., Phos., Puls.

Sneezing predominates, Ammon Phos., Cepa., Sab.

Sharp frontal headache, Bry., Nux.

Suborbital pain, Sang., Sulph.

Laryngeal coughing, Spongia, Caust., Bell., Phos., Hepar.

Cough thick, nausea, Ipecac.

Difficult expectoration, Kali bich.

Greenish expectoration, night sweat, Merc.

Pneumonia is threatened, Ant-tart.

Dry bronchial cough, Bell., Nux.

Night cough, Cham., Puls.

Predominant night cough, Conii.

Expectoration bloody, Phos., Dros.

Hæmoptysis, Acon., Bell., Ipecac.

Cough worse after eating, Nux.

Cough worse after inspiring cold air, Rumex.

Cough worse after entering house, Verat.

Dry cough, with dyspnœa, Bell.

Dyspnœa severe, Ipec., Phos.

Snoring respiration, can't expectorate, Ant tart.

Cough provokes vomiting, Dros.

Diarrhœa with vomiting, epidemic form, Verat., Ars., Carbo. veg., China.

If weakness predominates, with periodicity, Acon., next Ars.

Pains, loins, limbs, neck, Eup. perfol.

Red turgescent face, Bell.

Rheumatic cases; Bell. Rhododendron, Bry., Rhus., Ruta.

Pain in left thorax, Ranun-bulb.

Pneumonia cases, Bry., Phos., Ant.-tart.

Resolution tardy, Caust., Strych., Phos., Ant. Sulphuratum.

Pleuritic form of lagrippe, Bry., Sulph., Canth.—B. H. Lawson, in *Med. Counselor*.

Medicine.

SIGNIFICANCE OF SEXUAL PERVERSION IN DISEASE.

The intimate relation between the mind and the sexual nature of the individual has been noted by all investigators, and we are indebted to a few who have been brave enough to give to the world the results of this careful investigation: but a vast field remains unexplored, or at least our literature has not been especially enriched by contributions along these lines.

The subject must be approached from both the physical and the pschical points of view and the investigator must be possessed of a judicial temperament, if you will allow that designation, because much that will be discovered may be perverted to demonstrate either position held.

It is conceded that mind is supreme and that the body is but the manifestation of the combined action of the conscious or will mind and the subconscious or involuntary (vital) mind. It is further conceded by most investigators that the province of the subconscious mind is to direct the action of the vital energies, unreasoning and practically automatic, like a machine. Accepting this conclusion we would expect the human machine to be perfect in its operation, *provided* the mechanism started out perfect in its development and an environment was secured that was adapted for the perfect working of a delicately poised machine. The fact that in the great majority of instances there is a perversion, more or less serious in character, is so self evident as to become axiomatic, so we have only to inquire for the causes that contribute to this almost universal state to be confronted with all shades of opinions, depending almost entirely upon the mental grasp of the investigator.

We find *three* possible sources of perversion independent of the real victim and only *one* that can be charged directly to the action of the *conscious* mind, and the significance of this must be taken into consideration when we come to consider means for the correction of same. In the order in which they appear let us consider these causes and then try to find the *relative* importance of each.

In the first place, we must study the history of the progenitors, for the purpose of determining their ability to beget healthy offspring. In the second place, determine the influence of environment upon mother during the period of gestation and lactation. In the third place, get an accurate idea of the method of education employed during the period of childhood; and last, but not least, the environment during the stage of adolescence.

If it can be shown that both father and mother were normally healthy both mentally and physically and that the environment during the period of gestation ideal, we may assume that the child started out upon the sea of experience with a fair chance for the normal development of a body capable of perfectly sustaining the functional activities of the subconscious mind. If there is any sexual perversion it must be charged to the *deliberate acceptance by the conscious mind of suggestions more or less pernicious in character*. In other words the education has been faulty and most of the blame rests upon those who had control of the same. Fortunately all cases of sexual perversion who arrive at the age of mental responsibility without any serious perversion are easily cured, and the means of cure lies largely within and dependent upon the *will* of the sufferer, *supplemented* by intelligent *suggestions* from a wise counsellor and the use of such remedial agents as are best indicated for each individual case. Note the significance of the relative order in importance of the agencies to be employed for the correction of the perversion: Self—suggestion from competent advisor or teacher—suitable remedies. The victim can correct the entire perversion if his will power is positive enough and he desires to make full use of the same. If he *desires* a restoration to health and is *willing* to follow the *suggestions* of his advisor, there need be no great difficulty in giving positive assurance of a satisfactory result *without* remedies. But if the *sexual* perversion is only secondary to the *mental* perversion, and the patient only seeks relief from physical discomforts of the sexual perversion, so that he may again gratify his perverted desires, the physician will do well to bring to aid the most carefully selected remedy in strict accord with the *law of similars*.

At this point the attention of the physician is called to this significant fact, namely: These obstinate cases will as a rule disclose a history which dates back to a constitutional inheritance, in which the *fundamental* cause must be removed before the promise of a cure can be made with any degree of certainty.

(To be continued.)

H. W. Pierson.

PRO AND CON.*

As the years pass, more reverently do I bow before the memory and accomplishments of that inspired prophet genius who proclaimed to the world the dogma, "Similia Similibus Curantur." Even as the Inspired Nazarene felt the pulsing of divine principle, fearlessly voiced it, and as fearlessly lived it, leaving its vital working for the leading of souls heavenward, the noble, indefatigable discoverer of Homoeopathy felt, voiced and lived the principles of physical redemption. *Ecce Homo.* Is it strange that, as the great truths of Jesus proved so far above the common ability to follow, that after many centuries of its professed teaching, not one church of today proclaims it full and true? That only in isolated minds does its virtue obtain and save? Then it is not strange at all that the great truths that Hahnemann gave mankind should fall upon stony ground, and obtain root only in here and there a mind capable of assimilating them. The tares grow with the wheat until the harvest. Not in its vast bulk is the homoeopathic materia medica to be valued, but here and there stands a shining golden head of grain. At its root, its sap, its ruddy bloom, vibrate eternal principles which no unskillful or ignorant harvesting can prevent working to perfection in harmony with eternal thought. Should the golden grain be trodden under foot and dragged in the mire, its virtue remains unsullied. It is but mis-used. "Consider the lilies, how they grow." The unsullied flower, from the reeking filth and muck. How true, that "Solomon in all his glory was not arrayed like one of these." It is not difficult to grasp the truth of that lesson—that not in the quantity of material profession however elegant in property, loud in utterance or servile in practice, rests man's uplifting spiritually, but in his conformity to eternal principles. In medicine the same holds good. Not in material quantity, color, taste or power rests curative action, but in the assimilation of dynamic principle in medicine with dynamic principles in man, producing a new birth of health.

Is not this truth in medical practice of sufficient value to stimulate its earnest support? Why should it be dragged in the mud of charlatanry and gross hypocrisy? Is it not so degraded in college, pharmacy and private practice? It is so degraded when a professor of materia medica who has been privileged to bear the master's message, Similia Similibus Curantur, descends to teach his students to administer quinine in material doses in the onset of malarial fever. It is so degraded in pharmacy when the mixture or compound tablet is offered as a lure or snare to the weak-minded or unprincipled. It is so degraded when the patient is knowingly treated with the unhomoeopathic medicine. The college that denominates itself homoeopathic by so doing promises on its honor to teach its students nothing but homoeopathy. The pharmacy bidding for homoeopathy patronage, by so doing promises on its honor to keep to the principles of homoeopathic supply. The physician claiming to be homoeopathic nominally pledges himself, on his honor, to practice homoeopathy. These, by willingly retreating from their positions of honor, to the position of unhomoeopathic measures, drag themselves in the mire of falsehood and deceit, and cast obloquy upon the school they profess to support.

I have assumed, or affirmed, in the relation of medicine to disease in the process called cure, a dynamic property. Hahnemann looked upon the physical

*Read at meeting of International Hahnemannian Association.

body as only a product and vehicle of the inner life. How he was touched to a consciousness of this I do not pretend to know. He broke away from the traditional attitude, which arrayed medicine in bulk against disease bulk, and promulgated a theory which cannot be supported upon any other basis than one which recognizes in the curative action of remedies a subtle spirit power, God given, that dynamically restores the spiritual or soul poise of the inner being, to whom the outer body is but a means to an end. On this basis rests his carefully built materia medica. Without recognition of this, he must remain but partially understood. From this starting point, along the lines he marked out to be followed, we should be continuing the work he commenced. A glance at or study of other methods, even the latest chemical efforts, discloses the old old story of the pitting of so much drug against so much disease. The arguments and assumption of allopath, in its support of a voluminous materia medica, which averaged the past year the addition of new remedies weekly, has not abated one jot from its original stand, when homoeopathy was born. It continues to claim the necessity of saturating the human body with medicine to the endurance point, and that the *amount* of medicine is what cures the disease. Unfortunately we have among those who call themselves homoeopaths many who are inoculated with allopathic principles so far as to claim the same thing. Fortunately for the preservation of truth, a minor portion of those flying the banner of Similia follow in the footsteps of Hahnemann, endeavoring to preserve his platform, open to the possibility that he may have made some mistakes in the application of principles, yet convinced that in principle and theory he erred not. These aim, not to follow his leading only, but to seek the working out of the problems he left unsolved. No complaints come from those faithful ones regarding the flaws of omission in our materia medica. If there are heard complaints that certain symptoms are erroneous or that certain provings are full of faults, it is not the Hahnemannian who complains, and flies to quinine or morphine for solace. If a remark is heard that in a potency above the 12th or 30th no medicine exists, and that the giving of high potencies is foolishness, it is the one of little experience who makes that remark, or one who slyly shakes hands with allopathy, while ostensibly claiming to be a homoeopath.

The Organon of homoeopathic truth stands indisputable. Any effort to add to that truth by any other than Organon rules must fail to give proper results. While such clinical material is valuable, it fails to become established authoritative truth until provings corroborate it. It is impossible to mix allopathic and homoeopathic principles. The result is chaos. Likewise is the mixture of homoeopathic and allopathic practices chaotic. There can be no serving of two masters, or gathering of figs from thistles. The homoeopathic result is vitally linked with homoeopathic procedure. The pith of success is the true materia medica, allied with true homoeopathic principles in practice. To promote success there must be proper organization, conservative effort in preservation of our materia medica, and elimination of dross. How shall these factors be assured?

It is difficult for a minority to control in any movement where principle is the chief issue. In Hahnemann's own day he had cause to deplore the lack of principle in the practice of a majority of those claiming to follow his leading. The condition of homoeopathy now is much the same as then, as far as the fact of many professing homoeopathics making a caricature of homoeopathic principles is concerned. A letter reached me recently from a magazine editor whom I had rebuked for slurring homoeopathy in an editorial, who claimed to do no more than a professor in a so-called homoeopathic college had done, and he quoted the professor as saying: "He could recognize no difference between religion and faith, plus infinitesimals; and religion and faith, minus infinitesimals." This remark is a fair specimen of the position of that contingent following the movement in homoeopathy, which has never been Hahnemannian in principle, and therefore could not be homoeopathic in practice. These elements can never aid us in organization, in purifying our materia medica or in the uplifting of the honor of homoeopathy in practice, because wherever that element is found, in college, pharmacy or the ranks of private physicians, it is opposed to the essential principles of our faith. But for a faithful minority our honor would have been utterly blasted, and our literature lost in a sea of trash. And it is that faithful minority to whom we must look for future preservation. We are slurred for valuing our watch word, "Similia Similibus Curantur;" for waiting upon the single remedy, and for using potencies in which the microscope fails to find a material portion of drug. All this opposition is massed against our glorious materia medica, for that materia medica is indissolubly hinged with Similia, single remedy and dose.

Thus we come to value the integrity of our materia medica, in like manner as we value our homoeopathy. The necessity of preserving homoeopathy goes hand in hand with the necessity of preserving our materia medica. Those only who value the principles of homoeopathy as Hahnemann taught them are interested in the preservation of our materia medica as he taught and valued it, and they are the only ones which will work for that purpose. These must cling together and work together. Their position must be distinctly outlined as different from that of pseudo-homoeopathy which departs from homoeopathic principle. If such division in our ranks result in an open rupture, that result must be accepted, and two homoeopathics come before the world, the answer to the query, "Which is right?" to be the survival of the fittest. Let me not be misunderstood here. I do not value as any distinction between homoeopaths as Hahnemannian and non-Hahnemannian, the question of potency. If I incline to the higher, I would leave to my colleague the privilege of using the lower should he choose. But as regards the choice of remedy by the strict rule of Similia, and use of the single remedy, with dose regulated by the rules that Hahnemann gave, these should be rigidly held to as principles of true homoeopathy.

Unfortunately we cannot prevent the establishment of colleges calling themselves homoeopathic, which will disseminate unhomoeopathic teaching. I suppose they teach what they believe, graduating physicians who believe what they have been taught to be homoeopathy. The public cannot discriminate. From the ranks of these pseudo-homoeopaths comes the literature in form of essay or book which tends to contradict the true materia medica. Upon these same pseudo-homoeopaths, and the demand they create for false homoeopathic literature, the pharmacy depends for excuse to sell such literature and hand in hand with such literature goes the demand for many other unhommopathic things.

I do not know what the final issue will be. Adherence to the true materia medica and true homoeopathy demands such careful discriminative procedure and trial that the common mind is not as yet fitted to accept it. It is so arrayed, from the very beginning, against materiality of thought that it is a courageous mind which will espouse it in opposition to the gross materiality of the age. But I doubt not, the only way to preserve it is to practice it as Hahnemann practiced it, conserving the materia medica as he conserved it, and keeping faithful to the principles of Similia.

W. W. GLEASON.

Provincetown, Mass.

PAIN.

The word pain is from the Latin *pœna*, a fine or punishment. It suggests a violation of, or some precept governing, physiological processes. It also suggests some form of suffering, some distress of body. The first thing that comes to the mind of the suffering one is the cause; how or by what cause cometh the offence—"How have I offended thee?" The causes of pain may be many. They may be pressure, heat, cold, congestion, effusion of the fluids of the body, gases, retention of fluids or gases, to overeating or drinking, to indigestible foods, to drugs or alcoholic drinks. Again it may be due to traumatism from tight clothing, surgical dressings, bandages, or to disease states, such as abscesses, enlarged glands or ves els, to the occlusion of vessels due to diseased processes or by pressure, or to diseased organs themselves. Pain may be due also to states of the blood, such as lithic conditions, gouty states, gouty concretions. It may originate from the central nervous system, from the ganglia or from peripheral irritation; it may be local or general. The cause may lie at the seat of pain or it may be reflex. The reflexes of the body are great bugaboos to the young practitioner, it is so difficult for him to understand the phenomena of reflex action. The reflex centers in men are the rectum, sexual organs and prostate gland. In women, rectum, ovaries, uterus and external sexual organs. Each of those named points of reflex have their own peculiar phenomena, and they furnish a broad field for study and research to the physician. Where pain is due to reflex origin, it is usually accompanied with more or less nervous phenomena, and is generally worse when thinking about it, and it can be brought more or less under the control of the will. Quite frequently when pain is of nervous origin it is increased by light pressure and modified by firm pressure. Often the pain ceases while in conversation with the patient or when the mind is called to something else or the attacks of pain return from some slight cause or mental disturbance. It is difficult for some physicians to associate a severe pain located on the vertix with a uterine irritation, or a pain in the heel with the spinal cord. Yet nature's plan is to refer all it can to the periphery of the body and thus protect the internal organs. Again reflexes may be referred from one organ to another, as is seen in the vomiting of pregnancy; a severe nausea may often prevent an expulsive pain.

The good Homoeopath looks deeper and further than to external causes for pain. Many of the socalled predisposing cases are only secondary.

Strictly speaking, pain can originate from four causes only. Studying them from the light thrown on them by Hahnemann's miasmatic theory as to the cause of disease in general, they are traumatic, psoric, syphilitic and sycotic.

The traumatic pain is easily diagnosed by its soreness, tenderness and local traumatic symptoms; but the pains due to miasmatic origin are a life study for the student of miasmatics. The pains of syphilis are usually referred to the bony structures or their coverings. Otherwise we have no pain unless it be due to pressure from growths or internal organs. The pains of syphilis are lancinating, boring, shooting or dull, heavy. Above all, *they are persistent, continuous*, and *always worse at night and from heat.* They are concomitants of the night and of darkness. The patient longs for the light of day, and dreads the coming of the night.

The pains of psora are < in the winter months, > in the summer, the reverse to syphilis. They are also < from cold and > from heat. The sycotic pains are < from dampness or moisture in general, and better from motion. Syphilis says keep me cool; psora, keep me warm; sycosis, keep me dry. Syphilitic pain dreads the coming of the night and the summer; psora, the coming of the winter and the cold; sycosis, the falling barometer and the coming storm. A falling barometer makes the syphilitic patient's bones ache; a sycotic, joints and muscles or tendons and sheaths. Pains may assume any degree of intensity, from an unpleasant sensation of the part, to that of a tonic, even to contortion, to coma or convulsion. Pains may assume almost any sensation, such as pinching, pricking, drawing, tearing, rending, burning, stinging, lancinating, twisting, boring, digging, etc. They are dull in bones, sharp and shooting in the periosteum or pleura. They are dull, heavy and numbing in nerve trunks; sharp shooting and often tingling in the peripheral endings. They are forerunners in syphilis of tertiary changes, osteo or periosteal involvement or gummatous changes. If syphilis involves the joints it is usually a single joint, but it has preference for long bones and for osteo-periosteal surfaces.

When sycosis involves a joint, especially if of inflammatory origin, the pains usually begin with a slight stiffness of the part, then grow intense, gradually increasing in severity until the whole joint is involved and the suffering becomes agonizing. The pains are worse by motion, but there is such a desire to move that the patient cannot keep still, hence the relief of sycotic pains by motion. Suddenly the inflammation and the pains subside, but no sooner does the suffering patient find the desired relief when another joint becomes involved, with a repetition of all the former symptoms. This is not true of psora or syphilis; in fact, psora does not involve the joints. Pains are prophets of times and seasons, of light and darkness, of heat and cold, of a rising and falling barometer and temperatures, of moon changes, and planetary formulas, the rising and setting of the sun, of the four winds of heaven and of electrothermal phenomena. They tell of offended organs, by overwork, by overeating or over-indulgence; of a rebellion within the life, of heredity or acquired physiological degeneracy. To suppress a pain by sedatives or by local measures is to cover up the phenomena that lead to true causes, which often establish a new disease of a more profound nature and much more dangerous to life.

Cure a pain by changing the perverted life force, through the law of similia, and you will magnify and glorify all the physiological processes of that organism.

J. H. Allen.

92 State st., Chicago.

Nursing.*

OBSTETRICAL OPERATIONS.

Continued from July Number.

Lecture No. 10.

Embryotomy.

Ladies: It is sometimes necessary to destroy the child or to dismember its body and to bring it away piecemeal. This is known as embryotomy. Because the head presents most frequently it is most often pierced by such operations, and hence the most frequent variety of embrotomy is craniotomy.

The patient is placed in the dorsal posture and anesthetized, the doctor's instruments and other appliances being in readiness. A plentiful supply of antiseptic solution for a douche must also be ready. During the extraction of the child the physician will require a plentiful supply of hot antiseptic fluid, as it is often necessary to wash out the brain before the body is delivered. Lacerations often occur, and instruments and appliances must be in readiness for closing them. The strictest antiseptic precautions must be taken both before and after embryotomy, as many of these cases have been long in labor, and some of them are infected before they enter a hospital or before the operation is done.

Delivery by Abdominal Section.

It is believed that Julius Cæsar was extracted from his mother by abdominal incision, and hence delivery in this way has been commonly called Cesarean section. By this operation are meant the opening of the abdomen; the opening of the uterus; the extraction of the child, its placenta, cord, and membranes; and the closure of the uterus or in some cases its removal. The mother is exposed to dangers of hemorrhage and septic infection, while the child may be injured if the operation be not performed. In most of these cases the mother is in a sound and aseptic condition before the operation is undertaken. Hence the operation is a good test of the asepsis of the operator and his assistants, for if infection follows it comes most probably through his carelessness or ignorance. In order that Cesarean section may be successful the operation must proceed absolutely smoothly. The child is born very quickly after the abdomen is opened, and should delay occur at this moment the life of the child may be lost and the mother may be brought into great danger. Hence those who assist in this operation must understand what is expected of them, and must do it carefully and promptly.

To prepare a patient for Cesarean section, she should be under observation for at least a week. The intestinal canal must be thoroughly emptied. The patient's skin must be made active by a daily warm bath. The diet should be limited to liquids or to very limited simple and easily digestible food, and an abundance of water should be taken. The physician in charge will examine the patient's urine to know whether the kidneys are acting properly. If she has a cough, this must be reported to the physician, and any other abnormalities about the patient. It is better that the patient should be at rest during the greater part of the time. She can usually be made comfortable in bed, and

* Course of Lectures delivered in the Nurses Training School of Maryland Homoeopathic Hospital, by H. S. Douglass, M. D., Baltimore, Md.

this will avoid unnecessary fatigue. The nurse should encourage the patient in every way and tell her the good results obtained by this operation. In most cases in the hands of good operators mother and child recover. Attention must also be given to the breasts and nipples, because the mother can nurse her child after the operation in most cases. The breasts and nipples should be washed thoroughly with castile soap and warm water, and the nipples anointed daily with sterile olive oil or an ointment which the physician may order.

The operator should give precise and in most cases written directions for the antiseptic preparation of the patient. Most operators order that the abdomen should be thoroughly scrubbed with castile soap and water and brush, that the hair above the pubes be shaved and the hair about the labia be trimmed short with scissors curved upon the flat; and that the parts be douched thoroughly with boiled water, then scrubbed with alcohol and with bichlorid solution [1:2000]. Others prefer the use of green soap and alcohol; and some employ a poultice of green soap, which is worn by the patient for eight or ten hours. Some operators prefer lysol or carbolic acid. After the abdomen has been prepared an antiseptic dressing is applied large enough to extend from the tip of the sternum to the pubes. This is bandaged upon the patient by a many tailed bandage. Such preparation should be made at least twenty-four hours before the operation and the dressing worn during that time. Just before the commencement of the operation and often while the patient is being anesthetized, the abdomen may be prepared again in the same manner or as the obstetrician may direct. In some cases vaginal disinfection is also practiced. This is done by a copious vaginal douche of tincture of green soap [two ounces to one pint of boiled water]. The mucous membrane is thoroughly scrubbed with pieces of gauze or cotton held in uterine dressing forceps. A copious douche of hot boiled water is then given, and after this a douche of bichlorid solution [1:2000]. In some cases the operator applies a dressing of surgical gauze as well. A bichlorid napkin is worn over the vulva until the time of operation.

Whenever possible Cesarean section should be performed in the aseptic operating room of a modern hospital. This, however, is often not possible, so many of these operations must be done in private houses. If an ordinary room must be used and there is time to prepare it, carpets and curtains should be taken away, and the floor and as much as possible thoroughly scrubbed with soap and water. After this a thorough scrubbing with mercuric chloric solution [1:500] should be practiced. An operating table may be improvised by using one or two kitchen tables which have been thoroughly scrubbed. Pitchers and basins or metal vessels to be used must be thoroughly cleansed by scrubbing with soap and boiling water, or preferably by boiling. Sheets, towels, and linen to be used must be sterilized by boiling for at least thirty minutes. A half dozen large bottles or small jugs should be filled with tight corks, so that they may be filled with hot water and applied about the patient. Before the time of operation some reliable person must see that plenty of hot water is available. The room must also be heated, and an open stove or wood fire is the best heat available. If furnace heat is employed, operating-table should be placed as far as possible from the furnace register, and over the register there should be tacked several layers of cheesecloth or bichlorid gauze to arrest the dust. Over the bottom windowsash sheets or newspapers should be tacked if there is a possibility that any one may look into the room. Several small tables or a number of chairs with flat, hard bottoms are needed in addition to the operating table.

The nurse must personally be sure that she is in an aseptic condition. She must not come to a Cesarean case from any contagious or infectious disorder, should thoroughly cleanse herself by a daily bath for several days before the operation, and should have the hair thoroughly washed. Her clothing should be absolutely clean, the finger-nails trimmed smooth and short, and there should be upon the hands no sore spot or pimple containing pus or other suppurating surface. If the case be done in a hospital, instruments, dressings, and ligatures will be sterilized in the hospital apparatus. If the operation be done in a private house, the nurse must choose perfectly clean vessels in which the instruments can be boiled and kept. Fortunately, she will rarely be obliged to do this, as the operator will usually bring with him apparatus for sterilizing.

The part which the nurse takes in this operation will depend considerably upon the number of assistants present. The operator usually requires an assistant who helps him in the operation. Another physician gives the anesthetic. Another assistant receives the child at the moment of its birth, sees that it breathes properly, and ties and cuts the umbilical cord. An experienced and self-possessed nurse is perfectly competent to do this, and this part is often given to a good nurse. A nurse or physician should watch the needles and ligatures, keeping the needles threaded without interruption. The same assistant may help with the sponges if assistants are not abundant. It is better if possible to have one nurse or one physician give entire attention to sponges and dressings.

Skillful operators can perform the operation in private houses with the assistance of two physicians and one nurse. To do this the operator must prepare his needles, sutures and ligatures, sponges and dressings before the operation actually commences. The nurse must take the child and give it the first care which it requires. To do this she prepares a warm blanket or sheet, and standing at the operator's side as he directs, she hold the sheet or blanket open in her arms. The operator, when the uterus is opened, removes the child quickly, with its placenta, cord, and membranes, and puts the mass into the sheet. The nurse then ties the umbilical cord, cuts it, wipes the child's mouth and eyes, holds it head downward, and assists its respiration in the manner which we have described. After the child has been separated from the mother and has breathed, it should be turned upon its right side, wrapped in a warm blanket, and given to the care of some intelligent person, who will watch its breathing and notify the obstetrician if the child is not breathing well. If this duty is assigned to another, the nurse must assist with dressings, needles, sutures, and ligatures as desired, remembering to observe strictly antiseptic precautions. Her hands and arms must have been made thoroughly aseptic before touching sponges, instruments, sutures, ligatures, and needles. If by accident during the operation she touches any article which is not aseptic, she must at once again cleanse her hands and arms. If placed in charge of sponges, she must know how many gauze pads and sponges she has, and be able to assert that all have been returned. She must also have knowledge of the number of needles and instruments employed.

So soon as the operation is over it will be her duty to supply promptly hot bottles, blankets, clean linen, and stimulants. She must be ready to give rectal injections of stimulants if desired. She must obtain from the obstetrician written orders regarding the treatment of the patient. If she is required with the patient, she must not neglect the mother to clean the doctor's instruments. Nurses sometimes make grave mistakes in neglecting a patient to clean the doctor's instruments promptly and thus enable him to leave the case.

The after-care of a case of Cesarean section consists in the very careful following of the written orders given by the doctor. The nurse may be required to give rectal injections of stimulating or nutritious substances immediately after the operation. Hypodermic injections of sedative medicines are sometimes used. Nothing shall be given by the mouth without the distinct order of the doctor, and liquid food is usually employed with these patients for the first week or ten days. When the patient has reacted well from the operation and desires to see the child, it may be shown to her, and she may attempt to nurse it. If she does well, she should nurse the child afterward at regular intervals. It is usual to move the bowels thoroughly two or three days after the operation. Enemas of saline, glycerine, turpentine, and soapsuds are usually employed at first. Later, castor oil, olive oil with turpentine and soapsuds, or soapsuds only are usually given. It may be necessary to give this injection as high in the bowel as possible, using a long, soft rectal tube and inserting it very gently.

When the nurse is left alone with the patient she should watch carefully the condition of the pulse, taking the temperature at regular intervals as directed by the doctor. Should the pulse become rapid, or should the patient complain of pain in the abdomen, or should the abdomen become distended, the nurse must notify the physician at once. For the first twenty-four hours after the operation the patient must remain absolutely still. The nurse must exercise the greatest watchfulness, and must be prepared to go without sleep during this time. The child, fortunately, will not require much care, as it usually sleeps the greater part of the time. It must be put to the breast as ordered, and given water from a medicine dropper or a teaspoon in addition.

When the patient does well the stitches are removed at the end of ten days or two weeks; the patient is allowed light diet at about the same time; she may turn freely upon her side at the end of first week or ten days, and is able to sit up in bed at the end of two or three weeks. She is usually allowed to leave her bed at the end of the first three or four weeks, and is thought to be recovered in a month or six weeks after the operation.

Next week we will resume our studies of obstetric operations.

OBSTETRICAL OPERATIONS.

Lecture No. 11.

Ladies: This evening we will finish our studies of obstetrical operations.

A very important obstetric operation for the health of the mother consists in closing lacerations of the cervix, pelvic floor, or perineum. In some cases these injuries cannot be avoided, and if they be promptly repaired the patient recovers and remains in excellent health. If, however, they are not repaired, the patient may suffer indefinitely as a result.

Instruments for the repair of lacerations, with suture material, should be sterilized and kept in readiness for each case of labor. The repair of lacerations is usually done as soon as possible after the birth of the child. In some stitches are inserted before the placenta is expelled, although in most cases the physician delays until the womb is completely emptied. If the operation will be long and painful, an anesthetic is given if the patient is in good condition. If the physician does not wish to give an anesthetic because of the feeble condition of the patient, it may be omitted. The patient is placed upon her back at the edge of the bed or table, and her limbs supported by a sheet, as already described in speaking of the use of the forceps. If possible, a Kelly pad should be employed, and a rubber sheet should be placed over the edge of the bed and a slop jar beneath the sheet. The physician will require an antiseptic solution in a sterile basin, with sponges of gauze, his instruments within convenient reach, a plentiful supply of hot water, and an antiseptic solution of the strength desired for a viginal douche if necessary. The nurse's duties during the operation consist in preparing her hands suitably, supplying sponges and antiseptic fluid to keep the parts clean, in threading needles as required and assisting the anesthetizer, and in having ready clean dressings to use after the operation is completed.

The care of the stitches after the closure of the laceration is an important matter. Unfortunately, the genital tract is not like the skin in an abdominal incision. It cannot be protected by a heavy antiseptic dressing, nor can the parts be closed up absolutely, because they are likely to be soiled by discharges from the bowels and bladder. Stitches must be cleansed at regular intervals with such material as the obstetrician may direct. Care must be taken that the stitches do not become infected, and thorough surgical cleanliness is requisite in looking after them. Unless other directions be given, the nurse may cleanse the stitches as follows: She should first prepare a basin of antiseptic solution, usually mercuric chlorid [1:8000 to 1:4000]. A receptacle for the soiled dressing should be at hand, and also clean dressings for application. Beneath the patient should be placed a douche-pan or bed-pan, or a folded sheet or towels, to receive antiseptic fluid. The patient's limbs should be separated and wrapped with sheets or blankets. The nurse should cleanse her hands by scrubbing them with soap and water only, and then in mercuric chlorid solution [1:2000]. Having prepared a basin of antiseptic fluid containing sponges of gauze or sterile cotton, she should first allow the antiseptic fluid to flush the parts very freely, hold a handful of gause or cotton from the basin above the parts. Should there be secretions or discharges present, these should be carefully wiped off with the gauze and the parts made clean. Dipping the left hand then into the bichlorid solution, she should separate the labia with the thumb and fingers, and then flush off the tissues again with the gauze held in the right hand. The fluid should be allowed to fall into the vagina, and thus the stitches will be thoroughly flushed. The nurse should not rub the stitches nor pull upon them, and under no circumstances should she insert her finger or any instrument within the vagina without the doctor's orders. When the parts have been flushed clean a fresh dressing should be applied. In some cases the physician will order an antiseptic powder to be sprinkled into the vagina after the cleansing.

Stitches are usually removed about ten days after their insertion. The nurse should have the patient lie upon her back at the edge of the bed or table, her limbs suitably protected and placed on chairs. A basin of antiseptic fluid with gauze or cotton sponges should be ready. The external parts should be cleansed as if the patient were about to receive a douche. The instruments of the obstetrician should be boiled and his hands made aseptic. A good light should be available, and a candle is often useful. After the stitches have been removed the perineum is cleansed with an antiseptic solution and a clean dressing is applied.

Cases are ocasionally seen in which the patient during the lying-in period complains of much irritation about the stitches. This sometimes arises from the fact the stitches catch in the dressing, and when the patient moves a pull is made upon the stitch, which is painful. It is sometimes useful in these cases to apply sterile glycerine to the tissues in which the stitch is embedded. This may be done under antiseptic precautions. If, when the nurse cleanses the stitches, she sees pus forming about them, she must notify him. If the stitch begins to cut into the surrounding tissues, it is an indication that the time for its removal has come, and the doctor must be informed of the fact.

When septic infection develops interference must be practiced as soon as possible. The washing out of the uterus with either a douche tube or a curette is usually necessary. This must be done under antiseptic precautions, the tube and instruments first thoroughly boiled, and the patient's tissues made as aseptic as possible before the operation. Antiseptic precautions are taken by the physician and nurse; an anesthetic is often given, although omitted in some cases. Under a good light the physician will usually inspect the parts, and then, dilating the uterus if needed, he will introduce a douche-tube or curette and thoroughly wash out the interior of the womb. Unless bleeding occurs nothing will be placed within the womb. In some cases the uterus is tamponed with iodoform gauze. If ulcers are found in the vagina or pelvic floor, strong antiseptic solutions are applied to them.

In almost all cases puerperal septic infection can be prevented, and this occurrence must be looked upon in most cases as resulting from some omission or wrong doing of those who care for the patient. When it does occur it is very important that the patient be properly cared for, as her recovery will depend very much upon the nursing which she receives.

The prevention of puerperal sepsis requires the strict observance of those antiseptic precautions invariably practised by careful surgeons. The nurse should consider each pregnant and parturient patient as a surgical patient, and, so far as antiseptic precautions are concerned, an abortion or labor must be treated as a surgical operation. By this we mean that in attending a case of abortion or labor the nurse must exercise strict antiseptic precautions regarding herself, the instruments, appliances, dressings, and the external genital organs of the patient.

The symptoms of puerperal sepsis are fever, with tenderness in the abdomen, a large, soft womb, and usually an altered condition of the lochial discharge. In sepsis the patient has been attacked by germs which will destroy her blood and exhaust her vitality unless she can resist them. In this contest she requires all the assistance which proper nourishment, stimulus, and surgical help can give her. Puerperal sepsis sometimes begins with chill. At other times the temperature rises steadily from the first to the third or fourth day. The pulse is rapid, and there is usually constipation or diarrhœa.

The nurse must report to the attending physician a chill, rise of temperature, or a rise of the pulse rate of the patient. Nurses must not be deceived by a slight sensation of chilliness which is often felt immediately after labor. This is very different from the distinct rigor characteristic of puerperal sepsis.

When the physician sees his patient he will usually find it necessary to examine not only the external surface of the body, but also the condition of the genital tract. The nurse must prepare an antiseptic solution, plenty of hot water and dressings, and place the patient on her back across the bed. It is usual to wash out the birth canal as thoroughly as possible either before or after such an examination. The nurse must have ready the appliances and solution for a douche; and if an intra-uterine douche be given there will be needed normal salt solution or an abundance of hot sterile water. After the examination vaginal douches may be ordered at regular intervals. These must be given with the antiseptic precautions already described.

The patient will usually be ordered glycerine and saline enemas. The diet will be liquid; and if there is much pain in the abdomen the nurse may be ordered to place upon the abdomen a turpentine stupe, with or without an ice-bag. In some cases hot applications are made. To prepare a turpentine stupe for such a case, a piece of flannel is selected large enough to cover the abdomen from the pubes to the epigastrium. This should be folded in two thicknesses, and should be wrung out of one pint of water to which has been added one tablespoonful of spirits of turpentine. This is then laid smoothly upon the abdomen, and over it is placed one thickness of flannel, and upon this an ice-bag or hot water-bag. The choice is left to the attending physician. Such an application is clean, easily removed, does not blister if carefully watched, and relieves pain in most cases. If the action of the turpentine is not well borne, it may be removed and the ice-bag or hot water-bag be used alone.

The question of feeding in these cases is of the utmost importance. Milk must usually be peptonized to be readily absorbed. Rapid peptonisation by the cold process gives the best results. Milk-foods, such as junket, koumiss, buttermilk, and custards, should be used freely. Broths and soups, beef-juice, white of egg water, raw eggs beaten up with whiskey or sherry, are also needed. If fever be very high and thirst great, small quantities of cool drinks at frequent intervals are required. The best and simplest ice cream and ices are occasionally useful if taken partially melted. The nurse must employ every expedient to secure the taking of food. The patient should not be asked what she desires, but nourishment should be brought to her at favorable intervals and without delay or argument.

The use of alcoholic stimulants is very important in septic cases. Wines are seldom employed extensively, as they are rarely pure and often disturb digestion. The best quality of whiskey and brandy is usually employed. A thoroughly septic patient will often consume enormous quantities of alcoholic stimulants without the least sign of intoxication. Stimulants may usually be given with water, and as a beverage to quench thirst. Better results are obtained in the long run by giving food and stimulants seperately than by combining alcohol with articles of diet. In addition to alcoholic stimulants the nurse may be ordered to administer tonic and stimulating medicines, occasionally by hypodermic injection.

Operative treatment may become necessary during puerperal sepsis. Washing out of the womb, curetting the uterus, incision into the vagina or into the abdomen to empty an abscess, or abdominal section followed by the removal of diseased organs may be performed. The nurse must prepare for these operations as is usually done. The preparation for Cæsarean section already given may be followed if other orders are not received. Septic patients are often annoyed by diarrhœa. The discharges may be irritating in character. Unless the patient be well cared for, much suffering and the formation of a bed-sore may occur. Strict cleanliness, with frequent changing of the dressing and the use of healing ointments, will keep the patient in good condition.

In some cases bed-sores form very easily. Bathing with alcohol or alcohol and alum, the use of rubber adhesive plaster, the use of ice, and turning the patient frequently upon the side may all be employed. With some patients, lying directly upon a blanket is one of the best preservatives of bed-sore. The use of rubber sheeting or rings is objectionable because of its heating and and irritating properties. It is better to use ample dressings and little rubber material about the patient. The mattress used in puerperal septic infection should be burned at the termination of the case.

A most important matter in this connection is the care which the nurse must take of herself. A scratch, a cut, or a neglected hang-nail on her hands may result in infection, in serious illness or death. The constant demand upon her strength and the anxious and depressing nature of the case make such patients difficult to attend. It is necessary to wean the child, and this adds to the nurse's cares. She must be very cautious in the care of her hands, and rubber gloves are excellent in dressing a patient. The use of a simple healing lotion or ointment, applied thoroughly upon the hands and around the nails before retiring, will prove of great value. She must be careful to take a regular allowance of fresh air and sleep and to maintain her nutrition in every way possible. She must be very careful regarding the avoidance of infection in the eyes. Antiseptic solutions sometimes spatter into the eyes, setting up severe irritation. Septic fluids may also gain access to the eyes. The nurse must not rub her eyes while attending a septic case. Should smarting and redness occur, she should consult an opthalmologist at once.

Such patients require two or more nurses. It is impossible for one nurse to give mother and child proper treatment without sacrificing their good and her own health. The case is so serious and so much depends upon the patient's nursing that two or more nurses should be in attendance. The physician must decide whether one nurse should take exclusive care of the mother and the other of the child, or whether they shall alternate. It is usually better to have one nurse to do the surgical dressing for the mother, and the other nurse to dress the umbilicus and bathe the child, as care must be taken that the child does not become infected at the umbilicus or in the eyes or mouth.

In our next lecture we will discuss some of the complications of the lying-in period.

INTESTINAL OBSTRUCTION IN LABOR—FATAL PERFORATION.

Champetier de Ribes and Daniel [*Comptes Rendus de la Soc. d'Obstet. de Gyn. et de Pediat. de Paris*, December, 1901] sums up the literature of intestinal obstruction in labor. Out of a score of cases the cause of the obstruction was independent of the labor in all but two. Vinay, Gottscheld, and Spencer Wells have reported cases where there was a direct relation. De Ribes and Daniel's case was in a laundress aged 31. She had undergone three years earlier an operation for tubal pregnancy, and becoming pregnant on this occasion she entered hospital before term, as advised when she recovered from the operation. Ten days after admission the uterine contraction began; within a few minutes the patient was seized with a violent pain of another kind in the left side of the abdomen. The temperature was 101 degrees; labor was very easy and spontaneous, and all seemed well. Symptoms of peritonitis set in on the third day, the signs of obstruction reappearing. On the fifth day she died; a coil of sigmoid was seen to be gangrenous; the intestine was pressed on lower down by a pelvic abscess. Purulent and fæcal fluid was found in the peritoneal cavity. A strong band of adhesion passed from the fundus to the sigmoid flexure, and there were other bands; they seem to have been stretched or torn during labor, and some fæcal matter set up the suppuration. The adhesions, however, were sufficient to obstruct the intestine, the colon sloughed, and general septic peritonitis followed.—*Brit. Med. Jour.*

Correspondence.

LARGE VS. SMALL COLLEGES.

It seems to me, Mr. Editor, that the last word has not been said on the question raised in your journal, under the following heading: Can a College with a Teaching Force of Thirty Be Considered a Small One? It is twice too large. The time is coming when a radical change will be made in our present methods of teaching, probably the private college will go out of existence entirely. One reason for this is that a man engaged in active professional work cannot teach any department of medicine as it *should* be taught; he cannot give the time needed. Closely related to this fact, is the disastrous, or at all events the lamentable, compromise of dividing up a department among three or more men. Thus good men of the first rank can not, in the nature of things give as comprehensive and thorough instruction as one man can, even if less gifted than any one of the three. Take my own department, surgery, and see the difference. How many hours a week do the three or four men associated in this chair, in a private school, collectively, give? Not more than one hour each, exclusive of their clinics. In my college, I have nine hours' class work a week, for nine months in the year, with clinic hours *ad libitum*. Does it not stand to reason that one man, if at all competent, can give better work in every way, than if his department were divided up among three or more?

The school of the future *must*, it would seem in the very nature of things, be a state school, with a faculty of *teachers*, not "stock owners," and with one man at the head of each department, with such assistants, for quizzing, laboratory demonstrations etc., as the size of the classes calls for. The difference between the value of teaching from a faculty of thirty and one of sixty is infinitisimal, the efficiency increasing as the number diminishes, until we reach, say, fifteen, when at a bound the value rises enormously. We might as well commence to accustom ourselves to the idea that our private schools, in obedience to the laws of sound evolution, must go out of existence, unless so generously endowed that they are actually independent of student patronage. The cost of laboratory equipment alone is so enormous, if adequate, that no purely private school can possibly compete with a state institution. It is a fact, easily demonstrated, that a single state school has a larger equipment for laboratory work than all the colleges of homœopathic medicine combined have in Chicago.

If it is meant by "*small colleges*" a small class of students, other questions come up. Good teaching is not possible when the number of students reach above a certain limit, say 150, unless the number of demonstrators and assistants is so large that no one of them has oversight over more than twenty or twenty-five. In fact, there has been a movement looking toward limiting the admission to schools in a New England college, I think making 200 the maximum.

The whole question, therefore, I think, may be summed up something like this: The school of the future will require matriculates to enter with chemistry, botany, histology, and physiology, together with general descriptive anatomy finished in schools of science, and with a degree in arts or science. The schools will be state institutions, or sufficiently endowed to put them on a level with state colleges in equipment and income. The faculty will be a body of teachers, not in active practice, their practical work being found in hospitals, laboratories and consultations. There will not be more than twelve or fifteen heads of departments. Much that is now taught will be conducted in pre matriculate colleges, and still more in post-graduate schools and polyclinics. The classes will be limited to, say 200 as a maximum. The fact must be admitted that no medical college can meet its expenses from student fees; it must have a support entirely independent of student patronage.

JAMES G. GILCHRIST,
Iowa City, Iowa.

Editorial.

HERING-DUNHAM.

Two names that stand for the best in Homoeopathy. Two names that were selected as sponsors for two medical colleges whose declaration of principles put Homoeopathy in the foreground, but gave to every other department of medical training its relative place. Surgery and all mechanical means logically occupy the same position to dynamic means that the body occupies toward the mind. Homoeopathy has been taught as more logical, more scientific, than any other theory ever advanced for the treatment of the sick. The aims and purposes of both colleges have been one and the same and there has been no good or valid reason for the existence of the two colleges in the same city. Experience is an expensive teacher, but the truths thus taught are never forgotten.

The prospect of an immediate merger of the two colleges into one strong institution is very favorable. Everything has been agreed upon except the details and will go into effect before the beginning of the next session. The plan of consolidation being the combining of the two names, thus securing all the prestige and influence that has been divided in the past. In addition to this the two faculties will be combined in such a manner that every department may be strengthened and rounded out until it will equal that of any similar institution in the country.

Chicago is the greatest Homoeopathic center in the world and there is nothing to prevent the new college taking a much higher place in the professional world than either one could hope to attain alone. In union is strength, but the union must be so thoroughly cemented together that no one can detect the point of contact. Let the two charters be surrendered and a new one issued so that the union be basic in principle, and then burn out all factional spirt in the intense flame of undying Truth, and from the purified result build up a new faculty in which self and selfish interests shall be forgotten in the zeal and enthusiasm for the cause of Homoeopathy and no power on earth can successfully resist its onward progress. Truth will conquer and Homoeopathy will prevail.

The new name of the institution will be Hering-Dunham Medical College and Post Graduate School of Homoeopathics. By the consolidation, it becomes an innovation in university experience by being selected as *the* medical department of Midland University—a corporate name representing the close affiliation of eight or ten separate colleges under one corporate name. This combination enables each college to have all the benefits of concentration and systematic promotion at a minimum expense to each, that in and of itself means much for Homoeopathy and more for the new institution in particular.

Dr. J. T. Kent will be Dean of the combined faculty and Dr. H. C. Allen, President of the Board of Trustees. Drs. Waring and King will act as Registrars during the current year or until all the details of the consolidation have been completed. Dr. L. A. L. Day will be Treasurer of the Board of Trustees.

The college year will begin September 15th with a reception at which the new faculty will become acquainted and the students from the separate institutions made to feel that the change has been made solely for their benefit.

Let the profession respond with redoubled zeal, thus showing their appreciation of this effort to make Homoeopathy the most comforting word sick can hear. Every reader of the Advocate can secure a student if the right effort is put forth.

MEDICAL ETHICS.

It is a remarkable fact that Homoeopathy has never had an exponent who equalled Hahnemann either as an investigator or aggressive fighter of existing forms of medical practice. Little wonder that he aroused bitter antagonism in view of the fact that his teaching were not only diametrically opposed to the views held by the medical profession throughout the world but were so far in advance of the generally accepted scientific standard that but few could appreciate the logical significance of his principles. He was so aggressive in his writings that they dare not ignore him and so logical in his arguments that they could not answer him, so were compelled to resort to the usual method of ignorance and bigotry—brute force. He was driven from place to place—a most fortunate thing for Homoeopathy, because in that way Truth was promulgated over a wide stretch of territory. The machinery of government was brought into operation and those most potent weapons, ridicule and ostracism, employed. It is a high compliment to Homoeopathy that from the very beginning its growth has been fostered by means of the fierce opposition developed in every community in which its standard has been planted. Weak, inferior minds have never been attracted to its cause, but many times these noble souls have been made to suffer bitter persecution closely verging upon the border lines of criminal practice through refusal to render assistance when human life was in imminent danger.

The attention of the profession is being called to the distressing circumstances under which Dr. Stephenson of Dunedin, New Zealand, lost a patient during confinement because physicians of the dominant school refused to come to his aid for no other reason than he was an exponent of Homoeopathy. The subject must be viewed from all sides before we can get at the merits of the case.

Does the blame rest upon the expression of man's limitations—the code of ethics—or upon the men back of the code? Ignorance lies at the foundation of the whole matter. Bigotry is another name expressing the same. Selfishness is a twin sister to ignorance and the two together have caused much suffering through all ages. At the same time we are indebted to the selfish instincts for much of the advancement witnessed on all sides.

The code of ethics places all practitioners who proclaim *exclusiveness* in their practice in the same class and deny to them the "privileges" of consultation upon the basis that there can be no common ground upon which the consultants may stand and view the case. The dominent school claims that everything in the domain of science is common property and that medicine is both a science and an art, but prove their *bigotry* and *exclusiveness* by limiting all application of the art to their own particular interpretation, denying to all others the same rights and privileges.

Anatomy, physiology, pathology, biology, chemistry and, to a certain degree, bacteriology conform to the requirements of a science which, according to the *Century Dictionary*, is "knowledge gained by systematic observation, experiment and reasoning,"with definite, fixed *laws* governing their manifestations. These laws have been discovered by systematic observation, experiment and reasoning. They furnish common ground upon which every practitioner of medicine may stand. To this list may be added sanitation and preventive medicine. All physicians are now compelled to acquire knowledge of all these branches of medical science before they enter upon the systematic observation, experiment and reasoning of the action of *foreign* substances in the treatment of the sick.

At the time when the code of ethics was formulated there was no standard whereby the qualifications of a medical practitioner could be determined, and the code was adopted to protect those who were willing to devote the time necessary for the acquiring of suitable knowledge of the science of medicine. The colleges were in the hands of the dominant school, so it was natural to assume that they were better qualified for judging of qualifications of practitioners worthy of their recognition.

In the natural course of time, many changes have taken place and medicine and the medical profession have in a measure kept pace with investigation along other lines. To the degree in which bigotry has given place to actual knowledge do we find the restrictions and safeguards of the past yielding to the spirit of common brotherhood. Homoeopathy stands for law, but how many of its adherents *know* enough about the law and its *practical* workings to *demonstrate* its truth? We are all finite and the qualifications of the best but limited, hence the necessity for holding out the hand to anyone in need and let the mantle of charity cover the sins of omission as well as commission.

DECREASED BIRTH RATE IN THE UNITED STATES.

That the birth rate among native born American women has fallen to an even lower ebb than that among French women seems to be borne out by statistics. Previous to 1830, up to which time there was no considerable number of immigrants, the average birth rate according to records of the decennial censuses during 40 years, was 34.65 per cent. This rate, notwithstanding the influx of fecund foreigners, was reduced to 20.87 per cent in 1900.

In Europe the number of births per thousand, excluding still births, are: In Russia, 48.5; Austria; 37.2; Prussia, 36.9; Italy, 36.3; England, 30.3; France, 22.4.

In 1894 there were in Massachusetts, New Hampshire, Michigan, Rhode Island and New Jersey, 22.1 births to each thousand. The native born per thousand in Massachusetts from 1893 to 1897 were 17; foreign born, 52.2. Michigan, native born, 14.1; foreign, 50.

According to the above paragraph it appears that the French women are more prolific than their sisters in favored parts of the United States.

The immense difference between the fecundity of native born American women and foreign born is shown by the birth record of Massachusetts in 1900. The native born population of that state for that year was 1,959,022, the number of births being 23,000. The foreign born population was 846,324, to which were born 36,062 children; that is, thirty per cent of the entire population produced nearly fifty per cent of the total number of children born during that year.

The number of children to each marriage in Russia 5.5; Austria, 4.1; Prussia, 4.2; Italy, 4.4; England, 3.9; France, 2.1; Missouri, 1885 to 1895, native 2.1; foreign, 3.8; Michigan, 1890 to '94, native, 2.1; foreign, 4.1; Massachusetts, 1885, native, 2.7; foreign 4.5.

The birth rate among college women is the lowest of any groups, only 1.3 children to each married graduate.

That these figures are appalling to every student, and especially to the physician, is self evident.

What are the causes? Every physician is more or less familiar with many or all of them. It is not because native born women are growing weaker or less able to bear children. The reverse is true. The simple fact is that the average American wife does not want children.

Why?

Because they are in her way, interfere with her social plans, especially if she is rich or well-to-do.

Woman's desire to be "independent" leads her into all trades and professions, thereby preventing many marriages. If one of these business or professional women consummates a marriage, the bearing of children would take her away from her "business" or profession, so conception is prevented; if occuring, abortion is too often resorted to.

Our educational system is wrong. All the efforts of the system in vogue is to teach girls accomplishments, not to instruct them in practical matters, nor the beauty of maternity, nor how to keep a house in order.

Another item that militates against the rearing of a family by a struggling young couple is the expense of a confinement, which, in its entirety, hardly ever falls below $100.

The physician is doing his part in curing the sick, making it possible for many who would otherwise be unable to bear children to do so. But there is a great work of education that must be done with the young girls, some of which can be done by the family physician, but most of it must fall on the minister, the teacher and the mother. Different ideas must be instilled into the minds of the youth—other objects besides the ability to shine in society must be held up as the ne plus ultra of a girl's existence.

THE LEAVEN IS WORKING.

The editor of the Medical Times thinks the recent meeting of the American Medical Association showed that there "is a tremendous upheaval going on in the direction of liberal progressive medicine." As an instance of this change of feeling, as compared with a decade ago, Dr. Hare's earnest condemnation of large and long continued doses of Digitalis and other drugs was unquestioned. His insistance upon the individualism of cases also met with no opposition.

The editor of the Times also pays a deserved tribute to the superiority of homœopathy in the following paragraphs:

We were sorry not to have heard more on the subject of drugs and their uses, and it is a mistake to report cases without reasons for the use of remedies employed. It is not enough in these days to say that "the usual treatment was employed," we want to know the dose as well as the indications upon which it was given, then these reports may be made of real service.

Therapeutics has not kept pace with pathology, the latter subject being far in advance of the former. When the subject of the remedy shall be studied with all the analytical care accorded to diagnosis, then we shall be able to do far more in the direction of cure than can be done at present.

Personals and News Items.

Medical colleges in the United States graduated more than 5,500 students during the past year.

Dr. Replogle now occupies the office of the late Dr. T. C. Duncan, Reliance Building, 100 State street, Chicago.

Dr. W. E. Ledyard, lately of Berkeley, Cal., has removed to Sunol Glen, Alameda Co., Cal., where he is pleasantly located and apparently doing well.

Dr. L. M. Stanton of New York City has removed from 132 West 58th st., to 205 West 57th st.

GOOD HOMŒOPATHIC READING is found in back numbers of the ADVOCATE. Complete volumes 1896 to 1901, mailed on receipt of $1.00 a volume. Ten numbers, not consecutive, fifty cents. Address Hahnemann Publishing Co., 6704 Lafayette ave.

The Chicago Homœopathic Medical College is to be congratulated on securing the services of Dr. J. J. Thompson as associate professor Medical Gynecology. The Doctor's success in practice as well as his ability to impart his knowledge to others makes him a valuable acquisition.

It is raining honors upon the head of Dr. Charles Lowry of Topeka, Kansas. Not only is he president of the State Homœopathic Medical Society, but is also a member of the State Board of Health, and has been appointed a delegate to the Tuberculosis Congress to be held in New York City.

West Liberty, Ohio, a town of over a thousand people, offers an excellent field for a homœopath. Dr. D. B. Hale is unable to attend to the practice he has established there during the past twenty-four years, on account of continued illness. There is a popular demand for a homœopath, and Dr. Hale will be glad to help anyone looking for a good location.

GOOD MEDICAL LITERATURE, cheap, can be obtained, in the shape of complete volumes of MEDICAL ADVANCE, for years 1893, '94 and '95. $1.00 a volume, postpaid, while they last. Ten numbers, not consecutive, for fifty cents. Odd numbers of issues of the 70s and 80s at six cents a number. Address, Hahnemann Publishing Co., 6704 Lafayette ave.

Dr. Ernest P. Mills of Olathe, Kans., has been honored by appointment as county physician of Johnson county.

The American Institute of Phrenology, incorporated 1866, opens its next session, September 3, 1902. For particulars apply to the Secretary, M. H. Piercy, care of Fowler & Wells Co., 24 East 22d st., New York.

GOOD HOMŒOPATHIC READING is found in back numbers of the ADVOCATE. Complete volumes 1896 to 1901, mailed on receipt of $1.00 a volume. Ten numbers, not consecutive, fifty cents. Address Hahnemann Publishing Co., 6704 Lafayette ave.

Color to Chicago's title of medical "Vienna of America" is given by the fact that both the American Institute of of Homœopathy and the American Medical Association came to this medical metropolis to select their presidents, Drs. Cobb and Billings.

Drs. Menninger, Swan and Harding, all of Topeka, are working hard to have the new Kansas hospital for the insane at Parsons placed under homœopathic management. For the good of this unfortunate class it is to be hoped that their efforts may be successful.

Dr. Woodbury, Commissioner of Street Cleaning in New York City, recently undertook to determine the number and kind of microorganisms floating in the atmosphere of the town. A number of gelatin plates was prepared and exposed for a time at different levels above the street in various parts of the town. The result was unsatisfactory—not because no microbes were found, but because there were so many that the plates were simply a mass of colonies so thickly crowded together that it was impossible to distinguish them. Other experiments are now being made with briefer exposure of the plates.

Materia Medica Miscellany.

Hypericum.—Sometimes a vicious dog will take hold of an individual through the thumb, or through the wrist and run one of his great teeth through the radial nerve or some of its branches in the hand. You may not find in the earlier stages the symptoms of Hypericum, but they develop gradually, and you will have them to treat later on. Do not cut the arm off, but cure it. We cure all these injuries with medicines—punctured, incised, contused or lacerated wounds, painful wounds. A wound sometimes will yawn, swell up; no tendency to heal, look dry and shiny on the edges; red, inflamed; burning, stinging, tearing pains; no healing process. That wound needs Hypericum.—*The Critique.*

Strophanthus.—The actions and the medical uses of Strophanthus, which is perhaps the most important of the cardiotonic drugs after Digitalis, are summed up as follows: (1) It cannot be compared to Digitalis in the constancy of its effects. Nevertheless, in certain cases it succeeds when Digitalis has failed, and it is of value in replacing Digitalis during the periods of treatment in which that drug is suspended for the purpose of avoiding its cumulative effect. (2) It has no marked action upon either the vessels or the arterial pressure. It is, therefore, preferable to Digitalis in all cases in which arterial tension is evidently a source of embarrassment to an enfeebled heart. (3) The dosage is very irregular. In order to avoid its toxic effects, and at the same time secure its real benefits, it should be given in progressively increasing doses, till the physiological indication has been fulfilled. There are only two preparations of value, namely, the extract and Strophanthin; the tincture is very unreliable. The extract is to be given in doses of from one to six milligrams, severals times a day, its effect being watched. The dose of Strophanthin is one-tenth as large.—*Medical Era*

Crude Petroleum for Fecal Impaction.—Physicians of the oil regions have found out by experience (*Amer. Med.*) that the common crude oil as it comes from the wells is the best solvent known for the disintegration of hardened fecal masses, so that they may become movable. There is no fecal mass which it will not penetrate and soften. One quart of the oil should be introduced through a colon tube and allowed to remain for twelve hours. There is usually no trouble about its retention. This treatment has been found to succeed after the most energetic use of water and sweet oil and glycerine failed to give relief.

Cinnamon Water as an Antiseptic.—Oil of cinnamon (*Med. World*) in aqueous solution acts like magic as a local disinfectant. In a recent wound of any kind, after stitching or whatever may be needed, keep a compress wet with cinnamon water constantly applied until healing is complete, which usually takes place without suppuration. It takes the place of corrosive sublimate, and everything else. It is pleasant to use, cleanly, non-toxic, safe, and cheap. As a douche after parturition it is ideal, not often requiring to be used more than two or three times. I add three or four drops of the oil of cinnamon to two quarts of warm water, and direct it to be used as often as there is any scent to the lochia. In nasal catarrh it serves well, and in fact wherever a germicide and disinfectant is wanted.

Tuberculinum should not be given lower than the 30th, preferably in higher potencies, and in frequent doses. According to Dr. Nebel it is contra-indicated in the aged, in arterio-sclerosis, in nephritis unless preceded by other remedies, and in children with dry, harsh skin.

Antimonium crudum is an excellent remedy for the vocal cords. When, after laryngitis or fatigue of the voice, a singer has a harsh and badly pitched voice, this remedy will certainly give suppleness to the vocal cords [Cartier]. Cough worse coming into a warm room, with burning and itching of the chest. Loss of voice from becoming overheated.

Ipecacuanha.- Dr. Cartier says that this is the remedy for hoarseness more or less complete in inflammatory laryngititis. It rapidly dissipates hoarseness at the end of a cold. Nearly no cough, but complete aphonia. I have happened to give Ipecac 30 several times every half hour, resting the voice several hours. When the voice returns and the cough increases, we must stop Ipecac. Its place is in inflammatory aphonia.

Secale is the only drug that presents lesions akin to those observed in locomotor ataxia, a slow degeneration of the posterior columns of the spinal cord; impossibility of standing with the eyes closed, girdle pains, absence of the knee jerk; formication, anæsthesia and severe pains.—W. E. Boericke in *Med. Century.*

Magnesium Dioxide.—A discovery has been made recently which is claimed to be a remarkable achievement in chemistry and of considerable therapeutic value. Dr. Friedrich Elias, a Berlin scientist, has succeeded in evolving by a chemical process of his own devising, a magnesium dioxide (MgO^2) which he asserts is capable of emitting a large amount of diffusible oxygen throughout the system. This preparation, which is not a synthetic product, occurs as an impalpable white powder, tasteless, colorless, odorless, non-astringent, non-irritant, non-toxic, and insoluble in water. Dr. Henry Leffman, Professor of Chemistry in the Woman's Medical College, Philadelphia, and Vice President of the British Society of Public Analyses, has analyzed magnesium dioxide and makes the statement with regard to its composition that it contains no barium, strontium, or calcium compounds. It is free from sodium dioxide and caustic potash — therefore possesses no caustic properties. It is also declared to be capable of exuding large quantities of diffusible assimilable oxygen. It is claimed that this preparation exerts beneficial effects in the treatment of diseases arising from deficient oxidation. If magnesium dioxide be as easily absorbed by the capillaries as is stated to be the case by those who have tested it clinically, it should prove a therapeutic remedy of much value.—*Med. Record.*

Tua-Tua.—This a plant employed against leprosy in Honolulu (*Phar. Journal,* February 15, 1902) is probably *Jatropha gossypifolia,* Linnæus, Natural Order *Euphorbiaceæ.* In 1868, Pompa, in his collection of indigenous medicinal plants, described Tua-Tua, and stated that a decoction of leaves, to which a little salt was added, was excellent for "pain in the stomach." The decoction was recommended in dropsy; the milky juice obtained by cutting the young twings was employed as a cure of ulcers in the mouth. This plant also grows in Brazil, in Mexico, in British Guiana, and in the Niger districts.

Cranberries.—The pure, fresh juice of raw cranberries, given freely, either undiluted or with an equal part of water, is recommended by Goriansky as an excellent means of relieving the thirst in fever, and moreover, is markedly antipyretic. In the thirst and vomiting peculiar to cholera it is even more effective. In fifty cases in which ice and narcotics failed to make the slightest impression, cranberry juice, in small but repeated doses, rapidly checked both vomiting and nausea.—*Med. Times.*

Sterilized Grape Juice as Medicine.—The cost which the grape cure necessitates places it beyond the means of most people. E. Ivanhoff (*Sem. Med.*, Feb. 5, 1902) replaces it with expressed grape juice, which can be taken about half an hour or an hour before breakfast in doses of from four to eight ounces, corresponding usually to two hundred or four hundred grams of grapes. The liquid must be preserved in bottles carefully corked and kept in a cold place. It must be warmed slightly before taken in order to make its effects more active. As soon as the dose has been absorbed the patient should take a little walk or other exercise. The author has successfully treated in this manner a number of cases of chronic bronchitis, nephritis and intestinal atony. He also employs it with equal success as a general tonic for convalescents from typhoid fever and severe forms of grippe. In two case of organic heart disease, in one of aneurism accompanied with renal congestion and edema of the lower extremities and abdomen, this grape juice proved especially useful by reason of its diuretic action. The author thinks that this juice can be advantageously substituted for the grape cure, not only because it is more convenient, but also because it is exempt from the ordinary objections to grapes, namely, irritation of the teeth and the mucous membrane of the mouth, and occasionally indigestion from fermentation after eating the fruit.

Medorrhinum is a nosode prepared from the gonorrhœic *virus*. It is a great antisycotic remedy. It is useful in removing the constitutional effects of maltreated and suppressed gonorrhœa. Its antirheumatic property is very well marked. It is useful for persons suffering from gout and rheumatism. In throat affections its usefulness is clear. There is a sensation as if she had taken a severe cold. Throat is full of thick, gray and bloody mucus from posterior nares. Severe pains in renal region, so it is useful in renal colic, intense pain in ureters, with a sensation of passage of calculus. Menses profuse, flow dark and clotted and offensive. When best selected remedy fails to relieve or permanently cure.

Bovista is prepared from a fungus. Adapted to old person and dwarfs whose growth is stunned. In diseases of the skin and sexual organs of females. Menses flow only at night, not in the day time. Blood dark and clotted with pains. Leucorrhœa before and after menses. Persons suffering from tettery eruptions both dry and humid.

Coca.—Erythroxylon Coca. Useful in extreme prostration from mental and physical strain of a busy life. Persons with exhausted nerves and brains. Melancholy from nervous exhaustion. Longing for alcoholic liquors and tobacco. Want of breath in those engaged in athletic sports.—*Indian Hom. Review.*

Bean Tea.—Made from the dry pods of the common garden bean will, according to Dr. Ralph St. J. Perry (Surgical Clinic), cure cystitis. Here is part of what he says of a remedy which, no doubt, is so little used because it is cheap and has been overlooked in the chase after *new* remedies: Some years ago I had a case of cystitis which needed all my efforts to cure. Also those of several other medical gentlemen. One of my old lady friends who knew of the case suggested the use of a tea made of the dry pods of the common bean. I smiled the smile of superior medical knowledge; she backed her advice up by competent medical authority, and I tried the remedy. It worked like a charm. Not only in that case but in several others since then, I now keep dried bean pods in stock. My venerable friend, told me that she had been subject to attacks of bloody inflammation of the bladder for years, but that she was now able to control the disease in twenty-four hours by using the bean-pod tea. She had first learned of the remedy from a family doctor book. This book is the Encyclopedia of Health and Home, published in Chicago in 1884, and the medical portion is edited by George P. Wood, M. D., and E. H. Ruddock, M. D. Wood and Ruddock are looked upon as pretty good authorities. In the chapter on Cystitis there is the following: "In this disease it is seldom necessary that any remedy should be administered except a tea made of the pods or hulls of the common bean. It is to be drank freely three to six times a day, from which a speedy cure can be expected."

Hyoscine for Morphine and Alcohol Habits.—Some months ago I received a letter from Dr. Lott, of Cameron, Texas, stating that he was using massive doses of Hyoscine in the treatment of various forms of drug habit with very great success, and asking if I could not give any information in regard to what was to him a purely empirical plan of treatment. I asked him to write a paper on the subject, which he did and which was published in the *Therapeutic Gazette* for February, 1902. Since then I have tried the plan in six cases with extraordinary results from the following points of view:

I. The patients can take massive doses at a time, as much as 1/4 grain hypodermically, with no evil effects on any vital function.

2. They suffer very slightly, if at all, from the immediate withdrawal of the morphine.

3. And the more surprising, the desire for the drug is largely, if not entirely, dissipated after a few days.

It is a noteworthy fact that all the patients subjected to this method of treatment that I have seen, have expressed themselves as feeling well, when asked questions about their own sensations, and had no serious disorder of the heart or other organs. It is also a noteworthy fact that in some of them the dryness of the tongue passed away after the first 24 or 48 hours, so that they suffered not at all from the symptom. While as a rule they do not care to take solid food, I have never had any difficulty in getting them to take liquids in adequate quantities, both for the purpose of flushing the kidney and giving liquid nourishment.

In still another case, a comparatively young woman who for a number of months had taken 1/3 of a grain of morphine hypodermically every three hours, and at least a pint of whiskey in each 24 hours, was also given very large doses of Hyoscine. For a period of three days Hyoscine delirium with mental wandering was very marked, and she says that for those three days she had very little recollection of what took place. Within ten days of the beginning of the treatment, no morphine or alcohol at all having been given, the patient while still receiving these massive doses of Hyoscine began to pass from under their influence, her tongue became moist, her mind clear and she herself expressed surprise that she no longer had any desire for either morphine or whiskey. Twelve days after the treatment began she asked for solid food and on the thirteenth day complained to me that her appetite was ravenous and that she could not remember when she had had such an insatiable desire for food. During the last four days of these twelve, her mental condition was exceedingly bright and cheerful and she is now progressing rapidly towards what I hope will be a permanent cure. In her case morphine had not been taken for the relief of pains, but in gradually-increased quantities for the relief of nervousness.—H. A. Hare, in *Medical News.*

Purification of Drinking Water by Boiling.—Bizzozozero states, in a German periodical, that most people object to purifying water by boiling for various reasons. He gives the most important objections as follows:

1. The water loses its air, and is not digestible.

2. The water loses its free carbonic acid gas, which normally gives it a piquant taste.

3. There is a loss of lime salts, which are necessary to our nutrition.

4. Boiling gives water a specific unpleasant taste.

Bizzozozero takes up these objections one at a time. He shows that the air can easily be re-introduced into water after boiling merely by shaking it for a minute or two. He shows that the amount of carbonic acid gas normally present in drinking water is entirely too small to impart any taste at all to it. The lime salts in the water are quite unnecessary, as they are supplied better in the food. He claims that no specific unpleasant taste occurs if the water is boiled in clean glass or enamelled ware receptacles and cooled off rapidly afterwards. He considers this the best all-round method for sterilizing drinking water.—*Med. Times.*

According to the Eclectic Medical Journal there are 8,149 eclectic physicians in the United States. Illinois leads with 903, Indiana and New York being next in order with 690 and 656 respectively.

TO DISTINGUISH BETWEEN SMALLPOX AND CHICKENPOX.

A writer in the "*Lancet,*" referring to the prevalence of smallpox in London, and the difficulty sometimes in mild cases of differentiating between this disease and chickenpox, calls attention to a well known method by which this object can be attained. The vesicles in chickenpox are unilocular, while in smallpox they are multilocular, the practical result of this pathological fact being that, if a chickenpox vesicle be pricked with a needle, its contents can be completely evacuated, and the cell will collapse; whereas in smallpox, if you make twenty pricks with a needle, the vesicle will not collapse, because, being multilocular, it is impossible to empty it.

Book Reviews.

Smallpox—Illustrated by Dr. Geo. H. Fox and published by Lippincott & Co. Price $3.00.

Naturally there is a feeling of uncertainty whenever a case of smallpox is examined. There is so much depending upon the diagnosis that we hesitate and generally give the patient the benefit of the doubt until the suspicions have been confirmed by an expert.

The physician has an expert in his possession as soon as he becomes familiar with the contents of this very practical work. It consists of Two Parts in heavy paper covers, Atlas style, with *colored pictures taken from life*, illustrating the physical appearance from the very first day through the intervening stages up to the thirtieth day.

The text is plain and the whole scope of the work eminently *practical*. Altogether there are forty-three colored lithographic plates covering every imaginable variety and phase of the disease.

The price has been placed so low that it ought to be in the hands of every medical practitioner.

Dictionary of Materia Medica by John H. Clarke, M. D., and published by the Homœopathic Publishing Co., London.

This is the most ambitious work on Materia Medica since the publication of the Guiding Symptoms by Hering, containing over 2500 large octavo pages. The author has drawn upon all known and reliable sources for information and there will be found incorporated in this great work practically all that appears in the larger works, and in addition much that is new and otherwise would be exceedingly difficult to find. The experience of Burnett and Cooper alone adds much to the value of the book.

Each remedy is considered under each of the following sub-heads: Clinical; characteristics; relations; Causation symptoms. The reader therefore has five separate view points from which he can study the remedy.

The author promises a complete Concordance Repertory to complete the set. This will add greatly to the value because no other repertory can be a complete index to any but its own particular work.

We have taken the liberty of printing in the body of the July ADVOCATE the study of *Bacillinum* and in this number will be found *Pyrogenium*, as illustrative of the peculiar claims this new work has upon the medical profession.

Diseases of the Lungs by Prof. A. L. Blackwood. Published by Halsey Bros. Co., Chicago.

This is a *practical* book. All theories and speculative ideas have been eliminated and facts have been arranged in such a simple manner that the practical features of the etiology, pathology, symptomology, diagnosis, prognosis and *homœopathic* treatment of the different diseases involving lung tissue are brought out in a very attractive style.

The simplicity of expression is one of the most attractive features and the general tone bears evidence of actual knowledge. The book will be a helpful guide to the differential study of both disease and remedy and is worthy the distinctive title of *Homœopathic Treatment*, although the name does not appear between the covers of the book.

Bœnninghausen's Characteristics and Repertory, a practical working manual of Materia Medica, by C. M. Boger, M. D.

This work is an unabridged complication of the contents of Bœnninghausen's Characteristics, Pocket-book, Intermittent Fever, Whooping Cough, Domestic Physician, Sides of the Body, Kindred

Remedies, Table of Aggravations and Ameliorations, Apsoric and Antipsoric Repertories arranged in the form of a manual for ready reference. The pathogenesis of every remedy is characteristically epitomized as well as may be, the repertory is very voluminous, covering a large part of the materia medica; seventeen new remedies have been added, including the best proven of the later drugs. No clinical symptoms have been admitted to the *new* text, and all additions have been properly designated The completed volume will contain approximately 900 pages. Every chapter closes with an index of its appropriate aggravations, ameliorations and concomitants.

It is our understanding that this valuable work will only be published after the profession have shown their appreciation by giving orders for a sufficient number of copies to pay for the actual cost of publication, and therefore suggest that our readers desiring this valuable work when completed notify Dr. Boger at Parkersburg, W. Va. The price is placed at $6.50, in buckram binding, and at least 250 copies must be subscribed for before work can be commenced. There ought to be little difficulty in securing that many orders from the readers of the ADVOCATE alone, because there is no single work on Materia Medica that gives as practical a combination as we find promised in this work.

We published in July in the department of Materia Medica, a study of *Selenium*, in order that our readers may obtain something of an idea of the comprehensive understanding Bœnninghausen had of our materia medica.

Minor Surgery and Bandaging by Henry R. Wharton, M. D. Published by Lea Brothers & Co.

This work has passed through four editions, and the fifth comes out enlarged and thoroughly revised with over 500 illustrations many of which are half tone engravings.

The book is complete in every detail, seems to be simple and practical in its demonstrations. We feel like congratulating the author upon the improved appearance of this last edition. It tells of the popularity of the book in better language than we can select.

The Phrenological Journal.—The September number of the Phrenological Journal contains an interesting article on "Making the Mind King," illustrated with portraits of Lord Kelvin. The question is asked "Shall We Work and Live Without Talking?" by F. G. Fairfield. "How Shall We Study the Mind through the Brain and Skull" is an article that is illustrated by the life and work of the late John Mackey. Health Problems are discussed by Dr. E. P. Miller, and C. H. Shepard and the late Dr. M. L. Holbrook, and an illustrated article on "Physiognomy" by C.T. Parks, completes a fine number. 10c. monthly, $1.00 per year. Fowler & Wells Co., 24 East 22d St., New York.

Messrs. Bœricke & Tafel have in press a new work, *Diagnosis*, by Dr. Clarence Bartlett, from whose stenographic notes Farrington's *Clinical Materia Medica* was published and who, later, wrote the neurological section of Goodno's *Practice*. When published this new work on medical diagnosis will constitute one of the largest and certainly the most complete ever published on that branch of medical science; it will include every important modern diagnostic fact, and still at once place the members of our school beyond the need of referring to old school textbooks on the subject, for they will have the best one in their own ranks. The book will probably run between 1000 and 1100 pages and have a most thorough index. Ready in October.

The Hahnemannian Advocate

A MONTHLY HOMŒOPATHIC MAGAZINE.

H. W. PIERSON, B. S., M. D., Editor, 800 Marshall Field Building, Chicago.
HAHNEMANN PUBLISHING CO., Publisher, 6704 Lafayette Ave., Chicago.
BENJ. F. SWAN, Business Manager.

Subscription price of the magazine in the United States, Canada, Mexico, the island possessions and Cuba, $2.00 a year, payable in advance; in Great Britain, continental Europe, India and other countries members of the postal union, [illegible] a year to be paid in advance. Unless otherwise specified subscriptions will begin with January issue of the year in which order is received. Remittances should be made payable to the HAHNEMANN PUBLISHING Co., 6704 Lafayette Ave., Chicago.

Address all articles intended for publication and books for review to the editor. All business and other communications should be sent to the Hahnemann Publishing Co.

Vol. xii. Chicago, September, 1902. No. 9

Materia Medica.

TUBERCULINUM.*

Tuberculin of Koch. A glycerine extract of a pure cultivation of tubercle bacilli (human). Liquid attenuations.

CLINICAL.—Acne. Albuminuria. Appendicitis. Asthma. Bones, caries of. Bronchitis. Catarrhal pneumonia. Chilblains. Cornea, opacity of; ulceration of. Dentition. Erysipelas. Erythema. Hæmaturia. Hæmoptysis. Headache. Heart, affections of; palpitation of. Influenza. Leprosy. Leucorrhœa. Lungs, œdema of. Lupus. Mania. Menses too early. Nephritis. Night-terrors. Œdema glottidis. Paralysis. Phthisis. Pleurisy. *Pneumonia, acute.* Tuberculosis.

Characteristics—I consider it best to reserve the name *Tuberculinum* for this preparation of Koch, as it is universally known by that name. Burnett's "*Bacillinum*" is now accepted as the name of the original homoeopathic preparation, and though its originator, Swan, named it *Tuberculinum*, it owes its present position in therapeutics to Burnett, and it will simplify matters if we make the term *Bacillinum* cover the homoeopathic nosode and *Tuberculinum* the preparation of Koch. When Koch's *Tuberculinum* was first launched the medical papers were teeming with reports of cases undergoing the injection for various diseases. Of the reported effects, curative and pathogenetic, I made a collection. These will be found in *H. W.*, xxiv. 155. I have there given the authority for the observations and the nature of the cases in which the effects were observed. These symptoms will be found arranged in the Schema, and each symptom has appended to it the initial of the observer, or an indication of the disease from which the patient was suffering when the observation was made. Koch's own observations are marked (K); Virchow's, (V); Jonathan Hutchinson's, (H); Ewald's, (E); Albrand's, (A); Watson Cheyne's, (W C); Lenox Brown's, (L B). The names of other observers are given in full. Lupus cases are marked (lps.); observations made on a leper (lpr.). In *Four Belge d'H*, 1894, 236, Mersch published a pathogenesis of *Tub.* compiled main-

*Clark's Dictionary of Medicine.

ly from the same sources as mine but giving some additional symptoms. These I have included and marked (M). A few cured symptoms are put in brackets. The undistinguished symptoms are from a proving by Nebel, of Montreux (H. W., xxxv. 397). The provers were tuberculous individuals, mostly workpeople, and only pathogenetic symptoms are recorded. *Tub.* 30 was used, the preparation having been obtained from Hausmann's Pharmacy, St. Gall. I do not find any appreciable difference between the action of *Tub.* and that of *Bac.* My own impression is that they are practically identical, and that the one will answer to the indications of the other. Nebel has used *Tub.* in exactly the same way as Burnett and others have used *Bac.*, on the indications Burnett laid down and with Burnett's results. In *H W.* for May, June, and July, 1901, I have copied from *H. R.* of the same year articles by Nebel giving his experiences with *Tub.*: (1) Boy, 13, had diphtheria with fearful headache extending from neck to vertex, with swelling in back of neck and occiput, due, it was supposed, to an affection of the middle ear. Seven weeks passed without improvement. Paracentesis of the tympanum resulted in the evacuation of pus for a day or two. Nebel found the face bloated; strawberry tongue coated white at the root; mastoids not sensitive to even strong pressure. Swelling of occiput and neck down to fifth dorsal vertebra. The head is held fixed sideways towards the middle of the clavicle. If the boy wants to move his head he has to seize it with both hands and turn it slowly, with painful distortion of facial muscles, until it reaches the position desired. Even the slightest pressure on first, second, or third cervical vertebra was very painful; the skin on them was reddened and the periosteum was swollen; glands in neck enlarged. Tuberculosis of atlas and second and third vertebræ consequent on diphtheria was diagnosed. *Tub.* 1m. was given, five grains, during the day. Two days after the dose the boy could move his head more freely, the swelling of the neck diminished, appetite returned, and in a short time he was able to get up and run about. Five weeks after the dose, the swelling had altogether gone, and the boy's condition was altogether changed. (2) Swelling of tibiæ two inches below the knee, in a lady who had had a cough for twenty years. Cured chiefly with *Tub.* 1m. This patient had offensive sweat in axillæ, strawberry tongue, lack of appetite. Distaste for milk, constipation, and bad sleep. [Mau, of Kiel, treated the following cases with *Bac.* (*H. W.*, xxxvi. 316)—I introduce them here for comparison: (1) Vigorous man, tall and of well-developed appearance, was very liable to get pneumonia in cold weather, and spent the winter in some sanatorium or other in order to escape. His father had died of pneumonia, his mother of consumption, and a sister was consumptive. He perspired much, took much fluid nourishment, partly alcoholic. Sleep poor. Almost constant fever. Enlarged glands. Three months' treatment with *Bac.* removed all the symptoms, and, moreover, made his tissues less watery and reduced his corpulence somewhat. (2) A distinguished author, 50, complained of dreadful pains in the head, almost total insomnia, and great debility. His brother and sisters had mostly died of dropsy of the brain; he himself had congestion of the right lung, due probably to healed cavities, as he has frequently had hæmorrhages. For this he had had a lengthened treatment in the South, and had been pronounced cured of consumption. Softening of the brain and loss of reason were now feared. The headache was attended with a sensation as if his head was being tightly squeezed behind with an iron ring. Hands trembling; but he was most uneasy from a sensation in his back as if his clothes were moist. In less than a month, under *Bac.*, the headache, insomnia, and sensation in the back had all vanished. Another patient of Mau's, a child, had "screaming out in sleep and great restlessness at night," which were cured, along with peevish, irritable, taciturn disposition. In 1892 B. S. Arnulphy (*Clinique*, xvi. 629) began giving *Tub.* 6x and 8x trituration internally in tubercular cases, acute and chronic, and with encouraging success, but with at times undesired aggravations; with 12x and 30x these were avoided. In one case, originating in grippe, both apices were affected, the right one breaking down; and abundant pleuritic effusion on the left side. Six weeks' treatment with *Tub.* brought about recovery, and seen a year later the patient was quite well except for retraction of the left side. Arnulphy considers (*Clinique*, xvii. 86) that *Tub.* is frequently the remedy for bronchitis, catarrhal pneumonia, lobular pneumonia, tubercular pleurisy, parenchymatous nephritis, and grippe. He gives (*Clinique*, xvii. 457) two cases of acute lobular pneumonia with characteristic symptoms and high temperatures quickly resolved by *Tub.* One was in a boy of three who received the 12x; the other was a man, 78, being a sufferer from chronic bronchial catarrh. The latter was taken with grippe, pneumonia developed, and he was in a very serious state. *Tub.* 30x made an almost immediate change for the better, and recovery followed. Arnulphy relates that in this case an abundant perspiration took place (the skin had been dry) during the night; and he has observed this in all cases of pneumonia when *Tub.* acted favorably. I have found *Tub.* 30, 100, 200, and im the best general antidote to the chronic effects of influenza poisoning. B. G. Clark (*H. W.*, xxix. 349) reports the case of a lady, 60, who had had for some time a mild form of tuberculosis of the skin of the face, and more recently a small growth (lupus) on the side of the nose on a line with the inner canthus of left eye. It had grown much in six months. *Tub.* 200 F. C., six powders given, one to be dissolved in twelve teaspoonfuls of water, one teaspoonful every two hours. The six powders were taken in this way on successive days. On the fifth day the growth began to dry up. On the tenth day it fell off. Another dose of *Tub.* was given after this with marked improvement to the older affection of the face. A curious use has been made of *Tub.* by Jauregg, of Vienna, in a case of insanity (*H. W.*, xxx. 106). Having observed that cases of insanity are always benefited by an attack of an acute infectious disease, especially if it is accompanied with high fever, the idea occurred to him of utilizing the fever produced by Koch's *Tuberculin* injections. He tried it on some patients, and though the decidedly favorable symptoms soon disappeared after the fever subsided, still there was a *steady clearing of the confused sensorium.* Insanity is very frequently a manifestation of the consumptive taint, and there is something more than a pyrexial power in *Tub.* [Burnett has cured with *Bac.* a case of insanity, being led to give it by a ringworm like eruption on the body.] Among the *Peculiar Sensations* noted under *Tub*, are: As if the brain were squeezed with an iron ring. As if the teeth were jammed together and were too many for the mouth. Of mucus in the throat; of a tumor in the throat. Pressure in stomach going to throat as if the clothes were too tight. As if the clothes on the back were wet (*Bac.*). Fatigue, faintness, profuse debility are frequent symptoms. Great weakness in the limbs after dinner; this at times amounts to paralysis. The circulation is always disturbed, chills and flushes alternating. "Shivering when beginning to sleep" is a peculiar and interesting symptom; also "cold feet in bed," which is common in persons of low and vital reaction. "Sensitive to music" was observed in one of Nebel's patients; another had pains in the region of the appendix vermiformis, which should lead to serviceable action in appendicitis cases. The symptoms are: < By slightest exertion (it = excessive fatigue; sweat). Walking = pains in loins (fatigue). Raising himself up = palpitation. Every movement = sticking in chest and back. Rubbing = itching to change place. < Morning (much purulent expectoration; sickness and nausea; loss of appetite; thirst; fatigue). < From 10 to 3 p. m. (frontal headache). < Evening (heat in head; cough preventing sleep; severe pains in breast at beginning of menses]. < Evening in bed (itching; feet cold). < Night (sweat; from 3 a. m. sleep disturbed). <Beginning to sleep) shivering). < After dinner (flushing; drowsiness). Sensitive to music.

Relations.—[Burnett recommends to give the Tuberculinum high if there is a strong tubercular element in the case; if that element is small, 30 is better]. *Compare:* Bacillinum (including Tuberculinum of Swan), Bacil. test., Aviaire. In tubercular meningitis, Iodf. Irregular distribution of circulation; constitutional remedies, Pso., Med., Syph. Thuja. Sensation of an iron band compressing brain (Thuj. hoop round forehead). Sensitive to music, Thuj., Phthisis, Insanity, Thyroid. Pain in region of appendix, Ir. t., Ars., Lach. Pains in breasts at menses, Con., Calc. *Compatible:* Hydrast., "it actually seems to fatten up tuberculous patients" (Burnett; confirmed by Nebel), Calc., Calc. Iod., Calc. ph., Phos., Thuj. Sep., Puls. Sensitive to music, Aco., Amb., Nat. c., Nux, Pho. ac., Sep., Thuj., Vio. o. (> by music, Trn.).

Symptoms.

1. *Mind.*—Anxiety, gloomy, melancholy humor. — Has lost melancholy expression she formerly had (Ipr.).—Is disposed to whine and complain; dejected mind, anxiety.—She is very sad. —Nervous irritation; aversion to labor. —Indifferent — Forgetful.—Aversion to all labor, especially mental work.—Sensibility to music.—Does not like to be disturbed by people; trembling of hands.

2. *Head.*—Vertigo: especially in morning; heavy with obscuration of eyes; is obliged to lean on something; by bending down, especially by rising after bending down; with palpitations; with headache; with nausea; with headache in morning; after dinner.—Great heat in head; flushes of heat after dinner; sensation of heat in head in evening.—Headache: deep in forehead; deep in temples; on vertex with sensation of heat; from neck to forehead; in morning, passing away in afternoon.—Sensation of heaviness on vertex.—Headache with vertigo.—Piercing pain in forehead from 10 a.m. to 3 p.m.—Headache in evening; in afternoon.—Frontal headache in morning.—Headache with rushing in ears.—Headache in morning with bleeding of nose.—Headache from neck to forehead; burning, piercing.—Colossal hyperæmia of pia mater and brain substance; extreme engorgement of vessels on the surface, internally dusky red; tubercles presented no retrogressive changes (arachnitis.—V.) —(Sensation as if brain squeezed with iron band.—*Bac.*)

3. *Eyes.*—Swollen lids; headache with swollen lids in morning.—Right eye much swollen, conjunctiva inflamed (Ips.).—Dullness and heaviness of eyes; darkness before eyes.—Obscuration of

vision with vertigo.—Opens right eye (which had been closed. — W. C).—Breaking down of cicatrices of old corneal ulcers (Stoker).—Clearing of corneal opacity the result of old tuberculous corneitis (Stoker). Tuberculosis of eyelids, small, grey and yellow nodules, existing in conjunctiva of outer sections of lids, increased in size, ran together, then suddenly disappeared(A).—Phlyctenulæ appeared where none existed before (Maschke).—Conjunctivitis; herpes on lids (M).—Amblyopia with irregularity and complete paralysis of pupils (in an alcoholic).

4. *Ears.*—Tinnitus (Ips.).—Rushing in ears with heavy head.—Sticking pain from pharynx to ears.—Headache with rushing in ears and pressure on vertex.—Great aching in ears and teeth.

5. *Nose.* — Coryza. — Secretion of mucus from nose, viscid, yellow green.—Increased secretion of mucus, with frontal headache.—Aching of ears and teeth with coryza in evening, with headache.—Bleeding of nose.—Comedones on nose, surrounded with minute pustules (Ips.).—The nose, which used to feel "hot and burning," has lost this sensation (Ips.).

6. *Face.*—Œdematous, pale face.—Clonic convulsions of musculus orbicularis inferior, acute.—Convulsions in region of facial muscle, especially buccinator.—In one case the inflammation of the lupus (on face) presented unquestionable erysipelas of a rather severe type, and the patient was for some time in danger (H).—Flushing of cheek of same side as lung affected during the reaction (Borgherini). Upper lip and nose become swollen during the first two or three reactions, the lip becoming cracked on inner surface (W C).—Herpes on lips and eyelids (Heilferich).—After the tenth injection his left moustache, which was kept cut to prevent scabs from gathering, ceased to grow, every hair fell out, and for a month the left upper lip was perfectly denuded of hair, and had all the appearance when seen under a lens of being depilated; however, the hairs began to grow well before he left the Home (Ips., Hine).

7. *Teeth.*—Vague toothache.—Teeth felt loose (Ips.). "Feeling as if the teeth were all jammed together and too many for his head" (Ips.).—Sordes on teeth (Ips.).—Inflammation of gums, scurvy-like.—Gums turgescent, felt swollen (Ips.).

8. *Mouth.*—Tongue foul, furred.—Tongue much coated (Ips.).—Coating on soft palate and tongue (M).—Taste: salty, purulent.—Aphthæ on tongue and buccal mucosa.—Tongue dry (Ips.).—Dryness of lips.—On lips black blisters.—Palate: granulations enormously swollen and vascular (Ips.).—Breath offensive (M).

9. *Throat.*—Aching in pharynx and larynx. — Scratching in pharynx. — Tickling in throat exciting cough.—Sensation of mucus in throat.—Sensation of a tumor in throat.—Dryness in throat; tonsillitis; general inflammatory condition of pharyngeal mucous membrane (M).— Retropharyngeal abscess (M).—Burning pain in throat.—Sensation of constriction in throat; in larynx.—Heaviness and sensation of rattling in throat.—Aching extending from throat to ears.—Dysphagia increased; later diminished (in laryngeal phthisis.—I. B).

10. *Appetite.*—Loss of appetite, especially in morning.—Thirst: extreme, day and night; burning in morning.

11. *Stomach.*—Eructations and sensation of fullness over stomach.—Nausea, vomiting (K, 6h.).—Vomited severely with > to headache (Ips.).—Nausea and vomiting, nausea with efforts to vomit with colic and diarrhœa.—Transitory sickness and vomiting after dinner.—Vomiting after every meal.—

Nausea and sickness in morning with heaviness in stomach region.—Pressure in stomach, going to throat, as if the clothes were too tight.—Cramping pain in stomach.—Nausea with pains in umbilical region with diarrhœa.—Nausea with racking and stirring in stomach and increased thirst.—Sickness in stomach and pressing.—Nausea in morning. —Sticking pains in stomach region.

12. *Abdomen.*—Cramping pains in stomach and abdomen.—Sensation of constriction in abdomen.—Colic with diarrhœa and heaviness in stomach.—Colic with great thirst.—Fatigue and sickness in region of stomach and abdomen; sticking pains deep in spleen; severe pain in region of liver.—Aching (sticking) in region of liver, spleen, ovaries, spermatic cord, testicles (especially left), in hip-joints, in rectum.—Pains in region of appendix vermiformis. —Mass of enlarged glands, in right iliac fossa much smaller (W C).—Six pustules at different parts of skin of back and abdomen, and after discharging have healed (W C).—Discrete papular rash over chest and abdomen (W C).—Perforating ulcer in intestines (V).

13. *Stool and Anus.*—Obstipation; stool hard, dry with wind and colic.—Diarrhœa with pinching and burning pains.—Pressure and constriction in rectum.—Pain in rectum.—Itching sensation in anus.

14. *Urinary Organs.*—Diminished quantity of urine.—Is obliged to urinate very often, especially during changes of weather.—One tenth albumen in height of reaction; disappeared afterwards (W C).—Specific gravity of urine increases from 1016 to 1023 with an excess of urates and ropy mucus.—Peptonuria in man, 33 (Maregliano).—Hæmaturia with renal pain (M).—Excess of urates (M).—Abundant viscid mucous discharge.

15. *Male Sexual Organs.*—Pains in testicles, and cord of left side.

16. *Female Sexual Organs.*—Severe pains in breast in evening at beginning of menstruation.—Menstruation with pains in lumbo-sacral and ovarian region.—Sticking pain in lower abdomen; pains in lumbo-sacral region < when walking.—Weakness in genital region; painful menstruation.—Blood lumpy, menstruation lasting more days than usual; menstruation antepones eight days. —Burning pains in external genitals; sharp leucorrhœa; pains in sacral and ovarian region to hip-joints.—Sensation of heat in genitalia externa, with increased leucorrhœa.—Cramps in uterine region with pains in sacral and ovarian region.—Menstruation returns fourteen days after parturition.

17. *Respiratory Organs.*—Decided effect in laryngeal cases, mostly beneficial (I. B).—After ten injections, larynx markedly affected, inflammatory swelling and ulceration (I. B).—General infiltration of mucous membrane of larynx, high red color, brighter than normal (I. B).—Enormous swelling of arytenoids appeared (I. B).—Tuberculous outgrowths (I. B).—Exfoliation at right vocal cord, appearance extravasated below its posterior part (I. B).—Hyperæmia of cords intensified and covered with minute ulcerating points.—Cough and expectoration lasting four months, from a wetting (removed, no bacilli found).—Sensation of pressure on chest —Cough and sputa.—Irritating cough, < in night.—Little cough in night with aching in side and blood-tinged sputa. —Severe cough in evening with pains below mammæ on right side.—Inclination to cough (K, 3 to 4h).—Severe cough with muco-purulent secretion in morning.—Cough prevents him sleeping in evening.—Cough, secretion of phlegm, especially by walking, with

sticking pains in lungs and palpitation. —A sort of whooping-cough. — Dry cough; in night.—Cough with viscid mucus.—After much cough sensation of mucus in pharynx, mucous secretion being easily ejected.—Expectoration diminished (Heron). — Palpitation and pains in back with cough.—Crackling rales at right shoulder behind (lps.).—Copious watery expectoration usually seen during the reaction (Wilson).—With every increase of dose he suffered from asthmatic fits, lasting from three to seven hours.—Extreme rapidity of respirations without dyspnœa, 60 to 90 in the minute; if the patient is spoken to, the rapid breathing ceases at once (as with a dog panting in the sun.—Heron).—Is obliged to take deep inspirations; dyspnœa. — Difficulty in breathing speedily increased (K, 3 to 4h.). — Marked feeling of suffocation (lpr.).

18. *Chest.*—Sensation of pressure in chest.—Heat in chest (M).—Sticking pain in chest, especially at the apex of left lung.—Sensation of constriction in the præcordial region.—Pains in both sides of chest going to back.—Pains in left side.—Sticking in side. — Nightly pains on chest.—Sticking pains: in lungs; in left side, pains between scapulæ.—Aching in side in night.—Sticking pain in chest, on right and left.—Sticking pain in left side in morning and afternoon—Sticking pain in lungs when laughing. — Pain in axilla, especially when elevating arm.—Sticking pain: in lungs with cough and palpitation. — Pressure in chest, sticking pain on both sides of chest, in back.—Palpitation, caused by deep inspirations, aching in back with pains under ribs.—Pains in subclavicular region with cough.—Sticking pain in left lung.—Pain from clavicles to throat.—Pain in apex pulmonis radiating to axilla and arm. Sticking pain in chest and in back, < from every movement.—Pain in left lung to axilla. —Pain on left side going to back.—Pain in left apex and in region of the spleen.—Severe pain in back, in axilla and arms.—Pains in left side, must take deep inspiration.—Bronchitic sounds in both lungs (W C).—Dullness right apex (L B).—Sudden, profuse hæmoptysis, ends fatally (E).—Developed a cavity on side opposite to that first affected (E).—New deposit of tubercles on pleura (E).—Surface of old pulmonary cavities showed unusually intense redness of granulation layers (V). — Hæmorrhagic infiltration of the walls (V).—Recent hæmorrhage observed in the cavities.—In fatal cases of ulcerative phthisis the lungs especially and also the pleuræ, showed extensive and severe recent changes—pleurisy, for the most part very severe, simple and tuberculous, frequently hæmorrhagic, and not infrequently bilateral (V). — Caseous pneumonia or caseous hepatisation—the lung appearing like blood-pudding studded with pieces of lard; (the patient, an architect, 33, had six injections, the last four weeks before death. At the beginning he had induration of one apex only. The treatment was suspended because of persistent fever and infiltration of lower lobe.—V). — Catarrhal pneumonia was found, but it differed from ordinary catarrhal pneumonia (in which the alveoli when squeezed out have a gelatinous appearance) in that the contents of the alveoli were very watery and turbid—a turbid infiltration; it resembles a phlegmonous condition (V).—Soft hepatisation, which differs from ordinary catarrhal hepatisation in that in the midst of the patches foci of softening become developed, leading to rapid breaking down and excavation (V). —Development of fresh tubercles: small tubercles giving rise to new ulcers have suddenly appeared, especially in pleura, pericardium, and peritoneum (V).—

Metastasis, bacilli mobilized (V).—Abscesses in the lungs (V).—Perforating abscesses in respiratory organs (V).

19. *Heart.* — Palpitation early in morning.—Sensation of heaviness and pressure over heart.—Palpitation with cough and sticking pains in lungs.—By deep inspirations severe palpitation.—Aching in heart.—Palpitation in night, < when raising himself up.—Palpitation with pain in the back.—Death from paralysis of heart (Libbertz).

20. *Neck and Back.*—Glands in neck and scars swollen and very tender, various points about them showing yellow fluid under epidermis (Ips.).—Scars in neck softer and flatter; no lupus nodules now perceptible [Ips.].—Glands cannot now be felt, except the largest, which is now reduced to size of a pea [Ips.].—Cervical glands much smaller [W C].—Aching like needle-pricks in the back.—Prickly feeling in skin of back [Ips.].—Weakness in lumbo-sacral region.—Sticking pain over both scapulæ; pain in region of spleen; vague pains in back and on chest, with sensation of pressure.—Sticking in back.—Pain in back with palpitation.—[Sensation on his back as if the clothes were moist. — *Bar.*]—Three red patches on left side of back became much deeper [Ipr.].—Violent reaction, during which severe pains in loins < by pressure; [case of Addison's disease; two injections given.—Pick.]—Tuberculosis of sacrum greatly improved [Kurz].

21. *Limbs.*— Sensation of formication in arms and legs.—Great weakness in limbs after dinner.—Sensation of fatigue and faintness in all limbs.—Pains in limbs, fatigue [K, 3 to 4h. after injection].—Pains in limbs [K, 2nd d.].—Pains in ulnar nerve and calves of legs and knees, left great toe much affected, and became very red and turgid [Ipr.].—Trembling of limbs [in an alcoholic].—Twitching in the limbs [M].

22. *Upper Limbs.*—Aching in forearms; vague, sticking pain.—Diminution of inflammation above elbow joint; disappearance of abscess over olecranon; sinus connected with radius discharging freely a thick yellow pus [W C].—Sensation of luxation with severe pains in right carpal joint; < by effort to move it; ceasing by rest.—Trembling of hands.

23. *Lower Limbs.* — During night pain referred to right knee; right leg rotated in and flexed slightly at hip and knee; movement of right hip-joint free; 1 p.m., left hip much more painful and tender, more flexed, abducted and rotated out (disease of left hip in girl of five.—B. M. T.].—Aching in the hip-joints. — Pain in right knee without swelling [Heron, a non-tubucular case]. The knee became easily movable and could be bent to a right angle [tuberculous affection of right knee].—Swelling and tenderness of both knee-joints [Heron].— Tenderness in right ankle-joint [Heron].

24. *Generalities.*—Feeling of fatigue [K, 2d and d.].—Malaise, depression, headache, somnolence, oppression of breathing, tightness of chest, nausea [Ips.].—General fatigue in morning; sensation of faintness; great weakness in lower extremities, especially from knees down to feet.—Terribly tired, so that she can scarcely walk.—General excessive fatigue after a short walk, so that he must lean on his companion.—Emaciation [lost six pounds in fourteen days, twenty pounds in five weeks].—In parts affected throbbing pain.—Leucocytosis; diminution of oxyhæmoglobin [M].—Oxyhæmoglobin first diminished then increased [Henoque]. — Feeling well, but decidedly losing flesh [Ips.]—Acts principally by very acute irritation of internal organs [affected in the same way as in external organs], causing intense redness and great swelling [V].—Actual

inflammatory processes [not mere hyperæmias], and especially active proliferations, occur to an intense degree, in [1] edges of existing ulcers; in [2] neighboring lymphatic glands, especially bronchial and mesenteric [V].—Lymphatic glands present a quite unusual degree of enlargement, and notably that form of medullary swelling, characteristic of acute irritations, which is caused by rapid proliferation of the cells in the interior of the glands [V].—Leucocytosis: various infiltrations of white blood corpuscles over affected parts, especially round the tubercles themselves [V].—Enormous dangerous swellings in parts near ulcers [even where the surface of the ulcer becomes clean], causing dangerous constriction [V].—Phlegmonous swelling resembling erysipelatous œdema of glottis and retropharyngeal abscess [V] —Where tubercle is associated with any other specific disease, reaction is so slight as to be scarcely discernible [Heron].—Syphilitic cases are refractory to reaction [Heron].—Children bear the treatment well [Wendt].

25. *Skin.* — Erythematous eruption like measles or scarlatina [M].—Erythema with subcutaneous indurated nodules [M].—Great bronze patches on the forehead and temples. — Bronze finger-points as if touched by *Argentum nitricum.*—Itching all over the body in the evening in bed; changing place after rubbing.—"Rash on chest and abdomen similar, patient says, to what came out when disease first appeared" [Ips.]. Rash on abdomen and back, commencing very red; speedily becoming brownish, resembling ordinary skin eruption of secondary syphilis [L B].—Œdematous condition of upper lip.—Œdematous condition of eyelids.—Nose swollen, tense, erysipelatous-looking epidermis in lupus patch raised by yellow fluid.—In two cases, at least during the febrile action, old chilblains became again inflamed [H].—Slight attack of jaundice [several cases.—W C].—Site of injection slightly painful and red [K, 2d d.].—Erythematous blush confined to lupus parts, which were the seat of throbbing pain.—It has repeatedly caused general erythematous eruptions on the skin, and, in some, nodular effusions into the cellular tissue [H].

26. *Sleep.*—Great desire for sleep; drowsiness during day; after dinner.—Inclination to sleep in mornings.—Shivering when beginning to sleep.—Cold feet in bed.—Troubled sleep; sleeplessness;—Sleep disturbed from 3 a.m.—Sleeplessness on account of constant coughing. — Many dreams; disturbed sleep, interrupted by fearful dreams; gloomy dreams; dreams of shame; cries out in dreams.

27. *Fever.*—Shivering, when beginning to sleep; cold feet in bed.—Freezing and heat alternately; cold and heat for moments.—Violent attack of ague, lasting almost an hour [K, 3h.].—Freezing on the back in evening.—Freezing during the whole day.—Sensation of heat in evening in bed.—Flush of heat from back to head.—Feverish, nausea, thirsty, with headache, no vomiting [Heron].—Flushes of heat after eating.—High temperature, abating in twelve hours [K].—Lowering of temperature after each injection [Heron].—Lowering of temperature before a rise [Heron]. — Temperature seven hours after injection, 103.8 degrees, accompanied by thirst, rigor, increased cough, headache, and pains in joints [Heron]. Sweat in the night.—Much sweat, especially on head in night.—Profuse sweat after light exertion.—A little walk and slight efforts produce sweats.—Short sweats in morning, while awaking.—Profuse sweats during slight exertion.

INSANITY—LACHESIS.

A simple relief from pain, or uncomfortable symptoms does not always signify a cure. Before a case, especially a chronic case, is pronounced *cured* there should be no return of the symptoms for at least one year, for as long as symptoms return, though in a very slight and almost imperceptible form, the miasm that gave rise to the disease has not been wholly eradicated and under favorable conditions will start the disease afresh.

It is very exasperating, in mental diseases particularly, to notice a return of the evil, though slight it may be, and for this reason have waited more than one year before reporting this case of so much interest to me. I hope I may so present it as to make it interesting to you also.

A farmer came to me in the spring of 1900, and complained bitterly of the deportment of his wife now growing old, attributing her peculiar actions to mere meanness and jealousy. For some years she had kept the family—a large one—in a state of turmoil, and uncertainty as to what might happen. These "spells" always being worse in the early months of the year, March, April and May, and at the time of the farmer's visit to my office [in June], matters had about reached their limit. This poor woman moaned about the indifference of her church friends towards her, and daily upbraided her husband for a supposed love he had for his daughters more than for her; with such a spirit in the home there is little peace.

As to her physical ills there is not much to say. She complained at times of severe occipital headache often extending to the vertex. This headache was usually worse in the morning, though it often remained with her all day.

The woman had passed her climacteric, and apart from this headache and occasional twinges of rheumatism was in a fair state of health. There were no pathological changes discernable, her appetite was fair and bowels regular.

I prescribed for her, but made the very common mistake of changing remedies too soon and repeating too frequently, trusting to luck rather than to well established laws in the treatment of this case. The result was patch work with very little palliation until the changing seasons brought about the usual amelioration.

In the month of April, 1901, her husband came again and with tears in his eyes complained bitterly of his wife's temper and jealousy. He then spoke freely and frankly of sending her to an insane asylum, for he began to think she was rapidly going insane. She had already made some fruitless attempts to leave home, without any apparent cause, except the morbid idea that her husband and children were opposed to her and wished her in some other part of the world. I knew this to be erroneous, for her husband is disposed to be rather indulgent, and her children very obedient.

I requested the husband to bring his wife to my office and I would try to affect a reconciliation. In a few days she came and appeared to be somewhat surprised that family matters should be presented to the physician. *She* was right in all things, but her family and church were in error and must apologize for wrongs committed against her, though she could name no direct breach of domestic or ecclesiastical decorum. But she was not always in this morbid state of mind, was so at certain seasons only, then afterward she seemed to feel badly for the thoughts she had had, and the words she used. In her sane mo–

ments she was all that could be desired in a wife and mother.

She was of medium height, rather sparely built, of sallow complexion, dark hair and blue eyes and during these attacks had a blank expression.

After looking her over carefully, I concluded that the less said the better. I assured them both that matters would soon be better, for storms do sometimes arise, but do not last always.

Lachesis seemed so clearly pictured in her case that I gave her a dose of the cm potency on the tongue and a liberal *Placebo* to take home with her.

In a few weeks the husband returned saying that, apart from the first few days after taking the medicine, she was improving every day. They had now less discord and when she said little about her supposed enemies. A *Placebo* was again administered and I saw the woman no more until the winter of 1901 when I prescribed for a slight attack of rheumatism. When spring came this year I supposed her troubles would return, but heard nothing until the month of July when her oldest daughter came to see me on her own account and remarked, "Mother has had no trouble since you gave her that little medicine last spring. It doesn't seem possible that so little medicine can do so much good."

This was a case of periodical insanity, and in a few more years it would have been continual. There was no attempt at suggestive therapeutics for the reason that, having made a failure the year previous I preferred to rest wholly upon the efficiency of the indicated remedy. What it did has been told, and though I see some one or more of the family each week not a word is said, as there used to be, about the mother's peculiarities.

G. E. Dienst.

Naperville, Ill.

MENSTRUAL MELANCHOLY CURED.

A lady of twenty five has suffered a long time from melancholic depression during her menses. When I was called to see her, anguish and depression had lasted four days.

She is emaciated and anemic. Her thinness is very great, especially in the thorax. Abnormal sounds are occasionally heard in the apices of lungs.

Hallucinations: She saw her lover lying in her bed; she fancied herself a great actress, singing in slow, solemn tones fragments from Wagner's operas; she thought she was exceptionally beautiful and that she was a countess. She would be quiet for a few minutes and then rise suddenly, furiously attacking the members of her family. She talked constantly and was restless and sleepless.

She received *Hyos*[1m] that acted favorable for two days. As the quieting influence of that remedy passed off, *Platin*[1m] was given, and acted tolerably well.

On the fourth day of my treatment an aggravation of all the symptoms set in: She danced on her bed, struck the walls with her head and hands and also attacked her nurse; talked obscurely and begged for sexual gratification. Preparations were made to send her to a lunatic asylum.

She was given *Tuberculinum*[1m] one dose. In half an hour she lay in a deep sleep which continued 24 hours. She then awoke very much weakened, but her understanding was unclouded. Since then no trace of the former menstrual melancholy has returned. She has also fully recovered physically.

A. McNeil.

San Francisco, Cal.

HEADACHE—PHOSPHORUS.

Mrs. K. has had headaches for several years. Some of these spells will last for three or four weeks and often will not be free from headache for more than a week before another spell comes on. These spells start with flashes of light before the eyes and then pain of a dull aching character settles over and back of the eyes. The only relief she can get is from cold applications and the only aggravation is from a bright light. With all of this there is a severe burning in the vertex. No other symptoms could be gotten from the patient. She is 34 years old and the mother of three children. The menstruation and labors have been normal in every respect and have not had anything to do with aggravation or amelioration of the headache. Setting opposite each symptom the remedies that produce it and then taking a summary, we have the following:

Burning on vertex: Agar., Arn., Ars., Aur., Bapt., Bry., Calc. c., Calc. ph., Carbo veg., Caust., Chin. s., Coc. c., Con., Cup., Dulc., Glon., Graph., Helon., Hyper., Lach., Merc., Nat. m., Nat. sul., Phos., Phos. ac., Podo., Ran. sc., Raph., Saba., Sep., Stann., Sul., Zinc.

Flashes before the eyes: Bell., Benz. ac., Brom., Calc. c., Caust., Ced., Coca, Croc., Dig., Fl. ac., Glon., Merc. i. f., Nat. c., Op., Phos., Phys., Puls., Secale, Spong., Stram., Tabac., Tarent., Valer.

Headache > cold applications: Acon., Aloe., Ant. t., Ars., Asar., Aur. m., Bell., Bry., Bufo, Calc. c., Calc. ph., Caust., Cham., Chin. s., Cinnab., Cycl., Euph., Euphr., Ferr., Glon., Ind., Iod., Lac. c., Lach., Merc. c., Merl., Myric., Nat. m., Phos., Plant., Seneg., Spig., Stram., Zinc.

Headache < bright light: Calc. c., Hep., Nat. m., Phos., Sil.

Summary: Calc. c., Phos.

As this patient is dark, tall and slender, we gave a dose of *Phosphorus*^{mm}. There was a gradual decline of the symptoms for three weeks and since that time for the past several months there has not been a single headache or anything suggestive of a headache.

Naperville, Ill. G. E. DIENST.

AN OLD GONORRHEA CURED.

A young lady who, through a sexual indiscretion and a gonorrhœal, lascivious brute, acquired gonorrhœa. She, not knowing the real nature of the trouble, thought it only leucorrhœa and was treated for it by the "scientific" school. After four years of this treatment, with no result except a partial suppression of this discharge, she applied to me and although prescribing carefully, I only made a partial success. Thinking there was some ancient history, untold, by persistent effort I gleaned the truth, and then proceeded to get at the bottom of the trouble as can only be done with homœopathic remedies. First, I antidoted the gonorrhœal poison by *Medorrhinum*^{1m}. Allowing two weeks to intervene, I then antidoted nitrate of silver—which had been used locally—with the 1m potency. Again waiting two weeks, I antidoted *Kali* permanganate — which also had been used locally—with the effect of nearly suppressing the discharge, or at least holding it down to a slight then, irritating, excoriating, offensive, muco-purulent flow. The antidotal potency here used was cm. In two weeks restored the discharge to its original profuse condition. Then I followed with *Thuja*^{mm} and *Natrum sulph*^{1m} completed the cure.

How often we are puzzled by just

such conditions. Careful prescribing only palliates, and we wonder why is not the cure made when the accuracy of the indication and the application of the remedy is used. This serves to illustrate the *why*. We do not get down deep enough under the cause of the original disease. Yet how many do not believe in antidotal prescribing. For myself, my best work has been done by first clearing out the drugs; then, after having secured the therapeutic right of way, it is easy enough for the indicated remedy to do the work.

A. G. Downer,

Princeton, Ill.

HINTS FOR USE OF COMMON AND UNCOMMON REMEDIES.

In my eye and ear practice find a great many cases of acute conjunctivitis; symptoms are heat, roughness of lids, slight tenderness, aggravated by wind and bright light. *Aconite* 3x is specific in a short time.

Also, so many cases of twitching of lids, trembling or a fluttering feeling, as patients term it—and here *Agaricus* 3x is a magical specific.

I again want to call the attention of the profession to corn pollen as a remedy for hay fever and fall colds. It is a wonderful remedy. I make it out of corn husks, silks, leaves and top, and have it potentized to 30x. I am very much pleased with it and would like to send grafts to any who will use it and report. I have already sent it out to physicians from Michigan to Texas.

I had an interesting case of Rhus poisoning in a man. All allopathic physicians suppressed it with a lead lotion by antidoting lead and then by antidoting Rhus with a high potency given me by Dr. Nash, of Cortland, N. Y., and giving *Psorum*[cm] rapidly cured. In rhus poisoning we have such a stirring up of the psora in some individuals that after the *Rhus* is given one is forced to attack the psora to complete the cure.

A friend of mine asked me to look at his horse that was profusely salivating or "slobbering," no doubt from the effect of white clover or something else it had eaten. I gave him a 10 grain powder of *Mercurius*[3x] to be dissolved in half a pail of water, of which horse drank and was cured in thirty-six hours. I am wondering if any allopathic veterinarians could cure any quicker. Also on a horse of my own, I am reducing a hard lump on his jaw, due, no doubt, to an ulcerated tooth, with *C. Flour*[3x]. The action is truly wonderful, the lump or exostose is as hard as ivory.

A. G. Downer.

Princeton, Ill.

THE INJURIOUS EFFECT OF CHLOROFORM UPON THE KIDNEYS.

In the *Journal des Praticiens*, No. 15, 1902, Renaut asserts that young animals with a good resistant power die rapidly from chloroform. They die in syncope, and at autopsy the heart is found in diastole.

But there is one very important point upon which the author lays a particular stress; even in case a syncopal attack could be avoided, a lesion of the kidneys is always present.

If pieces of kidneys taken from an animal that died from chloroform are hardened and fixed by proper reagents, the border of the epithelial cells in the convoluted tubes is destroyed. This observation is, according to Renaut, of extreme importance, as the border of the epithelial cells is to the kidney what the rods and cones are to the eye, which being destroyed will render the eye blind. The kidney therefore losing that border can no more serve as a filter. The integrity of the epithelial cells is absolutely indispensable for a good function of the kidneys. Twenty-five years ago Heidenhain attributed to those cells the property of eliminating urea. We know now that the function of the cells with their intact border is secretion. They extract from the blood certain products. The renal secretion will therefore depend upon the integrity of the cells of the tubules. This important function is impaired by chloroform, when administered as an anesthetic, but the cell is capable of recuperating. It is therefore evident that in surgical operations the kidneys will be injured for certain time. This fact should always be taken into consideration before an operation. An examination of the condition of the kidneys should be made in every case before surgery intervenes.

In view of this fact anesthesia with ether is preferable to that with chloroform. The author has etherized patients a great many times whose hearts were in diseased conditions, also cases of diabetes or albuminuria, and he never witnessed untoward effects. What is to fear with ether is only asphyxia or syncope. He is therefore entirely in favor of ether, which presents only one inconvenience, namely, a tendency to vomit for several hours after the administration. This inconvenience can be avoided if the so-called by him "interrupted method" is employed. The last consists first of bringing on a complete narcosis, so that the reflexes are lost. Then the mask is removed and the patient is allowed to breathe air. As soon as he wakes up, the ether is readministered, and so on. This mode of administration can be prolonged as long as desired. In one case he kept the patient under ether during two hours. He arrives at the conclusion that ether is the best anesthetic; it does not injure the heart or kidney, while with chloroform one risks a mortal syncope and renal insufficiency.—*Therapeutic Gazette.*

SIGNIFICANCE OF SEXUAL PERVERSION IN DISEASE.

(Continued from August.)

In many cases, a careful examination will reveal some mechanical defect in the development of the genetalia. This does not come about by chance, and the patient is not *cured* by the correction of the mechanical defect. The *exciting* cause may be removed, but the *fundamental* cause will be found in some perversion of the *vital* force reflected through the *sympathetic* nervous system.

It is a recognized fact that the ganglionic or sympathetic nervous system is the medium of communication between the cells of the body and the vital force; but comparatively few observers have even hinted at the possible identity of the vital force of Hahnemann with the *subconscious* mind. A still smaller number have dared look for a local habitation for the subconscious mind because of a mistaken idea of its function, but for the sake of argument we believe it can be demonstrated that the subconscious mind or vital force is located in the cerebellum.

The size of the cerebellum is in exact proportion to the physical vitality of the individual; e.g., with a large cerebellum in an infant you may promise a a proportionate physical development with strong sexual instincts. Idiots, as a rule, have a large cerebellum. From the cerebellum go out all the *sensory* and *involuntary motor* fibres. Distributed throughout the body are innumerable *ganglia* all of these connected by means of nerve fibres thus forming a complete network through which impressions may be conveyed to and received by the subconscious or mechanical mind, and the proper response transmitted to the cell or group of cells involved.

The subconscious mind is void of all reasoning power but, as Hahnemann so vividly described, in § 9 of the *Organon*, "animates the material body, rules with unbounded sway, and retains all the parts of the organism in admirable, harmonious, vital operation as regards both sensations and functions, *so that one indwelling, reason gifted mind can freely employ this living, healthy instrument for the highest purposes of our existence.*"

With a large cerebellum, we naturally expect a well developed sexual apparatus perfectly adapted for the normal function of the reproduction of the species and if the conscious or reasoning brain is properly developed, you will find a healthy body, well nourished and all the processes of *alimentation, assimilation* and *reproduction* working in harmony.

It follows that a perversion of any of these functions in an organism, with a large cerebellum must be due to an abnormal development of the mental faculties through inheritance or environment. We must therefore carefully study the objective as well as the subjective symptoms for the purpose of determining the cause primary as well as the fundamental. It is only by means of this thorough analysis that we can hope to reach a true interpretation of the abnormal manifestations; and the successful treatment. Sexual perversion depends in a large measure upon a comprehensive knowledge of the relative importance of these varied factors.

When we come to a consideration of the various phases of sexual perversion the significance of the above outlines will be more clearly brought, especially in connection with the treatment.

As a rule you will find sexual perversion associated with anemia. This anemia may be brought about by an environment in which suitable nutrition cannot be supplied the body, but in the majority of cases the *fundamental* cause dates back to the beginning of the new organism and can be changed to a defect in the development. This defect may originate in the cerebellum and *all* the functions of the organism show perversion or there may have been transmitted to the offspring the direct fruits of a vicious life in the form of sycosis or syphilis. In rare instances you will find a perversion planted upon a healthy base. This is so rare, however, that it need be entertained only after a careful search has failed to disclose a sufficient cause.

It is clear to our mind that the *fundamental* cause for all sexual perversion rests upon a constitutional base and that it is *general* as *specific* but this is only the beginning, the providing of a susceptible soil in which all seed sown is liable to bring forth imperfect fruit. In no part of the organism will you find greater evidence of perversion than in the brain itself. The degree of convexity of the inferior occipital fossae shows the development of the cerebellum. When it is full and prominent you have reason for expecting great vitality and a corresponding rounding out of the body with well nourished tissues and normal functional activity of all the functions of the body. If you find a perversion in the sexual sphere, it will be along the line of increased activity—

excesses and a corresponding low mentality. It is a perversion brought about by the fact that there was but little control exercised by the will or reason. It is not disease and not amenable to treatment. The animal instincts predominate over the mental. If you find the occipital region negative or actually concave in the infant, you will see at a glance that a positive development must be developed before you can promise any great vitality or physical endurance for that child. Every function and organ will show will show improvement. Too little vitality to *maintain* functional activity, leaving out the assurance of growth. Food cannot be digested and if predigested will be assimilated only with difficulty. It is in these subjects that you find anemia, marasmus, rickets, scrofula, etc., etc. Hahnemann gave to this condition the general term of psora and it is generally known that nothing but deep constitutional remedies are indicated. Some stop short of the real significance and say that the cause is a deficiency of lime salts or iron in the blood, but the cause back of it all is the *inability to assimilate through lack of vitality*—the subconscious mind is diverted from its legitimate cause and impairment of function logically follows. Here again Hahnemann's theory of the nature of disease harmonizes with the most advanced thought of the present day.

The perversion is not altogether limited to the lower brain. The seat of the mental faculties is as dependent upon transmitted tendencies as any other part of the organism, while the future development is largely dependent upon the *direct* action of the "reason gifted mind" or the *indirect* action of some other mind. If the mental faculties are deficient or perverted at birth and the environment is pernicious we have two prominent factors which tend to perpetuate the evil results of a previous existence.

To summarize:

(1). The *fundamental* cause for the great majority of all forms of sexual perversion lies in a disturbance or deflection of the vital energies through the subconscious mind.

(2). This disturbing influence has been inherited.

(3). It is either general or specific.

(4). The *exciting* cause will be found in some defective *local* development that is dependent upon the *constitutional* derangement or the pernicious influence of the mental faculties.

(5). Treatment must be directed to the constitution, the mind and the environment. Local treatment of whatever nature can never be *curative*.

(To be continued).

H. W. Pierson.

THE SYMPTOMS OF THE PATIENT IN URGENT CASES.

Probably the most trying cases to a conscientious physician are those where the actual needs of the case, as well as the insistance of "interested friends" of the patient, demand speedy amelioration. Severe suffering, the patient being in great distress; hemorrhages from lungs, bowels, uterus or elsewhere; convulsions; zymotic states; collapse; cases where the vital organs are threatened, as a cardiac neuralgia and acute inflammation of kidneys,—these are disorders in whose presence one feels if something be not soon done to check the onward march, the consequences will be disastrous and opportunity for help soon be past.

Confronted with such cases the physician realizes a responsibility in his or her actions, and wishes most earnestly to make every stroke tell definitely in results that will relieve the distress and suspense. Friends and patient, if still able, demand that "something be *done*," "*something, anything* for relief."

If there is anything in a physician's experience that wears on the vitality and saps the reserve strength, it is attendance on these case . To be master of the occasion the physician must keep a cool, calm demeanor and to be master of the case, must keep clear perception and judgment, unprejudiced by overwrought sympathies.

Those not privileged in well trained observation are apt to deplore the attempt to find distinguishing symptoms by which to select an individual remedy. They are often heard to say "such patients have time to die, while you seek to discover their individual remedies." But it is in such urgent cases, when the patient declares "I can't stand it much longer," when the friends exhort the speediest, possible relief, that the homœopathic physician feels grateful to Providence and to his instructors for the God-given principles that lead to the selection of a remedy according to the image of the patient, the remedy which, when administered, subdues the the severity of the whole case, giving respite, but strength, to the patient and rest to the anxious friends. As one little boy explained to his companion, "you hardly know you are taking medicine, you just feel better right off."

Those not trained to observe the patient are apt to be bewildered at the idea of using anything but "heroic measures" for these heroic cases. The greatest hero is the one who drives the sword deep to the heart of the dragon, not halting nor wavering till he gets close enough to bury the blade to the hilt and vanquish the foe bodily.

While not ignorant of the terrors of the slashing tail and the sharp fangs and claws of the enemy that threaten the victim, the slayer must penetrate deeper than these. Guided by the lines that determine the form, he must recognize every feature and aim at the center which keeps these all at play, the very heart of the dragon.

The lines portraying the clear image of the particular case are the *symptoms of the patient.* The iliac pain; signs of local inflammation and digestive system disturbances [swelling, fever, thirst, coated tongue] are found in appendicitis cases, generally; but the intense *heat of the body; bright red face and skin; extreme sensitiveness to light, to touch, to jar*, and aggravation of all symptoms *from 3 p.m. to midnight;* restlessness and < *from exposing the body outside the covers*, saying *Belladonna* patient, or the *craving for quiet* and rest; all *pains* < *from motion; headache and nausea* < *raising the head; dull congested face; heat with chilliness especially on moving;* thirst for frequent large quantities of water; > lying on painful side; *irritability on being disturbed, and great drowsiness*, saying *Bryonia* patient. These groups of symptoms tell nothing of the nature of the disease action, but tell much of the patient, clearly portraying his characteristics.

No matter how severe the cardiac distress or the cholera symptoms, nor how violent the attacks of convulsions, a little attentive observation will detect *peculiarities* of the patient that in one case resemble *Arsenicum*, in another, *Cactus*, in another *Arg. nit.*, in others *Pulsatilla*, in others, *Cuprum, Camphor, Calcarea, Stramonium* or *Sulphur* etc.

These symptoms of the individual patient serve as beacon lights to the physician. He quails not before the fury of the storm, he quakes not though surrounded by the rocks, [the violent features of the case]. When he can detect these *symptoms of the patient*, he knows his course and guides the patient to safety, assured that when the disorder within is turned to order, the patient in his inner parts firmly directed toward cure, all these violent manifestations will melt away and the sufferer will bask in the sunshine of restored order.

Assured, that guided by these *symptoms of the patient* and as by beacon lights and compass, he can apply his sudden and motive power so as to carry the voyage safely, promptly, into quiet waters and deep channels.

Why should this captain pilot, the physician, devote his energies to pouring oil on the billows and dashing waters where they happen to be heaviest, now on this side, now on that? Why should he concern himself to measure the size or the distance of the rocks that threaten destruction? Why should he seek to change the character of the water dashing about or seek to discover where lie the wrecks of other craft scattered beneath the surface? Why should he worry and bestow himself to parley with these evidences of violence [*the symptoms that characterize the disease*], temporizing for short respites, when there are guides by observing which he can escape the neighborhood of such damages.

It is the confidence of possessing true compass and strong rudder and the presence of distinct signals to be sighted that cheers the homœopathic physician and makes it possible for him to go serenely into the presence of urgent cases and undertake their management with favorable prognosis. Everytime he does rely on these characterizing symptoms and the remedies they indicate, he has the satisfaction of sailing over quiet waters, while other attempts to deal with the individual urgent features, leaves the victims floundering in the menace of hidden or perceptible dangers, battling till the storm has passed and they can only float exhausted, or succumb.

JULIA C. LOOS.

Harrisburg, Pa.

THE HOMŒOPATHY OF THE OLD MASTERS.*

At the present day with so fearful a mania among the American people to be the Heroes of Surgical Operations, there are perhaps, a few, who would prefer to be cured, or be permitted to die a natural death, rather than to be sacrificed on the operating table, with the certainty of being disfigured or a cripple. To such few rational, judicious people, I would like to say that there is a better, easier, safer and less expensive way, that is not attended with loss of time, organ, function, or time from business or pleasure—it is by curing the diseases that make the morbid conditions and growths.

To see how it is done, please read the following:

By request of many citizens and my patrons, I will give some brief statements of the principles and methods taught and practised by the Founder, and by the Old Masters of Homœopathy, and which at the present day are carried out by their few faithful followers: I adhere closely to the teachings as found in their writings and as verified in my own practice, which I trust will be correctly understood by any unprejudiced reader, though my explanation may differ widely from those given by some eminent physicians. My ideas

*Read before the American Hahnemannian Association at Narragansett Pier, July 1, 1902.

are drawn from the works of the Old Masters, and my own experience; if others have different opinions, it is no fault of mine.

Homœopathy is the system of laws and rules of Therapeutics, for selecting the curative remedy in each particular case by the symptoms; according to this we must diagnose the *remedy*, in preference to the uncertain name of *disease;* which is, to find the remedy that is Homœopathic in the case.

Homœopathy does not mean small doses; neither do small doses mean Homœopathy. Hence, to say, it is Homœopathic when the dose is small, is a mistake.

It means that the remedy has been proven to produce similar symptoms on healthy persons; then it is Homœopathic to the Symptoms in the case.

The so-called Homœopathic Specifics, that are on the market labelled to cure certain diseases are misnamed, or, more correctly speaking, are frauds.

The laws of Homœopathy require the remedy to be Homœopathic to the symptoms in the case.

The laws of Homœopathy regard all local manifestations—affections of the head, eyes, heart, throat or any other organ, such as corns, piles, dyspepsia, tumors, carbuncles, cataract, and cancer—are all produced by an invisible disease (the cause), hence the remedy that is Homœopathic to the symptoms will remove the cause, and cure it, and the healthy action of the system will soon remove the morbid growth, or stop its growing.

All strong, or what is called innocent, home medicines produce sick symptoms, mislead the physician, and damage the patient by retarding the cure.

All local treatments, such as salves, ointments, plasters, or medicated washes, etc., tend to suppress the disease and fasten it on internal organs, which cause trouble of some other kind, in the future, more difficult to cure than the first.

Taking laxatives always defeats the cure of constipation or other diseases.

The laws of Homœopathy require but one carefully selected remedy be used at a time. Mixing or alternating creates confusion and retards recovery.

To get the proper remedy, the physician must learn all about the case; must learn all symptoms of every kind that indicate a departure from health; for they are the guides by which to select the remedy that is curative in the case.

With careful examinations, selecting the remedy by the symptoms, if correctly given by the patient, surgical operations will seldom be required, except in cases of accident.

When prescriptions are hastily made, the patient suffers the consequences afterwards, innocently.

Surgical operations may remove morbid growths, but never cure the diseases that make them, which remain, and seldom fail to cause similar or other more pernicious conditions in after life.

Cutting open abscesses, carbuncles, felons, or any suppurating sores, inoculates the fresh-cut flesh with septic matter, causes blood-poison to develop in after years, endangers life, retards recovery, leaves an unsightly scar, and often other pernicious conditions, which will not follow, if the disease is cured and the abscess is allowed to open in a natural way. Also there will be less pain, less suffering, less loss of time from business or pleasure, better complexion, and the cure more lasting, and, more than all, little or no scars of disfigurement.

With Homœopathic treatment carefully selected, patients do not take cold so readily, do not get sick so often, nor suffer so much nor so long. They enjoy better health after recovery, and lose no time in getting rid of the depressing effect of the strong and injurious drugs.

The remedy that is Homœopathic to the case, will never fail to give curative effects; but the patient may, and often does, fail to tell all the symptoms, and the hasty prescriber may, and often does fail to find the indicated remedy. Hence, there will be a failure to cure, through no fault of the laws of Homœopathy, but through negligence in taking the case, and the patient does not get the remedy that is Homœopathic to the symptoms.

If you want to be sick all the time, or to be the hero of a surgical operation for the glory of the surgeon—tell your complaints to everybody; take everybody's advice; and take all the medicine they all recommend (the more, the better). Employ a surgeon, and a specialist for each part, take the advice of each, and take all the medicines they prescribe, and you will surely be successful; but

If you are sick and want to get well—choose a physician, who studies his case and prescribes by the symptoms. Take your remedies exactly as directed. Follow strictly all written or oral instructions; take no other medicine of any kind; report frequently to your physician all changes of symptoms, either for better or worse. Eat, drink, work and sleep in moderation. Don't tell your complaints to your friends, nor listen to a rehearsal of theirs. Give proper time for medical effects; don't expect a few small doses to cure a case in a day or a week, that has resisted other treatments for months or years. Yet many cures are made with a single dose of the appropriate remedy, while other cases may require months. If the first doses develop some suppressed disease or effects of accumulated drugs of months' or years' standing, and make you sick for a few hours or days, it assures good results. Suspend treatment a while and then renew—there will be no danger. Homœopathy differs from all other methods of treatment in the selection of remedies, as it is a system of natural laws. Hence, consultations with physicians of other schools are useless; for they do not try to learn the laws of Homœopathy; and do not know the reasons why such small doses are so effective. They cannot know the medicines, and it is not probable they can know what effects to look for. They cannot understand that the Old Masters of Homœopathy take no opinions or dogmas, but must have every thing proved. They deal with facts.

You must adhere to the law to attain success.

W. L. Morgan, M. D.
Baltimore, Md.

PRACTICAL HOMŒOPATHY.

Were it not for practical homœopathy, that which has been proven practical every day and week and month and year for over a century, there would not be a school recognized the world over by that name today.

Anything which is practical is necessarily proven in practice. That which is not practical, after a short time, demonstrates its impracticability, and becomes obsolete, and gives place to the next new fad or fancy, be it in therapeutics or mechanics. How nicely this is demonstrated by the two dominant schools of therapeutics today. The allopathic school uses one series of drugs today, which are lauded to the skies as being the only proper and ethical treatment to be recognized; and only tomorrow or next week or, perchance, next month or next year a new regime is sprung upon the profession by its leaders, and they *ante* up to a man. It's like a lot of sheep following the bell weather over hill and dale, finally coming to the home fold again to get their regular "feed" at the same old trough, with the same mortality ratio, except, perchance, when a venturesome member has turned aside from following the leader and has grazed in the rich pastures of homœopathy, where the forage is so rich and tempting that when they do partake of it and it becomes assimilated—tried, and found practical—the mortality ratio is changed and is much reduced.

What lesson is to be learned from this? It teaches that homœopathy is *practical*, and recognition of the fact is becoming more general as the system is becoming more generally understood.

Now, in comparison with the everlasting therapeutics of the allopathic school, let us turn to the steadfastness of the homœopathic profession. Its members are guided by a law—nature's only therapeutic law—which has been demonstrated to be the only practical method of *curing* the sick. "Similia Similibus Curantur" [let likes be cured by likes]. How simple and yet how practical! This law never varies. Aconite, Belladonna, Arsenicum, Nux vomica etc. are used just as much today as formerly; only their range has been extended to some new remedies and symptoms not at first proven, but which have been found and added to our priceless materia medica.

What about the new remedies? They are proven at the first opportunity, and added to our list, and, when used according to the law of similars, are purely homœopathic and found practical.

One of the most practical features of homœopathy is the very fact that we have discovered the means by which we demonstrate and establish the true remedial place and value of any drug or chemical in existence, and when the similar set of symptoms appear in the sick we know it, know that we have found the place where that particular drug will prove curative. This fact proves the practability of the law of similars.

I have on many occasions been surprised by the rapid effects of the properly chosen remedy. Will cite the effect of Cantharis in relieving the terrible pain from scalding urine which comes only a few drops at a time and is so corrosive as to cause the patient to be willing to go to any extreme for relief, which is the constant desire. I have had one dose put a patient in such comfort that he could go to the theater or other place of amusement within less than an hour after taking. Who has not seen the magic effect of Ipecac in relieving nausea, or Bell., Bry., Nux or Puls., in headaches?

Now the homoeopathic use of these and other drugs demonstrates the practicability of our system, and he who investigates carefully will always be rewarded by straying from the old beaten track of allopathy and following the law of Similia Similbus Curantur.

A. M. DUFFIELD.

Huntsville, Ala.

SPOTTED FEVER.

This disease has been recognized in certain mountainous districts of Montana and Idaho for twenty years, and though its history and clinical symptoms have been described, the first report on its pathology and ætiology has lately been made by Wilson and Chowning (*Journ. Am. Med. Asso.*, July 19, 1902). (See also Dr. Wm. A. Glasgow's article in the June ADVOCATE, entitled "A Peculiar Disease"—Black Fever). The disease is characterized by an acute onset with chills and fever, an eruption extending over the entire body, beginning as a macular rash which later becomes of a spotted or marbled character and subsides in several weeks, followed by a general desquamation. There are moderate anæmia, tender and enlarged spleen. Constipation is usually present. The urine is reduced in amount and contains a small percentage of albumin. As complications, gangrene, hypostatic pneumonia and articular rheumatism often occur. The prognosis is bad, especially if the eruption is marked. In a series of six autopsies, the only gross lesions found were a much enlarged spleen with distended and thinned capsule, subcapsular hæmorrhages in the kidneys, slightly enlarged and pale liver, and some congestion of the meninges and viscera. Sections show a capillary congestion throughout, with many of the red cells containing parasites. Fatty degeneration of the liver and acute parenchymatous nephritis were found. Blood preparations during life showed a marked poikilocytosis and anæmia.

In studying the ætiology of the disease the following facts have appeared to be of most significance: (1) The definitely limited locality in which the disease occurred; (2) the season (March to July); (3) the symptoms and lesions indicating a specific infection; (4) no evidence of transmission directly from one patient to another; (5) no signs pointing to the digestive, respiratory, or genito urinary tracts as avenues of infection; (6) in all cases examined, small wounds of the skin were noticed, said to have been made by the bites of ticks. Bacteriological examinations showed no bacteria of any ætiologic significance. Examination of the blood, both before and after death, showed the presence of an amœba like organism in the red cells which varied greatly in form, size and staining reaction at various stages of its development. In marked contrast to the small number of infected cells in the circulating blood, is the great number of infected cells in the congested capillaries in the tissues removed at autopsy, where from 1 to 5 per cent. of the red cells contained each a large parasite. This is especially marked in the lung, spleen, liver and kidney. The organism resembles in its smaller form that of Texas fever, yet is as a rule, larger, and exhibits active amœboid movements. The absence of pigment would apparently separate it from the malarial group and place it with that of Texas fever. Inoculation experiments made with rabbits showed the presence of the organism in the blood within twenty-four hours, and on successive days for two weeks. The authors advance the hypothesis that the disease is conveyed to man by the tick. The facts which support this view are, (1) that the disease has been known to prevail only during the period of the active life of this insect; (2) the occurrence of spotted fever in isolated cases in sharply limited regions would indicate that the carrier traveled slowly and not widely; (3) all hæmatozoa of warm-blooded animals pass at least one phase of their development within the body of some host, usually an insect or arachnoid; (4) the organism of Texas fever in cattle is conveyed through the bite of ticks, and the germ of spotted fever seems closely related; (5) all the patients observed were known to have been bitten by ticks. The authors believe the intermediate host is probably one of the lower mammals, such as the gopher.—*Medical News.*

DO NO HARM.

The following from the *Therapeutic Gazette* contains so much good advice for the writer's brethren, and, we believe, for a great many homoeopaths, that we deem it worthy of repetition in the ADVOCATE.

A Fact in Treatment.

Some years ago a well known practitioner of this country wrote an article for one of the medical journals and gave it the title of "Nil Nocere," which may be translated "Do no harm." We fear that this axiom when applied to medicine did not make the impression upon the mind of the medical profession which it deserves, for there can be no doubt that far too often physicians administer drugs for the relief or removal of symptoms which are not sufficiently harmful to require relief, or give medicines with the object of curing a disease which is incurable except by nature's methods. It is not recognized that many maladies must run their course, and that the function of the physician is to guide the patient through the illness and not to attempt to arrest the storm or to modify its peculiarities, although he may very frequently with advantage control manifestations and results which if they were uncontrolled might result deleteriously. In no disease does it behoove the physician to take greater precaution that his treatments in no way produces evil result than in typhoid fever, a malady which must of necessity run a certain course, which cannot be aborted, and which at most can only be modified in the severity of its manifestations. A similar statement may be made in regard to pneumonia. For this reason we have read with much interest a brief article by Dr. Cheney, of San Francisco, in which he speaks of the methods which should be instituted in the lobar pneumonia in infants, and in which, after pointing out that the disease is one which runs a definite course, he indicates the remedies which may be employed to modify symptoms which are thought to be dangerous, but more than all, emphasizes the fact that infants in particular *suffer more from vigorous medication in some instances than they do from the disease itself.*

It is never to be forgotten that in addition to the influence of a medicine upon the particular symptoms for which it is given, it may influence the digestive tract, the kidneys, or the bowels, or even the heart and lungs, in a way which is undesirable, and care should be taken when deciding upon the employment of a remedy that its contra-indications do not become a factor of greater importance than the indications for its use.

THE DIFFERENCE.

"The "regular" doctors are regularly at work hunting microbes and giving them names, and calling them the *germs of diseases*, but that does not cure the patient.

The Old Masters of Homoeopathy have a system of laws by which they find the remedy that is homoeopathic in each case individually; that cures the patient and clears away the microbes.

The self-styled "regular" doctors, very regularly use very fine, up-to-date instruments to hunt microbes and give them jaw breaking names, and call them the germs of diseases, to make themselves famous, just as Old Father Adam did when he gathered all things together and gave them names and planted germs of diseases in the human race, and he has been famous ever since.

Master Samuel Hahnemann discovered the *laws* and *methods* for finding the remedy by the symptoms that are homoeopathic to, and curative in, the case; cures the patient without naming the disease or fighting microbes.

Now we ask, which is the humbug?

W. L. MORGAN.

Nursing.*

COMPLICATIONS OF THE LYING IN PERIOD.

Lecture No. 12.

Ladies: This evening we will take up some of the more common complications of the lying in period; and first, we will look at, briefly, some complications with the breasts.

The flow of the milk may be excessive or deficient. In the first instance the patient is annoyed by having her clothing and the bed soiled by the constant leaking of milk. To prevent this the nurse should keep the breasts abundantly covered with sterile gauze, which will soak up the excess, and the patient's diet will be altered as the physician shall direct. It is usual in these cases to withhold liquids, cereal foods, cocoa, and some of the vegetables, and to give the patient a diet poor in liquids, in starches, and in sweets. The most strict cleanliness must be observed in these cases, to avoid the retention and decomposition of milk in the clothing or upon the body. The supply usually diminishes when the patient gets up and is able to be about. In such cases much can be done to regulate the flow by the administration of one of the following remedies:

Acetic acid — Secretion abundant. Breasts greatly and painfully distended with milk.

Phytolacca—Excessive flow of milk, causing exhaustion.

Calcarea carb., Uranium, Pulsatilla; secretion too abundant.

Too little milk may be the result of lack of physical development or vigor in the mother, or may be caused by depressing mental influences or by improper diet. Worry will produce almost entire cessation of the secretion of milk, and great and sudden mental shock often produces the same result. Hence the nurse must be careful not to depress the mind of a nursing patient, but to encourage and comfort her in every way in her power. When the secretion of milk is deficient the nurse can assist it

* Course of Lectures delivered to the Nurses Training School at Maryland Homoeopathic Hospital, by H. S. Douglass, M. D., Baltimore, Md.

by massaging the breast, by following strictly the diet ordered by the doctor, by encouraging the patient, and by causing the child to nurse at regular intervals and as completely as possible. If the patient be encouraged to believe that the secretion of milk will not fail, much will be done to help to bring about the desired result.

Secretion deficient—Milk scanty or absent; despairing sadness: Agnus castus.

Deficiency of milk with over-sensitiveness: Asafœtida.

Scanty secretion of milk: Bryonia.

Mammæ seem distended, but milk scanty: Calcarea carb.

Little milk in mild, tearful women, presenting no morbid symptoms: Pulsatilla.

Milk scanty or vitiated; child refuses it: Mercurius.

Scanty milk, with debility and great apathy: Phos. acid.

The secretion is not established; stinging in the breasts: Secale.

Insufficiency of milk, or entire failure to appear: Urtica urens.

Milk watery and thin: Calc. phos.

Milk thin, blue; patient sad and despairing on waking: Lachesis.

Milk yellow and bitter, child refuses the breast: Rheum.

Abnormal conditions in the breast often arise which require careful attention to prevent the development of serious mischief.

Caked breasts are caused by failure of the milk to escape properly through the nipple. Sometimes it seems as if the outer skin of the breast is so firm that it will not yield and permit the flow of milk. In other cases the breasts are so full that it is impossible to obtain milk from them. This condition is a serious one, because if the accumulation cannot be relieved, and should infective bacteria be contained in the breast, an abscess will form. The sensible use of the breast bandage will do much to prevent this condition. The application of a poultice made of the root of Phytolacca decandra is very useful. Massage is an excellent help, and must be done by first washing the breast with soap and water and making the hands of the nurse aseptic. Sterile olive oil, as warm as the patient can conveniently bear it, is then taken to lubricate the skin of the breast. The nurse should rub from below upward, and from the outer border of the breast toward the nipple. The rubbing must be light in touch, gentle but thorough and steady, and may be continued from ten to twenty minutes. The best test of the success of this massage is the relief which the patient experiences. Massage should be practiced just before the regular time for the child to nurse. After this, if a breast pump be cautiously applied, a little milk will be extracted. If then the child is put to the breast, it will probably succeed in removing a considerable quantity of milk.

A frequent cause of caked breast and abscess is found in diseased or abnormal nipples. Such a condition can usually be remedied during pregnancy. If not, however, and if the nipple can be drawn out sufficiently for the child to grasp it, other conditions can usually be overcome. To draw out the nipple, the mouth of the child is undoubtedly the best apparatus. Next to this is some form of breast pump, which should be carefully cleansed after use. Its glass portion should be frequently boiled, and when not in use it should be kept in a saturated solution of boric acid. The breast pump must be used very gently, to prevent bruising and injuring the glandular structure. The nipple may be drawn out with a heated bottle, by heating the bottle in water, emptying it rapidly, inverting it and applying it over the nipple. As the bottle cools the nipple will be drawn through the neck of the bottle. When the nipples are not only depressed, but also deeply inverted, so that cup-like depressions are formed, the patient cannot nurse. Great care is requisite in keeping these depressions perfectly clean, as milk may accumulate and undergo decomposition in them.

In other cases the covering of the nipple is so sensitive that vigorous suction by the infant removes the superficial cells and causes the part to become sore. In these case the child must nurse through a nipple-shield. The nipple shield must be kept thoroughly clean by boiling, and when not in use it should be kept in a saturated solution of boric acid. When the nipples are sensitive they must be cleansed with the greatest care. Sterile olive oil, an ointment of Lanoline containing Boric acid, Castor oil, and Bismuth subnitrate are often employed as external applications.

Cracks and fissures may occur, and may be so deep as to cause bleeding at the time of nursing. For this condition strict antiseptic cleansing and the use of the nipple shield are usually sufficient. If infection occurs, then an abscess of the breast usually follows.

Nurses should observe any sore or ulcerated spot upon the nipples. Syphilitic women sometimes have sores upon the nipple, and occasionally a woman with a tubercular breast has such a condition. This must be at once reported to the physician, and it will very likely result in stopping the nursing of the child.

When the patient complains of pain in some portion of the breast, and that portion is found hard and firm and resisting, and when this does not soften with the method of treatment already described, a breast abscess is threatened. When pus actually forms the temperature rises as high as 103 or 104 degrees. The breast is sensitive to pressure, and over the hard area a red or pinkish color of the skin is seen. Such symptoms must at once be reported to the physician.

When pus has actually formed, the breast must be incised and the abscess emptied and drained. Some physicians apply hot fomentations to hasten the breaking down of the infected material. The operation of opening and draining the breast should be done under ether. The patient is prepared by abstinence from solid food and by purgation. The nurse must have ready an abundance of hot water, antiseptic solutions, ether, several breast bandages or binders, antiseptic gauze and cotton, and stimulants. A rubber sheet will be required, and if possible a kidney shaped pus-basin should be employed. An abundance of old linen may also be needed.

The breast is prepared for incision by washing thoroughly with soap and hot water, then rinsing with hot boiled water, and then washing with mercuric-chlorid solution [1:2000]. The physician's instruments should have been sterlized by boiling. A supply of sterile towels should be available, on which gauze may be cut in convenient strips. The patient's clothing should be removed from the chest, and her shoulders and the sound breast protected by a soft, thin blanket, and by clean linen. The physician will require a syringe for washing out the abscess cavity. A small glass piston syringe is very convenient for this purpose, while some prefer to use a fountain-syringe. The nurse must have ready such a syringe and solution as may be ordered. If care be taken, the patient's bed need not be soiled but without this, fluid is very apt to find its way into the center of the bed, requiring a complete change.

These cases need a daily dressing for varying periods, and the nurse must have ready the solution and dressing materials which the doctor may desire. Recovery from this condition is often tedious and prolonged, the abscess cavity being slow in healing. In neglected cases the abscess may burst spontaneously, or the pus may burrow beneath the breast or into the armpit and several openings may occur. In very severe cases it is necessary to make a few incisions and remove all of the infected gland tissue. Dressings are usually kept in place by a breast binder. If the child is to nurse from the healthy breast, the physician may prefer to use a broad roller bandage of flannel, which can be so applied that the nipple of the healthy breast is not included in the bandage. Nurses in attendance upon a case of breast abscess must remember to cleanse their hands with great care, lest they infect the infant or the genital tract of the mother, or some portion of their own body.

Insanity may attack the pregnant and puerperal woman in several forms. Of course, the most common is melancholia, while acute mania may develop. In these cases the patient often seeks to destroy herself, and endeavors to kill the child. Hence the nurse must be exceedingly cautious in the general management of these patients. Such cases occur among women in whom there is a family history of insanity, or in women who are exceedingly nervous or who have had some great calamity come upon them during pregnancy. If the disease be hereditary, the patient's chance for recovery is not a very good one; and if the child dies, the mother is less likely to recover. If, however, the patient has previously been strong and well, the chance for recovering is a good one if time and patience be used in the treatment. If the child survives, as the acute stage passes away the mother will find comfort in its care.

Restraint and absolute quiet are necessary during the acute stage; if the disorder develops during pregnancy, the patient may become actively maniacal during labor. She would then require anesthesia. After the birth of the child the mother must not be trusted to nurse it. Should the supply of milk be ample, an effort may be made to have the mother nurse it, but with the closest watchfulness lest the attempts to do it injury. When convalescent and quiet an out door life is best adapted for the mother's complete recovery. Her feeling for the child should be encouraged in every possible way, and her general health built up and made thoroughly good.

It is in these mental cases that homoeopathy has won some of its most brilliant results; but as the prescribing of remedies must naturally fall into the hands of an experienced prescriber, we will omit the mention of any drugs.

The nurse must remember the absolute uncertainty attending upon patients of unsound mind. The child is never safe in the presence of the mother in these cases unless a protector be at hand. The mother should never be left alone lest she attempt to destroy herself. The nurse must also have in mind her own safety, and not consent to go into situations where the patient could destroy both nurse and herself. The nurse can be of the greatest service to the patient, and in many cases she will have the satisfaction of seeing the patient's reason return and her affection for the child develop in a natural and most salutary manner.

In our next lecture we will take up the subject of feeding the infant.

Surgery.

SEPTICEMIA AND THE CURETTE.

To attempt to break up an old established custom in any line of life is, at best, a thankless job, and one likely to call down harsh criticism upon the head of the daring iconoclast.

To attempt to uproot old prejudices existing in favor of a certain line of practice, is to invite from some adverse criticism of the harshest kind. The only recompense for this is a logical refutation of, or concurrence in, the argument advanced on the part of other members of the profession.

This latter is what I hope for, and if I provoke a discussion, or start a line of thought in the minds of half of the readers of this article, I shall have achieved all I started out to do.

Curetting the uterus to remove fragments of after birth or other debris has been taught in our medical schools from time immemorial, and it is firmly fixed in the receptive and retentive mind of every medical student that the first move following any such abnormal uterine condition, is to cleanse the uterus by means of the curette.

That the organ should be thoroughly and aseptically cleansed admits of no argument, but that the work should be done with the curette, I deny most emphatically.

The majority of cases of death following the decomposition of fœtus or placenta in utero are caused by the use of the curette, and I hold that septicemia may be avoided if a more rational procedure be resorted to.

The condition of the uterus containing septic matter is one of great congestion; the thickened walls being coated internally and over the os with a thick, brown, tenacious mucus.

The congestion is active, and therefore the more dangerous in the event of the admission of septic matter into the circulation.

If the curette is used, denuding the walls of their protective covering, an immediate vaccination takes place with a septic virus, septicemia following in an incredibly short space of time [chemical metamorphosis is marvelously rapid in the circulatory system] and death quickly ensues.

If without using the curette, we can remove the septic matter from the uterus without disturbing the mucous covering, and enable the uterus of itself to expel the coating, we shall have taken a long step forward in the treatment of this class of uterine cases.

The uterus, by reason of its congestion may be made to perform a self-cleansing act by exciting the exudation of the serum of the blood into its cavity, thereby washing itself out, and expelling all septic matter instead of absorbing it.

This process of exosmosis is induced by a properly combined alkaline solution at a temperature above 100 degrees and a strict avoidance of bi chloride, carbolic acid, formaldehyde, or any antiseptic of an acid reaction or astringent nature, which would coagulate the fibrine and albumen of the blood.

My method of procedure is as follows:

First—The gentle removal of whatever fragments are lying in the uterine cavity, by means of forceps, care being taken not to tear from the walls any adherent piece.

Second—The gentle flushing of the uterine cavity with the alkaline solution [110 degrees], the reservoir containing the fluid being not more than two feet above the level of the hips.

If the flushing could be continuously

administered for a few hours [say two or three], the conditions would be more speedily reduced to normal, but the discomfort of the position of the patient [on a douche pan] prevents this, and a flushing once every two hours with one quart of solution is about the limit of treatment.

For flushing the uterus, I use a small dilating uterine douche, and there is no danger of fallopian colic or salpingitis.

The first flushing is frequently followed by contractile pains and expulsion of any previously adherent pieces, together with much of the mucus.

The remedy indicated by the totality of symptoms repeated every hour till desired effect is produced will contract uterus and alleviate pain.

The bowels should be moved freely, by enema.

During the interval between douches, the patient should be kept on her back with the hips sufficiently raised to permit the retention in the vagina of as much of the alkaline solution as it will hold.

The rapidity with which this treatment will reduce temperature, relieve pain, stop vomiting and remove offensive odor is marvelous to one who has not tried it. Sometimes two flushings are sufficient to cleanse the uterus thoroughly, vaginal douches being all that are needed subsequently to complete the work.

Uterine congestion is especially relieved, and the uterine discharge changes from brown, thick, bad smelling mucus, to a thin transparent one, accompanied or followed by more or less of a flow of blood.

A reduction in the frequency of the flushing is desirable as soon as a tendency to return to normal conditions begins to be observed, as it frequently will within twenty-four hours. Then simple vaginal douches every three hours with an occasional uterine flushing if symptoms indicate it.

The action of exosmosis [and endosmosis, for there is every reason to believe in the absorption of some of the fluid] is what is desired to relieve the existing congestion, as in a bronchitis, pneumonia, congestion of kidney, congestion of any mucous membrane, etc., and is the most rational means of restoring to normal condition.

I do not wish to be understood as decrying the use of that most valuable instrument, the curette, but only the abuse of it to-wit: its employment under such conditions as make it practically a sharp weapon loaded with septic matter, dangerous beyond the poisoned arrow of the Malay, or the fang of the cobra, and utterly opposed to our modern ideas of antisepsis.

H. PLYMPTON.

Brooklyn, N. Y.

Editorial.

CURED BY FAITH.

For the purpose of illustrating the power of the mind over the body and at the same time impressing upon the mind of the physician the importance of giving due consideration to this phase of the disease the following incident is recorded:

Nearly a year ago was called on consultation to a young lady suffering apparently from a severe *functional* derangement of the heart and general circulation. *The body seemed well nourished*, but there was an *absence* of desire for food or drink. Obstinate constipation. Scanty and very painful menstruation. *Depression* marked with complete *apathy* and a settled *conviction* that she *could not be healed with medicine. Hopeless.* Could not arouse the slightest enthusiasm, but would *passively* do anything that was directed.

A careful record was made and a thorough study for the remedy. The indications *seemed* clearly defined, but the lack of co-operation added to the previous history led me to my first error, *a guarded prognosis*. An explanation should be made at this time with reference to the last statement. The patient had implicit confidence in my ability to cure her *at the very beginning* and undoubtedly would have *responded at once* to the suggestion that *she would be well in a short time* if I had not mistaken the report for a more serious condition, and been correspondingly guarded in my prognosis. The *indefinite* promise of help was taken to mean that the case was *hopeless* and the golden opportunity was lost, never to be regained.

Absence of results only served to confirm the opinion formed at the very beginning, so that subsequent efforts to impress *positive* suggestions would be met with the statement that it might be true but appearances didn't seem to justify; conviction was started in her mind that she could be *healed by prayer as soon as her faith was strong enough.* This belief gained in power by constant dwelling upon the idea until it became the one thought uppermost in her mind. It called for action and a number of her friends were invited to come in and unite their prayers with her own. Her prayer was for *immediate* results, and she went to her bed *fully expecting* that her *sleep* would be *restful*, that her *bowels* would move *naturally* and that her *menstruation would be painless* and normal in every other way. Everything came about as she expected. She believes a miracle has been performed and is correspondingly happy.

The facts are before us and must be faced. The significance of the same are not appreciated by the mass of the profession and they see many of their patrons desert them and become *ardent, enthusiastic* followers of some cult or man who possesses much less real merit but has learned the fact that the *mind has almost absolute control over the functional activities of the body.* Let the mind become perverted or possessed with a pernicious idea and the body will suffer in a corresponding way. Bear in mind it is *functional* derangements that may be traced to this *mental* disturbance. Keep another fact as prominent before you, viz: the *disturbing cause may be within or it may come from without.* The predominating characteristic is fear, timidity, lack of confidence, apathy, indifference etc., and may be manifested through anxiety, depression, cowardice, apprehension etc.

As a rule the origin is deep seated

oftimes being a legacy inherited from progenitors and fostered by environment, and cannot be corrected in a day; but more frequently then we care to acknowledge, the cause is easily recognized and may be traced to a definite time, place or event.

The effects are almost without number, running the entire gamut of *functional* derangements, from headache to cold feet, and include susceptibility to draft, dampness, cold, heat, nervous dyspepsia, chronic constipation, menstrual derangements, hysteria etc., etc. Every case must be carefully analyzed, the *physical* examination thorough, so that both the *fundamental* and the *exciting* causes may be determined and the *functional* separated from the *organic*.

The physician must become master of the situation at the very start. Every moment of delay is dangerous. The first impression is the golden opportunity and if not utilized may be lost forever. *He must know* many failures may be traced to lack of thoroughness at the very beginning.

We all know of the varied means employed by the charletan to secure the undivided attention of his audience and how some public speakers can carry a mixed audience with them from beginning to the end. This principle is recognized in every case and means to that end employed.

Remedies selected in accordance with homeopathic indications have almost miraculous power in correcting mental perversions, but their efficacy is greatly increased when patient, physician and remedy are working in unison.

ERRATA.

On page 210, June issue of the ADVOCATE, in Dr. Loos' article on "Is there Any Value in Medicine?", first column, ninth line from the bottom, "*Sulphur*[cm]" should be stricken out. Second column, fourth line from the bottom, strike out the same words.

This mistake was not made by Dr. Loos, but was due to the ignorance of the proofreader of medical terms.

ED.

Personals and News Items.

Dr. F. W. Winter has removed from Arlington, Neb., to Adams, Gage Co., Neb.

The universities at Tokio and at Moscow will next year open their doors to women.

Dr. B. G. Clark, of New York City, announces his removal from 162 W. 122 street to 25 W. 74th street.

GOOD HOMOEOPATHIC READING is found in back numbers of the ADVOCATE. Complete volumes 1896 to 1901, mailed on receipt of $1.00 a volume. Ten numbers, not consecutive, fifty cents. Address Hahnemann Publishing Co., 6704 Lafayette ave.

Dr. Frank M. Hallock, for many years located at Plainfield, N. J., has removed to 134 West Sixty-fifth street, New York City.

To increase the bodily warmth when chilly from exposure, breathe very deeply and rapidly, and the temperature will be quickly raised.

Dr. V. H. Hallman of Hot Springs, Ark., has removed to elegant quarters, rooms 205, 206 and 207 Arkansas National Bank building.

Forty-nine of the sixty-six candidates for certificates from the Wisconsin Board of Medical Examiners were successful, as a result of the July test.

Dr. Geo. M. Cooper of Philadelphia, Pa., has removed from 1628 Mt. Vernon street to 1621 Chestnut street, adding one more to the already large number of physicians located on that thoroughfare.

The American Institute of Phrenology, incorporated 1866, opens its next session, September 3, 1902. For particulars apply to the Secretary, M. H. Piercy, care of Fowler & Wells Co., 24 East 22d st., New York.

By Australia's passage in 1901 of a law making it obligatory, in order to practice medicine there, to have taken a five-year course, graduates of American medical colleges will hereafter be excluded from practicing their profession in that country.

Is there anything in the following, which we clip from an exchange:

Boy or Girl—Which Will It Be?—If the expectant mother walks slowly, flat-footed, has sunken eyes, and craves oysters, it will be a boy. If she walks quickly, with elastic gait, has full eyes and craves sweetmeats it will be a girl.

The next annual meeting of the Missouri Valley Homœopathic Medical and Surgical Association will be held at Lincoln, Neb., Oct. 22–23. Besides the papers on subjects purely medical, a prominent minister will have something to say on the "Relation of the Clergy to the Physician." Dr. Bailey will tender the visitors a reception and banquet at his sanitorium.

On Wednesday, October 22d, Dr. William A. Glasgow, of Missoula, Montana, will be married to Maud Ironside at the home of the bride's mother in Camden, N. J. After Nov. 11 the Doctor will resume his growing practice in Missoula.

GOOD MEDICAL LITERATURE, cheap, can be obtained, in the shape of complete volumes of the MEDICAL ADVANCE, for years 1893, '94 and '95. $1.00 a volume, postpaid, while they last. Ten numbers, not consecutive, for fifty cents. Odd numbers of issues of the 70s and and 80s at six cents a number. Address Hahnemann Publishing Co., 6704 Lafayette ave.

The Illinois State Board of Health has drawn up a schedule of minimum requirements for the regulation of medical colleges. The conditions of admission to lecture courses are: (1) A certificate of moral character, and (2) evidence of preliminary education, of which a high school diploma represents the minimum requirement. Admission to advanced standing is based upon an equivalence of work done in other institutions recognized by the State Board. The curricula of the medical schools are to embrace four years of instruction aggregating at least forty months. The branches of medicine to be embraced in the course of instruction must include at least the following: (1) Anatomy, (2) Physiology, (3) Chemistry, (4) Materia Medica and Therapeutics, (5) Theory and Practice of Medicine, including Ophthalmology, Otology, Dermatology and Neurology, (6) Pathology and Bacteriology, (7) Surgery, including Orthopædic Surgery, (8) Obstetrics, (9) Gynæcology, (10) Hygiene, (11) Medical Jurisprudence (Forensic Medicine). The regulations also prescribe dissection, lectures, clinical courses, and regular attendance on the part of the student.

GOOD HOMŒOPATHIC READING is found in back numbers of the ADVOCATE. Complete volumes 1896 to 1901, mailed on receipt of $1.00 a volume. Ten numbers, not consecutive, fifty cents. Address Hahnemann Publishing Co., 6704 Lafayette ave.

The appointment of Dr. Johannes Orth, Professor of Pathological Anatomy at the University of Göttingen, as successor to the late Dr. Virchow in the chair of pathological anatomy and as director of the Pathological Institute in the University of Berlin, was announced September 25 Dr. Orth was for many years Virchow's assistant.

SOUTHERN MEETING ANNOUCEMENT.

The next meeting of the Southern Homœopathic Medical Association will occur in Louisville, Oct. 21, 22 and 23. This meeting will be the pleasantest in the history of the association and the largest in point of attendance. The local committee are working like beavers and pressure is being brought to get the largest possible attendance from all points accessible to Louisville. The grand historic old Galt House will be headquarters. This is the largest hotel in the city and contains assembly rooms and many conveniences for such a convention. It is now run on the European plan and rooms can be obtained for $1.50 per day and lodgers can eat where they please, though the cuisine of the Galt House is unsurpassed anywhere. This is the house of which Dickens said in his American notes, "We were as well housed and fed as though in the heart of London."

Visiting members are requested to bring their wives and daughters, and even their sisters, their cousins and their aunts with them, as amusement features will not be overlooked, including a trolley ride through one of the most beautiful cities in the world, and a wagon ride through Cherokee park, a sylvan retreat of rare beauty, containing the grandest of beech groves. There will also be a reception and musicale at the residence of Dr Monroe and other social features. The scientific part of the meeting is being thoroughly attended to by the chairmen of bureaus, but the local committee of arrangement is most anxious that our brethren of the north, east and west come and enjoy a few days of southern hospitality.

A. LEIGHT MONROE, Chairman.

Correspondence.

VACCINE VIRUS KILLS MULES.

EDITOR HAHNEMANNIAN ADVOCATE,

Dear Sir:—Apropos to the vaccination fight I have here, I enclose a clipping from a local paper showing the effect of scientific (?) vaccination on a bunch of mules. It is not necessary to add that this *telling effect* has made an impression on this community also. "If vaccination will kill a mule I want none of it in me," is a comment often heard now.

Some pretty dodging was done by witnesses and counsel for the defendants in the interest of "Science," but that *backwoods Arkansaw jury* thought that "whoever killed them mules ort to pay fur 'em! We ha'int got no use fur 'science' that'll kill a feller's mules!"

Mann-Tankersley Drug Co. feel

pretty sore over the affair as you may guess.

Yours "for the war,"
WELLS LEFEVRE.

Pine Bluff, Ark.

Following is the clipping from the Pine Bluff paper:

The suit of J. T. Cheairs & Sons, of Winchester, against the Mann-Tankersley Drug company, of this city, is attracting much attention in the Jefferson circuit court here just now. The case was called Wednesday morning and all that day witnesses were examined. Many of them are here from other places to testify in the case and several expert medicine men and veterinarians are also in attendance giving the jury their views on the subjects discussed.

Cheairs & Sons sues the local drug company for the value of eight head of of stock, they attempting to hold the local concern responsible for eight head of stock, which, they claim died after being vaccinated with vaccine points, sold them through the Mann-Tankersley company by Parke, Davis & Co., a prominent medicine house of Detroit, Mich. Mr. Charles M. Woodruff, a stockholder in the Detroit company, is in the city to hear the case argued. He is also a prominent attorney and member of the Detroit bar. Mr. E. C. Lawrence, traveling representative of Parke, Davis & Co., is also in the city as a witness.

The cross-examination of witnesses is still in progress. The case will in all probability go to the jury this afternoon.

Later—The jury in case of J.T.Cheairs & Sons against the M·nn-Tankersley Drug company, after being out about two hours, Thursday afternoon, returned a verdict for the plaintiff in the sum of $512.50. The plaintiffs sued the company for eight head of stock or their value—over eight hundred dollars—but the jury gave them only a few dollars over five hundred.

Materia Medica Miscellany.

Acetic acid.—Dr. Gaetano's tests have convinced him that a 20 per cent alcoholic solution of acetic acid is the most efficient disinfectant at our command for the treatment of wounds. In addition to its power of antisepsis, this mixture presents the very great advantage of making the wound as dry as possible, which in itself renders invasion by germs unlikely.

Ammonia—Antidote for Formaldehyde.—In view of the fact that this chemical is coming more and more into general use as a disinfectant and antiseptic, cases of poisoning from it will become more frequent. We have [*Merck's Archives*] an easily accessible and reliable antidote in ammonia water a few drops well diluted or the aromatic spirit or a solution of ammonium acetate.

Strophanthus.—Dr. Royal, from a study of strophanthus, concludes that its place as a cardiac tonic is in cases where the heart has been weakened by alcohol, tea, or tobacco, or stiffened by rheumatism. He finds fractions of a drop of the tincture produce sure as well as safe results.—*N. Am. Journ. of Hom.*

Conium.—A railway engineer, aged 78, came to Dr. McIntyer for treatment of paresis of the neck of the bladder, from which he had suffered for six years. Tracing the trouble to the long continued jolting of the locomotive, and learning that there was some pain in the lumbar spine, Dr. McIntyer gave him Conium 3x. From occasional weekly courses of this remedy improvement soon set in, and evenuated in about five months in a complete cure. —*Hom. Recorder.*

Helleborus.—In the lack of reaction is Helleborus most always indicated, says Dr. Mohr, of Philadelphia, no matter what the disease is. As soon as a couple of doses are given the vital powers seem fanned into action, new and stronger reaction appears, and the patient goes on to rapid recovery.—*Medical Century.*

Kali phosphoricum.—The action of Kali phos. on the nervous system is being utilized by our alienists. Dr. Taylor finds it of great value where the patient has been "acting queer" for a long time; when the brain has been gradually growing weaker, causing loss of memory, lack of interest in everything, carelessness in business, jealousies, suspicions, and more or less insomnia. This condition may result from domestic troubles, or any cause which exhausts the nervous energy.—*The Clinique.*

Cocoanut for Tapeworm.—The use of the common cocoanut for tapeworm is not generally known. A writer in the Medical Summary advices the eating of cocoanut to the exclusion of all other diet for two or three days. He claims that the worm will come away entire in every case without the use of a cathartic. If this simple measure be found available, it will be an important addition to the therapeutics of this condition.—*Chicago Medical Times.*

Ferrum picricum—Warts.— Miss H., age 35, had been troubled for several years with warts on her hands. On the little finger of right hand there were two very large and rather painful warts which had existed for about three years; and on the middle finger of the left hand there were three similar growths. Patient wished to try medicinal treatment, as she told me the warts had been on two occasions removed by electric cautery, but began to grow again within a month after each operation and were soon as bad as ever. The warts were extremely sensitive, aching always worse during night. Patient being of the type described by Dr. Cooper as peculiarly responsive to the action of Ferrum picricum (namely of dark complexion and "bilious"), on May 5 1901, I prescribed that remedy in the third decimal tincture every six hours. After continuing the medicine for three months the warts became much less prominent and sensitive; in another three months they had entirely disappeared and there has never been any recurrence. The general health of patient has also much improved.—*A. Pullar, in Homo. World.*

Colocynthis. It has been well said that *pain* is the principal and most essential indication of *Colocynthis*. In the digestive system it plays an important part in the treatment of colic, when the pains are of a *griping* or *cutting* nature, and in dysenteric diarrhea, in which the colic is *severe*. In the nervous system it is indicated in neuralgic hemicrania (in which there is a sensation as if the head were in a vice, and there is present a *cutting, burning*, or *pressive* pain in the eyeball); in facial neuralgia (left side chiefly), accompanied with toothache and headache (the pains being of a *stitching, tearing* character); and in sciatica (the pain being of a *lancinating* nature, and *darting* down the leg from the hip to the foot. I came recently across a case, that of a young lady, who was suffering from stitching and colicky pains in the left ovary, which was greatly inflamed and very tender to the touch.

She stated that the pains were almost unbearable, and extended through the left groin down the leg as far as the left knee. A week's treatment of *Colocynthis* 2 minims, every three hours for the first few days, and three times daily afterwards, speedily removed the pain and inflammation, and restored the ovary to a normal and healthy condition. — *Homo. World.*

Skin Grafting with Callus Shavings, in Blood.—Mary M., age 60 years, Irish. Diagnosis. Ulcer in leg. Patient admitted to hospital, March 3, 1902. She has a large varicose ulcer situated over the tibia, about 3½ by 2 inches. This condition had existed for nine years, and during that time in spite of all treatment employed had never entirely healed. It had been skin grafted in the old way, three times successfully. At the time of entering the hospital the patient suffered so severely from pain that at times she would cry out. She was put to bed, secretions regulated, the ulcer cleaned up by means of a dermal curette, and dressed for the first twenty-four hours with a Thiersch pack. On the morning of March 5th, after the surface had been thoroughly cleaned up, a bovine-pure pack was applied and kept wet with the bovinine for twenty-four hours.

On the morning of the 7th, I determined to employ grafts secured from a callus on the small toe, in order to demonstrate the technique of this mode of skin-grafting to five visiting physician. The mode of procedure was as follows: The callus was thoroughly scrubbed up, and the external layers scraped off. Then thin sections of the layers next to the true skin were obtained by means of a very keen razor. Nine of these were deposited on the ulcerous surface. Over these were laid strips of perforated rubber tissue, then strips of plain bi sterilised gauze saturated in bovinine, and a bandage applied. The nurse was instructed to keep the dressings wet with bovinine pure. This dressing was removed on the 14th, and it was found, much to the delight and astonishment of the visiting physicians, that out of the nine grafts employed eight were firmly adherent and in a healthy growing condition. The ninth had become displaced and was removed. The wound was now dressed with bovinine pure; the dressings being kept wet, and changed once in twenty four hours. Co incident with the local dressings, from the outset, the patient had been given a wineglassful of bovinine in milk alternating with wine and beer every three hours. On March 24th, she was discharged cured, the entire surface having become covered with new healthy skin.

This experiment has been employed frequently enough by me to demonstrate that where the technique is carefully followed it will in the majority of cases yield the most gratifying results. A point of interest in this case and a usual one, is that from the day of the first dressing of the bovinine up to the time the patient was discharged, she was relieved of all pain.

T. J. BIGGS.

Cocculus.—Cocculus is a very valuable medicine in various nervous affections, such as certain forms of hemiplegia, and paralytic stiffness, accompanied by a sense of heaviness, and by a loss of motor power in the lower limbs, with giddiness, and a feeling of lightness in the head. I have witnessed its good effects upon a patient who had suffered for several months from loss of power in the lower limbs, moving them only with considerable difficulty, and who, when standing erect, became giddy, disposed to be sick, light-headed. This patient quite recovered through a few weeks' perseverence with the tincture. Nervous affections, such as hysterical hemiplegia, choreic hemiplegia, and epileptic hemiplegia may likewise be usefully treated with Cocculus. I have seen well-marked cases of hysterical paralysis—where the sensibility and the muscular power are both impaired—yield quickly to this drug; and cases, in particular, which have been accompanied by menstruous irregularities, and by spasms attacking different organs. Some of those epileptic cases which are attributable to onanism likewise derive benefit from Cocculus.—M. E. Douglass, in *Am. Phy.*

Populus monilifera.—Some years ago, when drugs were hard to obtain in Arkansas, where I was located, and the people were suffering from the various forms of malarial manifestations, I sought to discover some antidote for the poison; and in that connection my attention was called to the antiperiodic properties of the *cotton wood bark*—Populus monilifera.

I found that by using a strong infusion I could soon cure any form of intermittent fever, and chronic and irregular forms could be thoroughly cured with it; and the pathological lesions of liver, spleen, and kidneys removed, and their physiological functions restored. I soon learned from clinical observation that the well known tendency to relapse, so often observed after quinine treatment, was overcome. In fact, I found that I had a powerful and reliable therapeutic agent, but I labored under the inconvenience of the large doses of the infusion, in order to get its therapeutic effect. But notwithstanding this, I have often cured grave forms of the disease with this agent only. There is one thing right here I wish to state: it is not likely to produce defective hearing so much complained of when the quinine treatment is used. Now I do not wish to be understood that I wish to detract from the honors justly belonging to quinine; but if I have made a discovery that we have an antidote which is American, I think it my duty as an American physician, to point it out.

Let us continue by saying that as year after year passed, I often had to resort to what I called the Alter Specific [*i. e.*, cotton wood bark tea], and finally a very severe form of malarial manifestation became common in my territory, to which quinine seemed to be poison. I refer to what we call malarial hematuria. I concluded then to try the cotton wood bark in this form, and from the first case on I had no trouble in controlling the hematuria, causing the icteroid color of the skin to disappear, and saved my patient.

I wish to call attention to some things which serve as a foundation for my claims to be the discoverer of a specific for the last mentioned form of malarial pathological conditions. I have very often cured my patient with the Alter Specific, and ordered that for a few days quinine be taken; and have often been called back in haste in less than an hour after the ingestion of the first dose of quinine, on account of the hematuria from the kidneys. After considering such clinical evidence as the above (and this I have observed often) I was forced to the conclusion that I discovered a specific. I have had trouble sometimes to get enough retained in the stomach on account of the irritation of that organ.

I thought for some time that I would keep the matter secret, but as my discovery came around rather as the result of circumstances, and not on account of my great knowledge of medical plants, or my work, I do not think that I am entitled to any special honor. Still I would like to contribute to the success of my profession and the better treatment of the sick. This is the first time I have revealed what the Alter Specific is made from. In 1899, I wrote an article to the *Medical World*, on the "Alter Specific," which was published in the March number of that year.

I will conclude by giving you my idea of the physiological effects: Cardiac stimulant, diaphoretic, diuretic, stimulant to hepatic cells, a promoter of physiological metabolism under pathological conditions, induced by malarial toxemia; promoting elimination of disintegrated material, it is a specific for material hematuria; also one of our most powerful antiperiodics, possessing advantages over quinine. It will not cause deafness; it will not cause abortion, but in malaria conditions of the pregnant, it will prevent abortion, soothe the pains often brought on by malarial poison in the pregnant uterus. There are other valuable properties which I have observed since I first began using the Populus monilifera some 26 or 27 years ago.—W. M. Alter in *Eclectic Med. Journal.*

What Homœopathy Needs.—What we need most is *a Reformation not a Reproving.* The immense bulk of our present materia medica is a check rather than an incentive to the introduction of new drugs. We have already too many partially proven and not-at-all-confirmed drugs. Why add to the number?

There are at present some twelve thousand practitioners engaged upon the reconfirmation of the drug symptoms as now recorded. There have not been twelve good provings of a useful sort in the past twelve years. Why waste further energy, time and money on this elusive proposition?

These twelve thousand reconfirmators are urged by fame, by scientific skill, by bread and butter demands to make their work good. The reprovers are urged by fame, by science, and held back by bread and butter demands; which side will gain most ground?

No one wishes to make himself sick by the experimental use of drugs. The whole business is much like volunteering in time of war; only the very patriotic and the very thoughtless volunteer; so with drugs; we prefer to try them on those in whom we have but slight interest—to let our wife's cousins enlist, as Josh Billings said.

Hence we return to the place from which we started; what we most need in the present is not a reproving of drugs but a reconfirmation of recorded symptoms.

The rejuvenation of therapy according to similars demands this sort of work. Year by year it is dropping back because we let these golden grains slip carelessly through our fingers.

What is wanted, is a comprehensive practical plan for gathering them together, preserving them, and rendering them available.—M. W. Vandenburg, M. D., in *Clinical Reporter.*

Book Reviews.

Transactions of the American Institute of Homœopathy for 1902.

Credit to whom credit is due. A remarkably fine volume appears as the work of the last session of the institute. An exceptional corps of officers, noted for their systematic habits, accuracy and promptness. This volume appears at an earlier date and seems remarkably free of errors and fuller in detail than any report appearing for a number of years. The members have the privilege of reading the same in connection with the valuable discussion before it shall have appeared in the various magazines. A volume of 860 pages filled with interesting and valuable contributions of current literature are well worth the price paid for annual dues. This is as it should be and will be a powerful incentive for future growth of the institute.

Practical Diagnosis, the Use of Symptoms and Physical Signs in the Diagnosis of Diseases, by Hobart A. Hare, M. D., and published by Lea Brothers & Co.

This is the *fifth* edition within six years and has been thoroughly revised. It is hardly necessary to add anything to the above notice, because the works of Prof. Hare are very favorably known throughout the country, but we cannot let the opportunity pass for presenting one of the *characteristics* of this work. The author *begins with symptoms and explains their possible meaning* in such a way as to throw direct light upon the symptomatology of many diseases as well as the pathologic effects from the use of many drugs. This alone commends this work to our favorable consideration.

Principles and Practice of Gynecology, by E. C. Dudley, M. D. Published by Lea Brothers & Co.

For all practical purposes this *third* edition of an already recognized standard work on gynecology is a new work since the subject matter has been so thoroughly revised as to present a different appearance from the preceding one.

To those who are not familiar with this work, we can say that Dr. Dudley is one of the most conservative gynecologists in the country. He is professor of gynecology in Northwestern University Medical School and has been a close observer and a practical teacher for many years.

There are 760 pages in addition to 22 full pages in colored plates and monochromes. The text is illustrated by 474 engravings. The publishers being very liberal in their preparation of the book for the market.

The book is divided into five parts instead of following the usual order and everything is considered under its proper head, e.g.:

Part I is devoted to General Principles and 136 pages are given to the Physiological periods in the life of a woman; septic infection and aseptic technique; diagnosis; local treatment; minor operations; major operations; drainage; after treatment; relation of dress to diseases of women. To local treatment is only given six pages and particular emphasis is given to the unsatisfactory results from indiscriminate local treatments. His work is that of the surgeon and must be reviewed from that standpoint and still that same conservative spirit is manifest throughout the entire work. Systematic treatment is urged whenever possible and largely along practical common sense lines. Of course the medicinal indications would be of no value to the homoeopathist, but with that exception the book abounds in valuable information.

The same general order is followed in each of the five sections. Part II being given over to Inflammation and kindred disorders. Part III, Tumors, Tubal Pregnancy and Malformations. Part IV, Traumatisms. Part V, Displacements. Part VI, Disorders of Menstruation and Sterility.

Physical Diagnosis of Thorax and Abdomen, by Egbert LeFevre, M. D., and published by Lea Brothers & Co.

Dr. LeFevre is professor of Clinical Medicine in Bellevue Hospital Medical College of New York and a careful study of his book gives the reader abundant proof that he is a natural and an interesting teacher. The secret of his success in the present product of his brain is the recognition that the average student is always looking for the "*Why*" and in every instance this seems to occupy equally prominent place with the *description* of the varied sounds and physical signs to be discovered by the varied means to be employed in securing accurate knowledge of that which lies within.

There are only about 450 pages and these are illustrated by 74 engravings and 12 monochrome plates.

The book is certainly worthy a place in the library of every student and many practitioners will refer to it in preference to the older and more established works.

From no other periodical can so sane and accurate a view of current politics be gained as from the *Review of Reviews*. The October number of that publication is noteworthy for its clear and full editorial exposition of the issues involved in this fall's campaign, the effect of Speaker Henderson's retirement, the meaning of the tariff agitation in the Middle West, and President Roosevelt's attitude on the trust question. The President's remarkable speaking tours through New England, in the South, and to the West as far as Indianapolis—where an abrupt ending was necessitated by the abscess on the President's leg — are described and pictured for the reader more comprehensively than in most daily and weekly journals In fact, this record of the year's campaigning up to date is something unique in our periodical literature. It includes a survey of State political activities, East, West, North and South. Neither Josiah Quincy's conservative leadership of the Massachusetts Democrats nor Tom Johnson's capture of the Ohio Democratic organization, on behalf of the pro Bryan radicals, is ignored. The editor of the *Review* has added another chapter to the unequaled "History of Our Own Times" that he is writing month by month.

A succinct and unbiased statement of the point at issue in the famous "Pious Fund" case now before The Hague arbitrators will be found in Mr. W. T. Stead's article, entitled "The United States and Mexico at the Opening of The Hague Court," in the October *Review of Reviews*. It is an interesting fact that the first case to be arbitrated by the Hague tribunal should be brought to it by two American nations, and that the matter involved should be the disposition of church funds. Portraits of the arbitrators accompany Mr. Stead's article.

As usual, the October *Success* is chock full of good things for young and old. Among other instructive articles the following cannot help but prove of benefit to the reader:

Good Citizenship, Henry C. Lodge; Farming the Ocean, John R. Spears; The Magic Forest, (Fiction.) Chapters III., IV. and V., S. E. White; How American Captains of Industry Are Made, R. H. Thurston; The First Century of Ohio's Statehood, D. F. St. Clair; Look for the Beautiful, J. L. Brooks; To Those Who Pay too Much for Success; The Story of My Boyhood Days, E. T. Jeffery; The Making of an Orator, H. M. Dowling; The Wonders of Chinese Tangrams, S. Loyd; The Supreme Court's New Justice; The Heroism of Coal Miners, F. A. Smink; The Wealth of Economy, W. Mathews; An Interview with Paul Kruger, H. S. Morrison; Psychurgy, (Interview with E. Gates,) E. L. Sherwood; Why Women Study Law, Mrs. T. Sutro; The New President of Princeton; How to Become an Honest Millionaire, R. Waters; A Devoted Slave, (A True Story), Rufus R. Wilson; The Evolution of the Sleeping Car, Cy Warman; The Light of the Future, H. Maxim; The World of Science, A. E. Bostwick.

The Hahnemannian Advocate

A MONTHLY HOMŒOPATHIC MAGAZINE.

H. W. Pierson, B. S., M. D., Editor., 809 Marshall Field Building, Chicago.
Hahnemann Publishing Co. Publisher, 6704 Lafayette Ave., Chicago.
Benj. F. Swab, Business Manager.

Subscription price of the magazine in the United States, Canada, Mexico, the island possessions and Cuba [illegible] a year, payable in advance; in Great Britain, continental Europe, India and other countries, members of the postal union, [illegible] a year to be paid in advance. Unless otherwise specified subscriptions will begin with January issue of the year in which order is received. Remittances should be made payable to the Hahnemann Publishing Co., 6704 Lafayette Ave., Chicago.

Address all articles intended for publication and books for review to the editor. All business and other communications should be sent to the Hahnemann Publishing Co.

Vol. xii. Chicago, October, 1902. No. 10

Materia Medica.

SULPHUR—LYCOPODIUM—THUJA.

Edna M., 16 years of age. Sickly and puny from birth. Undersized, appearing like a child of ten. Awkward in gait as if her limbs would hardly support her body. Vaccinated when five years of age. Vaccination did not take, passed through whooping cough when six, and measles when eight. Severely sick with both ailments and recuperated very slowly from both. Was sent to school at the usual age, but was so backward in learning she was soon taken out of school and never went back. Never enjoyed playing with other children. Could not keep up with them in their sports, but has always been kept out of doors all possible, and enjoyed being out in the air. Always physically backward, yet ate reasonably well, and sometimes has a voracious appetite. For many years she has been in the hands of physicians and has swallowed pounds of iron, sulphur, potassium, magnesia and soda, in tonics, alteratives, etc., without benefit.

Symptoms — Quarrelsome, peevish. Wants to be alone daytimes, but afraid to be alone nights. Cheerful at times; melancholy at times. Timid at all times. Often angry without due cause. Very weak memory. Always irritable. Is careless about exposing her person but does not purposely expose it. Muttering spells. Likes to attend religious meetings for the sake of excitement, but does not grasp their significance. Obstinate at times. Very rapid speech. Starting during sleep. Restless during menses particularly, but so also at other times. At times seems stupid, especially mornings soon after rising. Weeping spells during sleep, without waking. Sometimes averse to talking at all.

Sensorium—Dizzy after rising mornings. Sometimes dizzy when she wakes in the morning with eyes closed. Dizzy when stooping.

Head — Nodular lumps on scalp. Feeling of fulness or enlargement of the head evenings, (says her head feels big). Falling out of hair. Headache on waking mornings, (could not get her to describe the headache). Will only say "it thumps and thumps."

Nose — Catarrhal condition dating from the attack of measles before men.

tioned, not much discharge, more a dry irritative condition with scabs and crusts inside the nose; worse if awake nights. What slight discharge there is at times is greenish and somewhat purulent. Ulceration of edges of nostrils.

Face—Red and rough. Many comedones.

Eyes—Agglutination of lids on waking mornings. Pus exudes from between lids during sleep. Granulated lids. Sclerotic inflammation. Weak eyes. Objects appear to her to move up and down. Swollen upper lids. Excessive lachrymation in open air. Vision myopic with diplopia.

Ears—Fetid discharge, offensive and purulent. Little hard nodules in rims of ears. Complains of hearing noises at night, as of pounding, or like the rumbling of cars. Complains of right ear hurting her at times.

Teeth—Very darkly discolored; greenish black. Grinding of teeth in sleep.

Voice—Weak. At times nasal.

Respiration—During sleep somewhat asthmatic. Short. Rapid, thirty-four to the minute. In sleep the breathing is intermittent. Holds breath in sleep at times a full three quarters of a minute. Heart seems acting nominally.

Cough—Hacking dry cough the latter part of the day, and worse in bed at night. Coughs in sleep without waking. Aggravation of cough as soon as she lies down in bed at night. Complains that something tickles her throat.

Desires—Wants much cold drinks, as lemonade, or water, or tea. Dislikes hot drinks.

Stomach—Eructations after eating and especially after cold drinks. Eructations sometimes empty, sometimes of food or drink. Foul breath. Nausea when stomach is empty.

Sleep — Wakes frequently. Sometimes sleepless for hours. Dreams bad dreams as if much excited, and wakens frightened. Drowsy after dinner.

Skin—Warts, many on hands which bleed easily. Many on trunk and back.

Stools—Constipation at times with lumpy, knotty stools. Sometimes offensive, yellow, watery stools.

Urine—Dysuria with straining. Urine clear like water.

Genitals—Swelling of genitals. Warts on external parts. Menses frequent, scanty. Menses watery at times, thick at times.

Extremities — Awkward gait. Cold hands and feet. Cracking in joints on movement. Red spots on arms and legs. Frequent small boils on legs. Trembling of hands and feet. Twitching of arms and legs when angry or excited.

This case presents nothing new to the homœopath as to symptoms, or course, nor anything unique as to treatment, but it seems to illustrate quite well Hahnemannic method and its superiority over expectant treatment. It shows how a human life may be handicapped from birth by disease, and how, retarded in development physically and mentally, that life may be led from darkness to light, from dwarfed apathetic non-usefulness to a fair degree of power in competition with its fellows.

A careful study of the case showed a close correspondence of the symptoms with three remedies, namely: Lycopodium, Sulphur and Thuja. The first two of these remedies are powerful antipsorics, and the last is the king of antisycotics. Hahnemann's rule regarding precedence of treatment when Sycosis and Psora are combined, was to treat the Psora first; therefore the first choice among these three remedies must be between Lycopodium and Sulphur. Another rule is not to precede Sulphur with Lycopodium in the beginning of treatment. So the first remedy given was Sulphur and as the case was a very chronic one it was given in high potency.

June 10. Sulphur^{cm} three doses two hours apart. No improvement was immediately expected. Necessarily the fight with deep seated disease must be a long fight.

Aug. 12. Another dose of Sulphur was given, and no change had taken place in the symptoms. This time, according to the rule to change the potency and to alternate a lower with higher potency when repeating remedy, the 10 m was given, one dose.

Oct. 7. As yet no response from the remedy. Sulphur^{cm}.

Dec. 1. The child's mother came with her and gave what she called "a bad report." The child now has more violent fits of temper.

Is very restless nights.

Wakes from sleep oftener in frightened dreams.

Has skipped a menstrual period and red blotches are appearing on many parts of body.

She stumbles in walking.

She is more peevish.

Has spells when she must go into open air for breath.

Has much running from nose.

Coughs all the time, sometimes raising blood in sprays.

Has itching all over body.

Twitching of limbs very bad, sometimes amounting to jerking.

She sees visions of persons in the dark of the bed room which frighten her.

Is sick to her stomach after meals.

Has ravenous appetite with foul breath all the time.

Placebo was given, for these aggravated symptoms pointed strongly to the stirring up of the system by the antipsoric remedy. Here was unmistakable homœopathic aggravation, the first step of the curative process.

Jan. 29. The child was again seen. The mother was more anxious than ever. Every day the child has screaming spells from severe colic caused by incarceration of flatus in the bowels, and is much constipated. Has had one period of menses, commencing Jan. 22, and ending the 26th, the blood being pale, with much itching of the genitals. There is offensive sweating of the feet. There has appeared an eruption of yellow spots on chest, back and legs. The mother says the girl once had a similar eruption several years previous, which was "cured" by zinc salve. Evidently we are reaching the foundation of the disease, thanks to potentized Sulphur which is actively at work, so its action was not disturbed.

Feb. 23. Passed another menstrual period, Feb. 15 to 20, with blood yet too pale, but having more color than formerly. Itching of genitals not so severe. Yellow eruption fading away. No more blood with cough. Cough not so severe nor so continuous. Breathes easier. Respirations which were thirty-four to the minute at commencement of treatment now twenty eight to the minute, and deeper. Coryza much less. Colic has ceased. Stools difficult. Otherwise the same. Mother thinks her girl is better. Placebo.

April 13. About the same as last seen. The action of the Sulphur was evidently waning, and now the important second choice of remedy must be made. As none of the natural followers of Sulphur seemed appropriate, the rule of Hahnemann in such cases, to intervene a Sycotic remedy, was followed. The symptoms (need not here be repeated) were well covered by Thuja, which was given in the 30th.

May 1. No material change in symptoms. Menses came on April 10, and ceased the 15th. Blood quite pale and offensive. It seemed proper again now to give Sulphur and it was administered in the 50 m.

May 30. Mother calls with the girl saying that "she flows all the time a very little, just enough to stain the underclothing a little." This commenced the 18th. Examination revealed the fact that figwarts on the vaginal membrane were exuding blood. The girl's legs now twitch badly, but she seems to walk with less awkwardness. A severe choreic affection of the arms, hands and head, has developed. These parts are in almost continual motion, except during sleep. Sleeps better except when she gets turned on the left side when she will be very restless and talk out in sleep. In the early morning hours will complain of feeling very cold and thirsty; this is followed by sweat on the parts covered by the bed clothes. Perspiration is greasy and strong smelling. More asthmatic breathing than formerly during sleep. Cough increased again. Raises green purulent looking matter. Glands of neck (cervical) swollen and tender. More cheerful than formerly and does not anger so readily. Is not so obstinate. Notices other children more, and plays with them more readily than formerly. The nodular swellings on the scalp are almost gone. Does not weep in her sleep now. Doesn't have so many bad dreams. Seldom dizzy mornings. Hair does not fall so readily, and new hair is growing all over the scalp. Not so much trouble with the eyes. Thinking the girl's nervous system might be relieved of some strain by some proper glasses, I examined her eyes with the following result:

O. D. V. A. six-ninths, with Minus 2.50 D. S. was normal.

O. S. V. A. six-tenths, with Minus 2.75 D. S. was normal.

No astigmatism in either eye.

I furnished her the above glasses to be worn contantly. Medicine was left to work undisturbed.

July 10. Menses came on May 31, and lasted until June 6, with much better color. Bleeding of the figwarts ceased a *few* days after I last saw her. The warts on hand are withering away. Warts on genitals are gone. The eyes are nearly free from agglutination and lachrymation. She now takes considerable interest in books, and is learning to read. Is brighter every way, seldom gets angry, is less obstinate. A good growth of hair is coming on the scalp. The teeth are better color, not so dark. She eats well and bowels are moving easily and quite regularly. Does not have diarrhea spells. Is not dizzy at all. No more thumping headaches. Walks quite well and strongly, and the choreic affection has almost ceased. Voice not so nasal and much stronger. Respirations twenty-four to the minute. Thirst for cold drinks has ceased. Will now take warm drinks with meals. Placebo.

Aug. 15. Improving every way. Is a different girl from what she was fourteen months back. Has grown plumper and stronger and taller. Teeth are now as good color and as regular as need be. Warts nearly gone. Takes interest in general matters like other girls. Is fully interested in books and is gaining knowledge rapidly under private teacher. The general symptoms are all relieved, but now has a thick pimply eruption on face and about all the larger joints. Sulphur^{cm}

From this time on she gained steadily, and while she was under surveillance for another year, she took no more medicine for the chronic complaints. She grew rugged and strong, a brand snatched from the burning, and, thanks to specific treatment, remains strong and able as most young women. She has regained mental strength to match the renovated physique, and holds her own in competition with her mates in a business college.

W. W. GLEASON, M. D.

Provincetown, Mass.

THE TOTALITY OF SYMPTOMS.*

Mr. President, and Members of the Texas State Medical Association, Ladies and Gentlemen:

Although I have been a member of this Association for more than a year, and for more than 10 years a resident of this state, I never before had the pleasure of meeting with this body.

It gives me pleasure now to greet you all as friends and brothers and I am glad to look into the faces of those who have troubles similar to my own. In fact, you are homœopathic to my case, and to be here with you and exchange trials and triumphs with you will add years to my monotonous life.

The first three or four years of my professional life were spent in northeast Missouri, with no other homœopathist within thirty miles of me. Well do I remember how I used to long for even a look at a homœopathic physician. I remember one came through our town once and casually dropped in to see me. I stood good for his night's lodging and other little necessities, and sent him on his way rejoicing. (He spent most of his time rejoicing anyway, but I am glad to know that most all homœopathists are sober and useful m·n).

I came up here to learn something, as well as to offer what I might in the interests of *pure* homœopathy. When I say *pure* homœopathy, I do not mean the high-potency man, nor the low potency man, but that method of procedure in harmony with the teachings of Hahnemann.

Pathological prescribing does not come in this line. I am sorry that so many of our physicians have almost, if not entirely, fallen into this rut. *There is nothing Homœopathic* that does not have for its base, *The Totality of Symptoms*, and that is my theme today.

It is deplorable that only a minority of the homœopathic physicians of the United States recognize the fact that sickness is *only* due to *morbidly disturbed vital force*. This vital force is unseen, yet it dominates our every act, and its condition is only observed by its effect upon the body which it inhabits.

It has been observed that the vital force or spirit like dynamis which animates our bodies is very susceptible to external influences and easily becomes deranged or sick, and manifests itself upon our bodies in various signs or symptoms, and those signs and symptoms are the only language of the disease which appeals to the intelligent physician for a remedy.

The aches, the pains, the sensations and all abnormal feelings of our patient, taken as a whole, constitute the totality of symptoms upon which, with their modalities, we are to base our prescription. If we believe in the sufficiently verified truth, promulgated by our immortal Hahnemann, that *like cures like*, then it is our duty to seek the remedy which has been well proven to produce upon the healthy the symptoms of our patient. Our whole Materia Medica consists of provings of drugs, or the symptoms they are capable of producing upon the healthy human being. All these provings, and all the laborious work and suffering required to obtain these provings are for naught, if they are to be set aside as obsolete, as they are by many who use our good name.

I am afraid a majority of the homœopathists today are seeking for their remedy among obscure pathological conditions, when they should know that there is nothing in the teachings of Hahnemann, Hering, Bœnninghausen,

*Read before the Texas Medical Association.

Lippe, Farrington or any of our other great masters, that teaches them to prescribe thus. On the contrary, all those old sages of homœopathy have taught us to prescribe for the totality of symptoms, or to give our patient a remedy which would be capable of making a well person similarly sick.

Suppose you are called to the bedside of a man who is reported to be very sick. You are told to go as quickly as possible. You walk into the room and find a strong man lying on the bed in a great state of excitement. His face is red as blood. Pupils greatly dilated. He is delirious and hard to control. He bites and strikes and tries to get up and jump out of the window. Before he became delirious he complained of a fearful throbbing headache. He became sick all at once and grew rapidly worse. The cause of his sickness was a mystery to all his household. Now will anyone kindly tell me the pathological condition present here? And if you successfully guess it, what rule of procedure have you in making your prescription that anywhere near approaches similia? Any student of homœopathy who would not have given that man Belladonna, upon the symptoms alone, regardless of any other knowledge, is not worthy to practice our noble art.

Why would you give him Belladonna? *Because*, when you were studying your Materia Medica, you remembered distinctly that Belladonna produced that very picture, hence would promptly cure it.

There is the key to the *whole* situation. We must *study* our Materia Medica, and study it unceasingly, so that when we go to the bedside of a patient and carefully take all his symptoms from head to foot, regardless of his pathological state, we may be able to select the remedy capable of producing the *totality of his symptoms*.

When I was practicing in Missouri I was called to a small town in the northeast corner of the state to see a lady who was at the point of death with what the allopathists called "pleuro-pneumonia." Suppose their diagnosis was correct; where do you find in homœopathy a remedy for pleuro-pneumonia?

I ask you, Ladies and Gentlemen, what would even the most rank homœopathic pathologist give for pleuro-pneumonia? I am very much inclined to say that he who attempts to prescribe homœopathically for that case, without taking *the totality of symptoms*, is a fraud, and the truth, or the light, has never dawned upon him.

I copy from my note book her chief symptoms: Her husband met me at the train and told me he thought I was too late to do his wife any good; that there had been three of the be t allopathic physicians in almost constant attendance for four days; that she had not eaten nor slept for a week and that opiates had entirely failed to give her rest.

As I entered the room, the first thing I did was to excuse eight of her overly kind neighbors, who were accommodatingly breathing all the oxygen from the available atmosphere. Then I paid my respects and careful attention to the patient. She was lying on the right side with a small pillow under her right breast and was afraid to move a muscle. Even the act of breathing caused her sharp, excruciating pains in her right lung. She was better lying on the painful side, because in that position her right lung was kept quieter. She had considerable fever and was extremely thirsty for large drinks of cold water. She was constipated and very dizzy when rising from lying. Whispering, she asked me if I could give her any relief.

Knowing my Materia Medica and having a thorough knowledge of the drug that is capable of producing the totality of her symptoms, I said, "Yes," in quite a positive tone of voice. Gentlemen of this convention, I did not care a snap whether her lungs were engorged or dry as a bone, whether hepatization had taken place or would take place. In fact, her pathological state had nothing to do with *me* or my prescription.

Why did I give her Bryonia? Simply and solely because it was capable of producing the *totality of her symptoms.* I got a letter from her husband twenty-four hours later, stating that his neighbors and every one else who knew of it, thought I had performed a miracle. After taking the second dose (they were given 30 minutes apart) she went to sleep, rolled over on her back and slept beautifully for eight hours. The nurse was tempted to awaken her, thinking she might sleep into death. How happy they all were when she awoke and ate heartily and with a relish, and was almost entirely free from pain. She made a rapid and uneventful recovery.

Now, in order to still further demonstrate what I mean, I will describe another case to which I was called five weeks later:

Lady suffering severely with pain in right ovary. Perhaps the diagnostician would call it "ovarian neuralgia," but that knowledge was no good whatever to me, for I knew of no remedy for ovarian neuralgia. I proceeded in my usual manner to objectively and subjectively take the totality of her symptoms. She was lying on her right side with a small book under the region of her right ovary. She was somewhat comfortable when lying still in that position, but the least motion caused sharp excruciating pains. She had a little fever, was very thirsty for large cold drinks, constipated, and dizzy when rising from lying. She had had ten or twelve of these spells in that many years and each succeeding one was harder than the former. It generally took her, assisted by old Dr. Brown, about a week to recover, but a few doses of Bryonia[m] settled the whole thing in less than five hours.

Why did I give her Bryonia? Simply because Bryonia can produce similar symptoms.

Now the symptoms of these two cases were exactly alike, yet the pathological prescriber is hardly likely to give the same remedy for pleuro-pneumonia that he would for ovarian neuralgia. These cases demonstrate most beautifully our great law. Such verifications fill us with enthusiasm and encourage us to "hew close to the line," never forgetting that the greatest achievements are wrought by those who the most faithfully carry out the teachings of Hahnemann.

My dear brothers, those of you who are living in doubt, and drifting into the sea of experiment and uncertainty, having no infallible law upon which you can base your professional actions, I would ask you to come back. Come back to "Similia Similibus Curantur," the great law of homœopathy, and one that is as everlasting and unchangeable as gravity or any of the other laws of God.

Learn the symptoms of drugs. Take the *symptoms* of your patient and prescribe according to our law, and ever remember that there is no rule under heaven to guide the homoeopathist in his prescriptions, except that based upon *the totality of symptoms.*

F. L. Griffith, M. D.

Austin, Texas.

A CURE BY CURARE.

July 2, 1902. Fraulein von H. of Jaagpad in Gouda, Holland, consulted me. She is unmarried and twenty-five years old.

The following is the history of her case:

She was received into the Academische Krankenhaus at Leyden in November, 1897, and operated on for prolapsus ani. As a result of this operation, which did not cure the falling of the rectum, there developed very soon after a traumatic neurosis, the symptoms of which were the following: As soon as Fraulein von H. lay down to sleep in the evening there occurred a complete paralysis of *all* the voluntary muscles. She could not see, speak nor move a muscle in the slightest degree; her eyes were closed; her hearing more acute than normal. The family said "she was apparently dead." This condition would last half an hour, more or less. Gradually she revived, with rumbling in the abdomen, rising from below upward.

Fraulein von H. had such attacks, increasing in frequency from 1897, at first two or three times a week, then four, later five and six, and finally, from February to July, 1902, she had one every evening.

It is not necessary to say that every kind of treatment had been tried, but all without any benefit.

I do not hesitate to confess that I saw but little hope for a cure, and, certain it is that she left my office without any such assurance. I am skeptic in matters of science and have no desire to pose as a psycho-therapeutist. There had already been much psychical treatment in her case.

I gave Curare, 6th trit. (Schwab) every evening some time before going to sleep. She took one-half of a very small teaspoonful of the powder.

July 26, she returned. I was indiscreet enough to begin my consultation in such a way as to betray my lack of confidence in being able to cure her. She then said that she was very much better, the attacks returning only after long intervals and then were only rudimentary. She was happy, and I was surprised. I ordered the same medicine to be continued.

August 16, she returned. She had been more than two weeks entirely free from an attack. Ordered the medicine to be discontinued. She was cured! What I had anticipated occurred. She begged earnestly to continue the powders or, at least, to let her keep them on hand to avert a possible return. Said she would rather travel without money than without the powders.

August 25, she still continued well. I inquired on all sides and learned that she was really cured and was full of admiration for the medicine. An allopathic physician of this place called the cure, which was indisputable, "an autosuggestion from the powders;" not suggestion by me, for he knows my suggestive ability or lack of it, rather. I call it a cure produced by a putting in practice of the beneficent law, *Similia Similibus Curantur*.

This may be discussed and questioned. I consider it a contribution to the action of the arrow poison of the Indians of which there is not, to my knowledge, complete physiological provings in the homœpathic sense. It is a pity I despaired of curing her or I would have observed the patient more frequently and more objectively during her complete muscular paralysis. Repentance, however, comes too late. My excuse is that my time was fully claimed by my practice.

A. C. A. Hoffman, M. D.

Gouda, Holland, Aug. 27, 1902.

The editor (Allg. Hom. Zeitung) adds a very valuable differentiation from Nux vom., which it resembles much, viz., the reflex action is diminished or abolished, while with Nux it is increased.

Editor Hahnemannian Advocate: This is from the *Allg. Hom.* Zeitung, and translated by me. Although the dose and repetition are not to my mind, yet it is valuable.

A. McNeil, M. D.

San Francisco, Cal.

CLINICAL CASES—ASTHMA.

Mr. D., aged 36, under sized, dark hair, black eyes; an active and energetic business man living on the West side. Mr. D. came to me six months ago suffering from quite a severe form of bronchial asthma of six years' standing.

The history of his case revealed healthy parents and a good family history in general. When a boy an attack of itch had been suppressed by sulphur ointment locally applied, and which never appeared again. He had been quite well up to six years ago when he caught a heavy cold on his lungs and was threatened with pneumonia. The cold gradually grew better, to be followed within a few months by the asthmatic trouble. He was compelled to sleep in a chair many nights, especially during the winter months or following acute colds, which he says came frequently. He takes cold so easily and it is invariably followed by an attack of the asthma, so he dreads the cold or the approach of cold weather. He is much better during the summer months, especially when the weather is warm and dry. His appetite is good, and he sleeps well until 1 o'clock in the morning, when he is usually awakened by difficult breathing and is compelled to sit up. Much thirst usually accompanies the asthmatic attacks following colds. He breathes better by leaning over the back of a chair, like Kali carb.; but his cough is easy and loose, with expectoration of much mucus which relieves. The 1 a. m. aggravation at night seems to be quite a constant symptom. Arsenicum[dm] was given, which afforded much relief, but did not cure the case.

The case was again taken, but he seemed so absolutely free from all symptoms outside of the asthmatic grouping that I felt quite discouraged in retaking his case; but the following symptoms were taken into consideration:

1.—Dread of cold;

2.—Worse during winter months;

3.—Takes cold easily;

4.—The suppressed eruption.

5.—He was always hungry, never satisfied.

From this concise little grouping Psorinum[cm] was selected, which promptly cured the case.

Case 2. Mr. D, aged 33, dark hair and eyes, but fair and ruddy complexion. He was strongly motive in temperament, somewhat impulsive in his makeup.

This patient had always taken quinine and allopathic medicines. Asthma of four years' standing, which has been very severe from the first, <, of course, after each fresh cold. His colds usually began in the head, and in a day or two passed down upon the lungs, ending in a severe bronchial cough often lasting for weeks. He had slept fully half the time in a Morris chair, always awakened at 1 o'clock at night, and compelled to sit up the remainder of the night. His breathing was difficult, laborious, tiresome, exhausting. In the morning he was completely exhausted often drenched with a cold, clammy perspiration. Mentally there was much anxiety as soon as the difficult breathing began. Thirst for small drinks of water was a constant symptom. He had lost twenty pounds of flesh during the past forty days.

The promptness of the return of the attacks each night was indeed remarkable, always at the stroke of 1 o'clock. There were many other symptoms in the case equally as characteristic, but I do not now recall them. Arsenicum^{dmm} in water during an attack, but only a few spoonfuls of the preparation was taken when he fell asleep.

This case continued to improve for one week, when he was taken with one of his dreadful colds and bronchial coughs. I never recollect having seen a strong man like my patient suffer as he did from a cold.

The remedy was continued, but his symptoms grew decidedly worse. There was great heaviness and weight in the chest; cough loose, but almost constant, < in the morning and evening; < lying down; throat sore, painfully so; aphonia almost complete; talking is difficult and painful and aggravates the cough very much. Patient is quite discouraged and contemplates a trip to Mexico.

Phosphorus^{cm} one dose, followed by a gradual improvement. Third week of treatment, aphonia almost gone, cough only very slight, throat and lungs much better.

Has taken Phosphorus only seven days. Treatment continued. Twelfth day chest symptoms gone, but a new phenomena presents itself for consideration which explains many things and reveals the whole mystery of his asthma. He is now suffering with a severe case of hemorrhoids, which bleed profusely. They are in the nature of severe hemorrhages. On questioning my patient more particularly I find this was the condition that existed prior to his asthma four years ago. For years he suffered from bleeding piles, as he called them, and for which he was operated on only to have them return, to be followed by a prolonged course of local treatments, which, as he expressed it, dried them up. Now, as he recalls the history of his case, the asthma developed soon after, and since that time he has had no trouble with the piles.

Treatment continued, which will no doubt cure the case completely.

The history of this case adds one more proof to Hahnemann's theory of the cause of asthma, for he says asthma is always due to some suppression or other. Here is a case of tubercular origin, and we know that it is the tubercular and sycotic patients who suffer most from suppressed diseases. The new bond with the life force is always a deeper bond than with the former, as is clearly seen in this case. The life force was eliminating the products of disease at a remote point in the organism and through an eliminative channel, thus protecting that organism from the inroads of a deep acting and malignant process. But some false healer of the sick, who knows not these processes of the living organism, and, from his lack of knowledge of the great and wonderful art of healing, turns the tide of that process, and thus a live saving process is turned into a death dealing one, and the organism is engulfed in the tempest and tidal wave of that process. Indeed, it is pathetic to know and see so many of our own physicians who have embraced homœopathy as a profession deal so carelessly and unscientifically with the most valuable thing on this planet, *human life.*

Hahnemann's theory of disease is the only true theory, and his dealings with the life forces the only true ones, for he works with the physiological processes of the organism, and never against them. The only thing that can assist us in a cure, with any system of medicine, is the life force, through these physiological processes. So, let us study along the lines of true physiological action and never turn our forces, no matter what there may be, against them.

J. H. ALLEN, M. D.

Chicago.

THE TWO COHOSHES.*

The Blue and the Black. Caulophyllum and Cimicifuga. Rheumatism and Uterus. Man and Woman.

When I have a general similarity of the two cohoshes I think of Caulophyllum in rheumatism, and, hence, in men's diseases; and of Cimicifuga in uterine troubles, and, hence in women's diseases.

This is not to say that Cimicifuga may not be used for men, or Caulophyllum for women. It merely says that for a quick distinction, in order to have a range finder, I have, after a number of years of confusion and trouble, arbitrarily separated the two cohoshes in this way. (I am speaking now to general practitioners, and am not lecturing to a class of undergraduates.)

If you will carefully study the two cohoshes, as you did at college, if not since, you will see running through them a general similarity. You have found that the head-symptoms of the one cohosh are so much like those of the other cohosh, that, like the old woman's test of good lye, the spoon will float—or sink—she wan't quite certain—that you are perplexed to know which of the cohoshes is which, and which isn't.

This is one of the greatest difficulties of our materia medica—this frequent and unhappy general similarity in allied departments of the human body. After spending some time tracing out in Caulophyllum, let us say, the headache, you feel confident that now you have that headache anchored high and dry beyond all peradventure of doubt; and yet, on a following occasion, when you take up the study of Cimicifuga you are amazed at the similarity in general lines.

Take that most excellent little brochure, Bell's Diarrhœa, and note how the same general peculiarities of bowel disease appear in the great majority of the remedies. If you study Bryonia for a while until you thoroughly understand that peculiar autumnal diarrhœa, and then turn to Colchicum or Colocynth, or other allied remedies, you can find your same autumnal diarrhœa with a mere shade of difference. The same is true of rheumatism, of typhoid fever, of coughs, of sleep, of sleeplessness, of urinary and uterine difficulties—in fact, as we old hands know, it runs through all individual department of the therapeutic list—a stubborn fact which all the more emphasizes the rule, if I may not, in a loud voice, call it a law—that as homœopaths we must not deal with disease names, or disease entities, but with the whole man or woman.

All are but parts of one stupendous
whole,
Whose body Nature is, and God the
soul.

My use of the two cohoshes has become very much of the nature of empiricism, based, of course, on a long and patient study of the two remedies from a homœopathic standpoint. But after a run of years of general practice, un-

* Read at the American Institute of Homœopathy, at Cleveland, Ohio.

consciously the homoeopathic remedies have ranged themselves in groups and classes, and if one is not ultra careful and a constant student, he will find himself driving along in ruts and grooves from which it will be most difficult to extricate himself.

If I touch a case of rheumatism, I find myself instinctively questioning my patient along the line of a half-dozen rheumatic remedies; fitting my patient to my Procrustean bed, rather than fitting the metaphorical couch to the patient.

No one knows better than myself that this is not homœopathic prescribing; but unless one is constantly engaged in study, or teaching a class of students, who look up to him from the depths of their praise-worthy innocence, and take everything that falls from his lips as and for gospel truth, and strive faithfully to give back the exact words in quiz, the general physician will find himself straying after the bread and butter essentials, and very much inclined to leave the fine spun theories and philosophies with the medical college professors, who, in order to vary the monotony of the century old materia medica, will oft times strives after odd symptoms, odd statements, odd results, picked up here and there in their reading, but not in their practice.

For a long while after I left my dear alma mater I thought only of Cimicifuga for the ante-parturient state. I had been taught that this remedy given in the 200th, a few disks each morning in the seventh month, would work that most wonderful of wonders, the strengthening of the circular fibers of the uterus, and thus shorten the hours of actual labor—just as Pulsatilla, given a few hours preceding the hour of supreme travail, would secure and insure a proper presentation, and as well assist in strengthening the longitudinal fibers of that same uterus. I had the implicit faith of the Scriptures, which is capable of moving a mountain; but after laboring with that mountain in labor for a number of years, and no special advantage accruing from the promised remedial effects of Cimicifuga, I fell away from the letter of the law and found myself straying in other pastures—to my homœopathic confusion be it told—but with good results. Now, when I have a case of obstetrics in prospect, somewhere in the eighth month, I direct that the expectant mother provide herself with an ounce package of squaw-root — Caulophyllum — the dry herb, and each morning, for a month, make for herself a cup of tea and drink as hot as bearable. Thus far this has helped me in my cases, though I could not prove it even "if Bill Jones was alive." My swans may all have been just ordinary geese, notwithstanding. But this I do know, that whereas under the former treatment with the 200ths, I had met with undesirable results and prolonged labors, now I have but little trouble even with primiparæ.

If I am in doubt as to the difference between the two cohoshes I apply my empirical rule of rheumatism and uterus—man and woman. For if I have the well-described rheumatism of the small joints I lean to Caulophyllum for either sex; which general distinction, of course, fails me when I come to Cimicifuga. There I have only the general conditions to save me from confusion and dismissal. Then I take up the head symptoms, and the sexual symptoms—for I find Cimicifuga a most excellent remedy in the seminal emissions—and this I have taken from the Eclectics, giving it in 10 to 30 drops after meals. For sleeplessness in either sex I know of nothing at this writing which will equal Cimicifuga—always adding, "if indicated," and it usually is in nervous, easily excited, ill nourished people who have overdone in mental work—while Caulophyllum devotes itself pretty much to the physical overdoing.

The classical symptoms of mental depression, "blueness" almost to distraction and suicide, so well described in the books as a cloud descending and enveloping the patient in Cimicifuga, is a very real one, and most precious indication. It has always been associated in my mind with that sensation reported from the obstetric patient, where chloroform has been administered to the obstetrical degree and the woman says: "I see you, Doctor, I hear you, I know what you are doing; but you have put a curtain between me and my pains." Cimicifuga drops a curtain—a "pall," it is called—between the patient and her right-mindedness. She knows what she is doing, but she is powerless to help herself out of her cloud of disheartenment and trouble.

I have found Cimicifuga a master-key to unlock the lumbar district when we have that troublesome lumbago of the parturient woman, and as well the unparturient man. But in the latter instance you will find some thing wrong in his sexual department as a primary source of his lumbago. In such cases I help out matters, in the male, with a cold compress to the lower part of the spine, and as men, as a rule, take most unkindly and profanely to cold water applied to the body, internally or externally, I always instruct the wife to see that it is properly applied. I am a little fearful of cold water to the parturient woman.

In the woman I find Cimicifuga a sovereign remedy "worth a guinea a bottle" in rheumatism, unless some other remedy is clearly indicated. In Cimicifuga I govern myself mainly by the cramping pains in the groins and back and legs, with the pall-like depression—and the general soreness and bruisedness—which latter might cause one to stray off into the arnica fields, except that Cimicifuga lacks the foulness and blue and yellow color of arnica.

The book says that in Cimicifuga there is soreness from over exertion, as in gymnastics, dancing, skating and the like. Unless, however, I have other distinct and clear cut symptoms calling for this remedy, I turn most confidently to Caulophyllum, because I have learned that Cimicifuga is more likely to be of a lazy disposition physically, while Caulophyllum is inclined to be active. In a general way I distinguish the two remedies in rheumatism by the cramping and twisting and squeezing pains of Cimicifuga, and the general soreness in Caulophyllum—the pains in the wrists and fingers, the ankles and toes, where they can't hold on to a cup or a pen, can't stand without turning the ankle. The latter, too, has a Pulsatilla symptom, in that the pains fly from point to point. But Caulophyllum is more often indicated in dark complexioned people of intense irritability, tears being a rare commodity, and good nature at a large premium.

One other empirical use of Calophyllum which has given me excellent satisfaction has been in thrush, that most troublesome complaint in mother and babe. I have found that 20 to 60 drops of a low dilution in a glass of warm water applied upon a swab to the visible sores will produce prompt amelioration, and I give internally in doses of the 12th or 30th once every four or five hours. Those of you who have run the gamut from boracic acid to sage tea and back to hydrozone and permanganate of potash will appreciate this little practical point.

I like Caulophyllum much better than Cimicifuga when abortion threatens. Of course in such danger I do not use the tea or the lower numbers. Then I employ the homœopathic attenuations and follow closely the homœopathic landmarks. For a time I was afraid to give the tea to the parturient woman, fearful of precipitating trouble. But I have used it now for a number of years and have had no accident. It is needless to add that I would not give this or any other possible abortifacient to a woman who has had former mishaps. I have discovered long before this time that there is a good deal in medicine beside medicine. And it is well to mix your medicines "with brains, Sir!"

In conclusion of my rambling remarks—for I have not attempted to lecture this audience on the differences between the two cohoshes, but only to point out a few special lines in one department for which both are used most often, I will say that I use Caulophyllum for rheumatic troubles in either sex, as a range-finder; and Cimicifuga when I have a general rheumatism in the gentler sex—meaning thereby God's last, best gift to man—woman.

FRANK KRAFT, M. D.

Cleveland, O.

CURED BY SULPHUR.

Jan. 4, 1902. Wm. W., aged 22 years, jammed thumb of his right hand in machinery while working in a shop, the day before Christmas.

A few days ago a pustule came on dorsum of ring finger of the same hand. He pricked it with a needle; suppuration followed. Allopathic doctor applied a flax seed poultice; condition grew <.

Present condition, finger and thumb a suppurating sore, hand swo'len, pain extends up arm.

As I proceeded to take this case the young man said:

He was well, always had been well, nothing the matter with him. (Some people don't know when they are sick).

My first symptom was, Couldn't heal a sore.

I asked, "How is your appetite?" The reply was, "First class." "For every meal?" "Oh, no; don't care anything about breakfast, and just as sure as 11:25 comes in the morning I have a hungry, gone feeling in my stomach."

I now had three legs to my stool:

Can't heal a sore.

No appetite for breakfast.

Hungry, gone feeling in stomach at 11:25 every morning.

In addition to this I learned that he was tired in the morning when he got up; that he used to dream of falling; thirst, drinks a great deal of water.

Upon these symptoms I gave Sulphur ^{mm}. The third day after the pus and blood poured out as if the lance had been used.

The pain ceased the next day, I washed the sores daily with a week solution of Boracic acid for cleansing purposes, as I have learned from experience that this does not interfere with the internal treatment. The sores began to heal rapidly from below upward and from without in.

Jan. 21. The hand was nearly healed, so that the bandage could be taken off from the finger, and by February 4th, the hand was entirely well; and, of course, the patient, who claimed he was not sick, was much better in a general way. I anticipate that under allopathic treatment this young man would have lost his hand.

JOSEPHINE HOWLAND, M. D., H. M.

Auburn, N. Y.

GRATIOLA.*

Gratiola officinalis. Hedge Hyssop. "The Herb of Grace." *N. O.* Scrophulariaceæ (grows in moist places). Tincture of fresh plant before flowering.

Clinical.—Cholera. Coccygodynia. Constipation. Cramps. Diarrhea. Dropsy. Eyes, affections of. Gastralgia. Gout. Hemorrhoids. Headache. Hydrocephalus. Hypochondriasis. Hysteria. Mania. Masturbation. Mesenteric glands, affection of. Neuralgia. Nymphomania. Tetanus. Vision, disordered.

Characteristics.—*Gratiola* is one of the most important members of the great Scrophulariaceæ group—*Digit.*, *Euphrat.*, *Tabac.*, *Scroph.*—and should be carefully studied with these. A large proportion of the effects of *Gratiola* are expended on the gastro intestinal tract. It is an inodorous plant, of bitter taste, and very poisonous, causing violent colic, diarrhœa, bloody stools, enteritis, jaundice, trembling of extremities, convulsions, cramps, excitement and disordered condition of the sexual powers, and death. Symptoms of a fully developed, rapid attack of Asiatic cholera are produced. On the other hand, the mind is strongly affected. Peevishness, ill humor; irresolute; hysterical; cerebral affections without fever. It is useful in mental troubles from overweening pride. Teste considers *Gratiola* the *Chamomilla* of chronic diseases. There is < during and after eating: vertigo during and after a meal. Hunger after a meal with feeling of emptiness. The diarrhœa is yellowish, gushing, watery, as though rushing from a hydrant. There is also vomiting of yellowish fluid. Summer diarrhœa from excessive drinking of water whether cold or hot. Soreness, burning or irritation of anus follows the stools. Two excellent cures with *Gratiola* have been recorded by C. W. Sonnenschmidt (*H. R.*, xi. 547). (1) Mrs. C., 53, attacked in June with diarrhea; yellow, watery, frothy stools gushing out with force. Severe cutting pains in abdomen; rumbling of flatulence. Occasional nausea and vomiting. *Coloc.* and *Ipec.* failed to relieve; then on close inquiry it was elicited that "a cold feeling in the abdomen" had been a feature throughout. *Grat. off.* 3, cured promptly. (2) A three-weeks' old infant was attacked with diarrhea and colic. There were two or three passages in quick succession, and then an interval of an hour or two. Passages green or yellow, watery, *frothy*, expelled suddenly; nausea, vomiting, severe pain *before* stools, relieved after, for a short time. *Cham.*, *Coloc.*, *Verat.* failed and *Grat.* rapidly cured. It also removed in this case "redness around anus, and on one side an abrasion of half an inch in extent, which caused some oozing of blood." E. E. Case (*Med. Adv.*, xxix 343) cured a woman, aged 50 of hemorrhoids with the following symptoms: (1) Constipation, difficult stools. (2) External piles from any exertion and after stool. (3) Biting, stinging tension in tumors. (4) During stool, a sensation as if the rectal membrane was torn. (5) After stool, all the nerves of the pelvis seem in a high state of tension; the flesh on the perineum feels as if torn from the bone. [Compare "Wrenching pain in coccyx."] Sleepless before midnight; peevish; melancholy. *Grat*[cm] cured.

Cooper has used it with great success in a case of gouty acidity with great constipation; and in the constipation of cancer. He regards it as "the vegetable antacid." It is said to have formed the basis for a once famous nostrum for

* Clarke's Dictionary of Medicine.

gout, "Eau Medicinale." Indications are: Constant sinking but cannot eat; bitter taste. The affection of the solar plexus is very marked; cramps beginning at pit of stomach, and pains radiating therefrom; anxiety; gnawing; empty feeling; rolling about in epigastric region. Urine is diminished, reddish, turbid. Buvier, says Teste, saw four cases of nymphomania in females to whom herb-doctors had given injections of a decoction of freshly gathered *Gratiola*. Burnett considers it specific in female masturbation and nymphomania. A number of pains are experienced in the coccyx. Chilly; shuddering on entering a warm room. Heat ascending to face, with redness and increased external warmth. Constant vaporous exhalation from body. Sensations: as if brain contracted; as if head grew smaller; as if brain would fall forward; as if sand in eyes; as if throat contracted; as if a stone rolling from side to side in stomach. The left side is more affected than the right. The head and eye symptoms are of the first importance. Rush of blood to head with vanishing of sight I consider a keynote. With *Gratiola*[30] I cured this symptom in a patient: "Sometimes everything seems to assume a yellowish tint, and occasionally, when I have been taking notes, a rush of blood to my head seems to shut the book from my sight and for the moment I have been unable to follow the speaker by writing although I could by thought." Motion $<$; rest $>$. $>$ In open air; $<$ in warm room (some headaches, and vertigo have the opposite modality). Coffee = neuralgia.

Relations.—*Antidoted by:* Caust., Bell., Euphorb., Nux v. *It antidotes:* Iodum. *Compare:* Apis, Bell., Helleb., Cham., Nux v., Elat., Pod. Hunger after meals with feeling of emptiness, Lauro., Calc., Cascaril., Chi., Cin.; (emptiness after *stool*, Petrol.); vanishing of sight and headache, Gels.; botanical, Dig., Tab., Euphr., Scroph.

Causation.—Abuse of coffee.

Symptoms.

1. *Mind.*—Serious, taciturn, absorbed in reverie.—Self concentration.—Irresolute, want of perseverance.—Ill humor, tired of life, apprehensive of the future; hysteria; hypochondriasis.—Loquacity and gaiety.

2. *Head.*—Whirling vertigo on shutting the eyes.—Vertigo when reading, and when seated, as if the head were waving backwards and forwards.—Headache, with nausea and drowsiness.—Intoxicated feeling during and after a meal.—Rush of blood to the head and feeling as if intoxicated in whole brain.—Violent rush of blood to head, with throbbing in forehead amounting to vertigo, with blackness before the eyes; $<$ by motion, especially riding, increasing even to loss of consciousness, only disappearing after several hours' sleep.—Pressive headache, especially in the forehead and occiput.—Lancinating and pulsative headache.—Sensation of heaviness in the forehead, as if the brain would fall forward, with stoppage of the nose.—Sensation as if the head were shrinking from contraction of the brain.—Sudden attack; sudden vibration in the head, which suspends the senses of sight and hearing.—The headache is $<$ when rising from a seat, during movement, and while walking in the open air.—The head is very sensitive to cold.—Heat in the head, on raising the head.—Tightness in the forehead with wrinkles in the skin.

3. *Eyes.*—Itching, quivering, and sensation of weakness in eyelids.—Itching of eyelashes.—The eyes feel dry and as if sand were in them.—Burning pain and pressure on the eyes.—Eyes watery and weak when reading.—Mist before eyes, when reading or writing.—Myopia on reading.—Sees distant objects better

than near ones.—While writing, or looking at light objects, sight suddenly vanishes; > by closing eyes, but constantly returns.—All objects seem white on opening the eyes, even green trees and turf.

4. *Ears.*—Tearing and shootings in ears.—Itching of the ears.

5. *Nose.*—Frequent sneezings, with shootings in left side of the chest and of the hypochondria.—Stoppage of the nose.—Smarting-itching in left nostril.—Pressure at upper part of nose.

6. *Face.*—Burning heat and redness of the face.—Tingling burning in malar bones.—Sensation of tension in the face; it feels swollen.—Swelling of upper lip (every morning, with stinging).—Tearing on one side of face—Painful crack in left side of chin

7. *Teeth.*—Nocturnal tearing or piercing in the molars.—Sensation of cold in the teeth.

8. *Mouth.*—Accumulation of much saliva in the mouth.—Accumulation of clear water in the mouth.—Mouth bitter and clammy.—Tongue rough, covered with mucus.—Fetid breath in the morning after waking.

9. *Throat.*—Pressure in throat, as from thick mucus.—Accumulation of mucus in throat.—Pain in throat obliging one to swallow constantly; the swallowing is difficult, as if the throat were contracted; < during empty deglutition.—Stinging in throat (left side).—Tingling, roughness, and scraping in throat.—Phlegm in throat, with inability to throw it off.

10. *Appetite.*—Gnawing, as from hunger after eating.—Constant sinking at epigastrium, but cannot eat.—Hunger, sometimes with loathing and horror of all food.—Increased thirst.

11. *Stomach.*—Bitter or sweetish risings.—Ineffectual efforts to eructate, with pressure from stomach to throat, which suspends respiration.—Empty or cold feeling in stomach—Hiccough.—Regurgitation of bitter water.—Constant nausea, with retching.—Nausea, with cold in the abdomen.—Vomiting, with stoppage of the nose.—Bilious vomiting, or vomiting of acid or bitter substances.—Uneasiness, and sensation of fulness in stomach.—Pressure on the stomach after a meal, with nausea.—Searching and digging in the stomach, with inclination to vomit.—Pressure on the epigastrium after a meal, as from a stone; which moves back and forth.—The sufferings of the stomach and of the epigastrium are often accompanied by nausea, or ineffectual efforts at eructation.—Paroxysms of inclination to vomit, > by eructations.—Rolling about in epigastrium.

12. *Abdomen.*—Shooting pains in the abdomen.—Beatings in left hypochondrium (heating pain, burning).—Pressive pain in abdomen, with pinchings (in umbilical region), which force the patient to bend double (> by the emission of flatulence).—Inflation of the abdomen.—Flatulent and pressive colic, with nausea and disagreeable risings.—Rumbling, with nausea, eructation, and vertigo.—Feeling of coldness in abdomen, lasting half an hour.

13. *Stool and Anus.*—Urgent and fruitless want to evacuate.—Constipation.—Fæces, hard, scanty, and tenacious, expelled with great effort.—Nocturnal slimy diarrhea, with tenesmus.—Diarrhea: stools, watery yellow-green, succeeded by burning at the anus; green frothy, coming out with great force.—Stools with burning and protrusion of large stinging, burning tumors.—Passage of fæces without being conscious of it.—Discharge of ascarides.—Pain, as from excoriation in the rectum.—Burning pain in the rectum, during and after the evacuation.—Shootings, itching, smarting, and throbbing in the anus.—Blind hemorrhoids.

14. *Urinary Organs.* — Diminished secretion of urine.—Scanty and reddish urine, which becomes turbid on standing, with cloudy sediment.—Burning in the urethra during and after micturition.

15. *Male Sexual Organs.*—Stitches in left spermatic cord, ascending through the abdomen up to the chest.—Painful rigidity of the penis after pollutions.—Drawing pain in glans.

16. *Female Sexual Organs.*—Catamenia premature, too profuse, and of too long duration. — Masturbation. — Nymphomania.—Irritable condition of sexual organs, with congestions.—Shootings in right breast, < on rising, during menses.

17. *Respiratory Organs.*—Dry cough, excited by a sensation of roughness in the chest, especially in the morning or at night.—Nocturnal cough, with pain as from excoriation in the trachea, oppression of the chest and shivering.—Choking when ascending.

18. *Chest.*—Heat in the chest, then the head and hands, with redness of the face.—Pressure on the chest.—Shootings in the chest on breathing.—Pimples on the chest, which burn after having been scratched.

19. *Heart.*—Palpitation of the heart.—Violent palpitation, particularly immediately after a stool, and with oppression of the chest.

20. *Neck and Back.*—Sensation as if the neck were seized with the hands.—Darting from the left scapula to the shoulder and mamma.—Sticking pain in lower dorsal vertebræ; in right kidney.—Bruised pain in loins.—Painful cramps in coccyx.—Pressive or wrenching pain in coccyx after stool.

22. *Upper Limbs.*—Rheumatic pains in the shoulders, arms, fingers, particularly in elbow and wrist-joint.—Itching in the palm of the right hand.

23. *Lower Limbs.*—Bruised pain in the thigh, after a short walk.—Lancinating tearing in tibia when sitting, disappearing when walking. — Smarting itching on the tibia.—Shootings in legs and feet.

24. *Generalities.* — Tearing in the limbs. — Tetanus, with full consciousness while lying down after a meal, followed by a deep sleep with emission of semen; bruised feeling of the body, back and left arm on waking.—The majority of symptoms appear at night, or when sitting, and after rising from a seat, or in the open air: contact > them.—Great langour and prostration.—Great loquacity and gaiety.

25. *Skin.*—Itching, with burning after scratching — Running and corrosive eruptions, which resemble scabies.

26. *Sleep.* — Irresistible drowsiness with yawning.—Great drowsiness, with frequent yawning and inclination to lie down, especially in the afternoon.—Deep sleep, like stupor.

27. *Fever.*—Pulse small, intermittent.—Great tendency to chilliness.—Chilliness in a warm room, during sleep, after an evacuation; with the hair standing on end.—Heat ascending to the face, with redness and increased external warmth. Constant vaporous exhalation from the body.

TWO CASES OF TETANUS TREATED WITH RHUS TOX.

While talking with a friend of mine in Cleveland last June, about reporting our cases in the journals he said, "We should report our failures as often as we do our successes." I wish to follow his advice in recording two cases which I treated last July. Tatanus was quite prevalent in certain parts of Iowa during the four months of June, July, August and September, which were wet.

On July 14th, Mr. W. F., aged 50, a farmer by occupation, came to my office stating that the day before, while endeavoring to save some hogs from being drowned, he was standing on the side of a box, which was on a farm-wagon, when his foot slipped letting him down about five feet. He landed upon a plank in which was a nail, point upward, which passed through his rubber boot into the ball of the great toe of the left foot, penetrating the bone. He continued to work in the water without removing his boot until night. The next morning there was pain running from the foot to the body; redness, especially along the course of the blood-vessels and lymphatics. He had been chilly several times and there was some stiffness of all the muscles of the body. As he had been at work in the water, and as this stiffness caused pain on motion, I gave him Bryonia. The next morning I was sent for. I found the man had been very restless all night; had two quite marked chills, followed by perspiration. The stiffness had increased so that it was almost impossible for him to move. About eight o'clock in the morning spasms of the muscles of the calves of the affected leg had begun and had been repeated every fifteen minutes causing excruciating pain. The pulse was 130; temperature 99.5 There was a good deal of drawing of the head backward as well as rigidity of the muscles of the jaw. Because the wound was in the tendons, because of the stiffness I gave the patient Rhus tox[6] and although the temperature was about eighty-five, I had him wrapped in flannels and hot applications placed around him. The Rhus was repeated every thirty minutes. Ten hours later the spasms had ceased and the stiffness was materially improved, the pulse 108. The following day he was still better and made a complete though tedious recovery, there following a good deal of ostitis with slight suppuration. I forgot to mention that upon my first visit I opened the wound through the periosteum to the bone, making a free incision.

Case 2. Two weeks later I was called to see E. W., aged 20, who, while fooling with a revolver, accidentally shot himself through the tendonous portion of the right leg, the ball passing through the leg. The leg was dressed by a physician of the dominant school with all aseptic precautions; forty eight hours afterwards, I was told, rigors began and six hours later trismus was quite marked. When I saw him he was lying over a cot so that his knees could rest upon the floor, his head drawn back almost at right angles with the spine; every once in about ten minutes would come a fearful convulsion; the stools were diarrheaic. The old school physician had given him strychnia, hypodermically. My other case being fresh in mind I gave him Rhus tox[6] two drops every half hour; having him wrapped up as I did the other. Four hours brought no result. Six hours more and as the patient was growing worse I gave an unfavorable prognosis, the result of which was the calling of an old school physician who took the patient to the hospital that night and operated the next day. The man died about a few hours after the operation. The operation consisted in making a free incision of all the muscles to the bone immediately over the wound. Why did Rhus work in the first case and fail completely in the second, is the question that has puzzled me ever since, for the group of symptoms, except for severity, were in my judgment the same in both case. Perhaps some of the readers of your journal can answer.

GEORGE ROYAL, M. D.
Des Moines, Iowa.

Medicine.

THE MOLECULAR THEORY AND SUBSTANTIALISM.

In connection with the article printed in *Good Health*, from Dr. J. H. Kellogg, entitled "New Glimpses into the Unknown," perhaps, this resume of the Substantial Philosophy vs. the Molecular Theory may be of interest to your readers. While it has been contemptuously ignored by the adherents of the Molcular theory, the more recent discoveries are forcing physicists to admit that earlier conclusions do not wholly harmonize with later revealed facts. We need not be surprised to find, some day, that the wise men, instead of classing X-rays and thought rays with air sound waves, expressing them as violations of vibratory motion (Crooke's table of ratios puts thought at *9,223,052 billions vibrations per second*) will turn about and perceive that sound, light etc., are to be classified with thought, all being various forms of simple substance with the properties herein enumerated. This is the view consistent with the Vital Force doctrine, the conception which has revolutionized the logic of disease and medicinal action, making it rational and thinkable.

Dr. Kellogg's article, in full, here follows:

New Glimpses into the Unknown.

The remarkable discoveries in physics that have been made within the last few years are a great shock to the self-complacency of those philosophers who have imagined that the atomic theory and the Darwinian hypothesis solved all the mysteries of matter, dead and living. The atomic theory though serving the chemist a useful purpose as a working hypothesis, has for many years been growing weak in its knees as a lucid explanation of phenomena. The discoveries made in relation to light and electricity have shown clearly enough that there must be something associated with matter quite different from ordinary atoms and molecules as understood by the atomic theory. The ether hypothesis has helped to piece out, but this, too, has fallen short. Now the X-ray and the Becquerel ray, and other phenomena, are brought forward with an array of phenomena which quite unsettle things for the chemist and physicist, and leave us all at sea respecting the ultimate constitution of things.

The discovery of light that could penetrate such opaque objects as a hardwood plank, two or three inches thick, and even thin sheets of metal, was sufficiently startling; but then the X-ray was produced by the electrical current, and we have become accustomed to look upon electricity as a sort of scientific wizard, and to expect new and startling things from those engaged in the study of this agent. It was not long, however, before the discovery was made that the X-ray, while opening to view the most obscure nooks and corners of the body, even penetrating the largest bones, and revealing the movements of the heart and lungs, and thus rendering the greatest service to surgeons and physicians, was at the same time a powerful agent for mischief, causing deep sloughs of the skin when too long applied, which showed great obstinacy in healing. But then this very baneful property was soon turned to good account in the treatment of certain parasitic skin diseases, particularly lupus, or tubercular disease of the skin.

But now comes the surprising discovery that the X-ray is not the result of any human invention, that it is not dependent upon electrical machines nor electricians, but that it is widely produced in nature, that the aurora borealis may be a manifestation of this marvelous force emanating from the sun.

The discovery has been made that there are earthly substances closely resembling lime or chalk in appearance, which as found in nature and without manipulation of any sort, are constantly giving off X-ray in great quantities.

Two of the substances, barium and uranium, have long been known to chemists; but a new substance, radium, has recently been discovered, which possesses this property to an extent ninety times as great as any previously known.

The new element possesses light in itself. It seems to be, in fact, a sort of crystallized or solidified light. A few grains of it shut up in a closed glass tube give off a light of sufficient intensity to enable one to read a book. A mass as big as an apple would serve as a table lamp; and a ceiling covered with it would secure perpetual daylight in a room.

Professor Thompson and others have shown that these luminous earths give off minute corpuscles which are less than one thousandth part as large as the molecules of hydrogen, heretofore supposed to be the smallest of all existing atoms. These corpuscles, or particles, are continually flying off into space at a speed almost equal to that of light, or nearly 180,000 miles a second. So small are these particles, however, that the ceiling of a room twenty feet square would, according to Professor Becquerel, give off only one two-hundredth of a grain of radium in one thousand years. Supposing the amount required to cover such a ceiling to be one hundred thousand grains, the supply of light would not cease or diminish in less than one hundred million years.

A wonderful property of this light is that, while it is given off by a cold body, it is capable of heating the objects on which it falls. The writer has seen a piece of platinum glowing at a white heat under these wonderful rays. They produce chemical effects as do the sun's rays. Many other astonishing properties have been pointed out.

These observations throw a new light upon the constitution of things. We no longer need think of the sun as a big bonfire, likely to burn out some day, and leave the solar system to freeze up. It has been noted that radium or X-ray corpuscles will combine with nothing on the earth, but fly away into space. Who knows that this luminous matter is not being continually given back to the sun as fast as it is given out?

The spectacle of light and heat coming out of a cold, opaque body like chalk, opens a field for scientific speculation not likely to be soon exhausted. It may be that the scientific world will discover at last that the inspired word which declares, "God is light" is a simple statement of a profound and fundamental scientific fact. The discoveries of Becquerel, Currie, and Sequin in relation to the emanations from metals open new and most wonderfully interesting fields for thought, and give hints of greater discoveries, whole new fields of discoveries, yet to follow. At last we may be able to see clearly the deep philosophy of Paul's declaration, "In him we live and move, and have our being."

The Molecular theory has been taken as a positive basis in scientific teaching and speculation since its advancement, and upon it are raised all doctrines, by it are explained all phenomena, commonly observed in the world of science of today. While it is thus used as though it were known to be absolutely true, yet the foremost scientists say in speaking of it that it is only *theory*, supposed to be true, which may yet prove to be false; that while it is used as a basis of all calculation, it may be wrong; thus showing that it is not entirely demonstrated and is not accepted as infallible, only the best at hand.

If any fact can be demonstrated to be at variance with the elements of the theory, it can not then be accepted as an adequate law of nature.

Some points in the theory have been attacked and questioned and these points must be harmonized and fully explained before the theory fulfills the requirements of a basic law of the world's phenomena.

(a) The Molecular theory affirms that all substances are composed of minute particles, *indivisible* units. In the elements these are called atoms. In substances formed by combination of elements, these atoms combine to form molecules. Elements are composed of atoms, *incapable of division*. Compounds are formed of molecules, *units incapable of further subdivision*.

(b) It further states that these molecules are always in motion, not closely in contact, but in motion, striking against each other, maintaining a continual bombardment and motion within the limits of the mass of substance.

(c) The distance between these molecules is said to be equal to many times their diameters, but in their velocity they strike upon each other and rebound by the force of the contact.

(d) The motion of the molecules is said to be kept up by the change of temperature. This change of temperature results from the varying force and rebound of the ether particles, all the space between the molecules being filled with ether.

(e) The original cause of the molecular motion and the cause and origin of the motion of ether particles are left without explanation, considered intrinsic, inherent, but the *theory offers no origin for it*.

(f) When a mass is compressed into smaller volume, as in compression of air (for example) the theory asserts that there is no change in the molecules themselves; they are forced closer together, the inter-molecular spaces are lessened and the molecules come in contact more often, with greater rapidity and force and thus, the motion being increased, the heat is increased.

(g) The forces of heat, light, sound etc. are said to be *different kinds of motion* of molecules, one form of motion being convertible into the other.

These are the main elements of the Molecular theory. But these bring up several points which the theory does not satisfactorily explain to a rational mind.

(a) It has been freely demonstrated that substances may be divided beyond the limits of the "indivisible atom" or molecule. A measured quantity may be mixed with water or other substance, in definite proportion, say 1-100th, and part of this may be further mixed, 1 part to 100, of the same dividing substance (water), as the division may be continued until by calculation in 1 100 part there there would be none of the original substance. Yet such a substance is demonstrated to be present by the action of this mixture upon other things. It has different effects from those of water alone; it shows different results under the influence of electricity etc. For water alone it has the effects of that original substance in different degree. Hence the *divisibility* of *substance* is *not* to be *limited* as by the Molecular theory.

Consider next the statement regarding the constant molecular motion.

(b) By a physical known law, when two bodies meet, forcibly striking together, and rebound, the rebound depends upon the elasticity of the bodies. The parts which come in contact are forced to change their positions relative to the mass, a sort of indentation occurs as they meet, and the rebound is due to these parts re-assuming their former positions relative to the body. That is, the parts of the body "a" change posi tion and again resume the positions they sustained to each other before the body "b" came in contact. There is thus compression of parts with consequent indentation and subsequent expansion.

(c) If the parts of the molecules change position in relation to each other, the molecule must be further divisible, or no compression and indentation could occur and there could be no rebound. The theory states they are indivisible, therefore they must be, admittedly, inelastic.

(e) If the inelastic bodies come continually in contact with each other, they adhere, coming together with great force. The continual collision would thus gradually diminish the motion, in time destroy it, neutralizing it by contact, and the bodies adhering would at length become at rest in contact. If masses contain molecules in continual motion, how can the mass, made of these molecules—moving parts—be at rest? What fixes the limit of the motion and maintains the mass in the self same, unchanging shape, the same outline? There is no explanation. There is no explanation of the maintainance of molecular motion without extraneous force.

(f) If compressing a mass is bringing molecules closer together, when the particles have bombarded each other and come to rest in contact, being inelastic, no compressibility would be possible.

(g) No motion being present among the particles, there would be no possibility of forces exerted in the mass—no heat, light, motion, electricity, magnetism—if these forces are forms of motion of the molecules.

Large masses are known to be more stable than small ones. In a large mass, there being greater number of molecules, there would be more motion. Why would this not make the mass more unstable?

Until these discrepancies in the Molecular theory are corrected and elucidated, until all phenomena within its scope can be harmoniously conformant to its principle and all parts of the theory are consistent, and only mutually but with the *known laws* demonstrated to be true, the Molecular theory is not sufficient as a basis of reasonable philosophy, and some doctine must be sought that will more adequately explain phenomena as they exist.

(a) Such a doctrine has been formulated and applied to the phenomena of the world—by the term SUBSTANTIALISM. This supposes that substances are *infinitely divisible* beyond the limit of material calculation.

(b) That as substances in mass are at rest, except by the application of extraneous forces, what is true of the whole is true of the parts composing it, and the *particles are at rest.*

(g) That forces of different kinds are forms of *immaterial substance,* delegated agencies, with power to move matter, derived from the first fountain of all force, first cause of all things.

That all motion in material substances is the result of the action upon them of these immaterial substances, usually termed *forces*—heat, light, electricity, magnetism, sound, gravity etc.

This whole doctrine rests upon the possibility of the existence of two kinds of substances, one *material,* the other *immaterial.* The first is that usually known as matter, apparent to the senses, having all the physical properties of matter, such as form, size, weight etc. The second is not recognizable by the senses, manifest to the senses only by its effects upon material substances; known to the thought, reason, the unseen elements, acting on, in and through the seen.

This immaterial substance or *simple substance,* recognized only by the understanding, belongs more to the realm of thought, embraces such existing entities as life, will etc. It cannot be manipulated or demonstrated in any way to the senses, save by its *power and influence on material substance;* as in electricity, nothing is apparent of it until it acts on masses, which it may propel with great power and controls, even through other masses.

It is subject to change, i.e., it may exist in order or in disorder. It is endowed with influx and subject to all laws of influx, namely, it follows the course always of least resistance; it is continuous from source to ultimate. As in a chain of links connecting two objects, if one link is broken, or severed, there is no connection between first and last; if one link is weak, no part of the chain is stronger than that link; if connection is severed, the disturbance breaks all connection between the last and first, but up to the point of severence it continues. So if the influx of simple substance or immaterial substance is disturbed and connection broken, the influx ceases from the point of severance on to that which was the ultimate.

It is endowed with formative intelligence, controls material formation, its ultimates are in material substances, its source is the first cause of all formation.

There cannot be predicated of it, *weight, space, time,* it is not *subject to the laws of time, space, weight.*

It occupies material substance without displacement of the material.

It has only quality, as expressed by degrees, it exists from highest to lowest degree, from innermost to outermost; only quality can be predicated of it.

It is subject to reduction from that in which it exists, but being thus reduced is not subject to restitution, cannot be restored as it was.

It is subject to reduction from that in which it exists, but being thus reduced is not subject to restitution, cannot be restored as it was.

It may exist as discrete, compound and complex. Different forms of immaterial substance may exist separately from each other, (1); or may act together as compound, two or more act in unison, (2); or they may be complex, one form dominating another or others, (3); in such cases each exists from the highest to the lowest degrees, yet harmoniously, with no discordant disturbance.

Such is the nature of simple substance and of such is each force supposed to be, acting upon material substance, occupying matter, and otherwise subject to the above conditions.

Explained by this doctrine, the phenomena of the world follow harmoniously the conditions of the doctrine and corroborate such reasoning with but one great mystery—the original cause—from which all originates while minor details need not be set aside as unexplicable in its lights, but all consistent and complete, more satisfactory than the uncertainties and inconsistencies of the Molecular theory to a reasoning mind that demands something definite and tenable.

JULIA C. LOOS.

Harrisburg, Pa.

SIGNIFICANCE OF SEXUAL PERVERSION IN DISEASE.

(Continued from September).

From certain well established facts we have drawn conclusions that seem to have a bearing upon disease manifestations in general more important than usually recognized by the profession. They not only clear up many of the perplexing questions in their etiology but suggest a line of treatment that offers great inducements to the patient, but persistent, student of the healing art.

It is not our purpose to discuss the ethical questions involved, but to take the facts as we find them and seek to determine their significance from a medical standpoint, in the light of modern investigation.

In analyzing these facts, an exhaustive study is impossible, because a single proposition would demand more space than can be given to the entire subject, hence the suggestive character of its presentation.

Matter is always acted upon. The force is always dynamic in character. Before there can be an act there must be the desire for the same. Before there can be a perversion of the sexual function there must be a perverted desire. It therefore becomes necessary for us to consider the factors entering into the normal

Sexual Desire.

It is a part of the general plan of creation that the production of living organisms shall be dependent upon the combined acts of the male and female; and every female is so formed that she must be acted upon by the male. In the lower forms of life the process seems to be dependent upon forces acting from without, but as we advance in the scale of development this outside influence gives place to a form of mental direction, known as instinct, through which the female indicates her desire and invites the union with the male.

When we come to the highest form of development as shown in man, new factors enter into the process through the complicated combination of mental faculties. A longer period is required for the development of these mental faculties and few are the safeguards thrown around these growing minds during this important period of adolescence; and such safeguards as have been employed have tended to such a perversion of the original plan that a free and full discussion of this all important subject is restricted to medical publications, while the entire world have a morbid—a perverted—craving for knowledge.

Fascinating as would be a discussion of this phase of the subject, we cannot digress from our purpose of dealing with the facts as we find them, leaving the causes for some future discussion. The first fact that we wish to consider in this connection is the reversal of the original order in which the female invited the male to come to her. This carries a deeper and more significant meaning than appears upon the surface and is one of the logical products of the artificial and utterly unnatural plan evolved by man for the development of the race, which has as its basic principle well expressed in the declaration—Might makes right, and the survival of the fittest.

It may be true that man was designed to be the leader and that to him was entrusted the life principle, but facts do not seem to justify the conclusion that this gives to him the right to make of woman, a slave, subject to his wish and selfish desire; although the perversion can not be attributed so much to this cause as to the home training, or lack of the same, generally prevalent throughout the civilized world.

The necessary development incident to the process of reproduction is proportionate to the importance of the object to be created, e.g., the lowest forms of animal and vegetable life reproduce after their kind within a few moments after their own birth, while with man, in a generic sense, many years of development are required before it is possible for even the lowest grades of the species to be reproduced.

It is worthy of more than passing notice that as soon as the *normal* female has completed the necessary preparation for the reproduction of her species *she is ready to assume the responsibility.* The same may be said of the male. This normal state ends with the lowest type of the genus man. Up to this stage in the evolution of man, *sexual* desire occupied a subordinate place in the functional activities of the race; the *desire was made manifest by the female and satisfied when impregnation took place.* There was no concealment, no false modesty, no mental anguish, no perversion. During the period of reproduction, followed by that of lactation, there was no desire and all the surplus vitality was directed, by the sub-conscious mind, to the perfecting of the physical organism of the newly created offspring; and as a rule, all physical defects could be traced to *causes from without*; and great care was therefore taken to protect the child from *external* disturbances if the species being propagated was of sufficient value.

As soon as the *mental* factor entered into the equation, a *disturbing* element is recognized and *perversion* becomes the rule. It was no idle fancy, no mere accident that secured the incorporation of that singular passage in the second chapter of Genesis: "*But of the tree of the knowledge of good and evil thou shalt not eat of it: for in the day that thou eatest of it thou shalt surely die.*"

It is a significant fact that the knowledge of right and wrong is one of the very first mental faculties to be developed; and the employment of this prerogative determines the elevation or perversion of its future life. Note the order: sexual activity begins with and is co-exist with life itself; sexual perversion is practically unknown so long as the subconscious mind is undisturbed in its action; structural changes may come about by reason of defective or deficient nutrition, exposure or mechanical injuries, but *sexual perversion always comes from within, and is mental in character.*

A little knowledge is dangerous and for thousands of years the human race has been suffering from the misdirected efforts of this reason gifted mind. The physician who would see permanent results follow his treatment of all disease manifestations must give due prominence to the mental phase of the disease, and while the treatment may be directed to the removal of every disturbing influence from without, the mind must be diverted from its usual trend and positively occupied with something else.

Those who have not learned to appreciate the importance of the mental factor in every phase of disease manifestation will do well to carefully follow these suggestions to their logical conclusion, because it not only harmonizes with Hahnemann's dynamic theory of disease but opens up a broad and very profitable field for investigation.

As we stated in the beginning, all sexual perversion may be traced to a mental origin. We may go farther and state that this origin, directly or indirectly, is selfish—the gratification of selfish desire regardless of its effect upon others

—and leads us back to the basic principle of certain cults, who fail to note the difference between a half truth and half of the truth that sin and disease are synonymous terms.

The sexual instinct is purely animal and in its *normal* state becomes a reliable index of the vitality of the organism. Its functional activity is easily satisfied so long as there is no restraint but as soon as the gratification of its normal desire is restricted, the selfish faculties seem to combine and raise that function out of its legitimate sphere and make of it a center around which all else radiates. This does not apply to sexual perversion alone, but points to the beginning of a diversion of the vital force from its general oversight, and focuses it upon some particular function at the expense of the rest of the economy.

H. W. PIERSON.

(To be continued)

FADS IN MEDICINE.

Not every medical man is capable of becoming a faddist, but the number who manifest marked ability in this direction is by no means small.

Representative men of the faddist persuasion are found in all branches of medicine and surgery, with a particular tendency to become manifest in the most recent medical and surgical discoveries.

That we may not wander in uncertain paths in this brief paper, let us define, first of all, in what a fad consists.

"A fad," says the Century Dictionary, "is a trivial fancy adopted and persued for a time with irrational zeal."

"A matter of no importance, or *an important matter improperly understood*, taken up and urged with more zeal than sense."

These definitions will cover most of the ground occupied by medical and surgical fads.

We are all too well acquainted with certain surgical fads. The appendicitis fiend, who would operate for every suspicion of trouble in that region, however slight, or even when there are no indications of anything abnormal, would operate to remove the normal appendix vermiformis for fear of possible trouble.

This faddist may be set down as "having more zeal than sense."

Next in order is the orificial faddist, who derives all the ills to which flesh is heir, from "impingement of terminal nerve filaments," whatever that may mean. He also must be set down as not far behind his appendical brother. His idea may not be altogether a "trivial fancy," but it is at best an "important matter imperfectly understood," and he is very prone to urge it with "more zeal than sense."

Many other fads there are in surgery, too well known and too potent to need mention.

There are faddists in diseases of the eye, of the ear, of the throat, of the chest, of the heart and circulation, of the liver, the kidneys, the digestive tract, the lymphatic system, the brain and spinal cord, the skin, faddists in diet, in climate, in environment, in any of the narrow fields to which the medical man may restrict himself. They look at disease and all abnormal manifestations from the single standpoint of their own special fad.

This most naturally leads to an "imperfect understanding" of the situation, and the relative value of their favorite theme.

The faddist looks at his favorite topic through the small end of the microscope, and all other claims to recognition through the large end.

The faddist is a prejudiced man; he remains prejudiced because he prefers to be so. He renders himself ridiculous in the eyes of sensible people, because he pursues his theme with "more zeal than sense."

What is the cure for this condition? Evidently there is no better cure than the most natural one—*publicity*. Let each dog have his day and he will ultimately execute himself with the superbundance of tether. If weeping were needed, tears would never cease to flow for the self-slain faddist.

Fads in giving drugs; fads in treatment; fads assigned for "imperfectly understood" causes of disease; fads in the use of drugs; fads in withholding drugs.

The medical man should above all things *not* be a faddist. His views of morbid changes, of the means and methods of relief, of the inter-relationship of all parts of the "whole machine," should be as free as possible from bias, prejudgment and narrowness. Unfortunately the opposite state of mind too often prevails. One result of this condition of things is an immense amount of silly, zealous expositions of the causes and cures of disease with which medical literature teems today. The "medical-boiler" man, the "medical-scrub-brush" man, the "electrical vibrationist," the "dietary fiend," the "sun-cure," "water-cure," "grape-cure," "osteopathic cure," "mind-cure," "absent-treatment-cure," are all grades and varying degrees of "zeal without sense."

Doubtless there is a grain of sense in a bushel of chaff in all of these, and scores of other fads. They are all too often *trivial fancies* adopted and pursued with irrational zeal; and at best they are "important matters imperfectly understood, taken up and urged with more zeal than sense."

M. W. VanDenburg, M. D.

Mt. Vernon, N. Y.

Nursing.*

FEEDING OF THE INFANT.

Lecture No. 13.

Ladies: It is a great advantage to mother and child to have the child fed by the mother. For the mother, it produces vigorous contractions of the womb and greatly hastens her recovery. For the child, it avoids indigestion and is the best hope that the child will survive. Every effort, then, should be made to establish and continue nursing. This, however, may wholly or partially fail. A mother may be so debilitated that very little milk can form, and the child be in danger of failure from lack of nourishment. It may be better to assist the mother by partially feeding the child, while allowing it to take what the mother can supply.

In these cases the best results are obtained by having the mother nurse during the night and early morning. When she is at rest a quantity of milk sufficient for several meals for the child will accumulate, and her rest at night must be taken advantage of for this purpose. Milk for the child should be prepared in the forenoon, and if the mother nurses the infant during the night and in the early morning a fresh supply of cow's

*Course of Lectures delivered to the Nurses Training School at Maryland Homoeopathic Hospital, by E. K. [illegible], M. D., Baltimore, Md.

milk will be ready to supplement the mother's nursing.

It must be remembered that it is not the part of a trained nurse to prescribe food for an infant. The physician should prescribe the food as he would prescribe medicine, giving written or printed directions for its preparation, and these orders the nurse must follow.

In mixed feeding, physicians often prefer to use cow's milk partially digested. Materials for peptonizing and pancreatizing milk are furnished for this purpose, and printed directions are given for this process. In peptonizing and pancreatizing milk care must be taken that the milk is not bitter. If it is heated too long with the ferment, digestion goes so far that compounds are formed which in the body are produced in the small intestine. These compounds are very soluble, but bitter and unpleasant to the taste. Peptonized or pancreatized milk must be heated as short a time as possible to bring it to the change desired. It then remains perectly sweet and agreeable to the taste. In mixed feeding only milk and milk mixtures are necessary, as the child is too young for some of the articles of food which may be used to advantage later.

In selecting bottles the nurse must choose those of medium size with rounded surfaces, and having short necks upon which a rubber nipple may conveniently be placed. Under no circumstances should a bottle having a rubber tube and nipple be employed. Round bottles of medium size are very convenient, as the child can grasp them better when taking its food. Bottles must be cleaned by boiling in a solution of sodium bicarbonate, rinsing thoroughly with boiled water, and keeping in a saturated solution of boric acid. A brush for cleansing bottles can be obtained at house-furnishing shops. If a bottle becomes coated with a layer of albuminoid material, it may be necessary to employ a strong alkali or at times use shot in cleansing the bottle.

The best quality of black rubber nipples should be obtained, and care should be taken that the holes of the nipples are not too large. The nipples should be turned inside out to be cleaned with soap and water. They may also be boiled, and should be kept in boric acid solution when not in use.

The artificial feeding of an infant is a matter in which the faithful and intelligent co operation of the nurse is of the utmost importance. In her own field, she can do quite as much as the physician to bring about the successful growth of the child. She must necessarily have the confidence of the mother as well as that of the physician.

As milk is the food usually chosen, the nurse must know something of the composition and care of milk. The milk of cows is usually selected. The mixed milk coming from several sound, healthy cows of ordinary breed, fed on clean pasture, should be selected. It is well to avoid fine breeds of cattle, as the milk is often excessively fat, and such cattle easily become tuberculous. Good milk, like good wine, when poured into a glass and the glass tipped to one side should leave a distinct film on the empty side of the glass. Sound cow's milk is neutral or but very slightly acid or alkaline in reaction, has the characteristic odor of fresh milk, and has a dense white color. So soon as milk is obtained at the house it should be put upon ice, and under no circumstances should a bottle be opened unless the entire contents of the bottle or jar are to be used. If only part of the contents of the bottle is required, the remainder must be used in cooking, when it can be boiled or scalded.

To keep and prepare milk properly for a child, the nurse must have exclusive charge of the refrigerator in which the milk is kept. Nothing but milk should be kept in it. In addition to a nursery refrigerator, apparatus for pasteurizing or sterilizing milk must be at hand. The Arnold sterilizer is a good one. From a reliable druggist milk-sugar must be obtained in convenient quantities, lime-water, and litmus paper. Brushes for cleaning the bottles, bottles and nipples, as already described, must be procured. The nurse will require a vessel holding from one to two pints, which can be kept exclusively for the purpose of mixing the milk and of such a character that it can be made absolutely clean.

The physician will prescribe that the child should have so many ounces of such a mixture at certain intervals. Multiplying the number of ounces in each feeding by the number of feedings, the nurse ascertains readily the total amount required. It is well to provide one or two extra bottles, as one bottle may become broken or the child may take a little from it and refuse the rest, and the milk cannot be used. The physician must distinctly state whether he does or does not wish the milk to be boiled before it is taken. It is usual not to heat milk beyond the point of scalding for a few moments. This is practically pasteurizing the milk. Strictly speaking, heating the milk to 167 degrees for six minutes is termed pasteurizing it. To sterilize milk, it is brought to the boiling point, 212 degrees, and continued at this point for from twenty minutes to one half hour. It is seldom necessary to prepare milk but once in twenty four hours. If the milk be perfectly sound, and the nurse is absolutely clean with the utensils employed, and if the ice-chest be a good one and absolutely clean, pasteurized milk will keep readily for twenty-four hours or more. Sterilized milk will keep much longer. In the majority of cases pasteurized milk is preferred, because sterilized milk does not always nourish the child. After the whole quantity has been prepared it should then be put through a glass funnel into the number of bottles selected, so that each bottle contains the number of ounces of the mixture to be taken at each meal. The bottles are then to be corked with cotton which has been made sterile by baking or steaming. The bottles are then placed upon ice until time for feeding. When a bottle is required it is taken from the ice and warmed in a basin of water until it feels slightly warm to the hand, the cotton stopper is removed, and a nipple taken from the boric acid solution is placed upon the bottle. It is then given to the child to nurse. For warming a bottle at night a suitable apparatus can be procured at any house-furnishing shop, which can be placed upon a gas fixture. By scrupulous cleanliness and aseptic precautions on the part of the nurse very much can be done to provide proper nutrition for the child.

Cases sometimes arise in which the advice of a competent physician can not be immediately obtained. Under such circumstances the nurse must do as well as possible for the infant until a physician can arrive. To make one quart of food for an average healthy infant the following may be used:

Milk, 2¼ ounces.
Cream, 5¼ "
Lime-water, 1⅗ "
Milk-sugar, 1⅗ "
Water to make one quart.

For a premature or feeble child, the following may be used:

Milk, 1⅜ ounces.
Cream, 2⅝ "
Lime-water, 1½ "
Milk-sugar, 1 "
Water to make one quart.

In addition to milk prepared under

precise directions, predigested milk is often used. Physicians may dilute milk with barley water or oatmeal water. The nurse must be able to prepare either of these in a suitable manner.

In making either, the best quality of meal or grain should be used, and should be boiled until completely and very thoroughly softened. It is not desired that the infant should obtain any of the harder or irritating portions of the grain. Accordingly it must be made softer than when eaten by adults. The gruel should be strained through sterile cheese cloth or gauze, and the fluid so obtained may be used to dilute the child's milk. This may be added to a bottle containing milk, cream, lime water, and milk-sugar without making an unpalatable mixture.

Beef-juice is sometimes added to the bottle of a young child, or in cases of illness may be given to the child instead of milk. It is prepared by selecting a good piece of steak, broiling it on both sides quickly before a hot fire, and then squeezing the juice with a lemon-squeezer. Children sometimes take this better when a little salt is added to it. White-of-egg water is prepared by beating up the white of a fresh egg with four to six ounces of pure water. This may be sweetened with sugar of milk to an agreeable taste.

Cases are sometimes seen in which it is almost impossible to induce the child to nurse through a bottle. Food must then be given by a medicine-dropper or by a spoon. It is hard to maintain strict asepsis with such feeding, but the nurse can at least be absolutely clean, and this is often sufficient.

Nurses must be cautioned to avoid giving to children mixtures for colic. The nurse must not be deceived in imagining that the child has colic because it cries. Its diaper may be wet, or a pin or some portion of its clothing may be irritating the skin. Thirst is often mistaken, and several teaspoonfuls of water will often cause a crying child to be quiet. Gentle massage of the abdomen is very useful in these cases to aid in the expulsion of gas. In the absence of medical attendance the nurse should content herself with emptying the child's rectum with an injection of warm soap suds, and with giving the child water as hot as it will take it, to which are added a few drops of essence of peppermint. Further treatment should come from the physician.

It is a great convenience to a physician in treating an artificially fed child if the nurse will record the number of feedings and the amount of food actually taken. In this way an accurate idea is gained of the amount of nourishment which the child is really obtaining.

Nurses should be familiar with the appearance of the stools in breast fed and artificially fed infants. In healthy breast fed children, when digestion has become established, the stools are bright yellow, two or three in twenty-four hours, and the consistence of a soft paste. When the infant is fed upon cow's milk the stools are lighter in color, thick, and more tenacious. Sometimes a distinct curd can be seen. The healthy infant's discharges are neutral or slightly acid. If strong acidity be present, or if the stools are markedly alkaline in reaction, some disorder of digestion is present. Should the stools be green with mucus, blood, or pus, the nurse must report at once to the physician.

It is often necessary to form proper habits of eating and sleeping in the infant. The usual tendency of the new born infant is to sleep during the day and remain awake during the night. This must be broken up by waking the child during the day at regular intervals and feeding it. It should be fed at night at its regular time only; and if it be made comfortable and given plenty of water, it may be allowed to cry for a time until it learns that it will not be taken up.

Editorial.

RECIPROCITY.

It is an old adage that "all work and no play makes Jack a dull boy," and it is equally true that all work and no play is hardly in accord with the principles of reciprocity.

Members of the medical profession have the reputation of being philanthrophists, and philanthropy and business are not very close of kin. It would seem as though the public would appreciate a kind and generous act and that people would take pleasure in showing their appreciation in some palpable manner, but a careful investigation of the ruling spirit which directs the affairs of mankind in general ignores everything that cannot be measured by a purely business standard, and that a man or woman who depends upon the gratitude of others for his or her remuneration has no right to criticize that seeming indifference which really means that they are doing unto others as they expect others to do unto them.

It is almost an unheard of thing for a business man who is a debtor to send an inquiry to another business man who is the creditor regarding the non-presentation of a statement of account. The whole thought and attention of the debtor business man is directed to his end of the proposition, and, until a statement is rendered, no thought or consideration is given to the matter. The physician, as a philanthropist, is out of harmony with his environment, and until he recognizes the fact that his services have value he has no right to expect anyone else to place a value upon them higher or greater than his own acts would indicate. The physician who combines his professional skill with the shrewdness of the man of business shows by his every act that his services have a real value, and does not hesitate in placing a value upon every service rendered. This value may be fictitious and out of all proportion to the services rendered, but the public has the privilege of accepting the service or not, and, as a rule, accepts the estimate made by the physician, and makes consistent effort to reciprocate. In other words, the business physician who renders a prompt statement for every service given is more certain to secure prompt payment for the same than is the man who has the reputation of waiting upon the convenience of his patrons. With the majority of men every dollar of their income is disposed of in some way or other, and the man who awaits the convenience of the general public will find that date extended into the dim, distant future.

The present is an intensely commercial age, and everything is measured by its practical utility. Our schools and universities are adjusting their curriculums to meet the demands of the day. With this spirit of commercialism all services rendered assume a higher monetary value, because no other measure of compensation is used as a gauge than that of their practical utility. The physician must learn this lesson early in his professional life, and while he may be denied some satisfaction of withholding from the right hand the knowledge of what the left hand is doing, he will find greater opportunities for combining all of his faculties in the undivided pleasure of giving, with a whole heart, where it will be more thoroughly appreciated.

All of which leads up to a practical application of the principle of reciprocity that we have felt impelled for many months to make. This is no personal matter, but the discussion of a principle that is fundamental in character and lies at the bottom of much of the lack of appreciation shown to the medical profession as a body.

For the past ten years we have freely given to the profession services more or less valuable, without any hope of other compensation than that which comes from the knowledge of having done good. As a rule, the profession has accepted our services at the same valuation placed by us upon them. But being surrounded by an environment of commercialism we have, necessarily, caught the spirit of the times, and have firmly resolved that in the future we will carry our services to the market which shows an appreciation most thoroughly in accord with our own judgment. What we give we will give with our whole heart, and for what we sell we shall expect ample compensation.

In the past we have given our services in editing of this magazine, without price and would have been perfectly satisfied with the reception given to the same; but, unfortunately, we have put up good money to satisfy the demands of business men with whom we have been associated, and have been compelled to accept part payment in that form of compensation which, too often, came at the convenience of our subscribers. It was through this school of experience that we learned the character of medicine that is being given to many patrons of the medical profession.

This is an age of reciprocity, as well as an age of commercialism, and there is no necessity for any business physician to ask for time or accommodation in the payment of any of his obligations. If you belong to the class and have difficulty in making both ends meet, put the responsibility where it belongs and make every effort to adjust your business policy, so it will harmonize with that prevailing throughout the country.

For the past six years the ADVOCATE has been managed by the Hahnemann Publishing Co., and for the past year the publishing, or business, department has been separate and distinct from the editorial department. The manager brings to our notice the fact that there are outstanding, at the present writing $1,200.00 in accounts, nearly all of which have been formally acknowledged as legitimate, and for all of which value received has been rendered. Various have been the pleas made for extension of the time of payment of the same. But the time has now come when this state of affairs must cease, and everyone who would enjoy the feast spread before its readers from month to month must pay for the same or be denied admittance.

For fear it might seem as it our subscription list was largely made up of *philanthropists*, we desire to state that about four-fifths of our subscribers give abundant evidence of good business qualifications; but the margin between the expenditures and the resources of the magazine is so small that the disposition of the other fifth determines the interest of the management in its publication, and gives to the adage, "all work and no play" a practical and a painful application to those most intimately concerned.

There is no question but that every subscriber to the ADVOCATE could pay his obligation in full within the next thirty days if he will bring into play his business ability. Do this.

THE DOCTOR AND THE MAN.

During the past year homœopathic physicians located south of Mason and Dixon's line have had, in very many instances, a hard struggle to obtain recognition. In fact, nearly all who have located in that part of the country have had to do missionary work. But the self-sacrifice and hard struggle, like conscientious work done in any good cause, is bearing fruit, and most of our subscribers and followers of Hahnemann generally have made themselves necessary to the communities of their adoption, and are reaping the rewards, in a financial way, which are their due.

It has been the policy of the ADVOCATE to help these missionaries in every way possible, and as this was, in a majority of cases, a wise business policy is evidenced by receipts for subscription, and on other accounts in some instances of four or five years' standing, received during the present year. These physicians are making a reputation for manhood for themselves and upbuilding the cause of homœopathy.

Recently, in the locality above referred to, it became necessary to make a draft on one whose subscription we had been carrying for about six years. We say "it became necessary" advisedly, as we had sent the "Doctor" numerous statements showing the condition of his account, to none of which he deigned the courtesy of a reply. The draft was received by the bank, and endorsed by one of its officers as follows: "No good; never pays; no use to present."

Such is the only representative of homœopathy in a thriving little city. How the people must love the cause and its representative there!

A physician cannot succeed in the South, nor anywhere else, unless he is also a business man, with all that goes with the title. S.

Materia Medica Miscellany.

Xanthoxylum in Leucorrhœa.—S. C. Ghose, M. D., in the Recorder, has formulated the following indications for the use of this remedy: Watery, acrid, bloody leucorrhea; profuse menses; the flow is very copious, profuse discharge of hot, dark clotted blood; pains down the anterior of thighs; intense heat and burning in the stomach, aggravated by any hot application; the pains and burning are so very great that the patient rolls on the floor. I used Xanthoxylum in many cases of leucorrhea, but the majority of the cases revealed that the discharge was profuse rather than scanty, painful rather than painless cases; the pains were very excruciating and appeared down the anterior of thighs; intense burning and heat were not prominently marked in all my patients and the symptoms grew worse at night.—*Am. Physician.*

Hydrastis Canadensis in Ulceration of the Tongue.—U. N., aged 47, a journeyman tailor, had, for three months, on the dorsum of the tongue an oval ulcer an inch long and half an inch broad, not deep, granular in appearance, grey colored, with a thick yellow secretion. Single fissures towards the edges of the tongue; pricking pains on eating and on movement of the organ; glands not enlarged; no history of syphilis; pressure in the pit of the stomach with darting pains up through the œsophagus; cough with expectoration of yellow-white, tough mucus.

Hydrastis ix, gtt. iii. t. d. internally, and a penciling of the ulcer and the fissures with a solution of the matrix tincture in glycerine (1 in 10) morning and evening was the treatment adopted. Cured the ulcer in two months, and with the help of Phosphorus[3x] at the close of the case the whole train of symptoms disappeared.—Dr. Oscar Hanson in *Hom. World.*

Actea in Neurasthenia. J. W. Ellis, M. D., in Journal of the British Hom. Society, says: I have frequently found this drug of service in patients with neurasthenia where muscular exhaustion was a prominent symptom, with much pain about the cervical region, with inability to hold up the head for any length, or when there is a constant attempt to get rid of the feeling of fatigue or aching by drawing the head backward upon the spine. Whenever, too, there is asthenopia with hyperæsthesia of the retina, we may give Actea with expectation of relief of the symptoms. In the sexual sphere, at least in women, the drug has analogies with Ferrum, and we must not forget in this connection, that "key-note" symptom of Actea, infra-mammary pain, which so frequently accompanies congestion or irritation of the pelvic organs, such as is so frequently present in women suffering from nervous prostration. In another form of muscular disturbance I have found Cuprum metallicum and Cuprum aceticum of great service. I allude, of course, to those cases where muscular spasm is a marked feature of the case, spasm which may vary from the fibrillary flickering of the eyelids to severe and persistent cramps. Both preparations should, I think, be given in fairly high dilution—the sixth or twelfth centesimal, if we are to get the best results from their administration.—*Am. Physician.*

Psorinum.—A. L. Blackwood, M.D., in *Med. Visitor*, says: Some of my most happy results in medicine have come from the use of this remedy. And yet I believe it to be one that is not generally employed by physicians, but there is no reason why it should not be, when antitoxin and other products of disease are being so extensively used.

It should be studied in cases where there are evidences of an underlying dyscrasia, and as a result the apparently indicated remedy does not act, or its results are of but short duration and the patient is again as bad as ever. In other cases the apparently indicated remedy has no effect upon the patient, and it is demanded to arouse the vital forces. In this class of cases by careful inquiry into the clinical history there is usually some disease from which recovery has not been complete, or there is some underlying dyscrasia that is indicated by glandular enlargements or cutaneous exhibitions. The skin eruptions are usually herpetic in character and are attended by great itching, which is made worse by the warmth of the bed. The skin may appear all right, but more frequently it is of a dirty, greasy appearance, as though the patient had never bathed. If there is any discharge it is very offensive, which is true also of the perspiration; and all the discharges might be compared to carrion. The discharges from the bowels are of so foul an odor that it is impossible to remain in the room. They are profuse, watery, brown, or black; worse at night.

It also relieves a constipation that is attended with great straining at stool.

Following some acute disease that has greatly reduced the patient he is prostrated, suffering from night sweats, hopeless, and does not react from the acute disease and the chances appear to be poor for a recovery. The patient is chilly and desires to be wrapped up, especially about the head. There is dry, hacking cough with a thick, yellow, offensive sputa.—*Am. Physician.*

Eight Remedies in Rheumatism.—According to the Homœopathic Journal of Obstetrics the following remedies are among the most important:

Aconite may be thought of early in the attack. There is restlessness, fever, and involvement of the joints; this remedy is of special importance when the cause of an attack can be directly traceable to a chilling of the body.

Belladonna is specially indicated when there are febrile symptoms; general malaise, aching all over the body, sore throat and stiff neck. There are painful spots that are sore on gentle pressure, yet firm pressure is tolerated. Pains gradually increase, suddenly decline and appear elsewhere. The pains are cutting, tearing and lightning like through the joints.

Bryonia is useful in either muscular or articular rheumatism. The swollen joints are very sensitive to the touch; the slightest motion is intolerable; the joints are hot and shining, and the skin looks as if it had been stretched over them; heat applied externally affords relief; the Bryonia patient differs from the Rhus tox. one, in that he is made worse from the slightest motion, while with Rhus, the patient is continually moving about.

Mercurius has the tearing pain that is not relieved by sweating; the pains are worse at night, and from the warmth of the bed; the joints look swollen and pale. There may be gastric disturbance, with coated tongue, taking the imprints of the teeth; a foul breath. There may be extension to the heart, lungs and pleura.

Pulsatilla has the changeableness and tendency to shift about from joint to joint; there is aggravation from warmth, and relief from cold. There is relief from motion, and in the cool, open air. The joints are very sensitive, but without any visible signs of inflammation.

Rhus toxicodendron patients cannot bear cold air; the pain and stiffness are made worse on commencing to move, but continued motion brings relief. This remedy has a wider range of usefulness in rheumatism than any other remedy. The Rhus patient is made better by dry, warm, external applications.

Apis is useful when the pains are of a stinging or burning character; there is much œdema of affected parts, and synovitis.

Arnica is most useful to rheumatism that has been brought on from exposure to dampness, cold weather, and where there has been excessive muscular strain; the parts feel sore and bruised; the patient has a dread of being touched; the urine is scanty and high colored; the patient is chilly in bed; there is great internal heat and sour sweats.—*The Critique.*

Treatment of Acute Articular Rheumatism.–The author advises the following remedies to be selected: Aconite, Verat. viride, Colchi., Ars.

The first two are of constant utility during the first week. The high fever, the flow of blood to the head and the cerebral symptoms may render necessary the use of Belladonna.

If the muscles of the chest and abdomen are attacked as in some severe cases, Bryonia is indicated, while Nux vomica is useful for the muscles of the back.

Quite rarely the author has had occasion to advise Chamo., Sanguinaria, Ferrum carb., Pulsatilla, Rhus tox., and he does not hesitate to give alternately three or even four medicines at half-hour interval in medium potencies—3rd or 4th.

Veratum viride is frequently indicated; its properties resemble those of

Aconite and of Gelsemium which, nevertheless, cannot take its place.

Veratrum viride reduces fevers whose rapid progress becomes menacing and acts moreover, instantly, thus distinguishing it from Aconite and Belladonna. But the most astonishing action of Verat. viride is upon the pericardium and threatened paralysis of the heart.

In certain cases we see its power develop gradually, and the action of the heart reinforced little by little.

We notice, moreover, its beneficent influence upon the stomach, which in serious cases of acute articular rheumatism is impeded in its functions.

While using these medicines we must at the same time avoid the use of bouillon, white bread and of too highly seasoned food. Meat should be given only once a day, veal, either roasted or boiled, must be entirely forbidden, fowls and game are preferable. Fruits, especially apples, are recommended. The treatment is to be completed by Sulphur 30th. If thirst is excessive let Curare 1st be added.

Steam baths are to be avoided. However, we must not expect to cure every case. There are some which will resist this treatment. There are gaps in our knowledge.—Dr. M. Picard in Leipziger popul. Zeitschrift fuer Homœopathie.

Skin Grafting with Skin Scrapings, in Blood.—Anna H.; age 12 years; American. Diagnosis, burn of right hand. Patient was admitted to hospital March 8th, 1902. As a result of the burn she had on the back of her hand an ulcerous surface 2 by 1½ inches very painful, and in spite of three months treatment had refused to heal. It was impossible in this case to secure skin-grafts, and as I wished to demonstrate to the visiting physicians who were present the efficiency of *skin scrapings* as a means of bringing about a rapid healing of small surfaces where grafts could not be obtained, with an ordinary vaccinating comb I secured skin scrapings from the little patient's arms, legs and back. These were deposited within the periphery and dressed as in the other case. The dressing was kept wet with bovinine pure until the morning of the 16th, at which time it was removed and to the delight of the visiting physicians as before, the surface was found to be almost entirely healed, there remaining unhealed only a small space about the size of a ten cent piece, in the center. The wound was now dressed with bovinine pure the nurse ordered to change it every 24 hours. Internally the patient had been getting a teaspoonful of bovinine every two hours in peptonized milk. March 24th, she was discharged cured.

T. J. Biggs.

Borax—a test of its purity—Put a little in the bowl of a spoon, pour on a little vinegar, and if it foams the least bit return it to the dealer of whom it was purchased with a request for the pure article or the money you paid for the stuff. It has a liberal percentage of soda in its manufacture, and will not do the work of pure borax, is injurious to the skin and delicate fabrics.

Natrum mur. Dr. Krichbaum, in the *Advance*, says: In intermittent fever this remedy has scored some of its greatest victories. It is suited to those cases occurring near shoals or rapids or where stagnant water is found. Especially too do we find it indicated after the abuse of quinine, or after eating much salt pork.

The chill starts about 10 or 11 a.m. every day, every other day, every third day, or fourth day. Begins at the extremities, which become very blue. There is throbbing pain in the head, the face is flushed and there may be be delirium. Thirst for cold water during the entire attack. The cold is not ameliorated by heat or by applying bed covers, but he wants cold drinks. The teeth chatter, he tosses about, bones ache as if they would break, and vomiting often ensues.

In the fever he is almost scorched, so intense is the heat.

The sweat relieves the bone pains first, then gradually the headache disappears, and the attack is over. This is strongly Natrum muriaticum.

In the great malarial districts of our country this remedy is a giant of colossal proportions. For this one phase of humanity's ills it is well worth exhaustive study. I have merely outlined some of its ramifications and marked characteristics.—*Am. Physician.*

Personals and News Items.

Unvaccinated persons are not allowed to vote in Norway.

More than eighty per cent. of the present cost of the world's governments is caused by wars, past, present and prospective.

In West Australia the disproportion of the sexes is so very great that there are only 64,000 females in a population of 168,000.

On October 1, Dr. Charles Deady, the eye, ear and naso-pharynx specialist, removed to 151 W. 73d street, New York city where he can be consulted from 9 a. m. to 1 p. m.

Dr. J. H. Allen of this city has been making provings of Tritica repens (couch grass), a remedy useful in many forms of bladder trouble. If any of the brethren wish a sample of the potencies, it can be obtained by making a request of the Doctor, 92 State st.

The Japanese dentist does not frighten his patient with an array of steel instruments. All his operations in tooth-drawing are performed by the thumb and forefinger of one hand. The skill necessary to do this is acquired only after long practice, but when once it is obtained, the operator is able to extract half a dozen teeth in about thirty seconds without once removing his fingers from the patient's mouth. The dentist's education commences with the pulling out of plugs which have been pressed into soft wood; it ends with the drawing of hard pegs which have been driven into an oak plank with a heavy mallet.—*Exchange.*

For nearly a year past, many of the doctors and dentists of this country have been victimized by a very clever swindler who has passed under several aliases among them, R. G. Stearns, R. L. Nelson, and others. He claims to represent The Success Company, publishers of the *Success* magazine, and takes orders for numerous magazines comprised in the Success Clubbing Offers. He works very rapidly, jumping from town to town, and always among doctors and dentists. All the money he obtains is appropriated, and the magazines are never ordered or received. Every effort has been made by the Success Company to apprehend this swindler, but so far without success. The Success Company requests us to notify all doctors and dentists that its representatives always bear a special dated card of introduction, and to patronize no others. It also offers a reward of $50.00 for any information which will lead to the apprehension of this swindler. He is described as follows:

From 23 to 25 years old; 5 ft. 8 in. in height; medium build; weight about 150 lbs.; dark hair (almost black) of medium length, very curly about the temples; dark gray eyes (almost hazel); rather sallow complexion, with scattered dark brown freckles; face unusually round for man of so light build; clothes not shabby, but far from new, and much worn. Black coat and vest, gray trousers (hard twisted goods), with small stripe; black derby hat, much worn; old style turndown collar, with made tie. General untidy appearance for a man in the soliciting business.

Good Medical Literature, cheap, can be obtained, in the shape of complete volumes of Medical Advance, for years 1893, '94 and '95. $1.00 a volume, postpaid, while they last. Ten numbers, not consecutive, for fifty cents. Odd numbers of issues of the 70s and 80s at six cents a number. Address, Hahnemann Publishing Co., 6704 Lafayette ave.

Austin, Texas, Oct. 17, 1902.

Editor Hahnemannian Advocate—The Texas Homœopathic Medical Association held its annual meeting at Dallas on Oct. 8 and 9. This body has been increasing its membership in a gratifying way. We are also pleased to note that in the matter of reciprocity between Examining Medical Boards, we are falling into line with the East, the Illinois board having agreed to recognize the Texas license where the applicant is a graduate of a college in regular standing and has passed the examination of the Texas Homœopathic Board.

Very truly yours,
Julia H. Bass, M. D.
Sec'y Texas Hom. Med. Asso.

[The facts noted in Dr. Bass' communication are gratifying to the editor of the Advocate as well as to homœopaths everywhere, and the increased popularity of the followers of Hahnemann in Texas and the south is due, in a great measure, to the noble work so perseveringly carried on by the exponents of Similia there.—Ed.]

Good Homœopathic Reading is found in back numbers of the Advocate. Complete volumes 1896 to 1901, mailed on receipt of $1.00 a volume. Ten numbers, not consecutive, fifty cents. Address Hahnemann Publishing Co., 6704 Lafayette ave.

Book Reviews.

The Physician's Visiting List (Lindsay & Blakiston's) **for 1903-4** is now ready for distribution. This is the fifty second successive year of its publication. Published by P. Blakiston's Son & Co., Philidelphia.

The Physician's Visiting List for 1908-'04 is a small, neat, compactly-made, strongly-bound pocket book, with leather cover, gilt edges, tuck, pocket, and rubber tipped pencil, made up to hold 25 to 100 patients' records per day, week or month, dated and undated, with pages for special memoranda and tables for ready reference. It is a book of original entry; a simple, plain statement of a year's work that may be kept with a minimum of labor. It is the ideal book for the physician. In addition to the numerous other valuable features for which this work is noted, attention is directed to two new features, the pages on Incompatibility (chemic, pharmaceutic and therapeutic), and the page on Immediate Treatment of Poisoning.

Price of the book, sire above described, is $1.00 postpaid.

Dr. Gould's Biographic Clinics—It is a peculiar fact that the letters and other writings of DeQuincey, Carlyle, Darwin, Huxley and Browning, liberal as they are with references to the continued ill-health of those great writers, have not before this suggested to the medical profession an opportunity for research into the causal factors of those physical conditions. That the opportunity has not until now been recognized in its proper light is evidenced by the hitherto total absence of any work dealing with this subject. Dr. George M. Gould's Biographic Clinics, (P. Blakiston's Son & Co., Philadelphia) which is devoted to this neglected subject should, therefore, prove a most unique and valuable contribution to biographical and medical literature. The work is announced for publication in December.

Dr. Gould has gathered from the biographies, writings and letters of the five named men every reference to their ill-health. Each endured, as is well known, a life of suffering which made almost every day a torment and by which their work and worth as an asset of the nation and civilization was conditioned and often rendered morbid. The cause of their affliction was an utter mystery to their physicians. No explanation explained, and no cure cured. Dr. Gould has gone into the "why" of this very thoroughly and the conclusion reached by him, from logic and from a careful summary of the clinical symptoms, is that each of the writers suffered from eyestrain, and that scientific correction of their ametropia would have transformed their lives of mystery into lives of happiness. A history of the discovery of astigmatism and eyestrain, with a discussion of its indications and responsibilities, completes the work. It is interestingly written, and will undoubtedly meet with a ready sale among medical men and those interested in the works and lives of the quintette of great writers.

The ADVOCATE is in receipt of the *Success* calendar for 1903. The calendar is in form of a folder, a leaf for each month. The upper two-thirds of each leaf is occupied by a reproduction of the *Success* title pages during 1902. For instance, on the page assigned to the January calendar is a picture of "Young Roosevelt on the Frontier;" Feb., "Lincoln as a Rail Splitter;" May, "Out of Debt at Last," etc. Like everything else emanating from success, it is first-class as a work of art.

On the reverse side of each calendar page is a synopsis of what *Success* has done and is doing in the way of providing, entertaining, instructive and inspiration producing literature for over three millions of readers.

How our readers can obtain *Success*, and other good periodicals, is set forth in our ad entitled "Your Magazine Money."

The Denver Chemical Manufacturing Co., is sending a unique little Christmas folder and calendar to every physician in the United States, Canada and England, advertising the virtues of Antiphlogistine, a full page advertisement of which appears in this issue. Besides stating for what diseases the remedy should be given, the physician is warned to use from the "Original Package" only, a fac simile of which appears in two places on the folder.

The Hahnemannian Advocate

A MONTHLY HOMŒOPATHIC MAGAZINE.

H. W. PIERSON, B. S., M. D., Editor., 809 Marshall Field Building, Chicago.
HAHNEMANN PUBLISHING CO. Publisher, 6704 Lafayette Ave., Chicago.
BENJ. F. SWAB, Business Manager.

Subscription price of the magazine in the United States, Canada, Mexico, the island possessions and Cuba $1.50 a year, payable in advance; in Great Britain, continental Europe, India and other countries members of the postal union, $2.00 a year to be paid in advance. Unless otherwise specified subscriptions will begin with January issue of the year in which order is received. Remittances should be made payable to the HAHNEMANN PUBLISHING CO., 6704 Lafayette Ave., Chicago.

Address all articles intended for publication and books for review to the editor. All business and other communications should be sent to the Hahnemann Publishing Co.

Vol. xii. Chicago, December, 1902. Nos. 11 and 12

DOUBLE NUMBER.

Materia Medica.

PULSATILLA, SILICEA, CALCAREA CARBONICA, HEPAR SULPHURIS, CALCAREUM, GRAPHITES, PHOSPHORUS.*†

Common Characteristics. — The drugs which make up this group, act principally on the vascular apparatus. All the symptoms which they have in common, seem to depend upon a small number of primordial phenomena (such as impeded respiration, engorgement of the air passages, tumultuous or irregular beating of the heart, etc.) all of which indicate a disturbed condition of the vascular sphere; hence we have,

Throbbings here and there, isochronous with the pulse.

Blackness and diminished fluidity of the blood.

Swelling of the veins and capillary engorgement, constituting a sort of ill-conditioned plethora.

Diminution of the vital heat and action.

Congestion of blood to the head, and engorgement of its sinuses.

Sensation of heaviness and fulness in the brain.

Pain of the same kind, accompanied sometimes with apoplectic shocks, either in the centre of the brain, or, which is more frequent, in the right side.

Vertigo and cloudiness as in complete apoplexy, especially when the atmospheric pressure is below the ordinary standard, as is the case at the approach of storms, on the summit of mountains, and more generally on elevated regions.

Paroxysms of comatose somnolence, as in asphyxia (by charcoal, for instance), after a meal (which increases frequency of the pulse), in the afternoon or evening.

Dulness of the senses.

Swelling of the eyes and lachrymal glands; lachrymation.

Stickiness and bilious bitterness of the mouth and throat, with swelling of

*Ferr. muriat., Cham. vulg. and Gadus will very probably, one day, be added to the analogues of Pulsatilla; but, at all events, Chamomilla will always remain the type of a group, on account of its possessing several symptoms which appertain neither to Pulsatilla nor its analogues.

†Teste's Materia Medica, edition of 1854.

the salivary glands, salivation (at the commencement of the action of the drugs), frequently loss of thirst, and in some cases aversion to liquid food, as if one had an instinctive dread to increase the excessive fulness of the vessels.

Aversion to fat food, and especially to real fat.

Fulness at the stomach and in the whole abdomen, which is doubtless owing to the venous engorgement of the liver, of the portal system, pancreas, etc.

Nausea, rancid eructations, watery and bilious vomiting.

Suppression of the biliary secretion, hence: constipation, colorless clay-colored stools; stools consisting of undigested food; or (as I believe, a secondary and ulterior effect:) excessive secretion of bile, and especially of intestinal mucus; hence result:

Soft stools, and a passive diarrhea, without colic, which seems to ease the patient rather than to weaken him, and continues for an indefinite period.*

Venous or catarrhal engorgement of the genito-urinary apparatus.

Sort of numbness, torpor of the genital organs, with absence of erections and pleasurable sensation (especially among women) during an embrace, or else permanent sexual excitement.†

Heaviness of the uterus.

Delay of the menses in spite of evident symptoms of a flow of blood towards the uterus; the menstrual blood is black, coagulated, impoverished, and the menses are generally either too early or too late.

Discharge of blood from the vagina between the menses.

Passive metrorrhagia.

Milky leucorrhea.

Fluent coryza preceded by stoppage of the nose, and generally by irritation in the throat.

Angina, with puffing up of the pharyngeal or tracheal mucous membrane.

Loose cough preceded by dyspnœa, pains and oppression at the chest.

Pains in the chest as from an abscess.

Obstinate catarrh, which terminates in some cases in suppuration; hæmoptysis; ulceration of the lungs.

Heaviness of all the extremities.

Pain in the extremities as from an abscess.

Wandering pains, generally distensive; pains which cut short the breathing.

Blueish redness of some parts, but without increase of the temperature of these parts.

Varices.

Petechiæ.

Red papulous blotches on the skin (especially on the sides of the head, in the face, on the neck, chest).

Infiltration of the feet.

Abscess (whitlow) at the extremities.

Nightmare.

One is obliged to lie with the head much higher than the rest of the body.

Pains which manifest themselves principally in the parts upon which one is not lying, but aggravated breaking out of these pains, in shifting one's position, in the parts upon which one had been lying, etc.

Pulsatilla and its analogues will be found in several other groups, especially in the one which has Ipecacuanha for its type.

Hepar sulphuris, which terminates the series of the analogues of Pulsatilla, is the drug which is farthest removed from the sphere of action of Pulsatilla. The symptoms of Hepar seem to partake of the character of its two constituent ele-

*As in phthisicky patients, for instance.

†Probably owing to the compression of the cerebellum by the blood which flows to it in excessive quantity and remains there, as is the case in certain forms of asphyxia; this is perhaps the cause of the sexual excitement with which phthisicky persons are so often troubled.

ments, sulphur and lime. This is the reason why it is an antipsoric, although I have not mentioned it among the group *Sulphur;* it holds an intermediate rank between the Sulphur and Pulsatilla group.

CORRESPONDING DISEASES.

Affections of men and women of a plethoric and at the same time feeble constitution, (the plethoric condition prevailing first) organic diseases of the heart, arteries or veins, (aneurisms, varices, etc.) passive congestions with swelling, without any increase of heat in the affected parts; cutaneous abscesses: diseases of the air passages; acute or chronic catarrh; pulmonary engorgement; pneumonia; abscess in the lungs; tuberculous phthisis; Cerebral apoplexy, (especially on the right side), with numbness, convulsions or paralysis of the extremities of the opposite side; vertigo; headache; periodical headache, especially when the paroxysm takes place immediately before or after, or during the menstrual period; ophthalmia; cataract; amaurosis, (especially of the right eye); varicose condition of the veins of the cornea and sclerotica; epiphora; lachrymal fistula; indigestion from eating meat or fat; bilious, petechial, purple and miliary fever; typhus; typhoid fever; chronic constipation; lienteria; diarrhœa without colic; nightly diarrhœa; prolapsus of the rectum; piles; cystitis; catarrh of the bladder; stricture of the urethra; pains in the loins; swelling of the right testicle; metritis; various affections of pregnant woman; amenorrhœa; dysmenorrhœa; passive hæmorrhages from the womb; leucorrhœa, (thin or milky); impotence; sterility; cancer of the breast; measles, rash (on the chest); wandering erysipelas; red tetters in the face (acne rosacea); tetters on the sides of the head, (with falling of the hair) adipose cysts; rheumatism, (especially at the neck, shoulders, at the small of the back, in the hips and knees); wandering gout; ulcers (at the extremities); panaritia; warts; various kinds of intellectual derangements.

Pulsatilla, *anemone;* small herbaceous plant of the genus *anemone*, family *ranunculaceæ*, class polyandria polygynia.

This plant grows in most countries of central Europe, on arid and bare hills, or in sandy woods. It is recognized by its leafless stems, which are about three inches high, furnished with an indented sheath under the flowers. These are terminal, large, composed of five petals, which are straight, hairy on the outside, without chalice, and enclosing in the midst of stamina and numerous pistils, seeds which are surmounted by a long silky extremity.

Pulsatilla is usually considered identical with the anemone of the meadows. Some botanists, however, protest against such a confusion, and Mr. Spark, among others, goes so far as to make two different genera of these two plants.* This seems to me superfluous; for, the only difference which exists between pulsatilla and the other variety, is this, that, in the former, the petals, instead of being straight, are bent back at their tops. The medicinal properties of these two plants seem to be the same, except what difference may be derived from the localities where they grow.

The leaves of the recent Pulsatilla, its stem and root have an acrid, burning and nauseous taste. Its juice draws blisters, to the extent, it is said, of causing gangrene, if allowed to remain in contact with the part for a sufficient length of time; but these properties are, in a great measure, lost by desiccation, and ruminating animals, such as sheep and goats, eat the dry Pulsatilla, if mixed with other herbs, without aversion or inconvenience.

We are indebted to Stœrck, for a knowledge, if not of the physiological effects, at least, some of the therapeutic properties of Pulsatilla.†

Empirical applications.—Stœrck em-

*Dict. univers. d'hist. natur. article anemone.

†See libell. de usu pulsat. nigricantis medico, Vindeb. 1771, in 8vo. Stœrck used for his experiments the anemone of the meadows, which is very common in the neighborhood of Vienna, where the Pulsatilla on the contrary, is scarce.

ployed Pulsatilla, especially, in chronic affection of the eyes (cataract, amaurosis, spots on the cornea). Among his twenty cases, the most remarkable, is that of a young girl, who had been afflicted with amaurosis of both eyes since her infancy, and whose sight he restored in two months. He prescribed Pulsatilla in two different forms, namely, as extract internally, and a dry powder externally, which was blown into the eye. This process of insufflation, at first caused an acute pain, and a profuse flow of tears; after which, the pains which had existed previous to the lachrymation, diminished as soon as it commenced, and finally disappeared with it.

It seems to me that Stœrck did not properly appreciate the action of Pulsatilla in the diseases of the genito urinary apparatus.

According to him, this drug had antisyphilitic properties, and he ascribes to them the cures of syphilitic conditions, which he says, were affected with Pulsatilla, such as ulcers at the pudendum, at the tongue and in the throat; nocturnal arterial pains, (one of the most characteristic symptoms of Pulsatilla), caries of bones, and lastly condylomata. All this may be, but were all these various morbid conditions really syphilitic? This is not shown conclusively by the Vienna physician. Most of Stœrck's cures are accounted for by the physiological action of Pulsatilla. No homœopath will wonder that he should have cured with the extract of Pulsatilla: 1st a foul ulcer at the foot with serpiginous tetters at the neck and shoulder; 2d, a paralysis of the right arm, of five years standing; 3d, a paralysis of the thighs; 4th, a white swelling at the knee; 5th, lastly, melancholia.

Murray,* mentions the physicians who repeated Stœrck's experiments with more or less success. Bergius tried Pulsatilla without success in a case of amaurosis, which is not astonishing.† Bonnet was more fortunate. With Pulsatilla he cured tetters, which had resisted all other means of treatment.‡ In 1808, Dr. J. de Raum, published several cases, showing the good effects of Pulsatilla in asthma and whooping cough,§ against which diseases we Homœopaths frequently employ it, in accordance with the principle similia similibus.

In our time, Pulsatilla has been totally abandoned by allopathic physicians, who, for the most part, do not even seem to know that any of their predecessors has ever made use of this drug. Trousseau and Pidoux do not even mention it in their traite de therapeutique.**

Homœopathic applications. — "Pulsatilla will be found the more useful, the more the physical symptoms to which this plant is most adapted, are accompanied by a disturbed condition of the feelings, a tendency to silent grief, or to a sad and resigned mood, especially if, during health, the patient was of a benevolent and mild disposition, (even inconsistent and frivolous). It is, therefore, particularly suitable to lymphatic temperaments, and not very suitable to men of decision and rapid action, even when disposed to be benevolent.

"A favorable indication is, when the patient complains of chilliness every

* Appar. Medic., vol. III., p. 90, etc.

† Mat. Medic., p. 491.

‡ Ancien Journ. de Medec., vol. LVIII., p. 475.

§ Meme collection, vol. XVI., p. 604.

** See the pathogenesis of Pulsatilla in Hahnemann's Mat. Med. Pur., vol. III., of the numerous provings left to us by Hahnemann, that of Pulsatilla seems to be the one to which he has contributed himself more than to any other; it is one of the most interesting and most characteristic provings of his Mat. Med.

now and then, with absence of thirst.

"Pulsatilla suits females with delaying menses, or when it takes them a long time to fall asleep in the evening, or when they feel worse in the evening. It is a good remedy for ailments arising from the use of pork."*

To this I add, that the general action of Pulsatilla seems to correspond to the immediate or consecutive effects of fat food, not generally understood, but of real fat; in the same way as arsenic corresponds to the consequences arising from the abuse of raw food, and Nux vomica to the effects of rich viands and strong spirits; I say, moreover, that Pulsatilla is particular suitable to persons who, by the relative predominance of the adipose tissue in their constitution, by the whiteness of their flesh, the roundness of their forms, the mildness of their disposition, and their fitful mood, exhibit all the marked features of the female sex; that this drug is particularly indicated when the moral and physical symptoms of the disease are very changeable, that is to say, when there are frequent alternations of sadness and mild gaiety, of redness and paleness of the face, of shuddering and heat, of dryness and moisture of the skin, and finally, when the pains frequently shift without any apparent cause.†

Pulsatilla has been tried for almost every disease, but principally for diseases characterized by the following affections:

Symptoms caused by the abuse and improper use of Sulphur, Mercury, Cinchona or Chamomilla, (especially sulphur-springs) sadness; disposition to cry or laugh without any apparent cause; aversion to any kind of work; lassitude with heaviness of the whole body; uneasiness concerning one's health or business; want of decision; disposition to be afraid (of ghosts) in the evening or at night; anxiety, with apprehension of near death; anxiety, in the evening in bed, as if threatened by an attack of apoplexy; anxiety with beating at the heart and trembling of the extremities; here and there painful arterial pulsations, perceptible to contact; prominent veins, on the hands for instance, even without heat of the skin; varices; heat and redness of the cheeks, very frequently of the right cheek only, followed by coldness and paleness, paroxysms of fainting setting in with sudden heat, profuse sweat in the face, obscuration of sight as by a cloud and trembling of the extremities; internal pains here and there, as from some abscess; pains which cut off the breath, although they are seated in other parts than the air passages; wandering pains, with swelling of the affected parts; blueish redness of certain parts, without increase of heat, and even with coldness; chilblains; chilliness; fever, generally with coldness followed by dry heat, or chills alternating with the heat at short intervals, especially at sunset, or in the afternoon; loss of thirst during the chill, and thirst only during the heat, and then only when it is very considerable, or the thirst is only felt during the sweaty stage; disposition to sweat on making the least effort; sweat, in some cases, on one side of the body only, generally the right side; somnolence, which is sometimes irresistible, either in the evening or afternoon; restless sleep at night, with dry heat; frequent waking; disagreeable, frightful dreams; insomnia, with strange and confused ideas crowding upon one; pains which manifest themselves principally on the side on which one is not lying, quieted sometimes by lying on the affected side: co-

*Loc. Cit.

†Every physician knows that not one of these indications is to be taken in an absolute sense.

matose sleep with loud dreaming; profuse and sometimes fetid sweat during sleep; smarting itching not appeased by scratching, especially on the chest, (above the sternal region) on the sides of the neck, and in the face; red papulous blotches; measles; wandering erysipelas; eruption in consequence of an indigestion from grease, especially pork; alternating symptoms, most frequently aggravated by a sitting posture, sometimes by a recumbent posture, less frequently by gentle exercise, but almost always by passing from a cool air into the warm air of the room.

Vertigo recurring in paroxysms in the afternoon, especially in the evening, less frequently in the morning, when sitting, stooping, raising one's eyes, or even when walking: oppressive, tensive, throbbing headache, with sense of fulness in the head as from an indigestion, or a sensation of emptiness as after a night's watching or as after an excess at table; single acute shocks in the right half of the brain; stitches proceeding from the occiput and passing through the whole head; nocturnal headache with nausea; throbbing and pulling headache, which is alleviated by pressure with the hand; small pustules on the hairy scalp, filled with pus; bloating of the eyes; itching in the eyes; congestion of the vessels of the sclerotica; ophthalmia; deep-seated pains in the orbits; cloudiness of sight; cataract; amaurosis; photophobia; flickering of flames before the eyes, especially in the open air; rush of blood towards the organs of hearing; buzzing in the ears; acute otorrhea; stoppage of the ears; sense of tension in the face; abscess at the root of the nose; swelling of the salivary glands; toothache, with sense of fulness in the gums, which manifests itself especially in the afternoon or evening, generally aggravated by warm drinks and alleviated by cold water, although the reverse likewise takes place, but much less frequently; coated tongue without the sensation of taste; foul, herby taste, or taste of spoiled flesh, rancid grease or pus in the mouth, in the morning; bitter taste in the mouth after eating; aversion to butter or milk; all kinds of food seem bitter or too salt; tenacious mucus coating the inner mouth and throat as with a fur; want of appetite; loss of thirst; nausea and desire to vomit, as if one had drank oil; nausea, with profuse salivation and headache; hiccough after eating; aversion to tobacco smoke; eructation after having eaten pastry, tasting of rancid grease or old tallow; vomiting, with violent straining of a sour, greenish phlegm burning the pharynx like fire, in the evening after eating and going to bed; heaviness at the stomach; beatings in the epigastrium, which are isochronous with the pulse; bellyache, when walking; flatulent colic after eating, especially in the evening; pain as from an abscess, under the false ribs, extending to the sacrum; pinching, griping, bellyache, as if diarrhea would set in; bellyache after stool; typhoid fever; frequent soft stools mixed with mucus bilious diarrhea (especially at night) diarrhea without any pain; stools consisting of whitish substances;* constipation, blind or fluent piles; acute sensitiveness to contact over the whole hypogastric region; pressure and stitches in the vesical region as as if wind were incarcerated there; tenesmus if the bladder; discharge of watery urine; stricture of the urethra; brown urine, with gelatinous or brick dust sediment; mucous discharge from the urethra and swelling of the right testicle; itching at the prepuce and scrotum; sexual excitement, morning and evening; tensive drawing pains in the uterine and

*All the drugs belonging to the Pulsatilla group, have alternately an excessive secretion and a deficiency of bile in the duodenum, which causes white, clay-colored stools.

lumbar regions, resembling labor-pains; delay of the menses; suppression of the menses by a fright; premature menses; insufficient menses which flow only in the day time; difficult menses, although profuse, with blackish and coagulated blood; spasmodic pains in the lower abdomen, nausea, stricture at the throat, flow of water in the mouth, cloudiness, desire for stool; numbness of the abdominal extremities during the menses; stitches in the chest during the menses; milky leucorrhea.

Coryza with loss of smell in the nose; purulent discharge from the right nostril; nosebleed during the coryza; catarrhal angina, with headache, moist and burning skin, and absence of thirst; acute bronchitis; cough especially in the evening and at night, with profuse expectoration; cough when one is extended in bed, and disappearing in a sitting posture; engorgement of the lungs; rusty sputa; pneumonia; hæmoptysis; constriction at the base of the chest; purulent expectoration with hectic fever; paroxysm of suffocation, especially while lying down; rush of blood to the heart; with paroxysms of anguish; swelling of the breasts as if the milk were setting in; acute rheumatism, with or without swelling at the nape of the neck, at the right side of the neck and at the right shoulder; stitches between the shoulders; painful stiffness in the back; painful lameness at the sacrum, aggravated by motion; rheumatism with sensation of heaviness at the right shoulder; paralysis of the right arm; luxation pain in the hip, especially when the menses delay; painful lameness of the lower extremities; weakness of the knees which causes one to stagger, even without vertigo; swelling around the ankles; ulcers at the instep; boring in the heels; pain at the soles of the feet, apparently in the periosteum, with insensibility of the soft parts.

Many practitioners make a wrong use of Pulsatilla in amenorrhea and dysmenorrhea. They seem to imagine that Pulsatilla is indicated whenever these symptoms exist in any disease, and they prescribe it accordingly. What is still worse, is the practice of undertaking to combat a disease, which breaks out shortly before menstrual period, by hastening the appearance of the menses by means of Pulsatilla. Pulsatilla is only suitable in amenorrhea when there is an evident tendency of the blood to the uterus, and in dysmenorrhea when the little blood which flows out, is black and coagulated.

Chamomilla, Sulphur, Coffea and the the Vomic nut are the principal antidotes of Pulsatilla. But when the improper use of this drug affects the air passages, Calcarea phosphorata seems, according to my experience, to be the most suitable antidote.

Silicea.—*Silicea, oxyde of silicum, decarbonized white pebble.*—Although in some of the older treatises on Materia Medica, mention is made of Silicea and its compounds, under the vague denomination of terræ siliceæ, yet there is such a complete absence of all allopathic documents relative to the use of this drug, that we may safely consider it as a new element in the practice of medicine, due to our peculiar art. Indeed, of what use could have been a mineral to allopathic physicians, that seems inert in the form in which it exists in nature? I say, seems inert, for I am not sure that a finely pulverized pebble, if introduced into the alimentary canal, is without any effect whatever. This experiment might not be attended with any important result, but it has yet to be made.

Rapou, in his History of Homoeopathy, calls Sepia the "Pulsatilla of chronic diseases;" it is Silicea which should be considered in this light. There are few drugs that are as intimately related to each other as Pulsatilla and Siliçea.

I have even been tempted to suppose that Silicea might be a constituent portion of the active elements of Pulsatilla, a supposition which will not appear unfounded if we consider that Pulsatilla and all the other varities of anemone, are fond of sandy bottom, and may, on this account, readily incorporate the leading principle of the soil in their own constitution. But I admit that this is a very bold hypothesis, which is not even based upon facts furnished by a chemical analysis of the plant.*

Be this as it may, if we compare attentively, and symptom by symptom, the pure effects of silex to those of Pulsatilla, we are struck with their resemblance to each other, which is sometimes complete. But it is in the clinical results obtained with these drugs, that their perfect analogy is most strikingly evidenced.

Silicea corresponds to the chronic form of such diseases as Pulsatilla cures when acute; rush of blood to the head, more particularly in the right temple, and at the vertex; headache every day; photophobia; lachrymation; loss of taste; aversion to fat food, with rancid or oily taste in the mouth; catarrhal affections of the air passages; lateral swelling of the nape of the neck, right side; rheumatic pain at the right shoulder, in the back and sacrum; numbness of the limbs; pain as from chilblains or whitlows; suppression of the menses with beating of the heart; swelling of the lower abdomen, etc. The symptoms of Silicea differ, however, from those of Pulsatilla in this, that they are more constant, more deepseated, and last longer. For instance, the mucous secretions caused by Pulsatilla, become easily purulent under the action of Silicea. Silicea exhibits likewise, two series of phenomena, which, at different degrees and in different forms, belong to most other powerful drugs; these are, first, a sort of internal sinking, accompanied with a sort of canine hunger, a desire to restore one's strength by eating, etc., and secondly, nervous crises, of a more or less strange character, and apparently connected with this sense of exhaustion. It has seemed to me, at least, that this coincidence between a craving for food and the nervous derangements was, in all purely nervous affections, one of the most reliable indications for Silicea. And I have likewise observed that all nervous affections in which this drug exists with the best chances of success, are such as are either roused again or aggravated when, by some accidental circumstance, by caprice or by the requirements of a system, patients were condemned to excessive abstinence from food.

These, together with the thirst and the predominance of the symptoms in the morning on waking, or rather in the

*Pulsatilla has been analysed several times, especially by Vauquelin and Schwartz, but these chemists have contented themselves with the immediate results of their analysis, neglecting the discovery of the real constituents of the plant. A white, crystalline, insipid, inflammable substance which they termed anemonine, was considered by them the active principle of the plant, and engaged their particular attention. Does anemonine contain Silicea? I do not know.

It would be interesting to inquire whether white burgundy, that has a bouquet of flint, and which the vine-dressers of the Côte d'or drink every morning in order to remove the phlegm, does not contain Silicea. I am not, by any means, convinced of the efficacy of this white wine in removing disease which the peasants of Burgundy term "pituite," (phlegm); but what I am, on the contrary, convinced of, is that this wine causes the disease. Any other wine, it may be objected, will cause the same effect. This may be. Nevertheless it is positive that the chemical properties of drugs depend, to a certain extent, upon the chemical composition of the soil in which they grow. Who will assert that these properties do not, in part at least, result from the salts of lime and others inherent in the various soils, and naturally dynamised by the process of assimilating growth?

afternoon or evening, are the principal differences between Silicea and Pulsatilla. But, in their general action upon the vascular system. these two drugs either act alike, or, at any rate, similarly. It might be said, however, that Silicea affects the capillary system more specifically than does Pulsatilla.

Another observation which I regret having limited to a few experiments only, has led me to believe that the effects of Silicea are the more strikingly analogous to those of Pulsatilla, the lower the dilutions with which the provings were instituted.

According to Hahnemann, (see his Chronic Diseases, Vol. III.,) Silicea is principally indicated by the following symptoms. A comparison of the pure effects of Pulsatilla to those of Silicea, goes to show that Pulsatilla is indicated by the same morbid conditions:

Tendency to anger; ill-humor; aversion to work; excessive excitability; chagrined and irritated on the least provocation; discouraged; agitated; want of memory; malaise while reading and writing; inability to think; dizziness; sort of intoxication in the evening; vertigo, obliging one to hold on to something: heat in the head; headache on getting heated; headache from the nape of the neck to the vertex, hindering sleep; headache every day; tearing in the forehead, with heat in the morning; heaviness in the forehead from noon till evening; pulling pain in the head; pain in the head, as if it would burst; pulsative headache; megrim; tearings and stitches in the eyes and facial bones; sweat about the head in the evening; humid and itching crusts on the head; tuberculous elevations on the scalp; falling out of the hair; presbyopia; photophobia; blindness by the light of day; cataract; black spots floating before the eyes; a sort of gray veil before the eyes; amaurosis; sparks before the eyes; weakness of the eyes; the letters look blurred when reading at candle light; sudden paroxysms of blindness; one has to use spectacles to read and write; lachrymal fistula; lachrymation in the open air; tearing in the eyes; agglutination of the lids in the morning; redness of the eyes, with pain in the canthi; inflamed eyes; noise in the ears; hardness of hearing; boring pain in the ears; stitches in the ear from within outwards; eruption of pimples on the nose; redness at the tip of the nose; eruption of pimples in the nose; painful sensation of dryness in the nose; stoppage of both nostrils; loss of smell; nose bleed; cracking of the skin of the face; heat in the face; osseous swelling on the lower jaw; pulling and stitch in the lower jaw, at night; stiffness in the neck, preventing one from closing the jaws; ulceration at the vermilion border of the lower lip; tetter on the chin; swelling of the sub-maxillary glands; digging and stitch in the teeth; tearing pain in the teeth and cheek, night and day; shocks in the teeth when sucking at them with the tongue; tearing toothache which strikes to the ear when eating; bleeding of the gums; dryness in the mouth; smarting at the tongue; loss of taste; mucus in the mouth, constantly; bitter mouth, in the morning; eructations; eructations which are sour or taste as of rancid grease; eructations which taste of the food one had eaten; nausea in the morning; constant nausea and vomiting; nausea after every heating exercise; nausea after eating: vomiting after drinking; nausea every morning, with pain in the head and eyes when turning them; inability to digest meat; desire to vomit with shuddering; a good deal of thirst, he loathes every thing he eats; aversion to boiled things; aversion to meat; the child refuses the breast and vomits as soon as it takes it; heaviness at the stomach; heaviness at the stomach after drinking rapidly; pain at the pit of the stomach when pressing upon it; tightness in the pit of the stomach; pain at the stomach, after eating; it had existed for years; fulness after eating; hardness and swelling in the hepatic region; hardness and swelling of the abdomen on the right side and in the middle, above the navel, with hardness when touching it; tension and hardness of the abdomen; heat in the lower abdomen; borborygmi in the abdomen when stirring with the body; shifting of flatulence; difficult emission of flatulence; painful inguinal hernia; pinchings in the abdomen; cutting pains in the abdomen; cutting in the hypogastrium without diarrhœa; colic from constipation; bellyache, with diarrhea; worm fever in scrofulous children; several fæcal stools a day; constipation; indolence of the bowels; retention of the stools, with frequent unsuccessful urgings; itching at the anus; frequent urination; wetting the bed at night; no sexual desire and weakness of the sexual organs; frequent involuntary attacks of lascivious ideas; excessive sexual desire; itching at the prepuce; profuse menses; menstrual suppression of several months' standing; too early and too scanty menses; discharge of blood from uterus during the period of nursing; acrid, excoriating leucorrhea; leucorrhea when urinating; leucorrhea with cutting colic in the umbilical region; itching at the vulva.

Suppressed sneezing; excessive or too frequent sneezing; stoppage of the nose for years; dry stoppage of the nose; frequent coryza; coryza, after which a chronic stuffing of the nose ceases; hoarseness; asthma during work; asthma during a rapid walk, loud breathing when walking rapidly; loss of breath when lying on the back; loss of breath when stooping; loss of breath when running, coughing; cough, with purulent expectoration; cough, with mucous expectoration; suffocative cough at night; oppression of the chest; oppression of the chest when coughing or sneezing; beating in the sternum; stitches from the chest to the back; stitches under the left ribs; pain in the loins; spasmodic pulling in the sacrum, which obliges one to lie down and does not allow one to rise again; stitches in the back; tearing in the back; lameness at the trunk; stitch in the loins, when sitting or lying; contusive pain between the shoulder-blades; weakness in the sacrum, back and nape of the neck; glandular swellings at the nape of the neck; painful numbness in the arm on which one is lying; heaviness at the arm; inability to hold the arm raised a long time; weakness and trembling of the arm, after performing some slight manual labor; pulling pain in the arm; rheumatism in the arms; incipient paralysis at the fore-arm; the hand drops the object which it seizes; stitches in the wrist joint at night, extending along the arm; formication in the fingers; pains in the finger-joints in pressing upon them; stiffness and want of strength in the fingers; whitlow; pulling and stiffness in the legs; pressure in the muscles of the thigh; swelling of the knee; pulling pains in the legs; numbness of the calves; numbness of the feet, in the evening; cramps in the calves, in the evening, after working; stitch in the ankle when pressing the foot to the ground; cold feet; sweaty feet; suppression of the sweat on the feet; and cold feet; fetid smell of the feet; swelling of the feet; voluptuous and furious itching when slightly scratching a little spot on the sole of the foot; hard and painful cutaneous tubercles on the sole of the foot; corns; stitches in the corns; ulceration at the big toe, with stinging pain, vascular excitement and thirst after drinking a little wine; tendency to spraining joints; sweat during a slow walk; tendency to taking cold when uncovering the feet; foul smell of the ulcers; itching all over the body, on the legs, with ill look; itching ulcer on the thigh and at the ankle; carbuncle; stitches in every joint, at night; twitchings in the limbs, day and night, epilepsy; rheumatism in the arms and legs; numbness in the extremities; weakness in the extremities, in the evening; painful feeling of weariness in the evening; nervous debility; general prostration; tendency to faint away when remaining lying on one side; drowsiness in the afternoon; frequent yawning; one remains awake late, in the evening, in bed; slight sleep at night; many dreams and frequent waking; a good many dreams every night; disturbing dreams; snorting during sleep; night-sweats; frightful visions at night; dryness of the nose at night; frequent shuddering every day; profuse and sour night-sweat.

Until recently, Silicea has been principally used in chronic diseases; but there are also many acute maladies where it is sometimes indicated. I use Silicea as often and as successfully as any drug. In the following affections I have used it with marked benefit. 1st Measles, when first breaking out with thirst, pressive headache and dizziness in the morning. 2d. Cerebral apoplexy, with loss of consciousness, preceded (for three or four days) by a stupefying headache, deep-seated stitches in the right parietal region, and dull, heavy and crampy pains in the arms, and followed by an almost complete paralysis of the motor and sentient nerves of the left arm and left lower limb, in a young woman of short stature, very fat, blond hair, white and rose-colored skin, a lively and irascible temperament, and mother of four children, the youngest of whom she was yet nursing. I was called to this patient on the morning after the paralytic stroke, and Silicea removed in two days all the symptoms, including the headache, which still existed. 3d. *Metrorrhagia* of six weeks standing, in the case of a fat and robust woman of a brown complexion. This woman, who was a washer-woman at Grenille, and whom I saw only three or four times at my office, attributed her sickness to her constantly standing in cold water. *Silicea* arrested hæmorrhage almost immediately, and effected such an improvement in one week, that I scarcely knew her again the second week; she did not take any other medicine. 4th. *Sterility*, with descension of the uterus, anteversion and slight induration of the neck of the uterus, scanty and painful menses, which come every month some seven or eight days sooner; pulsative pain in the right ovarian region, incapaciating her from standing; unpleasant heat on the skin of the hypogastric region, whilst the feet and knees feel icy-cold, especially at night; complete absence of the thrill during an embrace, without, however, experiencing any aversion to sexual intercourse, in a very brown complexioned but thin lady. I may feel disposed to publish this case in extenso, some time or other. Silicea, which was administered for three months without an interruption, but in various dilutions, produced a regular, progressive amelioration, which never ceased until the moment when the patient became pregnant.* 5th. *Miscarriage*. A young woman, of blond hair, lively, easily impressed, who had been married for some ten months, was in the eighth month of pregnancy. For some days past she had felt a dullness about the head, and a dull pain at the lumbar region. After a somewhat long walk, and a little unpleasant excitement, she was suddenly

*She had been married for two years, and had already been under homœopathic treatment the previous year, but without deriving any perceptible benefit from it.

seized with violent pains in loins, which soon increased to real labor pains. The uterine contractions could be felt distinctly; a little rose-colored blood appeared at the vulva. Silicea arrested the symptoms immediately, and the lady went her full term. 6th. *Constant pressive headache* from above downwards, (over the whole head), with intermittent itching at the vulva, without any other apparent symptoms, in the case of a lady of forty years, blood hair, apathetic, very fat, and rosy complexion. 7th. *Chronic affections of the heart.*

As a general rule, and contrary to the opinion which a number of homœopathic physicians seem to entertain, Silicea is particularly suitable to lymphatico-sanguine individuals, rather than to persons who are simply lymphatic or cachectic. A remarkable contrast exists in this respect between Sepia and its two analogues. I have observed in several instances that sepia, copaiva or alumina produced bad effects on persons to whose temperament Silicea was especially adapted, and who had, indeed, been cured by Silicea. Nevertheless there are certain chronic maladies which it may be proper to treat alternately with Silicea, Sepia and Alumina; but such a combination never suits persons of a sanguine or a sanguine-nervous temperament. The use of Sepia, like Arsenic or Mercurius, always presupposes a condition of hyposthenia, if I may so express myself, in the affections for which it is prescribed; the reverse is generally the case with the remedies of the group Pulsatilla.

Sulphur antidotes Silicea, as it does Pulsatilla; but Hepar sulphuris corresponds much more completely to the symptoms of Silicea.

Graphites.—*Plumbago, Percarburet of Iron;* now-a-days, it is considered as pure, or almost pure carbon, that is to say, carbon with which atoms of native iron are mixed, but not combined in the minutest proportions. "The first idea of making use of this substance as a drug (see Hahnemann's Chronic Disease, Vol. II) is due to Doctor Weinhold, who was led to it during his voyage in Italy, by the workmen in a looking glass factory, who employed it externally for tetters. He imitated them, and described the results which he obtained. From this period, and perhaps even before the publication of Weinhold's memoir,* Ruggieri employed Graphites internally and externally, in the cases for which it is recommended by the German physician. Some time after, in 1812, Hufeland related, in the the third report of the Polyclinical Institute of Berlin, the case of a lady of forty-one years, who was cured by the internal and external use of Graphites of an acne rosacea, which had defied all the means of treatment that had been employed until then. In 1817 and '18, the same author published several other cases of the same kind."

As regards French allopathic physicians, I am not aware that any of them, except Doctor Marc, have ever employed Graphites. Marc† published several cases tending to confirm the experience of Weinhold, Ruggieri, and Hufeland concerning the efficacy of this drug in various cutaneous affections. But, according to Hahnemann's judicious remark, it is a mistake to suppose that the use of Graphites is limited to the treatment of a few kinds of tetters.‡

The more one studies the pathogenesis of Graphites, the more one must feel convinced of the many points of contact

*Graphites considered as a remedy for tetters, (in German), Leipsic, 1809. 2d edit., Meissen, 1812.

†Bibliotheque Medicale, vol. XLV., p. 109.

‡See the pathogenesis of Graphites in Hahnemann's Chronic Diseases, vol. II., p. 2[illegible]

it has with Pulsatilla and (perhaps more particularly) with Silicea. Graphites, for instance, has the following symptoms in common with Pulsatilla and Silicea:

Anxious, changeable, wavering mood; aversion to work; vertigo with cloudiness; sort of intoxication in the morning; sense of fullness or emptiness in the head; drowsiness in the day-time; single, acute, deep shocks in the right half of the brain; flickering before the eyes; suspension of the visual power; photophobia; lachrymation in the air; foul smell in the nostrils; purulent coryza; wandering heat in the face; red, papulous eruptions, or resembling flea-bites, in the face and over the whole body; bitter taste in the mouth; aversion to liquid food; thirst (less frequently); nausea in the morning; rancid eructation; aversion to fat food; pressure and beating in the epigastrium; soft, thin, tape shaped, incomplete and frequent stools; pain in the abdomen after stool; swelling of the lower abdomen; piles; tenesmus of the bladder, followed by flow of watery urine; amenorrhea and dysmenorrhea, watery leucorrhea, swelling of the right testicle; itching and swelling of the right half of the scrotum; sexual excitement; no thrill during an embrace; impotence; catarrhal engorgement of the air-passages; palpitation of the heart; arterial throbbings here and there; pains as from deep-seated abscesses; swelling of the veins; wandering pains; pains in the parts upon which one is not lying; weakness in the extremities, with heaviness in the affected parts; hemiplegia; rheumatism at the nape of the neck, with swelling of the right side of the neck; painful lameness at the scrotum; swelling of the feet; sweat at night, having the odor of urine; drowsiness in the day time; sleep is disturbed by dreams, etc. These affections seem to be the same for the three drugs. The reader will have to decide for himself, agreeably to the totality of the symptomatic indications, which of them requires a preference in a given case.

I doubt not that Graphites can be usually employed both in acute and chronic affections. I have never used it in measles, but I believe that in certain cases of measles Graphites may be found more efficacious than any other drug.

"When chronic constipation and a delay of the menstrual show of several days are prominent symptoms, Graphites is often required."

According to Hahnemann, Arsenic and Nux vomica are its antidotes.

Calcarea carbonica.—*Carbonate of Lime.*

It is quite natural that the almost complete insolubility of this salt was an obstacle to its being used as a drug by the older physicians. Nevertheless several substances, such as chalk, egg-shells, oyster-shells, or the concretions which are known by the name of crabs' eyes, are in reality, mere varieties of the carbonate of lime, and have formerly enjoyed a certain celebrity in therapeutics. This is not the place to inquire into the real or supposed merits of these substances as remedial agents; moreover, they were scarcely ever prescribed without being combined with other drugs, so that it would be impossible to determine their genuine effects upon the organism. But there is one calcareous preparation which might, in some respects, be considered a substitute for our Calcarea carbonica, and the uses and effects of which are pretty well known; I mean lime water. I do not pretend to say that lime water and the carbonate of lime are identical in their action; but, if Hahnemann considered the acetate and carbonate of lime so nearly alike that he deemed it proper to range their symptoms side by side in a common pathogenesis,* we may certainly be allowed to believe that the difference between the action of lime-water and of carbonate of lime cannot be very great. What justifies this hypothesis is the fact, that, when lime water remains exposed to the air for a while, a pellicle of sub-carbonate of lime is very speedily formed by the absorption of the carbonic acid. It is, therefore, interesting to us homœopaths to inquire how far the empirical applications of this drug coincide with the pathogenesis of the carbonate.

Lime water seems to have been employed in medicine from the remotest antiquity. Hippocrates mentions it in several of his works, especially in the second book on epidemics, 5th section, and lauds it for several diseases, especially lepra. Fabricius d' Aquapendente recommended it for encysted dropsy. According to Gmelin,† Monro prescribed it internally and externally for scald-head. Hell for soft and suppurating warts, and in general for humid chronic exanthema.‡ Girtenner for old gonorrhœa. Jæger for ulcerated whitlows. Morton,§ Boerhaave,‖ and Graham** considered lime water as one of the best remedies for scrofulous or scorbutic ulcerations of the mouth, the genital organs and extremities. These physicians used lime water, as they expressed it, as a desiccative, an astringent, a dissolvent, and an antiseptic (doubtless because they had remarked that it arrested the fetid smell of ulcers, which is, indeed, one of its effects in some cases). Hence they recommended it in chronic diarrhœa, ulcerated cancer, gangrene, etc. In many cases, according to Gmelin,†† phlegm (or probably the chronic catarrh of the air passages) has been known to yield to the prolonged use of this drug: a statement which was afterwards confirmed by Monginot, who maintained that lime water had been of great use to him in whooping cough.‡‡ Lime water has, lastly, been praised in rheumatic and arthritic affections, in worm and intermittent fevers.

It is to be remarked, that the warmest advocates of lime water, notwithstanding all the good effects which they said it had in the above named affections, were all agreed on the following points: 1st, that it was only suitable in the chronic forms of these affections. 2d, that it was counter indicated by inflammatory fever, or by acute inflammation of some important organ. 3d, that it had unpleasant effects on individuals of a dry constitution and disposed to spasms. 4th, lastly, that it was able to do mischief at the commencement of dysentery, or when there was a sanguineous congestion of the head or kidneys.§§ Most of these counter indications evidently reposed only on allopathic prejudices. If an improperly administered dose of lime water produced, in a single case, spasms, fever, congestion of the head or kidneys (and such a thing might and must have happened), it was supposed deleterious in all cases where such symptoms existed.

Now-a-days, lime water has lost its former charm, and is scarcely used for any other purpose than to transform uric acid calculi into soluble urate of

*The symptoms of the acetate are marked with asterisks.
†Appar. Med. vol. I., p. 11, etc.
‡See symptoms, 1475, and foll. of Calc. carb.
§Opera Medica, edit of Geneva, p. 148.
‖Elem. chem., vol. II., p. 316.
**Med. observ. by a societ. of phys., London, 6 vol., vol. I., p. 286.
††Loc. Cit., p. 12.
‡‡Journ. gener. de med., Vol. XLIV., p. 890.
§§Gmelin, loc. cit., p. 23.

lime, an iatro-chemical proceeding, the success of which I dare not warrant. A few physicians, however, among whom I should mention Dr. Bretonneau, have tried to improve, in their practice, some of the traditional uses of lime water. Bretonneau uses it in chronic diarrhœa, especially when ulcerations of the lesser intestines, and especially of the rectum, may be suspected.

This is a short synopsis of the history of lime water, which is, I dare say, little known to allopathic physicians, but which, no doubt, suggested to Hahnemann the idea of proving the oyster-shell for the purpose of determining the pure effects of lime, which may be found recorded in the first volume of his Chronic Diseases.

Calcarea is frequently, but contrary to rule, employed empirically, in chronic diseases, even by homœopathic physicians, in the hope of modifying, they know not how, an old or congenital diathesis. A few successes do not justify such a mode of proceeding, which I must reject. I know that the carbonate of lime, phosphorus, phosphoric acid, and all other substances which enter largely into the composition of the human body, exercise a deep and pervasive action on the organism; but this is, it strikes me, an additional reason why it should not be administered at random.

As a general rule, lime, when it is indicated by the symptoms, suits blond and fat children, of a peevish and whining mood, having a certain appearance of vigor, or in whom the process of ossification takes place with difficulty; fat youths, adults of both sexes, with fair complexions, blue eyes, disposed to sub-acute catarrhal affections and chronic rheumatism. Women with white skins, mild or listless dispositions, whose menstruation is generally too early and profuse, and who, after a meal, or during a walk in a somewhat cool air, are attacked with heat in the face and redness at the tip of the nose; lastly, aged persons of both sexes, with dry, southern constitutions, yellowish complexions, having been troubled with tetters formerly, and being subject to attacks of peevishness, neuralgia or gout. It is especially in affections characterized by one or more of the following symptoms, that the carbonate of lime has been found efficacious.

Depression of spirits; peevishness, or weeping without any apparent cause; tendency to start, apprehension of near death; excessive sensitiveness; egotism; laziness; indifference for every thing, fatigue after walking ever so little; great sensitiveness to the cold; sweat after the least effort; dryness and roughness of the skin; furfuraceous tetters; warts on the extremities, and even in the face; papulous red spots on different parts of the body; lipomata; anxiety and shuddering towards evening; drowsiness early in the evening; frequent waking at night; sleeplessness; restlessness in bed; disturbing dreams; paroxysms of epilepsy in the night; tertian fever in the afternoon or evening, with heat before the chill. The head feels generally dull, as if a board were pressing against the forehead, with difficulty of thinking; vertigo in ascending an eminence; deep and sudden pain in the right half of the brain when stooping; dizziness and trembling in the morning, after leaving the bed; heaviness and pressure at the forehead, obliging him to close his eyes; headache caused by the least mental exercise; boring pain at the forehead; pulsative headache at the occiput; beating in the centre of the brain; hammering headache after a walk in the open air; flashes of heat about the head; headache and noise in the head, with heat about the cheeks; icy coldness at the right side of the head; sweat about the head in the evening;

falling out of the hair; itching of the eyes; sw ing of the eyes; congestion of the vessels of the eye; stitches in the eyes; deep seated pain, proceeding from the bottom of the right orbit, as if the ball of the eye would be crushed from behind forward; photophobia; lachrymation in the morning, in the open air; lachrymal fistula; obscuration of sight after eating or when reading; hemiopia; muscæ volitantes, or a sort of opaque gauze before the eyes; sensation as if electrical sparks started out of the eyes, (even in darkness;) agglutination of the eyelids during the night, and still more during the morning slumber; stitches in the ear; discharge of pus from the ears; cracking in the ear when swallowing; beatings in the ears; ringing in the ears; buzzing in the ears; noise in the ears, with hardness of hearing; noise in the ears, ending in a report; dulness of hearing; pains at the nose; stoppage of the nostrils by a yellow and fetid pus; bleeding of the nose; foul smell from the nose; smell of manure in the nose; pain in the face; itching and eruption in the face; freckles; itching, and itching pimples in the beard; eruption around the mouth; pain in the sub-maxillary glands; toothache after a cold drink; pulling and stinging toothache, day and night, excited again or aggravated by cold or warmth; digging and smarting in the teeth; difficult teething of children; painful swelling of the gums; ready bleeding of the gums; dryness of the tongue, night or morning, on waking; ranula; accumulation of mucus in the mouth and throat; bitter mouth, in the morning; want of appetite; loss of appetite, with constant thirst; aversion to warm food, especially warm meat; urging hunger in the morning; hunger shortly after having eaten; insatiable hunger; heat of the skin after eating; rush of blood to the head and face, sometimes with palpitation of the heart, after eating; eructations after eating; bitter eructations; sour eructations immediately after taking milk; heaviness of the stomach, before breakfast, and after eating; heaviness at the pit of the stomach, (with thirst) at night; spasms of the stomach; pinching, lancing or cutting pain at the pit of the stomach; sensitiveness of the epigastric region, which does not allow one to wear tight clothes; swelling of the epigastric region, with pressive pain; tension in both hypochondria; pressive, lancing pain in the abdomen, without diarrhœa; cutting pain in the upper part of the abdomen; cutting colic in the lower abdomen, in the afternoon, with vomiting of the food that had been taken a few hours previously; coldness in the lower abdomen; swelling and hardness of the lower abdomen; shifting of flatulence; constipation; scanty and hard stools; soft, thin and frequent stools; stools consisting of undigested food; chronic diarrhœa without bellyache; stools white as clay; involuntary discharge of liquid stool; protrusion of the piles, with burning pain, when going to stool; violent, fetid diarrhœa, at night or towards morning, with prolapsus of the rectum, enormous pressure on the anus and the genitals, which are swollen, constant and painful erections, excessive anguish;* prostration and painful weariness after stool; itching and ascarides in the rectum; tenesmus of the bladder, or rather, frequent emission of urine; discharge of blood from the urethra; blood urine; lascivious fancies; deficiency of sexual desire; weakness of the genital organs; absence of thrill during an embrace; stitches and burning in the male genital organs during the ejaculation of the semen; pressive pain in the vagina; pressure on the uterus;

*In the case of a man of sixty-six years, of a dry and nervous constitution, afflicted with tetters and the gout, Calcarea arrested these alarming symptoms very soon.

symptoms of miscarriage; stitches at the vulva, varices on the labia majora, uterine hemorrhage; premature and profuse menses; cutting colic during the menses, acrid leucorrhea previous to the menses.

Stuffing in the nose, especially in the morning; excessive coryza; chronic coryza; purulent coryza; hoarseness; excessive phlegm on the chest; cough in the evening, in bed; cough all night, during sleep; cough in the morning; dry cough; yellow and fetid sputa; heaviness at the stomach when coughing; oppression on the chest; loss of breath when stooping; stitches in the side of the chest during motion; heat in the chest; palpitation of the heart at night; stitches in the region of the heart; formication in the pectoral muscles; swelling of the breasts; stiffness of the nape of the neck; swelling of the cervical glands; pain in the loins; liability to attacks of lumbago, either by making an effort, or by exposure to a draught of air; pressive pain in the right arm; rheumatic pain in the arms at night; weariness in the arms; paralytic weakness of the hands; swelling of the hands; sweat on the hands; arthritic nodes on the hands and feet; numbness of the fingers, even in warmth; heaviness of the extremities, and particularly of the feet; spasms in the nates; stitches in the thighs; varices at the thighs; numbness of the legs when sitting; stiffness of the legs; cramps in the legs; ulcers at the legs; stitches and tearing in the knee; pulling in the knees; swelling of the (right) knee; heat at the sole of the foot; swelling of the soles of the feet; cold feet in the evening; sweaty feet; numb feet in the evening; sensitiveness of the big toes; stitches in the corns.

The Calcarea pains are most generally felt while lying in bed, or while sitting; they are felt in the parts upon which the body had been lying for a time.

In some respects, there exists a sort of negative relation between the symptoms of Mercurius solubilis, or rather between those of nitric acid and the symptoms of Calcarea. This contrast has struck me several times, and it is the more remarkable for this reason, that nitric acid is one of the best antidotes of Calcarea.

Phosphorus. A simple body which was discovered in 1673, by Brandt, an alchymist of Hamburgh, and shortly after by Kunkel, in Saxony, and by Robert Bayle, in England.

Phosphorus is a solid substance, colorless, transparent, flexible, luminous in the dark, exhaling an odor sui generis which has been compared to that of garlic. Fusible at 43 degrees of the centigrade thermometer, it is very volatile, and has such a strong affinity for oxygen that, when exposed to the open air, it burns in any temperature, disengaging a white smoke of phosphoric acid, which shines in the dark. It is insoluble in water, but tolerably soluble in alcohol, ether, fat and volatile oils. Phosphorus, which exists in large quantities in nature combined with oxygen and lime, is never found in a free state. It is extracted from urine, and still more generally from the bones of animals, the solid portion of which consists, as is well known, for the most part, of phosphate of lime.

Empirical Applications.—As soon as Phosphorus had been discovered, attempts were made to use it as a drug. Kunkel made it into his so-called luminous pills, which he used for various chronic diseases, and some years after, Kramer, physician to the Elector of Saxony, pretended having cured with Phosphorus, as by enchantment, several cases of dementia, epilepsy and malignant fevers.

Bayle has collected in the second volume of his bibliotheque de therapeutique a very considerable number of cases successfully treated with Phosphorus in Germany and France, but especially in the former country, from the time of Kramer to that of Lœbenstein-Lebel, or from 1738 to 1815. The principal cases—there are not less than a hundred in all, in this learned compilation—are taken from the reports of Mentz, Morgenstern, P. J. Hartmann, Bœnnekenius, Weickard, Conrad, Alphonse Leroy, Jacquemin, Hufeland, Coindet, Odier, Lobstein, Frank, Crell, Midy, Poilroux, Pilger and Lœbenstein-Lebel.*

The following diseases were treated by these practitioners:

1st. Twenty five cases of continuous fever (of the kind generally termed typhoid, putrid, ataxic, adynamic, etc.); the principal symptoms being: increase of temperature, more or less accelerated pulse, delirium, coma, various nervous symptoms, petechial, miliary or purple eruptions, (almost always on the chest and neck,) restlessness or prostration, foul odor of the excretions frequently; and lastly, in most cases, at the period when the use of Phosphorus was decided upon, precursory signs of approaching death, such as feeble, imperceptible pulse, cold extremities, loss of sensibility and cessation of the action of the senses.

2d. Six cases of bilious fever.

3d. Three cases of tertian intermittent, having been unsuccessfully treated with Cinchona and other remedies.

4th. Six cases of general œdema following putrid fevers, with excessive prostration, coldness of the extremities, small pulse, interruption of the sensual perceptions, etc.

5th. A case of measles of a suspicious nature, with disappearance of exanthem, (which the Phosphorus brought out again) dyspnœa, anxiety in the præcordia, etc.

6th. Two cases of pneumonia (left lung) accompanied with ataxic symptoms.

7th. Two cases of very serious pleurisy, the symptoms of which unfortunately are described incompletely.

8th. A case of croupy disease.

9th. A case of chronic ophthalmia.

10th. A case of chronic rheumatism of the legs, (described incompletely).

11th. Two cases of cerebral apoplexy, one of them accompanied by convulsions of the right arm and right lower extremity, and the other case having been several times aggravated by bleeding.

12th. Two cases of hydrocephalus.

13th. Two cases of periodical headache; in one case the attacks came on almost every ten days, in a nervous and delicate female whose menstruation was irregular; the other case was of a gouty nature.

14th. A sort of catalepsy coming on after confinement, and which ceased after the breaking out of miliaria.

15th. Two cases of convulsions, incompletely described.

16th. Two cases of epilepsy.

17th. One case of mania.

18th. Five cases of paralysis, among which two cases came on after an attack of gout.

19th. A well marked case of gutta sereno, the cure of which cannot be attributed to any other agency than that of Phosphorus.

20th. A case of amenorrhœa.

21st. An obstinate case of cardialgia.

22d. A case of asthenia senilis, in a man of eighty years, who used other medicines at the same time.

23d. Three cases of gout, with swelling of the joints and typhus, the cure being accompanied with profuse sweat and emission of urine.

24th. A case of chronic lead poisoning.

*Lœbenstein-Lebel, recherches et observations sur le phosphore, Strasburgh 1815.

25th. A case of chlorosis.

The following cases were not cured, but a temporary relief, which was sometimes most extraordinary, was experienced under the administration of Phosphorus: Two cases of purple and petechial typhus; a case without any particular name (by Alphonse Leroy) with evident symptoms of agony, and the fatal termination of which was kept off for a fortnight; a case of bilious fever; a case of paralysis; a case of anasarca; and one case of ascites.

The other cases, related by Bayle, were treated with Phosphoric acid; we shall recur to them in time and season.

There is no doubt that the cases which were unsuccessfully treated by these physicians, are much more numerous than the cures. This, however, only shows that Phosphorus is, no more than any other drug, a panacea for all diseases, and that it cures only such cases as correspond to its remedial virtues. Let allopathic physicians study Bayle's cases as I have done, pen in hand, draw up a list of the symptoms of these cases, compare these symptoms with the pure effects of Phosphorus on the healthy organism, and they will soon learn why Phosphorus cured in some and failed in other cases. Unfortunately such a comparison could not have been instituted before the drug had been experimented with, and this is the reason why Phosphorus, in spite of the cures it had effected, has fallen into disuse among allopathic physicians to such a degree that it is not even mentioned in their modern treatises of therapeutics.

Bayle, who is not a homœopath, (which I am at a loss to comprehend, after having read his treatise) sums up the therapeutic action of Phosphorus as well as could be expected of an observer who is not accustomed to the Hahnemannian mode of investigation. He says: "Phosphorus is indicated, 1st, in every disease where death has become imminent in consequence of the deep-seated injury inflicted upon the vital forces, without the structure of the organs being much altered. We see this state of things in all severe continuous fevers, when they have attained their last stage, be they caused by some miasm, such as typhus, plague, etc., or by a spontaneous alteration of the blood, as in the socalled adynamic or putrid fevers. In such cases, Phosphorus reanimates the vitality, furnishes nature the means of effectually resisting the disease, and eliminating, by the natural excretory outlets of the system, the material causes of the disease. Phosphorus is indicated, 2d, in all acute exanthemata when the eruption had disappeared quite suddenly, with aggravation of the symptoms, (measles, variola, scarlatina, miliaria, erysipelas, low fevers, with exanthem;)* 3d, in malignant pustule, when the low fever has reached its acme, and the strength seems on the point of becoming extinct. 4th, in gout and chronic rheumatism, which nature relieves or cures by profuse sweat or urine. 5th, in all morbid conditions, where it is proper to excite these secretions, and, at the same time, to stimulate the vitality in a speedy and energetic manner."†

Homœopathic applications.—I infer from the clinical observations of homœopathic physicians, and from mine in

*Bayle's remark, which is often founded so far as measles, purple-rash, miliaria, petechiæ, and some forms of erysipelas are concerned, is much less applicable to variola and scarlatina. As a general rule, Phosphorus is only useful in retrocession of exanthemata when static symptoms and derangements in the region of the heart and the air-passages spring up in consequence of these retrocessions.

†Loc. Cit., p. 124. (See the pathogenesis of Phosphorus in Hahnemann's Chronic Diseases, vol. III.)

particular, that Phosphorus, when it is indicated by the symptoms of the disease, is principally suitable to adults of both sexes and to old men (much rather than to children) of a lymphatico-sanguine-nervous temperament, fair complexion, sensitive disposition, lively and quick perceptions, inclined to corpulence, or else thin and slender, with a narrow chest, and what is generally termed, a phthisicky habit. Here follows a list of the symptoms, a majority of which is taken from Hahnemann, against which Phosphorus has been used with the best effect:

Sadness, weeping, or involuntary laughter, want of decision, indifference for one's own family; aversion to society, in general; tendency to start; irascible disposition; timidity; aversion to work; paroxysms of anxiety, with embarrassed respiration; bitter eructations, and heat in the hands; anxiety, especially in the evening, with palpitation of the heart, and trembling of the extremities; pulsations in different parts of the body; vertigo of various kinds, stupefying headache; rush of blood to the head; headache in the morning; pulsations in the brain; sudden shock in the brain, (when stooping) stitches in the side of the head, externally; itching about the head, falling off of the hair, heat and smarting in the outer canthi in the eyes, inflammation of the eyes, with heat and pressive pain, lachrymation in the open air, photophobia, dimness of sight, hemeralopia, myopia, every object looks as of a grayish color, cataract, glaucoma, black spots hovering before the eyes, difficulty of opening the lids, nightly agglutination of the lids, beating in the ears, buzzing in the ears, difficulty of hearing the human voice, nose-bleed, bad smell from the nose, want of smell, earthy complexion, redness and heat of the cheeks, tearing in both jaws, at night; toothache in the morning, when eating; lancing toothache every night, until two o'clock, bitterness of the mouth, excoriation in the inner mouth; mucus in the mouth, dryness in the throat, day and night, a good deal of phlegm in the morning, slimy taste in the mouth, cheesy taste in the mouth, loss of taste; eructations, spasmodic eructations, sour eructations, absence of thirst; thirst in the middle of the day, nausea in the morning; obstinate or periodical hiccough; hunger after eating; nausea after eating; canine hunger; nausea after having eaten sour things; burning in the hands after eating; laziness and drowsiness after eating, heaviness at the stomach after eating, with vomiting of the ingesta; sort of tightness of the cardia, causing a rising of food that had just been swallowed; sensitiveness of the pit of the stomach, formication in the pit of the stomach, rancid regurgitations, difficulty of digesting milk, flatulence after dinner, bellyache in the morning, in bed, borborygmi, gurgling in the abdomen, inguinal hernia, violent urging before stool, tearing in the abdomen, with violent urging to stool, discharge of blood during stool, diarrhœa of phthisicky patients, discharge of pieces of tænia, itching at the anus, internal and external piles, discharge of mucus from the anus, tension in the urethra, smarting in the urethra when urinating, hot urine, burning twitching in the urethra, erection in the evening, excessive desire for an embrace, too rapid ejaculation of the semen, frequent emissions, stitches in the vagina, extending to the uterus, too profuse and watery menses, megrim at the period of the menses, leucorrhœa.

Stuffing of the nose, fatiguing dryness in the nose, constant discharge of mucus from the nose, smarting in the throat, mucous sputa, tickling in the throat, which excites a cough, chronic cough, cough excited by laughter, cough with vomiting, cough with pain in the chest and hoarseness, cough during the night, with stitches in the larynx, difficulty of breathing, noisy respiration, pressure on the chest, chronic stitches in the side, smarting pain in the chest, pain in the left side of the chest, when resting upon it, palpitation of the heart when sitting, palpitation of the heart during the least movement, spasms of the pectoral muscles, swelling of the breasts, (especially the left) contusive pain in the back, stiffness of the nape of the neck, swelling of the neck, pain in the arm when raising it, tearing stitches in the arms and shoulder-blades, heat in the hands, with swelling of the veins, trembling of the hands, pulsative pain in the buttocks, spasms in the glutei muscles, stitch in the hip striking to the chest, pulling pain in the knees, twitchings in the calves, exostosis at the tibia, cold feet at night, smarting pains at the soles of the feet when walking, shocks in the feet in the day time and at night before falling asleep, rheumatism in the extremities, numbness of the ends of the fingers and toes, round, papulous, yellow spots on the chest and lower abdomen, brown spots on the body, drowsiness in the day time, drowsiness in the morning, difficulty of falling asleep, in the evening, sleep full of dreams, frightful dreams, cold in bed, every evening, dry heat, without thirst, in the evening, in bed, transitory heat, sweat in the morning.

Sulphur, Chamomilla, Carbo veg. and Viola, are most generally employed with Phosphorus, at least in chest affections.

I do not believe that the antidotes which Jahr points out in his Manual, Camph., Coff., Nux vom. and wine, will prove of much avail. Chamom. may, perhaps, neutralize the action of Phosphorus with tolerable speed.

Hepar sulphuris calcareum. *Sulphuret of lime.*—This compound exists in nature, but the homœopathic preparation is obtained artificially, by calcinating in closed vessels equal parts of purified flowers of sulphur, and finely pulverized oyster shells.

The therapeutic history of this substance is very short. At first it was only used externally against the itch, rheumatism, gout, goitre and scrofulous swellings. G. L. Hoffman and Stoll, among others, recommended it very strongly for the two last named affections.* In 1794, Hahnemann, who is quoted by Gmelin, proposed to use it internally to arrest mercurial salivation. A few years after this, it was tried for asthma and pulmonary phthisis. This was one of the happiest applications that could have been made of this drug. I believe that this idea is due to Dr. Busch, of Strasburgh. In the first period of the disease, Busch prescribed the extract of Aconite, and Hepar sulphuris in the subsequent periods. He states that by means of this empirical proceeding, he has effected several cures of confirmed pulmonary phthisis.†

Professor Bang, of Copenhagen, pretends having arrested by the same means an incipient pulmonary phthisis, (which is very vague).‡

In our time, Dr. Harel de Tancrel, pretends curing pulmonary phthisis by means of a mixture of extract of Aconite and Hepar sulphuris. Such assertions are only imperfectly justified by the physiological action of Hepar. There are some forms of phthisis the symptoms of which correspond to Hepar, and which may, therefore, be

*Gmelin, appar. medic., vol. 1., p. 164.

†Recherch. sur la nature et le traitem. de la phthisie pulm., par. J. J. Busch, in 8vo., 1800.

‡Bullet. des sc. med. de Ferussac, vol. I, p. 218.

cured by means of this drug; but in other forms of this disease, Hepar would be out of place and might do harm. Experience shows this every day.*

According to Hahnemann, Hepar has been used with success in the following morbid conditions:

Dissatisfaction with one's self and others; unpleasant recollections; dreamy, atrabilious mood, a sort of ferocious spleen, as though one could murder a man in cold blood, (even in persons who are generally of a benevolent and merry disposition);† boring pain at the root of the nose, every morning, from seven o'clock until noon, smarting pain above the eye, every evening, stitches in the eyes, photophobia, discharge of fetid pus from the ear, erysipelas of the face, with prickling tension, dryness of the throat, scraping in the throat, with difficulty of talking, but not of swallowing, canine hunger, eruptions, paroxysms of nausea, with coldness and paleness, swelling and pressure at the epigastric region, frequent stomach ache, constrictive pain in the lower abdomen, stitches in the left side of the abdomen, shifting of flatulence, difficult emission of flatulence, in the morning, emission of urine during sleep at night, mucous discharge from the urethra, deficient sexual desire, absence of erections, feeble erections during an embrace, discharge of prostatic fluid while urinating after hard stool, considerable delay of the menses, leucorrhœa and excoriations of the vulva, cough, violent cough in the evening, in bed, spasmodic constriction of the chest, after talking, cancerous ulcer at the breast, with a lancinating, burning pain, and an odor as of old cheese, tearing pain in the arm, pulling in the back, between the shoulders, fetid sweat in the axillæ, cyst at the point of the elbow, numbness of the fingers, pulling pains in the extremities, especially in the morning, on waking, weakness and trembling after smoking, yawning, liability to sweating in the day time, transitory heat with sweat.

Hepar is frequently indicated in the diseases of children. In is antidoted by Silicea, Chamomilla, and especially by Belladonna.

*See the pathogenesis of this drug in Hahnemann's Chronic Diseases, vol. II., p. 283.

†These symptoms are not mentioned by Hahnemann; but I have seen them yield so often under the action of Hepar, that I look upon them as characteristic effects of this drug.

SPASMODIC STRICTURE OF THE PYLORUS.

There are books and books and books on almost every subject in medicine. But I have spent some time in searching for something bearing on this subject without being able to find anything. Yet I take it that no thinking man will deny the existence of such a condition.

The stomach has been termed "the musculo-membranous receptaculum," and this is quite appropriate, since it is membranous in appearance and function, while in structure it is muscular. But the circular muscular fibres are all with which we have to deal in the present discussion, although it will be necessary to direct attention to the mucous membrane and some of its abnormalities as possible causes.

The circular fibres form a uniform coat over the whole of the stomach, but are much more abundant at the pyloric extremity, where they form a ring-like band which projects into the canal, to form the body of the so-called pyloric valve, the mucous membrane covering its surface assisting to complete the valve-like sentry that stands guard to prevent the escape of anything not previously provided with proper passports in the shape of perfect preparation.

This sentry, like those of all well regulated armies, is under the command of superiors, and has very strict orders to permit nothing to pass except on giving the proper pass-word. He is all right and treats everybody well, so long as no one attempts to practice fraud on him, by presenting false credentials, but frequent attempts of this kind finally render him irritable, and he is liable to cause trouble, and refuse at times to permit the passage of any. And when he becomes too tyranical we are obliged to consult his superiors for relief. Therefore the first and most important thing for us to do is to learn who is in command and where he may be found.

Since this sentry is composed of muscles its commander is some nerve, but which one? We are told in the works on anatomy that the nerves of the stomach are terminal branches of the right and left pneumogastric, the former being distributed to the back and the latter upon the front part of the organ. Also that a great many sympathetic branches are distributed to it.

This is so indefinite as to seriously impair its usefulness in our inquiry. But we learn from other sources that there are some plexuses lying between the muscular coats which resemble Auerbach's plexuses in other portions of the alimentary tract, and have the same functions. Indeed they are Auerbach's plexuses, and as such, preside over peristaltic action of the stomach and are in immediate command of this sentry. But when we make our complaint to them we learn that they are acting on the orders of ranking officers. Who are they?

We must ascertain this by exclusion. We know that all sentries at the external orifices of the body are under the command of the cerebro-spinal system. But on inquiry we are told that these are more or less voluntary, and since this troublesome sentry is not, it must belong to some other command. True there are cerebro-spinal fibres all about it, but there is no voluntary power that can change its action in the least. But we must not overlook the frequent communications between the cerebro-spinal and the sympathetic systems, or we may be misled in our search for the ranking officer in this case.

But before we go any further in our search for him, let us inquire into the true or ultimate cause of this fellow's irritability and arrogance, since he is only a sentry any way. The neighborhood where he is stationed receives its common sensation through the pneumogastrics. The frequent attempts on the part of indigested food to run the blockade, so to speak, of the pylorus, finally results in more or less distension of that part of the stomach situated immediately above this organ, and this forcible distension produces stretching or pulling on the pneumogastric nerve fibres, causing an uncomfortable sensation, if not pain, in those fibres. Since in all cases nature has made pain a mentor and rest the cure, there is reflected from these fibres to those of the sympathetic, via the solar plexus, an impulse commanding rest for this part of the economy.

Therefore the real commander is the pneumogastric nerve. But when we go to that we are told that no relief can be expected so long as the source of irritation remains to attempt forced passage through the channel that is under quarantine regulations. We now turn our attention to Auerbach's plexuses which control the movements of the gastric walls, and hence seem to be responsible for these illegal attempts to run the blockade, and are told that the only business of this department is to keep things moving, and not to inspect the material to be passed through the channel, and we must look to the proper authorities for this. We now turn our attention to the mucous and other glands that are supposed to secrete the digestive juices, only to receive the information that they are doing the best that they possibly can with the material supplied, which is entirely inadequate to supply the demands, and digestion cannot be improved until more and better material can be had from which to extract the digestive secretions.

We next inquire who is in charge of this important department, and learn that it is the Meisner plexuses located beneath the mucous lining of the stomach. But when we inquire there we learn that it is impossible for them to extract material from that which does not contain it, or if it does contain the material, the machinery for its separation is so arranged that it does not extract it.

Inquiry leads us to another part of the sympathetic system, that presides over assimilation, or rather elimination.

Now after traveling all over the camp, we learn that the real cause of this irritability is in the sympathetic nervous system, all of which is in an abnormal condition, or a state of disorder, thus only proving what Hahnemann said many years ago, that sickness is not local but general, or words to that effect. There can be no such thing as purely a local disease.

Then why so much trouble to arrive at a correct diagnosis, when it is so easy to pronounce any case of indigestion with obstruction at the pyloric orifice cancer? Besides all that we need to do is to prescribe a remedy that covers a few of the superficial symptoms, that we call keynotes, and if it does not cure, we can say the case is incurable.

Because (1), it is not scientific, (2) the patient and friends have a right to know the probable termination, and, (3) it is not in accordance with Hahnemann's ideas of what constitutes the totality of symptoms.

He tells us that the physician must understand the following conditions:

"What is curable in disease in general, and in each individual case in particular; that is, the recognition of disease, (*indicatio*). He should clearly comprehend what is curative in drugs in general, and in each drug in particular; that is, he should possess a perfect knowledge of medicinal powers. He should be governed by distinct reasons, in order to insure recovery, by adapting what is curative in medicine to what he has recognized as undoubtedly morbid in the patient. Finally, when the physician knows in each case the obstacles in the way of recovery, and how to remove them, he is prepared to act thoroughly and to the purpose, as a true master of the healing art." Organon, section 3.

Now, how can we be prepared according to this without recognizing the tissues that are involved in each case? I leave the reader to answer.

The subject of this paper was suggested to me by a patient who came under my observation Nov. 20, 1902.

Dr. E. W. P., a dentist, aged 53, nervo-bilious temperament, with marked predominance of the nervous element.

Family history: Father died at the age of 79, of some acute form of heart disease.

Mother died at the age of 64 of paralysis.
Brothers, two living and well.
Sisters, one died aged 42 of consumption.

Personal: Never was sick a day until Sept., 1901, when he had an attack of acute indigestion brought on by eating cucumbers. This passed off and he remained well until July, 1902, when his stomach again became disordered without known cause. Nothing seemed to digest. He was always worse from eating hearty food, has lost 40 pounds since that time, and is growing worse all the time. Appetite good and food tastes good. At times there seems to be some obstruction that prevents the food from passing out of the stomach, while again it passes all right. Even liquids cannot escape when there is trouble of this nature. Food will lie for hours in the stomach, until it causes so much distress that he resorts to some means of emptying the stomach upwards. This gives immediate relief. The fermentation causes a slight nausea at times, but this is of no importance, being so slight.

All other organs are in perfect condition. There is much gas in the stomach after eating that usually is tasteless. *No pain* at any time in stomach, but a sense of pressure and a peculiar distressed feeling from gas.

Rumbling of gas in the abdomen at times. Stools regular as a rule, some diarrhœa from eating oysters a few days ago. Anus normal. Fever none.

Sleeps well all night. Thirst after he causes vomiting.

He has been examined and treated by several allopaths, who gave his trouble several names, two or three telling him that it is cancer, one that there was but one symptom lacking, the absence of hydro-chloric acid in the contents of the stomach. Analysis showed its absence. Of course the doctor did not look for the other digestive juices or he would most probably have found them also absent.

There is no tumor or soreness about the stomach. Not the least sensitiveness even to hard percussion over the stomach.

The history of the case pointing to previous druggings, and being unable to get a very clear picture for a remedy, I prescribed *Nux vomica*[c]

Nov. 28. Feels well. Had a little trouble with stomach on the night of the 26th. Prescription continued.

Dec. 3. Has had three hard days, stomach very sour, with much belching. Liquids and other food lay in the stomach for several hours, causing so much distress that he finally caused vomiting by irritating the throat, which gave relief. *No pain. Carbo. veg*[m] three doses, one a day.

Dec. 11. Feels very fine. Can eat with no distress following. Ate a baked potato yesterday, which gave no trouble. Would not know he had a stomach for several days. Has lost no weight, but on the contrary has gained about a pound. Had a normal stool each day. *Carbo. veg*[m] one dose.

This is undoubtedly a case of nervous indigestion, the undigested food causing irritation of the pyloric orifice of the stomach by continued attempt on the part of the muscular coats to force this unfit material through it. The consequent fermentation of the food resulted in the formation of gas and distention therefrom which further irritated the part, finally resulting in the only logical sequence, spasm of the pylorus, in an attempt to rest the part by force.

I am led to this conclusion by the fact that the obstruction is not constant, the absence of pain, vomiting, tumor or tenderness about the stomach, or any cancer cachexia. According to the best authorities hydro-chloric acid is present in some cases of cancer and frequently absent when there is no cancer. The consensus of opinion at present seems to be that the presence of an abundance of hydro-chloric acid contra-indicates cancer in cases of dilated stomach, but its absence is not diagnostic of cancer since it is also absent in chronic gastritis, fevers etc.

It does not take a great amount of reasoning to see that organic stricture of the pylorus could not disappear at times and completely close the orifice at other times. And pain is a very constant and marked symptom of cancer of the stomach or of any other organ or part of the body.

E. R. McINTYER, B. S., M. D.
Chicago.

Medicine.

MEDICAL AND SURGICAL EPIGRAMS.

The reason why there are so many poor men in the medical profession is because we give more time to the science of medicine than the science of collections.

There used to be such an individual as a "family" doctor, but nowadays folk use a physician as they do a borrowed umbrella.

Always be busy when an oily-tongued fellow approaches you; if you don't he will be, and nearly always to your detriment.

Ethics say "don't blow your own horn." But he who bloweth not his own horn, the same will not be blown.

Speaking about ethics reminds me of the fact that if you give an inch the other fellow will take an ell.

There is much sweet consolation in talking over a case with a confrere when he fully agrees with you, but never, looks you squarely in the face. Watch! You will get it where the bear wears his belt, sooner or later, at his hands.

The duty of a consultant is to tell the truth as he sees it. If you concur, do it honestly. Don't lose your patient for the sake of keeping a doctor's friendship.

A man who will charge less than five dollars for a consultation is too cheap to keep company with.

Some of the biggest (?) doctors in the country are the fellows who subscribe to one of the weekly almanacs.

It doesn't exalt a fellow in my estimation to see his medical books covered with dust and cob-webs.

A man who will not subscribe to some of the high-class medical journals, of which there are many, is too stingy to feed the horse which drags him to his dollars.

Business managers of the daily newspapers are wholly responsible for 95 per cent of quackery that exists. Let them refuse to sell quacks space and note results.

The unnatural laws of medicine and surgery have been practiced long enough. Let the pendulum swing back a little and start afresh.

The ancient method of bleeding is still in vogue—in and out of the profession.

The further a doctor sends his patients away, the more he is thought of by them. Why?

The man who lacks the moral courage to buy surgical instruments with which to do his work, is the man who will never become a surgeon.

Better is the surgeon who saves a finger than he who amputates a leg.

There has always been a big stink raised about iodoform, but without it a mightier stink may oft prevail.

The vermiform appendix is a very much abused organ and yet "Dr Epsoms" says he "knocks 'em out" for five cents. Too cheap to be safe every time!

A great many displeased delinquents remind me strongly of a case of "wind colic." The only relief they get is in growling.

How deliciously happy would the world be if it knew it did not possess a liver!

I would rather undertake to cure ten cases of syphilis than one case of hypertrophic rhinitis.

The maximum punishment that one can inflict on a "Rectal specialist" is to consult him for an ingrowing nail. They can't connect!

The man who is not in love with his profession will never be loved by the profession.

Rank poison is far preferable in surgery or medicine than rank ignorance.

Every medical institution of learning should establish a chair devoted exclusively to the art of collecting.

A doctor should be a success every day of his life. Evergy, ambition and applicability is the tripod upon which every one should firmly stand.

A miserable mistake is never a pardonable mistake.

One can't always be right, but one can always be sincere.—Lucien Lofton, M. D., in *Am. Jour. of Surg. and Gyn.*

Nursing.*

INTERRUPTED PREGNANCY.

Lecture No. 14.

Ladies: Pregnancy may be interrupted accidentally, or it may be necessary to bring on labor to save the life of the mother or child. Prematurely born children require especial care and very close attention. The most premature child that has been successfully raised was born after a gestation of twenty-six weeks. Usually, however, a child must be seven or eight months advanced to survive.

The dangers to which prematurely born children are exposed arise in the sudden change of temperature from the mother's womb to the external world, and in the difficulty in digestion which the feebleness of the child produces. When it is sure that the pregnancy is to terminate prematurely, artificial warmth for the child must be prepared and arrangements made to feed it.

Incubators are chambers, or boxes, kept at a comparatively high temperature, in which prematurely born children may be kept until they are sufficiently vigorous to endure the ordinary temperture. A simple and useful incubator is a wooden box having a glass lid which can be removed. About one fourth of the distance from the bottom of the box is a false bottom or berth, which covers three-fourths of the floor of the box. Beneath this berth or false bottom are placed cans or bottles containing hot water. They are introduced by drawing back a slide which covers the space between the bottom of the box and the berth. At one end is a square opening or air window, which may be wholly or partly covered by a slide. At one corner of the upper surface of the incubator is a tube to permit the escape of the heated air. A bed is made upon the false bottom with a blanket or pillow, and the child is placed upon this. The hot cans or bottles are put in the bottom, the air window is opened, air enters at the bottom, passing over the hot bottles, and escapes at the top through the air tube. A thermometer placed beneath the glass lid enables the nurse to read the temperature of the interior of the incubator. Such a simple apparatus costs but little, and the usual degrees of temperature required are readily obtained by re-filling of the hot

* Course of Lectures delivered to the Nurses Training School at Maryland Homœopathic Hospital, by H. H. Douglass, M. D., Baltimore, Md.

tles or cans at hourly intervals.

When it is not convenient to obtain and incubator an excellent substitute is found in the ordinary clothes basket, in the bottom of which hot cans or hot bottles may be placed, two or more rolls of blankets being put around the cans to make a floor, and to keep the child from coming in contact with the cans. A blanket should be so unfolded as to line the basket completely, and the child placed upon a thickly folded blanket, with its head slightly higher than the feet. Other heated cans or bottles may be placed between the basket and the blanket which lines it and thus the child may be kept thoroughly warm. The advantage of the clothes basket lies in the fact that the child can readily obtain an abundance of air, and in the ease with which it may be improved.

It is very important that the premature infant shall obtain abundant air no matter what apparatus is employed. The incubator or basket should never be placed upon the floor, but upon a table three or four feet above the floor. This is more convenient for the nurse, and gives the child a much better circulation of air. If the weather be cold, the basket should be placed in a room with an open fire, and the room should be freely ventilated. The doctor should prescribe the degree of temperature at which he wishes the child to be kept. This will range from 95 to 86 degrees in the majority of cases.

While it is of the greatest importance that artificial heat be supplied for the child, the most careful arrangements in this regard may be defeated by a little careless exposure. When a premature child is born it should at once be taken before an open fire, wrapped in blankets, and after it has breathed well it should be thoroughly oiled with sterile olive oil. The vernix caseosa and oil should be removed by rubbing the child's body with sterile cotton. If the scalp and face be soiled, they may be quickly sponged with [illegible] warm sterile water and quickly dried. The child should then be bandaged in [illegible] thin carded lamb's wool, a layer of from one-half to an inch thick being placed about the body and limbs, leaving the orifice of the excretory organs without any covering. This wool should be held in place by bandages of cheese-cloth, which are very light and very easily adjusted. A very thin flannel slip may then be placed on the child, although this is in most cases unnecessary. Over the orifice of the bladder and bowel a handful of sterile cotton or wool should be placed. The child should be laid in the incubator, and should not be removed without the doctor's orders.

When it is necessary to feed such a child the mother's breast should be pumped and the milk placed in a small cup in a basin of warm water. It should be taken at once to the child and dropped into the child's mouth from a medicine dropper. The doctor should prescribe the number of drams or drops which should be given, and the intervals of administration. When the mother has no nourishment for the child or when the milk is slow in forming, the doctor will prescribe other nourishment for it. Predigested milk diluted with barley water is often employed for this purpose.

Prematurely born children usually require stimulation. The physician will order the kind of stimulus and the dose, and this is best administered considerably diluted. Thus the child will obtain its nourishment, drink and stimulation at regular intervals. The discharges from the bladder and bowels are received upon the sterile cotton or gauze placed between the thighs and beneath the child, and this should be removed and the parts thoroughly dried with sterile cotton as often as necessary. By close attention it is possible to keep such an infant clean and in a thoroughly sound condition. Should the child become uneasy, the room may be warmed, the lid of the incubator removed, or the blanket covering the basket, and the bandages and wool removed gradually, the child's skin inspected, again rubbed with oil, and the wool and bandages replaced. The child should not be taken from the incubator if it can possibly be avoided. It is interesting to notice that such children cry but little, and seem more comfortable than children in the usual condition. This is probably due to their freedom from disturbance. When the temperature falls below the point of comfort the child will immediately cry. Should the temperature be too high the child will breathe rapidly and seem oppressed.

Such children should not be bathed in a tub until they have come to the full period of maturity, and have firmly established their health and vigor. They may be kept clean by sponge bathing when they are sufficiently strong. If care be taken to massage the breasts, and to use a breast pump regularly and gently, the mother will usually have a sufficient supply of milk.

We will now turn our attention to some of the more important disorders of children, which, I think, you should have some knowledge.

Infants may be much annoyed by constipation, and the condition may become difficult to remedy. It must not be allowed to continue, because straining and difficult defecation may bring about prolapse of the bowel and much suffering result. The constipation of an infant is a relative and not an absolute condition. Children have remained in perfect health who had but one bowel movement in two days. This, however, is the exception and not the rule. When the movements are hard, tough, and resisting when one examines them, and when the matter is ejected with difficulty, the child straining and crying during defecation, the condition demands active relief. The physician will see that the food is of proper quality. If the child be nursing, he may order a change in the diet of the mother. It is usual to employ a diet composed largely of vegetables, selected fruits, cereals, with a moderate quantity of sweet material and very little meat.

The nurse in such a case is often directed to give the child abdominal massage after the morning bath. The child is placed upon its back upon a blanket or upon the flannel bathing apron; the nurse's hands must be warm and clean, and the hand which is to be applied to the abdomen should be lubricated with sterile olive oil. The rubbing should begin at the lower portion of the right of the abdomen, and follow the course of the large intestine up upon the right side, across just above the umbilicus, and down upon the left side. This manipulation is usually very agreeable to the child, and will sometimes cause an attack of colic to cease. The pressure should be a gentle one, and the manipulation may be continued from ten to twenty minutes. Nurses are often directed to inject into the bowels in these cases an ounce of warm olive oil. The best syringe for this purpose is what is called the Infant's enema syringe, a moderately firm ball of rubber and a short nozzle. If a piston syringe is used, care must be taken that but little force is used. A Davidson syringe should not be used. It is practically impossible to introduce oil by means of a fountain syringe. If soap and water enemas are prescribed, the nurse should watch carefully for signs of irritation in the mucous membrane of the bowel. Some children bear soap and water enemas very badly. The injection of glycerine is not often practiced with infants.

The nurse may render the child great service by forming habits of regularity in the movements of the bowels. Morning and night should be the rule in infants, and if this be once established the adult will profit by it in later life. Constipation often shows itself by restlessness and fretfulness at night. If the attention of the physician be called to this, he will usually permit the nurse to empty the child's bowel just before the usual hour for putting it to bed. In this way discomfort may be avoided during the night to both mother and child. Nurses must not forget that the free use of water is as necessary in avoiding constipation with infants as in adults.

The best medicines for this condition are: Bryonia, Nux vomica and Opium.

When *bleeding* occurs *from the umbilicus*, the nurse may stop it for a moment by making pressure with sterile gauze at the point of bleeding. The physician must be immediately summoned. Hot water and antiseptic solutions must be in readiness. If the physician does not arrive promptly and pressure from a compress control the bleeding, the nurse may bandage a compress upon the umbilicus by a snugly fitting abdominal bandage. The case should not go, however, without the attendance of a physician.

After the umbilicus has healed a *protrution of the tissues* beneath the umbilical ring may occur. When the infant cries or coughs, a tumor about as large as the end of the little finger is forced outward. If this be carried back by the tip of the little finger, a small ring can be felt, which is the contracting umbilical ring. To prevent this protrusion, various sorts of pads and applications are used. A fairly efficient support is made by stitching sterile gauze into a pad an inch square. This is held in place by an abdominal binder of soft, elastic flannel. When difficulty is experienced in retaining a pad or retentive dressing adhesive plaster may be used. If such is the case, the nurse must take care that when the adhesive strips are changed, the child's skin beneath them is thoroughly cleansed with soap and water, and then with alcohol and water. Unless caution is exercised the skin may become sore. Circular pads cut from cardboard, coins covered with linen or surgeon's lint, or any smooth circular object may be tried as an appropriate support. The nurse may comfort the parents by informing them that few of these cases give rise to serious trouble or persist to adult life. When the case becomes chronic, the doctor may prescribe a hard rubber truss, held in position by an abdominal bandage.

During the first few weeks after birth, eruptions of various sorts are sometimes observed among infants. A small bright red eruption over almost the entire body, sometimes follows cleansing of the skin, especially if the child be too warmly clothed. An eruption of small blisters is mildly contagious, and in neglected cases with weak children may become serious. This is usually treated by the use of a very mild antiseptic powder or lotion. Chafing and excoriation about the genital organs and the anus are suggestive of constitutional taint, or result from neglect on the part of the nurse. If the diapers are not changed promptly and the child kept clean, such a condition readily arises. Irritating discharges from the bowels or bladder also form a cause. An eruption, at first dark red or brownish red, then fading to a copper color, is suggestive of constitutional disease, and must be at once reported to the attending physician. An eruption of dark, livid spots beneath the skin, becoming gradually larger, while the child has an abnormal temperature, with prostration and discharges of blood from the umbilicus, bowels, or mouth, is a serious symptom, and must be reported as soon as observed. Nurses must remember that dye stuffs in cloth may produce eruptions in children. The application to the body of an infant of a cheap quality of red flannel wrung out of hot water has often produced a deceptive eruption. The bites of insects must also be kept in mind in these cases. Usually the simplest treatment possible is ordered, bathing with alcohol and water or with boric acid solution, or by the use of simple ointment. The responsibility of the nurse consists very largely in detecting and promptly reporting the occurrence of such an eruption.

The next lecture closes this course, and we will conclude with the disorders of infants continued.

DISEASES OF THE NEW-BORN.

Lecture No. 13.

Ladies: Tonight we finish our course in this branch. There are a few diseases very important for us to consider, and they are diseases in which prompt action alone may save the child from death or permanent injury. The first I bring to your attention is *"Ophthalmia Neonatorum."*

By this is meant infection of the conjunctivæ in the eyes of infants resulting from the presence of a septic germ. The infective agent in many of these cases is the gonococcus, or germ causing gonorrhœa. This is peculiarly virulent, and blindness occurs in many of these patients. Other septic germs may cause ophthalmia, but the results are not so serious as in gonorrhœal infection. The signs of this disease are redness and swelling in the conjunctivæ, with the formation of pus, which accumulates in the corners of the eyes. The pus is usually thick and yellow in color. It is occasionally very thin, dark brown or reddish brown. When the child is recovering, a whitish mucous secretion is often present.

Unless the disorder be checked the inflammation spreads rapidly, the lids become swollen so that the eyes shut, the white of the eye becomes a bright and flaming red, the pupils are contracted, the discharge is a bright yellow, less thick and much more abundant, and the child frets and cries with distress, endeavoring to rub the eyes with the fingers. The inflammation goes on to the interior of the eye. The eyeball swells, and finally ulceration through some portion of the eye occurs, followed by shrinking of the eyeball and entire loss of vision. In cases which do not go so far the anterior portion of the eye becomes clouded and partially opaque from scar tissue. With this condition the child would have partial vision only.

The rate at which this inflammation progresses depends upon the kind of germ which attacks the eyes and the vigor and strength of the infant. If the gonococcus is present and the child a feeble one, blindness may result in two or three days. If a germ not so virulent attacks a strong and healthy child, treatment be instituted, the inflammation will be checked in forty-eight hours. The complete cure of this condition requires several weeks in most cases.

The nurse must remember that this is an active infection, and a particle of matter from the child's eyes introduced into her own will cause an active inflammation and may result in the loss of her sight. This matter, when introduced through a cut or pin prick into the finger, may set up a septic inflammation. If one eye only be infected, the other eye will become involved if the secretion passes from one to the other. The case must be treated then with promptness and with great care and thoroughness, to save the eyes of the child and to avoid danger to those who attend it.

Physicians usually employ the almost constant application of cold. Compresses the size of a half dollar are cut from surgeon's lint and laid upon a cake of ice placed in a pan or basin. The nurse sits with the child upon her lap or in a crib, applying an ice compress every five or ten minutes. To remove the secretion from the eyes, douching or washing with an antiseptic fluid is employed. A saturated solution of boric acid, mercuric chlorid (1:8000), normal salt solution, and sterile water are the fluids most often required. Special care must be taken that these fluids are of the proper strength, as an error in this particular might cause serious damage to the eyes. The way of making these applications differs with different physicians. Some prefer irrigation, while others cause the fluid to be dropped into the eyes from a medicine dropper. Of the two, irrigation is much more efficient, and is seldom injurious when carefully done. To make this application, if but one eye is affected, the other eye is covered with sterile gauze or cotton and a bandage placed over it. The nurse requires a rubber sheet, a slop-jar, a fountain syringe, a medicine dropper, the solutions ordered, several small bits of sterile gauze or cotton, and a little sterile oil or vaselin. The glass portion of the medicine dropper is separated from the rubber bulb, and is placed in the tube of the syringe to act as a nozzle. When the fluid has been placed in the bag, the latter is hung about four feet above the child. Having cleansed her hands thoroughly, the nurse spreads the rubber sheet upon her lap and takes the child with the infected eye lower than the bandaged one. If the child lies upon its side, the posture will be the best for this application. The fluid is allowed to run from the inner angle of the eye over the lids, passing downward and outward. Secretion is soon washed away, and if the child does not open the eye, the nurse must very gently separate the lids with the thumb and finger and wash the eye thoroughly. The eye must be washed in a careful manner so that absolutely no particle of secretion remains. When this has been accomplished, the eye should be dried with sterile cotton, and sterile olive oil or vaselin should be very lightly rubbed upon the outer surface of the lids to prevent the discharge from accumulating and contaminating the lids. The intervals of irrigation must be as short as is consistent with the child's general condition. Every half hour or every hour, while the inflammation is active, is not too frequent, and is often followed by great benefit. If bichlorid solutions are used, physicians often order that irrigation with normal salt solution be practiced immediately afterward. Nurses must take every precaution that the solution used does not spatter, as it might carry with it infected material.

In addition to irrigation, physicians make applications in some cases of strong antiseptic solutions for the rapid destruction of the infective germs, silver nitrate, 10 to 20 grains to the ounce. The physician will order the eye to be thoroughly cleansed by irrigation, and then separating the lids he will drop into the eye the silver solution. In other cases he may prefer to use a small, soft camel's hair pencil, dipping it in the silver solution and painting the infected surfaces with it. This is usually neutralized afterward by pouring normal salt solution into the eye.

Caution must be exercised that the secretions from the eyes or that irrigation fluid does not find its way into the mouth, ears, or nostrils. When both eyes are infected double labor falls upon the nurse. The inflammation is rarely of equal intensity and of equal duration, and hence the case is prolonged and trying. Whenever possible two nurses should be placed in charge of a case of ophthalmia. It is a physical impossibility for one nurse to continue the applications day and night. It is exceedingly important that treatment go on during the night, although it may not be so frequent as by day. A child will often sleep while compresses are placed upon the eyes, and in some cases irrigation but partially rouses the infant. The use of rubber gloves is advantageous for the nurse, as it diminishes the danger of infection. If, while caring for such a patient, the nurse experiences redness, smarting, or swelling in her own eye, she must report at once to a physician for treatment.

In children very badly nourished that are attacked with ophthalmia the destruction is sometimes very rapid. Perforation may occur, with the discharge of fluid from the chambers of the eye and the complete loss of vision. Under these circumstances the eye shrinks. In other cases the physician may find it necessary to remove the eye to lesson the danger of the other.

For some unknown reason, the breasts of new-born children become enlarged during the first two weeks after birth. A thin milky fluid may be present and considerable distension accompany it. It is usually necessary to do nothing for this condition, as it generally disappears in a few days. Should inflammation and suppuration occur, then the infected breast must be incised, and the abscess cavity washed out thoroughly and drained under antiseptic precautions.

Infants are sometimes seized with convulsions, and this condition is called the eclampsia of the new-born. Such a condition usually comes from some point of great irritation in the intestines, mouth, the skin, the genital organs, or in the brain itself. The convulsions are but a symptom whose cause must be discovered. A nurse can do but little for a child in convulsions without medical advise. Should the doctor fail to arrive promptly, she may put the child in a warm bath, placing a cloth wrung out of hot water on its head, and she may move the bowels by a copious injection of warm water or weak castile soap suds. When the doctor arrives, he will prescribe medicine to check the convulsions, and will endeavor to remove their cause. If the child be teething, it may be necessary to lance the gum. The nurse will sit, taking the child upon her lap, holding its hands with one hand while she draws the head of the child against her chest with the other hand placed against the forehead. In this way she can usually control a young infant. After the gums are lanced, should bleeding be excessive, ice is often applied, and a small bit of ice wrapped in an old handkerchief may be pressed firmly against the bleeding point. Soft, clean linen dipped in whiskey or brandy is sometimes applied. In other cases the nurse will be asked to wash out intestines very thoroughly, to remove decomposing food or intestinal secretions. Usually convulsions are indications of some serious condition, and require prompt and efficient treatment.

In the absence of the physician, the nurse is fully justified in giving one of the following remedies as indicated:

Belladonna—Is especially indicated when the paroxysms terminate in a lethargic state, or occur alternately with it; or else when the child wakes suddenly, as from fright, with haggard eyes, anxious and fixed look, as from alarm; dilated pupils; tetanic rigidity and coldness of the whole body, with burning in the hands and forehead; or else when the child wets the bed frequently.

Chamomilla—Convulsive jerkings of the arms and legs, with involuntary movements of the head, followed by drowsiness, with the eyes half open, and loss of consciousness, redness of one cheek, with paleness of the other, moaning, or frequent desire to drink.

Cina—Especially in children who have worms, or who wet the bed frequently, and where there are: Cramps in the chest, convulsive movements of the limbs, distension and hardness of the abdomen, frequent itching in the nose, cough resembling whooping cough, etc.

Coffea—Especially in weak, puny children, who are often attacked by these convulsions, without any other ailment.

Ignatia—Generally at the commencement of the treatment, especially when it is not clear whether the fits are caused by teething or by worms, or when the spasms return every day at the same hour, with jerking in some of the limbs, or in some of the muscles only, frequent flashes of heat, and perspiration either during or after the spasms; light sleep, from which the child awakes with a start, uttering piercing cries, with trembling of the whole body.

Opium—Especially when the fits are caused by fright, or when there are: Trembling of the whole body, tossing of the arms and legs, piercing cries during the fits; or else lethargy with loss of consciousness, distension of the abdomen, constipation, and ischuria.

Bromide of Camphor—Convulsions due to irritation of teething.

Now, in closing this course of lectures, just a few words in regard to exercise and air.

The muscular development of an infant can best be promoted by the nurse by the regular bathing of the child, with massage after morning bath. Abundant fresh air, suitable clothing, and in addition to this, proper food are most necessary. Young children during the winter should not be in the streets, but may be aired in an upper room by clothing the child properly and then opening the windows of the room. In mild weather the child should be out of doors as much as possible. When sunshine can fall upon the child it is most advantageous. Nurseries should be sunny, clean rooms, with abundant ventilation and without plumbing connecting with the sewer. The clothing should be so arranged as not to interfere in any degree with the child's movement. Skirts should not go much below the feet, as few skirts as possible should be worn, and the child should be encouraged to move its limbs.

Editorial.

LIBERALITY—AN ELEMENT OF DANGER.

Let there be no misunderstanding. Liberty has its place, and can find no more consistent advocate than the writer of these words; but taken outside its legitimate place and it becomes a stumbling block,— a rock of offense against which much wreckage accumulates.

Investigate everything — that means liberty. Investigate *without* prejudice. Investigate with a desire to find the good that exists in practically everything, but *hold fast to that alone which has been proven to be true*. Add to your knowledge from day to day such things, such facts, such truths as may be demonstrated, and hold all else in abeyance.

The great danger from liberality is the acceptances of theories upon some one else's say so without putting it to the test or demanding the demonstration. This is the liberality that acts like a boomerang and returning, knocks the few remaining props from under your foundation and leaves you floating about in a sea of uncertainty filled with the wreckage of similar lives.

It is dangerous to enter the field with liberality as your motto, unless you are prepared to subject everything to the rigid and severe test of scientific investigation, because you will find the field filled with those who have been attracted by the rich array of beautiful fancies and plausible theories. You will be fascinated; and, because of the desire from within, carried away with an idea that especially appeals to the ego and without making the slightest effort to stem the tide, allow yourself to be carried out to sea upon an exceedingly frail boat. Destruction stares you in the face and you begin to catch at straws.

Homœopathy is a science of medicine. It complies with all the requirements of a scientific proposition. Disease manifestations are cured—are removed—by remedies capable of producing similar disease manifestations in the healthy. That is the proposition and it becomes worthy of acceptance when its principles have been demonstrated. If you have accepted the theory without the demonstration you have given evidence of weakness which will become a source of danger. Demand the proof because when once clearly demonstrated you are in possession of a fact that can never be taken from you. Make of every case a scientific demonstration, in that all of the conditions are satisfied and then you will grow in strength, power and *positiveness*. You will know your limitations and having acquired habits of precision can venture out into the great unknown. It is a singular fact that the great scientists find so much close by their own doors that they have little time for promiscuous investigations, although their minds may be ever ready for the demonstration of truth wherever it may be found.

Homœopathy is not only a *science*, but careful investigation has invested it with a dignity and raised the application of its principles to an *art*. It is a great satisfaction to trace the finer lines and follow the application of its principles until it leads us on and up to results which seem almost beyond the possibilities of human power. This seeming impossibility becomes a matter of daily experience to the close and painstaking student. It gives to the art of healing a beauty, a charm, that satisfies the longings of an infinite soul. To be able to look into the mysteries of life and watch the unfolding and reforming of a perverted constitution under the beneficent influence of a remedial agent, selected under direction of the law of similars, gives an inspiration and nobility to the practice of medicine that raises it above the level of a trade and carries it into the realm of the highest and purest of the philosophies.

Having never tasted of the joys of such demonstrations there is no field of investigation that may not be entered with profit. If sufficient advancement has been made to furnish the key whereby many seeming mysteries may be unlocked revealing elements of truth which perfectly fit in with all other truths and thus add to the aggregate. Mental healing, electricity and kindred fields of investigation only tend to show the almost boundless limit of the applications of the principles of homœopathy and to strengthen one's faith in the efficacy of the potential remedy.

ONE DECADE IN JOURNALISM.

Ten years ago, circumstances made it possible for us to enter the field of medical journalism. We have worked hard to accomplish a certain object and now feel compelled to lay down the editorial pen in order that we may devote the time which has been required in securing and editing copy for a monthly publication to something of a more permanent nature.

As we look back over the past, mingled feelings of regret and pleasure come to us. Regret that we could do no more for the cause for which our life has been consecrated. Satisfaction in the fact that we have done our best with the limited means at our command. The profession has been loyal in its support and forbearing with its criticism. No one is more conscious of the elements that have tended to handicap our efforts than ourselves and no one can be more grateful for the support that, in a great measure, has covered up our own defects.

We wish to thank one and all for their contributions, and trust the efforts put forth have brought as rich a reward to them as our efforts have brought to us. We feel that this period of perparation —of apprenticeship — has been very profitable in many ways and would urge upon every member of the profession who has a desire to acquire anything like a comprehensive idea of the almost infinite possibilities contained within the limits of any single department of the science of medicine or the art of employing the same to set apart a portion of each day for the investigation and recording of results of that investigation for future use. No one can even guess at the value of such work until it has been thoroughly tested. It is only a step from this to that of putting upon paper the results of this investigation in such a way that the profession may get at the results. The reader gets *some* benefit from the simple reading, but nothing to be compared to the benefit gained by the original investigator. Another singular fact that will strike the general reader as incredible is this: *the busiest, the most successful physicians are the ones who find time for systematic research*. They are enabled by this thorough preparation to more quickly comprehend the nature of the manifestation and to determine the means required for the removal of the same. The extra skill developed by the study inspires confidence and thereby secures for him the most desirable clientele. It thereby pays, in a most practical manner, to devote the time necessary to the writing of articles for publication in your favorite magazine. It pays to become associated in an editorial capacity with any magazine which has a high aim and a definite purpose.

As we said in the beginning of this editorial, we lay down the editorial pen with this article with sincere regret and enter upon our prospective work with profound satisfaction that circumstances made it impossible for us to pass this probationary period upon such conscientious work as is demanded by the readers of the ADVOCATE; and that in a small measure at least the object has been accomplished for which we accepted the responsibilities of the position.

We had hoped to be able to announce a strong editorial staff ready to take up the work where we laid it down; but plans are not completed and it may be that a month or more will elapse before all the details will have been settled, when we hope to be able to announce the resumption of the work on a broader and a higher plane than heretofore attempted.

We regret exceedingly that there should be a break in the issue of the magazine, but it is thought wiser to suspend its publication than to begin a new year under one management and then make such a change as is contemplated. If the present plans materialize, we will become a regular contributor devoting all our energies along one line of investigation and relinquishing all care and responsibility for the other contributions or the publication of the same.

We can give you only a hint at this time, of the future policy of the magazine. Manuscript for a number of books are in a state of preparation and it is possible that the authors of the same will become associated together in such a manner that their books will appear in serial form in the same magazine and finally be offered to the profession in book form. This arrangement will give the readers of that magazine rare privileges, greater inducements to the conscientious writer than have been given under previous conditions.

Until this new proposition is presented to you, kindly hold your subscription in hand, for it will be one that will keep without spoiling. And now thanking you one and all for your loyal support, not only in contributions of papers, but money, we desire to remain,

Faithfully yours for Homœopathy,

H. W. PIERSON.

Obituary.

BUSHROD WASHINGTON JAMES

Died at his home in Philadelphia, January 6th, 1903 in the sixty-seventh year of his age.

Some six months ago he had a severe attack of pneumonia from which he never fully recovered and his death resulted from the anemia which undoubtedly preceded the attack of pneumonia and which resisted every means employed for its removal. Exact data of the precise form assumed has not been obtained.

During his active professional career he seemed wedded to his profession literally as he never took to himself a wife.

In 1859 he became a member of the American Institute of Homœopathy and throughout his life was an active and an honored member of that body, serving as president during the year 1884.

Since that time he frequently represented the Institute in the World's Congresses in London and Paris, one of his last services of an international nature being the American representative of the committee having charge of the raising of funds for building of a monument the memory of Hahnemann and placed over his grave in Paris, France.

A history of the American Institute is now passing through the presses of Boericke & Tafel and will soon be added to the list of books credited to him as author.

He was a descendant of a family of physicians, and a son of Dr. David James, a noted physician of the old school, who gave it up for homoeopathy after a practice of fourteen years.

Dr. Bushrod James was born in Philadelphia city. After gaining his degree of arts at the Central High School he entered the Homoeopathic Medical College and was graduated as a physician in 1857.

Not long afterwards he established a surgical infirmary, still in existence, adjoining his home. Through his founding of this, he assisted in the founding of the Children's Homoeopathic Hospital, of which he was president for five years, and a consulting physician for more than a score. He was one of the Hahnemann Hospital's Board of Advisers for many years. For thirty-five years he was a trustee of the Spring Garden Institute.

In the midst of these duties Dr. James found time for literary work. He was a world-wide traveler, having spent considerable time in Alaska, and two of his books concern that country. One is "Alaskana, or Legends of Alaska," written in the style of Longfellow's "Hiawatha." The other is "Alaska; Its Neglected Past and Brilliant Future." His last book was a romance called "The Political Freshmen," dealing with reform measures, and published only last year.

Dr. James was a member of the Masonic Veterans, Knights Templar, Union League, Franklin and Spring Garden Institutes, Society of American Authors, Pennsylvania Historical Society, Horticultural Society, Academy of Natural Sciences and Sons of the Revolution.

DR. TIMOTHY FIELD ALLEN.

Dr. Allen of New York, one of the best known homoeopaths in the U. S., and of world-wide reputation as a student of materia medica, died December 6. He was for many years dean of the New York Homoeopathic Medical College, and professor of materia medica.

He was the author of numerous works on botany and materia medica, and no homoeopathic library is complete without Allen's Handbook. Quite a large number of the leading bearers of the banner "Similia" have passed to their reward during this second year of the twentieth century. Helmuth, Talcott, Hughes, Ducherre, and now Allen.

DR. E. C. HOUSE.

The death of Dr. House, which occurred recently, is sincerely mourned in Canton, Ohio, his home, as well as by the members of the Northwestern Ohio Homoeopathic Society, of which he was president.

DR. A. W. WOODWARD.

Dr. A. W. Woodward of Chicago, one of the founders of the Chicago Homoeopathic Medical College, died November 9. He was one of the oldest and best known physicians in the city. For many years he occupied the chairs of Materia Medica and Clinical Therapeutics in the college which he was instrumental in founding.

Personals and News Items.

In France the physician's claim on the estate of a deceased patient has precedence of all others.

According to the Surgeon-General, the death rate in the army for the year ending June 30, 1902, was 13.94 per thousand.

An instance of marked virility is reported from Barnegat, N. J., where a man who remarried at the age of eighty-two years has had two children since, the youngest having just been born when the father was eighty-six years old.

Detroit had a hundred cases of small-pox on Dec. 10, that being the occasion of the Health Board getting busy making house to house vaccinations. Dr. E. J. Kendall's large and successful experience with this disease secured his appointment as a special number of the board. He keeps himself immune by taking high potencies of variolinum.

Conscientious work on the part of Dr. J. W. Mastin, associate editor of The Critique, will be rewarded by his advancement to the position of editor-in-chief, consequent upon the retirement of Dr. Samuel S. Smythe. The journal will, beginning with the January number, be issued on the first instead of the 15th of each month.

The New York Homoeopathic Medical College and Hospital has inaugurated a three weeks Practitioners' Course, commencing April 27th. This course is open to advanced students in medicine as well as graduates. It also aims as far as possible, to be a purely clinical course. The great hospital connections of this college will furnish clinical material that can be seen in no other city in this country. The college has the best equipped laboratory of any medical school, and in the Practitioners' Course there will be thirty-six hours of practical laboratory work in urinalysis. There will be forty-seven hours of operative work in surgery and gynecology. There will be personal bedside instruction at the Metropolitan Hospital of over one thousand beds. Every department of medicine and surgery will be covered. Above all, Homoeopathy will be taught throughout the whole course. A fee of twenty dollars covers the entire course or any part of it that may be desired, and includes a certificate of attendance. The class will positively be limited to one hundred. Read the advertisement of the course in this journal and for announcement, address Geo. W. Roberts, M. D., Secretary, 170 W. 59th Street, New York.

Good Medical Literature, cheap, can be obtained, in the shape of complete volumes of Medical Advance, for years 1893, '94 and '95. $1.00 a volume, postpaid, while they last. Ten numbers, not consecutive, for fifty cents. Odd numbers of issues of the 70s and 80s at six cents a number. Address, Hahnemann Publishing Co., 6704 Lafayette ave.

HAHNEMANNIAN ADVOCATE

Table of Contents.

www.ingramcontent.com/pod-product-compliance
Lightning Source LLC
Chambersburg PA
CBHW031057110726
47900CB00003B/960

* 9 7 8 3 7 4 1 1 7 0 9 5 9 *